Great Short Stories

from the World's Literature

Other Books by Charles Neider

Fiction

Naked Eye
The Authentic Death of Hendry Jones
The White Citadel

Biography

Susy: A Childhood

Criticism

Mark Twain
The Frozen Sea, a Study of Franz Kafka

Edited by Charles Neider

Short Novels of the Masters
Essays of the Masters
The Stature of Thomas Mann
The Complete Short Stories of Robert Louis Stevenson
Our Samoan Adventure, by Fanny and Robert Louis Stevenson
The Autobiography of Mark Twain
The Complete Short Stories of Mark Twain
The Complete Humorous Sketches and Tales of Mark Twain
The Complete Essays of Mark Twain
The Complete Novels of Mark Twain
The Complete Travel Books of Mark Twain
Mark Twain: The Adventures of Colonel Sellers
Mark Twain: Life as I Find It
Man against Nature
The Great West

Contents

Great Short Stories Revisited

In the two decades that have elapsed since the publication of the present volume many changes have occurred, social, literary and personal, which make the rereading of these stories an illuminating experience for me. There are first of all the changes in the spirit of the times. In 1950 we were five years out of World War II; the cold war was very cold; we were about to plunge into the war in Korea; there were considerably fewer human beings in an already crowded world; the earth's environment hadn't reached its present stage of dangerous pollution; our cities weren't in as desperate a condition as they are now in; our society wasn't as polarized as it is; the sexual revolution hadn't yet occurred; the rebellion of the young was still in the future; the strenuous efforts to desegregate the South were yet to come; the habit of political assassination hadn't yet taken hold in our country; and so on.

There have also been changes in literary fashion, partly due to the death of major literary figures. Bunin, Faulkner, Gide, Hemingway, Mann and Nexo were still alive twenty years ago. The reputation of members of the currently dominant Jewish school of writers (such as Mailer, Bellow, Malamud and Roth) hadn't been fully established. Nabokov's reputation hadn't been solidified. And the influence of new writers such as Updike and Capote wasn't yet felt.

Finally, my own tastes and preferences have undergone considerable change, not only because of the changes already mentioned but because of changes in myself, due to the difference be-

tween being thirty-five and fifty-five. What are my present re-
actions to these stories? Do they contain surprises? Disappoint-
ments? Revelations? Let us see.

Sholom Aleichem.   I still think this is a fine, vivid tale. I'm impressed by the author's quick yet rich effects. He seems to be saying, "We have no time to lose. This is a story, therefore you must
make your effects quickly and *leave*." There are two almost in-
commensurate views: the point of view of the adults (robbery,
fraud, sex: comedy) and that of the child (innocence: pathos).
The change from the adult to the child's world has been suggested
by the constant shifting of tense.

Balzac.   One receives an impression of great energy and of vast
narrative reserves. But the psychology of the soldier is thinner than
that of the panther. Everything is extremely romantic, reminding
one of the paintings of Delacroix: the setting in the Egyptian desert, the relations between man and beast, the plot. The tough old
soldier brings to mind Tolstoy's Cossacks from the latter's early
novel *The Cossacks*. Balzac's tale is memorably done; it is vivid,
vigorous and moving. There are sexual overtones in the relations
between the soldier and the panther, and at the end there's a suggestion of sodomy. The last line is the story's whole point. For the
soldier the experience of the desert was "it is God without mankind"; that is, "there is everything, and nothing" in the desert.

Bunin.   What a story this is! It's even better than I thought. My
estimation of Bunin's power as a writer and of his humanity is increased by rereading it. The story begins with exquisitely observed
nature details, continues simply and with pathos and ends with a
terrible murder, terrible because one poor beast of a man kills
another whom he calls "brother"; because both killer and victim are
at the end of their rope; and because the act is committed in drunkenness as well as in despair at being a social outcast. What is
most awful is that the victim has been so dehumanized in his beg-
gar-misery that he's incapable of resisting for his poor life's sake.
He's so far down on the social scale that he obeys orders even from
a slob of a *moujik*. The murderer has been destroyed by other
forces—liquor, self-pity, bad luck and an inner black rage. The
story ends with his running away into the fields but in one's mind

it continues; one imagines the young wife returning with her pail of milk, finding the body, sounding the alarm. It's a treacherous tale, beginning softly, poetically, and ending awfully. Bunin seems capable of capturing the minutest details: a baby's evanescent expression while sucking its mother's nipple, the delicate light on a pond at evening, the behavior of country dogs and sparrows. And everything is done with an absolute absence of false notes. The projection of the psychology of both the old beggar and the *moujik* is masterly.

Chekhov. This story is an old favorite of mine. The little boy is extremely well done even though one admits that some of his observations and remarks are beyond the usual nine-year-old's scope, especially the scope of one who is an orphan and who was raised in village poverty. The pathetic ending after the moving details gives one a sense of the hopelessness of so many Russian lives in that time. It is the same sense that Bunin's story gives of a nation dreadfully sick in spirit to allow its poor to endure such misery.

Defoe. Defoe handles a complex matter effortlessly and with a supple, inconspicuous style. The realism is completely persuasive; one is positive the apparition really occurred to Mrs. Bargrave. The details are so minute, so interwoven, so much a part of a complex pattern they give the impression of being beyond suspicion. One comes away with a profound respect for Defoe's intelligence. This is a ghost story without the usual overtones and suggestions of horror, for Mrs. Veal is a kindly spirit. In addition to the tale's credibility, the author's great triumph lies in the subtle psychological touches concerning Mrs. Veal, Mrs. Bargrave, Mrs. Veal's brother and even the narrator himself.

Dostoyevsky. How this makes one feel the sadness of the old Russia! There is irony in the author's "supposing" he made the story up, when the likelihood is he read or heard about the two deaths and imagined the details surrounding them. What he is talking so tellingly about is the terrible indifference among the comfortable classes to those who suffer from poverty, neglect, hardship and disease. The powers of empathy and humanity, as greatly exemplified by Dostoyevsky, seem to me even more important now than they did twenty years ago, when I was perhaps more intrigued by craftsmanship than I am now. Also, at fifty-five, death seems

a much closer reality than it did at thirty-five and one is consequently more involved and more moved by portrayals of it.

Faulkner. There is a mechanical quality here that I don't recall feeling twenty years ago. I know the story is powerful—I can
feel its power working on me. But I also sense the author pulling
at his little strings (particularly in the dialogue of the children) in
order to affect me. I sympathize with Nancy and I admire Faulkner's skill in setting down the Negroes' speech but I resent being
used. Faulkner is so intent on playing up the great (and he thinks
poignant but I suspect bathetic) contrast between the children's
innocence and the adults' sexuality and violence that he permits
the children's naïve questions and Nancy's assertions of her fears
and of her certainty of Jubah's lurking presence to become dan-
gerously repetitive. There's too much "art" here, therefore too little.
The first two sentences are a fair example. "Monday is no different
from any other week day in Jefferson now. The streets are paved
now," et cetera. The second "now" sounds mechanical and part of
an outmoded fashion. And because of repetition of words and
phrases the dialogue sounds stylized to the point of being strained.
The children, a sort of Greek chorus, are overdone. And the scene
in Nancy's cabin with them is too long.

Flaubert. To this tale too my reaction is not as favorable as
it once was. The story strikes me as being materialistic, as if the
author prepares to write by making up lists of *things* (and chiefly
exotic things). I imagine him collecting facts, names and details
that please him and marshaling them like a ledger-clerk. The style
is cold. There's a lack of creative excitement. His hand seems over-
played. In order to make the point that Julian was sadistic as a
youth he goes on endlessly to present his case; but we don't require so much cold "proof." The narrative at times seems to have
been reduced to a literary pointillism and the spirit, flow and inspiration to have vanished in this very famous story. My reaction
perhaps chiefly proves that I'm no longer awestruck by the name
Flaubert and am willing to commit lese majesty where he's concerned.

Goldsmith. This story is wonderfully fresh in irony, humor and
language. The disabled soldier is no doubt accurately drawn regarding his seemingly ridiculous love of a country that does its best

to humiliate and despise him; also regarding his fatalism. Both traits are similar to those of Russian peasant-soldiers of the last century as described brilliantly by Tolstoy. It must have been very painful to be socially sensitive, to witness flagrant but accepted inequities, yet to be almost wholly helpless to do anything about them. Goldsmith's views were quite different from those of his friend Samuel Johnson. The latter subscribed to the value of subordination, a system in which each person must accept his station in life in order to keep society strong and stable.

Hemingway. I read this intriguing and beautiful story on its first magazine appearance some thirty-five years ago. The recalled, italicized sections are brilliant and poetic but the famous Hemingway dialogue now seems to me stylized to the point of being self-indulgent. And it feels dated, a fact which is probably connected with Hemingway's death. He is no longer the exciting, partly mysterious, living literary force. There's self-pity and self-romancing behind Harry's bravado (as also behind Hemingway's). The scenes between Harry and his wife are rather too stylized for my present taste. But technically the tale is handled very gracefully and the italicized parts wonderfully set off the safari scenes and dialogue. And one certainly can't complain that the Hemingway of this period is boring. His intense excitement and curiosity about the life of action are pervasive and infectious.

Hoffmann and *Irving.* To my surprise I'm captivated by Hoffmann's tale. The tone is droll, delicious, modern, the comic invention superb, with a charming restraint. As for Irving's story, all the details are selected with a master's skill and care. The narrator's efforts to deduce the character of the stout gentleman from various and apparently changing clues are charming. The style is rich in idiom and the humor gentle and civilized. The ending is very apt. Any other would have been a letdown or melodramatic or strained. This one continues the mystery—and the joke, a joke played on the reader as well as on the narrator.

James and *Joyce.* James's story now strikes me as being too wordy. The very first sentence is full of abstractions doing poor service for things *seen*—"the face of nature well washed by last night's downpour and shining as with high spirits, good resolutions, lively intentions—the great glare of recommencement in short

fixed in his patch of sky." James compulsively repeats words: for
example, "books," "nothing," "leaving." And there's too much allit-
eration. The tale reminds me of the sentimental, effeminate excesses
of the pre-Raphaelites. Joyce's little story, on the other hand, written when he was a very young man, is so clear, so well observed
and so gently treated that it moves me once again. The language is
magical. The style is chaste, masculine, sober and beautiful.
James's reminds me of overheated, fetid, perfumed rooms and leads
me to wonder if James ever exercised.

Kafka and *Lawrence*. Kafka's story seems more transparent
than it used to and more deliberately expressionistic. Was it based
on a nightmare? It's powerful because of its sure selection of details: the girl being raped, the pigsty with the huge horses, the
young patient's wound, and so on. But possibly its nightmare tone
finds too much competition in the real nightmare of today's world.
At any rate the story doesn't strike me as being as strong and illuminating as it once did. Lawrence's story is amusing, skillful,
colorful and ironic. The nature touches—the sky, the garden, the
spring air, the birds—are, as always in Lawrence's work, delightful. The narrative tone is irreverent when compared with traditional narrative, which is supposed to wear a grave face. The author implies that both husband and wife are fools for tolerating
each other. The wife, it turns out, is less insipid than the husband: her claws show and she draws the secretary's blood; whereas
the husband remains aloof, remote, ineffectual—castrated. Lawrence suggests that because wife and husband are incapable of the
animal fury of the two blue birds they are less than vitally human.
I had rather expected to find the story dated after all these years
and am pleasantly surprised to see I was wrong.

Lu Hsün and *Maeterlinck*. Lu Hsün's moving, extremely well-
told story is a good example of how art, intelligence, profundity
and simplicity can cross such great barriers as language, nationality
and race. It's a biting portrait of human cruelty, stupidity and indifference to human suffering. Hsiang-lin Sao is mistreated by her
mother-in-law, by the customs of the time and place, by poverty,
by life itself; but Old Woman Wei, Fourth Aunt and Fourth Uncle
are hardly aware of her condition. Maeterlinck's story is even more
savage. The action is described brilliantly in great detail but with

almost no dialogue, causing the horrific events to seem eerily silent.

Mann and *Melville.*   Mann's story is a romantic and somewhat sentimental portrait of Schiller, the German poet and dramatist. It was written when Mann was a young man. It has been said of Mann that he identified himself with Goethe. I believe he was fascinated by Goethe but felt a spiritual kinship with Schiller. One senses autobiographical tones here. I seem to be more distant from the romantic mood than I once was and the story seems a bit too much like a closet drama for my present taste, but I still sense its power and beauty and I imagine it has much to say to struggling young writers working against the grain. Melville's style in the present tale seems now all flimflam, shilly-shally, highfalutin, with boring biblical allusions and lots of windy language. The sentence constructions are inverted, serpentine. Melville is language-drunk, as he was in *Moby Dick*, but here he has less to say and the language is less tolerable.

Pirandello and *Poe.*   Pirandello's is a superbly done if rather awful story. I'm impressed once again by the deft little psychological touches, the intense feeling for nature, the great economy, the poetic mood and the nightmare quality of the piece as a whole. The effect is Kafkaesque but without the use of expressionism. What's particularly impressive about Poe's story are the extreme precision of thought and the directness, clarity and verve with which the thought is expressed. The quality of mind and the modernity of the language take me by surprise. It's exciting to watch him deal with man's irrationality and perversity. In this he prefigured Dostoyevsky's efforts to illuminate the self-destructive side of man's nature. There is a special pleasure in confronting so sharp and penetrating an intelligence across the gulf of a century and a quarter.

Porter, Proust and *Pushkin.*   Porter's is still an astonishingly strong and beautiful story. Braggioni is well realized, better than Laura, who's a bit hazy. The present tense is effective and the observation of details faultless. It's hard to know how much of Proust's story is autobiographical and how much not, but it hardly matters. What matters is that even in so brief a piece there is explosive evidence of his genius: in the richness of allusion and metaphor, in the precise, uncannily accurate psychological analysis, in the effortless shifts from particular details to universal musings, in the incredible mixture of precise sensation and judicious, logical exploration. Pushkin's story is done with such vigor and economy it reminds one of Tolstoy. But the ending is weak. It turns out the undertaker was only dreaming. And the undertaker's last remark to his servant doesn't seem to end the tale. Why does he say, "Well, since that is the case, make tea as quickly as possible and call my daughters"? Why as quickly as possible? Why call the daughters?

Saint Exupéry and *Sartre*.   Saint Exupéry's is an extremely eloquent story by a man of great sensitivity and humanity moved by the events that overwhelmed his country in the last world war. In some respects it reads almost as if it were written yesterday. Sartre's is an overpowering tale about the Spanish Civil War, excellent in every way, with many hard details and with no fat at all. It is one of the best stories in the book. It is fierce, gripping. Its effect is tremendous. Ibbieta the narrator tells the fascists a lie that proves to be true, consequently Gris loses his life and Ibbieta's is spared. Such absurdity is related to Sartre's belief in the essential absurdity of existence: the existential farce of life.

Stevenson and *Svevo*.   Stevenson's tale of a schizoid murderer and of moral ambiguities owes a large debt to Dostoyevsky's Raskolnikov of *Crime and Punishment*, which Stevenson read in a French translation. Perhaps he had also read "Notes from Underground," Dostoyevsky's supreme projection of a split personality enchanted with human abysses. And he had read much of Poe, including "The Imp of the Perverse." It is still a fine story and the language is sonorous, striking, apt, deft, that of a master. The little touches in the Svevo story reveal an interestingly eccentric perspective but they do not seem to add up to a great deal; there is little plot, little movement. But the people say things so asinine as to make one smile. The tale's mordancy reminds one of the acid taste of life.

Tagore, Tolstoy and *Turgenev*.   I no longer relate strongly to so great a degree of romanticism as is evidenced in Tagore's story, with its lurid colors and its overtones of oriental filigree and scents, but I admire the author's strong talent. Tolstoy's tale is a lovely thing, simply done and with a wonderful, warm power of imagination. As for the Turgenev story, it makes you think how superb the Russian writers are. The human element, human relations of the most basic kind, are their stock in trade, their intimate knowledge, almost their religion. The portrait of the district doctor is brilliant. *He* tells the story, yet you are outside him, you can see how plain, parochial and in some ways small-minded he is. Yet he's also complex, with a sense of inferiority, a strong sense of duty and with his mind often on such important if seemingly vulgar matters as money.

Mark Twain, Unamuno and *Woolf.*   Mark Twain wrote this as propaganda against vivisection but I think now it was a mistake to do it from the dog's point of view, a decision which inevitably led to sentimentality. Some of the jokes, for example about the mother dog's use of long words to "put on the dog," are repetitious and ineffective. I no longer recall why I selected this particular story by a writer whom I greatly admire. The Unamuno piece I still like. And I still respect Virginia Woolf's talent but the present story seems to me overdone and too mannered, too indefinite. The reason, I suspect, is that there is not enough pressure of the unsaid trying to become the said.

What is perhaps most absorbing in the great majority of these stories is the richness of their detail. It is the detail which stirs our wonder at the world, excites our senses, reveals for us the quality and character of the personality that recorded or invented them, and projects us forcefully into the mimetic experience. I have chosen stories which are richest in this factor, and this may give the reader an untrue notion of its rarity. There are only too many stories that generalize. It is Defoe's sense of *things* that makes him the fascinating novelist. And it is the same sense of them that makes reports of certain true events approximate art. The boundary between art and such reports is a semi-artistic twilight from which great things may be salvaged.

We admire in great artists their power of invention, their seeming ability to rise beyond the gravitational sphere of their personality and simulate nature's effortless effects with their avoidance of monotony. I think it was Dostoyevsky who remarked of Tolstoy that his invention was as fertile as that of a dream. But what is the invention of a novelist compared to that of nature? Nature is not limited by modes of thought, language and the conventions of the novel. If we admire invention in artists, we are amazed by it in nature. Variations of surprise within the pattern of the known or the expected is the kind of invention that is common both to artists and to nature. But the artist selects, and it is his incalculable power of selection while simulating nature's effects that remains his mystery and his pride.

Charles Neider

Princeton, New Jersey
July 1971

◇◇◇*Sholom Aleichem (1859–1916). Pen name of Solomon Rabinowitz, one of the foremost modern Yiddish writers, who was born in Russia. He wrote a large number of stories and several novels and plays. His sketches of Tevye the dairyman were dramatized in the very successful Broadway musical comedy* Fiddler on the Roof.

THE PASSOVER GUEST

BY SHOLOM ALEICHEM

"I have a Passover guest for you, Reb Yoneh, such a guest as you never had since you became a householder."

"What sort is he?"

"A real Oriental citron!"

"What does that mean?"

"It means a 'silken Jew,' a personage of distinction. The only thing against him is—he doesn't speak our language."

"What does he speak, then?"

"Hebrew."

"Is he from Jerusalem?"

"I don't know where he comes from, but his words are full of *a's*."

Such was the conversation that took place between my father and the beadle, a day before Passover, and I was wild with curiosity to see the "guest" who didn't understand Yiddish, and who talked with *a's*. I had already noticed, in synagogue, a strange-looking individual, in a fur cap, and a Turkish robe striped blue, red, and yellow. We boys crowded around him on all sides, and stared, and then caught it hot from the beadle, who said children had no business "to creep into a stranger's face" like that. Prayers over, every one greeted the stranger, and wished him a happy Passover, and he, with a sweet smile on his red cheeks set in a round gray beard, replied to each one, "Shalom! Shalom!" instead of our Sholom. This "Shalom! Shalom!" of his sent us boys into fits of laughter. The beadle grew very angry, and pursued us with slaps. We eluded him,

From *Yiddish Tales*. (Translated by Helena Frank.) By permission of The Jewish Publication Society of America.

and stole deviously back to the stranger, listened to his "Shalom! Shalom!" exploded with laughter, and escaped anew from the hands of the beadle.

I am puffed up with pride as I follow my father and his guest to our house, and feel how all my comrades envy me. They stand looking after us, and every now and then I turn my head, and put out my tongue at them. The walk home is silent. When we arrive, my father greets my mother with "a happy Passover!" and the guest nods his head so that his fur cap shakes. "Shalom! Shalom!" he says. I think of my comrades, and hide my head under the table, not to burst out laughing. But I shoot continual glances at the guest, and his appearance pleases me; I like his Turkish robe, striped yellow, red, and blue, his fresh red cheeks set in a curly gray beard, his beautiful black eyes that look out so pleasantly from beneath his bushy eyebrows. And I see that my father is pleased with him too, that he is delighted with him. My mother looks at him as though he were something more than a man, and no one speaks to him but my father, who offers him the cushioned reclining-seat at table.

Mother is taken up with the preparations for the Passover meal, and Rikel the maid is helping her. It is only when the time comes for saying Kiddush that my father and the guest hold a Hebrew conversation. I am proud to find that I understand nearly every word of it. Here it is in full.

My father: "Nu?" (That means, "Won't you please say Kiddush?")

The guest: "Nu-nu!" (meaning, "Say it rather yourself!")

My father: "Nu-O?" ("Why not you?")

The guest: "O-nu?" ("Why should I?")

My father: "I-O!" ("You first!")

The guest: "O-ai!" ("*You* first!")

My father: "E-o-i!" ("I beg of you to say it!")

The guest: "Ai-o-ê!" ("I beg of you!")

My father: "Ai-e-o-nu?" ("Why should you refuse?")

The guest: "Oi-o-e-nu-nu!" ("If you insist, then I must!")

And the guest took the cup of wine from my father's hand, and recited a Kiddush. But what a Kiddush! A Kiddush such as we had never heard before, and shall never hear again. First, the Hebrew —all *a*'s. Secondly, the voice, which seemed to come, not out of his beard, but out of the striped Turkish robe. I thought of my comrades, how they would have laughed, what slaps would have rained down, had they been present at that Kiddush.

Being alone, I was able to contain myself. I asked my father the Four Questions, and we all recited the Haggadah together. And I was elated to think that such a guest was ours, and no one else's.

Our sage who wrote that one should not talk at meals (may he forgive me for saying so!) did not know Jewish life. When shall a Jew find time to talk, if not during a meal? Especially at Passover, when there is so much to say before the meal and after it. Rikel the maid handed the water, we washed our hands, repeated the benediction, mother helped us to fish, and my father turned up his sleeves and started a long Hebrew talk with the guest. He began with the first question one Jew asks another:

"What is your name?"

To which the guest replied all in *a*'s and all in one breath:

"Ayak Bakar Gashal Damas Hanoch Vassam Za'an Chafaf Tatzatz."

My father remained with his fork in the air, staring in amazement at the possessor of so long a name. I coughed and looked under the table, and my mother said, "Favele, you should be careful eating fish, or you might be choked with a bone," while she gazed at our guest with awe. She appeared overcome by his name, although unable to understand it. My father, who understood, thought it necessary to explain it to her.

"You see, Ayak Bakar, that is our Alef-Bes inverted. It is apparently their custom to name people after the alphabet."

"Alef-Bes! Alef-Bes!" repeated the guest with the sweet smile on his red cheeks, and his beautiful black eyes rested on us all, including Rikel the maid, in the most friendly fashion.

Having learned his name, my father was anxious to know whence, from what land, he came. I understood this from the names of countries and towns which I caught, and from what my father translated for my mother, giving her a Yiddish version of nearly every phrase. And my mother was quite overcome by every single thing she heard, and Rikel the maid was overcome likewise. And no wonder! It is not everyday that a person comes from perhaps two thousand miles away, from a land only to be reached across seven seas and a desert, the desert journey alone requiring forty days and nights. And when you get near to the land, you have to climb a mountain of which the top reaches into the clouds, and this is covered with ice, and dreadful winds blow there, so that there is peril of death! But once the mountain is safely crossed, and the land is reached, one beholds a terrestrial Eden. Spices, cloves, herbs, and every kind of fruit—apples, pears, and oranges, grapes, dates, and olives, nuts and quantities of figs. And the houses there are all built of deal, and roofed with silver, the furniture is gold (here the guest cast a look at our silver cups, spoons, forks, and knives), and brilliants, pearls, and diamonds bestrew the roads, and no one cares to take the trouble of picking them up, they are of no value there. (He was looking at my mother's diamond earrings, and at the pearls round her white neck.)

"You hear that?" my father asked her, with a happy face.

"I hear," she answered, and added: "Why don't they bring some over here? They could make money by it. Ask him that, Yoneh!"

My father did so, and translated the answer for my mother's benefit:

"You see, when you arrive there, you may take what you like, but when you leave the country, you must leave everything in it behind, too, and if they shake out of you no matter what, you are done for."

"What do you mean?" questioned my mother, terrified.

"I mean, they either hang you on a tree, or they stone you with stones."

The more tales our guest told us, the more thrilling they became, and just as we were finishing the dumplings and taking another sip or two of wine, my father inquired to whom the country belonged. Was there a king there? And he was soon translating, with great delight, the following reply:

"The country belongs to the Jews who live there, and who are called Sefardim. And they have a king, also a Jew, and a very pious one, who wears a fur cap, and who is called Joseph ben Joseph. He is the high priest of the Sefardim, and drives out in a gilded carriage, drawn by six fiery horses. And when he enters the synagogue, the Levites meet him with songs."

"There are Levites who sing in your synagogue?" asked my father, wondering, and the answer caused his face to shine with joy.

"What do you think?" he said to my mother. "Our guest tells me that in his country there is a temple, with priests and Levites and an organ."

"Well, and an altar?" questioned my mother, and my father told her:

"He says they have an altar, and sacrifices, he says, and golden vessels—everything just as we used to have it in Jerusalem."

And with these words my father sighs deeply, and my mother, as she looks at him, sighs also, and I cannot understand the reason. Surely we should be proud and glad to think we have such a land, ruled over by a Jewish king and high priest, a land with Levites and an organ, with an altar and sacrifices—and bright, sweet thoughts enfold me, and carry me away as on wings to that happy Jewish land where the houses are of pine-wood and roofed with silver, where the furniture is gold, and diamonds and pearls lie scattered in the street. And I feel sure, were I really there, I should know what to do—I should know how to hide things—they would shake nothing out of *me*. I should certainly bring home a lovely present for my mother, diamond ear-rings and several pearl necklaces. I look at the one mother is wearing, at her ear-rings, and I feel a great desire to be in that country. And it occurs to me that after Passover I will travel there with our guest, secretly, no one shall know. I will only speak of it to our guest, open my heart to him, tell him the whole truth, and beg him to take me there, if only for a little while. He will certainly do so, he is a very kind and approachable man, he looks at everyone, even at Rikel the maid, in such a friendly, such a very friendly way!

So I think, and it seems to me, as I watch our guest, that he has read my thoughts, and that his beautiful black eyes say to me:

"Keep it dark, little friend, wait till after Passover, then we shall manage it!"

I dreamt all night long. I dreamt of a desert, a temple, a high priest, and a tall mountain. I climb the mountain. Diamonds and pearls grow on the trees, and my comrades sit on the boughs, and shake the jewels down onto the ground, whole showers of them, and I stand and gather them, and stuff them into my pockets, and, strange to say, however many I stuff in, there is still room! I stuff and stuff, and still there is room! I put my hand into my pocket and draw out—not pearls and brilliants, but fruits of all kinds—apples, pears, oranges, olives, dates, nuts, and figs. This makes me very unhappy, and I toss from side to side. Then I dream of the temple, I hear the priests chant, and the Levites sing, and the organ play. I want to go inside and I cannot—Rikel the maid has hold of me, and will not let me go. I beg of her, and scream and cry, and again I am very unhappy, and toss from side to side. I wake—and see my father and mother standing there, half dressed, both pale, my father hanging his head, and my mother wringing her hands, and with her soft eyes full of tears. I feel at once that something has gone very wrong, very wrong indeed, but my childish head is incapable of imagining the greatness of the disaster.

The fact is this: our guest from beyond the desert and the seven seas has disappeared, and a lot of things have disappeared with him: all the silver wine cups, all the silver spoons, knives, and forks; all my mother's ornaments, all the money that happened to be in the house, and also Rikel the maid!

A pang goes through my heart. Not on account of the silver cups, the silver spoons, knives, and forks that have vanished; not on account of mother's ornaments or of the money, still less on account of Rikel the maid, good riddance! But because of the happy, happy land whose roads were strewn with brilliants, pearls, and diamonds; because of the temple with the priests, the Levites, and the organ; because of the altar and the sacrifices; because of all the other beautiful things that have been taken from me, taken, taken, taken!

I turn my face to the wall, and cry quietly to myself.

A PASSION IN THE DESERT

BY HONORE DE BALZAC

"The whole show is dreadful," she cried, coming out of the menagerie of M. Martin. She had just been looking at that daring specu-
lator "working with his hyena"——to speak in the style of the pro-
gram.

"By what means," she continued, "can he have tamed these animals to such a point as to be certain of their affection for——."

"What seems to you a problem," said I, interrupting, "is really
quite natural."

"Oh!" she cried, letting an incredulous smile wander over her
lips.

"You think that beasts are wholly without passions?" I asked her.
"Quite the reverse; we can communicate to them all the vices arising
in our own state of civilization."

She looked at me with an air of astonishment.

"Nevertheless," I continued, "the first time I saw M. Martin, I
admit, like you, I did give vent to an exclamation of surprise. I found
myself next to an old soldier with the right leg amputated, who had
come in with me. His face had struck me. He had one of those in-
trepid heads, stamped with the seal of warfare, and on which the
battles of Napoleon are written. Besides, he had that frank good-
humored expression which always impresses me favorably. He was
without doubt one of those troopers who are surprised at nothing,
who find matter for laughter in the contortions of a dying comrade,
who bury or plunder him quite light-heartedly, who stand intrepidly in the way of bullets; in fact, one of those men who waste no
time in deliberation, and would not hesitate to make friends with the

7

devil himself. After looking very attentively at the proprietor of the menagerie getting out of his box, my companion pursed up his lips with an air of mockery and contempt, with that peculiar and expressive twist which superior people assume to show they are not taken in. Then when I was expatiating on the courage of M. Martin, he smiled, shook his head knowingly, and said, 'Well known.'

"How 'well known'?" I said. "If you would only explain to me the mystery I should be vastly obliged."

"After a few minutes, during which we made acquaintance, we went to dine at the first restaurateur's whose shop caught our eye. At dessert a bottle of champagne completely refreshed and brightened up the memories of this odd old soldier. He told me his story, and I said he had every reason to exclaim, 'Well known.' "

When she got home, she teased me to that extent and made so many promises, that I consented to communicate to her the old soldier's confidences. Next day she received the following episode of an epic which one might call "The Frenchman in Egypt."

During the expedition in Upper Egypt under General Desaix, a Provençal soldier fell into the hands of the Mangrabins, and was taken by these Arabs into the deserts beyond the falls of the Nile.

In order to place a sufficient distance between themselves and the French army, the Mangrabins made forced marches, and only rested during the night. They camped round a well overshadowed by palm trees under which they had previously concealed a store of provisions. Not surmising that the notion of flight would occur to their prisoner, they contented themselves with binding his hands, and after eating a few dates, and giving provender to their horses, went to sleep.

When the brave Provençal saw that his enemies were no longer watching him, he made use of his teeth to steal a scimitar, fixed the blade between his knees, and cut the cords which prevented using his hands; in a moment he was free. He at once seized a rifle and dagger, then taking the precaution to provide himself with a sack of dried dates, oats, and powder and shot, and to fasten a scimitar to his waist he leaped onto a horse, and spurred on vigorously in the direction where he thought to find the French army. So impatient was he to see a bivouac again that he pressed on the already tired courser at such speed that its flanks were lacerated with his spurs, and at last the poor animal died, leaving the Frenchman alone in the desert. After walking some time in the sand with all the courage of an escaped convict, the soldier was obliged to stop, as the day had already ended. In spite of the beauty of an oriental sky at night, he felt he had not strength enough to go on. Fortunately he had been able to find a small hill, on the summit of which a few palm trees shot up into the air; it was their verdure seen from afar which had brought hope and consolation to his heart. His fatigue was so great that he lay down upon a rock of granite, capriciously cut out like a camp-bed; there he fell asleep without taking any precaution to defend himself while he slept. He had made the sacrifice of his life. His last thought was one of regret. He repented having left the Mangrabins, whose nomad life seemed to smile on him now that he was afar from them and without help. He was awakened by the sun, whose pitiless rays fell with all their force on the granite and produced an intolerable heat—for he had had the stupidity to place himself inversely to the shadow thrown by the verdant majestic heads of the palm trees. He looked at the solitary trees and shuddered—they reminded him of the graceful shafts crowned with foliage which characterize the Saracen columns in the cathedral of Aries.

But when, after counting the palm trees, he cast his eye around him, the most horrible despair was infused into his soul. Before him stretched an ocean without limit. The dark sand of the desert spread farther than sight could reach in every direction, and glittered like steel struck with a bright light. It might have been a sea of looking-glass, or lakes melted together in a mirror. A fiery vapor carried up in streaks made a perpetual whirlwind over the quivering land. The sky was lit with an oriental splendor of insupportable purity, leaving naught for the imagination to desire. Heaven and earth were on fire.

The silence was awful in its wild and terrible majesty. Infinity, immensity, closed in upon the soul from every side. Not a cloud in the sky, not a breath in the air, not a flaw on the bosom of the sand, ever moving in diminutive waves; the horizon ended as at sea on a clear day, with one line of light, definite as the cut of a sword.

The Provençal threw his arms around the trunk of one of the palm trees, as though it were the body of a friend, and then in the shelter of the thin straight shadow that the palm cast upon the granite, he wept. Then sitting down he remained as he was, contemplating with profound sadness the implacable scene, which was all he had to look upon. He cried aloud, to measure the solitude. His voice, lost in the hollows of the hill, sounded faintly, and aroused no echo—the echo was in his own heart. The Provençal was twenty-two years old;—he loaded his carbine.

"There'll be time enough," he said to himself, laying on the ground the weapon which alone could bring him deliverance.

Looking by turns at the black expanse and the blue expanse, the soldier dreamed of France—he smelt with delight the gutters of Paris—he remembered the towns through which he had passed, the faces of his fellow-soldiers, the most minute details of his life. His southern fancy soon showed him the stones of his beloved Provence, in the play of the heat which waved over the spread sheet of the desert. Fearing the danger of this cruel mirage, he went down the opposite side of the hill to that by which he had come up the day before. The remains of a rug showed that this place of refuge had at one time been inhabited; at a short distance he saw some palm trees full of dates. Then the instinct which binds us to life awoke again in his heart. He hoped to live long enough to await the passing of some Arabs, or perhaps he might hear the sound of cannon; for at this time Bonaparte was traversing Egypt.

This thought gave him new life. The palm tree seemed to bend with the weight of the ripe fruit. He shook some of it down. When he tasted this unhoped-for manna, he felt sure that the palms had been cultivated by a former inhabitant—the savory, fresh meat of the dates was proof of the care of his predecessor. He passed suddenly from dark despair to an almost insane joy. He went up again to the top of the hill, and spent the rest of the day in cutting down one of the sterile palm trees, which the night before had served him for shelter. A vague memory made him think of the animals of the desert; and in case they might come to drink at the spring, visible from the base of the rocks but lost farther down, he resolved to guard himself from their visits by placing a barrier at the entrance of his hermitage.

In spite of his diligence, and the strength which the fear of being devoured asleep gave him, he was unable to cut the palm in pieces, though he succeeded in cutting it down. At eventide the king of the desert fell; the sound of its fall resounded far and wide, like a sign in the solitude; the soldier shuddered as though he had heard some voice predicting woe.

But like an heir who does not long bewail a deceased parent, he tore off from this beautiful tree the tall broad green leaves which are its poetic adornment, and used them to mend the mat on which he was to sleep.

Fatigued by the heat and his work, he fell asleep under the red curtains of his wet cave.

In the middle of the night his sleep was troubled by an extraordinary noise; he sat up, and the deep silence around him allowed him to distinguish the alternative accents of a respiration whose savage energy could not belong to a human creature.

A profound terror, increased still further by the darkness, the silence, and his waking images, froze his heart within him. He almost felt his hair stand on end, when by straining his eyes to their utmost he perceived through the shadows two faint yellow lights. At first he attributed these lights to the reflection of his own pupils, but soon the vivid brilliance of the night aided him gradually to distinguish the objects around him in the cave, and he beheld a huge animal lying but two steps from him. Was it a lion, a tiger, or a crocodile?

The Provençal was not educated enough to know under what species his enemy ought to be classed; but his fright was all the greater, as his ignorance led him to imagine all terrors at once; he endured a cruel torture, noting every variation of the breathing close to him without daring to make the slightest movement. An odor, pungent like that of a fox, but more penetrating, profounder—so to speak— filled the cave, and when the Provençal became sensible of this, his terror reached its height, for he could no longer doubt the proximity of a terrible companion, whose royal dwelling served him for shelter.

Presently the reflection of the moon, descending on the horizon, lit up the den, rendering gradually visible and resplendent the spotted skin of a panther.

The lion of Egypt slept, curled up like a big dog, the peaceful possessor of a sumptuous niche at the gate of an hotel; its eyes opened for a moment and closed again; its face was turned toward the man. A thousand confused thoughts passed through the Frenchman's mind; first he thought of killing it with a bullet from his gun, but he saw there was not enough distance between them for him to take proper aim—the shot would miss the mark. And if it were to wake! —the thought made his limbs rigid. He listened to his own heart beating in the midst of the silence, and cursed the too violent pulsations which the flow of blood brought on, fearing to disturb that sleep which allowed him time to think of some means of escape.

Twice he placed his hand on his scimitar, intending to cut off the head of the enemy; but the difficulty of cutting the stiff, short hair compelled him to abandon this daring project. To miss would be to die for certain, he thought; he preferred the chances of fair fight, and made up his mind to wait till morning; the morning did not leave him long to wait.

He could now examine the panther at ease; its muzzle was smeared with blood.

"She's had a good dinner," he thought, without troubling himself as to whether her feast might have been on human flesh. "She won't be hungry when she gets up."

It was a female. The fur on her belly and flanks was glistening white; many small marks like velvet formed beautiful bracelets round her feet; her sinuous tail was also white, ending with black rings; the overpart of her dress, yellow like unburnished gold, very lissome and soft, had the characteristic blotches in the form of rosettes, which distinguish the panther from every other feline species.

This tranquil and formidable hostess snored in an attitude as graceful as that of a cat lying on a cushion. Her blood-stained paws, nervous and well-armed, were stretched out before her face, which rested upon them, and from which radiated her straight, slender whiskers, like threads of silver.

If she had been like that in a cage, the Provençal would doubtless have admired the grace of the animal, and the vigorous contrasts of vivid color which gave her robe an imperial splendor; but just then his sight was troubled by her sinister appearance.

The presence of the panther, even asleep, could not fail to produce the effect which the magnetic eyes of the serpent are said to have on the nightingale.

For a moment the courage of the soldier began to fail before this danger, though no doubt it would have risen at the mouth of a cannon charged with shell. Nevertheless, a bold thought brought daylight to his soul and sealed up the source of the cold sweat which sprang forth on his brow. Like men driven to bay who defy death and offer their body to the smiter, so he, seeing in this merely a tragic episode, resolved to play his part with honor to the last.

"The day before yesterday the Arabs would have killed me perhaps," he said; so considering himself as good as dead already, he waited bravely, with excited curiosity, his enemy's awakening.

When the sun appeared, the panther suddenly opened her eyes; then she put out her paws with energy, as if to stretch them and get rid of cramp. At last she yawned, showing the formidable apparatus of her teeth and pointed tongue, rough as a file.

"A regular *petite maîtresse*," thought the Frenchman, seeing her roll herself about so softly and coquettishly. She licked off the blood which stained her paws and muzzle, and scratched her head with reiterated gestures full of prettiness. "All right, make a little toilet," the Frenchman said to himself, beginning to recover his gaiety with his courage; "we'll say good morning to each other presently," and he seized the small, short dagger which he had taken from the Mangrabins. At this moment the panther turned her head toward the man and looked at him fixedly without moving.

The rigidity of her metallic eyes and their insupportable luster made him shudder, especially when the animal walked toward him. But he looked at her caressingly, staring into her eyes in order to magnetize her, and let her come quite close to him; then with a movement both gentle and amorous, as though he were caressing the most beautiful of women, he passed his hand over her whole body, from the head to the tail, scratching the flexible vertebrae which divided the panther's yellow back. The animal waved her tail voluptuously, and her eyes grew gentle; and when for the third time the Frenchman accomplished this interesting flattery, she gave forth one of those purrings by which our cats express their pleasure; but this murmur issued from a throat so powerful and so deep, that it resounded through the cave like the last vibrations of an organ in a church. The man, understanding the importance of his caresses, redoubled them in such a way as to surprise and stupefy his imperious courtesan. When he felt sure of having extinguished the ferocity of his capricious companion, whose hunger had so fortunately been satisfied the day before, he got up to go out of the cave; the panther let him go out, but when he had reached the summit of the hill she sprang with the lightness of a sparrow hopping from twig to twig, and rubbed herself against his legs, putting up her back after the manner of all the race of cats. Then regarding her guest with eyes whose glare had softened a little, she gave vent to that wild cry which naturalists compare to the grating of a saw.

"She is exacting," said the Frenchman, smilingly.

He was bold enough to play with her ears; he caressed her belly and scratched her head as hard as he could.

When he saw that he was successful, he tickled her skull with the point of his dagger, watching for the right moment to kill her, but the hardness of her bones made him tremble for his success.

The sultana of the desert showed herself gracious to her slave; she lifted her head, stretched out her neck, and manifested her delight by the tranquillity of her attitude. It suddenly occurred to the soldier that to kill this savage princess with one blow he must poignard her in the throat.

He raised the blade, when the panther, satisfied no doubt, laid herself gracefully at his feet, and cast up at him glances in which, in spite of their natural fierceness, was mingled confusedly a kind of good-will. The poor Provençal ate his dates, leaning against one of the palm trees, and casting his eyes alternately on the desert in quest of some liberator and on his terrible companion to watch her uncertain clemency.

The panther looked at the place where the date stones fell, and every time that he threw one down her eyes expressed an incredible mistrust.

She examined the man with an almost commercial prudence. However, this examination was favorable to him, for when he had finished his meager meal she licked his boots with her powerful rough tongue, brushing off with marvellous skill the dust gathered in the creases.

"Ah, but when she's really hungry!" thought the Frenchman. In spite of the shudder this thought caused him, the soldier began to measure curiously the proportions of the panther, certainly one of the most splendid specimens of its race. She was three feet high and four feet long without counting her tail; this powerful weapon, rounded like a cudgel, was nearly three feet long. The head, large as that of a lioness, was distinguished by a rare expression of refinement. The cold cruelty of a tiger was dominant, it was true, but there was also a vague resemblance to the face of a sensual woman. Indeed, the face of this solitary queen had something of the gaiety of a drunken Nero: she had satiated herself with blood, and she wanted to play.

The soldier tried if he might walk up and down, and the panther left him free, contenting herself with following him with her eyes, less like a faithful dog than a big Angora cat, observing everything, and every movement of her master.

When he looked around, he saw, by the spring, the remains of his horse; the panther had dragged the carcass all that way; about two-thirds of it had been devoured already. The sight reassured him.

It was easy to explain the panther's absence, and the respect she had had for him while he slept. The first piece of good luck emboldened him to tempt the future, and he conceived the wild hope of continuing on good terms with the panther during the entire day, neglecting no means of taming her, and remaining in her good graces.

He returned to her, and had the unspeakable joy of seeing her wag her tail with an almost imperceptible movement at his approach. He sat down then, without fear, by her side, and they began to play together; he took her paws and muzzle, pulled her ears, rolled her over on her back, stroked her warm, delicate flanks. She let him do whatever he liked, and when he began to stroke the hair on her feet she drew her claws in carefully.

The man, keeping the dagger in one hand, thought to plunge it into the belly of the too-confiding panther, but he was afraid that he would be immediately strangled in her last conclusive struggle; besides, he felt in his heart a sort of remorse which bid him respect a creature that had done him no harm. He seemed to have found a friend, in a boundless desert; half unconsciously he thought of his first sweetheart, whom he had nicknamed "Mignonne" by way of contrast, because she was so atrociously jealous that all the time of their love he was in fear of the knife with which she had always threatened him.

This memory of his early days suggested to him the idea of making the young panther answer to this name, now that he began to admire with less terror her swiftness, suppleness, and softness. Toward the end of the day he had familiarized himself with his perilous position; he now almost liked the painfulness of it. At last his companion had got into the habit of looking up at him whenever he cried in a falsetto voice, "Mignonne."

At the setting of the sun Mignonne gave, several times running, a profound melancholy cry. "She's been well brought up," said the light-hearted soldier; "she says her prayers." But this mental joke only occurred to him when he noticed what a pacific attitude his companion remained in. "Come, *ma petite blonde*, I'll let you go to bed first," he said to her, counting on the activity of his own legs to run away as quickly as possible, directly she was asleep, and seek another shelter for the night.

The soldier waited with impatience the hour of his flight, and when it had arrived he walked vigorously in the direction of the Nile; but hardly had he made a quarter of a league in the sand when he heard the panther bounding after him, crying with that saw-like cry more dreadful even than the sound of her leaping.

"Ah!" he said, "then she's taken a fancy to me; she has never met any one before, and it is really quite flattering to have her first love." That instant the man fell into one of those movable quicksands so terrible to travellers and from which it is impossible to save oneself. Feeling himself caught, he gave a shriek of alarm; the panther seized him with her teeth by the collar, and, springing vigorously backward, drew him as if by magic out of the whirling sand.

"Ah, Mignonne!" cried the soldier, caressing her enthusiastically; "we're bound together for life and death—but no jokes, mind!" and he retraced his steps.

From that time the desert seemed inhabited. It contained a being to whom the man could talk, and whose ferocity was rendered gentle by him, though he could not explain to himself the reason for their strange friendship. Great as was the soldier's desire to stay upon guard, he slept.

On awakening he could not find Mignonne; he mounted the hill, and in the distance saw her springing toward him after the habit of these animals, who cannot run on account of the extreme flexibility of the vertebral column. Mignonne arrived, her jaws covered with blood; she received the wonted caress of her companion, showing with much purring how happy it made her. Her eyes, full of languor, turned still more gently than the day before toward the Provençal who talked to her as one would to a tame animal.

"Ah! Mademoiselle, you are a nice girl, aren't you? Just look at that! so we like to be made much of, don't we? Aren't you ashamed of yourself? So you have been eating some Arab or other, have you? that doesn't matter. They're animals just the same as you are; but don't you take to eating Frenchmen, or I shan't like you any longer."

She played like a dog with its master, letting herself be rolled over, knocked about, and stroked, alternately; sometimes she herself would provoke the soldier, putting up her paw with a soliciting gesture.

Some days passed in this manner. This companionship permitted the Provençal to appreciate the sublime beauty of the desert; now that he had a living thing to think about, alternations of fear and quiet, and plenty to eat, his mind became filled with contrast and his life began to be diversified.

Solitude revealed to him all her secrets, and enveloped him in her delights. He discovered in the rising and setting of the sun sights unknown to the world. He knew what it was to tremble when he heard over his head the hiss of a bird's wing, so rarely did they pass, or when he saw the clouds, changing and many-colored travellers, melt one into another. He studied in the night time the effect of the moon upon the ocean of sand, where the simoom made waves swift of movement and rapid in their change. He lived the life of the Eastern day, marvelling at its wonderful pomp; then, after having revelled in the sight of a hurricane over the plain where the whirling sands made red, dry mists and death-bearing clouds, he would welcome the night with joy, for then fell the healthful freshness of the stars, and he listened to imaginary music in the skies. Then solitude taught him to unroll the treasures of dreams. He passed whole hours in remembering mere nothings, and comparing his present life with his past.

At last he grew passionately fond of the panther; for some sort of affection was a necessity.

Whether it was that his will powerfully projected had modified the character of his companion, or whether, because she found abundant food in her predatory excursions in the desert, she respected the man's life, he began to fear for it no longer, seeing her so well tamed.

He devoted the greater part of his time to sleep, but he was obliged to watch like a spider in its web that the moment of his deliverance might not escape him, if any one should pass the line marked by the horizon. He had sacrificed his shirt to make a flag with, which he hung at the top of a palm tree, whose foliage he had torn off. Taught by necessity, he found the means of keeping it spread out, by fastening it with little sticks; for the wind might not be blowing at the moment when the passing traveller was looking through the desert.

It was during the long hours, when he had abandoned hope, that he amused himself with the panther. He had come to learn the different inflections of her voice, the expressions of her eyes; he had studied the capricious patterns of all the rosettes which marked the gold of her robe. Mignonne was not even angry when he took hold of the tuft at the end of her tail to count her rings, those graceful ornaments which glittered in the sun like jewelry. It gave him pleasure to contemplate the supple, fine outlines of her form, the whiteness of her belly, the graceful pose of her head. But it was especially when she was playing that he felt most pleasure in looking at her; the agility and youthful lightness of her movements were a continual surprise to him; he wondered at the supple way in which she jumped and climbed, washed herself and arranged her fur, crouched down and prepared to spring. However rapid her spring might be, however slippery the stone she was on, she would always stop short at the word "Mignonne."

One day, in a bright mid-day sun, an enormous bird coursed through the air. The man left his panther to look at this new guest; but after waiting a moment the deserted sultana growled deeply.

"My goodness! I do believe she's jealous," he cried, seeing her eyes become hard again; "the soul of Virginie has passed into her body; that's certain."

The eagle disappeared into the air, while the soldier admired the curved contour of the panther.

But there was such youth and grace in her form! she was beautiful as a woman! the blond fur of her robe mingled well with the delicate tints of faint white which marked her flanks.

The profuse light cast down by the sun made this living gold, these russet markings, to burn in a way to give them an indefinable attraction.

The man and the panther looked at one another with a look full of meaning; the coquette quivered when she felt her friend stroke her head; her eyes flashed like lightning—then she shut them tightly.

"She has a soul," he said, looking at the stillness of this queen of the sands, golden like them, white like them, solitary and burning like them.

"Well," she said, "I have read your plea in favor of beasts; but how did two so well adapted to understand each other end?"

"Ah, well! you see, they ended as all great passions do end—by a misunderstanding. For some reason *one* suspects the other of treason; they don't come to an explanation through pride, and quarrel and part from sheer obstinacy."

"Yet sometimes at the best moments a single word or a look is enough—but anyhow go on with your story."

"It's horribly difficult, but you will understand, after what the old villain told me over his champagne.

"He said—'I don't know if I hurt her, but she turned round, as if enraged, and with her sharp teeth caught hold of my leg—gently, I daresay; but I, thinking she would devour me, plunged my dagger into her throat. She rolled over, giving a cry that froze my heart; and I saw her dying, still looking at me without anger. I would have given all the world—my cross even, which I had not got then—to have brought her to life again. It was as though I had murdered a real person; and the soldiers who had seen my flag, and were come to my assistance, found me in tears.'

" 'Well sir,' he said, after a moment of silence, 'since then I have been in war in Germany, in Spain, in Russia, in France; I've certainly carried my carcass about a good deal, but never have I seen anything like the desert. Ah! yes, it is very beautiful!'

" 'What did you feel there?' I asked him.

" 'Oh! that can't be described, young man. Besides, I am not always regretting my palm trees and my panther. I should have to be very melancholy for that. In the desert, you see, there is everything, and nothing.'

" 'Yes, but explain——'

" 'Well,' he said, with an impatient gesture, 'it is God without mankind.' "

◈◈◈*Ivan Bunin (1870–1953). Russian poet, novelist and short-story writer. Winner of the Nobel Prize, 1933. He translated Longfellow, Byron and Tennyson into Russian. He emigrated from Russia in 1919, taking up residence in France. During his lifetime he was called the most distinguished artist of contemporary Russian letters.*

AN EVENING IN SPRING

BY IVAN BUNIN

On St. Thomas' week, on a clear evening barely tinged with rose, at that enchanting time when the earth has just been freed from the snow, when, in the little hollows upon the steppes, underneath the young bare oaks, some gray, hardened snow still lingers, an old beggar was going from house to house in a certain village in the Eletz province,—of course, he had no hat, and there was a long linen wallet slung over his shoulder.

This village was a large one, but quiet, lying far out among the fields. And besides, it happened to be a quiet evening. There was nobody near the flooded, clayey pond, that one could not see the limits of; nor upon the level common where, in the shade of the huts and hayricks, this old man was walking. His head was bald, yet still black-haired; he held a long walnut staff in his hand, and looked like a primitive bishop. The common was of a clear, vivid green; the air was freshening; the pond, concavely-full, its tone that of a flashing flesh colour, was slightly crimson, and there was a certain beauty about it, despite a bottle-green block of ice, covered with rusty manure, that still floated about in it. Somewhere on the other side, warmly and caressingly lit up against the low-lying sun,—somewhere far-off, it seemed,—a child, strayed behind some corn-kiln or storehouse, was crying, and its plaintive, monotonous wailing was not unpleasant to the ear in the evening glow. . . . But the folk thereabouts were none too generous of alms.

There, at the entrance to the village, near an old, well-to-do farm, where age-old oaks covered with the nests of rooks stood beyond the three-roomed *izba* of dark-red brick, a young gray-eyed married woman had given something, but even that had been a trifle. She had been standing near the stone threshold amid the drying spring mire upon a hard-beaten path, holding a pretty little girl, whose little eyes did not show any glimmer of intelligence, perched in her arms; the child had on a little patchwork cap, and, pressing her close against her, the woman was dancing, stamping her bare feet, and, as she turned, her cotton skirt would swell out.

"There's an old man; I'll give you to him to put in his little wallet," she was saying through her teeth, her lips feasting on the little girl's cheeks:

> "I'm a-goin' to dance
> So's the floor will creak. . . ."

And, turning, completely around, she changed her voice to a ringing, coquettish tone, evidently imitative of some one:

"Old man, old man,—don't you need a little girl?"

The girl was not a bit frightened; she was calmly sucking a round cracknel, and the mother began coaxing the little girl, in all sorts of ways, to give it to the smiling beggar who had come up:

"Give it to him, my little babe, give it to him; for you and I are all, all alone on this whole farm; so we have nothing to give alms with. . . ."

And the little girl stolidly stretched out her short little arm, with the saliva-moistened cookie clenched in her little fist. And the beggar, smilingly shaking his head at other folks' happiness, took it and munched it as he went on his way.

He held his stick lightly, in readiness, as he went; now it would be a wicked, snarling watch-dog that would roll up in a ball underneath your feet,—and having rolled right up to you, would suddenly become quiet; or else a yellow, downy hound would ferociously tear the ground and throw it up with his hind feet, standing near a hayrick and growling, growling and gasping, with fiery eyes. . . . Upon approaching the little window of a hut, the beggar would make a humble bow and would tap lightly against the frame with his staff. But often no one would respond to this tap; many were still finishing up their sowing, finishing up their plowing, many were out in the fields. And his soul, the soul of a peasant from of old, even rejoiced in secret: the folks are out in the field . . . this is the time that feeds the whole year . . . no time for beggars. . . . And at times, on the other side of the panes upon which the beggar tapped, a fair-faced peasant woman carrying a child at breast in her arms, would lean over as she sat on a bench. Through the sorry little window, she appeared very big. Not at all abashed because the beggar could see her soft breast, as white as wheat-flour, she would wave him away with her large hand, covered with silver rings, while the infant, without letting the sweet nipple out of its mouth, lay back and looked up at her with its dark, clear eyes, scratching hard its bare little outspread legs, all dotted with pink from flea-bites. "God will give you alms,—don't be angry with us," the peasant woman would say calmly. As for the old women, each one of them would wrinkle up her face painfully, inevitably leaning out and complaining for a long time, constantly reiterating that she'd be glad as glad could be to give alms, but there wasn't anything . . . everybody was out in the fields . . . and to give without asking she was afraid, —she, being an old woman, had had her head bitten off long ago, as it was. . . . The beggar would agree with her, would say, "Well, forgive me, for the love of God," and would go on farther.

He had done thirty versts[1] that day, and was not a bit fatigued; only his legs had grown benumbed, dulled, and had begun to wobble. His long bag was half-filled with crusts and some odds and ends; while under the patched long coat, narrow belted and long skirted, under the sheepskin jacket and the much worn blouse, under the shirt next his skin, there had long been hanging upon his crucifix an amulet wherein were sewn ninety-two roubles in bills. And his soul was at rest. Of course, he was old, thin, all weather-beaten,—his mouth contracted, parched, until it was all black; his nose was like a bone; his neck all in wrinkles resembling cracks, criss-crossing one another, as though his neck were made of cork. But he was still spry. His eyes, which once upon a time had been black, were now rheumy and dimmed by thin cataracts; but still they could see not only the full-flooded pond, but, as well, the rose-ate tint upon its farther side, and even the clear, pale sky. The air

[1] A verst is about two-thirds of a mile. *Translator.*

was getting fresher; more loudly, but seemingly from a still greater distance, came the receding cry of the child; there was a scent of the chilling grass in the air. . . . Two pigeons soared together over the roofs, fell to the clayey little bank of the pond, and, raising their little heads, began to drink. . . . Just a little before, in a lonely farm near the great road, some women had grown generous and had given him a big piece of calico and a pair of good trousers,—oh, good as new, you might say; a young fellow that belonged to their farm had made them for himself, but he had been crushed in a pit, in the quarry where the *moujiks* had been digging for clay. Now the beggar was walking along and deliberating: should he dispose of them, or put them on himself, and throw away those he had on— which, by now, were really none too presentable,—near the edge of some field?

Having come to the end of the village, he entered a short little lane that led out into the steppe. And into his eyes glanced the many-rayed, fair-weather sun of April, sinking far beyond the plain, beyond the gray fallow-lands and the newly tilled fields of spring-corn. At the very end of the village, at a turn of the well-beaten, glistening road, leading to that distant, humble hamlet where the beggar was thinking of passing the night, stood a new hut, not large, well-roofed with new thatch, which was lemon-coloured and resembled a well-combed head. Keeping aloof from everybody, a man and his wife had settled here a year ago,—there were shavings and chips still knocking about here and there. They were a thrifty, hard-working, agreeable couple, and sold vodka on the sly. And so the beggar went straight toward his hut,—there was a possibility of selling the new trousers to its owner,—and besides, he liked just to enter it; he liked it because it seemed to be living some especial life, all its own, quiet and steadfast, standing at the end leading out of the village and gazing with its clear little windows upon the setting of the sun, while the skylarks were finishing their song in the chilling air. Near the blind wall that gave out upon the by-lane lay a shadow, but its front wall was gay. Last fall its owner had planted three acacia bushes beneath the little windows. Now they had taken root and were already downy with a yellowish verdure tender as that of a willow. Having skirted them, the beggar walked in through the entry into the main room.

At first, after the sunlight, he could not see anything, although the sun was looking in here as well, lighting up the blue transparent smoke floating over the table, that stood underneath a hanging tin lamp. To gain time while his eyes grew accustomed, he bowed and crossed himself for a long time in the direction of the new tinselled icon hanging in a corner. Then he laid down his bag and his staff on the floor near the door, and made out a large-bodied *moujik* in bast shoes and a tattered short sheepskin coat, sitting with his back to the door, on a stool near the table; the well-dressed mistress he saw sitting on a bench.

"The Lord's blessing be with you," said he, in a low voice, bowing once more. "Greetings of the holiday just past."

He wanted to sing the paschal *Christ Is Risen,* but felt that it would be out of place, and reflected:

"Well, I guess the master is not at home. . . . What a pity."

The mistress was not at all bad-looking, with a very shapely waist, with white hands,—just as though she were no mere peasant woman. She was in a gala-dress, as always; in a pearl necklace, in a blouse of coarse calico, with thin puffed-out sleeves, with an apron broidered in red and blue, in a skirt of indigo wool with terra-cotta checks, and in half-boots, rough but well-sewn and made to fit the foot, their heels shod with steel. With her neat head and clear face bent down, she was embroidering a blouse for her husband. When the beggar had greeted her, she raised her steady but unglittering eyes, threw an intent glance upon him, and nodded amiably. Then, with a light sigh, she laid her work aside, deftly stuck her needle in it, went toward the oven, her half-boots clacking over the wooden floor and her flanks swaying, and took a small bottle of vodka and a thick cup with blue stripes out of a little cupboard.

"I have gotten tired, though . . ." said the beggar, as if he was talking to himself,—both in apology for the vodka and because he was confused by the silence of the *moujik,* who had not turned around toward him.

Stepping softly in his bast shoes, humbly walking around him, the beggar sat down upon another stool, at an opposite corner of the table. As for the mistress, she put the cup and the small bottle before him, and went back to her work. Then this stalwart, tattered son of the steppes raised his head heavily,—there was a whole greenish demijohn standing before him,—and, narrowing his eyes, he fixed his gaze upon his humble bottle-companion. He may have been pretending just a trifle; but still, his face was inflamed; his eyes were drunken, filled with the dull glitter of tipsiness; the lips, grown soft and flabby, were half-open, as in a fever,—evidently, this was not the first day of his spree. And the beggar grew a little more wary, and carefully began filling his cup. "After all, now, he'll drink his and I'll drink mine. . . . This is a tavern, and we don't bother one another," he was thinking. He raised his head, and his mistily-black eyes, the colour of ripe sloe-thorn, as well as his whole visage, made rough and weather-beaten by the steppe, were void of all expression.

"Where was you tramping?" asked the *moujik,* roughly and crazily. "Have you come to steal, seeing as how all the folks are out in the fields?"

"Why should I be stealing?" the beggar replied, evenly and meekly. "I've had six children of my own, and my own house and goods. . . ."

"You're blind and you're blind, but, never fear, many's the feather and the twig you've carried to your nest!"

"Why should you be saying that? I've worked hard as could be for ten years in the quartz mines. . . ."

"That ain't work. That's. . . ."

"Don't you be saying anything out of the way," said the mistress, without elevating her voice, without raising her lashes, and bit off the thread. "I don't listen to anything unseemly. I ain't heard it from my husband yet."

"Well, that will do; I won't do it any more . . . lady!" said the *moujik.* " 'Scuse me . . . I'm after asking you," said he to the beggar, frowningly, "what can you get out of the ground, now, when it ain't been plowed nor sown?"

"Well, now, of course. . . . Whoever has the land, for example. . . ."

"Wait,—I'm smarter than you be!" said the *moujik* slapping the table with his palm. "Answer what you're asked: did you serve for a soldier?"

"I was a non-commissioned officer of the Tenth Grenadiers Regiment of Little Russia, under Count Rumiyantzev-Zadunaisky. . . . What else should I be doing but serving for a soldier?"

"Keep still, don't gabble more'n you're asked! What year was you took?"

"In 'seventy-six, in the month of November."

"Wasn't you ever at fault?"

"Never."

"Did you obey the officers?"

"There was no way of my doing otherwise. I had taken an oath."

"But what's that scar doing on your neck? Do you understand what I'm driving at now? I am testing him," said the *moujik*, with his eyebrows working surlily, but changing his commanding voice for a more simple one, and turning toward the mistress his crazed face, aureately illumined through the tobacco smoke by the sunset; "I may be poor, all right, but I've caught more than one fellow like that! I know enough to come in out of the rain!"

And again he put on a frown, looking at the beggar:

"Did you bow down before the Holy Cross and the Gospel?"

"That I have," answered the beggar, who had managed to take a drink, to wipe his mouth with his sleeve, to sit up straight again, and to impart to his face and his misty eyes a dispassionate expression.

The *moujik* surveyed him with glazed eyes.

"Stand up before me!"

"Don't raise any fuss. Am I talking to you, or am I not?" the mistress quietly intervened.

"Wait, for the love of God," the *moujik* waved her away—in vexation. "Stand up before me!"

"Honest to God, what are you up to . . ." the beggar began to mumble.

"Stand up, I'm telling you!" yelled the *moujik*. "I'm a-going to examine you."

The beggar stood up and shifted from foot to foot.

"Hands at the sides! So. Got a passport?"

"But are you an inspector, or something?"

"Keep still,—don't you dare to jaw back at me like that! I'm smarter than you be! I went all through this myself. Show it to me this minute!"

Hastily unhooking his long overcoat, then his sheepskin jacket, the beggar submissively rummaged within the bosom of his shirt for a long time. Finally he pulled out a paper wrapped up in a red handkerchief.

"Give it here," said the *moujik* abruptly.

And, unwrapping the little handkerchief, the beggar handed him a small frayed gray book, with a large wax seal. The *moujik* awkwardly opened it with his gnarled fingers and pretended to read it, putting it at a distance from him, leaning back, and looking at it for a long time through the tobacco smoke and the red light of the evening glow.

"So. I see now. Everything ship-shape. Take it back," he said, his parched lips moving with difficulty. "I am poor as poor can be; it's the second spring, you might say, that I'm neither plowing nor sowing; folks have done for me. . . . I fell down at his feet, the dog that he is. . . . And yet I'm beyond a price, you might say. . . . But you just tell me all that you've stolen, or else I'll kill you right off!" he yelled ferociously. "I know everything; I've gone through all sorts of things. . . . I've been boiled in pitch, you might say,— that's how I've suffered. . . . It is the Lord that gives us life, but any vermin can take it away. . . . Give the bag here, and that's all there is to it!"

The mistress merely shook her head, and leaned back from her embroidery, contemplating it. The beggar went toward the door and gave the *moujik* the bag, just as he had given him the passport. The *moujik* took it, and, as he laid it near him on the stool, he said:

"That's right. Now sit down,—let's chat a bit. I'll get to the bottom of all this here. I'll make an inspection of my own, don't you fret!"

And he became silent, staring at the table.

"Spring . . ." he muttered. "Ah, but what a sorrowful sabbath-day it is, that a man may not work in the fields. . . . Go on!" he cried out to some imagined person, trying to snap his fingers:

> "Oh, the lady starts to dance,
> And her fingers is all blue. . . ."

And he relapsed into silence. The mistress was smoothing down the embroidery with her thimble.

"I'm going out to milk the cow," said she, getting up from her seat. "Don't blow up the fire whilst I am out, or else you'll burn us out in your drunkenness."

The *moujik* came to with a start.

"Lordy!" he exclaimed, in hurt tones. "Little mistress! How can youse say that. . . . You've grown aweary for your husband, never fear?"

"That's none of your worry," said the mistress. "He's in town, on business. . . . He don't go traipsing around no inns."

"You'd go traipsing, too!" said the *moujik*. "Well, what would you have me do, now,—go out on the wayside, or what? You rich devils are all right. . . ."

The mistress, picking up a milk-pail, went out. It was growing dark in the hut; everything was quiet, and the roseate light was suffused in the soft, spring obscurity. The *moujik*, with his elbows on the table, was dozing, as he pulled at an extinguished, crudely made cigarette. The beggar was sitting peacefully, with never a sound, leaning against the dark partition, and his face was almost invisible.

"Do you drink beer?" asked the *moujik*.

"I do," came the low answer out of the dusk.

The *moujik* was silent for a while.

"We are vagabones, you and me," said he, morosely and meditatively. "Poor wayside rubbish. . . . Beggarmen. . . . I feel weary in your company!"

"That's right. . . ."

"But as for beer,—I like it," said the *moujik* loudly, after another silence. "She don't keep it, the carrion! Otherwise I would have drunk some beer . . . and would have had a snack of something. . . . My tongue's all soaked,—I want to eat. . . . I would have had a snack and drunk something. . . . Yes. . . . But she, the mistress, ain't got such a bad face! If I was harnessed up with one like her, I would. . . . All right, never mind, sit down, sit down . . . I got respect for the blind. Whenever a grand holiday used to come around, I would take twenty of these here blind men, now, and seat them at table,—you would have had to look and look to find another household like ours! And they would sing a stave for me, and make me a bow to boot. . . . Do you know how to sing staves? About Alexei, the Man of God? I do take to that stave. Pick up your cup,—I'll treat you to some of mine."

Having taken the cup from the beggar's hands, he held it up to the faint light of the evening glow and half-filled it. The beggar got up, made a low bow, drained the cup to the bottom, and again sat down. The *moujik* dragged the beggar's bag upon his knees, and, untying it, began to mutter:

"I sized you up at once . . . I've got enough money of my own, brother; you're no mate for me. . . . I go through my money in cold blood . . . I drink it away . . . I drink away a horse a year, and send a good ram up in smoke. . . . Aha! So you've run up against a bit of a *moujik*,—do you understand who I am? But still, I feel sorry for you. I understand! There's thousands of the likes of you roaming about in springtime. . . . There's mire, and sloughs, and never a path or a road,—but you've got to keep on going, bowing before everybody. . . . And you can't never tell whether they'll give you anything or no. . . . Eh, brother! Don't I understand you?" asked the *moujik* with bitter sorrow, and his eyes filled with tears.

"No, this time of the year is not so bad, it's all right," said the beggar quietly. "You walk along a field, over a big, abandoned tract that had once been planned for a road. . . . All alone, with never another soul nigh. . . . Then, too, there's the dear sun, and the warm weather. . . . True, there's many a thousand of the likes of me roaming about. Half of Russia is roaming so."

"I've drunk away two horses," said the *moujik*, raking the crusts out of the bag, pulling out a waistcoat, the calico, the trousers, and a bast shoe. "I'm goin' to go all through all your miserable pickings, and old rags. . . . Hold on! Pants! I must buy them from you, soon as I come into a little money. . . . How much?"

The beggar thought for a while.

"Why, I'd let it go for two. . . ."

"I'll give you three!" said the *moujik*, getting up, placing the trousers under him, and sitting down upon them. "They're mine! But where's the other shoe? It will pass for new,—that means you must have stolen it, for sure. But then, it's better to be thieving, than to be grieving your heart out in the springtime, the way I am a-doing now; to be perishing from hunger, to be coming to the end of your rope,—when you take the very least of the shepherds, and you'll find him at work. . . . I have drunk a horse away,—but a beastie like that is worth more nor any man. . . . But am I no plowman, no reaper? . . . And now you sing a stave, or I'll kill you right off!" he cried out. "I feel weary in your company!"

In a quavering, modest, but a practiced voice the beggar began to sing out of the obscurity:

"Once upon a time there lived and were two brethren—
Two blood-brethren, two brethren in God and Christ. . . ."

"Eh, two brethren in God and Christ!" the *moujik* chimed in, in a high-pitched and piteous tone, straining his voice.

The beggar, with even churchly chanting, continued:

"One dwelt in cold and poverty,
Rotting in his leprosy. . . ."

"And the o-ther was rich!" Out of tune, drowning out the beggar, with tears in his voice, the *moujik* caught up the song. "Put more heart in it!" he cried out, as his voice broke. "Grief has swallowed me up; all men are having a holiday, all men are sowing,—but here I be, biting the earth; it's the second spring that my mother earth has been barren. . . . Let me have your cup, or I'll kill you right off! Open the window for me!"

And again the beggar submissively gave him his cup. Then he started to open the window. Being new, it had swollen and would not yield for a long while. Finally it did yield, and flew open. A fresh, pleasant odor of the fields floated in. It was completely dark out there now, the roseate night glow had become extinguished, barely shimmering over the soft darkness of the quiet, joyous, fecundated field. One could hear the half-drowsy skylarks finishing their very last songs.

"Sing, Lazarus,—sing, my own brother!" said the *moujik*, extending a full cup to the beggar. "We're two of a kind, you and me. . . . Only what are you alongside of me? A vagabone! Whereas I am a working man, that gives food and drink to all those that suffer. . . ."

He sat down suddenly, losing his balance, and again dug into the bag.

"And what might you have here?" he asked, examining the calico, which had turned the faintest pink in the barely perceptible light of the evening glow.

"Oh, that's just so. . . . Some women gave it to me," said the beggar quietly, feeling everything floating before him from tipsiness, and that it was time to be going, and that it was necessary to extricate the trousers from underneath the *moujik* somehow.

"How can that be! You lie!" cried out the *moujik,* banging the table with his fist. "It's a shroud,—I can see! It's a grave-shroud!" he cried out with tears in his voice, and was silent for a while, hearkening to the abating songs of the skylarks. Then he shoved the bag away from him, and, shaking his tousled head, began to cry: "I have risen in my pride against God!" said he bitterly, weeping.

And then, straining himself, he began to sing loudly, keeping good time:

> "Oh my mother gave me birth and she guarded me,
> Though I now a sinner be, unforgivable!
> All the torments have I borne,
> All the sorrows have I borne,—
> Nowheres found I joy for me.
> Oh, my mother spoke to me
> And she cautioned me;
> If she only knew, if she only saw,
> She could never bear
> Such calamity. . . ."

"Oh, my soul is a sinner and a creeping thing!" he cried out wildly, weeping, and suddenly started clapping his palms with an eldritch laughter: "Beggarman, give me your money! I know you through and through; I feel you through and through,—give it to me! I know you have it! It can't be otherwise,—give it to me for love of the Lord God Himself!"

And, swaying, he arose, and the beggar, who had also arisen, felt his legs giving away from fear, felt a dull ache start in his thighs. The tear-stained face of the *moujik,* barely discernible in the twilight, was insane.

"Give it to me!" he repeated, in a voice suddenly grown hoarse. "Give it to me, for the Love of the Queen of Heaven! I can see, I can see,—you're grabbing at your bosom, at your undershirt; that means you've got it,—all your kind has! Give it to me,—it ain't of no use to you, anyway, whereas it will set me on my feet forever! Give it to me of your own will,—brother, don't lead me into sin!"

"Can't do it," said the beggar, quietly and dispassionately.

"What?"

"Can't do it. I've been saving for twenty years. Can't bring myself to do it."

"You ain't goin' to give it to me?" asked the *moujik* hoarsely.

"No . . ." said the beggar, barely audible but unshaken.

The *moujik* was silent for a long while. The beating of their hearts could be heard in the darkness.

"Very well," said the *moujik*, with an insane submissiveness. "I will kill you; I'll go and find me a stone and then kill you."

And, swaying, he went toward the threshold.

The beggar, standing erect in the darkness, made a sweeping and slow sign of the cross. As for the *moujik*, he, with his head lowered like a bull, was already walking about under the windows.

Then there came a crunching sound,—evidently he was pulling a stone out of the foundation.

And a minute later the door slammed again,—and the beggar drew himself up still more.

"For the last time I'm a-telling you . . ." the *moujik* mumbled out with his cracked lips, walking up to him with a big white stone in his hands. "Brother. . . ."

The beggar was silent. His face could not be seen. Swinging back with his left arm and catching the beggar by his neck, the *moujik* struck hard his shrinking face with the chill stone. The beggar tore away, backward, and, as he fell, catching the table with his bast shoe, he struck the back of his head against a stool, and then against the floor. And falling upon him, the *moujik*, squeezing the breath out of his chest, frenziedly began to batter in his throat with the stone.

Ten minutes later he was already far out in the dark, even field. There were many stars out; the air was fresh; the earth gave forth a metallic odor. Completely sobered up, he was walking so rapidly and lightly that he seemed capable of covering a hundred versts more. The amulet, torn off the beggar's crucifix, he was holding tightly clenched in his hand. Later, he flung it from him into a dark, freshly plowed field. His eyes were staring fixedly like an owl's; his teeth were tightly clenched, like a lobster's claws. Although he had looked for his cap for a long while, he had been unable to find it in the darkness; the chillness beat upon his bared head. His head seemed to him to be of stone.

◇◇◇*Anton Pavlovich Chekhov (1860-1904). Russian short-story writer and dramatist. He wrote more than a thousand stories, five full-length plays and a number of one-act plays. His literary art was casual and realistic, highly dependent on mood and atmosphere. His influence on short-story writers has been profound and widespread. He influenced James Joyce and Katherine Mansfield, among others.*

VANKA

BY ANTON PAVLOVICH CHEKHOV

Nine-year-old Vanka Zhukov, who had been apprentice to the shoemaker Aliakhin for three months, did not go to bed the night before Christmas. He waited till the master and mistress and the assistants had gone out to an early church-service, to procure from his employer's cupboard a small phial of ink and a penholder with a rusty nib; then, spreading a crumpled sheet of paper in front of him, he began to write.

Before, however, deciding to make the first letter, he looked furtively at the door and at the window, glanced several times at the sombre ikon, on either side of which stretched shelves full of lasts, and heaved a heart-rending sigh. The sheet of paper was spread on a bench, and he himself was on his knees in front of it.

"Dear Grandfather Konstantin Makarych," he wrote, "I am writing you a letter. I wish you a Happy Christmas and all God's holy best. I have no mamma or papa, you are all I have."

Vanka gave a look towards the window in which shone the reflection of his candle, and vividly pictured to himself his grandfather, Konstantin Makarych, who was nightwatchman at Messrs. Zhivarev. He was a small, lean, unusually lively and active old man of sixty-five, always smiling and blear-eyed. All day he slept in the servants' kitchen or trifled with the cooks. At night, enveloped in an ample sheep-skin coat, he strayed around the domain tapping

From *Best Russian Short Stories,* edited by Thomas Seltzer. (Translator unidentified.) By permission of Random House, Inc. Copyright 1925, by Modern Library, Inc.

with his cudgel. Behind him, each hanging his head, walked the old bitch Kashtanka, and the dog Viun, so named because of his black coat and long body and his resemblance to a loach. Viun was an unusually civil and friendly dog, looking as kindly at a stranger as at his masters, but he was not to be trusted. Beneath his deference and humbleness was hid the most inquisitorial maliciousness. No one knew better than he how to sneak up and take a bite at a leg, or slip into the larder or steal a muzhik's chicken. More than once they had nearly broken his hind-legs, twice he had been hung up, every week he was nearly flogged to death, but he always recovered.

At this moment, for certain, Vanka's grandfather must be standing at the gate, blinking his eyes at the bright red windows of the village church, stamping his feet in their high-felt boots, and jesting with the people in the yard; his cudgel will be hanging from his belt, he will be hugging himself with cold, giving a little dry, old man's cough, and at times pinching a servant-girl or cook.

"Won't we take some snuff?" he asks, holding out his snuff-box to the women. The women take a pinch of snuff, and sneeze.

The old man goes into indescribable ecstasies, breaks into loud laughter, and cries:

"Off with it, it will freeze your nose!"

He gives his snuff to the dogs, too. Kashtanka sneezes, twitches her nose, and walks away offended. Viun deferentially refuses to sniff and wags his tail. It is glorious weather, not a breath of wind, clear, and frosty; it is a dark night, but the whole village, its white roofs and streaks of smoke from the chimneys, the trees silvered with hoarfrost, and the snowdrifts, you can see it all. The sky scintillates with bright twinkling stars, and the Milky Way stands out so clearly that it looks as if it had been polished and rubbed over for the holidays. . . .

Vanka sighs, dips his pen in the ink, and continues to write:

"Last night I got a thrashing, my master dragged me by my hair into the yard, and belaboured me with a shoemaker's stirrup, because, while I was rocking his brat in its cradle, I unfortunately fell asleep. And during the week, my mistress told me to clean a herring, and I began by its tail, so she took the herring and stuck its snout into my face. The assistants tease me, send me to the tavern for vodka, make me steal the master's cucumbers, and the master beats me with whatever is handy. Food there is none; in the morning it's bread, at dinner, gruel, and in the evening bread again. As for tea or sour-cabbage soup, the master and the mistress guzzle that. They make me sleep in the vestibule, and when their brat cries, I don't sleep at all, but have to rock the cradle. Dear Grandpapa, for Heaven's sake, take me away from here, home to our village, I can't bear this anymore. . . . I bow to the ground to you, and will pray to God for ever and ever, take me from here or I shall die. . . ."

The corners of Vanka's mouth went down, he rubbed his eyes with his dirty fist, and sobbed.

"I'll grate your tobacco for you," he continued, "I'll pray to God for you, and if there is anything wrong, then flog me like the grey goat. And if you really think I shan't find work, then I'll ask the manager, for Christ's sake, to let me clean the boots, or I'll go instead of Fedya as underherdsman. Dear Grandpapa, I can't bear this anymore, it'll kill me. . . . I wanted to run away to our village, but I have no boots, and I was afraid of the frost, and when I grow up I will look after you, no one shall harm you, and when you die I'll pray for the repose of your soul, just like I do for mamma Pelagueya.

"As for Moscow, it is a large town, there are all gentlemen's houses, lots of horses, no sheep, and the dogs are not vicious. The children don't come round at Christmas with a star, no one is allowed to sing in the choir, and once I saw in a shop window hooks on a line and fishing rods, all for sale, and for every kind of fish, awfully convenient. And there was one hook which would catch a sheat-fish weighing a pound. And there are shops with guns, like the master's, and I am sure they must cost 100 rubles each. And in the meat-shops there are woodcocks, partridges, and hares, but who shot them or where they come from, the shopman won't say.

"Dear Grandpa, and when the masters give a Christmas tree, take a golden walnut and hide it in my green box. Ask the young lady, Olga Ignatyevna, for it, say it's for Vanka."

Vanka sighed convulsively, and again stared at the window. He remembered that his grandfather always went to the forest for the Christmas tree, and took his grandson with him. What happy times! The frost crackled, his grandfather crackled, and as they both did, Vanka did the same. Then before cutting down the Christmas tree his grandfather smoked his pipe, took a long pinch of snuff, and made fun of poor frozen little Vanka. . . . The young fir trees, wrapt in hoar-frost, stood motionless, waiting for which of them would die. Suddenly a hare springing from somewhere would dart over the snowdrift. . . . His grandfather could not help shouting:

"Catch it, catch it, catch it! Ah, short-tailed devil!"

When the tree was down, his grandfather dragged it to the master's house, and there they set about decorating it. The young lady, Olga Ignatyevna, Vanka's great friend, busied herself most about it. When little Vanka's mother, Pelagueya, was still alive, and was servant-woman in the house, Olga Ignatyevna used to stuff him with sugar-candy, and, having nothing to do, taught him to read, write, count up to one hundred, and even to dance the quadrille. When Pelagueya died, they placed the orphan Vanka in the kitchen with his grandfather, and from the kitchen he was sent to Moscow to Aliakhin, the shoemaker.

"Come quick, dear Grandpapa," continued Vanka, "I beseech you for Christ's sake take me from here. Have pity on a poor orphan, for here they beat me, and I am frightfully hungry, and so sad that I can't tell you, I cry all the time. The other day the master hit me on the head with a last; I fell to the ground, and only just returned to life. My life is a misfortune, worse than any dog's. . . . I send greetings to Aliona, to one-eyed Tegor, and the coachman, and don't let anyone have my mouth-organ. I remain, your grandson, Ivan Zhukov, dear Grandpapa, do come."

Vanka folded his sheet of paper in four, and put it into an envelope purchased the night before for a kopek. He thought a little, dipped the pen into the ink, and wrote the address:

"The village, to my grandfather." He then scratched his head, thought again, and added: "Konstantin Makarych." Pleased at not having been interfered with in his writing, he put on his cap, and, without putting on his sheep-skin coat, ran out in his shirtsleeves into the street.

The shopman at the poulterer's, from whom he had inquired the night before, had told him that letters were to be put into post-boxes, and from there they were conveyed over the whole earth in mail troikas by drunken post-boys and to the sound of bells. Vanka ran to the first post-box and slipped his precious letter into the slit.

An hour afterwards, lulled by hope, he was sleeping soundly. In his dreams he saw a stove, by the stove his grandfather sitting with his legs dangling down, barefooted, and reading a letter to the cooks, and Viun walking round the stove wagging his tail.

◇◇◇*Daniel Defoe (1660?-1731). He was born in London as the son of James Foe, a butcher, and changed his name to Defoe around 1703. One of the greatest natural writers in the language, he was extremely prolific, publishing more than 250 works.*

TRUE RELATION OF THE APPARITION OF ONE MRS. VEAL

BY DANIEL DEFOE

This thing is so rare in all its circumstances, and on so good authority, that my reading and conversation have not given me anything like it, It is fit to gratify the most ingenious and serious inquirer. Mrs. Bargrave is the person to whom Mrs. Veal appeared after her death; she is my intimate friend, and I can avouch for her reputation for these fifteen or sixteen years, on my own knowledge; and I can affirm the good character she had from her youth to the time of my acquaintance. Though, since this relation, she is calumniated by some people that are friends to the brother of Mrs. Veal who appeared to think the relation of this appearance to be a reflection, and endeavour what they can to blast Mrs. Bargrave's reputation and to laugh the story out of countenance. But by the circumstances thereof, and the cheerful disposition of Mrs. Bargrave, notwithstanding the ill usage of a very wicked husband, there is not yet the least sign of dejection in her face; nor did I ever hear her let fall a desponding or murmuring expression; nay, not when actually under her husband's barbarity, which I have been a witness to, and several other persons of undoubted reputation.

Now you must know Mrs. Veal was a maiden gentlewoman of about thirty years of age, and for some years past had been troubled with fits, which were perceived coming on her by her going off from her discourse very abruptly to some impertinence. She was maintained by an only brother, and kept his house in Dover. She was a very pious woman, and her brother a very sober man, to all appearance; but now he does all he can to null and quash the story. Mrs. Veal was intimately acquainted with Mrs. Bargrave from her childhood. Mrs. Veal's circumstances were then mean; her father did not take care of his children as he ought, so that they were exposed to hardships. And Mrs. Bargrave in those days had as unkind a father, though she wanted neither for food nor clothing; while Mrs. Veal wanted for both, insomuch that she would often say, "Mrs. Bargrave, you are not only the best, but the only friend I have in the world; and no circumstance of life shall ever dissolve my friendship." They would often condole each other's adverse fortunes, and read together *Drelincourt upon Death,* and other books; and so, like two Christian friends, they comforted each other under their sorrow.

Some time after, Mr. Veal's friends got him a place in the custom-house at Dover, which occasioned Mrs. Veal, by little and little, to fall off from her intimacy with Mrs. Bargrave, though there was never any such thing as a quarrel; but an indifferency came on by degrees, till at last Mrs. Bargrave had not seen her in two years and a half, though above a twelvemonth of the time Mrs. Bargrave hath been absent from Dover, and this last half-year has been in Canterbury about two months of the time, dwelling in a house of her own.

In this house, on the eighth of September, one thousand seven hundred and five, she was sitting alone in the forenoon, thinking over her unfortunate life, and arguing herself into a due resignation to Providence, though her condition seemed hard. "And," said she, "I have been provided for hitherto, and doubt not but I shall be still, and am well satisfied that my afflictions shall end when it is most fit for me." And then took up her sewing work, which she had no sooner done but she hears knocking at the door; she went to see who was there, and this proved to be Mrs. Veal, her old friend, who was in a riding habit. At that moment of time the clock struck twelve at noon.

"Madam," says Mrs. Bargrave, "I am surprised to see you, you who have been so long a stranger"; but told her she was glad to see her, and offered to salute her, which Mrs. Veal complied with, till their lips almost touched, and then Mrs. Veal drew her hand across her own eyes, and said, "I am not very well," and so waived it. She told Mrs. Bargrave she was going a journey, and had a great mind to see her first. "But," says Mrs. Bargrave, "how can you take a journey alone? I am amazed at it, because I know you have a fond brother." "Oh," says Mrs. Veal, "I gave my brother the slip, and came away, because I had so great a desire to see you before I took my journey." So Mrs. Bargrave went in with her into another room within the first, and Mrs. Veal sat her down in an elbow-chair, in which Mrs. Bargrave was sitting when she heard Mrs. Veal knock. "Then," says Mrs. Veal, "my dear friend, I am come to renew our old friendship again, and beg your pardon for my breach of it; and if you can forgive me, you are the best of women." "Oh," says Mrs. Bargrave, "do not mention such a thing; I have not had an uneasy thought about it." "What did you think of me?" says Mrs. Veal. Says Mrs. Bargrave, "I thought you were like the rest of the world, and that prosperity had made you forget yourself and me." Then Mrs. Veal reminded Mrs. Bargrave of the many friendly offices she did her in former days, and much of the conversation they had with each other in the times of their adversity; what books they read, and what comfort in particular they received from Drelincourt's *Book of Death*, which was the best, she said, on the subject ever wrote. She also mentioned Dr. Sherlock, and two Dutch books which were translated, wrote upon death, and several others. But Drelincourt, she said, had the clearest notions of death and of the future state of any who had handled that subject. Then she asked Mrs. Bargrave whether she had Drelincourt. She said, "Yes." Says Mrs. Veal, "Fetch it." And so Mrs. Bargrave goes upstairs and brings it down. Says Mrs. Veal, "Dear Mrs. Bargrave, if the eyes of our faith were as open as the eyes of our body, we should see numbers of angels about us for our guard. The notions we have of Heaven now are nothing like what it is, as Drelincourt says; therefore be comforted under your afflictions, and believe that the Almighty has a particular regard to you, and that your afflictions are marks of God's favour; and when they have done the business they are sent for, they shall be removed from you. And believe me, my dear friend, believe what I say to you, one minute of future happiness will infinitely reward you for all your sufferings. For I can never believe" (and clasps her hand upon her knee with great earnestness, which, indeed, ran through most of her discourse) "that ever God will suffer you to spend all your days in this afflicted state. But be assured that your afflictions shall leave you, or you them, in a short time." She spake in that pathetical and heavenly manner that Mrs. Bargrave wept several times, she was so deeply affected with it.

Then Mrs. Veal mentioned Doctor Kendrick's *Ascetic,* at the end of which he gives an account of the lives of the primitive Christians. Their pattern she recommended to our imitation, and she said, "their conversation was not like this of our age. For now," says she, "there is nothing but vain, frothy discourse, which is far different from theirs. Theirs was to edification, and to build one another up in faith, so that they were not as we are, nor are we as they were. But," said she, "we ought to do as they did; there was a hearty friendship among them; but where is it now to be found?" Says Mrs. Bargrave, "It is hard indeed to find a true friend in these days." Says Mrs. Veal, "Mr. Norris has a fine copy of verses, called *Friendship in Perfection,* which I wonderfully admire. Have you seen the book?" says Mrs. Veal. "No," says Mrs. Bargrave, "but I have the verses of my own writing out." "Have you?" says Mrs. Veal; "then fetch them"; which she did from above stairs, and offered them to Mrs. Veal to read, who refused, and waived the thing, saying, "holding down her head would make it ache"; and then desiring Mrs. Bargrave to read them to her, which she did. As they were admiring *Friendship,* Mrs. Veal said, "Dear Mrs. Bargrave, I shall love you forever." In these verses there is twice used the word Elysian. "Ah!" says Mrs. Veal, "these poets have such names for Heaven." She would often draw her hand across her own eyes, and say, "Mrs. Bargrave, do not you think I am mightily impaired by my fits?" "No," says Mrs. Bargrave; "I think you look as well as ever I knew you."

After this discourse, which the apparition put in much finer words than Mrs. Bargrave said she could pretend to, and as much more as she can remember—for it cannot be thought that an hour and three quarters' conversation could all be retained, though the main of it she thinks she does—she said to Mrs. Bargrave she would have her write a letter to her brother, and tell him she would have him give rings to such and such; and that there was a purse of gold in her cabinet, and that she would have two broad pieces given to her cousin Watson.

Talking at this rate, Mrs. Bargrave thought that a fit was coming upon her, and so placed herself on a chair just before her knees, to keep her from falling to the ground, if her fits should occasion it; for the elbow-chair, she thought, would keep her from falling on either side. And to divert Mrs. Veal, as she thought, took hold of her gown-sleeve several times, and commended it. Mrs. Veal told her it was a scoured silk, and newly made up. But, for all this, Mrs. Veal persisted in her request, and told Mrs. Bargrave she must not deny her. And she would have her tell her brother all their conversation when she had the opportunity. "Dear Mrs. Veal," says Mrs. Bargrave, "it is much better, methinks, to do it yourself." "No," says Mrs. Veal, "though it seems impertinent to you now, you will see more reasons for it hereafter." Mrs. Bargrave, then, to satisfy her importunity, was going to fetch a pen and ink, but Mrs. Veal said, "Let it alone now, but do it when I am gone; but you must be sure to do it"; which was one of the last things she enjoined her at parting, and so she promised her.

Then Mrs. Veal asked for Mrs. Bargrave's daughter. She said she was not at home. "But if you have a mind to see her," says Mrs. Bargrave, "I'll send for her." "Do," says Mrs. Veal; on which she left her, and went to a neighbour's to see her; and by the time Mrs. Bargrave was returning, Mrs. Veal was without the door in the street, in the face of the beast-market, on a Saturday (which is market-day), and stood ready to part as soon as Mrs. Bargrave came to her. She asked her why she was in such haste. She said she must be going, though perhaps she might journey till Monday; and told Mrs. Bargrave she hoped she should see her again at her cousin Watson's house before she went whither she was going. Then she said she would take her leave of her, and walked from Mrs. Bargrave, in her view, till a turning interrupted the sight of her, which was three-quarters after one in the afternoon.

Mrs. Veal died the seventh of September, at twelve o'clock at noon, of her fits, and had not above four hours' senses before her death, in which time she received the sacrament. The next day after Mrs. Veal's appearance, being Sunday, Mrs. Bargrave was

mightily indisposed with a cold and sore throat, that she could not
go out that day; but on Monday morning she sends a person to Captain Watson's to know if Mrs. Veal was there. They wondered at
Mrs. Bargrave's inquiry, and sent her word she was not there, nor
was expected. At this answer, Mrs. Bargrave told the maid she had
certainly mistook the name or made some blunder. And though she
was ill, she put on her hood and went herself to Captain Watson's,
though she knew none of the family, to see if Mrs. Veal was there
or not. They said they wondered at her asking, for that she had not
been in town; they were sure, if she had, she would have been
there. Says Mrs. Bargrave, "I am sure she was with me on Saturday
almost two hours." They said it was impossible, for they must have
seen her if she had. In comes Captain Watson, while they were in
dispute, and said that Mrs. Veal was certainly dead, and the es-
cutcheons were making. This strangely surprised Mrs. Bargrave,
when she sent to the person immediately who had the care of them,
and found it true. Then she related the whole story to Captain Watson's family; and what gown she had on, and how striped; and that
Mrs. Veal told her that it was scoured. Then Mrs. Watson cried
out, "You have seen her indeed, for none knew but Mrs. Veal and
myself that the gown was scoured." And Mrs. Watson owned that
she described the gown exactly; "for," said she, "I helped her to
make it up." This Mrs. Watson blazed all about the town, and
avouched the demonstration of truth of Mrs. Bargrave's seeing Mrs.
Veal's apparition. And Captain Watson carried two gentlemen immediately to Mrs. Bargrave's house to hear the relation from her
own mouth. And when it spread so fast that gentlemen and persons
of quality, the judicious and skeptical part of the world, flocked in
upon her, it at last became such a task that she was forced to go
out of the way; for they were in general extremely satisfied of the
truth of the thing, and plainly saw that Mrs. Bargrave was no hy-
pochondriac, for she always appears with such a cheerful air and
pleasing mien that she has gained the favour and esteem of all the
gentry, and it is thought a great favour if they can but get the relation from her own mouth. I should have told you before that Mrs.
Veal told Mrs. Bargrave that her sister and brother-in-law were just
come down from London to see her. Says Mrs. Bargrave, "How
came you to order matters so strangely?" "It could not be helped,"

said Mrs. Veal. And her brother and sister did come to see her, and entered the town of Dover just as Mrs. Veal was expiring. Mrs. Bargrave asked her whether she would drink some tea. Says Mrs. Veal, "I do not care if I do; but I'll warrant you this mad fellow"—meaning Mrs. Bargrave's husband—"has broke all your trinkets." "But," says Mrs. Bargrave, "I'll get something to drink in for all that"; but Mrs. Veal waived it, and said, "It is no matter; let it alone," and so it passed.

All the time I sat with Mrs. Bargrave, which was some hours, she recollected fresh saying of Mrs. Veal. And one material thing more she told Mrs. Bargrave, that old Mr. Bretton allowed Mrs. Veal ten pounds a year, which was a secret, and unknown to Mrs. Bargrave till Mrs. Veal told her.

Mrs. Bargrave never varies in her story, which puzzles those who doubt of the truth, or are unwilling to believe it. A servant in the neighbour's yard adjoining to Mrs. Bargrave's house heard her talking to somebody an hour of the time Mrs. Veal was with her. Mrs. Bargrave went out to her next neighbour's the very moment she parted with Mrs. Veal, and told her what ravishing conversation she had had with an old friend, and told the whole of it. Drelincourt's *Book of Death* is, since this happened, bought up strangely. And it is to be observed that, notwithstanding all the trouble and fatigue Mrs. Bargrave has undergone upon this account, she never took the value of a farthing, nor suffered her daughter to take anything of anybody, and therefore can have no interest in telling the story.

But Mr. Veal does what he can to stifle the matter, and said he would see Mrs. Bargrave; but yet it is certain matter of fact that he has been at Captain Watson's since the death of his sister, and yet never went near Mrs. Bargrave; and some of his friends report her to be a liar, and that she knew of Mr. Bretton's ten pounds a year. But the person who pretends to say so has the reputation to be a notorious liar among persons whom I know to be of undoubted credit. Now, Mr. Veal is more of a gentleman than to say she lies, but says a bad husband has crazed her; but she needs only present herself, and it will effectually confute that pretense. Mr. Veal says he asked his sister on her death-bed whether she had a mind to dispose of anything. And she said no. Now the things which Mrs. Veal's apparition would have disposed of were so trifling, and nothing of justice aimed at in her disposal, that the design of it appears to me to be only in order to make Mrs. Bargrave satisfy the world of the reality thereof as to what she had seen and heard, and to secure her reputation among the reasonable and understanding part of mankind. And then again, Mr. Veal owns that there was a purse of gold; but it was not found in her cabinet, but in a comb-box. This looks improbable; for that Mrs. Watson owned that Mrs. Veal was so very careful of the key of her cabinet that she would trust nobody with it. And Mrs. Veal's often drawing her hands over her eyes, and asking Mrs. Bargrave whether her fits had not impaired her, looks to me as if she did it on purpose to remind Mrs. Bargrave of her fits, to prepare her not to think it strange that she should put her upon writing to her brother, to dispose of rings and gold, which looks so much like a dying person's bequest; and it took accordingly with Mrs. Bargrave as the effect of her fits coming upon her, and was one of the many instances of her wonderful love to her and care of her, that she should not be affrighted, which, indeed, appears in her whole management, particularly in her coming to her in the daytime, waiving the salutation, and when she was alone; and then the manner of her parting, to prevent a second attempt to salute her.

Now, why Mr. Veal should think this relation a reflection—as it is plain he does, by his endeavouring to stifle it—I cannot imagine; because the generality believe her to be a good spirit, her discourse was so heavenly. Her two great errands were, to comfort Mrs. Bargrave in her affliction, and to ask her forgiveness for breach of friendship, and with a pious discourse to encourage her. So that, after all, to suppose that Mrs. Bargrave could hatch such an invention as this, from Friday noon to Saturday noon—supposing that she knew of Mrs. Veal's death the very first moment—without jumbling circumstances, and without any interest, too, she must be more witty, fortunate, and wicked, too, than any indifferent person, I dare say, will allow. I asked Mrs. Bargrave several times if she was sure she felt the gown. She answered modestly, "If my senses be to be relied on, I am sure of it." I asked her if she heard a sound when she clapped her hand upon her knee. She said she did not remember she did, but said she appeared to be as much a substance as I did who talked with her. "And I may," said she, "be as soon persuaded that your apparition is talking to me now as that I did not really see her; for I was under no manner of fear, and received her as a friend, and parted with her as such. I would not," says she, "give one farthing to make any one believe it; I have no interest in it; nothing but trouble is entailed upon me for a long time, for aught I know; and, had it not come to light by accident, it would never have been made public." But now she says she will make her own private use of it, and keep herself out of the way as much as she can; and so she has done since. She says she had a gentleman who came thirty miles to her to hear the relation; and that she had told it to a room full of people at the time. Several particular gentlemen have had the story from Mrs. Bargrave's own mouth.

This thing has very much affected me, and I am as well satisfied as I am of the best-grounded matter of fact. And why we should dispute matter of fact, because we cannot solve things of which we can have no certain or demonstrative notions, seems strange to me; Mrs. Bargrave's authority and sincerity alone would have been undoubted in any other case.

◈◈◈*Thomas de Quincey (1785-1859). English essayist, critic. He wrote the* Confessions of an English Opium Eater, *many essays and dream visions and a number of tales—all in an ornate prose marked by superb imagery. "Savannah-la-mar" is one of his recorded visions.*

SAVANNAH-LA-MAR

BY THOMAS DE QUINCEY

God smote Savannah-la-mar, and in one night, by earthquake, removed her, with all her towers standing and population sleeping, from the steadfast foundations of the shore to the coral floors of ocean. And God said,—"Pompeii did I bury and conceal from men through seventeen centuries: this city I will bury, but not conceal. She shall be a monument to men of my mysterious anger, set in azure light through generations to come; for I will enshrine her in a crystal dome of my tropic seas." This city, therefore, like a mighty galleon with all her apparel mounted, streamers flying, and tackling perfect, seems floating along the noiseless depths of ocean; and oftentimes in glassy calms, through the translucid atmosphere of water that now stretches like an air-woven awning above the silent encampment, mariners from every clime look down into her courts and terraces, count her gates, and number the spires of her churches. She is one ample cemetery, and *has* been for many a year; but, in the mighty calms that brood for weeks over tropic latitudes, she fascinates the eye with a *Fata-Morgana* revelation, as of human life still subsisting in submarine asylums sacred from the storms that torment our upper air.

Thither, lured by the loveliness of cerulean depths, by the peace of human dwellings privileged from molestation, by the gleam of marble altars sleeping in everlasting sanctity, oftentimes in dreams did I and the Dark Interpreter cleave the watery veil that divided us from her streets. We looked into the belfries, where the pendulous bells were waiting in vain for the summons which should awaken their marriage peals; together we touched the mighty organ-keys, that sang no *jubilates* for the ear of heaven, that sang no requiems for the ear of human sorrow; together we searched the silent nurseries, where the children were all asleep, and *had* been asleep through five generations. "They are waiting for the heavenly dawn," whispered the Interpreter to himself: "and, when *that* comes, the bells and the organs will utter a *jubilate* repeated by the echoes of Paradise." Then, turning to me, he said,—"This is sad, this is piteous; but less would not have sufficed for the purpose of God. Look here. Put into a Roman clepsydra one hundred drops of water; let these run out as the sands in an hour-glass, every drop measuring the hundredth part of a second, so that each shall represent but the three-hundred-and-sixty-thousandth part of an hour. Now, count the drops as they race along; and, when the fiftieth of the hundred is passing, behold! forty-nine are not, because already they have perished, and fifty are not, because they are yet to come. You see, therefore, how narrow, how incalculably narrow, is the true and actual present. Of that time which we call the present, hardly a hundredth part but belongs either to a past which has fled, or to a future which is still on the wing. It has perished or it is not yet born. It was, or it is not. Yet even this approximation to the truth is *infinitely* false. For again subdivide that solitary drop, which only was found to represent the present, into a lower series of similar fractions, and the actual present which you arrest measures now but the thirty-sixth-millionth of an hour; and so by infinite declensions the true and very present, in which we only live and enjoy, will vanish into a mote of a mote, distinguishable only by a heavenly vision. Therefore the present, which only man possesses, offers less capacity for his footing than the slenderest film that ever spider twisted from her womb. Therefore, also, even this incalculable shadow from the narrowest pencil of moonlight is more transitory than geometry can measure, or thought of angel can overtake. The time which *is* contracts into a mathematic point; and even that point perishes a thousand times before we can utter its birth. All is finite in the present; and even that finite is infinite in its velocity of flight towards death. But in God there is nothing finite; but in God there is nothing transitory; but in God there *can* be nothing that tends to death. Therefore it follows that for God there can be no present. The future is the present of God, and to the future it is that he sacrifices the human present. Therefore it is that he works by earthquake. Therefore it is that he works by grief. O, deep is the ploughing of earthquake! O, deep"—(and his voice swelled like a *sanctus* rising from the choir of a cathedral)—"O, deep is the ploughing of grief! But oftentimes less would not suffice for the agriculture of God. Upon a night of earthquake he builds a thousand years of pleasant habitations for man. Upon the sorrow of an infant he raises oftentimes from human intellects glorious vintages that could not else have been. Less than these fierce ploughshares would not have stirred the stubborn soil. The one is needed for the earth, our planet,—for earth itself as the dwelling place of man; but the other is needed yet oftener for God's mightiest instrument,—yes" (and he looked solemnly at myself), "is needed for the mysterious children of the earth!"

◇◇◇*Feodor Mikhailovich Dostoyevsky (1821-1881). The great Russian novelist and journalist, whose* The Brothers Karamazov *is often called the world's finest novel. Leo Tolstoy considered his* The House of the Dead *his best work. Others are* Crime and Punishment, The Idiot, The Possessed, *and numerous short stories and novellas, especially, among the latter,* Notes from Underground.

THE HEAVENLY CHRISTMAS TREE

BY FEODOR MIKHAILOVICH DOSTOYEVSKY

I am a novelist, and I suppose I have made up this story. I write "I suppose," though I know for a fact that I have made it up, but yet I keep fancying that it must have happened on Christmas Eve in some great town in a time of terrible frost.

I have a vision of a boy, a little boy, six years old or even younger. This boy woke up that morning in a cold damp cellar. He was dressed in a sort of little dressing-gown and was shivering with cold. There was a cloud of white steam from his breath, and sitting on a box in the corner, he blew the steam out of his mouth and amused himself in his dullness watching it float away. But he was terribly hungry. Several times that morning he went up to the plank bed where his sick mother was lying on a mattress as thin as a pancake, with some sort of bundle under her head for a pillow. How had she come here? She must have come with her boy from some other town and suddenly fallen ill. The landlady who let the "corners" had been taken two days before to the police station, the lodgers were out and about as the holiday was so near, and the only one left had been lying for the last twenty-four hours dead drunk, not having waited for Christmas. In another corner of the room a wretched old woman of eighty, who had once been a children's nurse but was now left to die friendless, was moaning and groaning with rheumatism, scolding and grumbling at the boy so that he was afraid to go near her corner. He had got a drink of water in the outer room, but could not find a crust anywhere, and had been on the point of wak-

(Translated by Constance Garnett.)

ing his mother a dozen times. He felt frightened at last in the darkness: it had long been dusk, but no light was kindled. Touching his mother's face, he was surprised that she did not move at all, and that she was as cold as the wall. "It is very cold here," he thought. He stood a little, unconsciously letting his hands rest on the dead woman's shoulders, then he breathed on his fingers to warm them, and then quietly fumbling for his cap on the bed, he went out of the cellar. He would have gone earlier, but was afraid of the big dog which had been howling all day at the neighbour's door at the top of the stairs. But the dog was not there now, and he went out into the street.

Mercy on us, what a town! He had never seen anything like it before. In the town from which he had come, it was always such black darkness at night. There was one lamp for the whole street, the little, low-pitched, wooden houses were closed up with shutters, there was no one to be seen in the street after dusk, all the people shut themselves up in their houses, and there was nothing but the howling of packs of dogs, hundreds and thousands of them barking and howling all night. But there it was so warm and he was given food, while here—oh, dear, if he only had something to eat! And what a noise and rattle here, what light and what people, horses and carriages, and what a frost! The frozen steam hung in clouds over the horses, over their warmly breathing mouths; their hoofs clanged against the stones through the powdery snow, and everyone pushed so, and—oh, dear, how he longed for some morsel to eat, and how wretched he suddenly felt. A policeman walked by and turned away to avoid seeing the boy.

There was another street—oh, what a wide one, here he would be run over for certain; how everyone was shouting, racing and driving along, and the light, the light! And what was this? A huge glass window, and through the window a tree reaching up to the ceiling; it was a fir tree, and on it were ever so many lights, gold papers and apples and little dolls and horses; and there were children clean and dressed in their best running about the room, laughing and playing and eating and drinking something. And then a little girl began dancing with one of the boys, what a pretty little girl! And he could hear the music through the window. The boy looked and wondered and laughed, though his toes were aching with the cold and his fingers were red and stiff so that it hurt him to move them. And all at once the boy remembered how his toes and fingers hurt him, and began crying, and ran on; and again through another window-pane he saw another Christmas tree, and on a table cakes of all sorts—almond cakes, red cakes and yellow cakes, and three grand young ladies were sitting there, and they gave the cakes to any one who went up to them, and the door kept opening, lots of gentlemen and ladies went in from the street. The boy crept up, suddenly opened the door and went in. Oh, how they shouted at him and waved him back! One lady went up to him hurriedly and slipped a kopeck into his hand, and with her own hands opened the door into the street for him! How frightened he was. And the kopeck rolled away and clinked upon the steps; he could not bend his red fingers to hold it right. The boy ran away and went on, where he did not know. He was ready to cry again but he was afraid, and ran on and on and blew his fingers. And he was miserable because he felt suddenly so lonely and terrified, and all at once, mercy on us! What was this again? People were standing in a crowd admiring. Behind a glass window there were three little dolls, dressed in red and green dresses, and exactly, exactly as though they were alive. One was a little old man sitting and playing a big violin, the two others were standing close by and playing little violins, and nodding in time, and looking at one another, and their lips moved, they were speaking, actually speaking, only one couldn't hear through the glass. And at first the boy thought they were alive, and when he grasped that they were dolls he laughed. He had never seen such dolls before, and had no idea there were such dolls! And he wanted to cry, but he felt amused, amused by the dolls. All at once he fancied that some one caught at his smock behind: a wicked big boy was standing beside him and suddenly hit him on the head, snatched off his cap and tripped him up. The boy fell down on the ground, at once there was a shout, he was numb with fright, he jumped up and ran away. He ran, and not knowing where he was going, ran in at the gate of some one's courtyard, and sat down behind a stack of wood: "They won't find me here, besides it's dark!"

He sat huddled up and was breathless from fright, and all at once, quite suddenly, he felt so happy: his hands and feet suddenly left off aching and grew so warm, as warm as though he were on a stove; then he shivered all over, then he gave a start, why, he must have been asleep. How nice to have a sleep here! "I'll sit here a little and go and look at the dolls again," said the boy, and smiled thinking of them. "Just as though they were alive! . . ." And suddenly he heard his mother singing over him. "Mammy, I am asleep; how nice it is to sleep here!"

"Come to my Christmas tree, little one," a soft voice suddenly whispered over his head.

He thought that this was still his mother, but no, it was not she. Who it was calling him, he could not see, but someone bent over and embraced him in the darkness; and he stretched out his hands to him, and . . . and all at once—oh, what a bright light! Oh, what a Christmas tree! And yet it was not a fir tree, he had never seen a tree like that! Where was he now? Everything was bright and shining, and all round him were dolls; but no, they were not dolls, they were little boys and girls, only so bright and shining. They all came flying round him, they all kissed him, took him and carried him along with them, and he was flying himself, and he saw that his mother was looking at him and laughing joyfully. "Mammy, Mammy; oh, how nice it is here, Mammy!" And again he kissed the children and wanted to tell them at once of those dolls in the shop window.

"Who are you, boys? Who are you, girls?" he asked, laughing and admiring them.

"This is Christ's Christmas tree," they answered. "Christ always has a Christmas tree on this day, for the little children who have no tree of their own . . ." And he found out that all these little boys and girls were children just like himself; that some had been frozen in the baskets in which they had as babies been laid on the doorsteps of well-to-do Petersburg people, others had been boarded out with Finnish women by the Foundling and had been suffocated, others had died at their starved mother's breasts (in the Samara famine), others had died in the third-class railway carriages from the foul air; and yet they were all here, they were all like angels about Christ, and He was in the midst of them and held out His hands to them and blessed them and their sinful mothers. . . . And the mothers of these children stood on one side weeping; each one knew her boy or girl, and the children flew up to them and kissed them and wiped away their tears with their little hands, and begged them not to weep because they were so happy.

And down below in the morning the porter found the little dead body of the frozen child on the woodstack; they sought out his mother too. . . . She had died before him. They met before the Lord God in heaven.

Why have I made up such a story, so out of keeping with an ordinary diary, and a writer's above all? And I promised two stories dealing with real events! But that is just it, I keep fancying that all this may have happened really—that is, what took place in the cellar and on the woodstack; but as for Christ's Christmas tree, I cannot tell you whether that could have happened or not.

◇◇◇*William Faulkner (1897–1962). Grew up in Oxford, Mississippi. Worked on a newspaper in New Orleans in the middle twenties, met Sherwood Anderson there and was influenced by him in style and subject matter. He wrote novels that portrayed the degeneracy of Southern genteel society, including* The Sound and the Fury, As I Lay Dying *and* Intruder in the Dust. *He was a prolific writer of novels and short stories and one of the most important American writers of his time.*

THAT EVENING SUN GO DOWN

BY WILLIAM FAULKNER

Monday is no different from any other week day in Jefferson now. The streets are paved now, and the telephone and the electric companies are cutting down more and more of the shade trees—the water oaks, the maples and locusts and elms—to make room for iron poles bearing clusters of bloated and ghostly and bloodless grapes, and we have a city laundry which makes the rounds on Monday morning, gathering the bundles of clothes into bright-colored, specially made motor-cars: the soiled wearing of a whole week now flees apparition-like behind alert and irritable electric horns, with a long diminishing noise of rubber and asphalt like a tearing of silk, and even the Negro women who still take in white peoples' washing after the old custom, fetch and deliver it in automobiles.

But fifteen years ago, on Monday morning the quiet, dusty, shady streets would be full of Negro women with, balanced on their steady turbaned heads, bundles of clothes tied up in sheets, almost as large as cotton bales, carried so without touch of hand between the kitchen door of the white house and the blackened wash-pot beside a cabin door in Negro Hollow.

Nancy would set her bundle on the top of her head, then upon the bundle in turn she would set the black straw sailor hat which she wore Winter and Summer. She was tall, with a high, sad face sunken a little where her teeth were missing. Sometimes we would go a part of the way down the lane and across the pasture with her, to watch the balanced bundle and the hat that never bobbed nor wavered, even when she walked down into the ditch and climbed out again and stooped through the fence. She would go down on her hands and knees and crawl through the gap, her head rigid, up-tilted, the bundle steady as a rock or a balloon, and rise to her feet and go on.

Sometimes the husbands of the washing women would fetch and deliver the clothes, but Jubah never did that for Nancy, even before father told him to stay away from our house, even when Dilsey was sick and Nancy would come to cook for us.

And then about half the time we'd have to go down the lane to Nancy's house and tell her to come on and get breakfast. We would stop at the ditch, because father told us to not have anything to do with Jubah—he was a short black man, with a razor scar down his face—and we would throw rocks at Nancy's house until she came to the door, leaning her head around it without any clothes on.

"What yawl mean, chunking my house?" Nancy said. "What you little devils mean?"

"Father says for you to come and get breakfast," Caddy said. "Father says it's over a half an hour now, and you've got to come this minute."

"I ain't studying no breakfast," Nancy said. "I going to get my sleep out."

"I bet you're drunk," Jason said. "Father says you're drunk. Are you drunk, Nancy?"

"Who says I is?" Nancy said. "I got to get my sleep out. I ain't studying no breakfast."

So after a while we quit chunking the house and went back home. When she finally came, it was too late for me to go to school. So we thought it was whiskey until that day when they arrested her again and they were taking her to jail and they passed Mr. Stovall. He was the cashier in the bank and a deacon in the Baptist church, and Nancy began to say:

"When you going to pay me, white man? When you going to pay me, white man? It's been three times now since you paid me a cent——" Mr. Stovall knocked her down, but she kept on saying,

"When you going to pay me, white man? It's been three times now since——" until Mr. Stovall kicked her in the mouth with his heel and the marshal caught Mr. Stovall back, and Nancy lying in the street, laughing. She turned her head and spat out some blood and teeth and said, "It's been three times now since he paid me a cent."

That was how she lost her teeth, and all that day they told about Nancy and Mr. Stovall, and all that night the ones that passed the jail could hear Nancy singing and yelling. They could see her hands holding to the window bars, and a lot of them stopped along the fence, listening to her and to the jailer trying to make her shut up. She didn't shut up until just before daylight, when the jailer began to hear a bumping and scraping upstairs and he went up there and found Nancy hanging from the window bar. He said that it was cocaine and not whiskey, because no nigger would try to commit suicide unless he was full of cocaine, because a nigger full of cocaine was not a nigger any longer.

The jailer cut her down and revived her; then he beat her, whipped her. She had hung herself with her dress. She had fixed it all right, but when they arrested her she didn't have on anything except a dress and so she didn't have anything to tie her hands with and she couldn't make her hands let go of the window ledge. So the jailer heard the noise and ran up there and found Nancy hanging from the window, stark naked.

When Dilsey was sick in her cabin and Nancy was cooking for us, we could see her apron swelling out; that was before father told Jubah to stay away from the house. Jubah was in the kitchen, sitting behind the stove, with his razor scar on his black face like a piece of dirty string. He said it was a watermelon that Nancy had under her dress. And it was Winter, too.

"Where did you get a watermelon in the Winter?" Caddy said.

"I didn't," Jubah said. "It wasn't me that give it to her. But I can cut it down, same as if it was."

"What makes you want to talk that way before these chillen?" Nancy said. "Whyn't you go on to work? You done et. You want Mr. Jason to catch you hanging around his kitchen, talking that way before these chillen?"

"Talking what way, Nancy?" Caddy said.

"I can't hang around white man's kitchen," Jubah said. "But

white man can hang around mine. White man can come in my
house, but I can't stop him. When white man want to come in my
house, I ain't got no house. I can't stop him, but he can't kick me
outen it. He can't do that."

Dilsey was still sick in her cabin. Father told Jubah to stay off
our place. Dilsey was still sick. It was a long time. We were in the
library after supper.

"Isn't Nancy through yet?" mother said. "It seems to me that she
has had plenty of time to have finished the dishes."

"Let Quentin go and see," father said. "Go and see if Nancy is
through, Quentin. Tell her she can go on home."

I went to the kitchen. Nancy was through. The dishes were put
away and the fire was out. Nancy was sitting in a chair, close to the
cold stove. She looked at me.

"Mother wants to know if you are through," I said.

"Yes," Nancy said. She looked at me. "I done finished." She
looked at me.

"What is it?" I said. "What is it?"

"I ain't nothing but a nigger," Nancy said. "It ain't none of my
fault."

She looked at me, sitting in the chair before the cold stove, the
sailor hat on her head. I went back to the library. It was the cold
stove and all, when you think of a kitchen being warm and busy
and cheerful. And with a cold stove and the dishes all put away, and
nobody wanting to eat at that hour.

"Is she through?" mother said.

"Yessum," I said.

"What is she doing?" mother said.

"She's not doing anything. She's through."

"I'll go and see," father said.

"Maybe she's waiting for Jubah to come and take her home,"
Caddy said.

"Jubah is gone," I said. Nancy told us how one morning she woke
up and Jubah was gone.

"He quit me," Nancy said. "Done gone to Memphis, I reckon.
Dodging them city *po*-lice for a while, I reckon."

"And a good riddance," father said. "I hope he stays there."

"Nancy's scaired of the dark," Jason said.

"So are you," Caddy said.

"I'm not," Jason said.

"Scairy cat," Caddy said.

"I'm not," Jason said.

"You, Candace!" mother said. Father came back.

"I am going to walk down the lane with Nancy," he said. "She says Jubah is back."

"Has she seen him?" mother said.

"No. Some Negro sent her word that he was back in town. I won't be long."

"You'll leave me alone, to take Nancy home?" mother said. "Is her safety more precious to you than mine?"

"I won't be long," father said.

"You'll leave these children unprotected, with that Negro about?"

"I'm going too," Caddy said. "Let me go, father."

"What would he do with them, if he were unfortunate enough to have them?" father said.

"I want to go, too," Jason said.

"Jason!" mother said. She was speaking to father. You could tell that by the way she said it. Like she believed that all day father had been trying to think of doing the thing that she wouldn't like the most, and that she knew all the time that after a while he would think of it. I stayed quiet, because father and I both knew that mother would want him to make me stay with her, if she just thought of it in time. So father didn't look at me. I was the oldest. I was nine and Caddy was seven and Jason was five.

"Nonsense," father said. "We won't be long."

Nancy had her hat on. We came to the lane. "Jubah always been good to me," Nancy said. "Whenever he had two dollars, one of them was mine." We walked in the lane. "If I can just get through the lane," Nancy said, "I be all right then."

The lane was always dark. "This is where Jason got scared on Hallowe'en," Caddy said.

"I didn't," Jason said.

"Can't Aunt Rachel do anything with him?" father said. Aunt Rachel was old. She lived in a cabin beyond Nancy's, by herself. She had white hair and she smoked a pipe in the door, all day long; she didn't work any more. They said she was Jubah's mother. Sometimes she said she was and sometimes she said she wasn't any kin to Jubah.

"Yes you did," Caddy said. "You were scairder than Frony. You were scairder than T. P. even. Scairder than niggers."

"Can't nobody do nothing with him," Nancy said. "He say I done woke up the devil in him, and ain't but one thing going to lay it again."

"Well, he's gone now," father said. "There's nothing for you to be afraid of now. And if you'd just let white men alone."

"Let what white men alone?" Caddy said. "How let them alone?"

"He ain't gone nowhere," Nancy said. "I can feel him. I can feel him now, in this lane. He hearing us talk, every word, hid somewhere, waiting. I ain't seen him, and I ain't going to see him again but once more, with that razor. That razor on that string down his back, inside his shirt. And then I ain't going to be even surprised."

"I wasn't scaired," Jason said.

"If you'd behave yourself, you'd have kept out of this," father said. "But it's all right now. He's probably in St. Louis now. Probably got another wife by now and forgot all about you."

"If he has, I better not find out about it," Nancy said. "I'd stand there and every time he wropped her, I'd cut that arm off. I'd cut his head off and I'd slit her belly and I'd shove——"

"Hush," father said.

"Slit whose belly, Nancy?" Caddy said.

"I wasn't scared," Jason said. "I'd walk right down this lane by myself."

"Yah," Caddy said. "You wouldn't dare to put your foot in it if we were not with you."

Dilsey was still sick, and so we took Nancy home every night until mother said, "How much longer is this going to go on? I to be left alone in this big house while you take home a frightened Negro?"

We fixed a pallet in the kitchen for Nancy. One night we waked up, hearing the sound. It was not singing and it was not crying, coming up the dark stairs. There was a light in mother's room and we heard father going down the hall, down the back stairs, and Caddy and I went into the hall. The floor was cold. Our toes curled away from the floor while we listened to the sound. It was like singing and it wasn't like singing, like the sounds that Negroes make.

Then it stopped and we heard father going down the back stairs, and we went to the head of the stairs. Then the sound began again, in the stairway, not loud, and we could see Nancy's eyes half way up the stairs, against the wall. They looked like cat's eyes do, like a big cat against the wall, watching us. When we come down the steps to where she was she quit making the sound again, and we stood there until father came back up from the kitchen, with his pistol in his hand. He went back down with Nancy and they came back with Nancy's pallet.

We spread the pallet in our room. After the light in mother's room went off, we could see Nancy's eyes again. "Nancy," Caddy whispered, "are you asleep, Nancy?"

Nancy whispered something. It was oh or no, I don't know which. Like nobody had made it, like it came from nowhere and went nowhere, until it was like Nancy was not there at all; that I had looked so hard at her eyes on the stair that they had got printed on my eyelids, like the sun does when you have closed your eyes and there is no sun. "Jesus," Nancy whispered. "Jesus."

"Was it Jubah?" Caddy whispered. "Did he try to come into the kitchen?"

"Jesus," Nancy said. Like this: Jeeeeeeeeeeeeeeesus, until the sound went out like a match or a candle does.

"Can you see us, Nancy?" Caddy whispered. "Can you see our eyes too?"

"I ain't nothing but a nigger," Nancy said. "God knows. God knows."

"What did you see down there in the kitchen?" Caddy whispered. "What tried to get in?"

"God knows," Nancy said. We could see her eyes. "God knows."

Dilsey got well. She cooked dinner. "You'd better stay in bed a day or two longer," father said.

"What for?" Dilsey said. "If I had been a day later, this place would be to rack and ruin. Get on out of here, now, and let me get my kitchen straight again."

Dilsey cooked supper, too. And that night, just before dark, Nancy came into the kitchen.

"How do you know he's back?" Dilsey said. "You ain't seen him."

"Jubah is a nigger," Jason said.

"I can feel him," Nancy said. "I can feel him laying yonder in the ditch."

"Tonight?" Dilsey said. "Is he there tonight?"

"Dilsey's a nigger too," Jason said.

"You try to eat something," Dilsey said.

"I don't want nothing," Nancy said.

"I ain't a nigger," Jason said.

"Drink some coffee," Dilsey said. She poured a cup of coffee for Nancy. "Do you know he's out there tonight? How come you know it's tonight?"

"I know," Nancy said. "He's there, waiting. I know. I done lived with him too long. I know what he fixing to do fore he knows it himself."

"Drink some coffee," Dilsey said. Nancy held the cup to her mouth and blew into the cup. Her mouth pursed out like a spreading adder's, like a rubber mouth, like she had blown all the color out of her lips with blowing the coffee.

"I ain't a nigger," Jason said. "Are you a nigger, Nancy?"

"I hell-born, child," Nancy said. "I won't be nothing soon. I going back where I come from soon."

She began to drink the coffee. While she was drinking, holding the cup in both hands, she began to make the sound again. She made the sound into the cup and the coffee sploshed out on to her hands and her dress. Her eyes looked at us and she sat there, her elbows on her knees, holding the cup in both hands, looking at us across the wet cup, making the sound.

"Look at Nancy," Jason said. "Nancy can't cook for us now. Dilsey's got well now."

"You hush up," Dilsey said. Nancy held the cup in both hands, looking at us, making the sound, like there were two of them: one looking at us and the other making the sound. "Whyn't you let Mr. Jason telefoam the marshal?" Dilsey said. Nancy stopped then, holding the cup in her long brown hands. She tried to drink some coffee again, but it sploshed out of the cup, on to her hands and her dress, and she put the cup down. Jason watched her.

"I can't swallow it," Nancy said. "I swallows but it won't go down me."

"You go down to the cabin," Dilsey said. "Frony will fix you a pallet and I'll be there soon."

"Won't no nigger stop him," Nancy said.

"I ain't a nigger," Jason said. "Am I, Dilsey?"

"I reckon not," Dilsey said. She looked at Nancy. "I don't reckon so. What you going to do, then?"

Nancy looked at us. Her eyes went fast, like she was afraid there wasn't time to look, without hardly moving at all. She looked at us, at all three of us at one time. "You member that night I stayed in yawls' room?" she said. She told about how we waked up early the next morning, and played. We had to play quiet, on her pallet, until father woke and it was time for her to go down and get breakfast. "Go and ask you maw to let me stay here tonight," Nancy said. "I won't need no pallet. We can play some more," she said.

Caddy asked mother. Jason went too. "I can't have Negroes sleeping in the house," mother said. Jason cried. He cried until mother said he couldn't have any dessert for three days if he didn't stop. Then Jason said he would stop if Dilsey would make a choco-late cake. Father was there.

"Why don't you do something about it?" mother said. "What do we have officers for?"

"Why is Nancy afraid of Jubah?" Caddy said. "Are you afraid of father, mother?"

"What could they do?" father said. "If Nancy hasn't seen him, how could the officers find him?"

"Then why is she afraid?" mother said.

"She says he is there. She says she knows he is there tonight."

"Yet we pay taxes," mother said. "I must wait here alone in this big house while you take a Negro woman home."

"You know that I am not lying outside with a razor," father said.

"I'll stop if Dilsey will make a chocolate cake," Jason said. Mother told us to go out and father said he didn't know if Jason would get a chocolate cake or not, but he knew what Jason was going to get in about a minute. We went back to the kitchen and told Nancy.

"Father said for you to go home and lock the door, and you'll be all right," Caddy said. "All right from what, Nancy? Is Jubah mad at you?" Nancy was holding the coffee cup in her hands, her elbow on her knees and her hands holding the cup between her knees. She was looking into the cup. "What have you done that made Jubah mad?" Caddy said. Nancy let the cup go. It didn't break on the floor, but the coffee spilled out, and Nancy sat there with her hands making the shape of the cup. She began to make the sound again, not loud. Not singing and not un-singing. We watched her.

"Here," Dilsey said. "You quit that, now. You get a-holt of yourself. You wait here. I going to get Versh to walk home with you." Dilsey went out.

We looked at Nancy. Her shoulders kept shaking, but she had quit making the sound. We watched her. "What's Jubah going to do to you?" Caddy said. "He went away."

Nancy looked at us. "We had fun that night I stayed in yawls' room, didn't we?"

"I didn't," Jason said. "I didn't have any fun."

"You were asleep," Caddy said. "You were not there."

"Let's go down to my house and have some more fun," Nancy said.

"Mother won't let us," I said. "It's too late now."

"Don't bother her," Nancy said. "We can tell her in the morning. She won't mind."

"She wouldn't let us," I said.

"Don't ask her now," Nancy said. "Don't bother her now."

"They didn't say we couldn't go," Caddy said.

"We didn't ask," I said.

"If you go, I'll tell," Jason said.

"We'll have fun," Nancy said. "They won't mind, just to my house. I been working for yawl a long time. They won't mind."

"I'm not afraid to go," Caddy said. "Jason is the one that's afraid. He'll tell."

"I'm not," Jason said.

"Yes you are," Caddy said. "You'll tell."

"I won't tell," Jason said. "I'm not afraid."

"Jason ain't afraid to go with me," Nancy said. "Is you, Jason?"

"Jason is going to tell," Caddy said. The lane was dark. We passed the pasture gate. "I bet if something was to jump out from behind that gate, Jason would holler."

"I wouldn't," Jason said. We walked down the lane. Nancy was talking loud.

"What are you talking so loud for, Nancy?" Caddy said.

"Who; me?" Nancy said. "Listen at Quentin and Caddy and Jason saying I'm talking loud."

"You talk like there was four of us here," Caddy said. "You talk like father was here too."

"Who; me talking loud, Mr. Jason?" Nancy said.

"Nancy called Jason 'Mister,'" Caddy said.

"Listen how Caddy and Quentin and Jason talk," Nancy said.

"We're not talking loud," Caddy said. "You're the one that's talking like father——"

"Hush," Nancy said; "hush, Mr. Jason."

"Nancy called Jason 'Mister' aguh——"

"Hush," Nancy said. She was talking loud when we crossed the ditch and stooped through the fence where she used to stoop through with the clothes on her head. Then we came to her house. We were going fast then. She opened the door. The smell of the house was like the lamp and the smell of Nancy was like the wick, like they were waiting for one another to smell. She lit the lamp and closed the door and put the bar up. Then she quit talking loud, looking at us.

"What're we going to do?" Caddy said.

"What you all want to do?" Nancy said.

"You said we would have some fun," Caddy said.

There was something about Nancy's house; something you could smell. Jason smelled it, even. "I don't want to stay here," he said. "I want to go home."

"Go home, then," Caddy said.

"I don't want to go by myself," Jason said.

"We're going to have some fun," Nancy said.

"How?" Caddy said.

Nancy stood by the door. She was looking at us, only it was like she had emptied her eyes, like she had quit using them.

"What do you want to do?" she said.

"Tell us a story," Caddy said. "Can you tell a story?"

"Yes," Nancy said.

"Tell it," Caddy said. We looked at Nancy. "You don't know any stories," Caddy said.

"Yes," Nancy said. "Yes I do."

She came and sat down in a chair before the hearth. There was some fire there; she built it up; it was already hot. You didn't need a fire. She built a good blaze. She told a story. She talked like her eyes looked, like her eyes watching us and her voice talking to us did not belong to her. Like she was living somewhere else, waiting somewhere else. She was outside the house. Her voice was there and the shape of her, the Nancy that could stoop under the fence with the bundle of clothes balanced as though without weight, like a balloon, on her head, was there. But that was all. "And so this here queen come walking up to the ditch, where that bad man was hiding. She was walking up the ditch, and she say, 'If I can just get past this here ditch,' was what she say. . . ."

"What ditch?" Caddy said. "A ditch like that one out there? Why did the queen go into the ditch?"

"To get to her house," Nancy said. She looked at us. "She had to cross that ditch to get home."

"Why did she want to go home?" Caddy said.

Nancy looked at us. She quit talking. She looked at us. Jason's legs stuck straight out of his pants, because he was little. "I don't think that's a good story," he said. "I want to go home."

"Maybe we had better," Caddy said. She got up from the floor. "I bet they are looking for us right now." She went toward the door.

"No," Nancy said. "Don't open it." She got up quick and passed Caddy. She didn't touch the door, the wooden bar.

"Why not?" Caddy said.

"Come back to the lamp," Nancy said. "We'll have fun. You don't have to go."

"We ought to go," Caddy said. "Unless we have a lot of fun." She and Nancy came back to the fire, the lamp.

"I want to go home," Jason said. "I'm going to tell."

"I know another story," Nancy said. She stood close to the lamp.

She looked at Caddy, like when your eyes look up at a stick balanced on your nose. She had to look down to see Caddy, but her eyes looked like that, like when you are balancing a stick.

"I won't listen to it," Jason said. "I'll bang on the floor."

"It's a good one," Nancy said. "It's better than the other one."

"What's it about?" Caddy said. Nancy was standing by the lamp. Her hand was on the lamp, against the light, long and brown.

"Your hand is on that hot globe," Caddy said. "Don't it feel hot to your hand?"

Nancy looked at her hand on the lamp chimney. She took her hand away, slow. She stood there, looking at Caddy, wringing her long hand as though it were tied to her wrist with a string.

"Let's do something else," Caddy said.

"I want to go home," Jason said.

"I got some popcorn," Nancy said. She looked at Caddy and then at Jason and then at me and then at Caddy again. "I got some popcorn."

"I don't like popcorn," Jason said. "I'd rather have candy."

Nancy looked at Jason. "You can hold the popper." She was still wringing her hand; it was long and limp and brown.

"All right," Jason said. "I'll stay a while if I can do that. Caddy can't hold it. I'll want to go home, if Caddy holds the popper."

Nancy built up the fire. "Look at Nancy putting her hands in the fire," Caddy said. "What's the matter with you, Nancy?"

"I got popcorn," Nancy said. "I got some." She took the popper from under the bed. It was broken. Jason began to cry.

"We can't have any popcorn," he said.

"We ought to go home, anyway," Caddy said. "Come on, Quentin."

"Wait," Nancy said; "wait. I can fix it. Don't you want to help me fix it?"

"I don't think I want any," Caddy said. "It's too late now."

"You help me, Jason," Nancy said. "Don't you want to help me?"

"No," Jason said. "I want to go home."

"Hush," Nancy said; "hush. Watch. Watch me. I can fix it so Jason can hold it and pop the corn." She got a piece of wire and fixed the popper.

"It won't hold good," Caddy said.

"Yes it will," Nancy said. "Yawl watch. Yawl help me shell the corn."

The corn was under the bed too. We shelled it into the popper and Nancy helped Jason hold the popper over the fire.

"It's not popping," Jason said. "I want to go home."

"You wait," Nancy said. "It'll begin to pop. We'll have fun then." She was sitting close to the fire. The lamp was turned up so high it was beginning to smoke.

"Why don't you turn it down some?" I said.

"It's all right," Nancy said. "I'll clean it. Yawl wait. The popcorn will start in a minute."

"I don't believe it's going to start," Caddy said. "We ought to go home, anyway. They'll be worried."

"No," Nancy said. "It's going to pop. Dilsey will tell um yawl with me. I been working for yawl long time. They won't mind if you at my house. You wait, now. It'll start popping in a minute."

Then Jason got some smoke in his eyes and he began to cry. He dropped the popper into the fire. Nancy got a wet rag and wiped Jason's face, but he didn't stop crying.

"Hush," she said. "Hush." He didn't hush. Caddy took the popper out of the fire.

"It's burned up," she said. "You'll have to get some more popcorn, Nancy."

"Did you put all of it in?" Nancy said.

"Yes," Caddy said. Nancy looked at Caddy. Then she took the popper and opened it and poured the blackened popcorn into her apron and began to sort the grains, her hands long and brown, and we watching her.

"Haven't you got any more?" Caddy said.

"Yes," Nancy said; "yes. Look. This here ain't burnt. All we need to do is——"

"I want to go home," Jason said. "I'm going to tell."

"Hush," Caddy said. We all listened. Nancy's head was already turned toward the barred door, her eyes filled with red lamplight. "Somebody is coming," Caddy said.

Then Nancy began to make that sound again, not loud, sitting there above the fire, her long hands dangling between her knees; all of a sudden water began to come out on her face in big drops, running down her face, carrying in each one a little turning ball of firelight until it dropped off her chin.

"She's not crying," I said.

"I ain't crying," Nancy said. Her eyes were closed. "I ain't crying. Who is it?"

"I don't know," Caddy said. She went to the door and looked out. "We've got to go home now," she said. "Here comes father."

"I'm going to tell," Jason said. "You all made me come."

The water still ran down Nancy's face. She turned in her chair. "Listen. Tell him. Tell him we going to have fun. Tell him I take good care of yawl until in the morning. Tell him to let me come home with yawl and sleep on the floor. Tell him I won't need no pallet. We'll have fun. You remember last time how we had so much fun?"

"I didn't have any fun," Jason said. "You hurt me. You put smoke in my eyes."

Father came in. He looked at us. Nancy did not get up.

"Tell him," she said.

"Caddy made us come down here," Jason said. "I didn't want to."

Father came to the fire. Nancy looked up at him. "Can't you go to Aunt Rachel's and stay?" he said. Nancy looked up at father, her hands between her knees. "He's not here," father said. "I would have seen. There wasn't a soul in sight."

"He in the ditch," Nancy said. "He waiting in the ditch yonder."

"Nonsense," father said. He looked at Nancy. "Do you know he's there?"

"I got the sign," Nancy said.

"What sign?"

"I got it. It was on the table when I come in. It was a hog bone, with blood meat still on it, laying by the lamp. He's out there. When yawl walk out that door, I gone."

"Who's gone, Nancy?" Caddy said.

"I'm not a tattletale," Jason said.

"Nonsense," father said.

"He out there," Nancy said. "He looking through that window this minute, waiting for yawl to go. Then I gone."

"Nonsense," father, said. "Lock up your house and we'll take you on to Aunt Rachel's."

" 'Twon't do no good," Nancy said. She didn't look at father now, but he looked down at her, at her long, limp, moving hands.

"Putting it off won't do no good."

"Then what do you want to do?" father said.

"I don't know," Nancy said. "I can't do nothing. Just put it off. And that don't do no good. I reckon it belong to me. I reckon what I going to get ain't no more than mine."

"Get what?" Caddy said. "What's yours?"

"Nothing," father said. "You all must get to bed."

"Caddy made me come," Jason said.

"Go on to Aunt Rachel's," father said.

"It won't do no good," Nancy said. She sat before the fire, her elbows on her knees, her long hands between her knees. "When even your own kitchen wouldn't do no good. When even if I was sleeping on the floor in the room with your own children, and the next morning there I am, and blood all——"

"Hush," father said. "Lock the door and put the lamp out and go to bed."

"I scared of the dark," Nancy said. "I scared for it to happen in the dark."

"You mean you're going to sit right here, with the lamp lighted?" father said. Then Nancy began to make the sound again, sitting before the fire, her long hands between her knees. "Ah, damnation," father said. "Come along, chillen. It's bedtime."

"When yawl go, I gone," Nancy said. "I be dead tomorrow. I done had saved up the coffin money with Mr. Lovelady——"

Mr. Lovelady was a short, dirty man who collected the Negro insurance, coming around to the cabins and the kitchen every Saturday morning, to collect fifteen cents. He and his wife lived in the hotel. One morning his wife committed suicide. They had a child, a little girl. After his wife committed suicide Mr. Lovelady and the child went away. After a while Mr. Lovelady came back. We could see him going down the lanes on Saturday morning. He went to the Baptist church.

Father carried Jason on his back. We went out Nancy's door; she was sitting before the fire. "Come and put the bar up," father said.

Nancy didn't move. She didn't look at us again. We left her there, sitting before the fire with the door opened, so that it wouldn't happen in the dark.

"What, father?" Caddy said. "Why is Nancy scared of Jubah? What is Jubah going to do to her?"

"Jubah wasn't there," Jason said.

"No," father said. "He's not there. He's gone away."

"Who is it that's waiting in the ditch?" Caddy said. We looked at the ditch. We came to it, where the path went down into the thick vines and went up again.

"Nobody," father said. There was just enough moon to see by. The ditch was vague, thick, quiet. "If he's there, he can see us, can't he?" Caddy said.

"You made me come," Jason said on father's back. "I didn't want to."

The ditch was quite still, quite empty, massed with honey-suckle. We couldn't see Jubah, any more than we could see Nancy sitting there in her house, with the door open and the lamp burning, because she didn't want it to happen in the dark. "I just done got tired," Nancy said. "I just a nigger. It ain't no fault of mine."

But we could still hear her. She began as soon as we were out of the house, sitting there above the fire, her long brown hands between her knees. We could still hear her when we had crossed the ditch, Jason high and close and little about father's head.

Then we had crossed the ditch, walking out of Nancy's life. Then her life was sitting there with the door open and the lamp lit, waiting, and the ditch between us and us going on, the white people going on, dividing the impinged lives of us and Nancy.

"Who will do our washing now, father?" I said.

"I'm not a nigger," Jason said on father's shoulders.

"You're worse," Caddy said, "you are a tattletale. If something was to jump out, you'd be scairder than a nigger."

"I wouldn't," Jason said.

"You'd cry," Caddy said.

"Caddy!" father said.

"I wouldn't," Jason said.

"Scairy cat," Caddy said.

"Candace!" father said.

◇◇◇*Gustave Flaubert (1821-1880). French novelist, noted for his objective, highly finished style. While his output was small his influence has been very great—on Mann, Joyce, Proust, and on almost every important writer who followed him.* Madame Bovary *is a realistic account of bourgeois life. Other works include* Salammbô, L'éducation sentimentale *and* Bouvard et Pécuchet.

THE LEGEND OF ST. JULIAN THE HOSPITALLER

BY GUSTAVE FLAUBERT

I

Julian's father and mother lived in a castle in the middle of the woods, on the slope of a hill.

The four towers at the corners had pointed roofs covered with plates of lead, and the base of the walls was supported on blocks of rock which sloped down to the bottom of a moat.

The pavement of the courtyard was as spotless as the flagstones of a church. Long gutter-pipes, in the shape of dragons with drooping jaws, spouted rainwater into a tank, and on the window-sills, in painted clap pots, bloomed sweet basil or heliotrope.

A second enclosure, formed by palings, included first an orchard of fruit-trees, then a garden-plot, with arrangements of flowers forming monograms, then an arbour with bowers in which to take the air, and a mall used for the pages' recreation. On the other side were the kennels, stables, bakehouse, wine-press, and barns. All round stretched a green grassy pasture, itself inclosed by a strong thorn hedge.

Things had been peaceful for so long that the portcullis was no longer in working order; the moats were full of water; swallows built their nests in the crevices of the battlements; and the archer who

From *Three Tales* by Gustave Flaubert. (Translated by Arthur McDowall.) By permission of Alfred A. Knopf, Inc. Copyright 1924 by Alfred A. Knopf, Inc.

paced the curtain-wall all day long used to retire into the watch-tower directly the sun got too strong, and sleep like a monk.

Inside, the iron-work everywhere gleamed; the rooms were protected against the cold by tapestries; and the cupboards overflowed with linen. Butts of wine were piled in the cellars, and oak chests creaked under the weight of money sacks.

In the armoury, between standards and heads of wild animals, were to be seen weapons of every age and every nation, from Amalekite slings and Garamantian javelins to Saracen broadswords and Norman coats of mail.

The main spit in the kitchen was capable of turning an ox; the chapel was sumptuous as a king's oratory. There was even, in a retired corner, a vapour-bath in the Roman style; but the noble lord denied himself the use of it, deeming it an idolatrous practice.

Wrapped always in a fox-skin robe, he would wander about his house, administer justice to his vassals, settle his neighbours' quarrels. In winter he would watch the snow-flakes falling, or have stories read to him. As soon as the first fine days came, he would set off on his mule along the lanes, by the edge of the springing corn, and would talk with the rustics and give them his advice. After many adventures he had taken to wife a maiden of high degree.

She was very fair, somewhat proud and sedate. The horns of her head-dress touched the lintels of the doorways; the train of her cloth dress trailed three feet behind her. Her household was ordered like a monastic establishment; every morning she dealt out their duties to her maidservants, saw to her preserves and salves, spun at her distaff or embroidered altar-cloths. In answer to her constant prayers, a son was born to her.

Then there were great rejoicings and a feast which lasted three days and four nights, by the light of torches, to the sound of harps, on thickstrewn leafage. The rarest spices were eaten, and fowls big as sheep; for amusement, a dwarf came out of a pasty; and, the supply of bowls becoming inadequate, for the crowd was continually increasing, it became necessary to drink from horns and from helmets.

The newly confined mother was not present at these festivities. She remained in her bed, quietly. One evening she awoke, and saw in a moonbeam which entered by the window, what looked like a moving shadow. It was an old man in a homespun gown, with a string of beads at his side, a wallet on his shoulder, looking altogether like a hermit. He drew near her bedside and said, without opening his lips:

"Rejoice, O mother! thy son shall be a saint!"

She was about to cry out; but, gliding along the moonbeam, he rose gently into the air and disappeared. The songs of the banquet broke forth more loudly. She heard the voices of angels, and her head sank back on the pillow, above which stood, set aloft, the bone of a martyr in a frame of carbuncles.

Next day all the servants, when questioned, declared that they had seen no hermit. Whether a dream or real, the thing must have been a communication from heaven; but she was careful to say nothing about it, fearing to be accused of vaingloriousness.

The guests departed at break of day; and Julian's father was standing outside the postern-gate, where he had just seen out the last of them, when suddenly a beggar rose up before him in the mist. He was a Bohemian with plaited beard, silver bracelets on both arms, and burning eyes. He stammered out with an inspired air these incoherent words:

"Ah! ah! your son! . . . much blood! . . . much glory! . . . ever happy! an emperor's family."

And stooping down to pick up his alms, he was lost to sight in the grass, and vanished.

The good lord of the castle looked to the right and to the left, and called with all his might. There was no one. The wind whistled, the morning mists drifted away.

He attributed this vision to the fact that his head was tired from having had too little sleep. "If I speak of it, I shall be laughed at," said he to himself. Nevertheless he was dazzled by the splendours destined for his son, although the promise was not a clear one, and he was even doubtful whether he had heard it.

The husband and wife hid their secrets from each other. But both doted on the child with equal love; and respecting him as marked out by God, they surrounded his person with infinite attentions. His couch was padded with the finest down; a lamp in the shape of a dove burned continually above it; three nurses rocked his cradle; and, snugly wrapped in his swaddling clothes, with his pink cheeks and blue eyes, his robe of brocade and cap loaded with pearls, he looked like a little child Jesus. He got his teeth without crying once.

When he was seven years old his mother taught him to sing. To make him brave his father hoisted him up on to a great horse. The child smiled with glee, and it was not long before he knew everything about a charger.

A very learned old monk taught him Holy Scripture, Arabic numeration and Latin, and how to make dainty paintings on vellum. They used to work together, at the very top of a turret, out of the way of noise.

When the lesson was over, they would go down into the garden, where, moving along step by step, they would study the flowers.

Sometimes there would be seen wending its way along the valley-bottom a string of packhorses, led by a man on foot, in Eastern garb. The lord of the castle, having recognized him as a merchant, would send a servant off to him. The stranger, taking heart, would turn aside from his path; and when brought to the parlour would draw forth from his coffers pieces of velvet and silk, goldsmiths' wares, aromatic perfumes, strange things whose uses were unknown; in the end the fellow would go off with much profit, and having suffered no violence.

Another time, a band of pilgrims would knock at the gate. Their wet clothes would smoke in front of the hearth; and when they had eaten their fill, they would tell the story of their travels: the roving of the ships over the foaming sea, the journeys afoot in the burning desert sands, the fierceness of the paynims, the caves of Syria, the Manger and the Sepulchre. Then they would give the young lord shells off their cloaks.

Often the lord of the castle would feast his old comrades in arms. While they drank they would recall their wars, the assaults on fortresses with the battering of engines and stupendous wounds. Julian, listening to them, would shout aloud; then his father had no doubt that he would later on be a conqueror. But at evening, coming out from Angelus, when he passed between the poor, waiting with bowed heads, he would dip into his purse with such modesty and such an air of nobility that his mother was sure she would eventually see him an archbishop.

His place in the chapel was at his parents' side; and however long the services were, he would remain on his knees on his prayer-stool, his cap on the floor and his hands folded.

One day, during Mass, he saw as he raised his head a little white mouse coming out of a hole in the wall. It ran along the first step of the altar, and after two or three excursions to right and left, ran back the same way. The next Sunday the thought that he might see it again disturbed him. It did come again; and every Sunday he waited for it, was irritated by it, conceived an aversion for it, and determined to get rid of it.

So, having shut the door and strewed crumbs of cake on the steps, he took up his stand before the hole with a wand in his hand.

At the end of a very long time a pink nose appeared, and then the whole mouse. He gave it a tap, and stood aghast at the sight of the tiny body which had ceased to move. A drop of blood stained the pavement. He wiped it away hastily with his sleeve, threw the mouse out and said nothing about it to anyone.

All sorts of little birds used to pick up the seeds in the garden. He conceived the idea of putting peas in a hollow reed. When he heard twittering in a tree, he would draw near softly, then raise his tube, puff out his cheeks, and the little creatures showered down on his shoulders so plentifully that he could not help laughing, pleased by his malicious trick.

One morning, as he was coming back by the curtain-wall, he saw on the ridge of the rampart a big pigeon preening itself in the sun. Julian stopped to look at it; the wall having a breach in it at that point, a chip of stone happened to be lying under his hand. He swung his arm, and the stone knocked down the bird, which fell plump into the moat.

He hurried to the bottom, tearing himself on the bushes, ferreting about more nimbly than a puppy.

The pigeon, with its wings broken, was still quivering, caught in the branches of a privet.

The persistency of its life irritated the boy. He set about strangling it; and the bird's convulsive struggles made his heart beat, and filled him with a savage, tumultuous delight. When it finally stiffened, he felt himself swooning.

That evening, during supper, his father declared that a boy of his age ought to learn venery; and he went and fetched an old manuscript book containing in questions and answers the whole pastime of the chase. In it a master demonstrated to his pupil the art of training dogs and reclaiming hawks, and of setting traps, how to recognize the stag by his fumet, the fox by his tracks, the wolf by his scratches, the best way of distinguishing their trails, how they are started, where their hiding-places are usually to be found, which are the most favourable winds, together with a list of the cries and the rules of the quarry.

When Julian was able to recite all these things by heart his father formed a pack for him.

In it there were to be found first twenty-four Barbary greyhounds, swifter than gazelles, but apt to run away; next seventeen couples of Breton dogs, red flecked with white, unshakable in their obedience to control, deep-chested and loud-baying. For attacks on boars, with their perilous doublings, there were forty griffons, as shaggy as bears. There were Tartary mastiffs, almost as big as donkeys, flame-coloured, broad-backed and straight-legged, designed for the pursuit of the aurochs. The black coats of the spaniels shone like satin, the yapping of the Talbots vied with the music of the beagles.

In a yard apart, rattling their chains and rolling their eyes, growled eight Alans, formidable beasts which fly at a rider's belly and are not afraid of lions.

All of them were fed on wheaten bread, drank out of stone troughs, and bore high-sounding names.

The falconry perhaps surpassed the pack; the noble lord, at great expense, had procured tiercels from the Caucasus, Babylonian sakers, German gerfalcons, and peregrine falcons captured on the cliffs bordering the chill seas in distant lands. They were lodged in a thatched outhouse, and, chained to the perch in order of size, had a grass-sod before them on which they were set down from time to time to get rid of their stiffness.

Bag-nets, fish-hooks, traps, and snares of all kinds were constructed.

Often they would go out into the country with fowling-dogs, which would quickly make a point. Then prickers advancing step by step, would cautiously spread an immense net over their impassive forms. They barked at a word of command; quails took wing; and the ladies of the neighbourhood, invited with their husbands, the children, the waiting-women, all would fling themselves upon them and catch them easily.

At other times drums would be beaten to start hares; foxes fell into pits, or a spring, uncoiling, would catch a wolf by the paw.

But Julian despised these easy contrivances; he preferred hunting far from anyone, with his horse and his hawk. This was nearly always a big Scythian tartaret, as white as snow. Its leather hood was surmounted by a plume, little golden bells quivered on its blue legs: and it sat steady on its master's arm while his horse galloped and the plains unfolded before him. Julian, slipping its jesses, would fly it suddenly; the fearless creature would rise straight as an arrow into the air; and two unequal specks would be seen turning, meeting, and disappearing in the depths of the blue. It would not be long before the hawk came down tearing a bird, and would return to settle on the gauntlet, with quivering wings.

Julian flew in this manner herons, kites, crows and vultures.

He loved to sound his horn and follow his dogs as they coursed along the hill-sides, leaped streams, and turned up again toward the woods; and when the stag began to moan under their bites he would fell it swiftly, and then delight in the fury of the mastiffs as they devoured it, cut in pieces upon its smoking hide.

On misty days he would go deep into a marsh to lie in wait for geese, otters, and young wild duck.

Three squires would be waiting for him at the foot of the steps at earliest dawn; and the old monk, leaning out of his dormer-window, would signal in vain to call him back; Julian did not turn round. He would go in the heat of the sun, in the rain, through the storm, drinking spring-water from the hollow of his hand, eating wild apples as he ambled along, resting if he was weary under an oak; and he would come home in the middle of the night, covered with blood and mud, with burrs in his hair and smelling of wild animals. He grew like them. When his mother kissed him, he accepted her embrace coldly, and seemed to be musing upon deep matters.

He killed bears with a knife, bulls with an axe, boars with a spear; once even, having nothing but a stick left, he protected himself against wolves which were gnawing corpses at the foot of a gallows.

One winter morning he set off before daylight, well equipped, a crossbow on his shoulder and a bundle of arrows at his saddle-bow.

His Danish jennet, followed by two terriers, stepped out at an even pace, its hoofs ringing on the ground. Drops of rime clung to his cloak, a violent wind was blowing. One side of the horizon cleared; and in the white light of dawn he saw some rabbits frisking at the mouth of their holes. The two terriers immediately dashed at them; and, now here, now there, swiftly broke their backs.

Soon he entered a wood. On the end of a branch a black-cock, benumbed by the cold, was asleep with its head under its wing. Julian, with a backward sweep of his sword, sliced off its feet, and without picking it up went on his way.

Three hours later he found himself on the peak of a mountain so high that the sky seemed almost black. Before him a rock like a long wall fell away, overhanging a precipice; and at the extreme end, two wild goats were looking down into the chasm. As he had not his arrows (for his horse was left behind), he took it into his head to go down to where they were; bent half double, barefoot, he at length reached the first goat, and drove his dagger home under its ribs. The second, terror-stricken, leapt into the void. Julian sprang forward to strike it, and, his right foot slipping, he fell on the corpse of the other, his head over the chasm and his arms outspread.

When he had come down to the plain again, he followed the line of some willows on the bank of a river. Cranes, flying very low, passed over his head from time to time. Julian knocked them down with his whip and did not miss one.

Meanwhile the warmer air had melted the hoar-frost, broad patches of mist were rising, and the sun came out. He saw, gleaming far in the distance, a frozen lake, looking like lead. In the middle of the lake was an animal which Julian did not know, a black-nosed beaver. In spite of the distance an arrow brought it down; and he was vexed at not being able to carry off the skin.

Then he went on into an avenue of tall trees, their tops forming, as it were, a triumphal arch at the entrance to a forest. A roe bounded out from a thicket; a buck appeared at a cross-roads; a badger came out of a hole; a peacock on the grass spread its tail;— and when he had slain them all, more roes presented themselves, more bucks, more badgers, more peacocks, and blackbirds, jays, polecats, foxes, hedgehogs, lynxes, an infinitude of animals, more numerous at every step.

They circled round him, trembling, with gentle, supplicating glances. But Julian did not weary of killing, by turns bending his crossbow, unsheathing his sword, thrusting with his cutlass, and he had no thought for anything, no recollection of anything whatsoever. He had been hunting in some indeterminate place, for an indefinite time, by the mere fact of his own existence, everything happening with the facility experienced in dreams. An extraordinary sight arrested him. A circus-shaped valley was filled with stags; and, crowded close together, they were warming each other with their breath, which could be seen smoking in the mist.

The hope of such carnage as that suffocated him with joy for some minutes. Then he dismounted, turned up his sleeves, and began to shoot.

At the whistle of the first arrow all the stags turned their heads at the same moment. Gaps appeared in the mass; plaintive cries arose, and a great tremor passed through the herd.

The lip of the valley was too high to cross. They bounded about the enclosure, seeking to escape. Julian aimed and shot; and the arrows fell like the streaks of rain in a storm. The maddened stags fought, reared, climbed on each other's backs; and their bodies, with their antlers entangled, formed a great mound, crumbling and shifting.

At length they died, lying on the sand with slavering muzzles, disembowelled, the heaving of their bellies growing less and less by degrees. Then all was still.

Night was drawing on; and behind the wood, through the spaces between the branches, the sky showed red like a sheet of blood.

Julian leant his back against a tree. He gazed wide-eyed at the vastness of the slaughter, not understanding how he had been able to do it.

On the other side of the valley, on the edge of the forest, he caught sight of a stag, a doe, and its fawn.

The stag, which was black and of huge size, had sixteen points and a white beard. The doe, as light in colour as dead leaves, was cropping the grass; and the dappled fawn, without impeding her movements, was feeding at her udder.

The crossbow hummed once more. The fawn was killed on the spot. Then the mother, looking up to the sky, gave a deep, heartrending, human bellow. Julian, exasperated, laid her low on the ground with a shot full in the breast.

The great stag had seen him and gave a bound. Julian shot his last arrow at him. It struck him on the forehead, and remained planted there.

The great stag did not appear to feel it; stepping over the dead bodies, it came on, ready to rush at him and disembowel him; and Julian retreated in unspeakable dread. The monstrous beast stopped; and with flaming eyes, solemn as a patriarch or a justiciary, a bell tinkling in the distance meanwhile, he repeated thrice:

"Accursed! accursed! accursed! One day, thou savage heart, thou shalt slay thy father and mother!"

His knees gave under him, his eyes closed gently, and he died.

Julian was dumbfounded, and then, overcome by sudden weariness, a feeling of disgust and vast sadness stole over him. His head in his hands, he wept long.

His horse was lost; his dogs had forsaken him; the solitude which enfolded him seemed menacing, full of vague perils. Then, impelled by a sudden terror, he set off across country, chose a path at random, and found himself almost at once at the castle gate.

That night he did not sleep. In the wavering light of the hanging lamp he kept on seeing the great black stag again. Its prophecy obsessed him; he struggled against it. "No! no! no! I cannot kill them!" Then he mused: "And yet, supposing I should want to? . . ." and he was afraid lest the Devil should inspire him with the desire to do it.

Throughout three months his mother in anguish prayed at his bedside, and his father walked ceaselessly up and down the passages, groaning. He summoned the most famous master-leeches, who prescribed quantities of drugs. Julian's sickness, they said, was caused by some baleful wind, or an amorous lust. But, in answer to all questions, the youth shook his head.

His strength returned; and he was taken out to walk in the courtyard, the old monk and the noble lord each supporting him with an arm.

When he was completely restored, he persistently refused to go hunting.

His father, wishing to cheer him, made him a present of a great Saracen sword.

It was at the top of a pillar, in a panoply. To reach it a ladder was required. Julian went up it. The sword was too heavy, and slipped from his fingers, and, as it fell, grazed so closely past the noble lord that his surcoat was cut by it; Julian thought he had killed his father, and swooned.

From that time on, he had a dread of weapons. The sight of a naked sword turned him pale. This weakness was a great grief to his family.

At length the old monk commanded him, in the name of God, his honour, and his forbears, to resume a nobleman's pursuits.

The squires used every day to amuse themselves with javelin-play. Julian quickly excelled in this. He could throw his into the neck of a bottle, break the pointers of a weather-vane, hit the nails in a door at a hundred paces.

One summer evening, at the hour when mist makes things indistinct, he was in the arbour in the garden, and suddenly saw, right at the farther end, two white wings fluttering on a level with the espalier. He never doubted that it was a stork; and he threw his javelin.

A heart-rending cry arose.

It was his mother, whose cap with its long lappets was left pinned to the wall.

Julian fled from the castle, and never appeared again.

II

He enlisted in a passing band of adventurers.

He experienced hunger and thirst, fevers and vermin. He grew accustomed to the din of affrays and the sight of dying men. The wind tanned his skin. His limbs were hardened by contact with armour; and as he was very strong, brave, sober and circumspect, he gained command of a company without difficulty.

At the outset of battles he would stir up his soldiers with a great wave of his sword. With a knotted rope he would climb the walls of citadels by night, rocked by the storm-wind, while the burning flakes from the Greek fire adhered to his cuirass, and boiling pitch and molten lead poured down from the battlements. Often his buck-ler was shattered by the crash of a stone. Bridges overladen with men gave way under him. Whirling his battle-mace he rid himself of fourteen horsemen. He overthrew in the lists all who came forward. More than twenty times he was believed dead.

Thanks to divine favour, he always came out safely, for he protected churchmen, orphans, widows, and especially old men. When he saw one walking before him, he would call out, in order to see his face, as if he had been afraid of killing him by mistake.

Fugitive slaves, peasants in revolt, portionless bastards, dauntless fellows of all kinds flocked to his banner, and he formed an army.

It grew. He became famous and sought after.

One after the other he succoured the Dauphin of France, the King of England, the Templars at Jerusalem, the Surena of the Parthians, the Negus of Abyssinia, and the Emperor of Calicut. He fought Scandinavians covered with fish scales, negroes armed with round shields of hippopotamus hide and mounted on red asses, gold-coloured Indians brandishing above their headbands great sabres brighter than mirrors. He defeated the Troglodytes and the Anthropophagi. He traversed regions so torrid that in the burning heat of the sun the hair caught fire of itself, like a torch; and others so glacial that the arms became detached from the body and fell to the ground; and lands where there were so many fogs that men walked surrounded by phantoms.

Republics in difficulties consulted him. At ambassadors' conferences he obtained unhoped-for conditions. If a monarch conducted himself too ill, he would arrive suddenly and remonstrate with him. He freed nations. He delivered queens imprisoned in towers. It was he, and none else, who struck down the Viper of Milan and the Dragon of Oberbirbach.

Now the Emperor of Occitania, triumphant over the Spanish Moslems, had taken as a concubine the sister of the Caliph of Cordova, and he had a daughter by her, whom he had brought up in Christian wise. But the Caliph, feigning a desire to be converted, came to visit him, accompanied by a numerous escort, massacred his whole garrison, and threw him into the deepest dungeon, where he treated him harshly, so as to extort treasures from him.

Julian hastened to his aid, destroyed the infidel army, besieged the town, killed the Caliph, cut off his head, and tossed it like a ball over the ramparts. Then he brought the Emperor forth from his prison, and set him on his throne again in presence of his whole court.

The Emperor, as the price of so great a service, presented to him, in baskets, great sums of money. Julian would have none of it. Thinking he wanted more, he offered him three-fourths of his wealth; he met with another refusal; then to share his kingdom; Julian thanked him and declined; and the Emperor was weeping with vexation, not knowing how to show his gratitude, when he clapped his hand to his brow, said a word in a courtier's ear; the curtains in some tapestry hangings were raised, and a maiden appeared.

Her great black eyes shone like two very soft lamps. A charming smile parted her lips. Her ringlets were caught among the precious stones in her open-necked gown, and her diaphanous tunic hinted at the youthful lines of her form. She was all dainty and dimpled, and slender-waisted.

Julian fell blindly in love, all the more because he had up till then led a life of great chastity.

So he received the Emperor's daughter in marriage, and with her a castle which she inherited from her mother; and the wedding over, the farewells were made, after endless compliments on both sides.

It was a white marble palace, built in the Moorish style, on a promontory in an orange grove. Terraces of flowers sloped away to the edge of a cove where pink shells crunched under foot. Behind the castle stretched a forest in the pattern of a fan. The sky was eternally blue, and the trees bowed now before the sea-breeze and now before the wind from the mountains which bounded the horizon in the distance.

The rooms, full of dusky shadows, were lighted by inlaid work on the walls. Tall columns, as slender as reeds, supported the arched cupolas, ornamented with reliefs in imitation of the stalactites in grottoes.

There were fountains in the halls, mosaics in the courtyards, festooned partitions, innumerable refinements of architecture, and everywhere such silence that one heard the rustle of a scarf or the echo of a sigh.

Julian went to war no longer. He rested in the midst of a people at peace; and every day a crowd passed before him, bending the knee and kissing hands in the Eastern fashion.

Clad in purple, he would linger leaning on his elbow in the recess of a window, calling to mind his old hunting days; and he would fain have been speeding over the desert after the gazelles and ostriches, hiding among the bamboos in wait for leopards, going through forests full of rhinoceros, or climbing to the top of the most inaccessible mountains to get a better aim at the eagles, and on blocks of ice in the sea fighting the polar bears.

Sometimes, in a dream, he would see himself, like Father Adam, in the midst of Paradise, among all the animals; by stretching out his arm he would cause them to die; or else they would file past, two by two, in order of size, from the elephants and lions to the stoats and ducks, as on the day when they went into Noah's ark. In the shadow of a cave he would hurl unerring javelins at them; others came on; there was no end to it; and he would wake with wild eyes rolling.

Princes among his friends invited him to the chase. He refused always, thinking by this sort of penance to avert the disaster; for it seemed to him that on the slaying of animals his parents' fate depended. But he suffered from not seeing them, and his desire became unbearable.

His wife, to entertain him, had ministrels and dancing-girls brought.

She would go about the country-side with him, in an open litter; or again, lying on the deck of a skiff, they would watch the fish straying through water clear as the sky. Often she would toss flowers in his face; crouching at his feet she would pick out tunes on a three-stringed mandolin; then, laying her clasped hands on his shoulder, she would say in a timid voice: "What ails you, dear lord?"

He would not answer, or would burst into sobs. At last one day he confessed his horrible thought.

She argued against it, reasoning very soundly; his father and mother were in all probability dead; if he did ever see them again, by what chance, for what purpose, should he be brought to commit such an abomination? Well, then, his fear was groundless, and he ought to take up hunting again.

Julian smiled as he listened, but could not bring himself to gratify his desire.

One evening in the month of August when they were in their chamber, she had just got into bed and he was kneeling down to pray, when he heard the yelp of a fox, and then light steps under the window, and in the gloom he got a glimpse of what looked like animal forms. The temptation was too strong. He took down his quiver.

She seemed surprised.

"It is in obedience to you!" he said; "at sunrise I shall be back."

Nevertheless she dreaded some disaster happening.

He reassured her, and went out, surprised at her inconsistent moods.

Shortly afterwards a page came to say that two strangers, in the absence of the lord of the castle, were asking urgently for the lady.

And soon there came into the room an old man and an old woman, bowed, dusty, in linen garments, each leaning on a stick.

They made bold to announce that they were bringing Julian news of his parents.

She leant down to hear them.

But, after exchanging a glance, they asked her if he still loved them, and if he ever spoke of them.

"Oh, yes!" said she.

Then they cried:

"Well, we are they!" and they sat down, being very weary and jaded with fatigue.

There was nothing to make the young wife sure that her husband was their son.

They gave her proof of it, by describing special marks which he had on his skin.

She sprang from her couch, called her page, and a meal was served to them.

Although they were very hungry they could hardly eat; and

she sat apart watching the trembling of their bony hands as they lifted the goblets.

They asked numberless questions about Julian. She answered each one, but was careful to keep silence with regard to the ominous idea concerning themselves.

Finding that he did not come back, they had set out from their castle, and they had been faring on their way for several years, following vague clues, without losing hope. So much money had been required for bridge tolls and in inns, for princes' dues and robbers' exactions, that their purse was absolutely empty, and they were now beggars. But what did it matter, since soon they would be embracing their son? They extolled his good fortune in having so charming a wife, and could not look at her and kiss her enough.

They were greatly astonished at the richness of their lodging; and the old father, examining the walls, asked why they bore the coat of arms of the Emperor of Occitania.

She replied:

"He is my father!"

Then he started, remembering the Bohemian's prophecy; and the old mother thought of the Hermit's words. Doubtless her son's glory was only the dawn of everlasting splendour; and both sat there agape in the glow of the chandelier, by which the table was lighted.

They must have been very handsome in their youth. The mother had not lost any of her hair, and its fine smooth loops, like slabs of snow, hung low on her cheeks; and the father, with his tall figure and great beard, looked like a statue in a church.

Julian's wife besought them not to wait for him. She saw them to bed herself, in her own bed, then shut the casement, and they fell asleep. It was on the point of daybreak, and outside the window the birds were beginning to sing.

Julian had crossed the park. He was walking through the forest at a vigorous pace, enjoying the softness of the grass and the balminess of the air.

The shadow of the trees lay on the moss. Sometimes the moon made patches of white in the glades, and he hesitated to go forward, thinking he saw a pool of water, or sometimes the surface of the quiet meres merged into the colour of the grass. Everywhere there was a great silence; and he could not discover any of the animals which, a few minutes before, had been wandering round his castle.

The wood grew thicker, the darkness profound. Gusts of hot wind blew, heavy with enervating odours. He kept sinking into heaps of dead leaves, and leant against an oak to pant a little.

Suddenly, behind his back, there leapt out a darker object, a wild boar. Julian had not time to seize his bow, and he was distressed by this as by a misfortune.

Then, when he had come out of the wood, he espied a wolf speeding along by a hedge.

Julian shot an arrow at him. The wolf stopped, turned its head to look at him, and set off again. It trotted along, keeping always at the same distance, stopping from time to time, and as soon as Julian aimed at it, beginning to run away again.

Julian crossed in this wise an endless plain, then some sand-hillocks, and at last found himself on a plateau overlooking a great stretch of country.

There were flat stones lying scattered among ruined vaults. He went stumbling over dead men's bones; here and there worm-eaten crosses stood at a mournful slant. But shapes began to move in the vague shadow of the tombs, and hyenas sprang up terrified and panting. Making a pattering noise with their claws on the stones, they drew near and sniffed at him, with their gaping jaws disclosing their gums. He unsheathed his sword. They went off all at once in every direction, and keeping up their hurried, halting gallop, were lost in the distance in a cloud of dust.

An hour later he met in a gorge a mad bull, with lowered horns, pawing the sand. Julian thrust at it with his lance beneath its dewlap. It shivered in pieces, as if the beast had been made of bronze; he shut his eyes, and waited for death. When he opened them again the bull had disappeared.

Then his soul fainted within him from shame. Some superior power was destroying his strength, and in order to turn back home he went into the forest again.

It was choked with creepers, and he was cutting them with his sword when a marten slipped suddenly between his legs, a panther bounded over his shoulder, a serpent reared itself in coils round an ash-tree.

In its foliage was a huge jackdaw, watching Julian; and here and there a number of great sparks appeared among the branches, as if the heavens had rained down all their stars into the forest. They were the eyes of beasts, wild cats, squirrels, owls, parrots, and monkeys.

Julian sent a shower of arrows among them, and the arrows, with their feathers, settled on the leaves like white butterflies. He threw stones at them, and the stones fell without touching anything. He cursed himself, longed to fight something, shouted out imprecations, choked with rage.

And all the animals he had pursued showed themselves again, making a narrow ring round him. Some were sitting on their haunches, others drawn up to their full height. He remained in the middle, frozen with terror, incapable of the slightest movement. By a supreme effort of will he took a step forward; the creatures perched on the trees spread their wings, those standing on the ground moved their limbs; and all of them went with him.

The hyenas went in front, the wolf and the boar behind. The bull, on his right, swung its head from side to side; and on his left the snake writhed through the grass, while the panther, arching his back, paced along, velvet-footed. He went as slowly as possible so as not to provoke them, and he saw, coming forth from the depths of the bushes, hedgehogs, foxes, vipers, jackals, and bears.

Julian began to run, and they ran too. The snake hissed, the foul beasts slavered. The boar rubbed his heels with its tusks, the wolf the palms of his hands with its whiskers. The monkeys pinched him and grimaced, the marten rolled on his feet. A bear knocked his hat off with its paw, and the panther disdainfully dropped an arrow which it was carrying in its mouth.

There was irony beneath the slyness of their demeanour. Watching him out of the corners of their eyes, they seemed to be brooding over some scheme of revenge the while; and, deafened by the buzzing of the insects, buffeted by birds' tails, suffocated by evil breaths, he walked on with his arms outstretched and his eyes closed like a blind man, without the strength to cry for mercy.

The crow of a cock rang out on the air. Others answered; it was day; and he recognized, beyond the orange-trees, the topmost roof of his palace.

Then, on the edge of a field, he saw, three paces away, some red partridges fluttering among the stubble. He unclasped his cloak and threw it over them like a net. When he had uncovered them, he found but one, and that one had been dead a long time, and was decomposed.

This disappointment exasperated him more than all the others. His thirst for carnage came on him again; and since animals were lacking he would fain have slaughtered men.

He ascended the three terraces, broke open the door with a blow of his fist; but at the foot of the stairs the memory of his beloved wife softened his heart. She was probably asleep, and he would come upon her unawares.

Taking off his sandals, he turned the lock gently and went in.

The leaded window panes dimmed the pale light of dawn. Julian caught his foot in some clothes on the floor; a little farther on he knocked against a side-table still laden with dishes. "I suppose she had something to eat," he said to himself; and he advanced toward the bed, which was hidden in the darkness at the end of the room. When he was beside it, in order to kiss his wife, he bent down over the pillow where the two heads were resting side by side. Then he felt against his lips the touch of a beard.

He started back, thinking he was going mad; but he came back to the bedside, and his fingers, groping about, came upon hair—very long hair. To convince himself that he was mistaken, he passed his hand slowly over the pillow again. It was certainly a beard this time, and a man! a man lying with his wife!

In a burst of ungovernable rage he leaped on them with his dagger; he stamped and foamed, yelling like a wild beast. Then he stopped. The victims, stabbed to the heart, had not even moved. He listened attentively to the rattle of their dying breath, which came almost in unison, and as it grew fainter, another in the distance took it up. Faint at first, the plaintive voice, long-drawn out, came nearer, swelled, became cruel; and he recognized with terror the bellowing of the great black stag.

And as he turned, he thought he saw, framed in the doorway, the wraith of his wife, a light in her hand.

The noise of the murder had brought her to the spot, and with a comprehensive glance she took in the whole situation, and fled in horror, dropping the torch.

He picked it up.

His father and mother were before him, lying on their backs with a hole in their breasts; and their faces, in their mild majesty, looked as if keeping some eternal secret. Splashes and pools of blood showed on their white skin, on the sheets, the floor, and all down an ivory Christ hanging in the alcove. The crimson glow of the stained glass, on which the sun was striking, lighted up the red splashes, and multiplied them all through the room.

Julian went toward the two dead bodies, telling himself, and trying to think, that it was not possible, that he had made a mistake, that inexplicable likenesses do occur sometimes. At last he stooped slightly to look at the old man closely, and he saw between the half-closed lids a dim eye that burned him like fire. Then he moved round to the other side of the couch, where the other body was lying, the white hair concealing part of the face. Julian slipped his fingers under the tresses of hair and lifted the head and gazed at it, holding it at arm's length, rigidly, while with his other hand he held the torch so as to give a light. Drops oozing from the mattress fell one by one on the floor.

At the end of the day he presented himself before his wife; and in a voice different from his usual one, he bade her in the first place not to reply to him, not to come near him, not even to look at him again; and that she must carry out, on pain of everlasting punishment, all his orders, which were irrevocable.

The burial was to be performed according to the instructions which he had left in writing on a prayer-stool in the chamber where the dead bodies lay. He was relinquishing to her his palace, his vassals, all his possessions, not even keeping his wearing apparel, and his sandals, which would be found at the top of the stairway.

She had obeyed God's will in bringing about his crime, and must pray for his soul, since henceforth he no longer lived.

The dead were buried with pomp in a monastery church three days distant from the castle. A monk, in a cloak with the cowl pulled over his head, followed the procession, far away from everybody else, and no one dared to speak to him.

He remained during mass prone in the midst of the doorway, his arms outspread in the shape of a cross, and his forehead in the dust.

After the burial he was seen to take the road leading to the mountains. He looked back several times, and at length disappeared.

III

He went away into the world, begging his bread.

He held out his hand for charity to horsemen on the roads, went up to harvesters and bent the knee before them, or stood motionless at the gates of courtyards; and his face was so sad that he was never refused alms.

In a spirit of humility he used to tell his story; and then everybody fled, making the sign of the cross. In villages through which he had already passed, as soon as he was recognized, the doors would be shut against him, threats were called out, and stones were thrown at him. The more charitable would set a bowl on their windowledge, and then close the shutter so as not to see him.

Rebuffed on all sides, he avoided men, and lived on roots and plants and chance fruit, and shell-fish which he sought for along the sea-shore.

Sometimes from the brow of a hill he would see below him a medley of crowded roofs, with stone spires, bridges, towers, and dark intersecting streets, whence a continual hum rose to his ears.

The craving to join in the life of other men would make him go down into the town. But the animal look of the faces, the noise of the different trades, the dullness of the conversations froze his heart. On feast days, when the great bell of the cathedral filled the whole populace with joy from daybreak, he would watch the inhabitants coming forth from their houses, and then the dancing in the market-places, the fountains of ale at the cross-roads, the damask awnings in front of the princes' houses, and, when evening had come, through the ground-floor windows, the long family tables where old grandsires sat with little children on their laps; he would be choked with sobs, and would turn away back to the country.

He gazed with transports of love at the colts in the pastures, the birds in their nests, the insects on the flowers; but at his approach they ran farther off, or hid affrighted, or flew away swiftly.

He sought out lonely places. But the wind brought to his ears, as it were, the sound of dying agonies; tears of dew as they fell on the earth reminded him of other and heavier drops. The sun every evening spread blood among the clouds; and every night in his dreams the murder of his parents began all over again.

He made himself a hair shirt with iron spikes in it. He climbed on his knees all the hills which had a chapel on their summit. But his relentless thought dimmed the splendour of tabernacles, tortured him through the mortification of the penance.

He did not rebel against God who had ordained his action, and yet he was in despair at having been capable of committing it.

He was filled with such horror of his own person that, hoping to free himself of it, he risked it in perilous ventures. He saved paralytics from fires, children from the depths of chasms. The abyss cast him up again, the flames spared him.

Time did not assuage his suffering, and it became unbearable. He made up his mind to die.

And one day, when he was at the brink of a spring, leaning over it to judge of the depth of the water, he saw facing him a gaunt old man, white-bearded and so wretched-looking that he could not restrain his tears. The other also wept. Without recognizing his own reflection, Julian vaguely recalled a face resembling the one before him. He gave a cry; it was his father; and he had no further thought of killing himself.

So, bearing the burden of memory, he journeyed through many lands; and drew near to a river which was dangerous to cross, because of its impetuosity and because there was a wide stretch of mud on its banks. No one for a long time past had dared to cross.

An old boat lay with its stern buried and its bows sticking up among the reeds. Julian examined it and found a pair of oars; and he conceived the idea of using his life in the service of others.

He began by constructing on the river bank a sort of causeway by which people could go down to the stream; and he broke his nails moving the huge stones, propped them against his body to carry them, slipped in the mud, sank in it, and very nearly perished several times over.

Then he mended the boat with wreckage, and made himself a hut with clay and tree-trunks.

When once the crossing was known, travellers presented themselves. They hailed him from the opposite bank, waving flags; Julian hastily leapt into his boat. It was very heavy; and they overloaded it with packs and baggage of all kinds, not counting the beasts of burden, which, kicking with fright, increased the confusion. He asked nothing for his trouble. Some gave him scraps of food from their wallets, or worn-out clothes which they did not want any longer. Brutes yelled out curses. Julian rebuked them gently, and they retaliated with insults. He contented himself with blessing them.

A little table, a stool, a bed of dead leaves, and three clay drinking-vessels were his sole furniture. Two holes in the walls served as windows. On one side, as far as the eye could see, stretched barren plains with wan-looking ponds here and there on their surface; and before him rolled the greenish waters of the great river.

In spring the damp earth smelt of rottenness. Then a mighty wind would raise the dust in whirling clouds. It penetrated everywhere, made the water muddy, gritted between the teeth. Later came clouds of mosquitoes, whose singing and biting never stopped day or night. Then followed cruel frosts, which made all things as stiff as stones and caused a frantic appetite for meat.

Months passed when Julian saw no one. Often he would close his eyes, and try in memory to get back to his young days;—and the courtyard of a castle would appear, with greyhounds on a flight of steps, servingmen in the armoury, and under a bower of vines a fair-haired youth between an old man wrapped in furs and a lady with a great horned head-dress; all at once the two dead bodies were before him. He would throw himself face downwards on his bed, and weeping, say over and over again:

"Ah, poor father and mother! poor mother!" and he would fall into a drowsy slumber in which the mournful visions still went on.

One night as he slept he thought he heard some one calling. He listened with all his ears, but could distinguish nothing save the roaring of the waves.

But the same voice began again:

"Julian!"

It came from the other bank, which seemed to him extraordinary, considering the width of the river.

The call came a third time:

"Julian!"

And the voice, crying aloud, had the sound of a church bell.

Lighting his lantern he went out of the hut. The night was filled with a raging hurricane. The darkness was profound, rent here and there by the white of leaping waves.

After a moment's hesitation Julian cast off the mooring-rope. The water immediately became still, the boat glided over it, and touched the other bank, where a man was waiting.

He was wrapped in a ragged linen cloth; his face was like a plaster cast, and his eyes redder than burning coals. On bringing the lantern near him, Julian saw that he was covered with a hideous leprosy; and yet in his bearing there was something of royal majesty.

Directly he got into the boat it sank strangely, borne down by his weight; a jerk brought it up again, and Julian started rowing.

At every pull the swirl of the waters lifted it by the bows. The water, blacker than ink, rushed furiously past its sides. It was hollowed into gulfs, and rose into mountains, and the craft leapt up and then sank again into depths where it turned about, tossed to and fro by the wind.

Julian leant forward, stretched out his arms, and, bracing his feet firmly, threw himself back with a wrench of the body so as to get more force. The hail lashed his hands, the rain streamed down his back, the violence of the wind caught his breath, and he stopped. Then the boat was swept along adrift. But, realizing that this was some important matter, some order that must not be disobeyed, he took up his oars again; and the rattle of the thole-pins broke in upon the din of the storm.

The little lantern was burning before him. Birds fluttering past hid it from time to time. But all the while he saw the eyes of the Leper, who was standing erect in the stern, motionless as a pillar.

And this went on for a long, long time!

When they had reached the hut Julian shut the door; and he saw him seated on the stool. The sort of shroud that covered him had slipped down to his hips; and his shoulders, breast and thin arms could not be seen for blotches of scaly pustules. His brow was furrowed by huge wrinkles. Like a skeleton, he had a hole where the nose should be; and from his bluish lips issued breath as thick as a mist and loathsome.

"I am hungry," said he.

Julian gave him what he had, an old flitch of bacon and the crust of a loaf of black bread.

When he had devoured them, the table, the dish and the knife-handle had the same spots on them as showed on his body.

Then he said: "I am thirsty."

Julian went and fetched his pitcher; and as he took it up, there arose from it a fragrant perfume which made his heart and nostrils dilate. It was wine; what a godsend! But the Leper stretched out his hand, and emptied the whole pitcher at a draught.

Then he said: "I am cold."

Julian, with his candle, set light to a bundle of bracken in the middle of the hovel.

The Leper drew near to warm himself, and squatting on his heels, he trembled in every limb, and grew weaker; his eyes no longer glowed, his ulcers became running sores; and in a dying voice he murmured: "Your bed!"

Julian helped him gently to drag himself to it, and even spread the sail of his boat over him to cover him.

The Leper moaned. The corners of his lips lifted, showing his teeth, his chest heaved as the dying breath came more and more quickly, and his belly, at each inhalation, was drawn in to the very backbone.

Then he closed his eyes.

"It feels like ice in my bones. Come close to me!"

And Julian, pushing the sail aside, lay down side by side with him on the dead leaves.

The Leper turned his head.

"Undress, so that I may get the warmth of your body!"

Julian took off his clothes; then, naked as on the day he was born, he got back into the bed; and he felt against his thigh the Leper's skin, colder than a snake and as rough as a file.

He tried to encourage him; and the other answered, gasping:

"Ah, I am dying! . . . Get closer, warm me! Not with your hands! no, your whole body!"

Julain laid himself right over him, mouth to mouth, breast to breast.

Then the Leper clasped him in his arms; and his eyes all at once became as bright as stars; his hair lengthened out like beams of the sun; the breath of his nostrils had the sweetness of roses; a cloud of incense rose from the hearth, the waves sang. Meanwhile a fullness of bliss, a superhuman joy came down like a flood into Julian's heart as he lay swooning; and the one in whose arms he was still clasped grew and grew, his head and his feet touching the two walls of the hovel. The roof flew off, the heavens unfolded; and Julian rose toward the blue, face to face with the Lord Jesus who was bearing him to Heaven.

And that is the story of Saint Julian the Hospitaller, more or less as it is to be found on a church window near my old home.

◇◇◇*André Gide (1869–1951). An extraordinarily active and v̶* *French man of letters, he wrote criticism, novels, novellas, pl̶* *travel books and journals. His works include* Strait Is the Gate, The Vatican Swindle, The Counterfeiters, The Immoralist, *his three volumes of journals and his books on* Oscar Wilde *and* Dostoyevsky. *He was awarded the Nobel Prize.*

MY MOTHER

BY ANDRE GIDE

I

When I had finished with school, my Mother decided to take me into "the world." But she had been uprooted from Rouen and brought to Paris, where she had never tried to get to know anyone, except some of our less distant cousins and the wives of a few of my Father's colleagues in the Faculty of Law. Moreover the world that seemed likely to interest me, the world of writers and artists, was not her world, and in it she would have felt out of place.

I have forgotten which salon it was that she took me to on this first occasion: probably our Saussine cousin's, to whose house in the Rue d'Athènes I went twice a week for dreary dancing-lessons. It was an At Home Day. I was introduced to a number of persons, and the talk was, like almost all talk at such social gatherings, a tissue of trifles and affectations. I was impressed not so much by the other ladies as by my Mother. I hardly recognized her. Usually so modest, so reserved and as it were frightened of her own opinions, in this drawing-room she seemed confident and, though not in the least self-assertive, absolutely at ease. It was as if she was throwing herself into a part, playing it exactly right, not indeed attaching any importance to it, but lending herself readily to the social comedy in which everything is pretense. It seemed to me even that among all the insipidities and sillinesses some particularly sensible comments

From *Modern French Short Stories.* (Translated by Raymond Mortimer.) By permission of New Directions.

hers broke rather disturbingly into the general conversation, deflating instantly all the absurd remarks and making them vanish back into thin air like ghosts at cockcrow.

I was filled with astonishment and admiration; and I told my Mother so, as soon as we were alone together, having escaped from this Vanity Fair. I was dining out that evening—I think with Pierre Louys. At any rate I remember leaving her at the corner of the Rue d'Athènes. But almost directly after dinner I came home, for I was impatient to see her. We were then living in the Rue de Commaille. The windows of our flat looked on to a garden that ran a long way back. (It is no longer there.) My Mother was on the balcony. She had taken off her finery, and I found her in her simple, dull, everyday clothes. It was the time of the year when the first acacias send out their scent. My Mother seemed pensive: she never liked talking about herself and no doubt it was the feeling of spring that now encouraged her to speak.

"Was it true, what you said when we left?" she began with great difficulty. "Do you really think so? Did I, well, was I as ladylike as the others?"

And, as I began to protest, she went on sadly: "If only your Father for once had told me so. . . . I never dared ask him, and it would have made all the difference to me to know, when we went out together, whether he. . . ."

She paused a moment. I watched her trying to keep back her tears. In a lower voice, hardly audible, she went on: "Whether he was pleased with me."

I fancy that those were her exact words: and they made me understand in a flash how many uncertainties, unspoken questions and unfulfilled hopes could persist, under the appearance of happiness, even in the closest union—for such my parents' marriage was in the eyes of everyone, including their son. What my Mother had waited for in vain was not a compliment from my Father: it was just the certainty that she had managed to seem worthy of him, that he had not been disappointed in her. But what my Father thought I never could tell any more than she; and that evening I realized that every soul takes away to the grave, where they will be for ever hidden, some secrets.

II

I loved everything in my Mother that was part of her nature. But it sometimes happened that her impulses were repressed by the conventions and by the durable twist that a bourgeois education too often leaves. (But this was not always the case: this I remember that she had the courage to defy the advice of all her family by going to nurse the La Roque farmers during an outbreak of typhus.) Such an upbringing is excellent where there are evil instincts to be curbed; but it is hostile also to the generous movements of the heart—and most deplorably. It restrains and deflects these, because it renders us calculating. Let me give an example.

My Mother told me she proposed to give a Littré dictionary to Anna Shackleton, an impoverished friend of ours whom I loved like a son. I was bursting with joy, when my Mother added: "The one I gave your Father is bound in morocco. I've decided that for Anna a grain binding would do."

I at once understood, what I had not known, that grain was much cheaper. In an instant all my joy was gone. And no doubt my Mother noticed this, for she continued very quickly:

"She won't know the difference."

No, no. The giving came from her nature, but not this mean little trick. And I was vexed also at her wishing to make me so to speak a party to it.

I have lost all memory of a thousand more important matters. Why did these few sentences of my Mother's imprint themselves so indelibly on my heart? Perhaps because I felt myself capable of the same thoughts, the same words, in spite of the violent disapproval they excited in me. Perhaps, too, I became conscious at this moment of the twist against which I should have to struggle, the twist I was so sad and astonished to detect in my Mother. Everything else was in key with her harmonious personality and therefore inconspicuous; and perhaps my memory seized on this trait, which was so unworthy of her, just because I could not recognize it as properly hers. What a warning to me! How strong the twist left by her upbringing must be, since it could thus occasionally predominate! But my Mother could not distinguish her natural impulses from her acquired characteristics, so closely was she surrounded by those who were similarly warped; above all she remained too nervous and uncertain of herself to make her nature take the upper hand. She kept to the end her respect for other people and their opinions; always anxious to improve, but accepting the conventional view of improvement; always making efforts to do better and never realizing, because she was too modest, that the best in herself was precisely what required from the least effort of will.

THE DISABLED SOLDIER

BY OLIVER GOLDSMITH

No observation is more common, and at the same time more true, than that one half of the world are ignorant how the other half lives. The misfortunes of the great are held up to engage our attention; are enlarged upon in tones of declamation; and the world is called upon to gaze at the noble sufferers: the great, under the pressure of calamity, are conscious of several others sympathising with their distress; and have, at once, the comfort of admiration and pity.

There is nothing magnanimous in bearing misfortunes with fortitude, when the whole world is looking on: men in such circumstances will act bravely even from motives of vanity: but he who, in the vale of obscurity, can brave adversity; who without friends to encourage, acquaintances to pity, or even without hope to alleviate his misfortunes, can behave with tranquillity and indifference, is truly great: whether peasant or courtier, he deserves admiration, and should be held up for our imitation and respect.

While the slightest inconveniences of the great are magnified into calamities; while tragedy mouths out their sufferings in all the strains of eloquence, the miseries of the poor are entirely disregarded; and yet some of the lower ranks of people undergo more real hardships in one day, than those of a more exalted station suffer in their whole lives. It is inconceivable what difficulties the meanest of our common sailors and soldiers endure without murmuring or regret; without passionately declaiming against providence, or calling their fellows to be gazers of their intrepidity. Every day is to them a day of misery, and yet they entertain their hard fate without repining.

With what indignation do I hear an Ovid, a Cicero, or a Rabutin complain of their misfortunes and hardships, whose greatest calamity was that of being unable to visit a certain spot of earth, to which they had foolishly attached an idea of happiness. Their distresses were pleasures, compared to what many of the adventuring poor every day endure without murmuring. They ate, drank, and slept; they had slaves to attend them, and were sure of subsistence for life; while many of their fellow creatures are obliged to wander without a friend to comfort or assist them, and even without shelter from the severity of the season.

I have been led into these reflections from accidentally meeting, some days ago, a poor fellow, whom I knew when a boy, dressed in a sailor's jacket, and begging at one of the outlets of the town, with a wooden leg. I knew him to have been honest and industrious when in the country, and was curious to learn what had reduced him to his present situation. Wherefore, after giving him what I thought proper, I desired to know the history of his life and misfortunes, and the manner in which he was reduced to his present distress. The disabled soldier, for such he was, though dressed in a sailor's habit, scratching his head, and leaning on his crutch, put himself into an attitude to comply with my request, and gave me his history as follows:

"As for my misfortunes, master, I can't pretend to have gone through any more than other folks; for, except the loss of my limb, and my being obliged to beg, I don't know any reason, thank Heaven, that I have to complain. There is Bill Tibbs, of our regiment, he has lost both his legs, and an eye to boot; but, thank Heaven, it is not so bad with me yet.

"I was born in Shropshire; my father was a labourer, and died when I was five years old, so I was put upon the parish. As he had been a wandering sort of man, the parishioners were not able to tell to what parish I belonged, or where I was born, so they sent me to another parish, and that parish sent me to a third. I thought in my heart, they kept sending me about so long, that they would not let me be born in any parish at all; but at last, however, they fixed me. I had some disposition to be a scholar, and was resolved at least to know my letters: but the master of the workhouse put me to business as soon as I was able to handle a mallet; and here I lived an easy kind of life for five years. I only wrought ten hours in the day, and had my meat and drink provided for my labour. It was true I was not suffered to stir out of the house, for fear, as they said, I should run away; but what of that? I had the liberty of the whole house, and the yard before the door, and that was enough for me. I was then bound out to a farmer, where I was up both early and late; but I ate and drank well; and liked my business well enough, till he died, when I was obliged to provide for myself; so I was resolved to go seek my fortune.

"In this manner I went from town to town, worked when I could get employment, and starved when I could get none; when, happening one day to go through a field belonging to a justice of the peace, I spied a hare crossing the path just before me; and I believe the devil put it into my head to fling my stick at it. Well, what will you have on't? I killed the hare, and was bringing it away, when the justice himself met me; he called me a poacher and a villain, and collaring me, desired I would give an account of myself. I fell upon my knees, begged his worship's pardon, and began to give a full account of all that I knew of my breed, seed, and generation; but though I gave a very true account, the justice said I could give no account; so I was indicted at the sessions, found guilty of being poor, and sent up to London to Newgate, in order to be transported as a vagabond.

"People may say this and that of being in jail, but, for my part, I found Newgate as agreeable a place as ever I was in in all my life. I had my belly full to eat and drink, and did no work at all. This kind of life was too good to last forever; so I was taken out of prison, after five months, put on board of ship, and sent off, with two hundred more, to the plantations. We had but an indifferent passage, for being all confined to the hold, more than a hundred of our people died for want of sweet air; and those that remained were sickly enough, God knows. When we came ashore we were sold to the planters, and I was bound for seven years more. As I was no scholar, for I did not know my letters, I was obliged to work among the negroes; and I served out my time, as in duty bound to do.

"When my time was expired, I worked my passage home, and

glad I was to see old England again, because I loved my country. I was afraid, however, that I should be indicted for a vagabond once more, so did not much care to go down into the country, but kept about the town, and did little jobs when I could get them.

"I was very happy in this manner for some time till one evening, coming home from work, two men knocked me down, and then desired me to stand. They belonged to a press-gang. I was carried before the justice, and as I could give no account of myself, I had my choice left, whether to go on board a man-of-war, or list for a soldier. I chose the latter, and in this post of a gentleman, I served two campaigns in Flanders, was at the battles of Val and Fontenoy, and received but one wound through the breast here; but the doctor of our regiment soon made me well again.

"When the peace came on I was discharged; and as I could not work, because my wound was sometimes troublesome, I listed for a landman in the East India Company's service. I have fought the French in six pitched battles; and I verily believe that if I could read or write, our captain would have made me a corporal. But it was not my good fortune to have any promotion, for I soon fell sick, and so got leave to return home again with forty pounds in my pocket. This was at the beginning of the present war, and I hoped to be set on shore, and to have the pleasure of spending my money; but the Government wanted men, and so I was pressed for a sailor, before ever I could set foot on shore.

"The boatswain found me, as he said, an obstinate fellow: he swore he knew that I understood my business well, but that I shammed Abraham, to be idle; but God knows, I knew nothing of sea-business, and he beat me without considering what he was about. I had still, however, my forty pounds, and that was some comfort to me under every beating; and the money I might have had to this day, but that our ship was taken by the French, and so I lost all.

"Our crew was carried into Brest, and many of them died, because they were not used to live in a jail; but, for my part, it was nothing to me, for I was seasoned. One night, as I was asleep on the bed of boards, with a warm blanket about me, for I always loved to lie well, I was awakened by the boatswain, who had a dark lantern in his hand. 'Jack,' says he to me, 'will you knock out the

French sentry's brains?' 'I don't care,' says I, striving to keep myself awake, 'if I lend a hand.' 'Then follow me,' says he, 'and I hope we shall do business.' So up I got, and tied my blanket, which was all the clothes I had, about my middle, and went with him to fight the Frenchman. I hate the French, because they are all slaves, and wear wooden shoes.

"Though we had no arms, one Englishman is able to beat five French at any time; so we went down to the door where both sentries were posted, and rushing upon them, seized their arms in a moment, and knocked them down. From thence nine of us ran together to the quay, and seizing the first boat we met, got out of the harbour and put to sea. We had not been here three days before we were taken up by the Dorset privateer, who were glad of so many good hands; and we consented to run our chance. However, we had not as much luck as we expected. In three days we fell in with the *Pompadour* privateer of forty guns, while we had but twenty-three, so to it we went, yard-arm and yard-arm. The fight lasted three hours, and I verily believe we should have taken the Frenchman, had we but some more men left behind; but unfortunately we lost all our men just as we were going to get the victory.

"I was once more in the power of the French, and I believe it would have gone hard with me had I been brought back to Brest; but by good fortune we were retaken by the *Viper*. I had almost forgotten to tell you, that in that engagement, I was wounded in two places: I lost four fingers off the left hand, and my leg was shot off. If I had had the good fortune to have lost my leg and the use of my hand on board a king's ship, and not aboard a privateer, I should have been entitled to clothing and maintenance during the rest of my life; but that was not my chance: one man is born with a silver spoon in his mouth, and another with a wooden ladle. However, blessed be God, I enjoy good health, and will for ever love liberty and old England. Liberty, property, and old England, for ever, huzza!"

Thus saying, he limped off, leaving me in admiration at his intrepidity and content; nor could I avoid acknowledging, that an habitual acquaintance with misery serves better than philosophy to teach us to despise it.

◇◇◇*Nathaniel Hawthorne (1804–1864). Born in Salem, Massachusetts, of a Puritan family. He ranks as one of America's greatest literary artists. He composed tales, novels and essays. He was a friend of Herman Melville, who admired him as man and writer.*

THE GRAY CHAMPION

BY NATHANIEL HAWTHORNE

There was once a time when New England groaned under the actual pressure of heavier wrongs than those threatened ones which brought on the Revolution. James II, the bigoted successor of Charles the Voluptuous, had annulled the charters of all the colonies, and sent a harsh and unprincipled soldier to take away our liberties and endanger our religion. The administration of Sir Edmund Andros lacked scarcely a single characteristic of tyranny: a Governor and Council, holding office from the King, and wholly independent of the country; laws made and taxes levied without concurrence of the people immediate or by their representatives; the rights of private citizens violated, and the titles of all landed property declared void; the voice of complaint stifled by restrictions on the press; and, finally, disaffection overawed by the first band of mercenary troops that ever marched on our free soil. For two years our ancestors were kept in sullen submission by that filial love which had invariably secured their allegiance to the mother country, whether its head chanced to be a Parliament, Protector, or Popish Monarch. Till these evil times, however, such allegiance had been merely nominal, and the colonists had ruled themselves, enjoying far more freedom than is even yet the privilege of the native subjects of Great Britain.

At length a rumor reached our shores that the Prince of Orange had ventured on an enterprise, the success of which would be the triumph of civil and religious rights and the salvation of New England. It was but a doubtful whisper; it might be false, or the attempt might fail; and, in either case, the man that stirred against King

James would lose his head. Still the intelligence produced a marked effect. The people smiled mysteriously in the streets, and threw bold glances at their oppressors; while far and wide there was a subdued and silent agitation, as if the slightest signal would rouse the whole land from its sluggish despondency. Aware of their danger, the rulers resolved to avert it by an imposing display of strength, and perhaps to confirm their despotism by yet harsher measures. One afternoon in April, 1689, Sir Edmund Andros and his favorite councillors, being warm with wine, assembled the red-coats of the Governor's Guard, and made their appearance in the streets of Boston. The sun was near setting when the march commenced.

The roll of the drum at that unquiet crisis seemed to go through the streets, less as the martial music of the soldiers, than as a muster-call to the inhabitants themselves. A multitude, by various avenues, assembled in King Street, which was destined to be the scene, nearly a century afterwards, of another encounter between the troops of Britain, and a people struggling against her tyranny. Though more than sixty years had elapsed since the pilgrims came, this crowd of their descendants still showed the strong and sombre features of their character perhaps more strikingly in such a stern emergency than on happier occasions. There were the sober garb, the general severity of mien, the gloomy but undismayed expression, the scriptural forms of speech, and the confidence in Heaven's blessing on a righteous cause, which would have marked a band of the original Puritans, when threatened by some peril of the wilderness. Indeed, it was not yet time for the old spirit to be extinct; since there were men in the street that day who had worshipped there beneath the trees, before a house was reared to the God for whom they had become exiles. Old soldiers of the Parliament were here, too, smiling grimly at the thought that their aged arms might strike another blow against the house of Stuart. Here, also, were the veterans of King Philip's war, who had burned villages and slaughtered young and old, with pious fierceness, while the godly souls throughout the land were helping them with prayer. Several ministers were scattered among the crowd, which, unlike all other mobs, regarded them with such reverence, as if there were sanctity in their very garments. These holy men exerted their influence to quiet the people, but not to disperse them. Meantime, the purpose of the Governor, in disturbing the peace of the town at a period when the slightest commotion might throw the country into a ferment, was almost the universal subject of inquiry, and variously explained.

"Satan will strike his master-stroke presently," cried some, "because he knoweth that his time is short. All our godly pastors are to be dragged to prison! We shall see them at a Smithfield fire in King Street!"

Hereupon the people of each parish gathered closer round their minister, who looked calmly upwards and assumed a more apostolic dignity, as well befitted a candidate for the highest honor of his profession, the crown of martyrdom. It was actually fancied, at that period, that New England might have a John Rogers of her own to take the place of that worthy in the Primer.

"The Pope of Rome has given orders for a new St. Bartholomew!" cried others. "We are to be massacred, man and male child!"

Neither was this rumor wholly discredited, although the wiser class believed the Governor's object somewhat less atrocious. His predecessor under the old charter, Bradstreet, a venerable companion of the first settlers, was known to be in town. There were grounds for conjecturing, that Sir Edmund Andros intended at once to strike terror by a parade of military force, and to confound the opposite faction by possessing himself of their chief.

"Stand firm for the old charter, Governor!" shouted the crowd, seizing upon the idea. "The good old Governor Bradstreet!"

While this cry was at the loudest, the people were surprised by the well-known figure of Governor Bradstreet himself, a patriarch of nearly ninety, who appeared on the elevated steps of a door, and, with characteristic mildness, besought them to submit to the constituted authorities.

"My children," concluded this venerable person, "do nothing rashly. Cry not aloud, but pray for the welfare of New England, and expect patiently what the Lord will do in this matter!"

The event was soon to be decided. All this time, the roll of the drum had been approaching through Cornhill, louder and deeper, till with reverberations from house to house, and the regular tramp of martial footsteps, it burst into the street. A double rank of soldiers made their appearance, occupying the whole breadth of the passage, with shouldered matchlocks, and matches burning, so as to present a row of fires in the dusk. Their steady march was like the progress of a machine, that would roll irresistibly over everything in its way. Next, moving slowly, with a confused clatter of hoofs on the pavement, rode a party of mounted gentlemen, the central figure being Sir Edmund Andros, elderly, but erect and soldier-like. Those around him were his favorite councillors, and the bitterest foes of New England. At his right hand rode Edward Randolph, our arch-enemy, that "blasted wretch," as Cotton Mather calls him, who achieved the downfall of our ancient government, and was followed with a sensible curse, through life and to his grave. On the other side was Bullivant, scattering jests and mockery as he rode along. Dudley came behind, with a downcast look, dreading, as well he might, to meet the indignant gaze of the people, who beheld him, their only countryman by birth, among the oppressors of his native land. The captain of a frigate in the harbor, and two or three civil officers under the Crown, were also there. But the figure which most attracted the public eye, and stirred up the deepest feeling, was the Episcopal clergyman of King's Chapel, riding haughtily among the magistrates in his priestly vestments, the fitting representative of prelacy and persecution, the union of church and state, and all those abominations which had driven the Puritans to the wilderness. Another guard of soldiers, in double rank, brought up the rear.

The whole scene was a picture of the condition of New England, and its moral, the deformity of any government that does not grow out of the nature of things and the character of the people. On one side the religious multitude, with their sad visages and dark attire, and on the other, the group of despotic rulers, with the high churchman in the midst, and here and there a crucifix at their bosoms, all magnificently clad, flushed with wine, proud of unjust authority, and scoffing at the universal groan. And the mercenary soldiers, waiting but the word to deluge the street with blood, showed the only means by which obedience could be secured.

"O Lord of Hosts," cried a voice among the crowd, "provide a Champion for thy people!"

This ejaculation was loudly uttered, and served as a herald's cry, to introduce a remarkable personage. The crowd had rolled back, and were now huddled together nearly at the extremity of the street, while the soldiers had advanced no more than a third of its length. The intervening space was empty—a paved solitude, between lofty edifices, which threw almost a twilight shadow over it. Suddenly, there was seen the figure of an ancient man, who seemed to have emerged from among the people, and was walking by himself along the centre of the street, to confront the armed band. He wore the old Puritan dress, a dark cloak and a steeple-crowned hat, in the fashion of at least fifty years before, with a heavy sword upon his thigh, but a staff in his hand to assist the tremulous gait of age.

When at some distance from the multitude, the old man turned slowly round, displaying a face of antique majesty, rendered doubly venerable by the hoary beard that descended on his breast. He made a gesture at once of encouragement and warning, then turned again, and resumed his way.

"Who is this gray patriarch?" asked the young men of their sires.

"Who is this venerable brother?" asked the old men among themselves.

But none could make reply. The fathers of the people, those of fourscore years and upwards, were disturbed, deeming it strange that they should forget one of such evident authority, whom they must have known in their early days, the associate of Winthrop, and all the old councillors, giving laws, and making prayers, and leading them against the savage. The elderly men ought to have remembered him, too, with locks as gray in their youth, as their own were now. And the young! How could he have passed so utterly from their memories—that hoary sire, the relic of long-departed times, whose awful benediction had surely been bestowed on their uncovered heads, in childhood?

"Whence did he come? What is his purpose? Who can this old man be?" whispered the wondering crowd.

Meanwhile, the venerable stranger, staff in hand, was pursuing his solitary walk along the centre of the street. As he drew near the advancing soldiers, and as the roll of their drum came full upon his ear, the old man raised himself to a loftier mien, while the decrepitude of age seemed to fall from his shoulders, leaving him in gray but unbroken dignity. Now, he marched onward with a warrior's step, keeping time to the military music. Thus the aged form advanced on one side, and the whole parade of soldiers and magistrates on the other, till, when scarcely twenty yards remained between, the old man grasped his staff by the middle, and held it before him like a leader's truncheon.

"Stand!" cried he.

The eye, the face, and attitude of command; the solemn, yet war-like peal of that voice, fit either to rule a host in the battle-field or be raised to God in prayer, were irresistible. At the old man's word and outstretched arm, the roll of the drum was hushed at once, and the advancing line stood still. A tremulous enthusiasm seized upon the multitude. That stately form, combining the leader and the saint, so gray, so dimly seen, in such an ancient garb, could only belong to some old champion of the righteous cause, whom the oppressor's drum had summoned from his grave. They raised a shout of awe and exultation, and looked for the deliverance of New England.

The Governor, and the gentlemen of his party, perceiving themselves brought to an unexpected stand, rode hastily forward, as if they would have pressed their snorting and affrighted horses right against the hoary apparition. He, however, blenched not a step, but glancing his severe eye round the group, which half encompassed him, at last bent it sternly on Sir Edmund Andros. One would have thought that the dark old man was chief ruler there, and that the Governor and Council, with soldiers at their back, representing the whole power and authority of the Crown, had no alternative but obedience.

"What does this old fellow here?" cried Edward Randolph, fiercely. "On, Sir Edmund! Bid the soldiers forward, and give the dotard the same choice that you give all his countrymen—to stand aside or be trampled on!"

"Nay, nay, let us show respect to the good grand-sire," said Bullivant, laughing. "See you not, he is some old round-headed dignitary, who hath lain asleep these thirty years, and knows nothing of the change of times? Doubtless, he thinks to put us down with a proclamation in Old Noll's name!"

"Are you mad, old man?" demanded Sir Edmund Andros, in loud and harsh tones. "How dare you stay the march of King James's Governor?"

"I have stayed the march of a King himself, ere now," replied the gray figure, with stern composure. "I am here, Sir Governor, be-

cause the cry of an oppressed people hath disturbed me in my secret place; and beseeching this favor earnestly of the Lord, it was
vouchsafed me to appear once again on earth, in the good old
cause of his saints. And what speak ye of James? There is no longer
a Popish tyrant on the throne of England, and by to-morrow noon,
his name shall be a byword in this very street, where ye would make
it a word of terror. Back, thou that wast a Governor, back! With
this night thy power is ended—to-morrow, the prison!—back, lest
I foretell the scaffold!"

The people had been drawing nearer and nearer and drinking in
the words of their champion, who spoke in accents long disused,
like one unaccustomed to converse, except with the dead of many
years ago. But his voice stirred their souls. They confronted the
soldiers, not wholly without arms, and ready to convert the very
stones of the street into deadly weapons. Sir Edmund Andros looked
at the old man; then he cast his hard and cruel eye over the multitude, and beheld them burning with that lurid wrath, so difficult
to kindle or to quench; and again he fixed his gaze on the aged form,
which stood obscurely in an open space, where neither friend nor
foe had thrust himself. What were his thoughts, he uttered no word
which might discover. But whether the oppressor were overawed
by the Gray Champion's look, or perceived his peril in the threatening attitude of the people, it is certain that he gave back, and ordered his soldiers to commence a slow and guarded retreat. Before
another sunset, the Governor, and all that rode so proudly with
him, were prisoners, and long ere it was known that James had
abdicated, King William was proclaimed throughout New England.

But where was the Gray Champion? Some reported that, when
the troops had gone from King Street, and the people were throng-
ing tumultuously in their rear, Bradstreet, the aged Governor, was
seen to embrace a form more aged than his own. Others soberly af-
firmed, that while they marvelled at the venerable grandeur of his
aspect, the old man had faded from their eyes, melting slowly into
the hues of twilight, till, where he stood, there was an empty space.
But all agreed that the hoary shape was gone. The men of that generation watched for his reappearance, in sunshine and in twilight,
but never saw him more, nor knew when his funeral passed, nor
where his gravestone was.

And who was the Gray Champion? Perhaps his name might be found in the records of that stern Court of Justice, which passed a sentence, too mighty for the age, but glorious in all after-times, for its humbling lesson to the monarch and its high example to the subject. I have heard, that whenever the descendants of the Puritans are to show the spirit of their sires the old man appears again. When eighty years had passed, he walked once more in King Street. Five years later, in the twilight of an April morning, he stood on the green, beside the meeting-house, at Lexington, where now the obelisk of granite, with a slab of slate inlaid, commemorates the first fallen of the Revolution. And when our fathers were toiling at the breastwork on Bunker's Hill, all through that night the old warrior walked his rounds. Long, long may it be, ere he comes again! His hour is one of darkness, and adversity, and peril. But should domestic tyranny oppress us, or the invader's step pollute our soil, still may the Gray Champion come, for he is the type of New England's hereditary spirit; and his shadowy march, on the eve of danger, must ever be the pledge, that New England's sons will vindicate their ancestry.

◇◇◇Heinrich Heine (1797-1856). German poet, born of Jewish parents. He was baptized a Christian in 1825. He was a radical, a critic of philosophy, a wit and an ironist. But he is chiefly famous as a lyrical poet. A Tale of Olden Time was originally designed to be the first chapter of a novel. The novel was never completed. Many of Heine's poems have received musical settings and are widely sung, prominent among them the Lorelei.

A TALE OF OLDEN TIME

BY HEINRICH HEINE

Above the Rhineland, where the great river's banks cease to smile, where mountain and cliff, with their romantic ruined castles, show a bolder bearing and a wilder, sterner majesty arises—there, like a fearful tale of olden times, lies the gloomy, ancient town of Bacharach. But these walls with the toothless battlements and blind lookouts, in whose gaps the wind blows and the sparrows nest, were not always so broken-down and crumbling. In the ugly unpaved alleys seen through the ruined gate there did not always reign that dreary silence broken only now and then by screaming children, bickering women, and lowing cows. These walls were proud and strong once, and through these alleys moved a fresh, free life, power and pomp, joy and sorrow, plenty of love, and plenty of hate.

Bacharach was once one of those municipalities which the Romans founded when they ruled along the Rhine. And, although subsequent times were stormy and the inhabitants later came under the overlordship of the Hohenstaufens and finally that of the Wittelsbachs, nevertheless they knew, after the example of other towns on the Rhine, how to maintain a fairly free commonwealth. It consisted of a combination of several corporate bodies, with those of the old patriciate and those of the guilds which again were subdivided according to their different trades—both striving for sole power. So that while outwardly they all stood firmly together,

From *Works of Prose* by Heinrich Heine, edited by Hermann Kesten. (Translated by E. B. Ashton.) By permission of the publishers, A. A. Wyn, Inc.

bound to common vigilance and defense against the neighboring robber-barons, internally their divergent interests kept them in constant dissension. There was therefore little neighborliness and much mistrust; even overt outbursts of passion were not infrequent. The Lord Warden sat on the high tower of Sareck; and, like his falcon, he swooped down whenever called for—and sometimes uncalled for. The clergy ruled in darkness by darkening the souls. One of the most isolated and helpless of bodies, gradually crushed by the civil law, was the small Jewish community which had first settled in Bacharach in Roman days, and later, during the Great Persecution, had taken in whole flocks of fugitive brothers in the faith.

The Great Persecution of the Jews began with the Crusades and raged grimly about the middle of the fourteenth century, at the end of the Great Plague which, like any other public disaster, was blamed on the Jews. It was asserted that they had brought down the wrath of God, and that they had poisoned the wells with the aid of the lepers. The enraged rabble, especially the hordes of the Flagellants—half-naked men and women who, lashing themselves for penance and chanting a mad song to the Virgin Mary, swept through the Rhineland and South Germany—murdered many thousands of Jews, tortured them, or baptized them by force. Another accusation, which even before that time, and throughout the Middle Ages until the beginning of the past century, cost them much blood and anguish, was the absurd tale, repeated ad nauseam in chronicle and legend, that the Jews would steal the consecrated wafer, stabbing it with knives until the blood ran from it, and that they would slay Christian children at the feast of the Passover, in order to use the blood for their nocturnal rite.

The Jews—sufficiently hated for their faith, their wealth, and their ledgers—were on this holiday entirely in the hands of their enemies, who could encompass their destruction with ease by spreading rumors of such an infanticide, perhaps even sneaking the bloody corpse of a child into a Jewish outcast's house, and then setting upon the Jews at their prayers. There would be murder, plunder, and baptism; and great miracles would be wrought by the dead child, whom the Church might even canonize in the end. Saint Werner is one of these saints; and it was in his honor that at

Oberwesel the great abbey was founded which is now one of the most beautiful ruins on the Rhine, and delights us so much with the Gothic splendor of its long, ogival windows, proudly soaring pillars, and stone-carvings, when we pass it on a gay, green summer day and do not know its origin. In honor of this saint, three more great churches were built along the Rhine and innumerable Jews abused or murdered. This happened in the year 1287; and in Bacharach, where one of Saint Werner's churches arose, the Jews also underwent many trials and tribulations. For two centuries afterwards they were spared such attacks of mob fury, although they were still harassed and threatened enough.

However, the more they were beset with hate from without, the more fond and tender grew the Bacharach Jews' domestic life, and the more profound their piety and fear of God. A model of godly conduct was the local rabbi, called Rabbi Abraham; a young man still, but famed far and wide for his learning. He was born in the town, and his father, who had been the rabbi there before him, had charged him in his last will to devote himself to the same calling and never leave Bacharach unless in deadly peril. This word, and a cabinet full of rare books, was all that was left him by his father, who had lived in poverty and learning. Nevertheless Rabbi Abraham was a very wealthy man now, being married to the only daughter of his late paternal uncle who had been a dealer in jewelry, and whose riches he had inherited. A few sly gossips kept hinting at that—as if the Rabbi had married his wife just for the money. But the women, contradicting in unison, had old stories to tell: how the Rabbi had been in love with Sarah—she was commonly called Lovely Sarah—long before he went to Spain, and how she had to wait seven years till he returned after he wed her against her father's will, and even without her consent, by means of the "betrothal ring." For every Jew can make a Jewish girl his lawful wife if he succeeds in putting a ring on her finger and saying at the same time: "I take thee for my wife, according to the laws of Moses and Israel!"

At the mention of Spain the sly ones used to smile in a knowing way; probably because of a dark rumor that while Rabbi Abraham had studied the holy law zealously enough at the high school of Toledo, he had also copied Christian customs and absorbed ways of free thinking, like the Spanish Jews who at that time had attained an extraordinary height of culture. In their hearts, though, those gossips hardly believed their own insinuations. For the Rabbi's life, after his return from Spain, had been extremely pure, pious, and earnest; he observed the most trivial rites with painful conscientiousness, fasted each Monday and Thursday, abstained from meat and wine except on the Sabbath and other holidays, and spent his days in study and prayer. By day, he expounded the Law to the students whom his fame had drawn to Bacharach; and by night he gazed on the stars in the sky, or into the eyes of Lovely Sarah. The Rabbi's marriage was childless, yet there was about him no lack of life or gaiety. The great hall in his house, which adjoined the synagogue, was open to the whole community. Here one came and went without ceremony, offered quick prayers, traded news, or took common counsel in hard times. Here the children played on Sabbath mornings while in the synagogue the weekly chapter was read; here one met for wedding and funeral processions, quarreled, and was reconciled; here those that were cold found a warm stove, and the hungry a well-spread table. Besides, there was a multitude of relatives surrounding the Rabbi; brothers and sisters with their wives and husbands and children, as well as both his and his wife's uncles and aunts and countless other kin—all of whom regarded him as the head of the family—made themselves at home in his house from dawn to dusk, and never failed to dine there in full force on the high holidays. In particular, such grand family dinners took place in the Rabbi's house at the annual celebration of the Passover, an age-old, wondrous festival which Jews all over the world still observe on the fourteenth day of the month of Nisan, in eternal memory of their redemption from Egyptian slavery in the following manner:

As soon as night falls, the mistress of the house lights the lamps, spreads the tablecloth, puts three pieces of the flat unleavened bread in its midst, covers them with a napkin, and on the pile places six little dishes containing symbolical food: an egg, lettuce, horseradish, the bone of a lamb, and a brown mixture of raisins, cinnamon, and nuts. At this table, the head of the house then sits down with all relations and friends, and reads to them from a very curious book called the Hagaddah, the contents of which are a strange mixture of ancestral legends, miraculous tales of Egypt, odd narratives, disputations, prayers, and festive songs. A huge supper is brought in halfway through this celebration; and even during the reading, at certain times, one tastes of the symbolical dishes, eats pieces of unleavened bread, and drinks four cups of red wine. This nocturnal festival is melancholically gay in character, gravely playful, and mysterious as a fairy tale. And the traditional singsong in which the Hagaddah is read by the head of the house, and now and then repeated by the listeners in chorus, sounds at the same time so awesomely intense, maternally gentle, and suddenly awakening, that even those Jews who have long forsaken the faith of their fathers and pursued foreign joys and honors are moved to the depths of their hearts when the old, familiar sounds of the Passover happen to strike their ears.

And so Rabbi Abraham once sat in the great hall of his house with his relations, disciples, and other guests, to celebrate the eve of the Passover. Everything in the hall was brighter than usual; over the table hung a gaily embroidered silk spread whose gold fringes touched the floor; the plates with the symbolic foods shone appealingly, as did the tall, wine-filled goblets adorned with the embossed images of many holy stories. The men sat in their black cloaks and black, flat hats and white ruffs; the women, in strangely glittering garments made of cloths from Lombardy, wore their diadems and necklaces of gold and pearls; and the silver Sabbath lamp cast its most festive light on the devoutly merry faces of old and young. Reclining, as custom enjoins, on the purple velvet cushions of a chair raised above the others, Rabbi Abraham sat reading and chanting the Hagaddah, while the mixed choir fell in or responded in the prescribed places. The Rabbi wore his black holiday garb. His noble, somewhat austere features seemed milder than usual; his lips were smiling out of the dark beard as if they had something fair to tell; and in his eyes was a light as of happy memories and visions of the future.

Lovely Sarah, seated beside him on a similar high velvet chair, wore none of her jewelry, being the hostess; only white linen enclosed her slender form and pious face. It was a touchingly beautiful face, just as always the beauty of Jewesses is of a peculiarly moving kind—a consciousness of the deep misery, the bitter scorn, and the evil chances wherein their kindred and friends live, brings to their lovely features a certain aching tenderness and observant loving apprehension that strangely charm our hearts. So, on this evening, Lovely Sarah sat looking constantly into her husband's eyes. But every now and then she also glanced at the quaint parchment book of the Hagaddah which lay before her, bound in gold and velvet: an old heirloom with wine stains of many years on it, which had come down from her grandfather's time and in which were many bold and brightly-colored pictures that even as a little girl she had so loved to look at on Passover evenings. They represented all kinds of Biblical stories, such as Abraham smashing his father's idols with a hammer; the angels coming to him; Moses killing Mizri; and the Pharaoh sitting in state on his throne, with the frogs giving him no rest even at table. Also she saw how Pharaoh drowned, thank God! and how the children of Israel went cautiously through the Red Sea; and how they stood open-mouthed before Mount Sinai, with their sheep, cows, and oxen; how pious King David played the harp; and finally how Jerusalem, with the towers and battlements of its Temple, shone in the glory of the sun!

The second cup of wine was poured, the faces and the voices of the guests grew brighter, and the Rabbi, taking a piece of the un-leavened bread and raising it in a gay greeting, read these words from the Hagaddah: "This is the bread our fathers ate in Egypt. Whoever is hungry, let him come and share it! Whoever is in want, let him come and celebrate the Passover! This year we are here; and the coming year, in the land of Israel! This year we are slaves; the coming year, free men!"

At this moment, the door of the hall opened and two tall, pale men entered, wrapped in very wide cloaks, and one of them said: "Peace be with you; we are men of your faith, on a journey, and wish to celebrate the Passover with you." And the Rabbi, quickly and kindly, replied, "Peace be with you. Sit down here by me." The two strangers promptly sat down at the table, and the Rabbi read on. Sometimes, while the others were saying the responses, he would throw an endearing word to his wife: alluding to the old joke that on this evening the head of a Jewish house considers him-self a king, he said to her, "Be happy, my Queen!" But she, smil-ing sadly, replied, "We have no Prince"—by which she meant the son of the house, whom a passage in the Hagaddah requires to question his father in certain prescribed words about the meaning of the festival. The Rabbi said nothing, only pointing with his finger to a picture just turned up in the Hagaddah, on which was shown very charmingly how the three angels came to Abraham, to announce to him that he would have a son by his wife Sarah, who with feminine cunning was listening to their talk from behind the tent-door. This little hint sent a threefold blush to the beautiful woman's cheeks; she cast her eyes down, and then lovingly raised them again to her husband, who sent on chanting the wondrous story of Rabbi Jesua, Rabbi Eliezer, Rabbi Azaria, Rabbi Akibah, and Rabbi Tarphon, who sat reclining in Bona-Brak and talked all night of the Children of Israel's exodus from Egypt, until their disciples came to tell them that it was daylight and the great morning prayer was being read in the synagogue.

Now, as Lovely Sarah was thus devoutly listening and continually looking at her husband, she noticed that his face suddenly froze in horrible distortion, the blood left his cheeks and lips, and his eyes stood out like balls of ice. But almost at the same instant she saw his features returning to their former calm and cheerfulness, his cheeks and lips growing red again, his eyes circling merrily—in fact, his whole being seemed seized by a mad gaiety that otherwise was quite foreign to his nature. Lovely Sarah was frightened as never before in her life. A chilling dread rose in her, due less to the signs of rigid terror which for a moment she had seen in her husband's countenance than to his present merriment, which gradually turned into rollicking exultation. The Rabbi moved his cap from one ear to the other, pulled and twisted his beard comically, sang the text of the Hagaddah as if it were a catch; and in the enumeration of the Egyptian plagues, when it is the custom to dip the forefinger in the full cup and shake the clinging drop of wine to the ground, the Rabbi sprinkled the younger girls with red wine and there was much wailing over spoiled collars, and ringing laughter. An ever more eerie feeling overcame Lovely Sarah, at this convulsively bubbling gaiety of her husband's; seized by nameless qualms, she gazed on the humming swarm of brightly illumined people, comfortably rocking to and fro, nibbling the thin Passover bread or sipping wine or gossiping or singing aloud, in the very happiest of moods.

The time for supper came and all rose to wash, and Lovely Sarah brought a great silver basin covered with embossed gold figures, which she held before each guest while water was poured over his hands. When she thus served the Rabbi, he winked at her significantly and quietly slipped out of the door. Lovely Sarah followed on his heels; hastily, the Rabbi grasped her hand and quickly drew her away through the dark alleys of Bacharach, quickly through the town gate, out onto the highway leading along the Rhine, toward Bingen.

It was one of those nights in spring which, though soft enough and starry, raise strange shivers in the soul. The fragrance of the flowers was deathly. The birds chirped as if glad to vex someone and yet vexed themselves. The moon cast malicious yellow stripes of light over the darkly murmuring river. The tall, bulky rocks of the cliffs looked like menacingly wagging giants' heads. The watchman on the tower of Castle Strahleck blew a melancholy tune, and with it, jealously chiming, tolled the little death-bell of Saint Werner's. Lovely Sarah still held the silver ewer in her right hand; her left was held by the Rabbi, and she felt that his fingers were icy and his arm was trembling. But she followed in silence, perhaps because she had long been accustomed to obey her husband blindly and without questioning—perhaps, too, because fear sealed her lips from within.

Below Castle Sonneck, opposite Lorch—about where the hamlet of Niederrheinbach stands now—a high cliff arches out over the bank of the Rhine. This Rabbi Abraham ascended with his wife, looked all about him, and stared up at the stars. Lovely Sarah, trembling and chilled by fears of death, stood with him and regarded the pale face on which pain, dread, piety, and rage seemed to flash back and forth in the ghostly light of the moor. But when the Rabbi suddenly tore the silver ewer from her hand and hurled it clanking down into the Rhine, she could no longer bear the awful anxiety—and crying out, "*Schadai* full of mercy!" she threw herself at his feet and implored him to lift the dark secret.

The Rabbi moved his lips soundlessly a few times, unable to speak; but finally he called out, "Do you see the Angel of Death? Down there he hovers over Bacharach. Yet we have escaped his sword. Praised be the Lord!" And in a voice still shaking with fright he told her how, reclining happily and chanting the Hagaddah, he had chanced to look under the table and there, at his feet, had seen the bloody corpse of a child. "Then I knew," added the Rabbi, "that our two late guests were not of the community of Israel, but of the assembly of the godless whose plan was to bring that corpse into our house by stealth, charge us with the murder, and incite the people to loot and murder us. I could not let on that I saw through the work of darkness; thereby I should have only speeded my destruction. Cunning alone could save our lives. Praised be the Lord! Have no fear, Lovely Sarah; our friends and relatives also will be saved. It was my blood after which the villains lusted; I have escaped them, and they will be content with my silver and gold. Come with me, Lovely Sarah, to another land; we will leave misfortune behind; lest it follow us, I threw the last of my possessions, the silver ewer, to it as a peace offering. The God of our fathers will not forsake us. Come, you are tired. Down there, Quiet William stands by his boat; he will row us up the Rhine."

Without a sound and as if her every limb were broken, Lovely Sarah sank into the Rabbi's arms. Slowly, he carried her down to the river bank, to Quiet William who, although a deaf-mute, was a handsome lad; he supported his old foster-mother, a neighbor of the Rabbi's, as a fisherman, and kept his boat at this point. It seemed, however, as if he sensed the Rabbi's intention or had, in fact, been waiting for him; for playing about his silent lips was the sweetest compassion, and his great blue eyes rested meaningly on Lovely Sarah as he carefully lifted her into the boat.

The glance of the dumb youth stirred Lovely Sarah from her daze. She suddenly realized that all her husband had told her was no mere dream; and streams of bitter tears poured down over her cheeks which now were as white as her garment. She sat in the center of the boat, a weeping marble image, while beside her sat her husband and Quiet William, both rowing earnestly.

Now, whether this is due to the oars' monotonous beat, or to the boat's rocking, or to the fragrance of those mountainous banks where joy grows, it always happens that somehow even the saddest will feel strangely calmed, when on a night in spring he is lightly borne in a light boat, on the dear, clear river Rhine. Truly, old, kind-hearted Father Rhine cannot bear to see his children weep. Hushing their tears he rocks them on his faithful arms, tells them his loveliest fairy tales and promises them his most golden treasures—perhaps even the hoard of the Nibelungs, sunk ages ago. Lovely Sarah's tears, too, flowed ever more gently; her greatest woes were playfully carried away by the whispering waves. The night grew less darkly awesome, and the native hills greeted her as in the tenderest farewell. Greeting kindlier than all was the Kädrich, her favorite mountain—and in the strange moonlight it seemed as if up there a damsel stood with anxiously outstretched arms, as if quick dwarfs were swarming out of their rock fissures, and a horseman racing up the mountainside at full gallop. Lovely Sarah felt like a little girl again, sitting once more in the lap of her aunt from Lorch and being told the pretty story of the bold knight who freed the poor damsel the dwarfs had kidnapped, and further true stories: of the queer Whispervale beyond, where the birds talk quite sensibly, and of Gingerbread-Land where the good, obedient children go, and of enchanted princesses, singing trees, crystal castles, golden bridges, laughing water sprites. . . . But in between all these pretty tales that were coming to life, ringing and gleaming, Lovely Sarah heard her father's voice angrily scolding poor Aunt for putting so much nonsense into the child's head! Soon it was as if she were being placed on the little stool before her father's velvet-covered chair, and he were smoothing her long hair with gentle fingers, smiling cheerfully, and rocking himself comfortably in his spacious Sabbath dressing-gown of blue silk. . . . It must be a Sabbath, for the flowered spread was on the table, all the silver in the room had been polished until it shone like mirror-glass, and the white-bearded sexton sat beside her father, chewing raisins and talking in Hebrew. Little Abraham also came in, with a perfectly huge book, and modestly asked his uncle for permission to interpret a chapter from the Holy Scripture, so that the uncle might convince himself that he had learned a great deal in the past week and thus deserved a great deal of praise and cakes. . . . Then, the little fellow put the book on the broad arm of the chair and explained the story of Jacob and Rachel—how Jacob raised his voice and wept aloud when he first saw his little cousin Rachel, how he talked with her so fondly by the well, how he had to serve seven years for her, and how quickly they passed, and how he married Rachel and loved her forever and ever. . . . All at once, Lovely Sarah remembered too that her father then exclaimed in a merry voice, "Won't you marry your cousin Sarah like that?" To which little Abraham gravely replied, "I will, and she shall wait seven years." Dimly, these pictures moved through the woman's soul; she saw how she and her little cousin—now grown so big, and her husband—played childishly together in the tabernacle, where they delighted in the gay wallpapers, flowers, mirrors, and gilded apples; how little Abraham would pet her ever more tenderly until he gradually grew bigger and surlier, and finally quite big and quite surly. . . . And at last she is sitting at home in her room, alone, on a Saturday evening; the moon shines brightly through the window, and the door flies open and her cousin Abraham, in travel clothes and pale as death, storms in and grasps her hand and puts a golden ring on her finger and says solemnly: "I hereby take thee for my wife, according to the law of Moses and Israel!" "But now," he adds, trembling, "now I must go away to Spain. Farewell—seven years you shall wait for me!" And he rushes off, and Lovely Sarah, crying, tells all that to her father. . . . He roars and rages: "Cut off your hair, for you are a married woman! —and wants to ride after Abraham to force him to write a letter of divorcement. But Abraham is over the hills and far away; the father comes home silently; and when Lovely Sarah helps him pull his boots off and soothingly remarks that Abraham would return after seven years, he curses, "Seven years you shall go begging!" and dies soon after.

So the old stories swept through Lovely Sarah's mind like a hurried shadow-play, with the images strangely intermingling; and between them appeared half-strange, half-familiar bearded faces, and great flowers with marvelously broad leaves. Then, too, the Rhine seemed to murmur the melodies of the Hagaddah, and its pictures rose out of the water, large as life but distorted—crazy pictures: the forefather Abraham anxiously smashed the idols which always hurriedly put themselves together again; Mizri defends himself fiercely against an enraged Moses; Mount Sinai flashes and flames; King Pharaoh swims in the Red Sea with his jagged golden crown clutched in his teeth; frogs with human faces swim after him, and the waves foam and roar, and a dark giant's hand emerges from them, threateningly. . . .

That, however, was the Bishop Hatto's Mouse Tower, and the boat was just shooting through the eddy of Bingen. It shook Lovely Sarah somewhat out of her reveries, and she looked at the hills along the shore, with the lights in the castles flickering atop them and moonlit night mists drawing past below. But suddenly she thought she saw there her friends and relatives rushing past in terror, with dead faces and white-flowing shrouds, along the Rhine. . . . Everything turned black before her eyes; a stream of ice poured into her soul, and as though sleeping she could just hear the Rabbi saying the night prayer over her, slowly and anxiously as it is said over people sick unto death, and dreamily she stammered the words: "Ten thousand to the left—ten thousand to the right—to guard the King from the dread of the night. . . ."

But, suddenly, all the invading gloom and terror vanished. The dark curtain was torn away from Heaven, and in view above came the holy city, Jerusalem, with its towers and gates; the Temple gleamed in golden splendor; in its forecourt Lovely Sarah saw her father in his yellow Sabbath dressing-gown, smiling cheerfully; from the round windows of the Temple, all her friends and relatives merrily greeted her; in the Holy of Holies knelt pious King David with purple mantle and glittering crown, and his song and harp rang sweetly. And blissfully smiling, Lovely Sarah fell asleep.

◈◈◈*Ernest Hemingway (1898–1961). American novelist and short-story writer. He was perhaps the foremost American writer of his time. See* Death in the Afternoon, *a book on bullfighting,* Green Hills of Africa, *an account of big-game hunting, the play and stories in* The Fifth Column and the First Forty-Nine Stories, *the short novel* The Old Man and the Sea, *and the novels* The Sun Also Rises, A Farewell to Arms, For Whom the Bell Tolls. A Moveable Feast *was published posthumously. He was awarded the Nobel Prize.*

THE SNOWS OF KILIMANJARO

BY ERNEST HEMINGWAY

Kilimanjaro is a snow-covered mountain 19,710 feet high, and is said to be the highest mountain in Africa. Its western summit is called the Masai "Ngàje Ngài," the House of God. Close to the western summit there is the dried and frozen carcass of a leopard. No one has explained what the leopard was seeking at that altitude.

"The marvelous thing is that it's painless," he said. "That's how you know when it starts."

"Is it really?"

"Absolutely. I'm awfully sorry about the odor though. That must bother you."

"Don't! Please don't."

"Look at them," he said. "Now is it sight or is it scent that brings them like that?"

The cot the man lay on was in the wide shade of a mimosa tree and as he looked out past the shade onto the glare of the plain there were three of the big birds squatted obscenely, while in the sky a dozen more sailed, making quick-moving shadows as they passed.

"They've been there since the day the truck broke down," he said. "Today's the first time any have lit on the ground. I watched the way they sailed very carefully at first in case I ever wanted to use them in a story. That's funny now."

"I wish you wouldn't," she said.

"I'm only talking," he said. "It's much easier if I talk. But I don't want to bother you."

"You know it doesn't bother me," she said. "It's that I've gotten so very nervous not being able to do anything. I think we might make it as easy as we can until the plane comes."

"Or until the plane doesn't come."

"Please tell me what to do. There must be something I can do."

"You can take the leg off and that might stop it, though I doubt it. Or you can shoot me. You're a good shot now. I taught you to shoot, didn't I?"

"Please don't talk that way. Couldn't I read to you?"

"Read what?"

"Anything in the book bag that we haven't read."

"I can't listen to it," he said. "Talking is the easiest. We quarrel and that makes the time pass."

"I don't quarrel. I never want to quarrel. Let's not quarrel any more. No matter how nervous we get. Maybe they will be back with another truck today. Maybe the plane will come."

"I don't want to move," the man said. "There is no sense in moving now except to make it easier for you."

"That's cowardly."

"Can't you let a man die as comfortably as he can without calling him names? What's the use of slanging me?"

"You're not going to die."

"Don't be silly. I'm dying now. Ask those bastards." He looked over to where the huge, filthy birds sat, their naked heads sunk in the hunched feathers. A fourth planed down, to run quick-legged and then waddle slowly toward the others.

"They are around every camp. You never notice them. You can't die if you don't give up."

"Where did you read that? You're such a bloody fool."

"You might think about some one else."

"For Christ's sake," he said, "that's been my trade."

He lay then and was quiet for a while and looked across the heat shimmer of the plain to the edge of the bush. There were a few

Tommies that showed minute and white against the yellow and, far off, he saw a herd of zebra, white against the green of the bush. This was a pleasant camp under big trees against a hill, with good water, and close by, a nearly dry water hole where sand grouse flighted in the mornings.

"Wouldn't you like me to read?" she asked. She was sitting on a canvas chair beside his cot. "There's a breeze coming up."

"No thanks."

"Maybe the truck will come."

"I don't give a damn about the truck."

"I do."

"You give a damn about so many things that I don't."

"Not so many, Harry."

"What about a drink?"

"It's supposed to be bad for you. It said in Black's to avoid all alcohol. You shouldn't drink."

"Molo!" he shouted.

"Yes Bwana."

"Bring whiskey-soda."

"Yes Bwana."

"You shouldn't," she said. "That's what I mean by giving up. It says it's bad for you. I know it's bad for you."

"No," he said. "It's good for me."

So now it was all over, he thought. So now he would never have a chance to finish it. So this was the way it ended in a bickering over a drink. Since the gangrene started in his right leg he had no pain and with the pain the horror had gone and all he felt now was a great tiredness and anger that this was the end of it. For this, that now was coming, he had very little curiosity. For years it had obsessed him; but now it meant nothing in itself. It was strange how easy being tired enough made it.

Now he would never write the things that he had saved to write until he knew enough to write them well. Well, he would not have to fail at trying to write them either. Maybe you could never write them, and that was why you put them off and delayed the starting. Well he would never know, now.

"I wish we'd never come," the woman said. She was looking at him holding the glass and biting her lip. "You never would have gotten anything like that in Paris. You always said you loved Paris. We could have stayed in Paris or gone anywhere. I'd have gone anywhere. I said I'd go anywhere you wanted. If you wanted to shoot we could have gone shooting in Hungary and been comfortable."

"Your bloody money," he said.

"That's not fair," she said. "It was always yours as much as mine. I left everything and I went wherever you wanted to go and I've done what you wanted to do. But I wish we'd never come here."

"You said you loved it."

"I did when you were all right. But now I hate it. I don't see why that had to happen to your leg. What have we done to have that happen to us?"

"I suppose what I did was to forget to put iodine on it when I first scratched it. Then I didn't pay any attention to it because I never infect. Then, later, when it got bad, it was probably using that weak carbolic solution when the other antiseptics ran out that paralyzed the minute blood vessels and started the gangrene." He looked at her. "What else?"

"I don't mean that."

"If we would have hired a good mechanic instead of a half baked kikuyu driver, he would have checked the oil and never burned out that bearing in the truck."

"I don't mean that."

"If you hadn't left your own people, your goddamned Old Westbury, Saratoga, Palm Beach people to take me on——"

"Why, I loved you. That's not fair. I love you now. I'll always love you. Don't you love me?"

"No," said the man. "I don't think so. I never have."

"Harry, what are you saying? You're out of your head."

"No. I haven't any head to go out of."

"Don't drink that," she said. "Darling, please don't drink that. We have to do everything we can."

"You do it," he said. "I'm tired."

Now in his mind he saw a railway station at Karagatch and he was standing with his pack and that was the headlight of the Simplon-Orient cutting the dark now and he was leaving Thrace then

*after the retreat. That was one of the things he had saved to write,
with, in the morning at breakfast, looking out the window and seeing snow on the mountains in Bulgaria and Nansen's Secretary asking the old man if it were snow and the old man looking at it and
saying, No, that's not snow. It's too early for snow. And the Secretary repeating to the other girls, No, you see. It's not snow and them
all saying, It's not snow we were mistaken. But it was the snow all
right and he sent them on into it when he evolved exchange of popu-
lations. And it was snow they tramped along in until they died that
winter.*

*It was snow too that fell all Christmas week that year up in the
Gauertal, that year they lived in the woodcutter's house with the big
square porcelain stove that filled half the room, and they slept on
mattresses filled with beech leaves, the time the deserter came with
his feet bloody in the snow. He said the police were right behind
him and they gave him woolen socks and held the gendarmes talking
until the tracks had drifted over.*

*In Schrunz, on Christmas day, the snow was so bright it hurt your
eyes when you looked out from the weinstube and saw every one
coming home from church. That was where they walked up the
sleigh-smoothed urine-yellowed road along the river with the steep
pine hills, skis heavy on the shoulder, and where they ran that great
run down the glacier above the Madlener-haus, the snow as smooth
to see as cake frosting and as light as powder and he remembered the noiseless rush the speed made as you dropped down like a
bird.*

*They were snow-bound a week in the Madlener-haus that time in
the blizzard playing cards in the smoke by the lantern light and the
stakes were higher all the time as Herr Lent lost more. Finally he
lost it all. Everything, the skischule money and all the season's profit
and then his capital. He could see him with his long nose picking
up the cards and then opening, "Sans Voir." There was always
gambling then. When there was no snow you gambled and when
there was too much you gambled. He thought of all the time in his
life he had spent gambling.*

*But he had never written a line of that, nor of that cold, bright
Christmas day with the mountains showing across the plain that
Barker had flown across the lines to bomb the Austrian officers' leave*

train, machine-gunning them as they scattered and ran. He remembered Barker afterwards coming into the mess and starting to tell about it. And how quiet it got and then somebody saying, "You bloody murderous bastard."

Those were the same Austrians they killed then that he skied with later. No not the same. Hans, that he skied with all that year, had been in the Kaiser-Jägers and when they went hunting hares together up the little valley above the saw-mill they had talked of the fighting on Pasubio and of the attack on Pertica and Asalone and he had never written a word of that. Nor of Monte Corno, nor the Siete Commum, nor of Arsiedo.

How many winters had he lived in the Voralberg and the Arlberg? It was four and then he remembered the man who had the fox to sell when they had walked into Bludenz, that time to buy presents, and the cherry-pit taste of good kirsch, the fast-slipping rush of running powder-snow on crust, singing "Hi! Ho! said Rolly!" as you ran down the last stretch to the steep drop, taking it straight, then running the orchard in three turns and out across the ditch and onto the icy road behind the inn. Knocking your bindings loose, kicking the skis free and leaning them up against the wooden wall of the inn, the lamplight coming from the window, where inside, in the smoky, new-wine smelling warmth, they were playing the accordion.

"Where did we stay in Paris?" he asked the woman who was sitting by him in a canvas chair, now, in Africa.

"At the Crillon. You know that."

"Why do I know that?"

"That's where we always stayed."

"No. Not always."

"There and at the Pavillion Henri-Quatre in St. Germain. You said you loved it there."

"Love is a dunghill," said Harry. "And I'm the cock that gets on it to crow."

"If you have to go away," she said, "is it absolutely necessary to kill off everything you leave behind? I mean do you have to take away everything? Do you have to kill your horse, and your wife and burn your saddle and your armour?"

"Yes," he said. "Your damned money was my armour. My Swift and my Armour."

"Don't."

"All right. I'll stop that. I don't want to hurt you."

"It's a little bit late now."

"All right then. I'll go on hurting you. It's more amusing. The only thing I ever really liked to do with you I can't do now."

"No. That's not true. You liked to do many things and everything you wanted to do I did."

"Oh, for Christ sake stop bragging, will you?"

He looked at her and saw her crying.

"Listen," he said. "Do you think that it is fun to do this? I don't know why I'm doing it. It's trying to kill to keep yourself alive, I imagine. I was all right when we started talking. I didn't mean to start this, and now I'm crazy as a coot and being as cruel to you as I can be. Don't pay any attention, darling, to what I say. I love you, really. You know I love you. I've never loved any one else the way I love you."

He slipped into the familiar lie he made his bread and butter by.

"You're sweet to me."

"You bitch," he said. "You rich bitch. That's poetry. I'm full of poetry now. Rot and poetry. Rotten poetry."

"Stop it. Harry, why do you have to turn into a devil now?"

"I don't like to leave anything," the man said. "I don't like to leave things behind."

It was evening now and he had been asleep. The sun was gone behind the hill and there was a shadow all across the plain and the small animals were feeding close to camp; quick dropping heads and switching tails, he watched them keeping well out away from the bush now. The birds no longer waited on the ground. They were all perched heavily in a tree. There were many more of them. His personal boy was sitting by the bed.

"Memsahib's gone to shoot," the boy said. "Does Bwana want?"

"Nothing."

She had gone to kill a piece of meat and, knowing how he liked to watch the game, she had gone well away so she would not disturb this little pocket of the plain that he could see. She was always thoughtful, he thought. On anything she knew about, or had read, or that she had ever heard.

It was not her fault that when he went to her he was already over. How could a woman know that you meant nothing that you said; that you spoke only from habit and to be comfortable? After he no longer meant what he said, his lies were more successful with women than when he had told them the truth.

It was not so much that he lied as that there was no truth to tell. He had had his life and it was over and then he went on living it again with different people and more money, with the best of the same places, and some new ones.

You kept from thinking and it was all marvellous. You were equipped with good insides so that you did not go to pieces that way, the way most of them had, and you made an attitude that you cared nothing for the work you used to do, now that you could no longer do it. But, in yourself, you said that you would write about these people; about the very rich; that you were really not of them but a spy in their country; that you would leave it and write of it and for once it would be written by some one who knew what he was writing of. But he would never do it, because each day of not writing, of comfort, of being that which he despised, dulled his ability and softened his will to work so that, finally, he did no work at all. The people he knew now were all much more comfortable when he did not work. Africa was where he had been happiest in the good time of his life, so he had come out here to start again. They had made this safari with the minimum of comfort. There was no hardship; but there was no luxury and he had thought that he could get back into training that way. That in some way he could work the fat off his soul the way a fighter went into the mountains to work and train in order to burn it out of his body.

She had liked it. She said she loved it. She loved anything that was exciting, that involved a change of scene, where there were new people and where things were pleasant. And he had felt the illusion of returning strength of will to work. Now if this was how it ended, and he knew it was, he must not turn like some snake biting itself because its back was broken. It wasn't this woman's fault. If it had not been she it would have been another. If he lived by a lie he should try to die by it. He heard a shot beyond the hill.

She shot very well this good, this rich bitch, this kindly caretaker and destroyer of his talent. Nonsense. He had destroyed his talent himself. Why should he blame this woman because she kept him well? He had destroyed his talent by not using it, by betrayals of himself and what he believed in, by drinking so much that he blunted the edge of his perceptions, by laziness, by sloth, and by snobbery, by pride and by prejudice, by hook and by crook. What was this? A catalogue of old books? What was his talent anyway? It was a talent all right but instead of using it, he had traded on it. It was never what he had done, but always what he could do. And he had chosen to make his living with something else instead of a pen or a pencil. It was strange, too, wasn't it, that when he fell in love with another woman, that woman should always have more money than the last one? But when he no longer was in love, when he was only lying, as to this woman, now, who had the most money of all, who had all the money there was, who had had a husband and children, who had taken lovers and been dissatisfied with them, and who loved him dearly as a writer, as a man, as a companion and as a proud possession; it was strange that when he did not love her at all and was lying, that he should be able to give her more for her money than when he had really loved.

We must all be cut out for what we do, he thought. However you make your living is where your talent lies. He had sold vitality, in one form or another, all his life and when your affections are not too involved you give much better value for the money. He had found that out but he would never write that, now, either. No, he would not write that, although it was well worth writing.

Now she came in sight, walking across the open toward the camp. She was wearing jodhpurs and carrying her rifle. The two boys had a Tommie slung and they were coming along behind her. She was still a good-looking woman, he thought, and she had a pleasant body. She had a great talent and appreciation for the bed, she was not pretty, but he liked her face, she read enormously, liked to ride and shoot and, certainly, she drank too much. Her husband had died when she was still a comparatively young woman and for a while she had devoted herself to her two just-grown children, who did not need her and were embarrassed at having her about, to her stable of horses, to books, and to bottles. She liked to read in the evening before dinner and she drank Scotch and soda while she read. By dinner she was fairly drunk and after a bottle of wine at dinner she was usually drunk enough to sleep.

That was before the lovers. After she had the lovers she did not drink so much because she did not have to be drunk to sleep. But the lovers bored her. She had been married to a man who had never bored her and these people bored her very much.

Then one of her two children was killed in a plane crash and after that was over she did not want the lovers, and drink being no anæsthetic she had to make another life. Suddenly, she had been acutely frightened of being alone. But she wanted some one that she respected with her.

It had begun very simply. She liked what he wrote and she had always envied the life he led. She thought he did exactly what he wanted to. The steps by which she had acquired him and the way in which she had finally fallen in love with him were all part of a regular progression in which she had built herself a new life and he had traded away what remained of his old life.

He had traded it for security, for comfort too, there was no denying that, and for what else? He did not know. She would have bought him anything he wanted. He knew that. She was a damned nice woman too. He would as soon be in bed with her as any one; rather with her, because she was richer, because she was very pleasant and appreciative and because she never made scenes. And now this life that she had built again was coming to a term because he had not used iodine two weeks ago when a thorn had scratched his knee as they moved forward trying to photograph a herd of waterbuck standing, their heads up, peering while their nostrils searched the air, their ears spread wide to hear the first noise that would send them rushing into the bush. They had bolted, too, before he got the picture.

Here she came now.

He turned his head on the cot to look toward her. "Hello," she said.

"I shot a Tommy ram," she told him. "He'll make you good broth and I'll have them mash some potatoes with the Klim. How do you feel?"

"Much better."

"Isn't that lovely? You know I thought perhaps you would. You were sleeping when I left."

"I had a good sleep. Did you walk far?"

"No. Just around behind the hill. I made quite a good shot on the Tommy."

"You shoot marvellously, you know."

"I love it. I've loved Africa. Really. If *you're* all right it's the most fun that I've ever had. You don't know the fun it's been to shoot with you. I've loved the country."

"I love it too."

"Darling, you don't know how marvellous it is to see you feeling better. I couldn't stand it when you felt that way. You won't talk to me like that again, will you? Promise me?"

"No," he said. "I don't remember what I said."

"You don't have to destroy me. Do you? I'm only a middle-aged woman who loves you and wants to do what you want to do. I've been destroyed two or three times already. You wouldn't want to destroy me again, would you?"

"I'd like to destroy you a few times in bed," he said.

"Yes. That's the good destruction. That's the way we're made to be destroyed. The plane will be here tomorrow."

"How do you know?"

"I'm sure. It's bound to come. The boys have the wood all ready and the grass to make the smudge. I went down and looked at it again today. There's plenty of room to land and we have the smudges ready at both ends."

"What makes you think it will come tomorrow?"

"I'm sure it will. It's overdue now. Then, in town, they will fix up your leg and then we will have some good destruction. Not that dreadful talking kind."

"Should we have a drink? The sun is down."

"Do you think you should?"

"I'm having one."

"We'll have one together. *Molo, letti dui whiskey-soda!*" she called.

"You'd better put on your mosquito boots," he told her.

"I'll wait till I bathe . . ."

While it grew dark they drank and just before it was dark and there was no longer enough light to shoot, a hyena crossed the open on his way around the hill.

"That bastard crosses there every night," the man said. "Every night for two weeks."

"He's the one makes the noise at night. I don't mind it. They're a filthy animal though."

Drinking together, with no pain now except the discomfort of lying in one position, the boys lighting a fire, its shadow jumping on the tents, he could feel the return of acquiescence in this life of pleasant surrender. She *was* very good to him. He had been cruel and unjust in the afternoon. She was a fine woman, marvellous really. And just then it occurred to him that he was going to die.

It came with a rush; not as a rush of water nor of wind; but of a sudden evil-smelling emptiness and the odd thing was that the hyena slipped lightly along the edge of it.

"What is it, Harry?" she asked him.

"Nothing," he said. "You had better move over to the other side. To windward."

"Did Molo change the dressing?"

"Yes. I'm just using the boric now."

"How do you feel?"

"A little wobbly."

"I'm going in to bathe," she said. "I'll be right out. I'll eat with you and then we'll put the cot in."

So, he said to himself, we did well to stop the quarrelling. He had never quarrelled much with this woman, while with the women that he loved he had quarrelled so much they had finally, always, with the corrosion of the quarrelling, killed what they had together. He had loved too much, demanded too much, and he wore it all out.

He thought about alone in Constantinople that time, having quarrelled in Paris before he had gone out. He had whored the whole time and then, when that was over, and he had failed to kill his loneliness, but only made it worse, he had written her, the first one, the one who left him, a letter telling her how he had never been able to kill it. . . . How when he thought he saw her outside the Regence one time it made him go all faint and sick inside, and that

*he would follow a woman who looked like her in some way, along
the Boulevard, afraid to see it was not she, afraid to lose the feeling
it gave him. How every one he had slept with had only made him
miss her more. How what she had done could never matter since
he knew he could not cure himself of loving her. He wrote this letter at the Club, cold sober, and mailed it to New York asking her
to write him at the office in Paris. That seemed safe. And that night
missing her so much it made him feel hollow sick inside, he wandered up past Taxim's, picked a girl up and took her out to supper.
He had gone to a place to dance with her afterward, she danced
badly, and left her for a hot Armenian slut, that swung her belly
against him so it almost scalded. He took her away from a British
gunner subaltern after a row. The gunner asked him outside and
they fought in the street on the cobbles in the dark. He'd hit him
twice, hard, on the side of the jaw and when he didn't go down
he knew he was in for a fight. The gunner hit him in the body, then
beside his eye. He swung with his left again and landed and the
gunner fell on him and grabbed his coat and tore the sleeve off
and he clubbed him twice behind the ear and then smashed him
with his right as he pushed him away. When the gunner went
down his head hit first and he ran with the girl because they heard
the M. P.'s coming. They got into a taxi and drove out to Rimmily
Hissa along the Bosphorus, and around, and back in the cool night
and went to bed and she felt as over-ripe as she looked but smooth,
rose-petal, syrupy, smooth-bellied, big-breasted and needed no pillow under her buttocks, and he left her before she was awake looking blousy enough in the first daylight and turned up at the Pera
Palace with a black eye, carrying his coat because one sleeve was
missing.*

*That same night he left for Anatolia and he remembered, later
on that trip, riding all day through fields of the poppies that they
raised for opium and how strange it made you feel, finally, and all
the distances seemed wrong, to where they had made the attack
with the newly arrived Constantine officers, that did not know a
god-damned thing, and the artillery had fired into the troops and
the British observer had cried like a child.*

*That was the day he'd first seen dead men wearing white ballet
skirts and upturned shoes with pompons on them. The Turks had*

*come steadily and lumpily and he had seen the skirted men run-
ning and the officers shooting into them and running then themselves and he and the British observer had run too until his lungs
ached and his mouth was full of the taste of pennies and they
stopped behind some rocks and there were the Turks coming as
lumpily as ever. Later he had seen the things that he could never
think of and later still he had seen much worse. So when he got
back to Paris that time he could not talk about it or stand to have
it mentioned. And there in the café as he passed was that American
poet with a pile of saucers in front of him and a stupid look on his
potato face talking about the Dada movement with a Roumanian
who said his name was Tristan Tzara, who always wore a monocle
and had a headache, and, back at the apartment with his wife
that now he loved again, the quarrel all over, the madness all over,
glad to be home, the office sent his mail up to the flat. So then the
letter in answer to the one he'd written came in on a platter one
morning and when he saw the handwriting he went cold all over
and tried to slip the letter underneath another. But his wife said,
"Who is that letter from, dear?" and that was the end of the beginning of that.*

*He remembered the good times with them all, and the quarrels.
They always picked the finest places to have the quarrels. And why
had they always quarrelled when he was feeling best? He had never
written any of that because, at first, he never wanted to hurt any
one and then it seemed as though there was enough to write without it. But he had always thought that he would write it finally.
There was so much to write. He had seen the world change; not
just the events; although he had seen many of them and had
watched the people, but he had seen the subtler change and he
could remember how the people were at different times. He had
been in it and he had watched it and it was his duty to write of it;
but now he never would.*

"How do you feel?" she said. She had come out from the tent now
after her bath.

"All right."

"Could you eat now?" He saw Molo behind her with the folding
table and the other boy with the dishes.

"I want to write," he said.

"You ought to take some broth to keep your strength up."

"I'm going to die tonight," he said. "I don't need my strength up."

"Don't be melodramatic, Harry, please," she said.

"Why don't you use your nose? I'm rotted half way up my thigh now. What the hell should I fool with broth for? Molo bring whiskey-soda."

"Please take the broth," she said gently.

"All right."

The broth was too hot. He had to hold it in the cup until it cooled enough to take it and then he just got it down without gagging.

"You're a fine woman," he said. "Don't pay any attention to me."

She looked at him with her well-known, well-loved face from *Spur* and *Town and Country*, only a little the worse for drink, only a little the worse for bed, but *Town and Country* never showed those good breasts and those useful thighs and those lightly small-of-back-caressing hands, and as he looked and saw her well-known pleasant smile, he felt death come again. This time there was no rush. It was a puff, as of a wind that makes a candle flicker and the flame go tall.

"They can bring my net out later and hang it from the tree and build the fire up. I'm not going in the tent tonight. It's not worth moving. It's a clear night. There won't be any rain."

So this was how you died, in whispers that you did not hear. Well, there would be no more quarrelling. He could promise that. The one experience that he had never had he was not going to spoil now. He probably would. You spoiled everything. But perhaps he wouldn't.

"You can't take dictation, can you?"

"I never learned," she told him.

"That's all right."

There wasn't time, of course, although it seemed as though it telescoped so that you might put it all into one paragraph if you could get it right.

There was a log house, chinked white with mortar, on a hill above the lake. There was a bell on a pole by the door to call the people in to meals. Behind the house were fields and behind the fields was the timber. A line of lombardy poplars ran from the house to the dock. Other poplars ran along the point. A road went up to the hills along the edge of the timber and along that road he picked blackberries. Then that log house was burned down and all the guns that had been on deer foot racks above the open fire place were burned and afterwards their barrels, with the lead melted in the magazines, and the stocks burned away, lay out on the heap of ashes that were used to make lye for the big iron soap kettles, and you asked Grandfather if you could have them to play with, and he said, no. You see they were his guns still and he never bought any others. Nor did he hunt any more. The house was rebuilt in the same place out of lumber now and painted white and from its porch you saw the poplars and the lake beyond; but there were never any more guns. The barrels of the guns that had hung on the deer feet on the wall of the log house lay out there on the heap of ashes and no one ever touched them.

In the Black Forest, after the war, we rented a trout stream and there were two ways to walk to it. One was down the valley from Triberg and around the valley road in the shade of the trees that bordered the white road, and then up a side road that went up through the hills past many small farms, with the big Schwarzwald houses, until that road crossed the stream. That was where our fishing began.

The other way was to climb steeply up to the edge of the woods and then go across the top of the hills through the pine woods, and then out to the edge of a meadow and down across this meadow to the bridge. There were birches along the stream and it was not big, but narrow, clear and fast, with pools where it had cut under the roots of the birches. At the Hotel in Triberg the proprietor had a fine season. It was very pleasant and we were all great friends. The next year came the inflation and the money he had made the year before was not enough to buy supplies to open the hotel and he hanged himself.

You could dictate that, but you could not dictate the Place Contrescarpe where the flower sellers dyed their flowers in the street and the dye ran over the paving where the autobus started and the old men and the women, always drunk on wine and bad marc;

and the children with their noses running in the cold; the smell of dirty sweat and poverty and drunkenness at the Café des Amateurs and the whores at the Bal Musette they lived above. The Concierge who entertained the trooper of the Garde Républicaine in her loge, his horse-hair-plumed helmet on a chair. The locataire across the hall whose husband was a bicycle racer and her joy that morning at the Crémerie when she had opened L'Auto and seen where he placed third in Paris-Tours, his first big race. She had blushed and laughed and then gone upstairs crying with the yellow sporting paper in her hand. The husband of the woman who ran the Bal Musette drove a taxi and when he, Harry, had to take an early plane the husband knocked upon the door to wake him and they each drank a glass of white wine at the zinc of the bar before they started. He knew his neighbors in that quarter then because they all were poor.

Around that Place *there were two kinds: the drunkards and the sportifs. The drunkards killed their poverty that way; the sportifs took it out in exercise. They were the descendants of the Communards and it was no struggle for them to know their politics. They knew who had shot their fathers, their relatives, their brothers, and their friends when the Versailles troops came in and took the town after the Commune and executed any one they could catch with calloused hands, or who wore a cap, or carried any other sign he was a working man. And in that poverty, and in that quarter across the street from a Boucherie Chevaline and a wine co-operative he had written the start of all he was to do. There never was another part of Paris that he loved like that, the sprawling trees, the old white plastered houses painted brown below, the long green of the autobus in that round square, the purple flower dye upon the paving, the sudden drop down the hill of the rue Cardinal Lemoine to the River, and the other way the narrow crowded world of the rue Mouffetard. The street that ran up toward the Panthéon and the other that he always took with the bicycle, the only asphalted street in all that quarter, smooth under the tires, with the high narrow houses and the cheap tall hotel where Paul Verlaine had died. There were only two rooms in the apartments where they lived and he had a room on the top floor of that hotel that cost him sixty francs a month where he did his writing, and from it he could see the roofs and chimney pots and all the hills of Paris.*

From the apartment you could only see the wood and coal man's place. He sold wine too, bad wine. The golden horse's head outside the Boucherie Chevaline where the carcasses hung yellow gold and red in the open window, and the green painted co-operative where they bought their wine; good wine and cheap. The rest was plaster walls and the windows of the neighbors. The neighbors who, at night, when some one lay drunk in the street, moaning and groaning in that typical French ivresse[1] that you were propaganded to believe did not exist, would open their windows and then the murmur of talk.

"Where is the policeman? When you don't want him the bugger is always there. He's sleeping with some concièrge. Get the Agent." Till some one threw a bucket of water from a window and the moaning stopped. "What's that? Water. Ah, that's intelligent." And the windows shutting. Marie, his femme de ménage, protesting against the eight-hour day saying, "If a husband works until six he gets only a little drunk on the way home and does not waste too much. If he works only until five he is drunk every night and one has no money. It is the wife of the working man who suffers from this shortening of hours."

"Wouldn't you like some more broth?" the woman asked him now.

"No, thank you very much. It is awfully good."

"Try just a little."

"I would like a whiskey-soda."

"It's not good for you."

"No. It's bad for me. Cole Porter wrote the words and the music. This knowledge that you're going mad for me."

"You know I like you to drink."

"Oh yes. Only it's bad for me."

When she goes, he thought, I'll have all I want. Not all I want but all there is. Ayee he was tired. Too tired. He was going to sleep a little while. He lay still and death was not there. It must have gone around another street. It went in pairs, on bicycles, and moved absolutely silently on the pavements.

---

[1] Drunkenness.

No, he had never written about Paris. Not the Paris that he cared about. But what about the rest that he had never written?

What about the ranch and the silvered gray of the sage brush, the quick, clear water in the irrigation ditches, and the heavy green of the alfalfa. The trail went up into the hills and the cattle in the summer were shy as deer. The bawling and the steady noise and slow moving mass raising a dust as you brought them down in the fall. And behind the mountains, the clear sharpness of the peak in the evening light and, riding down along the trail in the moonlight, bright across the valley. Now he remembered coming down through the timber in the dark holding the horse's tail when you could not see and all the stories that he meant to write.

About the half-wit chore boy who was left at the ranch that time and told not to let any one get any hay, and that old bastard from the Forks who had beaten the boy when he had worked for him stopping to get some feed. The boy refusing and the old man saying he would beat him again. The boy got the rifle from the kitchen and shot him when he tried to come into the barn and when they came back to the ranch he'd been dead a week, frozen in the corral, and the dogs had eaten part of him. But what was left you packed on a sled wrapped in a blanket and roped on and you got the boy to help you haul it, and the two of you took it out over the road on skis, and sixty miles down to town to turn the boy over. He having no idea that he would be arrested. Thinking he had done his duty and that you were his friend and he would be rewarded. He'd helped to haul the old man in so everybody could know how bad the old man had been and how he'd tried to steal some feed that didn't belong to him, and when the sheriff put the handcuffs on the boy he couldn't believe it. Then he'd started to cry. That was one story he had saved to write. He knew at least twenty good stories from out there and he had never written one. Why?

"You tell them why," he said.

"Why what, dear?"

"Why nothing."

She didn't drink so much, now, since she had him. But if he lived he would never write about her, he knew that now. Nor about any of them. The rich were dull and they drank too much, or they played too much backgammon. They were dull and they were repetitious. He remembered poor Julian and his romantic awe of them and how he had started a story once that began, "The very rich are different from you and me." And how some one had said to Julian, Yes, they have more money. But that was not humorous to Julian. He thought they were a special glamorous race and when he found they weren't it wrecked him just as much as any other thing that wrecked him.

He had been contemptuous of those who wrecked. You did not have to like it because you understood it. He could beat anything, he thought, because no thing could hurt him if he did not care.

All right. Now he would not care for death. One thing he had always dreaded was the pain. He could stand pain as well as any man, until it went on too long, and wore him out, but here he had something that had hurt frightfully and just when he had felt it breaking him, the pain had stopped.

He remembered long ago when Williamson, the bombing officer, had been hit by a stick bomb some one in a German patrol had thrown as he was coming in through the wire that night and, screaming, had begged every one to kill him. He was a fat man, very brave, and a good officer, although addicted to fantastic shows. But that night he was caught in the wire, with a flare lighting him up and his bowels spilled out into the wire, so when they brought him in, alive, they had to cut him loose. Shoot me, Harry. For Christ sake shoot me. They had had an argument one time about our Lord never sending you anything you could not bear and some one's theory had been that meant that at a certain time the pain passed you out automatically. But he had always remembered Williamson, that night. Nothing passed out Williamson until he gave him all his morphine tablets that he had always saved to use himself and then they did not work right away.

Still this now, that he had, was very easy; and if it was no worse as it went on there was nothing to worry about. Except that he would rather be in better company.

He thought a little about the company that he would like to have. No, he thought, when everything you do, you do too long, and do too late, you can't expect to find the people still there. The people all are gone. The party's over and you are with your hostess now.

I'm getting as bored with dying as with everything else, he thought.

"It's a bore," he said out loud.

"What is, my dear?"

"Anything you do too bloody long."

He looked at her face between him and the fire. She was leaning back in the chair and the firelight shone on her pleasantly lined face and he could see that she was sleepy. He heard the hyena make a noise just outside the range of the fire.

"I've been writing," he said. "But I got tired."

"Do you think you will be able to sleep?"

"Pretty sure. Why don't you turn in?"

"I like to sit here with you."

"Do you feel anything strange?" he asked her.

"No. Just a little sleepy."

"I do," he said.

He had just felt death come by again.

"You know the only thing I've never lost is curiosity," he said to her.

"You've never lost anything. You're the most complete man I've ever known."

"Christ," he said. "How little a woman knows. What is that? Your intuition?"

Because, just then, death had come and rested its head on the foot of the cot and he could smell its breath.

"Never believe any of that about a scythe and a skull," he told her. "It can be two bicycle policemen as easily, or be a bird. Or it can have a wide snout like a hyena."

It had moved up on him now, but it had no shape any more. It simply occupied space.

"Tell it to go away."

It did not go away but moved a little closer.

"You've got a hell of a breath," he told it. "You stinking bastard."

It moved up closer to him still and now he could not speak to it, and when it saw he could not speak it came a little closer, and now he tried to send it away without speaking, but it moved in on him so its weight was all upon his chest, and while it crouched there and he could not move, or speak, he heard the woman say, "Bwana is asleep now. Take the cot up very gently and carry it into the tent."

He could not speak to tell her to make it go away and it crouched now, heavier, so he could not breathe. And then, while they lifted the cot, suddenly it was all right and the weight went from his chest.

It was morning and had been morning for some time and he heard the plane. It showed very tiny and then made a wide circle and the boys ran out and lit the fires, using kerosene, and piled on grass so there were two big smudges at each end of the level place and the morning breeze blew them toward the camp and the plane circled twice more, low this time, and then glided down and levelled off and landed smoothly and, coming walking toward him, was old Compton in slacks, a tweed jacket and a brown felt hat.

"What's the matter, old cock?" Compton said.

"Bad leg," he told him. "Will you have some breakfast?"

"Thanks. I'll just have some tea. It's the Puss Moth you know. I won't be able to take the Memsahib. There's only room for one. Your lorry is on the way."

Helen had taken Compton aside and was speaking to him. Compton came back more cheery than ever.

"We'll get you right in," he said. "I'll be back for the Mem. Now I'm afraid I'll have to stop at Arusha to refuel. We'd better get going."

"What about the tea?"

"I don't really care about it you know."

The boys had picked up the cot and carried it around the green tents and down along the rock and out onto the plain and along past the smudges that were burning brightly now, the grass all consumed, and the wind fanning the fire, to the little plane. It was difficult getting him in, but once in he lay back in the leather seat, and the leg was stuck straight out to one side of the seat, where Compton sat. Compton started the motor and got in. He waved to Helen and to the boys and, as the clatter moved into the old familiar roar, they swung around with Compie watching for wart-hog holes and roared, bumping, along the stretch between the fires and with the last bump rose and he saw them all standing below, waving, and the camp beside the hill, flattening now, and the plain spreading, clumps of trees, and the bush flattening, while the game trails ran now smoothly to the dry waterholes, and there was a new water that he had never known of. The zebra, small rounded backs now, and the wildebeeste, big-headed dots seeming to climb as they moved in long fingers across the plain, now scattering as the shadow came toward them, they were tiny now, and the movement had no gallop, and the plain was as far as you could see, gray-yellow now and ahead old Compie's tweed back and the brown felt hat. Then they were over the first hills and the wildebeeste were trailing up them, and then they were over mountains with sudden depths of green-rising forest and the solid bamboo slopes, and then the heavy forest again, sculptured into peaks and hollows until they crossed, and hills sloped down and then another plain, hot now, and purple brown, bumpy with heat and Compie looking back to see how he was riding. Then there were other mountains dark ahead.

And then instead of going on to Arusha they turned left, he evidently figured that they had the gas, and looking down he saw a pink sifting cloud, moving over the ground, and in the air, like the first snow in a blizzard, that comes from nowhere, and he knew the locusts were coming up from the South. Then they began to climb and they were going to the East it seemed, and then it darkened and they were in a storm, the rain so thick it seemed like flying through a waterfall, and then they were out and Compie turned his head and grinned and pointed and there, ahead, all he could see, as wide as all the world, great, high, unbelievably white in the sun, was the square top of Kilimanjaro. And then he knew that there was where he was going.

Just then the hyena stopped whimpering in the night and started to make a strange, human, almost crying sound. The woman heard it and stirred uneasily. She did not wake. In her dream she was at the house on Long Island and it was the night before her daughter's début. Somehow her father was there and he had been very rude. Then the noise the hyena made was so loud she woke and for a moment she did not know where she was and she was very afraid. Then she took the flashlight and shone it on the other cot that they had carried in after Harry had gone to sleep. She could see his bulk under the mosquito bar but somehow he had gotten his leg out and it hung down alongside the cot. The dressings had all come down and she could not look at it.

"Molo," she called, "Molo! Molo!"

Then she said, "Harry, Harry!" Then her voice rising, "Harry! Please, Oh Harry!"

There was no answer and she could not hear him breathing.

Outside the tent the hyena made the same strange noise that had awakened her. But she did not hear him for the beating of her heart.

◇◇◇E. T. A. Hoffmann (1776-1822). *German artist, musician and novelist. A master of fantastic prose, Offenbach based his opera,* The Tales of Hoffmann, *on three of his stories.*

THE HISTORY OF KRAKATUK

BY E. T. A. HOFFMANN

Perlipat's mother was the wife of a king—that is, a queen; and, in consequence, Perlipat, the moment she was born, was a princess by birth. The king was beside himself for joy as he saw his beautiful little daughter lying in her cradle; he danced about, and hopped on one leg, and sang out, "Was anything ever so beautiful as my Perlipatkin?" And all the ministers, presidents, generals, and staff-officers, hopped likewise on one leg, and cried out, "No, never!" However, the real fact is, that it is quite impossible, as long as the world lasts, that a princess should be born more beautiful than Perlipat. Her little face looked like a web of the most beautiful lilies and roses, her eyes were the brightest blue, and her hair was like curling threads of shining gold. Besides all this, Perlipat came into the world with two rows of pearly teeth, with which, two hours after her birth, she bit the lord chancellor's thumb so hard that he cried out, "O gemini!" Some say he cried out, "O dear!" but on this subject people's opinions are very much divided, even to the present day. In short, Perlipat bit the lord chancellor on the thumb, and all the kingdom immediately declared that she was the wittiest, sharpest, cleverest little girl, as well as the most beautiful. Now, everybody was delighted except the queen—she was anxious and dispirited, and nobody knew the reason; everybody was puzzled to know why she caused Perlipat's cradle to be so strictly guarded. Besides having guards at the door, two nurses always sat close to the cradle, and six other nurses sat every night round the room; and what was most extraordinary, each of these six nurses was obliged

(Translated by William Makepeace Thackeray.)

to sit with a great tom-cat in her lap, and keep stroking him all night, to amuse him, and keep him awake.

Now, my dear little children, it is quite impossible that *you* should know why Perlipat's mother took all these precautions; but *I* know, and will tell you all about it. It happened that, once on a time, a great many excellent kings and agreeable princesses were assembled at the court of Perlipat's father, and their arrival was celebrated by all sorts of tournaments, and plays, and balls. The king, in order to show how rich he was, determined to treat them with a feast which should astonish them. So he privately sent for the upper court cook-master, and ordered him to order the upper court astronomer to fix the time for a general pig-killing, and a universal sausage-making; then he jumped into his carriage, and called, himself, on all the kings and queens; but he only asked them to eat a bit of mutton with him, in order to enjoy their surprise at the delightful entertainment he had prepared for them. Then he went to the queen, and said, "You already know, my love, the partiality I entertain for sausages." Now the queen knew perfectly well what he was going to say, which was that she herself (as indeed she had often done before) should undertake to superintend the sausage-making. So the first lord of the treasury was obliged to hand out the golden sausage-pit and silver saucepans; and a large fire was made of sandal-wood; the queen put on her damask kitchen-pinafore; and soon after the sausage soup was steaming and boiling in the kettle. The delicious smell penetrated as far as the privy-council-chamber; the king was seized with such extreme delight, that he could not stand it any longer. "With your leave," said he, "my lords and gentlemen"—jumped over the table, ran down into the kitchen, gave the queen a kiss, stirred about the sausage-brew with his golden scepter, and then returned back to the privy-council-chamber in an easy and contented state of mind. The queen had now come to the point in the sausage-making, when the bacon was cut into little bits and roasted on little silver spits. The ladies of honor retired from the kitchen, for the queen, with a proper confidence in herself, and consideration for her royal husband, performed *alone* this important operation. But just when the bacon began to roast, a little whispering voice was heard, "Sister, I am a queen as well as you, give me some roasted bacon, too"; then the queen knew it was Mrs. Mouserinks who was talking. Mrs. Mouserinks had lived a long time in the palace; she declared she was a relation of the king's, and a queen into the bargain, and she had a great number of attendants and courtiers underground. The queen was a mild, good-natured woman; and although she neither acknowledged Mrs. Mouserinks for a queen nor for a relation, yet she could not, on such a holiday as this, grudge her a little bit of bacon. So she said, "Come out, Mrs. Mouserinks, and eat as much as you please of my bacon." Out hops Mrs. Mouserinks, as merry as you please, jumped on the table, stretched out her pretty little paw, and ate one piece of bacon after the other, until, at last, the queen got quite tired of her. But then out came all Mrs. Mouserinks' relations, and her seven sons, ugly little fellows, and nibbled all over the bacon; while the poor queen was so frightened that she could not drive them away. Luckily, however, when there still remained a little bacon, the first lady of the bedchamber happened to come in; she drove all the mice away, and sent for the court mathematician, who divided the little that was left as equally as possible among all the sausages. Now sounded the drums and the trumpets; the princes and potentates who were invited rode forth in glittering garments, some under white canopies, others in magnificent coaches, to the sausage feast. The king received them with hearty friendship and elegant politeness; then, as master of the land, with scepter and crown, sat down at the head of the table. The first course was polonies. Even then it was remarked that the king grew paler and paler; his eyes were raised to heaven, his breast heaved with sighs; in fact, he seemed to be agitated by some deep and inward sorrow. But when the blood-puddings came on, he fell back in his chair, groaning and moaning, sighing and crying. Everybody rose from table; the physicians in ordinary in vain endeavored to feel the king's pulse: a deep and unknown grief had taken possession of him.

At last—at last, after several attempts had been made, several violent remedies applied, such as burning feathers under his nose, and the like, the king came to himself, and almost inaudibly gasped out the words, "Too little bacon!" Then the queen threw herself in despair at his feet: "Oh, my poor unlucky royal husband," said she, "what sorrows have you had to endure! but see here the guilty one at your feet; strike—strike—and spare not. Mrs. Mouserinks and her

seven sons, and all her relations, ate up the bacon, and—and—"
Here the queen tumbled backwards and in a fainting-fit! But the
king arose in a violent passion, and said he, "My lady of the bed-
chamber, explain this matter." The lady of the bedchamber explained as far as she knew, and the king swore vengeance on Mrs.
Mouserinks and her family for having eaten up the bacon which
was destined for the sausages.

The lord chancellor was called upon to institute a suit against
Mrs. Mouserinks and to confiscate the whole of her property; but
as the king thought that this would not prevent her from eating his
bacon, the whole affair was entrusted to the court machine and
watch maker. This man promised, by a peculiar and extraordinary
operation, to expel Mrs. Mouserinks and her family from the palace
forever. He invented curious machines, in which pieces of roasted
bacon were hung on little threads, and which he set round about
the dwelling of Mrs. Mouserinks. But Mrs. Mouserinks was far too
cunning not to see the artifices of the court watch and machine
maker; still all her warnings, all her cautions, were vain; her seven
sons, and a great number of her relations, deluded by the sweet
smell of the bacon, entered the watchmaker's machines, where, as
soon as they bit at the bacon, a trap fell on them, and then they
were quickly sent to judgment and execution in the kitchen. Mrs.
Mouserinks, with the small remnants of her court, left the place of
sorrow, doubt, and astonishment. The court was rejoiced; but the
queen alone was sorrowful; for she knew well Mrs. Mouserinks'
disposition, and that she would never allow the murder of her sons
and relations to go unrevenged. It happened as she expected. One
day, whilst she was cooking some tripe for the king, a dish to
which he was particularly partial, appeared Mrs. Mouserinks and
said, "You have murdered my sons, you have killed my cousins and
relations, take good care that the mouse, queen, does not bite your
little princess in two. Take care." After saying this, she disappeared;
but the queen was so frightened, that she dropped the tripe into the
fire, and thus for the second time Mrs. Mouserinks spoiled the dish
the king liked best; and of course he was very angry. And now you
know why the queen took such extraordinary care of princess Perlipatkin: was not she right to fear that Mrs. Mouserinks would ful-
fill her threat, come back, and bite the princess to death?

The machines of the machine-maker were not of the slightest use against the clever and cunning Mrs. Mouserinks; but the court astronomer, who was also upper-astrologer and star-gazer, discovered that only the Tom-cat family could keep Mrs. Mouserinks from the princess's cradle; for this reason each of the nurses carried one of the sons of this family on her lap, and, by continually stroking him down the back, managed to render the otherwise unpleasant court service less intolerable.

It was once at midnight, as one of the two chief nurses, who sat close by the cradle, awoke as it were from a deep sleep; everything around lay in profound repose; no purring, but the stillness of death; but how astonished was the chief nurse when she saw close before her a great ugly mouse, who stood upon his hind legs, and already had laid his hideous head on the face of the princess. With a shriek of anguish, she sprung up; everybody awoke; but Mrs. Mouserinks (for she it was who had been in Perlipat's cradle), jumped down, and ran into the corner of the room. The tom-cats went after, but too late; she had escaped through a hole in the floor. Perlipat awoke with the noise, and wept aloud. "Thank heaven," said the nurses, "she lives!" But what was their horror, when, on looking at the before beautiful child, they saw the change which had taken place in her! Instead of the lovely white and red cheeks which she had had before, and the shining golden hair, there was now a great deformed head on a little withered body; the blue eyes had changed into a pair of great green gogglers, and the mouth had stretched from ear to ear. The queen was almost mad with grief and vexation, and the walls of the king's study were obliged to be wadded, because he was always dashing his head against them for sorrow, and crying out, "O luckless monarch!" He might have seen how that it would have been better to have eaten the sausage without bacon, and to have allowed Mrs. Mouserinks quietly to stay underground. Upon this subject, however, Perlipat's royal father did not think at all, but he laid all the blame on the court watchmaker, Christian Elias Drosselmeier, of Nuremberg. He therefore issued this wise order, that Drosselmeier, should before four weeks restore the princess to her former state, or at least find out a certain and infallible means for so doing; or, in failure thereof, should suffer a shameful death under the ax of the executioner.

Drosselmeier was terribly frightened; but, trusting to his learning and good fortune, he immediately performed the first operation which seemed necessary to him. He carefully took Princess Perlipat to pieces, took off her hands and feet, and thus was able to see the inward structure; but there, alas! he found that the princess would grow uglier as she grew older, and he had no remedy for it. He put the princess neatly together again, and sunk down in despair at her cradle; which he never was permitted to leave.

The fourth week had begun,—yes, it was Wednesday! when the king, with eyes flashing with indignation, entered the room of the princess; and, waving his scepter, he cried out, "Christian Elias Drosselmeier, cure the princess, or die!" Drosselmeier began to cry bitterly, but little Princess Perlipat went on cracking her nuts. Then first was the court watchmaker struck with the princess's extraordinary partiality for nuts, and the circumstance of her having come into the world with teeth. In fact, she had cried incessantly since her metamorphosis, until someone by chance gave her a nut; she immediately cracked it, ate the kernel, and was quiet.

From that time the nurses found nothing so effectual as to bring her nuts. "O holy instinct of natural, eternal and unchangeable sympathy of all beings; thou showest me the door to the secret. I will knock, and thou wilt open it." He then asked permission to speak to the court astronomer, and was led out to him under a strong guard. These two gentlemen embraced with many tears, for they were great friends; they then entered into a secret cabinet, where they looked over a great number of books which treated of instinct, sympathies, and antipathies, and other deep subjects. The night came; the court astronomer looked to the stars, and made the horoscope of the princess, with the assistance of Drosselmeier, who was also very clever in this science. It was a troublesome business, for the lines were always wandering this way and that; at last, however, what was their joy to find that the princess Perlipat, in order to be freed from the enchantment which made her so ugly, and to become beautiful again, had only to eat the sweet kernel of the nut Krakatuk.

Now the nut Krakatuk had such a hard shell that an eight-and-forty-pound cannon could drive over without breaking it. But this nut was only to be cracked by a man who had never shaved, and never worn boots; he was to break it in the princess's presence, and then to present the kernel to her with his eyes shut; nor was he to open his eyes until he had walked seven steps backwards without stumbling. Drosselmeier and the astronomer worked without stopping three days and three nights; and, as the king was at dinner on Saturday, Drosselmeier (who was to have had his head off Sunday morning early), rushed into the room, and declared he had found the means of restoring the princess Perlipat to her former beauty. The king embraced him with fervent affection, promised him a diamond sword, four orders, and two new coats for Sundays. "We will go to work immediately after dinner," said the king in the most friendly manner, "and thou, dear watchmaker, must see that the young unshaven gentleman in shoes be ready with the nut Krakatuk. Take care, too, that he drink no wine before, that he may not stumble as he walks his seven steps backwards like a crab; afterwards he may get as tipsy as he pleases." Drosselmeier was very much frightened at this speech of the king's; and it was not without fear and trembling that he stammered out that it was true that the means were known, but that both the nut Krakatuk, and the young man to crack it, were yet to be sought for; so that it was not impossible that nut and cracker would never be found at all. In tremendous fury the king swung his scepter over his crowned head, and cried, with a lion's voice, "Then you must be beheaded, as I said before."

It was a lucky thing for the anxious and unfortunate Drosselmeier that the king had found his dinner very good that day, and so was in a disposition to listen to any reasonable suggestions, which the magnanimous queen, who deplored Drosselmeier's fate, did not fail to bring forward. Drosselmeier took courage to plead that, as he had found out the remedy and the means whereby the princess might be cured, he was entitled to his life. The king said this was all stupid nonsense; but after he had drunk a glass of cherry-brandy, concluded that both the watchmaker and the astronomer should immediately set off on their journey, and never return, except with the nut Krakatuk in their pocket. The man who was to crack the same was, at the queen's suggestion, to be advertised for in all the newspapers, in the country and out of it.

Drosselmeier and the court astronomer had been fifteen years on their journey without finding any traces of the nut Krakatuk. The countries in which they were, and the wonderful sights they saw, would take me a month at least to tell of. This, however, I shall not do: all I shall say is, that at last the miserable Drosselmeier felt an irresistible longing to see his native town Nuremberg. This longing came upon him most particularly as he and his friend were sitting together smoking a pipe in the middle of a wood; in Asia. "O Nuremberg, delightful city! Who's not seen thee, him I pity! All that beautiful is, in London, Petersburg, or Paris, are nothing when compared to thee! Nuremberg, my own city!" As Drosselmeier deplored his fate in this melancholy manner, the astronomer, struck with pity for his friend, began to howl so loudly that it was heard all over Asia. But at last he stopped crying, wiped his eyes, and said, "Why do we sit here and howl, my worthy colleague? Why don't we set off at once for Nuremberg? Is it not perfectly the same where and how we seek this horrid nut Krakatuk?" "You are right," said Drosselmeier; so they both got up, emptied their pipes, and walked from the wood in the middle of Asia to Nuremberg at a stretch.

As soon as they had arrived in Nuremberg, Drosselmeier hastened to the house of a cousin of his, called Christopher Zachariah Drosselmeier, who was a carver and gilder, and whom he had not seen for a long, long time. To him the watchmaker related the whole history of Princess Perlipat, of Mrs. Mouserinks, and the nut Krakatuk; so that Christopher Zachariah clapped his hands for wonder, and said, "O, cousin, cousin, what extraordinary stories are these!" Drosselmeier then told his cousin of the adventures which befell him on his travels: how he had visited the grand duke of Almonds, and the king of Walnuts; how he had inquired of the Horticultural Society of Acornshausen; in short, how he had sought everywhere, but in vain, to find some traces of the nut Krakatuk. During this recital Christopher Zachariah had been snapping his fingers, and opening his eyes, calling out, hum! and ha! and oh! and ah! At last, he threw his cap and wig up to the ceiling, embraced his cousin, and said, "Cousin, I'm very much mistaken, *very* much mistaken, I say, if I don't myself possess this nut Krakatuk!" He then fetched a little box, out of which he took a gilded nut, of a middling size. "Now," said he, as he showed his cousin the nut, "the history of this nut is this: Several years ago, a man came here on Christmas

Eve with a sackful of nuts, which he offered to sell cheap. He put the sack just before my booth, to guard it against the nut-sellers of the town, who could not bear that a foreigner should sell nuts in their native city. At that moment a heavy wagon passed over his sack, and cracked every nut in it except one, which the man, laughing in an extraordinary way, offered to sell me for a silver half-crown of the year 1720. This seemed odd to me. I found just such a half-crown in my pocket, bought the nut, and gilded it, not knowing myself why I bought it so dear and valued it so much." Every doubt with respect to its being the nut which they sought was removed by the astronomer, who, after removing the gilding, found written on the shell, in Chinese characters, the word Krakatuk.

The joy of the travelers was excessive, and Drosselmeier's cousin, the gilder, the happiest man under the sun, on being promised a handsome pension and the gilding of all the gold in the treasury into the bargain. The two gentlemen, the watchmaker and the astronomer, had put on their night caps and were going to bed, when the latter (that is, the astronomer) said, "My worthy friend and colleague, you know one piece of luck follows another, and I believe that we have not only found the nut Krakatuk, but also the young man who shall crack it, and present the kernel of beauty to the princess; this person I conceive to be the son of your cousin!" "Yes," continued he, "I am determined not to sleep until I have cast the youth's horoscope." With these words he took his night cap from his head, and instantly commenced his observations. In fact, the gilder's son was a handsome well-grown lad, who had never shaved, and never worn boots.

At Christmas he used to wear an elegant red coat embroidered with gold; a sword, and a hat under his arm, besides having his hair beautifully powdered and curled. In this way he used to stand before his father's booth, and with a gallantry which was born with him, crack the nuts for the young ladies, who, from this peculiar quality of his, had already called him "Nutcrackerkin."

Next morning the astronomer fell delighted on the neck of the watchmaker, and cried, "We have him,—he is found! but there are two things, of which, my dear friend and colleague, we must take particular care: first, we must strengthen the under-jaw of your excellent nephew with a tough piece of wood, and then, on returning home, we must carefully conceal having brought with us the young man who is to bite the nut; for I read by the horoscope that the king, after several people have broken their teeth in vainly attempting to crack the nut, will promise to him who shall crack it, and restore the princess to her former beauty,—will promise, I say, to this man the princess for a wife, and his kingdom after his death." Of course the gilder was delighted with the idea of his son marrying the Princess Perlipat and becoming a prince and king; and delivered him over to the two deputies. The wooden jaw which Drosselmeier had fixed in his young and hopeful nephew answered to admiration, so that in cracking the hardest peach-stones he came off with distinguished success.

As soon as Drosselmeier and his comrade had made known the discovery of the nut, the requisite advertisements were immediately issued; and as the travelers had returned with the means of restoring the princess's beauty, many hundred young men, among whom several princes might be found, trusting to the soundness of their teeth, attempted to remove the enchantment of the princess. The ambassadors were not a little frightened when they saw the princess again. The little body with the wee hands and feet could scarcely support the immense deformed head! The hideousness of the countenance was increased by a woolly beard, which spread over mouth and chin. Everything happened as the astronomer had foretold. One dandy in shoes after another broke teeth and jaws upon the nut Krakatuk, without in the slightest degree helping the princess, and as they were carried away half-dead to the dentist (who was always ready), groaned out—that was a hard nut!

When now the king in the anguish of his heart had promised his daughter and kingdom to the man who would break the enchantment, the gentle Drosselmeier made himself known, and begged to be allowed the trial. No one had pleased the princess so much as this young man; she laid her little hand on her heart, and sighed inwardly, Ah! if *he* were the person destined to crack Krakatuk, and be my husband! Young Drosselmeier, approaching the queen, the king, and the princess Perlipat in the most elegant manner, received from the hands of the chief master of ceremonies the nut Krakatuk, which he immediately put into his mouth,—and crack! crack!— broke the shell in a dozen pieces; he neatly removed the bits of shell which yet remained on the kernel, and then with a most profound bow presented it to the princess, shut his eyes, and proceeded to step backwards. The princess swallowed the kernel; and oh! wonderful wonder! her ugliness disappeared, and instead, was seen a form of angel beauty, with a countenance like lilies and roses mixed, the eyes glancing azure, and the full locks curling like threads of gold. Drums and trumpets mingled with rejoicings of the people. The king and the whole court danced upon one leg, as before, at Perlipat's birth, and the queen was obliged to be sprinkled all over with eau de Cologne, since she had fainted with excessive joy. This great tumult did not a little disturb young Drosselmeier, who had yet his seven steps to accomplish: however, he recollected himself, and had just put his right foot back for the seventh step, when Mrs. Mouserinks, squeaking in a most hideous manner, raised herself from the floor, so that Drosselmeier, as he put his foot backwards, trod on her, and stumbled,—nay, almost fell down. What a misfortune! The young man became at that moment just as ugly as ever was the princess Perlipat. The body was squeezed together, and could scarcely support the thick deformed head, with the great goggling eyes and wide gaping mouth. Instead of the wooden roof for his mouth, a little wooden mantel hung out from behind his back. The watchmaker and astronomer were beside themselves with horror and astonishment; but they saw how Mrs. Mouserinks was creeping along the floor all bloody. Her wickedness, however, was not unavenged, for Drosselmeier had struck her so hard on the neck with the sharp heel of his shoe, that she was at the point of death; but just as she was in her last agonies, she squeaked out in the most piteous manner, "O Krakatuk, from thee I die! but Nutcracker dies as well as I; and thou, my son, with the seven crowns, revenge thy mother's horrid wounds! Kill the man who did attack her, that naughty, ugly wicked Nutcracker!" Quick with this cry died Mrs. Mouserinks, and was carried off by the royal housemaid. Nobody had taken the least notice of young Drosselmeier. The princess, however, reminded the king of his promise, and he immediately ordered the young hero to be brought before him. But when that unhappy young man appeared in his deformed state, the princess put her hands before her and cried out, "Away with that nasty Nutcracker!" So the court marshal took him by his little shoulder and pushed him out of the door.

The king was in a terrible fury that anybody should ever think of making a nutcracker his son-in-law: he laid all the blame on the watchmaker and astronomer, and banished them both from his court and kingdom. This had not been seen by the astronomer in casting his horoscope; however, he found, on reading the stars a second time, that young Drosselmeier would so well behave himself in his new station, that, in spite of his ugliness, he would become prince and king. In the meantime, but with the fervent hope of soon seeing the end of these things, Drosselmeier remains as ugly as ever; so much so, that the nutcrackers in Nuremberg have always been made after the exact model of his countenance and figure.

◇◇◇*Washington Irving (1783-1859). Irving traveled widely and early
became famous as a sophisticated, conservative man of society and
wit as well as a brilliant author. He created the comic Dutch-
American scholar Diedrich Knickerbocker and wrote a burlesque*
History of New York, *which has been called "the first great book of
comic literature written by an American." He resided in England for
a while and there wrote* The Sketch Book, *which brought him fame
and intimacy with such men as Scott, Byron and Moore. He described a tour of the Western prairies, wrote an account of the fur-
trading activities of John Jacob Astor (with his nephew Pierre), a
biography of Oliver Goldsmith and a life of Washington.*

THE STOUT GENTLEMAN

A STAGE-COACH ROMANCE

BY WASHINGTON IRVING

I'll cross it though it blast me!

HAMLET

It was a rainy sunday in the gloomy month of November. I had been
detained, in the course of a journey, by a slight indisposition, from
which I was recovering; but was still feverish, and obliged to keep
within doors all day, in an inn of the small town of Derby. A wet
Sunday in a country inn!—whoever has had the luck to experience
one can alone judge of my situation. The rain pattered against the
casements; the bells tolled for church with a melancholy sound. I
went to the windows in quest of something to amuse the eye; but
it seemed as if I had been placed completely out of the reach of
all amusement. The windows of my bedroom looked out among tiled
roofs and stacks of chimneys, while those of my sitting-room commanded a full view of the stable-yard. I know of nothing more calculated to make a man sick of this world than a stable-yard on a
rainy day. The place was littered with wet straw that had been
kicked about by travellers and stable-boys. In one corner was a
stagnant pool of water, surrounding an island of muck; there were
several half-drowned fowls crowded together under a cart, among

164

which was a miserable, crest-fallen cock, drenched out of all life and spirit, his drooping tail matted, as it were, into a single feather, along which the water trickled from his back; near the cart was a half-dozing cow, chewing the cud, and standing patiently to be rained on, with wreaths of vapor rising from her reeking hide; a wall-eyed horse, tired of the loneliness of the stable, was poking his spectral head out of a window, with the rain dripping on it from the eaves; an unhappy cur, chained to a doghouse hard by, uttered something, every now and then, between a bark and a yelp; a drab of a kitchen-wench tramped backward and forward through the yard in pattens, looking as sulky as the weather itself; everything, in short, was comfortless and forlorn, excepting a crew of hardened ducks, assembled like boon companions round a puddle, and making a riotous noise over their liquor.

I was lonely and listless, and wanted amusement. My room soon become insupportable, I abandoned it, and sought what is technically called the travellers' room. This is a public room set apart at most inns for the accommodation of a class of wayfarers called travellers, or riders; a kind of commercial knights-errant, who are incessantly scouring the kingdom in gigs, on horseback, or by coach. They are the only successors that I know of at the present day to the knights-errant of yore. They lead the same kind of roving, adventurous life, only changing the lance for a driving-whip, the buckler for a pattern-card, and the coat of mail for an upper Benjamin. Instead of vindicating the charms of peerless beauty, they rove about, spreading the fame and standing of some substantial tradesman, or manufacturer, and are ready at any time to bargain in his name; it being the fashion nowadays to trade, instead of fight, with one another. As the room of the hostel, in the good old fighting-times, would be hung round at night with the armor of wayworn warriors, such as coats of mail, falchions, and yawning helmets, so the travellers' room is garnished with the harnessing of their successors, with box-coats, whips of all kinds, spurs, gaiters, and oilcloth covered hats.

I was in hopes of finding some of these worthies to talk with, but was disappointed. There were, indeed, two or three in the room; but I could make nothing of them. One was just finishing his breakfast, quarrelling with his bread and butter, and huffing the waiter;

another buttoned on a pair of gaiters, with many execrations at Boots for not having cleaned his shoes well; a third sat drumming on the table with his fingers and looking at the rain as it streamed down the window-glass; they all appeared infected by the weather, and disappeared, one after the other, without exchanging a word.

I sauntered to the window, and stood gazing at the people, picking their way to church, with petticoats hoisted midleg high, and dripping umbrellas. The bell ceased to toll, and the streets became silent. I then amused myself with watching the daughters of a tradesman opposite; who, being confined to the house for fear of wetting their Sunday finery, played off their charms at the front windows, to fascinate the chance tenants of the inn. They at length were summoned away by a vigilant, vinegar-faced mother, and I had nothing further from without to amuse me.

What was I to do to pass away the long-lived day? I was sadly nervous and lonely; and everything about an inn seems calculated to make a dull day ten times duller. Old newspapers, smelling of beer and tobacco-smoke, and which I had already read half a dozen times. Good-for-nothing books, that were worse than rainy weather. I bored myself to death with an old volume of the *Lady's Magazine*. I read all the commonplace names of ambitious travellers scrawled on the panes of glass; the eternal families of the Smiths, and the Browns, and the Jacksons, and the Johnsons, and all the other sons; and I deciphered several scraps of fatiguing inn-window poetry which I have met with in all parts of the world.

The day continued lowering and gloomy; the slovenly, ragged, spongy cloud drifted heavily along; there was no variety even in the rain: it was one dull, continued, monotonous patter—patter—patter, excepting that now and then I was enlivened by the idea of a brisk shower, from the rattling of the drops upon a passing umbrella.

It was quite *refreshing* (if I may be allowed a hackneyed phrase of the day) when, in the course of the morning, a horn blew, and a stage-coach whirled through the street, with outside passengers stuck all over it, cowering under cotton umbrellas, and seethed together, and reeking with the steams of wet box-coats and upper Benjamins.

The sound brought out from their lurking-places a crew of vagabond boys, and vagabond dogs, and the carroty-headed hostler, and that nondescript animal ycleped Boots, and all the other vagabond race that infest the purlieus of an inn; but the bustle was transient; the coach again whirled on its way; and boy and dog, and hostler and Boots, all slunk back again to their holes; the street again became silent, and the rain continued to rain on. In fact, there was no hope of its clearing up; the barometer pointed to rainy weather; mine hostess's tortoise-shell cat sat by the fire washing her face, and rubbing her paws over her ears; and, on referring to the Almanac, I found a direful prediction stretching from the top of the page to the bottom through the whole month, "expect—much —rain—about—this—time!"

I was dreadfully hipped. The hours seemed as if they would never creep by. The very ticking of the clock became irksome. At length the stillness of the house was interrupted by the ringing of a bell. Shortly after I heard the voice of a waiter at the bar: "The stout gentleman in No. 13 wants his breakfast. Tea and bread and butter, with ham and eggs; the eggs not to be too much done."

In such a situation as mine, every incident is of importance. Here was a subject of speculation presented to my mind, and ample exercise for my imagination. I am prone to paint pictures to myself, and on this occasion I had some materials to work upon. Had the guest upstairs been mentioned as Mr. Smith, or Mr. Brown, or Mr. Jackson, or Mr. Johnson, or merely as "the gentleman in No. 13," it would have been a perfect blank to me. I should have thought nothing of it; but "The stout gentleman!"—the very name had something in it of the picturesque. It at once gave the size; it embodied the personage to my mind's eye, and my fancy did the rest.

He was stout, or, as some term it, lusty; in all probability, therefore, he was advanced in life, some people expanding as they grow old. By his breakfasting rather late, and in his own room, he must be a man accustomed to live at his ease, and above the necessity of early rising; no doubt, a round, rosy, lusty old gentleman.

There was another violent ringing. The stout gentleman was impatient for his breakfast. He was evidently a man of importance; "well to do in the world"; accustomed to be promptly waited upon;

of a keen appetite, and a little cross when hungry; "perhaps," thought I, "he may be some London Alderman; or who knows but he may be a Member of Parliament?"

The breakfast was sent up, and there was a short interval of silence; he was, doubtless, making the tea. Presently there was a violent ringing; and before it could be answered, another ringing still more violent. "Bless me! what a choleric old gentleman!" The waiter came down in a huff. The butter was rancid, the eggs were overdone, the ham was too salt; the stout gentleman was evidently nice in his eating; one of those who eat and growl, and keep the waiter on the trot, and live in a state militant with the household.

The hostess got into a fume. I should observe that she was a brisk, coquettish woman; a little of a shrew, and something of a slammerkin, but very pretty withal; with a nincompoop for a husband, as shrews are apt to have. She rated the servants roundly for their negligence in sending up so bad a breakfast, but said not a word against the stout gentleman; by which I clearly perceived that he must be a man of consequence, entitled to make a noise and to give trouble at a country inn. Other eggs, and ham, and bread and butter were sent up. They appeared to be more graciously received; at least there was no further complaint.

I had not made many turns about the travellers' room, when there was another ringing. Shortly afterward there was a stir and an inquest about the house. The stout gentleman wanted the *Times* or the *Chronicle* newspaper. I set him down, therefore, for a Whig; or, rather, from his being so absolute and lordly where he had a chance, I suspected him of being a Radical. Hunt, I had heard, was a large man; "who knows," thought I, "but it is Hunt himself!"

My curiosity began to be awakened. I inquired of the waiter who was this stout gentleman that was making all this stir; but I could get no information: nobody seemed to know his name. The landlords of bustling inns seldom trouble their heads about the names or occupations of their transient guests. The color of a coat, the shape or size of the person, is enough to suggest a travelling name. It is either the tall gentleman, or the short gentleman, or the gentleman in black, or the gentleman in snuff-color; or, as in the present instance, the stout gentleman. A designation of the kind once hit on, answers every purpose, and saves all further inquiry.

Rain—rain—rain! pitiless, ceaseless rain! No such thing as putting a foot out of doors, and no occupation nor amusement within. By and by I heard someone walking overhead. It was in the stout gentleman's room. He evidently was a large man by the heaviness of his tread; and an old man from his wearing such creaking soles. "He is doubtless," thought I, "some rich old square-toes of regular habits, and is now taking exercise after breakfast."

I now read all the advertisements of coaches and hotels that were stuck about the mantelpiece. The *Lady's Magazine* had become an abomination to me; it was as tedious as the day itself. I wandered out, not knowing what to do, and ascended again to my room. I had not been there long, when there was a squall from a neighboring bedroom. A door opened and slammed violently; a chambermaid, that I had remarked for having a ruddy, good-humored face, went downstairs in a violent flurry. The stout gentleman had been rude to her!

This sent a whole host of my deductions to the deuce in a moment. This unknown personage could not be an old gentleman; for old gentlemen are not apt to be so obstreperous to chambermaids. He could not be a young gentleman; for young gentlemen are not apt to inspire such indignation. He must be a middle-aged man, and confounded ugly into the bargain, or the girl would not have taken the matter in such terrible dudgeon. I confess I was sorely puzzled.

In a few minutes I heard the voice of my landlady. I caught a glance of her as she came tramping upstairs—her face glowing, her cap flaring, her tongue wagging the whole way. "She'd have no such doings in her house, she'd warrant. If gentlemen did spend money freely, it was no rule. She'd have no servant-maids of hers treated in that way, when they were about their work, that's what she wouldn't."

As I hate squabbles, particularly with women, and above all with pretty women, I slunk back into my room, and partly closed the door; but my curiosity was too much excited not to listen. The landlady marched intrepidly to the enemy's citadel, and entered it with a storm: the door closed after her. I heard her voice in high windy clamor for a moment or two. Then it gradually subsided, like a gust of wind in a garret; then there was a laugh; then I heard nothing more.

After a little while my landlady came out with an odd smile on her face adjusting her cap, which was a little on one side. As she went downstairs, I heard the landlord ask her what was the matter; she said, "Nothing at all, only the girl's a fool." I was more than ever perplexed what to make of this unaccountable personage, who could put a good-natured chambermaid in a passion, and send away a termagant landlady in smiles. He could not be so old, nor cross, nor ugly either.

I had to go to work at his picture again, and to paint him entirely different. I now set him down for one of those stout gentlemen that are frequently met with swaggering about the doors of country inns. Moist, merry fellows, in Belcher handkerchiefs, whose bulk is a little assisted by malt-liquors. Men who have seen the world, and been sworn at Highgate; who are used to tavern-life; up to all the tricks of tapsters, and knowing in the ways of sinful publicans. Free-livers on a small scale; who are prodigal within the compass of a guinea; who call all the waiters by name, tousle the maids, gossip with the landlady at the bar, and prose over a pint of port, or a glass of negus, after dinner.

The morning wore away in forming these and similar surmises. As fast as I wove one system of belief, some movement of the unknown would completely overturn it, and throw all my thoughts again into confusion. Such are the solitary operations of a feverish mind. I was, as I have said, extremely nervous; and the continual meditation in the concerns of this invisible personage began to have its effect—I was getting a fit of the fidgets.

Dinner-time came. I hoped the stout gentleman might dine in the travellers' room, and that I might at length get a view of his person; but no—he had dinner served in his own room. What could be the meaning of this solitude and mystery? He could not be a radical; there was something too aristocratical in thus keeping himself apart from the rest of the world, and condemning himself to his own dull company throughout a rainy day. And then, too, he lived too well for a discontented politician. He seemed to expatiate on a variety of dishes, and to sit over his wine like a jolly friend of good living. Indeed, my doubts on this head were soon at an end; for he could not have finished his first bottle before I could faintly hear him humming a tune; and on listening I found it to be "God Save the King."

'Twas plain, then, he was no radical, but a faithful subject; one who grew loyal over his bottle, and was ready to stand by king and constitution, when he could stand by nothing else. But who could he be? My conjectures began to run wild. Was he not some personage of distinction travelling incog.? "God knows!" said I, at my wit's end; "it may be one of the royal family for aught I know, for they are all stout gentlemen!"

The weather continued rainy. The mysterious unknown kept his room, and, as far as I could judge, his chair, for I did not hear him move. In the meantime, as the day advanced, the travellers' room began to be frequented. Some, who had just arrived, came in buttoned up in box-coats; others came home who had been dispersed about the town; some took their dinners, and some their tea. Had I been in a different mood, I should have found entertainment in studying this peculiar class of men. There were two especially who were regular wags of the road, and up to all the standing jokes of travellers. They had a thousand sly things to say to the waiting-maid, whom they called Louisa, and Ethelinda, and a dozen other fine names, changing the name every time, and chuckling amazingly at their own waggery. My mind, however, had been completely engrossed by the stout gentleman. He had kept my fancy in chase during a long day, and it was not now to be diverted from the scent.

The evening gradually wore away. The travellers read the papers two or three times over. Some drew round the fire and told long stories about their horses, about their adventures, their overturns, and breaking-down. They discussed the credit of different merchants and different inns; and the two wags told several choice anecdotes of pretty chambermaids and kind landladies. All this passed as they were quietly taking what they called their night-caps, that is to say, strong glasses of brandy and water and sugar, or some other mixture of the kind; after which they one after another rang for "Boots" and the chambermaid, and walked off to bed in old shoes cut down into marvellously uncomfortable slippers.

There was now only one man left: a short-legged, long-bodied, plethoric fellow, with a very large, sandy head. He sat by himself, with a glass of port-wine negus, and a spoon; sipping and stirring, and meditating and sipping, until nothing was left but the spoon. He gradually fell asleep bolt upright in his chair, with the empty glass standing before him; and the candle seemed to fall asleep, too, for the wick grew long, and black, and cabbaged at the end, and dimmed the little light that remained in the chamber. The gloom that now prevailed was contagious. Around hung the shapeless, and almost spectral, box-coats of departed travellers, long since buried in deep sleep. I only heard the ticking of the clock, with the deep-drawn breathings of the sleeping topers, and the drippings of the rain, drop—drop—drop, from the eaves of the house. The church-bells chimed midnight. All at once the stout gentleman began to walk overhead, pacing slowly backward and forward. There was something extremely awful in all this, especially to one in my state of nerves. These ghastly great-coats, these guttural breathings, and the creaking footsteps of this mysterious being. His steps grew fainter and fainter, and at length died away. I could bear it no longer. I was wound up to the desperation of a hero of romance. "Be he who or what he may," said I to myself, "I'll have a sight of him!" I seized a chamber-candle, and hurried up to No. 13. The door stood ajar. I hesitated—I entered: the room was deserted. There stood a large, broad-bottomed elbow-chair at a table, on which was an empty tumbler, and a *Times* newspaper, and the room smelt powerfully of Stilton cheese.

The mysterious stranger had evidently but just retired. I turned off, sorely disappointed, to my room, which had been changed to the front of the house. As I went along the corridor, I saw a large pair of boots, with dirty, waxed tops, standing at the door of a bed-chamber. They doubtless belonged to the unknown: but it would not do to disturb so redoubtable a personage in his den: he might discharge a pistol, or something worse, at my head. I went to bed, therefore, and lay awake half the night in a terribly nervous state; and even when I fell asleep, I was still haunted in my dreams by the idea of the stout gentleman and his wax-topped boots.

I slept rather late the next morning, and was awakened by some stir and bustle in the house, which I could not at first comprehend; until getting more awake, I found there was a mail-coach starting from the door. Suddenly there was a cry from below, "The gentleman has forgotten his umbrella! Look for the gentleman's umbrella in No. 13!" I heard an immediate scampering of a chambermaid along the passage, and a shrill reply as she ran, "Here it is! here's the gentleman's umbrella!"

The mysterious stranger then was on the point of setting off. This was the only chance I should ever have of knowing him. I sprang out of bed, scrambled to the window, snatched aside the curtains, and just caught a glimpse of the rear of a person getting in at the coach-door. The skirts of a brown coat parted behind, and gave me a full view of the broad disk of a pair of drab breeches. The door closed—"all right!" was the word—the coach whirled off; and that was all I ever saw of the stout gentleman!

◇◇◇*Henry James (1843-1916). American novelist, short-story and novella
writer, dramatist, essayist, critic. One of the towering figures in
American literature. He was a facile, sensitive and prolific writer.
He spent most of his life in Europe, particularly in England, convinced that the American scene of his day was hostile to a talent
such as his. He was an extremely conscious artist and the master of
a subtle and complex prose. Hawthorne was one of his masters and
Flaubert and Turgenev were his friends.*

THE GREAT GOOD PLACE

BY HENRY JAMES

I

George Dane had opened his eyes to a bright new day, the face of
nature well washed by last night's downpour and shining as with
high spirits, good resolutions, lively intentions—the great glare of
recommencement in short fixed in his patch of sky. He had sat up
late to finish work—arrears overwhelming, then at last had gone to
bed with the pile but little reduced. He was now to return to it
after the pause of the night; but he could only look at it, for the
time, over the bristling hedge of letters planted by the early postman
an hour before and already, on the customary table by the chimney-
piece, formally rounded and squared by his systematic servant. It
was something too merciless, the domestic perfection of Brown.
There were newspapers on another table, ranged with the same rig-
our of custom, newspapers too many—what could any creature want
of so much news?—and each with its hand on the neck of the other,
so that the row of their bodiless heads was like a series of decapita-
tions. Other journals, other periodicals of every sort, folded and in
wrappers, made a huddled mound that had been growing for several
days and of which he had been wearily, helplessly aware. There
were new books, also in wrappers as well as disenveloped and
dropped again—books from publishers, books from authors, books

from friends, books from enemies, books from his own bookseller, who took, it sometimes struck him, inconceivable things for granted. He touched nothing, approached nothing, only turned a heavy eye over the work, as it were, of the night—the fact, in his high wide-windowed room, where duty shed its hard light into every corner, of the still unashamed admonitions. It was the old rising tide, and it rose and rose even under a minute's watching. It had been up to his shoulders last night—it was up to his chin now.

Nothing had *gone*, had passed on while he slept—everything had stayed; nothing, that he could yet feel, had died—so naturally, one would have thought; many things on the contrary had been born. To let them alone, these things, the new things, let them utterly alone and see if that, by chance, wouldn't somehow prove the best way to deal with them: this fancy brushed his face for a moment as a possible solution, just giving it, as so often before, a cool wave of air. Then he knew again as well as ever that leaving was difficult, leaving impossible—that the only remedy, the true soft effacing sponge, would be to *be* left, to be forgotten. There was no footing on which a man who had ever liked life—liked it at any rate as *he* had—could now escape it. He must reap as he had sown. It was a thing of meshes; he had simply gone to sleep under the net and had simply waked up there. The net was too fine; the cords crossed each other at spots too near together, making at each a little tight hard knot that tired fingers were this morning too limp and too tender to touch. Our poor friend's touched nothing—only stole significantly into his pockets as he wandered over to the window and faintly gasped at the energy of nature. What was most overwhelming was that she herself was so ready. She had soothed him rather, the night before, in the small hours by the lamp. From behind the drawn curtain of his study the rain had been audible and in a manner merciful; washing the window in a steady flood, it had seemed the right thing, the retarding interrupting thing, the thing that, if it would only last, might clear the ground by floating out to a boundless sea the innumerable objects among which his feet stumbled and strayed. He had positively laid down his pen as on a sense of friendly pressure from it. The kind full swish had been on the glass when he turned out his lamp; he had left his phrase unfinished and his papers lying quite as for the flood to bear them away in its rush. But there still on the table were the bare bones of the sentence—and not all of those; the single thing borne away and that he could never recover was the missing half that might have paired with it and begotten a figure.

Yet he could at last only turn back from the window; the world was everywhere, without and within, and the great staring egotism of its health and strength wasn't to be trusted for tact or delicacy. He faced about precisely to meet his servant and the absurd solemnity of two telegrams on a tray. Brown ought to have kicked them into the room—then he himself might have kicked them out.

"And you told me to remind you, sir—"

George Dane was at last angry. "Remind me of nothing!"

"But you insisted, sir, that I was to insist!"

He turned away in despair, using a pathetic quaver at absurd variance with his words: "If you insist, Brown, I'll kill you!" He found himself anew at the window, whence, looking down from his fourth floor, he could see the vast neighbourhood, under the trumpet-blare of the sky, beginning to rush about. There was a silence, but he knew Brown hadn't left him—knew exactly how straight and serious and stupid and faithful he stood there. After a minute he heard him again.

"It's only because, sir, you know, sir, you can't remember—"

At this Dane did flash round; it was more than at such a moment he could bear. "Can't remember, Brown? I can't forget. That's what's the matter with me."

Brown looked at him with the advantage of eighteen years of consistency. "I'm afraid you're not well, sir."

Brown's master thought. "It's a shocking thing to say, but I wish to heaven I weren't! It would be perhaps an excuse."

Brown's blankness spread like the desert. "To put them off?"

"Ah!" The sound was a groan; the plural pronoun, *any* pronoun, so mistimed. "Who is it?"

"Those ladies you spoke of—to luncheon."

"Oh!" The poor man dropped into the nearest chair and stared a while at the carpet. It was very complicated.

"How many will there be, sir?" Brown asked.

"Fifty!"

"Fifty, sir?"

Our friend, from his chair, looked vaguely about; under his hand were the telegrams, still unopened, one of which he now tore asunder. " 'Do hope you sweetly won't mind, today, 1.30, my bringing poor dear Lady Mullet, who's so awfully bent,' " he read to his companion.

His companion weighed it. "How many does *she* make, sir?"

"Poor dear Lady Mullet? I haven't the least idea."

"Is she—a—deformed, sir?" Brown enquired, as if in this case she might make more.

His master wondered, then saw he figured some personal curvature. "No; she's only bent on coming!" Dane opened the other telegram and again read out: " 'So sorry it's at eleventh hour impossible, and count on you here, as very greatest favour, at two sharp instead.' "

"How many does *that* make?" Brown imperturbably continued.

Dane crumpled up the two missives and walked with them to the waste-paper basket, into which he thoughtfully dropped them. "I can't say. You must do it all yourself. I shan't be there."

It was only on this that Brown showed an expression. "You'll go instead—"

"I'll go instead!" Dane raved.

Brown, however, had had occasion to show before that *he* would never desert their post. "Isn't that rather sacrificing the three?" Between respect and reproach he paused.

"*Are* there three?"

"I lay for four in all."

His master had at any rate caught his thought. "Sacrificing the three to the one, you mean? Oh I'm not going to *her*!"

Brown's famous "thoroughness"—his great virtue—had never been so dreadful. "Then where *are* you going?"

Dane sat down to his table and stared at his ragged phrase. " '*There* is a happy land—far far away!' " He chanted it like a sick child and knew that for a minute Brown never moved. During this minute he felt between his shoulders the gimlet of criticism.

"Are you quite sure you're all right?"

"It's my certainty that overwhelms me, Brown. Look about you and judge. Could anything be more 'right,' in the view of the envious world, than everything that surrounds us here: that immense array of letters, notes, circulars; that pile of printers' proofs, magazines and books; these perpetual telegrams, these impending guests, this retarded, unfinished and interminable work? What could a man want more?"

"Do you mean there's too much, sir?"—Brown had sometimes these flashes.

"There's too much. There's too much. But *you* can't help it, Brown."

"No, sir," Brown assented. "Can't *you?*"

"I'm thinking—I must see. There are hours—!" Yes, there were hours, and this was one of them: he jerked himself up for another turn in his labyrinth, but still not touching, not even again meeting, his admonisher's eye. If he was a genius for any one he was a genius for Brown; but it was terrible what that meant, being a genius for Brown. There had been times when he had done full justice to the way it kept him up; now, however, it was almost the worst of the avalanche. "Don't trouble about me," he went on insincerely and looking askance through his window again at the bright and beautiful world. "Perhaps it will rain—that *may* not be over. I do love the rain," he weakly pursued. "Perhaps, better still, it will snow."

Brown now had indeed a perceptible expression, and the expression was of fear. "Snow, sir—the end of May?" Without pressing this point he looked at his watch. "You'll feel better when you've had breakfast."

"I dare say," said Dane, whom breakfast struck in fact as a pleasant alternative to opening letters. "I'll come in immediately."

"But without waiting—?"

"Waiting for what?"

Brown at last, under his apprehension, had his first lapse from logic, which he betrayed by hesitating in the evident hope his companion might by a flash of remembrance relieve him of an invidious duty. But the only flashes now were the good man's own. "You say you can't forget, sir; but you do forget—"

"Is it anything very horrible?" Dane broke in.

Brown hung fire. "Only the gentleman you told me you had asked—"

Dane again took him up; horrible or not it came back—indeed its mere coming back classed it. "To breakfast today? It *was* today; I see." It came back, yes, came back; the appointment with the young man—he supposed him young—whose letter, the letter about—what was it?—had struck him. "Yes, yes; wait, wait."

"Perhaps he'll do you good, sir," Brown suggested.

"Sure to—sure to. All right!" Whatever he might do he would at least prevent some other doing: that was present to our friend as, on the vibration of the electric bell at the door of the flat, Brown moved away. Two things in the short interval that followed were present to Dane: his having utterly forgotten the connexion, the whence, whither and why of his guest; and his continued disposition not to touch—no, not with the finger. Ah if he might *never* again touch! All the unbroken seals and neglected appeals lay there while, for a pause he couldn't measure, he stood before the chimney-piece with his hands still in his pockets. He heard a brief exchange of words in the hall, but never afterwards recovered the time taken by Brown to reappear, to precede and announce another person—a person whose name somehow failed to reach Dane's ear. Brown went off again to serve breakfast, leaving host and guest confronted. The duration of this first stage also, later on, defied measurement; but that little mattered, for in the train of what happened came promptly the second, the third, the fourth, the rich succession of the others. Yet what happened was but that Dane took his hand from his pocket, held it straight out and felt it taken. Thus indeed, if he had wanted never again to touch, it was already done.

II

He might have been a week in the place—the scene of his new consciousness—before he spoke at all. The occasion of it then was that one of the quiet figures he had been idly watching drew at last nearer and showed him a face that was the highest expression—to his pleased but as yet slightly confused perception—of the general charm. What *was* the general charm? He couldn't, for that matter, easily have phrased it; it was such an abyss of negatives, such an absence of positives and of everything. The oddity was that after a minute he was struck as by the reflexion of his own very image in this first converser seated with him, on the easy bench, under the high clear portico and above the wide far-reaching garden, where the things that most showed in the greenness were the surface of

still water and the white note of old statues. The absence of everything was, in the aspect of the Brother who had thus informally
joined him—a man of his own age, tired distinguished modest kind
—really, as he could soon see, but the absence of what he didn't
want. He didn't want, for the time, anything but just to *be* there, to
steep in the bath. He was in the bath yet, the broad deep bath of
tillness. They sat in it together now with the water up to their
chins. He hadn't had to talk, he hadn't had to think, he had scarce
even had to feel. He had been sunk that way before, sunk—when
and where?—in another flood; only a flood of rushing waters in
which bumping and gasping were all. *This* was a current so slow
and so tepid that one floated practically without motion and without chill. The break of silence was not immediate, though Dane
seemed indeed to feel it begin before a sound passed. It could pass
quite sufficiently without words that he and his mate were Brothers, and what that meant.

He wondered, but with no want of ease—for want of ease was
impossible—if his friend found in *him* the same likeness, the proof
of peace, the gage of what the place could do. The long afternoon
crept to its end; the shadows fell further and the sky glowed deeper;
but nothing changed—nothing *could* change—in the element itself.
It was a conscious security. It was wonderful! Dane had lived into
it, but he was still immensely aware. He would have been sorry to
lose that, for just this fact as yet, the blest fact of consciousness,
seemed the greatest thing of all. Its only fault was that, being in
itself such an occupation, so fine an unrest in the heart of gratitude,
the life of the day all went to it. But what even then was the harm?
He had come only to come, to take what he found. This was the part
where the great cloister, enclosed externally on three sides and
probably the largest lightest fairest effect, to his charmed sense, that
human hands could ever have expressed in dimensions of length and
breadth, opened to the south its splendid fourth quarter, turned to
the great view an outer gallery that combined with the rest of the
portico to form a high dry loggia, such as he a little pretended to
himself he had, in the Italy of old days, seen in old cities, old con-
vents, old villas. This recalled disposition of some great abode of an
Order, some mild Monte Cassino, some Grande Chartreuse more
accessible, was his main term of comparison; but he knew he had

really never anywhere beheld anything at once so calculated and so generous.

Three impressions in particular had been with him all the week, and he could but recognise in silence their happy effect on his nerves. How it was all managed he couldn't have told—he had been content moreover till now with his ignorance of cause and pretext; but whenever he chose to listen with a certain intentness he made out as from a distance the sound of slow sweet bells. How could they be so far and yet so audible? How could they be so near and yet so faint? How above all could they, in such an arrest of life, be, to *time* things, so frequent? The very essence of the bliss of Dane's whole change had been precisely that there was nothing now to time. It was the same with the slow footsteps that, always within earshot to the vague attention, marked the space and the leisure, seemed, in long cool arcades, lightly to fall and perpetually to recede. This was the second impression, and it melted into the third, as, for that matter, every form of softness, in the great good place, was but a further turn, without jerk or gap, of the endless roll of serenity. The quiet footsteps were quiet figures; the quiet figures that, to the eye, kept the picture human and brought its perfection within reach. This perfection, he felt on the bench by his friend, was now more within reach than ever. His friend at last turned to him a look different from the looks of friends in London clubs.

"The thing was to find it out!"

It was extraordinary how this remark fitted into his thought. "Ah wasn't it? And when I think," said Dane, "of all the people who haven't and who never will!" He sighed over these unfortunates with a tenderness that, in its degree, was practically new to him, feeling too how well his companion would know the people he meant. He only meant some, but they were all who'd want it; though of these, no doubt—well, for reasons, for things that, in the world, he had observed—there would never be too many. Not all perhaps who wanted would really find; but none at least would find who didn't really want. And then what the need would have to have been first! What it at first had had to be for himself! He felt afresh, in the light of his companion's face, what it might still be even when deeply satisfied, as well as what communication was established by the mere common knowledge of it.

"Every man must arrive by himself and on his own feet—isn't that so? We're Brothers here for the time, as in a great monastery, and we immediately think of each other and recognise each other as such; but we must have first got here as we can, and we meet after long journeys by complicated ways. Moreover we meet—don't we? —with closed eyes."

"Ah don't speak as if we were dead!" Dane laughed.

"I shan't mind death if it's like this," his friend replied.

It was too obvious, as Dane gazed before him, that one wouldn't; but after a moment he asked with the first articulation as yet of his most elementary wonder: "Where is it?"

"I shouldn't be surprised if it were much nearer than one ever suspected."

"Nearer 'town,' do you mean?"

"Nearer everything—nearer every one."

George Dane thought. "Would it be somewhere for instance down in Surrey?"

His Brother met him on this with a shade of reluctance. "Why should we call it names? It must have a climate, you see."

"Yes," Dane happily mused; "without that—!" All it so securely did have overwhelmed him again, and he couldn't help breaking out: "*What* is it?"

"Oh it's positively a part of our ease and our rest and our change, I think, that we don't at all know and that we may really call it, for that matter, anything in the world we like—the thing for instance we love it most for being."

"I know what *I* call it," said Dane after a moment. Then as his friend listened with interest: "Just simply 'The Great Good Place.' "

"I see—what can you say more? I've put it to myself perhaps a little differently." They sat there as innocently as small boys confiding to each other the names of toy animals. " 'The Great Want Met.' "

"Ah yes—that's it!"

"Isn't it enough for us that it's a place carried on for our benefit so admirably that we strain our ears in vain for a creak of the machinery? Isn't it enough for us that it's simply a thorough hit?"

"Ah a hit!" Dane benignantly murmured.

"It does for us what it pretends to do," his companion went on;

"the mystery isn't deeper than that. The thing's probably simple enough in fact, and on a thoroughly practical basis; only it has had its origin in a splendid thought, in a real stroke of genius."

"Yes," Dane returned, "in a sense—on somebody or other's part—so exquisitely personal!"

"Precisely—it rests, like all good things, on experience. The 'great want' comes home—that's the great thing it does! On the day it came home to the right mind this dear place was constituted. It always moreover in the long run *has* been met—it always must be. How can it not require to be, more and more, as pressure of every sort grows?"

Dane, with his hands folded in his lap, took in these words of wisdom. "Pressure of every sort *is* growing!" he placidly observed.

"I see well enough what that fact has done to *you*," his Brother declared.

Dane smiled. "I couldn't have borne it longer. I don't know what would have become of me."

"I know what would have become of *me*."

"Well, it's the same thing."

"Yes," said Dane's companion, "it's doubtless the same thing." On which they sat in silence a little, seeming pleasantly to follow, in the view of the green garden, the vague movements of the monster—madness, surrender, collapse—they had escaped. Their bench was like a box at the opera. "And I may perfectly, you know," the Brother pursued, "have seen you before. I may even have known you well. We don't know."

They looked at each other again serenely enough, and at last Dane said: "No, we don't know."

"That's what I meant by our coming with our eyes closed. Yes—there's something out. There's a gap, a link missing, the great hiatus!" the Brother laughed. "It's as simple a story as the old, old rupture—the break that lucky Catholics have always been able to make, that they're still, with their innumerable religious houses, able to make, by going into 'retreat.' I don't speak of the pious exercises—I speak only of the material simplification. I don't speak of the putting off of one's self; I speak only—if one has a self worth sixpence—of the getting it back. The place, the time, the way were, for those of the old persuasion, always there—are indeed practically there for them as much as ever. They can always get off—the blessed houses receive. So it was high time that we—we of the great Protestant peoples, still more, if possible, in the sensitive individual case, over-scored and overwhelmed, still more congested with mere quantity and prostituted, through our 'enterprise,' to mere profanity—should learn how to get off, should find somewhere *our* retreat and remedy. There was such a huge chance for it!"

Dane laid his hand on his companion's arm. "It's charming how when we speak for ourselves we speak for each other. That was exactly what I said!" He had fallen to recalling from over the gulf the last occasion.

The Brother, as if it would do them both good, only desired to draw him out. "What you 'said'—?"

"To *him*—that morning." Dane caught a far bell again and heard a slow footstep. A quiet presence passed somewhere—neither of them turned to look. What was little by little more present to him was the perfect taste. It was supreme—it was everywhere. "I just dropped my burden—and he received it."

"And was it very great?"

"Oh such a load!" Dane said with gaiety.

"Trouble, sorrow, doubt?"

"Oh no—worse than that!"

"Worse?"

" 'Success'—the vulgarest kind!" He mentioned it now as with amusement.

"Ah I know that too! No one in future, as things are going, will be able to face success."

"Without something of this sort—never. The better it is the worse —the greater the deadlier. But my one pain here," Dane contin-ued, "is in thinking of my poor friend."

"The person to whom you've already alluded?"

He tenderly assented. "My substitute in the world. Such an un-utterable benefactor. He turned up that morning when everything had somehow got on my nerves, when the whole great globe indeed, nerves or no nerves, seemed to have appallingly squeezed itself into my study and to be bent on simply swelling there. It wasn't a question of nerves, it was a mere question of the dislodgement and derangement of everything—of a general submersion by our eternal too much. I didn't know *où donner de la tête*—I couldn't have gone a step further."

The intelligence with which the Brother listened kept them as children feeding from the same bowl. "And then you got the tip?"

"I got the tip!" Dane happily sighed.

"Well, we all get it. But I dare say differently."

"Then how did *you*—?"

The Brother hesitated, smiling. "You tell me first."

III

"Well," said George Dane, "it was a young man I had never seen —a man at any rate much younger than myself—who had written to me and sent me some article, some book. I read the stuff, was much struck with it, told him so and thanked him—on which of course I heard from him again. Ah *that*—!" Dane comically sighed. "He asked me things—his questions were interesting; but to save time and writing I said to him: 'Come to see me—we can talk a little; but all I can give you is half an hour at breakfast.' He arrived to the minute on a day when more than ever in my life before I seemed, as it happened, in the endless press and stress, to have lost possession of my soul and to be surrounded only with the affairs of other people, smothered in mere irrelevant importunity. It made me literally ill—made me feel as I had never felt that should I once really for an hour lose hold of the thing itself, the thing that did matter and that I was trying for, I should never recover it again. The wild waters would close over me and I should drop straight to the dark depths where the vanquished dead lie."

"I follow you every step of your way," said the friendly Brother. "The wild waters, you mean, of our horrible time."

"Of our horrible time precisely. Not of course—as we sometimes dream—of any other."

"Yes, any other's only a dream. We really know none but our own."

"No, thank God—that's enough," Dane contentedly smiled. "Well, my young man turned up, and I hadn't been a minute in his presence before making out that practically it would be in him somehow or other to help me. He came to me with envy, envy extravagant—really passionate. I was, heaven save us, the great 'success' for him; he himself was starved and broken and beaten. How can I say what passed between us?—it was so strange, so swift, so much a matter, from one to the other, of instant perception and agreement. He was so clever and haggard and hungry!"

"Hungry?" the Brother asked.

"I don't mean for bread, though he had none too much, I think, even of that. I mean for—well, what *I* had and what I was a monument of to him as I stood there up to my neck in preposterous evidence. He, poor chap, had been for ten years serenading closed windows and had never yet caused a shutter to show that it stirred. *My* dim blind was the first raised to him an inch; my reading of his book, my impression of it, my note and my invitation, formed literally the only response ever dropped into his dark alley. He saw in my littered room, my shattered day, my bored face and spoiled temper —it's embarrassing, but I must tell you—the very proof of my pudding, the very blaze of my glory. And he saw in my repletion and my 'renown'—deluded innocent!—what he had yearned for in vain."

"What he had yearned for was to *be* you," said the Brother. Then he added: "I see where you're coming out."

"At my saying to him by the end of five minutes: 'My dear fellow, I wish you'd just try it—wish you'd for a while just *be* me!' You go straight to the mark, good Brother, and that was exactly what occurred—extraordinary though it was that we should both have understood. I saw what he could give, and he did too. He saw moreover what I could take; in fact what he saw was wonderful."

"He must be very remarkable!" Dane's converser laughed.

"There's no doubt of it whatever—far more remarkable than I. That's just the reason why what I put to him in joke—with a fantastic desperate irony—became, in his hands, with his vision of his chance, the blessed means and measure of my sitting on this spot in your company. 'Oh if I could just *shift* it all—make it straight over for an hour to other shoulders! If there only *were* a pair!'—that's the way I put it to him. And then at something in his face, 'Would *you*, by a miracle, undertake it?' I asked. I let him know all it meant— how it meant that he should at that very moment step in. It meant that he should finish my work and open my letters and keep my engagements and be subject, for better or worse, to my contacts and complications. It meant that he should live with my life and think with my brain and write with my hand and speak with my voice. It meant above all that I should get off. He accepted with greatness—rose to it like a hero. Only he said: 'What will become of *you?*' "

"There was the rub!" the Brother admitted.

"Ah but only for a minute. He came to my help again," Dane pursued, "when he saw I couldn't quite meet that, could at least only say that I wanted to think, wanted to cease, wanted to do the thing itself—the thing that mattered and that I was trying for, miserable me, and that thing only—and therefore wanted first of all really to *see* it again, planted out, crowded out, frozen out as it now so long had been. 'I know what you want,' he after a moment quietly remarked to me. 'Ah what I want doesn't exist!' 'I know what you want,' he repeated. At that I began to believe him."

"Had you any idea yourself?" the Brother's attention breathed.

"Oh yes," said Dane, "and it was just my idea that made me despair. There it was as sharp as possible in my imagination and my longing—there it was so utterly *not* in the fact. We were sitting together on my sofa as we waited for breakfast. He presently laid his hand on my knee—showed me a face that the sudden great light in it had made, for me, indescribably beautiful. 'It exists—it exists,' he at last said. And so I remember we sat a while and looked at each other, with the final effect of my finding that I absolutely believed him. I remember we weren't at all solemn—we smiled with the joy of discoverers. He was as glad as I—he was tremendously glad. That came out in the whole manner of his reply to the appeal that broke from me: 'Where is it then in God's name? Tell me without delay where it is!' "

The Brother had bent such a sympathy! "He gave you the address?"

"He was thinking it out—feeling for it, catching it. He has a wonderful head of his own and must be making of the whole thing, while we sit here patching and gossiping, something much better than ever *I* did. The mere sight of his face, the sense of his hand on my knee, made me, after a little, feel that he not only knew what I wanted but was getting nearer to it than I could have got in ten years. He suddenly sprang up and went over to my study-table—sat straight down there as if to write me my prescription or my passport. Then it was—at the mere sight of his back, which was turned to me—that

I felt the spell work. I simply sat and watched him with the queerest deepest sweetest sense in the world—the sense of an ache that had stopped. All life was lifted; I myself at least was somehow off the ground. He was already where I had been."

"And where were you?" the Brother amusedly asked.

"Just on the sofa always, leaning back on the cushion and feeling a delicious ease. He was already me."

"And who were *you?*" the Brother continued.

"Nobody. That was the fun."

"That *is* the fun," said the Brother with a sigh like soft music.

Dane echoed the sigh, and, as nobody talking with nobody, they sat there together still and watched the sweet wide picture darken into tepid night.

IV

At the end of three weeks—so far as time was distinct—Dane began to feel there was something he had recovered. It was the thing they never named—partly for want of the need and partly for lack of the word; for what indeed was the description that would cover it all? The only real need was to know it, to see it in silence. Dane had a private practical sign for it, which, however, he had appropriated by theft—"the vision and the faculty divine." That doubtless was a flattering phrase for his idea of his genius; the genius was at all events what he had been in danger of losing and had at last held by a thread that might at any moment have broken. The change was that little by little his hold had grown firmer, so that he drew in the line—more and more each day—with a pull he was delighted to find it would bear. The mere dream-sweetness of the place was superseded; it was more and more a world of reason and order, of sensible visible arrangement. It ceased to be strange—it was high triumphant clearness. He cultivated, however, but vaguely the question of where he was, finding it near enough the mark to be almost sure that if he wasn't in Kent he was then probably in Hampshire. He paid for everything but that—that wasn't one of the items. Payment, he had soon learned, was definite; it consisted of sovereigns and shillings—just like those of the world he had left, only parted with more ecstatically—that he committed, in his room, to a fixed receptacle and that were removed in his absence by one of the unobtrusive effaced agents (shadows projected on the hours like the noiseless march of the sundial) that were always at work. The scene had whole sides that reminded and resembled, and a pleased resigned perception of these things was at once the effect and the cause of its grace.

Dane picked out of his dim past a dozen halting similes. The sacred silent convent was one; another was the bright country-house. He did the place no outrage to liken it to an hotel; he permitted himself on occasion to feel it suggest a club. Such images, however, but flickered and went out—they lasted only long enough to light up the difference. An hotel without noise, a club without newspapers—when he turned his face to what it was "without" the view opened wide. The only approach to a real analogy was in himself and his companions. They were brothers, guests, members; they were even, if one liked—and they didn't in the least mind what they were called—"regular boarders." It wasn't they who made the conditions, it was the conditions that made them. These conditions found themselves accepted, clearly, with an appreciation, with a rapture, it was rather to be called, that proceeded, as the very air that pervaded them and the force that sustained, from their quiet and noble assurance. They combined to form the large simple idea of a general refuge—an image of embracing arms, of liberal accommodation. What was the effect really but the poetisation by perfect taste of a type common enough? There was no daily miracle; the perfect taste, with the aid of space, did the trick. What underlay and overhung it all, better yet, Dane mused, was some original inspiration, but confirmed, unquenched, some happy thought of an individual breast. It had been born somehow and somewhere—it had had to insist on being—the blest conception. The author might remain in the obscure for that was part of the perfection: personal service so hushed and regulated that you scarce caught it in the act and only knew it by its results. Yet the wise mind was everywhere—the whole thing infallibly centred at the core in a consciousness. And what a consciousness it had been, Dane thought, a consciousness how like his own! The wise mind had felt, the wise mind had suffered; then, for all the worried company of minds, the wise mind had seen a chance.

Of the creation thus arrived at you could none the less never have said if it were the last echo of the old or the sharpest note of the modern.

Dane again and again, among the far bells and the soft footfalls, in cool cloister and warm garden, found himself wanting not to know more and yet liking not to know less. It was part of the high style and the grand manner that there was no personal publicity, much less any personal reference. Those things were in the world—in what he had left; there was no vulgarity here of credit or claim or fame. The real exquisite was to be without the complication of an identity, and the greatest boon of all, doubtless, the solid security, the clear confidence one could feel in the keeping of the contract. That was what had been most in the wise mind—the importance of the absolute sense, on the part of its beneficiaries, that what was offered was guaranteed. They had no concern but to pay—the wise mind knew what they paid for. It was present to Dane each hour that he could never be overcharged. Oh the deep deep bath, the soft cool plash in the stillness!—this, time after time, as if under regular treatment, a sublimated German "cure," was the vivid name for his luxury. The inner life woke up again, and it was the inner life, for people of his generation, victims of the modern madness, mere maniacal extension and motion, that was returning health. He had talked of independence and written of it, but what a cold flat word it had been! This was the wordless fact itself—the uncontested possession of the long sweet stupid day. The fragrance of flowers just wandered through the void, and the quiet recurrence of delicate plain fare in a high, clean refectory where the soundless simple service was a triumph of art. That, as he analysed, remained the constant explanation: all the sweetness and serenity were created calculated things. He analysed, however, but in a desultory way and with a positive delight in the residuum of mystery that made for the great agent in the background the innermost shrine of the idol of a temple; there were odd moments for it, mild meditations when, in the broad cloister of peace of some garden-nook where the air was light, a special glimpse of beauty or reminder of felicity seemed, in passing, to hover and linger. In the mere ecstasy of change that had at first possessed him he hadn't discriminated—had only let himself sink, as I have mentioned, down to hushed depths. Then had come the slow soft stages of intelligence and notation, more marked and more fruitful perhaps after that long talk with his mild mate in the twilight, and seeming to wind up the process by putting the key into his hand. This key, pure gold, was simply the cancelled list. Slowly and blissfully he read into the general wealth of his comfort all the particular absences of which it was composed. One by one he touched, as it were, all the things it was such rapture to be without.

It was the paradise of his own room that was most indebted to them—a great square fair chamber, all beautified with omissions, from which, high up, he looked over a long valley to a far horizon, and in which he was vaguely and pleasantly reminded of some old Italian picture, some Carpaccio or some early Tuscan, the representation of a world without newspapers and letters, without telegrams and photographs, without the dreadful fatal too much. There, for a blessing, he *could* read and write; there above all he could do nothing—he could live. And there were all sorts of freedoms—always, for the occasion, the particular right one. He could bring a book from the library—he could bring two, he could bring three. An effect produced by the charming place was that for some reason he never wanted to bring more. The library was a benediction—high and clear and plain like everything else, but with something, in all its arched amplitude, unconfused and brave and gay. He should never forget, he knew, the throb of immediate perception with which he first stood there, a single glance round sufficing so to show him that it would give him what for years he had desired. He had not had detachment, but there was detachment here—the sense of a great silver bowl from which he could ladle up the melted hours. He strolled about from wall to wall, too pleasantly in tune on that occasion to sit down punctually or to choose; only recognising from shelf to shelf every dear old book that he had had to put off or never returned to; every deep distinct voice of another time that in the hubbub of the world, he had had to take for lost and unheard. He came back of course soon, came back every day; enjoyed there, of all the rare strange moments, those that were at once most quickened and most caught—moments in which every apprehension counted double and every act of the mind was a lover's embrace. It was the quarter he perhaps, as the days went on, liked best; though indeed it only shared with the rest of the place, with every aspect to which his face happened to be turned, the power to remind him of the masterly general care.

There were times when he looked up from his book to lose himself in the mere tone of the picture that never failed at any moment or at any angle. The picture was always there, yet was made up of things common enough. It was in the way an open window in a broad recess let in the pleasant morning; in the way the dry air pricked into faint freshness the gilt of old bindings; in the way an empty chair beside a table unlittered showed a volume just laid down; in the way a happy Brother—as detached as one's self and with his innocent back presented—lingered before a shelf with the slow sound of turned pages. It was a part of the whole impression that, by some extraordinary law, one's vision seemed less from the facts than the facts from one's vision; that the elements were determined at the moment by the moment's need or the moment's sympathy. What most prompted this reflexion was the degree in which Dane had after a while a consciousness of company. After that talk with the good Brother on the bench there were other good Brothers in other places—always in cloister or garden some figure that stopped if he himself stopped and with which a greeting became, in the easiest way in the world, a sign of the diffused amenity and the consecrating ignorance. For always, always, in all contacts, was the balm of a happy blank. What he had felt the first time recurred: the friend was always new and yet at the same time—it was amusing, not disturbing—suggested the possibility that he might be but an old one altered. That was only delightful—as positively delightful in the particular, the actual conditions as it might have been the reverse in the conditions abolished. These others, the abolished, came back to Dane at last so easily that he could exactly measure each difference, but with what he had finally been hustled on to hate in them robbed of its terror in consequence of something that had happened. What had happened was that in tranquil walks and talks the deep spell had worked and he had got his soul again. He had drawn in by this time, with his lightened hand, the whole of the long line, and that fact just dangled at the end. He could put his other hand on it, he could unhook it, he was once more in possession. This, as it befell, was exactly what he supposed he must have said to a comrade beside whom, one afternoon in the cloister, he found himself measuring steps.

"Oh it comes—comes of itself, doesn't it, thank goodness?—just by the simple fact of finding room and time!"

The comrade was possibly a novice or in a different stage from his own; there was at any rate a vague envy in the recognition that shone out of the fatigued yet freshened face. "It has come to *you* then?—you've got what you wanted?" That was the gossip and interchange that could pass to and fro. Dane, years before, had gone in for three months of hydropathy, and there was a droll echo, in this scene, of the old questions of the water-cure, the questions asked in the periodical pursuit of the "reaction"—the ailment, the progress of each, the action of the skin and the state of the appetite. Such memories worked in now—all familiar reference, all easy play of mind; and among them our friends, round and round, fraternised ever so softly till, suddenly stopping short, Dane, with a hand on his companion's arm, broke into the happiest laugh he had yet sounded.

V

"Why it's raining!" And he stood and looked at the splash of the shower and the shine of the wet leaves. It was one of the summer sprinkles that bring out sweet smells.

"Yes—but why not?" his mate demanded.

"Well—because it's so charming. It's so exactly right."

"But everything *is*. Isn't that just why we're here?"

"Just exactly," Dane said; "only I've been living in the beguiled supposition that we've somehow or other a climate."

"So have I, so I dare say has every one. Isn't that the blest moral? —that we live in beguiled suppositions. They come so easily here, where nothing contradicts them." The good Brother looked placidly forth—Dane could identify his phase. "A climate doesn't consist in its never raining, does it?"

"No, I dare say not. But somehow the good I've got has been half the great easy absence of all that friction of which the question of weather mostly forms a part—has been indeed largely the great easy perpetual air-bath."

"Ah yes—that's not a delusion; but perhaps the sense comes a little from our breathing an emptier medium. There are fewer things *in* it! Leave people alone, at all events, and the air's what they take to. Into the closed and the stuffy they have to be driven. I've had too—I think we must all have—a fond sense of the south."

"But imagine it," said Dane, laughing, "in the beloved British islands and so near as we are to Bradford!"

His friend was ready enough to imagine. "To Bradford?" he asked, quite unperturbed. "How near?"

Dane's gaiety grew. "Oh it doesn't matter!"

His friend, quite unmystified, accepted it. "There are things to puzzle out—otherwise it would be dull. It seems to me one can puzzle them."

"It's because we're so well disposed," Dane said.

"Precisely—we find good in everything."

"In everything," Dane went on. "The conditions settle that—they determine us."

They resumed their stroll, which evidently represented on the good Brother's part infinite agreement. "Aren't they probably in fact very simple?" he presently enquired. "Isn't simplification the secret?"

"Yes, but applied with a tact!"

"There it is. The thing's so perfect that it's open to as many interpretations as any other great work—a poem of Goethe, a dialogue of Plato, a symphony of Beethoven."

"It simply stands quiet, you mean," said Dane, "and lets us call it names?"

"Yes, but all such loving ones. We're 'staying' with some one—some delicious host or hostess who never shows."

"It's liberty-hall—absolutely," Dane assented.

"Yes—or a convalescent home."

To this, however, Dane demurred. "Ah that, it seems to me, scarcely puts it. You weren't *ill*—were you? I'm very sure I really wasn't. I was only, as the world goes, too 'beastly well'!"

The good Brother wondered. "But if we couldn't keep it up—?"

"We couldn't keep it *down*—that was all the matter!"

"I see—I see." The good Brother sighed contentedly; after which he brought out again with kindly humour: "It's a sort of kinder-garten!"

"The next thing you'll be saying that we're babes at the breast!"

"Of some great mild invisible mother who stretches away into space and whose lap's—the whole valley—?"

"And her bosom"—Dane completed the figure—"the noble eminence of our hill? That will do; anything will do that covers the essential fact."

"And what do you call the essential fact?"

"Why that—as in old days on Swiss lakesides—we're *en pension*."

The good Brother took this gently up. "I remember—I remember: seven francs a day without wine! But alas it's more than seven francs here."

"Yes, it's considerably more," Dane had to confess. "Perhaps it isn't particularly cheap."

"Yet should you call it particularly dear?" his friend after a moment enquired.

George Dane had to think. "How do I know, after all? What practice has one ever had in estimating the inestimable? Particular cheapness certainly isn't the note we feel struck all round; but don't we fall naturally into the view that there *must* be a price to anything so awfully sane?"

The good Brother in his turn reflected. "We fall into the view that it must pay—that it does pay."

"Oh yes; it does pay!" Dane eagerly echoed. "If it didn't it wouldn't last. It has *got* to last of course!" he declared.

"So that we can come back?"

"Yes—think of knowing that we shall be able to!"

They pulled up again at this and, facing each other, thought of it, or at any rate pretended to; for what was really in their eyes was the dread of a loss of the clue. "Oh when we want it again we shall find it," said the good Brother. "If the place really pays it will keep on."

"Yes, that's the beauty; that it isn't, thank goodness, carried on only for love."

"No doubt, no doubt; and yet, thank goodness, there's love in it too." They had lingered as if, in the mild moist air, they were charmed with the patter of the rain and the way the garden drank it. After a little, however, it did look rather as if they were trying to talk each other out of a faint small fear. They saw the increasing rage

of life and the recurrent need, and they wondered proportionately
whether to return to the front when their hour should sharply strike
would be the end of the dream. Was this a threshold perhaps, after
all, that could only be crossed one way? They must return to the
front sooner or later—that was certain: for each his hour would
strike. The flower would have been gathered and the trick played—
the sands would in short have run.

There, in its place, *was* life—with all its rage; the vague unrest
of the need for action knew it again, the stir of the faculty that had
been refreshed and reconsecrated. They seemed each, thus confronted, to close their eyes a moment for dizziness; then they were
again at peace and the Brother's confidence rang out. "Oh we shall
meet!"

"Here, do you mean?"

"Yes—and I dare say in the world too."

"But we shan't recognise or know," said Dane.

"In the world, do you mean?"

"Neither in the world nor here."

"Not a bit—not the least little bit, you think?"

Dane turned it over. "Well, so is it that it seems to me all best to
hang together. But we shall see."

His friend happily concurred. "We shall see." And at this, for
farewell, the Brother held out his hand.

"You're going?" Dane asked.

"No, but I thought *you* were."

It was odd, but at this Dane's hour seemed to strike—his consciousness to crystallise. "Well, I am. I've got it. You stay?" he went
on.

"A little longer."

Dane hesitated. "You haven't yet got it?"

"Not altogether—but I think it's coming."

"Good!" Dane kept his hand, giving it a final shake, and at that
moment the sun glimmered again through the shower, but with
the rain still falling on the hither side of it and seeming to patter
even more in the brightness. "Hallo—how charming!"

The Brother looked a moment from under the high arch—then
again turned his face to our friend. He gave this time his longest
happiest sigh. "Oh it's all right!"

But why was it, Dane after a moment found himself wondering, that in the act of separation his own hand was so long retained? Why but through a queer phenomenon of change, on the spot, in his companion's face—change that gave it another, but an increasing and above all a much more familiar identity, an identity not beautiful, but more and more distinct, an identity with that of his servant, with the most conspicuous, the physiognomic seat of the public propriety of Brown? To this anomaly his eyes slowly opened; it was not his good Brother, it was verily Brown who possessed his hand. If his eyes had to open it was because they had been closed and because Brown appeared to think he had better wake up. So much as this Dane took in, but the effect of his taking it was a relapse into darkness, a recontraction of the lids just prolonged enough to give Brown time, on a second thought, to withdraw his touch and move softly away. Dane's next consciousness was that of the desire to make sure he *was* away, and this desire had somehow the result of dissipating the obscurity. The obscurity was completely gone by the time he had made out that the back of a person writing at his study-table was presented to him. He recognised a portion of a figure that he had somewhere described to somebody—the intent shoulders of the unsuccessful young man who had come that bad morning to breakfast. It was strange, he at last mused, but the young man was still there. How long had he stayed—days, weeks, months? He was exactly in the position in which Dane had last seen him. Everything —stranger still—was exactly in that position; everything at least but the light of the window, which came in from another quarter and showed a different hour. It wasn't after breakfast now; it was after —well, what? He suppressed a gasp—it was after everything. And yet—quite literally—there were but two other differences. One of these was that if he was still on the sofa he was now lying down; the other was the patter on the glass that showed him how the rain—the great rain of the night—had come back. It was the rain of the night, yet when had he last heard it? But two minutes before? Then how many were there before the young man at the table, who seemed intensely occupied, found a moment to look round at him and, on meeting his open eyes, get up and draw near?

"You've slept all day," said the young man.

"All day?"

The young man looked at his watch. "From ten to six. You were extraordinarily tired. I just after a bit let you alone, and you were soon off." Yes, that was it; he had been "off"—off, off, off. He began to fit it together: while he had been off the young man had been on. But there were still some few confusions; Dane lay looking up. "Everything's done," the young man continued.

"Everything?"

"Everything."

Dane tried to take it all in, but was embarrassed and could only say weakly and quite apart from the matter: "I've been so happy!"

"So have I," said the young man. He positively looked so; seeing which George Dane wondered afresh, and then in his wonder read it indeed quite as another face, quite, in a puzzling way, as another person's. Every one was a little some one else. While he asked himself who else then the young man was, this benefactor, struck by his appealing stare, broke again into perfect cheer. "It's all right!" That answered Dane's question; the face was the face turned to him by the good Brother there in the portico while they listened together to the rustle of the shower. It was all queer, but all pleasant and all distinct, so distinct that the last words in his ear—the same from both quarters—appeared the effect of a single voice. Dane rose and looked about his room, which seemed disencumbered, different, twice as large. It *was* all right.

◇◇◇*James Joyce (1882-1941). Irish novelist and short-story writer. Joyce is considered by some critics to be the most important writer of his time. During an almost life-long struggle with poverty, he also endured years of public indifference, attempts of publishers to censor his work, and the attacks of public censors. Sensitive, strong-willed, brilliant, a great linguist and scholar, his faith in himself strengthened him for a life of solitude and unending work. See* Dubliners, *a collection of stories,* A Portrait of the Artist as a Young Man, Ulysses, Finnegans Wake.

ARABY

BY JAMES JOYCE

North Richmond Street, being blind, was a quiet street except at the hour when the Christian Brothers' School set the boys free. An uninhabited house of two storeys stood at the blind end, detached from its neighbours in a square ground. The other houses of the street, conscious of decent lives within them, gazed at one another with brown imperturbable faces.

The former tenant of our house, a priest, had died in the back drawing-room. Air, musty from having been long enclosed, hung in all the rooms, and the waste room behind the kitchen was littered with old useless papers. Among these I found a few paper-covered books, the pages of which were curled and damp: *The Abbot,* by Walter Scott, *The Devout Communicant* and *The Memoirs of Vidocq.* I liked the last best because its leaves were yellow. The wild garden behind the house contained a central apple-tree and a few straggling bushes under one of which I found the late tenant's rusty bicycle-pump. He had been a very charitable priest; in his will he had left all his money to institutions and the furniture of his house to his sister.

When the short days of winter came dusk fell before we had well eaten our dinners. When we met in the street the houses had grown sombre. The space of sky above us was the colour of ever-changing violet and towards it the lamps of the street lifted their feeble lanterns. The cold air stung us and we played till our bodies glowed. Our shouts echoed in the silent street. The career of our play brought us through the dark muddy lanes behind the houses where we ran the gauntlet of the rough tribes from the cottages, to the back doors of the dark dripping gardens where odours arose from the ashpits, to the dark odorous stables where a coachman smoothed and combed the horse or shook music from the buckled harness. When we returned to the street light from the kitchen windows had filled the areas. If my uncle was seen turning the corner we hid in the shadow until we had seen him safely housed. Or if Mangan's sister came out on the doorstep to call her brother in to his tea we watched her from our shadow peer up and down the street. We waited to see whether she would remain or go in and, if she remained, we left our shadow and walked up to Mangan's steps resignedly. She was waiting for us, her figure defined by the light from the half-opened door. Her brother always teased her before he obeyed and I stood by the railings looking at her. Her dress swung as she moved her body and the soft rope of her hair tossed from side to side.

Every morning I lay on the floor in the front parlour watching her door. The blind was pulled down to within an inch of the sash so that I could not be seen. When she came out on the doorstep my heart leaped. I ran to the hall, seized my books and followed her. I kept her brown figure always in my eye and, when we came near the point at which our ways diverged, I quickened my pace and passed her. This happened morning after morning. I had never spoken to her, except for a few casual words, and yet her name was like a summons to all my foolish blood.

Her image accompanied me even in places the most hostile to romance. On Saturday evenings when my aunt went marketing I had to go to carry some of the parcels. We walked through the flaring streets, jostled by drunken men and bargaining women, amid the curses of labourers, the shrill litanies of shop-boys who stood on guard by the barrels of pigs' cheeks, the nasal chanting of street-singers, who sang a *come-all-you* about O'Donovan Rossa, or a ballad about the troubles in our native land. These noises converged in a single sensation of life for me: I imagined that I bore my chalice safely through a throng of foes. Her name sprang to my lips at moments in strange prayers and praises which I myself did not understand. My eyes were often full of tears (I could not tell why) and at times a flood from my heart seemed to pour itself out into my bosom. I thought little of the future. I did not know whether I would ever speak to her or not or, if I spoke to her, how I could tell her of my confused adoration. But my body was like a harp and her words and gestures were like fingers running upon the wires.

One evening I went into the back drawing-room in which the priest had died. It was a dark rainy evening and there was no sound in the house. Through one of the broken panes I heard the rain impinge upon the earth, the fine incessant needles of water playing in the sodden beds. Some distant lamp or lighted window gleamed below me. I was thankful that I could see so little. All my senses seemed to desire to veil themselves and, feeling that I was about to slip from them, I pressed the palms of my hands together until they trembled, murmuring: *"O love! O love!"* many times.

At last she spoke to me. When she addressed the first words to me I was so confused that I did not know what to answer. She asked me was I going to *Araby*. I forgot whether I answered yes or no. It would be a splendid bazaar, she said she would love to go.

"And why can't you?" I asked.

While she spoke she turned a silver bracelet round and round her wrist. She could not go, she said, because there would be a retreat that week in her convent. Her brother and two other boys were fighting for their caps and I was alone at the railings. She held one of the spikes, bowing her head towards me. The light from the lamp opposite our door caught the white curve of her neck, lit up her hair that rested there and, falling, lit up the hand upon the railing. It fell over one side of her dress and caught the white border of a petticoat, just visible as she stood at ease.

"It's well for you," she said.

"If I go," I said, "I will bring you something."

What innumerable follies laid waste my waking and sleeping thoughts after that evening! I wished to annihilate the tedious intervening days. I chafed against the work of school. At night in my bedroom and by day in the classroom her image came between me and the page I strove to read. The syllables of the word *Araby* were called to me through the silence in which my soul luxuriated and cast an Eastern enchantment over me. I asked for leave to go to the bazaar on Saturday night. My aunt was surprised and hoped it was not some Freemason affair. I answered few questions in class. I watched my master's face pass from amiability to sternness; he hoped I was not beginning to idle. I could not call my wandering thoughts together. I had hardly any patience with the serious work of life which, now that it stood between me and my desire, seemed to me child's play, ugly monotonous child's play.

On Saturday morning I reminded my uncle that I wished to go to the bazaar in the evening. He was fussing at the hallstand, looking for the hat-brush, and answered me curtly:

"Yes, boy, I know."

As he was in the hall I could not go into the front parlour and lie at the window. I felt the house in bad humour and walked slowly towards the school. The air was pitilessly raw and already my heart misgave me.

When I came home to dinner my uncle had not yet been home. Still it was early. I sat staring at the clock for some time and, when its ticking began to irritate me, I left the room. I mounted the staircase and gained the upper part of the house. The high cold empty gloomy rooms liberated me and I went from room to room singing. From the front window I saw my companions playing below in the street. Their cries reached me weakened and indistinct and, leaning my forehead against the cool glass, I looked over at the dark house where she lived. I may have stood there for an hour, seeing nothing but the brown-clad figure cast by my imagination, touched discreetly by the lamplight at the curved neck, at the hand upon the railings and at the border below the dress.

When I came downstairs again I found Mrs. Mercer sitting at the fire. She was an old garrulous woman, a pawnbroker's widow, who collected used stamps for some pious purpose. I had to endure the gossip of the tea-table. The meal was prolonged beyond an hour and still my uncle did not come. Mrs. Mercer stood up to go: she was sorry she couldn't wait any longer, but it was after eight o'clock and she did not like to be out late, as the night air was bad for her.

When she had gone I began to walk up and down the room, clenching my fists. My aunt said:

"I'm afraid you may put off your bazaar for this night of Our Lord."

At nine o'clock I heard my uncle's latchkey in the halldoor. I heard him talking to himself and heard the hallstand rocking when it had received the weight of his overcoat. I could interpret these signs. When he was midway through his dinner I asked him to give me the money to go to the bazaar. He had forgotten.

"The people are in bed and after their first sleep now," he said.

I did not smile. My aunt said to him energetically:

"Can't you give him the money and let him go? You've kept him late enough as it is."

My uncle said he was very sorry he had forgotten. He said he believed in the old saying: "All work and no play makes Jack a dull boy." He asked me where I was going and, when I had told him a second time he asked me did I know *The Arab's Farewell to his Steed*. When I left the kitchen he was about to recite the opening lines of the piece to my aunt.

I held a florin tightly in my hand as I strode down Buckingham Street towards the station. The sight of the streets thronged with buyers and glaring with gas recalled to me the purpose of my journey. I took my seat in a third-class carriage of a deserted train. After an intolerable delay the train moved out of the station slowly. It crept onward among ruinous houses and over the twinkling river. At Westland Row Station a crowd of people pressed to the carriage doors; but the porters moved them back, saying that it was a special train for the bazaar. I remained alone in the bare carriage. In a few minutes the train drew up beside an improvised wooden platform. I passed out on to the road and saw by the lighted dial of a clock that it was ten minutes to ten. In front of me was a large building which displayed the magical name.

I could not find any sixpenny entrance and, fearing that the bazaar would be closed, I passed in quickly through a turnstile, handing a shilling to a weary-looking man. I found myself in a big hall girdled at half its height by a gallery. Nearly all the stalls were closed and the greater part of the hall was in darkness. I recognised a silence like that which pervades a church after a service. I walked into the centre of the bazaar timidly. A few people were gathered about the stalls which were still open. Before a curtain, over which the words *Café Chantant* were written in coloured lamps, two men were counting money on a salver. I listened to the fall of the coins.

Remembering with difficulty why I had come I went over to one of the stalls and examined porcelain vases and flowered tea-sets. At the door of the stall a young lady was talking and laughing with two young gentlemen. I remarked their English accents and listened vaguely to their conversation.

"O, I never said such a thing!"

"O, but you did!"

"O, but I didn't!"

"Didn't she say that?"

"Yes. I heard her."

"O, there's a . . . fib!"

Observing me the young lady came over and asked me did I wish to buy anything. The tone of her voice was not encouraging; she seemed to have spoken to me out of a sense of duty. I looked humbly at the great jars that stood like eastern guards at either side of the dark entrance to the stall and murmured:

"No, thank you."

The young lady changed the position of one of the vases and went back to the two young men. They began to talk of the same subject. Once or twice the young lady glanced at me over her shoulder.

I lingered before her stall, though I knew my stay was useless, to make my interest in her wares seem the more real. Then I turned away slowly and walked down the middle of the bazaar. I allowed the two pennies to fall against the six-pence in my pocket. I heard a voice call from one end of the gallery that the light was out. The upper part of the hall was now completely dark.

Gazing up into the darkness I saw myself as a creature driven and derided by vanity; and my eyes burned with anguish and anger.

◇◇◇*Franz Kafka (1883-1924). German novelist and short-story writer. Kafka was born in Prague of a middle-class Jewish family. He studied law and worked for the Austrian civil service. He worked slowly and conscientiously, in a classically pure prose yet with a strong personal idiom. See the novels,* Amerika, The Trial *and* The Castle. *Also his diaries, published in two volumes, and the stories in* The Great Wall of China.

A COUNTRY DOCTOR

BY FRANZ KAFKA

I was in great perplexity; I had to start on an urgent journey; a seriously ill patient was waiting for me in a village ten miles off; a thick blizzard of snow filled all the wide spaces between him and me; I had a gig, a light gig with big wheels, exactly right for our country roads; muffled in furs, my bag of instruments in my hand, I was in the courtyard all ready for the journey; but there was no horse to be had, no horse. My own horse had died in the night, worn out by the fatigues of this icy winter; my servant girl was now running round the village trying to borrow a horse; but it was hopeless, I knew it, and I stood there forlornly, with the snow gathering more and more thickly upon me, more and more unable to move. In the gateway the girl appeared, alone, and waved the lantern; of course, who would lend a horse at this time for such a journey? I strode through the courtway once more; I could see no way out; in my confused distress I kicked at the dilapidated door of the year-long uninhabited pigsty. It flew open and flapped to and fro on its hinges. A steam and smell as of horses came out of it. A dim stable lantern was swinging inside from a rope. A man, crouching on his hams in that low space, showed an open blue-eyed face. "Shall I yoke up?" he asked, crawling out on all fours. I did not know what to say and merely stooped down to see what else was in the sty. The servant girl was standing beside me. "You never know what you're going to find in your own house," she said, and we both laughed. "Hey there, Brother, hey there, Sister!" called the groom, and two horses, enormous creatures with powerful flanks, one after the other, their legs tucked close to their bodies, each well-shaped head lowered like a camel's, by sheer strength of buttocking squeezed out through the door hole which they filled entirely. But at once they were standing up, with their long legs and their bodies steaming thickly. "Give him a hand," I said, and the willing girl hurried to help the groom with the harnessing. Yet hardly was she beside him when the groom clipped hold of her and pushed his face against hers. She screamed and fled back to me; on her cheek stood out in red the marks of two rows of teeth. "You brute," I yelled in fury, "do you want a whipping?" but in the same moment reflected that the man was a stranger; that I did not know where he came from, and that of his own free will he was helping me out when everyone else had failed me. As if he knew my thoughts he took no offense at my threat but, still busied with the horses, only turned round once towards me. "Get in," he said then, and indeed: everything was ready. A magnificent pair of horses, I observed, such as I had never sat behind, and I climbed in happily. "But I'll drive, you don't know the way," I said. "Of course," said he, "I'm not coming with you anyway, I'm staying with Rose." "No," shrieked Rose, fleeing into the house with a justified presentiment that her fate was inescapable; I heard the door chain rattle as she put it up; I heard the key turn in the lock; I could see, moreover, how she put out the lights in the entrance hall and in further flight all through the rooms to keep herself from being discovered. "You're coming with me," I said to the groom, "or I won't go, urgent as my journey is. I'm not thinking of paying for it by handing the girl over to you." "Gee up!" he said; clapped his hands; the gig whirled off like a log in a freshet; I could just hear the door of my house splitting and bursting as the groom charged at it and then I was deafened and blinded by a storming rush that steadily buffeted all my senses. But this only for a moment, since, as if my patient's farmyard had opened out just before my courtyard gate, I was already there; the horses had come quietly to a standstill; the blizzard had stopped; the moonlight all around; my patient's parents hurried out of the house, his sister behind them; I was almost lifted out of the gig; from their confused ejaculations I gathered not a word; in the sick room the air was almost unbreathable; the neglected stove was smoking; I wanted to push open a window; but first I had to look at my patient. Gaunt, without any fever, not cold, not warm, with vacant eyes, without a shirt, the youngster heaved himself up from under the feather bedding, threw his arms around my neck, and whispered in my ear: "Doctor, let me die." I glanced round the room; no one had heard it; the parents were leaning forward in silence waiting for my verdict; the sister had set a chair for my handbag; I opened the bag and hunted among my instruments; the boy kept clutching at me from his bed to remind me of his entreaty; I picked up a pair of tweezers, examined them in the candlelight and laid them down again. "Yes," I thought blasphemously, "in cases like this the gods are helpful, send the missing horse, add to it a second because of the urgency, and to crown everything bestow even a groom—" And only now did I remember Rose again; what was I to do, how could I rescue her, how could I pull her away from under that groom at ten miles' distance, with a team of horses I couldn't control. These horses, now, they had somehow slipped the reins loose, pushed the window open from the outside, I did not know how; each of them had stuck a head in at a window and, quite unmoved by the startled cries of the family, stood eyeing the patient. "Better go back at once," I thought, as if the horses were summoning me to the return journey, yet I permitted the patient's sister, who fancied that I was dazed by the heat, to take my fur coat from me. A glass of rum was poured out for me, the old man clapped me on the shoulder, a familiarity justified by this offer of his treasure. I shook my head; in the narrow confines of the old man's thoughts I felt ill; that was my only reason for refusing the drink. The mother stood by the bedside and cajoled me towards it; I yielded, and, while one of the horses whinnied loudly to the ceiling, laid my head to the boy's breast, which shivered under my wet beard. I confirmed what I already knew; the boy was quite sound, something a little wrong with his circulation, saturated with coffee by his solicitous mother, but sound and best turned out of bed with one shove. I am no world reformer and so I let him lie. I was the district doctor and I did my duty to the uttermost, to the point where it became almost too much. I was badly paid and yet generous and helpful to the poor. I had still to see that Rose was alright, and then the boy might have his way and I wanted to die too. What was I doing there in that endless winter! My horse was dead, and not a single person in the village would lend me another. I had to get my team out of the pigsty; if they hadn't chanced to be horses I should have had to travel with swine. That was how it was. And I nodded to the family. They knew nothing about it, and, had they known, would not have believed it. To write prescriptions is easy, but to come to an understanding with people is hard. Well, this should be the end of my visit, I had once more been called out needlessly, I was used to that, the whole district made my life a torment with my night bell, but that I should have to sacrifice Rose this time as well, the pretty girl who had lived in my house for years almost without my noticing her—that sacrifice was too much to ask, and I had somehow to get it reasoned out in my head with the help of what craft I could muster, in order not to let fly at this family, which with the best will in the world could not restore Rose to me. But as I shut my bag and put an arm out for my fur coat, the family meanwhile standing together, the father sniffing at the glass of rum in his hand, the mother, apparently disappointed in me—why, what do people expect?—biting her lips with tears in her eyes, the sister fluttering a blood-soaked towel, I was somehow ready to admit conditionally that the boy might be ill after all. I went towards him, he welcomed me smiling as if I were bringing him the most nourishing invalid broth—ah, now both horses were whinnying together; the noise, I suppose, was ordained by heaven to assist my examination of the patient—and this time I discovered that the boy was indeed ill. In his right side, near the hip, was an open wound as big as the palm of my hand. Rose-red, in many variations of shade, dark in the hollows, lighter at the edges, softly granulated, with irregular clots of blood, open as a surface mine to the daylight. That was how it looked from a distance. But on a closer inspection there was another complication. I could not help a low whistle of surprise. Worms, as thick and as long as my little finger, themselves rose-red and blood-spotted as well, were wriggling from their fastness in the interior of the wound towards the light, with small white heads and many little legs. Poor boy, you were past helping. I had discovered your great wound; this blossom in your side was destroy-

ing you. The family was pleased; they saw me busying myself; the
sister told the mother, the mother the father, the father told several
guests who were coming in, through the moonlight at the open door,
walking on tiptoe, keeping their balance with outstretched arms.
"Will you save me?" whispered the boy with a sob, quite blinded
by the life within his wound. That is what people are like in my
district. Always expecting the impossible from the doctor. They
have lost their ancient beliefs; the parson sits at home and unravels
his vestments, one after another; but the doctor is supposed to be
omnipotent with his merciful surgeon's hand. Well, as it pleases
them; I have not thrust my services on them; if they misuse me for
sacred ends, I let that happen to me too; what better do I want,
old country doctor that I am, bereft of my servant girl! And so they
came, the family and the village elders, and stripped my clothes
off me; a school choir with the teacher at the head of it stood before
the house and sang these words to an utterly simple tune:

> Strip his clothes off, then he'll heal us,
> If he doesn't, kill him dead!
> Only a doctor, only a doctor.

Then my clothes were off and I looked at the people quietly, my
fingers in my beard and my head cocked to one side. I was altogether composed and equal to the situation and remained so, although it was no help to me, since they now took me by the head
and feet and carried me to the bed. They laid me down in it next to
the wall, on the side of the wound. Then they all left the room; the
door was shut; the singing stopped; clouds covered the moon; the
bedding was warm around me; the horses' heads in the opened windows wavered like shadows. "Do you know," said a voice in my
ear, "I have very little confidence in you. Why, you were only blown
in here, you didn't come on your own feet. Instead of helping me,
you're cramping me on my death bed. What I'd like best is to scratch
your eyes out." "Right," I said, "it's a shame. And yet I am a doctor.
What am I to do? Believe me, it is not too easy for me either." "Am
I supposed to be content with this apology? Oh, I must be, I can't
help it. I always have to put up with things. A fine wound is all I
brought into the world; that was my sole endowment." "My young
friend," said I, "your mistake is: you have not a wide enough view.

I have been in all the sickrooms, far and wide, and I tell you: your wound is not so bad. Done in a tight corner with two strokes of the ax. Many a one proffers his side and can hardly hear the ax in the forest, far less that it is coming nearer to him." "Is that really so, or are you deluding me in my fever?" "It is really so, take the word of honor of an official doctor." And he took it and lay still. But now it was time for me to think of escaping. The horses were still standing faithfully in their places. My clothes, my fur coat, my bag were quickly collected; I didn't want to waste time dressing; if the horses raced home as they had come, I should only be springing, as it were, out of this bed into my own. Obediently a horse backed away from the window; I threw my bundle into the gig; the fur coat missed its mark and was caught on a hook only by the sleeve. Good enough. I swung myself on to the horse. With the reins loosely trailing, one horse barely fastened to the other, the gig swaying behind, my fur coat last of all in the snow. "Geeup!" I said, but there was no galloping; slowly, like old men, we crawled through the snowy wastes; a long time echoed behind us the new but faulty song of the children:

O be joyful, all you patients,
The doctor's laid in bed beside you!

Never shall I reach home at this rate; my flourishing practice is done for; my successor is robbing me, but in vain, for he cannot take my place; in my house the disgusting groom in raging; Rose is the victim; I do not want to think about it any more. Naked, exposed to the frost of this most unhappy of ages, with an earthly vehicle, unearthly horses, old man that I am, I wander astray. My fur coat is hanging from the back of the gig, but I cannot reach it, and none of my limber pack of patients lifts a finger. Betrayed! Betrayed! A false alarm on the night bell once answered—it cannot be made good, not ever.

◇◇◇*Heinrich von Kleist (1777-1811). German lyric poet and one of the chief dramatists of his time. He led an unhappy life which he ended with suicide.*

THE BEGGAR-WOMAN
OF LOCARNO

BY HEINRICH VON KLEIST

At the foot of the Alps, near Locarno in Upper Italy, stood once a castle, the property of a marquis; of this castle, as one goes southward from the St. Gotthard, one sees now only the ashes and ruins. In one of its high and spacious rooms there once lay, on a bundle of straw which had been thrown down for her, an old, sick woman, who had come begging to the door, and had been taken in and given shelter out of pity by the mistress of the castle. The Marquis, returning from the hunt, happened to enter this room, where he usually kept his guns, while the old woman lay there, and angrily ordered her to come out of the corner where the bundle of straw had been placed and to get behind the stove. In rising the old woman slipped on the polished floor and injured her spine severely; so much did she hurt herself that only with unspeakable agony could she manage to cross the room, as she was ordered, to sink moaning behind the stove and there to die:

Some years later the Marquis, owing to war and bad harvests, having lost most of his fortune, decided to sell his estates. One day a nobleman from Florence arrived at the castle which, on account of its beautiful situation, he wished to buy. The Marquis, who was very anxious to bring the business to a successful conclusion, gave instructions to his wife to prepare for their guest the above-mentioned room, which was now very beautifully furnished. But imagine their horror when, in the middle of the night, the nobleman, pale and distracted, entered their room, solemnly assuring them that his

From *Selected German Short Stories,* World's Classics Series. (Translated by E. N. Bennett.) Used by permission of Oxford University Press.

room was haunted by something which was not visible, but which sounded as if somebody lying on straw in one corner of the room got up and slowly and feebly but with distinct steps crossed the room to lie down moaning and groaning behind the stove.

The Marquis, horrified, he did not himself know why, laughed with forced merriment at the nobleman and said he would get up at once and keep him company for the rest of the night in the haunted room, and when the morning came he ordered his horses to be brought round, bade farewell, and departed.

This incident, which created a great sensation, unhappily for the Marquis frightened away several would-be buyers; and when amongst his own servants strangely and mysteriously the rumour arose that queer things happened in the room at midnight, he determined to make a definite stand in the matter and to investigate it himself the same night. For that reason he had his bed moved into the room at twilight, and watched there without sleeping until midnight. To his horror, as the clock began to strike midnight, he became aware of the mysterious noise; it sounded as though somebody rose from straw which rustled beneath him, crossed the room, and sank down sighing and groaning behind the stove. The next morning when he came downstairs his wife inquired what he had discovered; he looked round with nervous and troubled glances, and after fastening the door assured her that the rumour was true. The Marquise was more terrified than ever in her life, and begged him, before the rumour grew, to make a cold-blooded trial in her company. Accompanied by a loyal servant, they spent the following night in the room and heard the same ghostly noises; and only the pressing need to get rid of the castle at any cost enabled the Marquise in the presence of the servant to smother the terror which she felt, and to put the noise down to some ordinary and casual event which it would be easy to discover. On the evening of the third day, as both of them, with beating hearts, went up the stairs to the guest-room, anxious to get at the cause of the disturbance, they found that the watch-dog, who happened to have been let off his chain, was standing at the door of the room; so that, without giving a definite reason, both perhaps unconsciously wishing to have another living thing in the room besides themselves, they took him into the room with them. About eleven o'clock the two of them, two candles on the table, the Marquise fully dressed, the Marquis with dagger and pistol which he had taken from the cupboard beside him, sat down one on each bed; and while they entertained one another as well as they could by talking, the dog lay down, his head on his paws, in the middle of the room and slept. As the clock began to strike midnight the horrible sound began; somebody whom human eyes could not see raised himself on crutches in the corner of the room; the straw could be heard rustling beneath him; and at the first step the dog woke, pricked up his ears, rose from the ground growling and barking, and, just as though somebody were making straight for him, moved backwards towards the stove. At the sight the Marquise, her hair rising, rushed from the room, and while the Marquis, who had snatched up his dagger, called 'Who is there?' and received no answer, she, like a mad woman, had ordered the coach to be got out, determined to drive away to the town immediately. But before she had packed a few things together and got them out of the door she noticed that all around her the castle was in flames. The Marquis, overcome with horror, and tired of life, had taken a candle and set fire to the wooden panelling on all sides. In vain she sent people in to rescue the wretched man; he had already found his end in the most horrible manner possible; and his white bones, gathered together by his people, still lie in that corner of the room from which he once ordered the beggar-woman of Locarno to rise.

◇◇◇*Selma Lagerlöf (1858-1940). Swedish novelist and storyteller. Nobel Prize winner, 1909. First woman to be elected to the Swedish Academy. See* Jerusalem, The Outcast, Invisible Links.

THE OUTLAWS

BY SELMA LAGERLÖF

A peasant who had murdered a monk took to the woods and was made an outlaw. He found there before him in the wilderness another outlaw, a fisherman from the outermost islands, who had been accused of stealing a herring net. They joined together, lived in a cave, set snares, sharpened darts, baked bread on a granite rock and guarded one another's lives. The peasant never left the woods, but the fisherman, who had not committed such an abominable crime, sometimes loaded game on his shoulders and stole down among men. There he got in exchange for black-cocks, for long-eared hares and fine-limbed red deer, milk and butter, arrowheads and clothes. These helped the outlaws to sustain life.

The cave where they lived was dug in the side of a hill. Broad stones and thorny sloe-bushes hid the entrance. Above it stood a thick growing pine-tree. At its roots was the vent-hole of the cave. The rising smoke filtered through the tree's thick branches and vanished into space. The men used to go to and from their dwelling-place, wading in the mountain stream, which ran down the hill. No one looked for their tracks under the merry, bubbling water.

At first they were hunted like wild beasts. The peasants gathered as if for a chase of bear or wolf. The wood was surrounded by men with bows and arrows. Men with spears went through it and left no dark crevice, no bushy thicket unexplored. While the noisy battue hunted through the wood, the outlaws lay in their dark hole, listening breathlessly, panting with terror. The fisherman held out a whole day, but he who had murdered was driven by unbearable fear out

From *Invisible Links* by Selma Lagerlöf. (Translated by Pauline Bancroft Flach.) By permission of Doubleday & Co. Copyright 1899 by Pauline Bancroft Flach.

into the open, where he could see his enemy. He was seen and hunted, but it seemed to him seven times better than to lie still in helpless inactivity. He fled from his pursuers, slid down precipices, sprang over streams, climbed up perpendicular mountain walls. All latent strength and dexterity in him was called forth by the excitement of danger. His body became elastic like a steel spring, his foot made no false step, his hand never lost its hold, eye and ear were twice as sharp as usual. He understood what the leaves whispered and the rocks warned. When he had climbed up a precipice, he turned toward his pursuers, sending them gibes in biting rhyme. When the whistling darts whizzed by him, he caught them, swift as lightning, and hurled them down on his enemies. As he forced his way through whipping branches, something within him sang a song of triumph.

The bald mountain ridge ran through the wood and alone on its summit stood a lofty fir. The red-brown trunk was bare, but in the branching top rocked an eagle's nest. The fugitive was now so audaciously bold that he climbed up there, while his pursuers looked for him on the wooded slopes. There he sat twisting the young eaglets' necks, while the hunt passed by far below him. The male and female eagle, longing for revenge, swooped down on the ravisher. They fluttered before his face, they struck with their beaks at his eyes, they beat him with their wings and tore with their claws bleeding weals in his weather-beaten skin. Laughing, he fought with them. Standing upright in the shaking nest, he cut at them with his sharp knife and forgot in the pleasure of the play his danger and his pursuers. When he found time to look for them, they had gone by to some other part of the forest. No one had thought to look for their prey on the bald mountain-ridge. No one had raised his eyes to the clouds to see him practicing boyish tricks and sleep-walking feats while his life was in the greatest danger.

The man trembled when he found that he was saved. With shaking hands he caught at a support, giddy he measured the height to which he had climbed. And moaning with the fear of falling, afraid of the birds, afraid of being seen, afraid of everything, he slid down the trunk. He laid himself down on the ground, so as not to be seen, and dragged himself forward over the rocks until the underbrush covered him. There he hid himself under the young pine-tree's tangled branches. Weak and powerless, he sank down on the moss. A single man could have captured him.

Tord was the fisherman's name. He was not more than sixteen years old, but strong and bold. He had already lived a year in the woods.

The peasant's name was Berg, with the surname Rese. He was the tallest and the strongest man in the whole district, and moreover handsome and well-built. He was broad in the shoulders and slender in the waist. His hands were as well shaped as if he had never done any hard work. His hair was brown and his skin fair. After he had been some time in the woods he acquired in all ways a more formidable appearance. His eyes became piercing, his eyebrows grew bushy, and the muscles which knitted them lay finger thick above his nose. It showed now more plainly than before how the upper part of his athlete's brow projected over the lower. His lips closed more firmly than of old, his whole face was thinner, the hollows at the temples grew very deep, and his powerful jaw was much more prominent. His body was less well filled out but his muscles were as hard as steel. His hair grew suddenly gray.

Young Tord could never weary of looking at this man. He had never before seen anything so beautiful and powerful. In his imagination he stood high as the forest, strong as the sea. He served him as a master and worshiped him as a god. It was a matter of course that Tord should carry the hunting spears, drag home the game, fetch the water and build the fire. Berg Rese accepted all his services, but almost never gave him a friendly word. He despised him because he was a thief.

The outlaws did not lead a robber's or brigand's life; they supported themselves by hunting and fishing. If Berg Rese had not murdered a holy man, the peasants would soon have ceased to pursue him and have left him in peace in the mountains. But they feared great disaster to the district, because he who had raised his hand against the servant of God was still unpunished. When Tord came down to the valley with game, they offered him riches and pardon for his own crime if he would show them the way to Berg Rese's hole, so that they might take him while he slept. But the boy always refused; and if anyone tried to sneak after him up to the wood, he led him so cleverly astray that he gave up the pursuit.

Once Berg asked him if the peasants had not tried to tempt him to betray him, and when he heard what they had offered him as a reward, he said scornfully that Tord had been foolish not to accept such a proposal.

Then Tord looked at him with a glance, the like of which Berg Rese had never before seen. Never had any beautiful woman in his youth, never had his wife or child looked so at him. "You are my lord, my elected master," said the glance. "Know that you may strike me and abuse me as you will, I am faithful notwithstanding."

After that Berg Rese paid more attention to the boy and noticed that he was bold to act but timid to speak. He had no fear of death. When the ponds were first frozen, or when the bogs were most dangerous in the spring, when the quagmires were hidden under richly flowering grasses and cloudberry, he took his way over them by choice. He seemed to feel the need of exposing himself to danger as a compensation for the storms and terrors of the ocean, which he had no longer to meet. At night he was afraid in the woods, and even in the middle of the day the darkest thickets or the wide-stretching roots of a fallen pine could frighten him. But when Berg Rese asked him about it, he was too shy to even answer.

Tord did not sleep near the fire, far in in the cave, on the bed which was made soft with moss and warm with skins, but every night, when Berg had fallen asleep, he crept out to the entrance and lay there on a rock. Berg discovered this, and although he well understood the reason, he asked what it meant. Tord would not explain. To escape any more questions, he did not lie at the door for two nights, but then he returned to his post.

One night, when the drifting snow whirled about the forest tops and drove into the thickest underbrush, the driving snowflakes found their way into the outlaws' cave. Tord, who lay just inside the entrance, was, when he waked in the morning, covered by a melting snowdrift. A few days later he fell ill. His lungs wheezed, and when they were expanded to take in air, he felt excruciating pain. He kept up as long as his strength held out, but when one evening he leaned down to blow the fire, he fell over and remained lying.

Berg Rese came to him and told him to go to his bed. Tord

moaned with pain and could not raise himself. Berg then thrust his arms under him and carried him there. But he felt as if he had got hold of a slimy snake; he had a taste in the mouth as if he had eaten the unholy horseflesh, it was so odious to him to touch the miserable thief.

He laid his own big bearskin over him and gave him water, more he could not do. Nor was it anything dangerous. Tord was soon well again. But through Berg's being obliged to do his tasks and to be his servant, they had come nearer to one another. Tord dared to talk to him when he sat in the cave in the evening and cut arrow shafts.

"You are of a good race, Berg," said Tord. "Your kinsmen are the richest in the valley. Your ancestors have served with kings and fought in their castles."

"They have oftener fought with bands of rebels and done the kings great injury," replied Berg Rese.

"Your ancestors gave great feasts at Christmas, and so did you, when you were at home. Hundreds of men and women could find a place to sit in your big house, which was already built before Saint Olof first gave the baptism here in Viken. You owned old silver vessels and great drinking-horns, which passed from man to man, filled with mead."

Again Berg Rese had to look at the boy. He sat up with his legs hanging out of the bed and his head resting on his hands, with which he at the same time held back the wild masses of hair which would fall over his eyes. His face had become pale and delicate from the ravages of sickness. In his eyes fever still burned. He smiled at the pictures he conjured up: at the adorned house, at the silver vessels, at the guests in gala array and at Berg Rese, sitting in the seat of honor in the hall of his ancestors. The peasant thought that no one had ever looked at him with such shining, admiring eyes, or thought him so magnificent, arrayed in his festival clothes, as that boy thought him in the torn skin dress.

He was both touched and provoked. That miserable thief had no right to admire him.

"Were there no feasts in your house?" he asked.

Tord laughed. "Out there on the rocks with father and mother! Father is a wrecker and mother is a witch. No one will come to us."

"Is your mother a witch?"

"She is," answered Tord, quite untroubled. "In stormy weather she rides out on a seal to meet the ships over which the waves are washing, and those who are carried overboard are hers."

"What does she do with them?" asked Berg.

"Oh, a witch always needs corpses. She makes ointments out of them, or perhaps she eats them. On moonlight nights she sits in the surf, where it is whitest, and the spray dashes over her. They say that she sits and searches for shipwrecked children's fingers and eyes."

"That is awful," said Berg.

The boy answered with infinite assurance: "That would be awful in others, but not in witches. They have to do so."

Berg Rese found that he had here come upon a new way of regarding the world and things.

"Do thieves have to steal, as witches have to use witchcraft?" he asked sharply.

"Yes, of course," answered the boy; "everyone has to do what he is destined to do." But then he added, with a cautious smile: "There are thieves also who have never stolen."

"Say out what you mean," said Berg.

The boy continued with his mysterious smile, proud at being an unsolvable riddle: "It is like speaking of birds who do not fly, to talk of thieves who do not steal."

Berg Rese pretended to be stupid in order to find out what he wanted. "No one can be called a thief without having stolen," he said.

"No; but," said the boy, and pressed his lips together as if to keep in the words, "but if someone had a father who stole," he hinted after a while.

"One inherits money and lands," replied Berg Rese, "but no one bears the name of thief if he has not himself earned it."

Tord laughed quietly. "But if somebody has a mother who begs and prays him to take his father's crime on him. But if such a one cheats the hangman and escapes to the woods. But if someone is made an outlaw for a fish-net which he has never seen."

Berg Rese struck the stone table with his clenched fist. He was angry. This fair young man had thrown away his whole life. He could never win love, nor riches, nor esteem after that. The wretched striving for food and clothes was all which was left him. And the fool had let him, Berg Rese, go on despising one who was innocent. He rebuked him with stern words, but Tord was not even as afraid as a sick child is of its mother, when she chides it because it has caught cold by wading in the spring brooks.

On one of the broad, wooded mountains lay a dark tarn. It was square, with as straight shores and as sharp corners as if it had been cut by the hand of man. On three sides it was surrounded by steep cliffs, on which pines clung with roots as thick as a man's arm. Down by the pool, where the earth had been gradually washed away, their roots stood up out of the water, bare and crooked and wonderfully twisted about one another. It was like an infinite number of serpents which had wanted all at the same time to crawl up out of the pool but had got entangled in one another and been held fast. Or it was like a mass of blackened skeletons of drowned giants which the pool wanted to throw up on the land. Arms and legs writhed about one another, the long fingers dug deep into the very cliff to get a hold, the mighty ribs formed arches, which held up primeval trees. It had happened, however, that the iron arms, the steel-like fingers with which the pines held themselves fast, had given way, and a pine had been borne by a mighty north wind from the top of the cliff down into the pool. It had burrowed deep down into the muddy bottom with its top and now stood there. The smaller fish had a good place of refuge among its branches, but the roots stuck up above the water like a many-armed monster and contributed to make the pool awful and terrifying.

On the tarn's fourth side the cliff sank down. There a little foaming stream carried away its waters. Before this stream could find the only possible way, it had tried to get out between stones and tufts, and had by so doing made a little world of islands, some no bigger than a little hillock, others covered with trees.

Here where the encircling cliffs did not shut out all the sun, leafy trees flourished. Here stood thirsty, gray-green alders and smooth-leaved willows. The birch-tree grew there as it does everywhere where it is trying to crowd out the pine woods, and the wild cherry and the mountain ash, those two which edge the forest pastures, filling them with fragrance and adorning them with beauty.

Here at the outlet there was a forest of reeds as high as a man, which made the sunlight fall green on the water just as it falls on the moss in the real forest. Among the reeds there were open places; small, round pools, and water-lilies were floating there. The tall stalks looked down with mild seriousness on those sensitive beauties, who discontentedly shut their white petals and yellow stamens in a hard, leather-like sheath as soon as the sun ceased to show itself.

One sunshiny day the outlaws came to this tarn to fish. They waded out to a couple of big stones in the midst of the reed forest and sat there and threw out bait for the big, green-striped pickerel that lay and slept near the surface of the water.

These men, who were always wandering in the woods and the mountains, had, without their knowing it themselves, come under nature's rule as much as the plants and the animals. When the sun shone, they were open-hearted and brave, but in the evening, as soon as the sun had disappeared, they became silent; and the night, which seemed to them much greater and more powerful than the day, made them anxious and helpless. Now the green light, which slanted in between the rushes and colored the water with brown and dark-green streaked with gold, affected their mood until they were ready for any miracle. Every outlook was shut off. Sometimes the reeds rocked in an imperceptible wind, their stalks rustled, and the long, ribbon-like leaves fluttered against their faces. They sat in gray skins on the gray stones. The shadows in the skins repeated the shadows of the weather-beaten, mossy stone. Each saw his companion in his silence and immovability change into a stone image. But in among the rushes swam mighty fishes with rainbow-colored backs. When the men threw out their hooks and saw the circles spreading among the reeds, it seemed as if the motion grew stronger and stronger, until they perceived that it was not caused only by their cast. A sea-nymph, half human, half a shining fish, lay and slept on the surface of the water. She lay on her back with her whole body under water. The waves so nearly covered her that they had not noticed her before. It was her breathing that caused the motion of the waves. But there was nothing strange in her lying there, and when the next instant she was gone, they were not sure that she had not been only an illusion.

The green light entered through the eyes into the brain like a gentle intoxication. The men sat and stared with dulled thoughts, seeing visions among the reeds, of which they did not dare to tell one another. Their catch was poor. The day was devoted to dreams and apparitions.

The stroke of oars was heard among the rushes, and they started up as from sleep. The next moment, a flat-bottomed boat appeared, heavy, hollowed out with no skill and with oars as small as sticks. A young girl, who had been picking water-lilies, rowed it. She had dark-brown hair, gathered in great braids, and big dark eyes; otherwise she was strangely pale. But her paleness toned to pink and not to gray. Her cheeks had no higher color than the rest of her face, the lips had hardly enough. She wore a white linen shirt and a leather belt with a gold buckle. Her skirt was blue with a red hem. She rowed by the outlaws without seeing them. They kept breathlessly still, but not for fear of being seen, but only to be able to really see her. As soon as she had gone they were as if changed from stone images to living beings. Smiling, they looked at one another.

"She was white like the water-lilies," said one. "Her eyes were as dark as the water there under the pine-roots."

They were so excited that they wanted to laugh, really laugh as no one had ever laughed by that pool, till the cliffs thundered with echoes and the roots of the pines loosened with fright.

"Did you think she was pretty?" asked Berg Rese.

"Oh, I do not know, I saw her for such a short time. Perhaps she was."

"I do not believe you dared to look at her. You thought that it was a mermaid."

And they were again shaken by the same extravagant merriment.

Tord had once as a child seen a drowned man. He had found the body on the shore on a summer day and had not been at all afraid, but at night he had dreamed terrible dreams. He saw a sea, where every wave rolled a dead man to his feet. He saw, too, that all the islands were covered with drowned men, who were dead and belonged to the sea, but who still could speak and move and threaten him with withered white hands.

It was so with him now. The girl whom he had seen among the rushes came back in his dreams. He met her out in the open pool, where the sunlight fell even greener than among the rushes, and he had time to see that she was beautiful. He dreamed that he had crept up on the big pine-root in the middle of the dark tarn, but the pine swayed and rocked so that sometimes he was quite under water. Then she came forward on the little islands. She stood under the red mountain ashes and laughed at him. In the last dream-vision he had come so far that she kissed him. It was already morning, and he heard that Berg Rese had got up, but he obstinately shut his eyes to be able to go on with his dream. When he awoke, he was as though dizzy and stunned by what had happened to him in the night. He thought much more now of the girl than he had done the day before.

Toward night he happened to ask Berg Rese if he knew her name.

Berg looked at him inquiringly. "Perhaps it is best for you to hear it," he said. "She is Unn. We are cousins."

Tord then knew that it was for that pale girl's sake Berg Rese wandered an outlaw in forest and mountain. Tord tried to remember what he knew of her. Unn was the daughter of a rich peasant. Her mother was dead, so that she managed her father's house. This she liked, for she was fond of her own way and she had no wish to be married.

Unn and Berg Rese were the children of brothers, and it had long been said that Berg preferred to sit with Unn and her maids and jest with them than to work on his own lands. When the great Christmas feast was celebrated at his house, his wife had invited a monk from Draksmark, for she wanted him to remonstrate with Berg, because he was forgetting her for another woman. This monk was hateful to Berg and to many on account of his appearance. He was very fat and quite white. The ring of hair about his bald head, the eyebrows above his watery eyes, his face, his hands and his whole cloak, everything was white. Many found it hard to endure his looks.

At the banquet table, in the hearing of all the guests, this monk now said, for he was fearless and thought that his words would have more effect if they were heard by many, "People are in the habit of saying that the cuckoo is the worst of birds because he does not rear his young in his own nest, but here sits a man who does not provide for his home and his children, but seeks his pleasure with a strange woman. Him will I call the worst of men."—Unn then rose up. "That, Berg, is said to you and me," she said. "Never have I been so insulted, and my father is not here either." She had wished to go, but Berg sprang after her. "Do not move!" she said. "I will never see you again." He caught up with her in the hall and asked her what he should do to make her stay. She had answered with flashing eyes that he must know that best himself. Then Berg went in and killed the monk.

Berg and Tord were busy with the same thoughts, for after a while Berg said: "You should have seen her, Unn, when the white monk fell. The mistress of the house gathered the small children about her and cursed her. She turned their faces toward her, that they might forever remember her who had made their father a murderer. But Unn stood calm and so beautiful that the men trembled. She thanked me for the deed and told me to fly to the woods. She bade me not to be robber, and not to use the knife until I could do it for an equally just cause."

"Your deed had been to her honor," said Tord.

Berg Rese noticed again what had astonished him before in the boy. He was like a heathen, worse than a heathen; he never condemned what was wrong. He felt no responsibility. That which must be, was. He knew of God and Christ and the saints, but only by name, as one knows the gods of foreign lands. The ghosts of the rocks were his gods. His mother, wise in witchcraft, had taught him to believe in the spirits of the dead.

Then Berg Rese undertook a task which was as foolish as to twist a rope about his own neck. He set before those ignorant eyes the great God, the Lord of justice, the Avenger of misdeeds, who casts the wicked into places of everlasting torment. And he taught him to love Christ and His mother and the holy men and women, who with lifted hands kneeled before God's throne to avert the wrath of the great Avenger from the hosts of sinners. He taught him all that men do to appease God's wrath. He showed him the crowds of pilgrims making pilgrimages to holy places, the flight of self-torturing penitents and monks from a worldly life.

As he spoke, the boy became more eager and more pale, his eyes grew large as if for terrible visions. Berg Rese wished to stop, but thoughts streamed to him, and he went on speaking. The night sank down over them, the black forest night, when the owls hoot. God came so near to them that they saw his throne darken the stars, and the chastising angels sank down to the tops of the trees. And under them the fires of Hell flamed up to the earth's crust, eagerly licking that shaking place of refuge for the sorrowing races of men.

The autumn had come with a heavy storm. Tord went alone in the woods to see after the snares and traps. Berg Rese sat at home to mend his clothes. Tord's way led in a broad path up a wooded height.

Every gust carried the dry leaves in a rustling whirl up the path. Time after time, Tord thought that someone went behind him. He often looked round. Sometimes he stopped to listen, but he understood that it was the leaves and the wind, and went on. As soon as he started on again, he heard someone come dancing on silken foot up the slope. Small feet came tripping. Elves and fairies played behind him. When he turned round, there was no one, always no one. He shook his fists at the rustling leaves and went on.

They did not grow silent for that, but they took another tone. They began to hiss and to pant behind him. A big viper came gliding. Its tongue dripping venom hung far out of its mouth, and its bright body shone against the withered leaves. Beside the snake pattered a wolf, a big, gaunt monster, who was ready to seize fast in his throat when the snake had twisted about his feet and bitten him in the heel. Sometimes they were both silent, as if to approach him unperceived, but they soon betrayed themselves by hissing and panting, and sometimes the wolf's claws rung against a stone. Involuntarily Tord walked quicker and quicker, but the creatures hastened after him. When he felt that they were only two steps distant and were preparing to strike, he turned. There was nothing there, and he had known it the whole time.

He sat down on a stone to rest. Then the dry leaves played about his feet as if to amuse him. All the leaves of the forest were there: small, light yellow birch leaves, red speckled mountain ash, the elm's dry, dark-brown leaves, the aspen's tough light red, and the willow's yellow green. Transformed and withered, scarred and torn were they, and much unlike the downy, light green, delicately shaped leaves, which a few months ago had rolled out of their buds.

"Sinners," said the boy, "sinners, nothing is pure in God's eyes. The flame of his wrath has already reached you."

When he resumed his wandering, he saw the forest under him bend before the storm like a heaving sea, but in the path it was calm. But he heard what he did not feel. The woods were full of voices.

He heard whisperings, wailing songs, coarse threats, thundering oaths. There was laughter and laments, there was the noise of many people. That which hounded and pursued, which rustled and hissed, which seemed to be something and still was nothing, gave him wild thoughts. He felt again the anguish of death, as when he lay on the floor in his den and the peasants hunted him through the wood. He heard again the crashing of branches, the people's heavy tread, the ring of weapons, the resounding cries, the wild, bloodthirsty noise, which followed the crowd.

But it was not only that which he heard in the storm. There was something else, something still more terrible, voices which he could not interpret, a confusion of voices, which seemed to him to speak in foreign tongues. He had heard mightier storms than this whistle through the rigging, but never before had he heard the wind play on such a many-voiced harp. Each tree had its own voice; the pine did not murmur like the aspen nor the poplar like the mountain ash. Every hole had its note, every cliff's sounding echo its own ring. And the noise of the brooks and the cry of foxes mingled with the marvelous forest storm. But all that he could interpret; there were other strange sounds. It was those which made him begin to scream and scoff and groan in emulation with the storm.

He had always been afraid when he was alone in the darkness of the forest. He liked the open sea and the bare rocks. Spirits and phantoms crept about among the trees.

Suddenly he heard who it was who spoke in the storm. It was God, the great Avenger, the God of justice. He was hunting him for the sake of his comrade. He demanded that he should deliver up the murderer to His vengeance.

Then Tord began to speak in the midst of the storm. He told God what he had wished to do, but had not been able. He had wished to speak to Berg Rese and to beg him to make his peace with God, but he had been too shy. Bashfulness had made him dumb. "When I heard that the earth was ruled by a just God," he cried, "I understood that he was a lost man. I have lain and wept for my friend many long nights. I knew that God would find him out, wherever he might hide. But I could not speak, nor teach him to understand. I was speechless, because I loved him so much. Ask not that I shall speak to him, ask not that the sea shall rise up against the mountain."

He was silent, and in the storm the deep voice, which had been the voice of God for him, ceased. It was suddenly calm, with a sharp sun and a splashing as of oars and a gentle rustle as of stiff rushes. These sounds brought Unn's image before him.—The outlaw cannot have anything, not riches, nor women, nor the esteem of men.—If he should betray Berg, he would be taken under the protection of the law.—But Unn must love Berg, after what he had done for her. There was no way out of it all.

When the storm increased, he heard again steps behind him and sometimes a breathless panting. Now he did not dare to look back, for he knew that the white monk went behind him. He came from the feast at Berg Rese's house, drenched with blood, with a gaping axewound in his forehead. And he whispered: "Denounce him, betray him, save his soul. Leave his body to the pyre, that his soul may be spared. Leave him to the slow torture of the rack, that his soul may have time to repent."

Tord ran. All this fright of what was nothing in itself grew, when it so continually played on the soul, to an unspeakable terror. He wished to escape from it all. As he began to run, again thundered that deep, terrible voice, which was God's. God himself hunted him with alarms, that he should give up the murderer. Berg Rese's crime seemed more detestable than ever to him. An unarmed man had been murdered, a man of God pierced with shining steel. It was like a defiance of the Lord of the world. And the murderer dared to live! He rejoiced in the sun's light and in the fruits of the earth as if the Almighty's arm were too short to reach him.

He stopped, clenched his fists and howled out a threat. Then he ran like a madman from the wood down to the valley.

Tord hardly needed to tell his errand; instantly ten peasants were ready to follow him. It was decided that Tord should go alone up to the cave, so that Berg's suspicions should not be aroused. But where he went he should scatter peas, so that the peasants could find the way.

When Tord came to the cave, the outlaw sat on the stone bench and sewed. The fire gave hardly any light, and the work seemed to go badly. The boy's heart swelled with pity. The splendid Berg Rese seemed to him poor and unhappy. And the only thing he possessed, his life, should be taken from him. Tord began to weep.

"What is it?" asked Berg. "Are you ill? Have you been frightened?"

Then for the first time Tord spoke of his fear. "It was terrible in the wood. I heard ghosts and saw specters. I saw white monks."

" 'Sdeath, boy!"

"They crowded round me all the way up Broad mountain. I ran, but they followed after and sang. Can I never be rid of the sound? What have I to do with them? I think that they could go to one who needed it more."

"Are you mad tonight, Tord?"

Tord talked, hardly knowing what words he used. He was free from all shyness. The words streamed from his lips.

"They are all white monks, white, pale as death. They all have blood on their cloaks. They drag their hoods down over their brows, but still the wound shines from under; the big, red, gaping wound from the blow of the axe."

"The big, red, gaping wound from the blow of the axe?"

"Is it I who perhaps have struck it? Why shall I see it?"

"The saints only know, Tord," said Berg Rese, pale and with terrible earnestness, "what it means that you see a wound from an axe. I killed the monk with a couple of knife-thrusts."

Tord stood trembling before Berg and wrung his hands. "They demand you of me! They want to force me to betray you!"

"Who? The monks?"

"They, yes, the monks. They show me visions. They show me her, Unn. They show me the shining, sunny sea. They show me the fishermen's camping-ground, where there is dancing and merry-making. I close my eyes, but still I see. 'Leave me in peace,' I say. 'My friend has murdered, but he is not bad. Let me be, and I will talk to him, so that he repents and atones. He shall confess his sin and go to Christ's grave. We will both go together to the places which are so holy that all sin is taken away from him who draws near them.' "

"What do the monks answer?" asked Berg. "They want to have me saved. They want to have me on the rack and wheel."

"Shall I betray my dearest friend, I ask them," continued Tord. "He is my world. He has saved me from the bear that had his paw on my throat. We have been cold together and suffered every want together. He has spread his bear-skin over me when I was sick. I have carried wood and water for him; I have watched over him while he slept; I have fooled his enemies. Why do they think that I am one who will betray a friend? My friend will soon of his own accord go to the priest and confess, then we will go together to the land of atonement."

Berg listened earnestly, his eyes sharply searching Tord's face. "You shall go to the priest and tell him the truth," he said. "You need to be among people."

"Does that help me if I go alone? For your sin, Death and all his specters follow me. Do you not see how I shudder at you? You have lifted your hand against God himself. No crime is like yours. I think that I must rejoice when I see you on rack and wheel. It is well for him who can receive his punishment in this world and escapes the wrath to come. Why did you tell me of the just God? You compel me to betray you. Save me from that sin. Go to the priest." And he fell on his knees before Berg.

The murderer laid his hand on his head and looked at him. He was measuring his sin against his friend's anguish, and it grew big and terrible before his soul. He saw himself at variance with the Will which rules the world. Repentance entered his heart.

"Woe to me that I have done what I have done," he said. "That which awaits me is too hard to meet voluntarily. If I give myself up to the priests, they will torture me for hours; they will roast me with slow fires. And is not this life of misery, which we lead in fear and want, penance enough? Have I not lost lands and home? Do I not live parted from friends and everything which makes a man's happiness? What more is required?"

When he spoke so, Tord sprang up wild with terror. "Can you repent?" he cried. "Can my words move your heart? Then come instantly! How could I believe that! Let us escape! There is still time."

Berg Rese sprang up, he too. "You have done it, then—"

"Yes, yes, yes! I have betrayed you! But come quickly! Come, as you can repent! They will let us go. We shall escape them!"

The murderer bent down to the floor, where the battle-axe of his ancestors lay at his feet. "You son of a thief!" he said, hissing out the words, "I have trusted you and loved you."

But when Tord saw him bend for the axe, he knew that it was now a question of his own life. He snatched his own axe from his belt and struck at Berg before he had time to raise himself. The edge cut through the whistling air and sank in the bent head. Berg Rese fell head foremost to the floor, his body rolled after. Blood and brains spouted out, the axe fell from the wound. In the matted hair Tord saw a big, red, gaping hole from the blow of an axe.

The peasants came rushing in. They rejoiced and praised the deed.

"You will win by this," they said to Tord.

Tord looked down at his hands as if he saw there the fetters with which he had been dragged forward to kill him he loved. They were forged from nothing. Of the rushes' green light, of the play of the shadows, of the song of the storm, of the rustling of the leaves, of dreams were they created. And he said aloud: "God is great."

But again the old thought came to him. He fell on his knees beside the body and put his arm under his head.

"Do him no harm," he said. "He repents; he is going to the Holy Sepulcher. He is not dead, he is not a prisoner. We were just ready to go when he fell. The white monk did not want him to repent, but God, the God of justice, loves repentance."

He lay beside the body, talked to it, wept and begged the dead man to awake. The peasants arranged a bier. They wished to carry the peasant's body down to his house. They had respect for the dead and spoke softly in his presence. When they lifted him up on the bier, Tord rose, shook the hair back from his face, and said with a voice which shook with sobs—

"Say to Unn, who made Berg Rese a murderer, that he was killed by Tord the fisherman, whose father is a wrecker and whose mother is a witch, because he taught him that the foundation of the world is justice."

◇◇◇D. H. Lawrence (1885-1930). English poet, novelist, short-story writer. He was and is a controversial figure, whose first fame was secured with the publication of his second novel, Sons and Lovers. His style is fresh and poetic. He was particularly interested in the relations between men and women. He was an essayist and a painter. He wrote criticism and travel sketches. See The Rainbow, Women in Love, The Captain's Doll.

TWO BLUE BIRDS

BY D. H. LAWRENCE

There was a woman who loved her husband, but she could not live with him. The husband, on his side, was sincerely attached to his wife, yet he could not live with her. They were both under forty, both handsome and both attractive. They had the most sincere regard for one another, and felt, in some odd way, eternally married to one another. They knew one another more intimately than they knew anybody else, they felt more known to one another than to any other person.

Yet they could not live together. Usually, they kept a thousand miles apart, geographically. But when he sat in the greyness of England, at the back of his mind, with a certain grim fidelity, he was aware of his wife, her strange yearning to be loyal and faithful, having her gallant affairs away in the sun, in the south. And she, as she drank her cocktail on the terrace over the sea, and turned her grey, sardonic eyes on the heavy dark face of her admirer, whom she really liked quite a lot, she was actually preoccupied with the clear-cut features of her handsome young husband, thinking of how he would be asking his secretary to do something for him, asking in that good-natured, confident voice of a man who knows that his request will be only too gladly fulfilled.

The secretary, of course, adored him. She was *very* competent, quite young, and quite good-looking. She adored him. But then all his servants always did, particularly his women-servants. His men-servants were likely to swindle him.

When a man has an adoring secretary, and you are the man's wife, what are you to do? Not that there was anything "wrong"—if you know what I mean!—between them. Nothing you could call adultery, to come down to brass tacks. No, no! They were just the young master and his secretary. He dictated to her, she slaved for him and adored him, and the whole thing went on wheels.

He didn't "adore" her. A man doesn't need to adore his secretary. But he depended on her. "I simply rely on Miss Wrexall." Whereas he could never rely on his wife. The one thing he knew finally about *her* was that she didn't intend to be relied on.

So they remained friends, in the awful unspoken intimacy of the once-married. Usually each year they went away together for a holiday, and, if they had not been man and wife, they would have found a great deal of fun and stimulation in one another. The fact that they were married, had been married for the last dozen years, and couldn't live together for the last three or four, spoilt them for one another. Each had a private feeling of bitterness about the other.

However, they were awfully kind. He was the soul of generosity, and held her in real, tender esteem, no matter how many gallant affairs she had. Her gallant affairs were part of her modern necessity. "After all, I've got to *live*. I can't turn into a pillar of salt in five minutes just because you and I can't live together! It takes years for a woman like me to turn into a pillar of salt. At least I hope so!"

"Quite!" he replied. "Quite! By all means put them in pickle, make pickled cucumbers of them, before you crystallize out. That's my advice."

He was like that: so awfully clever and enigmatic. She could more or less fathom the idea of the pickled cucumbers, but the "crystallizing out"—what did that signify?

And did he mean to suggest that he himself had been well pickled and that further immersion was for him unnecessary, would spoil his flavour? Was that what he meant? And herself, was she the brine and the vale of tears?

You never knew how catty a man was being, when he was really clever and enigmatic, withal a bit whimsical. He was adorably whimsical, with a twist of his flexible, vain mouth, that had a long upper lip, so fraught with vanity! But then a handsome, clear-cut histrionic young man like that, how could he help being vain? The women made him so.

Ah, the women! How nice men would be if there were no other women!

And how nice the women would be if there were no other men! That's the best of a secretary. She may have a husband, but a husband is the mere shred of a man compared to a boss, a chief, a man who dictates to you and whose words you faithfully write down and then transcribe. Imagine a wife writing down anything her husband said to her! But a secretary! Every *and* and *but* of his she preserves for ever. What are candied violets in comparison!

Now it is all very well having gallant affairs under the southern sun, when you know there is a husband whom you adore dictating to a secretary whom you are too scornful to hate yet whom you rather despise, though you allow she has her good points, away north in the place you ought to regard as home. A gallant affair isn't much good when you've got a bit of grit in your eye. Or something at the back of your mind.

What's to be done? The husband, of course, did not send his wife away.

"You've got your secretary and your work," she said. "There's no room for me."

"There's a bedroom and a sitting-room exclusively for you," he replied. "And a garden and half a motor-car. But please yourself entirely. Do what gives you most pleasure."

"In that case," she said, "I'll just go south for the winter."

"Yes, do!" he said. "You always enjoy it."

"I always do," she replied.

They parted with a certain relentlessness that had a touch of wistful sentiment behind it. Off she went to her gallant affairs, that were like the curate's egg, palatable in parts. And he settled down to work. He said he hated working, but he never did anything else. Ten or eleven hours a day. That's what it is to be your own master!

So the winter wore away, and it was spring, when the swallows homeward fly, or northward, in this case. This winter, one of a series similar, had been rather hard to get through. The bit of grit in

the gallant lady's eye had worked deeper in the more she blinked.
Dark faces might be dark, and icy cocktails might lend a glow; she
blinked her hardest to blink that bit of grit away, without success.
Under the spicy balls of the mimosa she thought of that husband of
hers in his library, and of that neat, competent but *common* little
secretary of his, forever taking down what he said!

"How a man can *stand* it! How *she* can stand it, common little
thing as she is, I don't know!" the wife cried to herself.

She meant this dictating business, this ten hours a day intercourse,
à deux, with nothing but a pencil between them, and a flow of
words.

What was to be done? Matters, instead of improving, had grown
worse. The little secretary had brought her mother and sister into
the establishment. The mother was a sort of cook-housekeeper, the
sister was a sort of upper maid—she did the fine laundry, and looked
after "his" clothes, and valeted him beautifully. It was really an
excellent arrangement. The old mother was a splendid plain cook,
the sister was all that could be desired as a valet de chambre, a fine
laundress, an upper parlour-maid, and a table-waiter. And all eco-
nomical to a degree. They knew his affairs by heart. His secretary
flew to town when a creditor became dangerous, and she *always*
smoothed over the financial crisis.

"He," of course, had debts, and he was working to pay them off.
And if he had been a fairy prince who could call the ants to help
him, he would not have been more wonderful than in securing this
secretary and her family. They took hardly any wages. And they
seemed to perform the miracle of loaves and fishes daily.

"She," of course, was the wife who loved her husband, but helped
him into debt, and she still was an expensive item. Yet when she
appeared at her "home," the secretarial family received her with
most elaborate attentions and deference. The knight returning from
the Crusades didn't create a greater stir. She felt like Queen Eliza-
beth at Kenilworth, a sovereign paying a visit to her faithful subjects. But perhaps there lurked always this hair in her soup! Won't
they be glad to be rid of me again!

But they protested No! No! They had been waiting and hoping
and praying she would come. They had been pining for her to be
there, in charge: the mistress, "his" wife. Ah, "his" wife!

"His" wife! His halo was like a bucket over her head.

The cook-mother was "of the people," so it was the upper-maid daughter who came for orders.

"What will you order for tomorrow's lunch and dinner, Mrs. Gee?"

"Well, what do you usually have?"

"Oh, we want *you* to say."

"No, what do you *usually* have?"

"We don't have anything fixed. Mother goes out and chooses the best she can find, that is nice and fresh. But she thought you would tell her now what to get."

"Oh, I don't know! I'm not very good at that sort of thing. Ask her to go on just the same; I'm quite sure she knows best."

"Perhaps you'd like to suggest a sweet?"

"No, I don't care for sweets—and you know Mr. Gee doesn't. So don't make one for me."

Could anything be more impossible! They had the house spotless and running like a dream; how could an incompetent and extravagant wife dare to interfere, when she saw their amazing and almost inspired economy! But they ran the place on simply nothing!

Simply marvellous people! And the way they strewed palm-branches under her feet!

But that only made her feel ridiculous.

"Don't you think the family manage very well?" he asked her tentatively.

"Awfully well! Almost romantically well!" she replied. "But I suppose you're perfectly happy?"

"I'm perfectly comfortable," he replied.

"I can see you are," she replied. "Amazingly so! I never knew such comfort! Are you sure it isn't bad for you?"

She eyed him stealthily. He looked very well, and extremely handsome, in his histrionic way. He was shockingly well-dressed and valeted. And he had that air of easy *aplomb* and good humour which is so becoming to a man, and which he only acquires when he is cock of his own little walk, made much of by his own hens.

"No!" he said, taking his pipe from his mouth and smiling whimsically round at her. "Do I look as if it were bad for me?"

"No, you don't," she replied promptly: thinking, naturally, as a woman is supposed to think nowadays, of his health and comfort, the foundation, apparently, of all happiness.

Then, of course, away she went on the backwash.

"Perhaps for your work, though, it's not so good as it is for *you*," she said in a rather small voice. She knew he couldn't bear it if she mocked at his work for one moment. And he knew that rather small voice of hers.

"In what way?" he said, bristles rising.

"Oh, I don't know," she answered indifferently. "Perhaps it's not good for a man's work if he is too comfortable."

"I don't know about *that!*" he said, taking a dramatic turn round the library and drawing at his pipe. "Considering I work, actually, by the clock, for twelve hours a day, and for ten hours when it's a short day, I don't think you can say I am deteriorating from easy comfort."

"No, I suppose not," she admitted.

Yet she did think it, nevertheless. His comfortableness didn't consist so much in good food and a soft bed, as in having nobody, absolutely nobody and nothing, to contradict him. "I do like to think he's got nothing to aggravate him," the secretary had said to the wife.

"Nothing to aggravate him!" What a position for a man! Fostered by women who would let nothing "aggravate" him. If anything would aggravate his wounded vanity, this would!

So thought the wife. But what was to be done about it? In the silence of midnight she heard his voice in the distance, dictating away, like the voice of God to Samuel, alone and monotonous, and she imagined the little figure of the secretary busily scribbling shorthand. Then in the sunny hours of morning, while he was still in bed—he never rose till noon—from another distance came that sharp insect-noise of the typewriter, like some immense grasshopper chirping and rattling. It was the secretary, poor thing, typing out his notes.

That girl—she was only twenty-eight—really slaved herself to skin and bone. She was small and neat, but she was actually worn out. She did far more work than he did, for she had not only to take down all those words he uttered, she had to type them out, make three copies, while he was still resting.

"What on earth she gets out of it," thought the wife, "I don't know. She's simply worn to the bone, for a very poor salary, and he's never kissed her, and never will, if I know anything about him."

Whether his never kissing her—the secretary, that is—made it worse or better, the wife did not decide. He never kissed anybody. Whether she herself—the wife, that is—wanted to be kissed by him, even that she was not clear about. She rather thought she didn't.

What on earth did she want then? She was his wife. What on earth did she want of him?

She certainly didn't want to take him down in shorthand and type out again all those words. And she didn't really want him to kiss her; she knew him too well. Yes, she knew him too well. If you know a man too well, you don't want him to kiss you.

What then? What did she want? Why had she such an extraordinary hang-over about him? Just because she was his wife? Why did she rather "enjoy" other men—and she was relentless about enjoyment—without ever taking them seriously? And why must she take him so damn seriously, when she never really "enjoyed" him?

Of course she *had* had good times with him, in the past, before—ah! before a thousand things, all amounting really to nothing. But she enjoyed him no more. She never even enjoyed being with him. There was a silent, ceaseless tension between them, that never broke, even when they were a thousand miles apart.

Awful! That's what you call being married! What's to be done about it? Ridiculous, to know it all and not do anything about it!

She came back once more, and there she was, in her own house, a sort of super-guest, even to him. And the secretarial family devoting their lives to him.

Devoting their lives to him! But actually! Three women pouring out their lives for him day and night! And what did they get in return? Not one kiss! Very little money, because they knew all about his debts, and had made it their life-business to get them paid off! No expectations! Twelve hours' work a day! Comparative isolation, for he saw nobody!

And beyond that? Nothing! Perhaps a sense of uplift and importance because they saw his name and photograph in the newspapers sometimes. But would anybody believe that it was good enough?

Yet they adored it! They seemed to get a deep satisfaction out of it, like people with a mission. Extraordinary!

Well, if they did, let them. They were, of course, rather common, "of the people"; there might be a sort of glamour in it for them.

But it was bad for him. No doubt about it. His work was getting diffuse and poor in quality—and what wonder! His whole tone was going down—becoming commoner. Of course it was bad for him.

Being his wife, she felt she ought to do something to save him. But how could she? That perfectly devoted, marvellous secretarial family, how could she make an attack on them? Yet she'd love to sweep them into oblivion. Of course they were bad for him: ruining his work, ruining his reputation as a writer, ruining his life. Ruining him with their slavish service.

Of course she ought to make an onslaught on them! But how *could* she? Such devotion! And what had she herself to offer in their place? Certainly not slavish devotion to him, nor to his flow of words! Certainly not!

She imagined him stripped once more naked of secretary and secretarial family, and she shuddered. It was like throwing the naked baby in the dust-bin. Couldn't do that!

Yet something must be done. She felt it. She was almost tempted to get into debt for another thousand pounds and send in the bill, or have it sent in to him, as usual.

But no! Something more drastic!

Something more drastic, or perhaps more gentle. She wavered between the two. And wavering, she first did nothing, came to no decision, dragged vacantly on from day to day, waiting for sufficient energy to take her departure once more.

It was spring! What a fool she had been to come up in spring! And she was forty! What an idiot of a woman to go and be forty!

She went down the garden in the warm afternoon, when birds were whistling loudly from the cover, the sky being low and warm, and she had nothing to do. The garden was full of flowers: he loved them for their theatrical display. Lilac and snowball bushes, and laburnum and red may, tulips and anemones and coloured daisies. Lots of flowers! Borders of forget-me-nots! Bachelor's buttons! What absurd names flowers had! She would have called them blue dots and yellow blobs and white frills. Not so much sentiment, after all!

There is a certain nonsense, something showy and stagey, about spring, with its pushing leaves and chorus-girl flowers, unless you have something corresponding inside you. Which she hadn't.

Oh, heaven! Beyond the hedge she heard a voice, a steady rather theatrical voice. Oh, heaven! He was dictating to his secretary, in the garden. Good God, was there nowhere to get away from it!

She looked around: there was indeed plenty of escape. But what was the good of escaping? He would go on and on. She went quietly towards the hedge, and listened.

He was dictating a magazine article about the modern novel. "What the modern novel lacks is architecture." Good God! Architecture! He might just as well say: What the modern novel lacks is whalebone, or a teaspoon, or a tooth stopped.

Yet the secretary took it down, took it down, took it down! No, this could not go on! It was more than flesh and blood could bear.

She went quietly along the hedge, somewhat wolf-like in her prowl, a broad, strong woman in an expensive mustard-coloured silk jersey and cream-coloured pleated skirt. Her legs were long and shapely, and her shoes were expensive.

With a curious wolf-like stealth she turned the hedge and looked across at the small, shaded lawn where the daisies grew impertinently. "He" was reclining in a coloured hammock under the pink-flowering horse-chestnut tree, dressed in white serge with a fine yellow-coloured linen shirt. His elegant hand dropped over the side of the hammock and beat a sort of vague rhythm to his words. At a little wicker table the little secretary, in a green knitted frock, bent her dark head over her note-book, and diligently made those awful shorthand marks. He was not difficult to take down, as he dictated slowly, and kept a sort of rhythm, beating time with his dangling hand.

"In every novel there must be one outstanding character with which we always sympathize—with *whom* we always sympathize—even though we recognize its—even when we are most aware of the human frailties——"

Every man his own hero, thought the wife grimly, forgetting that every woman is intensely her own heroine.

But what did startle her was a blue bird dashing about near the feet of the absorbed, shorthand-scribbling little secretary. At least it was a blue-tit, blue with grey and some yellow. But to the wife it seemed blue, that juicy spring day, in the translucent afternoon. The blue bird, fluttering round the pretty but rather *common* little feet of the little secretary.

The blue bird! The blue bird of happiness! Well, I'm blest, thought the wife. Well, I'm blest!

And as she was being blest, appeared another blue bird—that is, another blue-tit—and began to wrestle with the first blue-tit. A couple of blue birds of happiness, having a fight over it! Well, I'm blest!

She was more or less out of sight of the human preoccupied pair. But "he" was disturbed by the fighting blue birds, whose little feathers began to float loose.

"Get out!" he said to them mildly, waving a dark-yellow handkerchief at them. "Fight your little fight, and settle your private affairs, elsewhere, my dear little gentlemen."

The little secretary looked up quickly, for she had already begun to write it down. He smiled at her his twisted whimsical smile.

"No, don't take that down," he said affectionately. "Did you see those two tits laying into one another?"

"No!" said the little secretary, gazing brightly round, her eyes half-blinded with work.

But she saw the queer, powerful, elegant, wolf-like figure of the wife, behind her, and terror came into her eyes.

"I did!" said the wife, stepping forward with those curious, shapely, she-wolf legs of hers, under the very short skirt.

"Aren't they extraordinarily vicious little beasts?" said he.

"Extraordinarily!" she re-echoed, stooping and picking up a little breast-feather. "Extraordinarily! See how the feathers fly!"

And she got the feather on the tip of her finger, and looked at it. Then she looked at the secretary, then she looked at him. She had a queer, werewolf expression between her brows.

"I think," he began, "these are the loveliest afternoons, when there's no direct sun, but all the sounds and the colours and the scents are sort of dissolved, don't you know, in the air, and the whole thing is steeped, steeped in spring. It's like being on the inside; you know how I mean, like being inside the egg and just ready to chip the shell."

"Quite like that!" she assented without conviction.

There was a little pause. The secretary said nothing. They were waiting for the wife to depart again.

"I suppose," said the latter, "you're awfully busy, as usual?"

"Just about the same," he said, pursing his mouth deprecatingly. Again the blank pause, in which he waited for her to go away again.

"I know I'm interrupting you," she said.

"As a matter of fact," he said, "I was just watching those two blue-tits."

"Pair of little demons!" said the wife, blowing away the yellow feather from her finger-tip.

"Absolutely!" he said.

"Well, I'd better go, and let you get on with your work," she said.

"No hurry!" he said, with benevolent nonchalance. "As a matter of fact, I don't think it's a great success, working out of doors."

"What made you try it?" said the wife. "You know you never could do it."

"Miss Wrexall suggested it might make a change. But I don't think it altogether helps, do you, Miss Wrexall?"

"I'm sorry," said the little secretary.

"Why should *you* be sorry?" said the wife, looking down at her as a wolf might look down half-benignly at a little black-and-tan mongrel. "You only suggested it for his good, I'm sure!"

"I thought the air might be good for him," the secretary admitted.

"Why do people like you never think about yourselves?" the wife asked.

The secretary looked her in the eye.

"I suppose we do, in a different way," she said.

"A *very* different way!" said the wife ironically. "Why don't you make *him* think about *you*?" she added slowly, with a sort of drawl. "On a soft spring afternoon like this, you ought to have him dictating poems to you, about the blue birds of happiness fluttering round your dainty little feet. I know *I* would, if I were his secretary."

There was a dead pause. The wife stood immobile and statuesque, in an attitude characteristic of her, half turning back to the little secretary, half averted. She half turned her back on everything.

The secretary looked at him.

"As a matter of fact," he said, "I was doing an article on the Future of the Novel."

"I know that," said the wife. "That's what's so awful! Why not something lively in the life of the novelist?"

There was a prolonged silence, in which he looked pained, and somewhat remote, statuesque. The little secretary hung her head. The wife sauntered slowly away.

"Just where were we, Miss Wrexall?" came the sound of his voice.

The little secretary started. She was feeling profoundly indignant. Their beautiful relationship, his and hers, to be so insulted!

But soon she was veering downstream on the flow of his words, too busy to have any feelings, except one of elation at being so busy.

Tea-time came; the sister brought out the tea-tray into the garden. And immediately, the wife appeared. She had changed, and was wearing a chicory-blue dress of fine cloth. The little secretary had gathered up her papers and was departing, on rather high heels.

"Don't go, Miss Wrexall," said the wife.

The little secretary stopped short, then hesitated.

"Mother will be expecting me," she said.

"Tell her you're not coming. And ask your sister to bring another cup. I want you to have tea with us."

Miss Wrexall looked at the man, who was reared on one elbow in the hammock, and was looking enigmatical, Hamletish.

He glanced at her quickly, then pursed his mouth in a boyish negligence.

"Yes, stay and have tea with us for once," he said. "I see strawberries, and I know you're the bird for them."

She glanced at him, smiled wanly, and hurried away to tell her mother. She even stayed long enough to slip on a silk dress.

"Why, how smart you are!" said the wife, when the little secretary reappeared on the lawn, in chicory-blue silk.

"Oh, don't look at my dress, compared to yours!" said Miss Wrexall. They were of the same colour, indeed!

"At least you earned yours, which is more than I did mine," said the wife, as she poured tea. "You like it strong?"

She looked with her heavy eyes at the smallish, birdy, blue-clad, overworked young woman, and her eyes seemed to speak many inexplicable dark volumes.

"Oh, as it comes, thank you," said Miss Wrexall, leaning nervously forward.

"It's coming pretty black, if you want to ruin your digestion," said the wife.

"Oh, I'll have some water in it, then."

"Better, I should say."

"How'd the work go—all right?" asked the wife, as they drank tea, and the two women looked at each other's blue dresses.

"Oh!" he said. "As well as you can expect. It was a piece of pure flummery. But it's what they want. Awful rot, wasn't it, Miss Wrexall?"

Miss Wrexall moved uneasily on her chair.

"It interested me," she said, "though not so much as the novel."

"The novel? Which novel?" said the wife. "Is there another new one?"

Miss Wrexall looked at him. Not for words would she give away any of his literary activities.

"Oh, I was just sketching out an idea to Miss Wrexall," he said.

"Tell us about it!" said the wife. "Miss Wrexall, *you* tell us what it's about."

She turned on her chair and fixed the little secretary.

"I'm afraid"—Miss Wrexall squirmed—"I haven't got it very clearly myself, yet."

"Oh, go along! Tell us what you *have* got then!"

Miss Wrexall sat dumb and very vexed. She felt she was being baited. She looked at the blue pleatings of her skirt.

"I'm afraid I can't," she said.

"Why are you afraid you can't? You're so *very* competent. I'm sure you've got it all at your finger-ends. I expect you write a good deal of Mr. Gee's books for him, really. He gives you the hint, and you fill it all in. Isn't that how you do it?" She spoke ironically, and as if she were teasing a child. And then she glanced down at the fine pleatings of her own blue skirt, very fine and expensive.

"Of course you're not speaking seriously?" said Miss Wrexall, rising on her mettle.

"Of course I am! I've suspected for a long time—at least, for some time—that you write a good deal of Mr. Gee's books for him, from his hints."

It was said in a tone of raillery, but it was cruel.

"I should be terribly flattered," said Miss Wrexall, straightening herself, "if I didn't know you were only trying to make me feel a fool."

"Make you feel a fool? My dear child!—why, nothing could be farther from me! You're twice as clever and a million times as competent as I am. Why, my dear child, I've the greatest admiration for you! I wouldn't do what you do, not for all the pearls in India. I *couldn't,* anyhow——"

Miss Wrexall closed up and was silent.

"Do you mean to say my books read as if——" he began, rearing up and speaking in a harrowed voice.

"I do!" said the wife. "*Just* as if Miss Wrexall had written them from your hints. I *honestly* thought she did—when you were too busy——"

"How very clever of you!" he said.

"Very!" she cried. "Especially if I was wrong!"

"Which you were," he said.

"How very extraordinary!" she cried. "Well, I am once more mistaken!"

There was a complete pause.

It was broken by Miss Wrexall, who was nervously twisting her fingers.

"You want to spoil what there is between me and him, I can see that," she said bitterly.

"My dear, but what *is* there between you and him?" asked the wife.

"I was *happy* working with him, working for him! I was *happy* working for him!" cried Miss Wrexall, tears of indignant anger and chagrin in her eyes.

"My dear child!" cried the wife, with stimulated excitement, "go *on* being happy working with him, go on being happy while you can! If it makes you happy, why then, enjoy it! Of course! Do you think I'd be so cruel as to want to take it away from you?—working with him? *I* can't do shorthand and typewriting and double-entrance book-keeping, or whatever it's called. I tell you, I'm utterly incompetent. I never earn anything. I'm the parasite on the British oak, like the mistletoe. The blue bird doesn't flutter round my feet. Perhaps they're too big and trampling."

She looked down at her expensive shoes.

"If I *did* have a word of criticism to offer," she said, turning to her husband, "it would be to you, Cameron, for taking so much from her and giving her nothing."

"But he gives me everything, everything!" cried Miss Wrexall. "He gives me everything!"

"What do you mean by everything?" said the wife, turning on her sternly.

Miss Wrexall pulled up short. There was a snap in the air and a change of currents.

"I mean nothing that *you* need begrudge me," said the little secretary rather haughtily. "I've never made myself cheap."

There was a blank pause.

"My God!" said the wife. "You don't call that being cheap? Why, I should say you got nothing out of him at all, you only give! And if you don't call that making yourself cheap—my God!"

"You see, we see things different," said the secretary.

"I should say we do!—*thank* God!" rejoined the wife.

"On whose behalf are you thanking God?" he asked sarcastically.

"Everybody's, I suppose! Yours, because you get everything for nothing, and Miss Wrexall's, because she seems to like it, and mine because I'm well out of it all."

"You *needn't* be out of it all," cried Miss Wrexall magnanimously, "if you didn't *put* yourself out of it all."

"Thank you, my dear, for your offer," said the wife, rising. "But I'm afraid no man can expect *two* blue birds of happiness to flutter round his feet, tearing out their little feathers!"

With which she walked away.

After a tense and desperate interim, Miss Wrexall cried:

"And *really*, need any woman be jealous of *me?*"

"Quite!" he said.

And that was all he did say.

◇◇◇*Lu Hsün (1881-1936). Chinese physician, educator, author. Sometimes called the Chinese Chekhov.*

BENEDICTION

BY LU HSÜN

I

The end of the year according to the lunar calendar is, after all, the right time for a year to end. A strange almost-new-year sort of atmosphere seems to overlay everything; pale grey clouds at evening, against which flash the hot little fires of crackers giving a thunderous boost to the kitchen god's[1] ascent into heaven. And as one draws into it the scene grows noisier, and scattered on the air is the sting of gunpowder.

On such a night I return to Lo Ching—my 'home town' as I call it, but in reality I have no home there at all. I stay with Lo Shih Lao-yeh, a relative one generation older than myself, a fellow who ought to be called 'Fourth Uncle,' according to the Chinese family way of reckoning. He is a *chien-sheng*,[2] and talks all the time about the old virtues and the old ethics.

I find him not much changed; a little aged of course, but still without a whisker. We exchange salutations. After the "How are you?" he tells me I've grown fat. With that done, he at once commences a tirade against the 'new party.' But I know that the phrase to him still means poor Kang Yu-wei,[3] and not the Renaissance, of which he probably has not even heard. We have at any rate nothing in common, and before long I am left alone in the study.

Reprinted by permission of Edgar Snow, translator.

[1] The kitchen god is supposed to report at this time to the Heavenly Emperor about the conduct of the family during the past year. He returns to earth after seven days.

[2] A *chien-sheng* is an honorary degree equivalent to the *hsiu-ts'ai*, but is purchased, whereas the latter is given only to scholars.

[3] A scholar who led in the attempted reform movement under the Emperor Kuang Hsu, towards the end of the Manchu dynasty. The movement was suppressed by the Empress Dowager.

Next day I get up very late, and after lunching go out to call on some relatives and friends. The day after is the same, and the day after that. None of them has changed much, each is a little older, and everywhere they are busily preparing for New Year prayers-of-blessing. It is a great thing in Lo Ching: every one exerts himself to show reverence, exhausts himself in performing rites, and falls down before the god of benediction to ask favours for the year ahead. There is much chicken-killing, geese-slaughtering, and pork-buying; women go round with their arms raw and red from soaking in hot water preparing such fowl. When they are thoroughly cooked they are placed on the altar, with chopsticks punched into them at all angles, and offered up as sacrifices at the sixth watch. Incense sticks and red candles are lighted, and the men (no women allowed) make obeisance and piously invite the blessing-spirits to eat away. And after this, of course, the crackers.

Every year it is that way, and the same in every home—except those of the miserable poor who cannot buy either sacrifices or candles or crackers—and this year is like any other. The sky is dark and gloomy, and in the afternoon snow falls—flakes like plum blossoms darting and dancing across a screen of smoke and bustle, and making everything more confused. By the time I return home the roof-tiles are already washed white, and inside my room seems brighter. The reflection from the snow also touches up the large crimson character, LONGEVITY, which hangs on a board against the wall. It is said to be the work of the legendary Chen Tuan Lao-tso. One of the scrolls has fallen down and is rolled up loosely and lying on the long table, but the other still admonishes me: "Understand deeply the reason of things, be moderate, and be gentle in heart and manner." On the desk under the window are incomplete volumes of the *K'ang Hsi Dictionary*, a set of *Recent Thoughts*, with collected commentaries, and the *Four Books*. How depressing!

I decided to return to-morrow, at the very latest, to the city.

The incident with Hsiang-lin Sao also has very much disturbed me. This afternoon I went to the eastern end of the town to visit a friend, and while returning I encountered her at the edge of the canal. The look in her staring eyes showed clearly enough that she was coming after me, so I waited. Although other folk I used to know in Lo Ching have apparently changed little, Hsiang-lin Sao was no longer the same. Her hair was all white, her face was alarmingly lean, hollow, and burnt a dark yellow. She looked completely exhausted, not at all like a woman not yet forty, but like a wooden thing with an expression of tragic sadness carved into it. Only the movement of her lustreless eyes showed that she still lived. In one hand she carried a bamboo basket: inside it was an empty broken bowl; and she held herself up by leaning on a bamboo pole. She had apparently become a beggar.

I stood waiting to be asked for money.

"So—you've come back?"

"Yes."

"That's good—and very timely. Tell me, you are a scholar, a man who has seen the world, a man of knowledge and experience"—her faded eyes very faintly glowed—"tell me, I just want to ask you one thing."

I could not, in ten thousand tries, have guessed what she would ask. I waited, shocked and puzzled, saying nothing.

She moved nearer, lowered her voice, and spoke with great secrecy and earnestness.

"It is this: after a person dies is there indeed such a thing as the *soul?*"

Involuntarily I shuddered. Her eyes stuck into me like thorns. Here was a fine thing! I felt more embarrassed than a schoolboy given a surprise examination, with the teacher standing right beside him. Whether there was such a thing as the 'soul' had never bothered me, and I had speculated little about it. How could I reply? In that brief moment I remembered that many people in Lo Ching believed in some kind of spirits, and probably she did too. Perhaps I should just say it was rather doubtful—but no, it was better to let her go on hoping. Why should I burden a person obviously on the 'last road' with even more pain? Better for her sake say yes.

"Perhaps," I stammered. "Yes, I suppose there is."

"Then there is also a *hell?*"

"Ah—hell?" She had trapped me, and I could only continue placatingly, "Hell? Well, to be logical, I dare say there ought to be. But, then, again—there may not be. What does it matter?"

"Then in this hell do all deceased members of a family come together again, face to face?"

"H'mm? Seeing face to face, eh?" I felt like a fool. Whatever knowledge I possessed, whatever mental dexterity, was utterly useless; here I had been confounded by three simple questions. I made up my mind to extricate myself from the mess, and wanted to repudiate everything I had said. But somehow I could not do so in the gaze of her intensely earnest and tragic eyes.

"That is to say . . . in fact, I cannot definitely say. Whether there is a soul or not in the end I am in no position to deny or affirm."

With that she did not persist, and, taking advantage of her silence, I strode away with long steps and hastened back to Fourth Uncle's home, feeling very depressed. I could not help thinking that perhaps my replies would have an evil effect on her. No doubt her loneliness and distress had become all the more unbearable at this time, when every one else seemed to be praying for benediction—but perhaps there was something else on her mind. Perhaps something that had recently happened to her. If so, then my answers might be responsible . . . for what? I soon laughed about the whole thing, and at my absurd habit of exaggerating the importance of casual happenings. Educators unquestionably would pronounce me mentally unbalanced. Hadn't I, after all, made it clear that all I could say was, "Cannot definitely say"? Even should all my replies be refuted, even if something happened to the woman, it could in no way concern me.

"Cannot definitely say" is a very convenient phrase. Bold and reckless youths often venture so far as to offer a positive opinion on critical questions for others, but responsible people, like officials and doctors,[1] have to choose their words carefully, for if events belie their opinion then it becomes a serious affair. It is much more advisable to say, "Cannot definitely say"; obviously it solves everything. This encounter with the woman mendicant impresses upon me the importance of that practice, for even in such cases the deepest wisdom lies in ambiguity.

Nevertheless, I continue to feel troubled, and when the night

---

[1] The author was formerly a doctor, having studied medicine in Japan.

is gone I wake up with the incident still on my mind. It is like an unlucky presentiment of a movement of fate. Outside the day is still gloomy, with flurrying snow, and in the dull study my uneasiness gradually increases. Certainly I must go back to the city to-morrow. . . . To be sure, there is still unsampled the celebrated pure-cooked fish-fins at Fu Shing Lou—excellent eating and very cheap at only a dollar a big salver. Has the price by now increased? Although many of my boyhood friends have melted away like clouds in the sky, there must remain, at least, the incomparable fish-fins of Lo Ching, and these I must eat, even though I eat alone. . . . All the same, I am returning to-morrow. . . .

Because I have so often seen things happen exactly as I predicted —but hoped against, and tried to believe improbable—so I am not unprepared for this occasion to provide no exception. Towards evening some of the family gather in an inner room, and from fragments of their talk I gather they are discussing some event with no little annoyance. Presently all the voices cease except one, that of Fourth Uncle, who thunders out above the thud of his own pacing feet:

"Not a day earlier nor a day later, but just at this season she decided upon it. From this alone we can see that she belongs to a species utterly devoid of human sense!"

My curiosity is soon followed by a vague discomfort, as if these words have some special meaning for me. I go out and look into the room, but every one has vanished. Suppressing my increasing impatience, I wait till the servant comes to fill my teapot with hot water. Not until then am I able to confirm my suspicions.

"Who was it Fourth Uncle was blowing up about a while ago?"

"Could it after all have been any other than Hsiang-lin Sao?" he replies in the brief and positive manner of our language.

"What has happened to her?" I demand in an anxious voice.

"Aged." [1]

"Dead?" My heart twinges and seems to jump back; my face burns. But he doesn't notice my emotion at all, doesn't even lift his

---

[1] The word 'die' and its synonyms are forbidden at this season, and 'aged' is commonly used to describe death. Ordinarily Chinese refer to the dead as 'not here,' or 'outside.'

head, so that I control myself to the end of further questioning.

"When did she die then?"

"When? Last night—or possibly to-day. I cannot definitely say."

"What did she die of?"

"What did she die of? Could it indeed be anything else than that she has been strangled to death by poverty?" His words are absolutely colourless, and without even looking at me he goes out.

My terror at first is great, but I reason that this is a thing which was bound to happen very soon, and it is merely an accident that I even know about it. I further reassure my conscience by recalling my non-committal "Cannot definitely say," and the servant's report that it was simply a case of "strangled to death by poverty." Still, now and then I feel a prick of guilt, I don't know exactly why, and when I sit down beside the dignified old Fourth Uncle I am continually thinking of opening a discussion about Hsiang-lin Sao. But how to do it? He still lives in a world of religious interdicts, and at this time of year these are like an impenetrable forest. You cannot, of course, mention anything connected with death, illness, crime, and so on, unless it is absolutely imperative. Even then such references must be disguised in a queer riddle-language in order not to offend the hovering ancestral spirits. I torture my brain to remember the necessary formula, but, alas, I cannot recall the right phrases, and at length have to give it up.

Fourth Uncle throughout the meal wears an austere look on his face. At last I suspect that he regards me also as "belonging to a species utterly devoid of human sense," since "neither a day earlier, nor a day later, but just at this season" I have put in an appearance. To loosen his heart and save him further anxiety I tell him that I have determined to return to-morrow. He doesn't urge me to stay very enthusiastically, and I conclude that my surmise was correct. And thus in a cheerless mood I finish my meal.

The short day is ended, the curtain of snow dropping over it earlier than usual even in this month, and the black night falls like a shroud over the whole town. People still busy themselves under the lamplight, but just beyond my window there is the quiet of death. Snow lies like a down mattress over the earth, and the still falling flakes make a faint *suh-suh* sound that adds to the intense loneliness and the unbearable melancholy. Sitting alone under the yellow rays of the rape-oil lamp, my mind goes back again to that blown-out flicker, Hsiang-lin Sao.

This woman who once stood among us in this house, thrown now, like an old toy, discarded by a child, on to the dustheap. For those who find the world amusing, for the kind for whom she is created, no doubt if they think about her at all it is simply to wonder why the devil she should so long have had the effrontery to continue to exist. Well, she has obliged them by disappearing at last, swept away thoroughly by Wu Chang,[1] and a very tidy job. I don't know whether there is such a thing as the 'soul' that lives on after death, but it would be a great improvement if people like Hsiang-lin Sao were never born, would it not? Then nobody would be troubled, neither the despised nor those who despise them.

Listening to the *suh-suh* of the leafy autumnal snow I go on musing, and gradually find some comfort in my reflections. It is like putting together an intricate puzzle, but in the end the incidents of her life fit together into a single whole.

II

Hsiang-lin Sao was not a native of Lo Ching. She arrived in early winter one year with Old Woman Wei, who bargained in the labour of others. Fourth Uncle had decided to change the servant, and Hsiang-lin Sao was Old Woman Wei's candidate for the job.

She wore a white scarf wrapped round her head, a blue jacket, a pale green vest, and a black skirt. She was perhaps twenty-six or twenty-seven, still quite young and rather pretty, with ruddy cheeks and a bronzed face. Old Woman Wei said that she was a neighbour of her mother's. Her husband had died, she explained, and so she had to seek work outside.

Fourth Uncle wrinkled up his brow, and his wife, looking at him, knew what he meant. He didn't like hiring a widow. But Fourth Aunt scrutinized her carefully, noting that her hands and feet looked strong and capable, and that she had honest, direct eyes. She impressed her as a woman who would be content with her lot, and not likely to complain about hard work; and so in spite of her husband's wrinkled brow Fourth Aunt agreed to give her a trial. For

[1] A sheriff-spirit who 'sweeps up' the soul at the last breath of life.

three days she worked as if leisure of any kind bored her; she proved very energetic and as strong as a man. Fourth Aunt then definitely hired her, the wage being five hundred cash[1] per month.

Everybody called her simply Hsiang-lin Sao, without asking for her surname. The Old Woman Wei was, however, a native of Wei Chia Shan (Wei Family Mountain), and since she claimed that Hsiang-lin Sao came from that village no doubt her surname also was Wei.[2] Like most mountaineers, she talked little, and only answered others' questions in monosyllables, and so it took more than ten days to pry out of her the bare facts that there was still a severe mother-in-law in her home; that her young brother-in-law cut wood for a living; that she had lost her husband, ten years her junior, in the previous spring; and that he also had lived by cutting firewood. This was about all people could get out of her.

Day followed day, and Hsiang-lin Sao's work was just as regular. She never slackened up, she never complained about the food, she never seemed to tire. People agreed that Old Lord Lo Shih had found a worthy worker, quick and diligent, more so in fact than a man. Even at New Year she did all the sweeping, dusting, washing, and other household duties, besides preparing geese and chickens and all the sacrifices, without any other help. She seemed to thrive on it. Her skin became whiter, and she fattened a little.

New Year had just passed when one day she came hurrying up from the canal, where she had been washing rice. She was much agitated. She said she had seen, on the opposite bank, a man who looked very much like her late husband's first cousin, and she was afraid he had come to take her away. Fourth Aunt was alarmed and suspicious. Why should he be coming for her? Asked for details, Hsiang-lin Sao could give none. Fourth Uncle, when he heard the story, wrinkled his brow and announced:

"This is very bad. It looks as though she has run away, instead of being ordered."

And, as it turned out, he was correct. She was a runaway widow. Some ten days later, when everybody was gradually forgetting

---

[1] This is about 50 cents. Wages for similar work would be from $2 to $6 per month.

[2] 'Sao' means 'sister-in-law.' The Chinese call a woman married to an eldest son by that son's given name, suffixed by 'Sao.' Thus, her husband's name was probably Wei Hsiang-lin.

the incident, Old Woman Wei suddenly appeared, accompanied by a woman who, she claimed, was Hsiang-lin Sao's mother-in-law. The latter seemed not at all like a tongue-bound mountaineer, but knew how to talk, and after a few courtesy words got to the subject of her business at once. She said she had come to take her daughter-in-law back home. It was spring, there was much to be done at home, and in the house at present were none but the very old and the very young. Hsiang-lin Sao was needed.

"Since it is her own mother-in-law who requests it, how can we deny the justice of it?" said Fourth Uncle.

Hsiang-lin Sao's wage, therefore, was figured out. It was discovered that altogether one thousand seven hundred and fifty cash were due. She had let the sum accumulate with her master, not taking out even a single cash for use. Without any more words, this amount was handed over to the mother-in-law, although Hsiang-lin Sao was not present. The woman also took Hsiang-lin Sao's clothes, thanked Fourth Uncle and left. It was then past noon. . . .

"*Ai-ya!* the rice? Didn't Hsiang-lin Sao go out to scour the rice?" Fourth Aunt, some time later, cried out this question in a startled way. She had forgotten all about Hsiang-lin Sao until her hunger reminded her of rice, and the rice reminded her of the former servant.

Everybody scattered and began searching for the rice basket. Fourth Aunt herself went first to the kitchen, next to the front hall, and then into the bedroom, but she didn't see a shadow of the object of her search. Fourth Uncle wandered outside, but he saw nothing of it either till he came near the canal. There, upright on the bank, with a cabbage near by, lay the missing basket.

Apparently not until then had anyone thought to inquire in what manner Hsiang-lin Sao had departed with her mother-in-law. Now eyewitnesses appeared who reported that early in the morning a boat, carrying a white canopy, anchored in the canal, and lay there idly for some time. The awning hid the occupants, and no one knew who was in it. Presently Hsiang-lin Sao came to the bank, and just as she was about to kneel down for water two men quickly jumped out, grabbed her, and forcibly put her inside the boat. They seemed to be mountain people, but they certainly took her against her will; she cried and shouted for help several times. Afterwards she was hushed up, evidently with some kind of gag. Nothing more happened until the arrival of two women, one of whom was Old Woman Wei. Nobody saw very clearly what had happened to Hsiang-lin Sao, but those who peered in declared that she seemed to have been bound and thrown on the deck of the cabin.

"Outrageous!" exclaimed Fourth Uncle. On reflection, however, he simply ended impotently, "But after all . . ."

Fourth Aunt herself had to prepare the food that day, and her son Ah Niu made the fire.

In the afternoon Old Woman Wei reappeared.

"Outrageous!" Fourth Uncle greeted her.

"What is this? How wonderful! You have honoured us once more with your presence!" Fourth Aunt, washing dishes, angrily shouted at the old bargain-maker. "You yourself recommend her to us, then you come with companions to abduct her from the household. This affair is a veritable volcanic eruption. How do you suppose it will look to outsiders? Are you playing a joke at our expense, or what is it?"

"*Ai-ya! Ai-ya!* I have surely been fooled and tricked. I came here to explain to you. Now how was I to know she was a rebel? She came to me, begged me to get her work, and I took her for genuine. Who would have known that she was doing it behind her mother-in-law's back, without in fact even asking for permission? I'm unable to look in your face, my lord and my lady. It's all my fault, the fault of a careless old fool. I can't look you in the face. . . . Fortunately, your home is generous and forgiving, and will not punish insignificant people like myself too strictly, eh? And next time the person I recommend must be doubly good to make up for this sin—"

"But—" interjected Fourth Uncle, who, however, could get no farther.

And so the affair of Hsiang-lin Sao came to an end, and indeed she herself would have been entirely forgotten were it not that the Fourth Aunt had such difficulty with subsequent servants. They were too lazy, or they were gluttonous, or in extreme cases they were both lazy and gluttonous, and in truth were totally undesirable, "from the extreme left to the extreme right." In her distress, Fourth Aunt always mentioned the exemplary Hsiang-lin Sao. "I wonder how she is living?" she would say, inwardly wishing that some misfortune would oblige her to return to work. By the time the next New Year rolled round, however, she had given up hope of ever seeing her again.

Towards the end of the holidays Old Woman Wei called one day to k'ou-t'ou[1] and offer felicitations. She had already drunk herself into semi-intoxication, and was in a garrulous mood. She explained that because of a visit to her mother's home in Wei Village, where she had stayed for several days, she was late this year in paying her courtesy calls. During the course of the conversation their talk naturally touched upon Hsiang-lin Sao.

"She?" the old woman cried shrilly and with alcoholic enthusiasm. "There's a lucky woman! You know, when her mother-in-law came after her here she had at that time already been promised to a certain Hu Lao-liu, of Hu Village. After staying in her home only a few days she was loaded again into the Flowery Sedan Chair and borne away!"

"*Ai-ya,* what a mother!" Fourth Aunt exclaimed.

"*Ai-ya,* my lady! You speak from behind a lofty door.[2] We mountaineers, of the small-doored families, for us what does it matter? You see, she had a young brother-in-law, and he had to be married. If Hsiang-lin Sao was not married off first, where would the family get money enough for the brother-in-law's presents to his betrothed? So you understand the mother-in-law is by no means a stupid woman, but keen and calculating. Moreover, she married the daughter-in-law to an inner mountain dweller. Why? Don't you see? Marrying her to a local man, she would have got only a small betrothal gift, but, since few women want to marry deep into the mountains, the price is higher. Hence the husband actually paid eighty thousand cash for Hsiang-lin Sao. Now the son of the family has also been married, and he gave his bride presents costing but five thousand cash. After deducting the cost of the wedding there still remained over ten thousand cash profit. Is she clever or not? Good figuring, eh?"

---

[1] The prostration made at this time in wishing greetings.
[2] That is, an upper-class family. It is not against the mother-in-law's tyranny that Fourth Aunt protests, but her lack of virtue in remarrying her widowed daughter-in-law.

"And Hsiang-lin Sao—she obeyed all right?"

"Well, it wasn't a question of obedience with her. Anybody in such a situation has to make a protest, of course. They simply tie her up, lift her into the Flowery Sedan Chair, bear her away to the groom's home, forcibly put the Flowery Hat on her head, forcibly make her *k'ou-t'ou* in the ancestral hall, forcibly 'lock her up' with the man—and the thing is done."

"*Ai-ya!*"

"But Hsiang-lin Sao was unusually rebellious. I heard people say that she made a terrific struggle. In fact, it was said that she was different from most women, probably because she had worked in your home—the home of a scholar. My lady, I have seen much in these years. Among widows who remarry I have seen the kind who cry and shout. I have seen those who threaten suicide. There is in addition the kind who, after being taken to the groom's home, refuse to make the *k'ou-t'ou* to Heaven and Earth, and even go so far as to smash the Flowery Candles used to light the bridal chamber! But Hsiang-lin Sao was like none of those demonstrators.

"From the beginning she fought like a tigress. She screamed and she cursed, and by the time she reached Hu Village her throat was so raw that she had almost lost her voice. She had to be dragged out of the sedan chair. It took two men to get her into the ancestral hall, and still she would not *k'ou-t'ou*. Only for one moment they carelessly loosened their grip on her, and, *ai-ya!* by Buddha's name! she knocked her head a sound whack on the incense altar, and cut a deep gash from which blood spurted out thickly! They used two handfuls of incense ash on the wound, and bound it up with two thicknesses of red cloth, and still it bled. Actually, she struggled till the very last, when they locked her with her husband in the bridal room, and even then she cursed! This was indeed a *protest*. *Ai-ya*, it really was!"

She shook her gnarled head, bent her gaze on the floor, and was silent.

"How was it afterwards?"

"They say she did not get up the first day, nor the second."

"Afterwards?"

"After that? Oh, she finally got up. At the end of the year she bore him a child, a boy. While I was at my mother's home I saw some people who had returned from Hu Village, and they had seen her. Mother and son were both fat. Above their heads was fortunately no mother-in-law. Her husband, it seems, is strong and a good worker. He owns his house. *Ai-ya,* she is a lucky one indeed."

From that time on Fourth Aunt gave up any thought of Hsianglin Sao's excellent work, or at any rate she ceased to mention her name.

III

In the autumn, two years after Old Woman Wei had brought news of Hsiang-lin Sao's extraordinary good luck, our old servant stood once more in person before the hall of Fourth Uncle's home. On the table she laid a round chestnut-shaped basket and a small bedding-roll. She still wore a white scarf on her head, a black skirt, a blue jacket, and 'moon-white' vest. Her complexion was about the same, except that her cheeks had lost all their colour. Traces of tears lay at the corners of her eyes, from which all the old brightness and lustre seemed washed away. Moreover, with her once more appeared Old Woman Wei, wearing on her face an expression of commiseration. She babbled to Fourth Aunt:

"So it is truly said, 'Heaven holds many an unpredictable wind and cloud.' Her husband was a strong and healthy man. Who would have guessed that at a green age he would be cut down by fever? He had actually recovered from the illness, but ate a bowl of cold rice, and it attacked him again. Fortunately she had the son. By cutting wood, plucking tea-leaves, raising silkworms—and she is skilled at each of these jobs—she could make a living. Could anyone have preducted that the child itself would be carried off by a wolf? A fact! By a wolf!

"It was already late spring, long after the time when anyone fears a wolf. Who could have anticipated this one's boldness? *Ai-ya!* And now she is left only her one bare body. Her late husband's elder brother-in-law took possession of the house, and everything in it, and he drove her out without a cash. She is, in fact, in the 'no-road no-destination' predicament, and can but return to beg you to take her in once more. She no longer has any connexions (such as a mother-in-law) whatever. Knowing you want to change servants,

I brought her along. Since she already knows your ways, it's certain she'll be more satisfactory than a raw hand."

"I was truly stupid, truly," said Hsiang-lin Sao in a piteous voice, and lifting up her faded eyes for a moment. "I knew that when the snow lies on the mountains the wild animals will sometimes venture into the valleys and will even come into the villages in search of food. I did not know that they could be so fierce long after the coming of spring. I got up early one morning, took a small basket of beans, and told little Ah Mao to sit in the doorway and string the beans. He was very bright, and he was obedient. He always listened to every word, and this morning he did so, and I left him in the door. I myself went behind the house to chop kindling and to scour rice. I had just put the rice in the boiler and was ready to cook the beans, so I called to Ah Mao. He didn't answer. I went round to the door, but there was no Ah Mao; only beans scattered on the ground. He never wandered to play, but I hurried to each door to ask for him. Nobody had seen him. I was terror-stricken! I begged people to help me hunt for him. All the morning and into the afternoon we moved back and forth, looking into every corner. Finally we found one of his little shoes hanging on a thorn bush. From that moment every one said that he had been seized by a wolf, but I would not believe it. After a little while, going farther into the mountains, we . . . found . . . him. Lying in a grassy lair was his body with the five organs missing.[1] But the bean basket was still tightly clutched in his little hand." Here she broke down, and could only make incoherent sounds, without stringing a sentence together.

Fourth Aunt had at first hesitated, but after hearing this story her eyes reddened, and she instantly told the widow to take her things to the servants' quarters. Old Woman Wei sighed with relief, as if she had just put down a heavy bundle. Hsiang-lin Sao quieted somewhat, and without waiting for a second invitation she took her bedding-roll into the familiar room.

Thus she once more became a worker in Lo Ching, and everybody still called her Hsiang-lin Sao, after her first husband.

But she was no longer the same woman. After a few days her mistress and master noticed that she was heavy of hand and foot, that

---

[1] Completely eviscerated.

she was listless at her work, that her memory was bad, and over her corpse-like face all day there never crossed the shadow of a smile. One could tell by Fourth Aunt's tone of voice that she was already dissatisfied, and with Fourth Uncle it was the same. He had, as usual, wrinkled his brow in disapproval when she had first arrived, but since they had been having endless difficulties with servants he had raised no serious objection to the re-employment of Hsiang-lin Sao. Now, however, he informed Fourth Aunt that, though the woman's case seemed indeed very lamentable, and it was permissible because of that to give her work, still she was obviously out of tune with Heaven and Earth. She must not, therefore, be allowed to pollute precious vessels with her soiled hands, and especially on ceremonial occasions Fourth Aunt herself must prepare all food. Otherwise the ancestral spirits would be offended and, likely as not, refuse to touch a crumb.

These ancestral sacrifices were, in fact, the most important affairs in Fourth Uncle's home, for he still rigidly adhered to the old beliefs. Formerly they had been busy times for Hsiang-lin Sao also, and so the next time the altar was placed in the centre of the hall and covered with a fine cloth she began to arrange the wine cups and bowls and chopsticks on it exactly as before.

"Hsiang-lin Sao," Fourth Aunt cried, rushing in, "never mind that. I'll fix the things."

Puzzled, she withdrew and proceeded to take out the candlesticks.

"Never mind that, either. I'll get the sticks," Fourth Aunt said again.

Hsiang-lin Sao walked about several times in a rather dazed manner, and ended up by finding nothing to do, for Fourth Aunt was always ahead of her. She went away suspiciously. She found the only use they had for her that day was to sit in the kitchen and keep the fire burning.

People in Lo Ching continued to call her Hsiang-lin Sao, but there was a different tone in their voices. They still talked with her, but smiled in a cool way, and with faint contempt. She did not seem to notice, or perhaps did not care. She only stared beyond them, and talked always about the thing that day and night clung to her mind.

"I was truly stupid, truly," she would repeat. "I only knew that

when the snow lies on the mountains the wild animals will sometimes venture into the valleys and will even come into the villages
in search of food. I did not know that they could be fierce long after
the coming of spring. . . ."

Retelling her story in the same words, she would end up sobbing
and striking her breast.

Every one who heard it was moved, and even the sneering men,
listening, would loosen their smiles and go off in depressed spirits.
The women not only forgot all their contempt for her, but at the
moment forgave her entirely for her black sins—remarrying and
causing the death not only of a second husband but also of his child
—and in many cases ended by joining with her in weeping at the
end of the tragic narrative. She talked of nothing else, only this
incident that had become the central fact of her life, and she told it
again and again.

Before long, however, the entire population of Lo Ching had
heard her story not once but several times, and the most generous
old women, even the Buddha-chanters, could not muster up a tear
when she spoke of it. Nearly everybody in the town could recite
the story word for word, and it bored them excessively to hear it
repeated.

"I was truly stupid, truly," she would begin.

"Yes, you only knew that when the snow lies on the mountains
the wild animals will sometimes venture into the valleys and will
even come into the villages in search of food. . . ." Her audience
would recite the next lines, cruelly cutting her short, and walk
away.

With her mouth hanging open, Hsiang-lin Sao would stand stupefied for a while, stare as if seeing some one for the first time, and
then drag away slowly as if weary of her continued existence. But
her obsession gave her no rest, and she ingenuously tried to interest
others in it by indirect approaches. Seeing a bean, a small basket, or
other people's children, she would innocently lead up to the tragedy
of Ah Mao. Looking at a child three or four years old, for instance,
she would say:

"If Ah Mao were still here, he would be just about that size."

Frightened by the wild light in Hsiang-lin Sao's eyes, the children signalled for a retreat by pulling on their mother's skirts. She

would therefore soon find herself alone again, and falter off until the next time. Pretty soon every one understood these tactics too, and made fun of her. When they saw her staring morosely at an infant they would look at her mockingly.

"Hsiang-lin Sao, if our Ah Mao were still here, wouldn't he be just about that big?"

Probably she had not suspected that her misery had long since ceased to afford any vicarious enjoyment for anyone, and that the whole episode had now become loathsome to her former sympathizers, but the meaning of this kind of mockery pierced her armour of preoccupation at last, and she understood. She glanced at the jester, but did not utter a word of response.

IV

Lo Ching never loses its enthusiasm for the celebration of New Year. Promptly after the twentieth of the Twelfth Moon the festivities begin.

Next year at this time Fourth Uncle hired an extra male worker, and in addition a certain Liu Ma, to prepare the chickens and geese. This Liu Ma was a 'good woman,' a Buddhist vegetarian who really kept her vow not to kill living creatures. Hsiang-lin Sao, whose hands were polluted, could only feed the fire and sit watching Liu Ma working over the sacred vessels. Outside a fine snow was matting the earth.

"*Ai-ya*, I was truly stupid," sighed Hsiang-lin Sao, staring despondently at the sky.

"Hsiang-lin Sao, you are back on the same trail!" Liu Ma interrupted, with some exasperation. "Listen to me, is it true you got the scar by knocking your forehead against the altar in protest?"

"Um-huh."

"I ask you this: If you hated it that much, how was it that later on you actually submitted?"

"I?"

"Ah, you! It seems to me you must have been half-willing, otherwise—"

"Ha, Ha! You don't understand how great were his muscles."

"No, I don't. I don't believe that strength such as your own was not enough to resist him. It is clear to me that you must have been ready for it yourself."

"Ah—*you!* I'd like to see you try it yourself, and see how long you could struggle."

Liu Ma's old face crinkled into a laugh, so that it looked like a polished walnut. Her dry eyes rested on Hsiang-lin Sao's scar for a moment, and then sought out her eyes. She spoke again.

"You are really not very clever. One more effort that time to really kill yourself would have been better for you. As it is, you lived with your second man less than two years, and that is all you got for your great crime. Just think about it: when you go into the next world you will be held in dispute between the spirits of your two husbands. How can the matter be settled? Only one way: Yen Lu-t'a, the Emperor of Hell, can do nothing else but saw you in half and divide you equally between the two men. That, I think, is a fact."

An expression of mingled fear and astonishment crept over Hsiang-lin Sao's face. This was something she had not considered before, had never even heard in her mountain village.

"My advice is that you'd better make amends before it is too late. Go to the Tu-ti Temple and contribute money for a threshold. This threshold, stepped on by a thousand, stepped over by ten thousand,[1] can suffer for you and perhaps atone for the crime. Thus you may avoid suffering after death."

Hsiang-lin Sao did not say a word, but felt intolerably crushed with pain. Next day dark shadows encircled her eyes. Right after breakfast she went off to the Tu-ti Temple to beg the priest to let her buy a new threshold. He stubbornly refused at first, and only when she released a flood of tears would he consider it. Then, unwillingly, he admitted that it might be arranged for twelve thousand cash.

She had long since stopped talking with the villagers, who shunned her and the tiresome narrative of Ah Mao's death, but news soon spread that there was a development in her case. Many people came now and inquisitively referred to the scar on her forehead.

"Hsiang-lin Sao, I ask you this: Why was it that you submitted to the man?"

---

[1] It is believed that the stone threshold acts as a kind of proxy body for the sinner, and every step on it is a blow subtracted from the total punishment awaiting him in Hell.

"Regrettable, regrettable," sighed another, "that the knock was not deep enough."

She understood well enough the mockery and irony of their words, and she did not reply. She simply continued to perform her duties in silence. Near the end of next year's service she drew the money due to her from Fourth Aunt, exchanged it for twelve silver dollars, and asked permission to visit in the west end of the town. Before the next meal she returned, much altered. Her face no longer seemed troubled, her eyes held some life in them for the first time in months, and she was in a cheerful mood. She told Fourth Aunt that she had bought a threshold for the temple.

During the Coming-of-Winter Festival she worked tirelessly, and on the day of making sacrifices she was simply bursting with energy. Fourth Aunt brought out the holy utensils, and Ah Niu carried the altar to the centre of the room. Hsiang-lin Sao promptly went over to bring out the wine cups and chopsticks.

"Never mind," Fourth Aunt cried out. "Don't touch them."

She withdrew her hand as if it had been burned, her face turned ashen, and she did not move, but stood as if transfixed. She remained standing there, in fact, until Fourth Uncle came in to light the offertory incense, and ordered her away.

From that day she declined rapidly. It was not merely a physical impoverishment that ensued, but the spark of life in her was dimmed almost to extinction. She became extremely nervous, and developed a morbid fear of darkness or the sight of anyone, even her master or mistress. She became altogether as timid and frightened as a little mouse that has wandered from its hole to blink for a moment in the glaring light of day. In half a year her hair lost all its colour. Her memory became so clouded that she sometimes forgot even to scour the rice.

"What has got into her? How has she become like that? It's better not to have her around," Fourth Aunt began saying in her presence.

But "become like that" she had, and there did not seem to be any possibility of improving her. They talked of sending her away, or of returning her to the management of Old Woman Wei. Nothing came of it while I was still in Lo Ching, but the plan was soon afterwards carried out. Whether Old Woman Wei actually took charge of her for a while after she left Fourth Uncle's home or whether she at once became a beggar I never learned.

I am awakened by giant crackers, and see yellow tongues of flame, and then immediately afterwards hear the sharp *pipipapao* of exploding gunpowder. It is near the Fifth Hour, and time for the prayers and blessings. Still only drowsily aware of the world, I hear far away the steady explosive notes, one after another, and then more rapidly and thickly, until the whole sky is echoing, and the whirling snowflakes, eddying out of little white balls themselves like something shot from above, hover everywhere. Within the compass of the medley of sound and gentle storm I feel somehow a nostalgic contentment, and all the brooding of the dead day and the early night is forgotten in the stir around me, lost in the air of expectancy that pervades these homes about to receive benediction. What a satisfaction it is to understand that the Holy Spirits of Heaven and Earth, having bountifully inhaled their fill of the offertory meat and wine and incense, now limp about drunkenly in the wide air. In such a mood they are certain to dispense boundless prosperity on the good people of Lo Ching!

◇◇◇*Maurice Maeterlinck (1862-1949). Belgian dramatist, poet, essayist. He is chiefly important as a symbolist playwright. Nobel Prize, 1911. The Massacre of the Innocents was his first published story, written when he was twenty-four. In its minuteness of detail and high polish it recalls the work of the old Dutch masters.*

THE MASSACRE OF THE INNOCENTS

BY MAURICE MAETERLINCK

On Friday the 26th of December about supper time, a little shepherd came into Nazareth crying terribly.

Some peasants who were drinking ale at the Blue Lion threw open the shutters to look into the village orchard, and saw the lad running across the snow. They recognized him as Korneliz' son, and shouted at him from the window: "What's the matter? Go to bed, you!"

But the boy answered in a voice of terror, telling them that the Spaniards had come, having already set fire to the farm, hanged his mother from a chestnut bough, and bound his nine little sisters to the trunk of a large tree. The peasants quickly came forth from the inn, surrounded the boy and plied him with questions. He went on to tell them that the soldiers were clad in steel armor and mounted on horseback, that they had seized the cattle of his uncle, Petrus Krayer, and would soon enter the wood with the sheep and cattle.

They all ran to the Golden Sun, where Korneliz and his brother-in-law were drinking ale, while the innkeeper hastened out into the village to spread the news of the approach of the Spaniards.

There was great excitement in Nazareth. Women threw open windows and peasants ran forth from their houses carrying lights which they extinguished as soon as they came to the orchard, where it was bright as midday, because of the snow and the full moon.

From *Great Short Stories of the World,* edited by Barrett H. Clark and Maxim Lieber. (Translated by Barrett H. Clark.) By permission of Maxim Lieber.

They gathered round Korneliz and Krayer in the public square before the inn. Many had brought pitchforks and rakes. They took counsel, speaking in tones of terror, out under the trees.

As they were uncertain what to do, one of them ran to fetch the curé, who owned the farm that was worked by Korneliz. He came forth from his house with the keys of the church, in company with the sacristan, while all the others followed him to the churchyard, where he proclaimed from the top of the tower that he could see nothing, either across the fields or in the wood, but there were red clouds in the direction of his farm. Over all the rest of the horizon the sky was blue and filled with stars.

After deliberating a long while in the churchyard, they decided to hide in the wood which the Spaniards were to come through, attack them if they were not too numerous, and recover Petrus Krayer's cattle and any booty they might have taken at the farm.

The men armed themselves with forks and spades while the women remained with the curé by the church. Looking for a favorable place for an ambuscade, the men reached a hilly spot near a mill at the edge of the wood, where they could see the fire glowing against the stars of night. They took up their position under some enormous oaks by the side of an ice-covered pond.

A shepherd, who was called the Red Dwarf, mounted to the top of the hill in order to warn the miller, who had already stopped the mill when he saw flames on the horizon. But he allowed the peasant to enter, and the two went to a window to look out over the countryside.

The moon shone down brightly upon the conflagration, and the men could see a long procession of people wending their way across the snow. After they had done watching, the Dwarf went down again to the others waiting in the wood. They could soon distinguish in the distance four riders behind a herd of cattle browsing over the fields. As they stood, clad in their blue breeches and red mantles, looking about by the pond's edge under trees made luminous by the heavy snowfall, the sacristan showed them a box-hedge, and behind this they crouched.

The Spaniards, driving before them flocks and cattle, made their way over the ice, and when the sheep came to the hedge and began nibbling at the greenery, Korneliz broke through, the others following him into the moonlight, armed with their forks. There was then a great massacre in the presence of the huddled sheep and cows, that looked on frightened at the terrible slaughter under the light of the moon.

When they had killed the men and their horses, Korneliz went out into the fields toward the blazing farm, while the others stripped the dead. Then they all returned to the village with the flocks and cattle. The women, who were looking out toward the dense wood from behind the churchyard walls, saw them coming out from among the trees and in company with the curé ran to meet them. They all returned dancing amid laughing children and barking dogs. As they made merry under the pear-trees, where the Dwarf had hung lanterns as for a kermesse, they asked the curé what ought to be done next. They decided to send a cart for the body of the woman who had been hanged and her nine little girls, and bring them all back to the village. The sisters of the dead woman and various other relatives got into the cart, and the curé as well, for he was old and very fat and could walk only with the greatest difficulty. They drove off into the wood, and in silence reached the wide open fields, where they saw the dead soldiers, stripped naked, and the horses lying on their backs on the shining ice among the trees. They went on toward the farm, which was still burning in the midst of the open fields.

When they reached the orchard of the burning house, they stopped short before the garden gate and looked upon the terrible tragedy. Korneliz' wife hung, naked, from the branches of a huge chestnut. He himself climbed up a ladder into the branches of the tree, below which his nine little girls awaited their mother on the lawn. Korneliz made his way through the arching boughs overhead when all at once, outlined against the bright snow, he caught sight of the crowd beneath, looking up at him. Weeping, he signed to them to come to his help, and they came into the garden, and the sacristan, the Red Dwarf, the innkeepers of the Blue Lion and the Golden Sun, the curé carrying a lantern, and several other peasants, climbed into the snow-covered chestnut to cut down the body of the hanged woman. The women took the body into their arms at the foot of the tree, as those other women once received Our Lord Jesus Christ.

She was buried on the following day, and for the next week nothing unusual occurred in Nazareth, but the next Sunday famished wolves ran through the village after High Mass, and the snow fell until noon. Then the sun came out and shone bright in the sky, and the peasants went home to dinner as usual, and dressed for Benediction.

At this time there was no one on the square, for it was bitter cold. Only dogs and chickens wandered here and there among the trees, and sheep nibbled at the triangular spot of grass, and the cure's maid swept the snow in the garden.

Then a troop of armed men crossed the stone bridge at the far end of the village, and pulled up at the orchard. A few peasants came out of their houses, but hurried back terror-stricken when they saw that the horsemen were Spaniards, and went to their windows to watch what was going to happen. There were thirty horsemen, in armor. They gathered round an old man with a white beard. Each horseman carried with him a foot-soldier dressed in yellow or red. These dismounted and ran over the snow to warm themselves, while a number of armored soldiers also dismounted.

They made their way toward the Golden Sun and knocked at the door. It was opened with some hesitancy, and the Spaniards entered, warmed themselves before the fire, and demanded ale. They then left the inn, taking with them pots, pitchers, and bread for their companions, and the old man with the white beard who stood waiting among his soldiers. As the street was still deserted, the commanding officer sent off some horsemen behind the houses to guard the village on the side facing the open country, and ordered the footmen to bring him all children two years old and under, as he intended to massacre them, in accordance with what is written in the Gospel of St. Matthew.

The men went first to the small inn of the Green Cabbage and the barber's hut, which stood close to each other in the central part of the street. One of them opened the pigsty and a whole litter of pigs escaped and roamed about through the village. The innkeeper and the barber came out of their houses and humbly inquired of the soldiers what was wanted, but the Spaniards understood no Flemish, and entered the houses in search of the children. The innkeeper had one who, dressed in its little shirt, was sitting on the dinner table, crying. One of the soldiers took it in his arms and carried it off out under the apple trees, while its parents followed weeping. The foot-soldiers next threw open the stables of the barrel-maker, the black-smith, and the cobbler, and cows, calves, asses, pigs, goats and sheep wandered here and there over the square. When they broke the windows of the carpenter's house, a number of the wealthiest and oldest peasants of the parish gathered in the street and advanced to-ward the Spaniards. They respectfully took off their caps and hats to the velvet-clad chief, asking what he intended to do, but he too did not understand their language, and one of them ran off to get the cure. He was about to go to Benediction, and was putting on his golden chasuble in the sacristy. The peasants cried, "The Spaniards are in the orchard!" Terror-stricken, he ran to the church door, fol-lowed by the choir-boys carrying their censers and candles. From the door he could see the cattle and other animals set loose from their stables wandering over the grass and snow, the Spanish horsemen, the foot-soldiers before the doors of the houses, horses tied to trees all along the street, and men and women supplicating the soldier who carried the child still clad in its shirt. He hastened into the churchyard, the peasants turning anxiously toward him, their priest, who arrived like a god covered with gold, out there among the pear trees. They pressed close about him as he stood facing the white-bearded man. He spoke both in Flemish and Latin, but the officer slowly shrugged his shoulders to show that he failed to understand.

The parishioners inquired of him in undertones, "What does he say? What is he going to do?" Others, seeing the curé in the orchard, emerged cautiously from their huts, and women hastily came near and whispered in small groups among themselves, while the soldiers who had been besieging the inn, came out again when they saw the crowd assembling in the square.

Then he who held the innkeeper's child by one leg, cut off its head with a stroke of the sword. The peasants saw the head fall, and the body bleeding on the ground. The mother gathered it to her arms, forgetting the head, and ran toward her house. On the way she stumbled against a tree, fell flat on the snow and lay in a faint, while the father struggled with the two soldiers.

Some of the younger peasants threw stones and wood at the

Spaniards, but the horsemen rallied and lowered their lances, the women scattered in all directions, while the curé with his other parishioners shrieked with horror to the accompaniment of the noises made by the sheep, geese, and dogs.

As the soldiers went off once more down the street, they were quiet again, waiting to see what would happen. A group went into the shop of the sacristan's sisters, but came out again without touching the seven women, who were on their knees praying within. Then they entered the inn of the Hunchback of St. Nicholas. There too the door was instantly opened in the hope of placating them, but when they appeared again in the midst of a great tumult, they carried three children in their arms, and were surrounded by the Hunchback, his wife and daughters, who were begging for mercy with clasped hands. When the soldiers came to their leader they laid the children down at the foot of an elm, all dressed in their Sunday clothes. One of them, who wore a yellow dress, got up and ran with unsteady feet toward the sheep. A soldier ran after it with his naked sword. The child died with its face on the earth. The others were killed near the tree. The peasants and the innkeeper's daughters took flight, screaming, and went back to their houses. Alone in the orchard, the curé fell to his knees and begged the Spaniards, in a piteous voice, with arms crossed over his breast, going from one to the other on his knees, while the father and mother of the murdered children, seated on the snow, wept bitterly as they bent over the lacerated bodies.

As the foot-soldiers went along the street they noticed a large blue farmhouse. They tried to break in the door, but this was of oak and studded with huge nails. They therefore took tubs which were frozen in a pond near the entrance, and used them to enter the house from the second story windows.

There had been a kermesse in this house: relatives had come to feast on waffles, hams, and custards. At the sound of the smashing of windows they crouched together behind the table, still laden with jugs and dishes. The soldiers went to the kitchen and after a savage fight in which many were wounded, they seized all the small boys and girls, and a little servant who had bitten the thumb of one soldier, left the house and closed the door behind them to prevent their being followed.

Those who had no children cautiously came forth from their houses and followed the soldiers at a distance. They could see them throw down their victims on the ground before the old man, and cold-bloodedly massacre them with lances or swords. Meanwhile men and women crowded the windows of the blue farmhouse and the barn, cursing and raising their arms to heaven as they contemplated the pink, red, and white clothes of their motionless children on the ground among the trees. Then the soldiers hanged the servant from the Half Moon Inn on the other side of the street. There was a long silence in the village.

It had now become a general massacre. Mothers escaped from their houses, trying to flee through vegetable and flower gardens out into the open country, but mounted soldiers pursued them and drove them back into the street. Peasants, with caps held tight between their hands, fell to their knees before the soldiers who dragged off their little ones, and dogs barked joyously amid the disorder. The curé, his hands raised heavenwards, rushed back and forth from house to house and out among the trees, praying in desperation like a martyr. The soldiers, trembling from the cold, whistled in their fingers as they moved about, or stood idly with their hands in their pockets, their swords under their arms, in front of houses that were being entered. Small groups in all directions, seeing the fear of the peasants, were entering the farmhouses, and in every street similar scenes were enacted. The market-gardener's wife, who lived in an old hut with pink tiles near the church, pursued with a chair two soldiers who were carrying off her children in a wheelbarrow. She was terribly sick when she saw her children die, and made to sit on a chair against a tree.

Other soldiers climbed into the lime trees in front of a farmhouse painted the color of lilacs, and made their way in by taking off the tiles. When they reappeared on the roof, the parents with extended arms followed them until the soldiers forced them back, finding it necessary finally to strike them over the head with their swords before they could shake themselves free and return again to the street below.

One family, who had concealed themselves in the cellar of a large house, stood at the gratings and wildly lamented, while the father desperately brandished his pitchfork through the grating.

Outside, an old bald-headed fellow sat on a manure-heap, sobbing to himself. In the square a woman dressed in yellow had fainted away, her weeping husband holding her up by the arms against a pear tree. Another woman, in red, clutched her little girl, whose hands had been cut off, and lifted the child's arms to see whether she could move. Still another woman was escaping toward the open country, the soldiers running after her among the haystacks, which stood out in sharp relief against the snow-covered fields.

Before the Four Sons of Aymon confusion reigned. The peasants had made a barricade while the soldiers encircled the inn, unable to effect an entrance. They were trying to climb up to the sign-board by means of the vines, when they caught sight of a ladder behind the garden gate. Setting this against the wall, they scaled it, one after another. But the landlord and his family threw down at them tables and chairs, cockery and cradles from the window, upsetting ladder and soldiers together.

In a wooden cottage at the outskirts of the village another group of soldiers came upon an old woman washing her children in a tub before the open fire. She was old and deaf, and did not hear them when they entered. Two soldiers carried off the tub with the children in it, while the bewildered old woman set off in pursuit, carrying the clothes which she had been about to put on the infants. Out in the village she saw traces of blood, swords in the orchard, smashed cradles in the open streets, women praying and wringing their hands over their dead children, and began to scream and strike the soldiers who had to set down the tub in order to defend themselves. The curé hurried over to her, his hands still folded over his chasuble, and entreated the Spaniards for mercy, in the presence of the naked children screaming in the tub. Other soldiers came up, bound the distracted mother to a tree, and went off with the children.

The butcher, having hidden his baby girl, leaned against the front of his shop with apparent unconcern. A foot-soldier and one of the armed horsemen entered his home and found the child in a copper pot. The butcher desperately seized a knife and rushed off in pursuit, but the soldiers disarmed him and suspended him by the hands from some hooks in the wall, where he kicked and wriggled among his dead animals until evening.

Round the churchyard a multitude gathered in front of a long low green farmhouse. The proprietor wept bitterly as he stood in his doorway. He was a fat, jolly-looking man, and happened to arouse the compassion of a few soldiers who sat near the wall in the sunlight, patting a dog. The soldier who was taking off his child made gestures as if to convey the meaning, "What can I do? I'm not to blame!"

One peasant who was being pursued leaped into a boat near the stone bridge, and, with his wife and children, rowed quickly across that part of the pond that was not frozen. The Spaniards, who dared not follow, walked angrily among the reeds by the shore. They climbed into the willows along the bankside, trying to reach the boat with their lances. Unable to do so, they continued to threaten the fugitives, who drifted out over the dark water.

The orchard was still thronged with people: it was there, in the presence of the white-bearded commanding officer, that most of the children were being murdered. The children who were over two and could just walk, stood together eating bread and jam, staring in wide-eyed wonder at the massacre of their helpless playmates, or gathered round the village fool, who was playing his flute.

All at once there was a concerted movement in the village, and the peasants made off in the direction of the castle that stood on rising ground at the far end of the street. They had caught sight of their lord on the battlements, watching the massacre. Men and women, young and old, extended their hands toward him in supplication as he stood there in his velvet cloak and golden cap like a king in Heaven. But he only raised his hands and shrugged his shoulders to show that he was powerless, while the people supplicated him in growing despair, kneeling with heads bared in the snow, and crying piteously. He turned slowly back into his tower. Their last hope had vanished.

When all the children had been killed, the weary soldiers wiped their swords on the grass and ate their supper among the pear-trees, then mounting in pairs, they rode out of Nazareth across the bridge over which they had come.

The setting sun turned the wood into a flaming mass, dyeing the village a blood red. Utterly exhausted, the curé threw himself down in the snow before the church, his servant standing at his side. They both looked out into the street and the orchard, which were filled with peasants dressed in their Sunday clothes. Before the entrances of many houses were parents holding the bodies of children on their knees, still full of blank amazement, lamenting over their grievous tragedy. Others wept over their little ones where they had perished, by the side of a cask, under a wheelbarrow, or by the pond. Others again carried off their dead in silence. Some set to washing benches, chairs, tables, bloody underclothes, or picking up the cradles that had been hurled into the street. Many mothers sat bewailing their children under the trees, having recognized them by their woolen dresses. Those who had no children wandered through the square, stopping by grief-stricken mothers, who sobbed and moaned. The men, who had stopped crying, doggedly pursued their strayed beasts to the accompaniment of the barking of dogs; others silently set to work mending their broken windows and damaged roofs.

As the moon quietly rose through the tranquil sky, a sleepy silence fell upon the village, where at last the shadow of no living thing stirred.

◈◈◈*Thomas Mann (1875–1955). German novelist, short-story writer, essayist, critic. Awarded the Nobel Prize in 1929. Mann ranks, with Proust and Joyce, among the three greatest men of letters of our time. He left Germany in protest against fascism and made his home for many years in the United States, where he became a citizen. See Stories of Three Decades, Buddenbrooks, The Magic Mountain, Joseph and His Brothers, Doctor Faustus.*

A WEARY HOUR

BY THOMAS MANN

He got up from the table, his little, fragile writing-desk; got up as though desperate, and with hanging head crossed the room to the tall, thin, pillar-like stove in the opposite corner. He put his hands to it; but the hour was long past midnight and the tiles were nearly stone cold. Not getting even this little comfort that he sought, he leaned his back against them and, coughing, drew together the folds of his dressing-gown, between which a draggled lace shirt-frill stuck out; he snuffed hard through his nostrils to get a little air, for as usual he had a cold.

It was a particular, a sinister cold, which scarcely ever quite disappeared. It inflamed his eyelids and made the flanges of his nose all raw; in his head and limbs it lay like a heavy, sombre intoxication. Or was this cursed confinement to his room, to which the doctor had weeks ago condemned him, to blame for all his languor and flabbiness? God knew if it was the right thing—perhaps so, on account of his chronic catarrh and the spasms in his chest and belly. And for weeks on end now, yes, weeks, bad weather had reigned in Jena—hateful, horrible weather, which he felt in every nerve of his body—cold, wild, gloomy. The December wind roared in the stove-pipe with a desolate god-forsaken sound—he might have been wandering on a heath, by night and storm, his soul full of unappeasable grief. Yet this close confinement—that was not good either; no

From *Stories of Three Decades* by Thomas Mann. (Translated by H. T. Lowe-Porter.) By permission of Alfred A. Knopf, Inc. Copyright 1936 by Alfred A. Knopf, Inc.

good for thought, nor for the rhythm of the blood, where thought was engendered.

The six-sided room was bare and colourless and devoid of cheer: a whitewashed ceiling wreathed in tobacco smoke, walls covered with trellis-patterned paper and hung with silhouettes in oval frames, half a dozen slender-legged pieces of furniture; the whole lighted by two candles burning at the head of the manuscript on the writing-table. Red curtains draped the upper part of the window-frames; mere festooned wisps of cotton they were, but red, a warm, sonorous red, and he loved them and would not have parted from them; they gave a little air of ease and charm to the bald unlovely poverty of his surroundings. He stood by the stove and blinked repeatedly, straining his eyes across at the work from which he had just fled: that load, that weight, that gnawing conscience, that sea which to drink up, that frightful task which to perform, was all his pride and all his misery, at once his heaven and his hell. It dragged, it stuck, it would not budge—and now again . . . ! It must be the weather; or his catarrh, or his fatigue. Or was it the work? Was the thing itself an unfortunate conception, doomed from its beginning to despair?

He had risen in order to put a little space between him and his task, for physical distance would often result in improved perspective, a wider view of his material and a better chance of conspectus. Yes, the mere feeling of relief on turning away from the battlefield had been known to work like an inspiration. And a more innocent one than that purveyed by alcohol or strong, black coffee.

The little cup stood on the side-table. Perhaps it would help him out of the impasse? No, no, not again! Not the doctor only, but somebody else too, a more important somebody, had cautioned him against that sort of thing—another person, who lived over in Weimar and for whom he felt a love which was a mixture of hostility and yearning. That was a wise man. He knew how to live and create; did not abuse himself; was full of self-regard.

Quiet reigned in the house. There was only the wind, driving down the Schlossgasse and dashing the rain in gusts against the panes. They were all asleep—the landlord and his family, Lotte and the children. And here he stood by the cold stove, awake, alone, tormented; blinking across at the work in which his morbid self-dissatisfaction would not let him believe.

His neck rose long and white out of his stock and his knock-kneed legs showed between the skirts of his dressing-gown. The red hair was smoothed back from a thin, high forehead; it retreated in bays from his veined white temples and hung down in thin locks over the ears. His nose was aquiline, with an abrupt whitish tip; above it the well-marked line of the brows almost met. They were darker than his hair and gave the deep-set, inflamed eyes a tragic, staring look. He could not breathe through his nose; so he opened his thin lips and made the freckled, sickly cheeks look even more sunken thereby.

No, it was a failure, it was all hopelessly wrong. The army ought to have been brought in! The army was the root of the whole thing. But it was impossible to present it before the eyes of the audience —and was art powerful enough thus to enforce the imagination? Besides, his hero was no hero; he was contemptible, he was frigid. The situation was wrong, the language was wrong; it was a dry pedestrian lecture, good for a history class, but as drama absolutely hopeless!

Very good, then, it was over. A defeat. A failure. Bankruptcy. He would write to Körner, the good Körner, who believed in him, who clung with childlike faith to his genius. He would scoff, scold, beseech—this friend of his; would remind him of the *Carlos,* which likewise had issued out of doubts and pains and rewritings and after all the anguish turned out to be something really fine, a genuine masterpiece. But times were changed. Then he had been a man still capable of taking a strong, confident grip on a thing and giving it triumphant shape. Doubts and struggles? Yes. And ill he had been, perhaps more ill than now; a fugitive, oppressed and hungry, at odds with the world; humanly speaking, a beggar. But young, still young! Each time, however low he had sunk, his resilient spirit had leaped up anew; upon the hour of affliction had followed the feeling of triumphant self-confidence. That came no more, or hardly ever, now. There might be one night of glowing exaltation—when the fires of his genius lighted up an impassioned vision of all that he might do if only they burned on; but it had always to be paid for with a week of enervation and gloom. Faith in the future, his guiding star in times of stress, was dead. Here was the despairing truth: the years of need and nothingness, which he had thought of as the painful testing-time, turned out to have been the rich and fruitful ones; and now that a little happiness had fallen to his lot, now that he had ceased to be an intellectual freebooter and occupied a position of civic dignity, with office and honours, wife and children—now he was exhausted, worn out. To give up, to own himself beaten—that was all there was left to do. He groaned; he pressed his hands to his eyes and dashed up and down the room like one possessed. What he had just thought was so frightful that he could not stand still on the spot where he had thought it. He sat down on a chair by the further wall and stared gloomily at the floor, his clasped hands hanging down between his knees.

His conscience . . . how loudly his conscience cried out! He had sinned, sinned against himself all these years, against the delicate instrument that was his body. Those youthful excesses, the nights without sleep, the days spent in close, smoke-laden air, straining his mind and heedless of his body; the narcotics with which he had spurred himself on—all that was now taking its revenge.

And if it did—then he would defy the gods, who decreed the guilt and then imposed the penalties. He had lived as he had to live, he had not had time to be wise, not time to be careful. Here in this place in his chest, when he breathed, coughed, yawned, always in the same spot came this pain, this piercing, stabbing, diabolical little warning; it never left him, since that time in Erfurt five years ago when he had catarrhal fever and inflammation of the lungs. What was it warning him of? Ah, he knew only too well what it meant—no matter how the doctor chose to put him off. He had no time to be wise and spare himself, no time to save his strength by submission to moral laws. What he wanted to do he must do soon, quickly, do today.

And the moral laws? . . . Why was it that precisely sin, surrender to the harmful and the consuming, actually seemed to him more moral than any amount of wisdom and frigid self-discipline? Not that constituted morality: not the contemptible knack of keeping a good conscience—rather the struggle and compulsion, the passion and pain.

Pain . . . how his breast swelled at the word! He drew himself up and folded his arms; his gaze, beneath the close-set auburn brows, was kindled by the nobility of his suffering. No man was utterly wretched so long as he could still speak of his misery in high-sounding and noble words. One thing only was indispensable; the courage to call his life by large and fine names. Not to ascribe his sufferings to bad air and constipation; to be well enough to cherish emotions, to scorn and ignore the material. Just on this one point to be naïve, though in all else sophisticated. To believe, to have strength to believe, in suffering. . . . But he *did* believe in it; so profoundly, so ardently, that nothing which came to pass with suffering could seem to him either useless or evil. His glance sought the manuscript, and his arms tightened across his chest. Talent itself— was that not suffering? And if the manuscript over there, his unhappy effort, made him suffer, was not that quite as it should be—a good sign, so to speak? His talents had never been of the copious, ebullient sort; were they to become so he would feel mistrustful. That only happened with beginners and bunglers, with the ignorant and easily satisfied, whose life was not shaped and disciplined by the possession of a gift. For a gift, my friends down there in the audience, a gift is not anything simple, not anything to play with; it is not mere ability. At bottom it is a compulsion; a critical knowledge of the ideal, a permanent dissatisfaction, which rises only through suffering to the height of its powers. And it is to the greatest, the most unsatisfied, that their gift is the sharpest scourge. Not to complain, not to boast; to think modestly, patiently of one's pain; and if not a day in the week, not even an hour, be free from it— what then? To make light and little of it all, of suffering and achievement alike—that was what made a man great.

He stood up, pulled out his snuff-box and sniffed eagerly, then suddenly clasped his hands behind his back and strode so briskly through the room that the flames of the candles flickered in the draught. Greatness, distinction, world conquest and an imperishable name! To be happy and unknown, what was that by comparison? To be known—known and loved by all the world—ah, they might call that egotism, those who knew naught of the urge, naught of the sweetness of this dream! Everything out of the ordinary is egotistic, in proportion to its suffering. "Speak for yourselves," it says, "ye without mission on this earth, ye whose life is so much easier than mine!" And Ambition says: "Shall my sufferings be vain? No, they must make me great!"

The nostrils of his great nose dilated, his gaze darted fiercely about the room. His right hand was thrust hard and far into the opening of his dressing-gown, his left arm hung down, the fist clenched. A fugitive red played in the gaunt cheeks—a glow thrown up from the fire of his artistic egoism; that passion for his own ego, which burnt unquenchably in his being's depths. Well he knew it, the secret intoxication of this love! Sometimes he needed only to contemplate his own hand, to be filled with the liveliest tenderness towards himself, in whose service he was bent on spending all the talent, all the art that he owned. And he was right so to do, there was nothing base about it. For deeper still than his egoism lay the knowledge that he was freely consuming and sacrificing himself in the service of a high ideal, not as a virtue, of course, but rather out of sheer necessity. And this was his ambition: that no one should be greater than he who had not also suffered more for the sake of the high ideal. No one. He stood still, his hand over his eyes, his body turned aside in a posture of shrinking and avoidance. For already the inevitable thought had stabbed him: the thought of that other man, that radiant being, so sense-endowed, so divinely unconscious, that man over there in Weimar, whom he loved and hated. And once more, as always, in deep disquiet, in feverish haste, there began working within him the inevitable sequence of his thoughts: he must assert and define his own nature, his own art, against that other's. Was the other greater? Wherein, then, and why? If he won, would he have sweated blood to do so? If he lost, would his downfall be a tragic sight? He was no hero, no; a god, perhaps. But it was easier to be a god than a hero. Yes, things were easier for him. He was wise, he was deft, he knew how to distinguish between knowing and creating; perhaps that was why he was so blithe and carefree, such an effortless and gushing spring! But if creation was divine, knowledge was heroic, and he who created in knowledge was hero as well as god.

The will to face difficulties. . . . Did anyone realize what discipline and self-control it cost him to shape a sentence or follow out a hard train of thought? For after all he was ignorant, undisciplined, a slow, dreamy enthusiast. One of Cæsar's letters was harder to write than the most effective scene—and was it not almost for that very reason higher? From the first rhythmical urge of the inward creative force towards matter, towards the material, towards casting in shape

and form—from that to the thought, the image, the word, the line—
what a struggle, what a Gethsemane! Everything that he wrote was
a marvel of yearning after form, shape, line, body; of yearning after
the sunlit world of that other man who had only to open his god-
like lips and straightway call the bright unshadowed things he saw
by name!

And yet—and despite that other man. Where was there an artist,
a poet, like himself? Who like him created out of nothing, out of his
own breast? A poem was born as music in his soul, as pure, primitive
essence, long before it put on a garment of metaphor from the visible
world. History, philosophy, passion were no more than pretexts and
vehicles for something which had little to do with them, but was at
home in orphic depths. Words and conceptions were keys upon
which his art played and made vibrate the hidden strings. No one
realized. The good souls praised him, indeed, for the power of feeling with which he struck one note or another. And his favourite
note, his final emotional appeal, the great bell upon which he
sounded his summons to the highest feasts of the soul—many there
were who responded to its sound. Freedom! But in all their exaltation, certainly he meant by the word both more and less than they
did. Freedom—what was it? A self-respecting middle-class attitude
towards thrones and princes? Surely not that. When one thinks of
all that the spirit of man has dared to put into the word! Freedom
from what? After all, from what? Perhaps, indeed, even from happiness, from human happiness, that silken bond, that tender, sacred
tie. . . .

From happiness. His lips quivered. It was as though his glance
turned inward upon himself; slowly his face sank into his hands.
. . . He stood by the bed in the next room, where the flowered curtains hung in motionless folds across the window, and the lamp shed
a bluish light. He bent over the sweet head on the pillow . . . a
ringlet of dark hair lay across her cheek, that had the paleness of
pearl; the childlike lips were open in slumber. "My wife! Beloved,
didst thou yield to my yearning and come to me to be my joy? And
that thou art. . . . Lie still and sleep; nay, lift not those sweet
shadowy lashes and gaze up at me, as sometimes with thy great,
dark, questioning, searching eyes. I love thee so! By God I swear
it. It is only that sometimes I am tired out, struggling at my self-

imposed task, and my feelings will not respond. And I must not be too utterly thine, never utterly happy in thee, for the sake of my mission."

He kissed her, drew away from her pleasant, slumbrous warmth, looked about him, turned back to the outer room. The clock struck; it warned him that the night was already far spent; but likewise it seemed to be mildly marking the end of a weary hour. He drew a deep breath, his lips closed firmly; he went back and took up his pen. No, he must not brood, he was too far down for that. He must not descend into chaos; or at least he must not stop there. Rather out of chaos, which is fullness, he must draw up to the light whatever he found there fit and ripe for form. No brooding! Work! Define, eliminate, fashion, complete!

And complete it he did, that effort of a labouring hour. He brought it to an end, perhaps not to a good end, but in any case to an end. And being once finished, lo, it was also good. And from his soul, from music and idea, new works struggled upward to birth and, taking shape, gave out light and sound, ringing and shimmering, and giving hint of their infinite origin—as in a shell we hear the sighing of the sea whence it came.

◇◇◇*Herman Melville (1819-1891). The great American novelist, author of Typee, Omoo, Mardi, Redburn, Moby Dick. A great stylist, symbolist. He also wrote sketches, stories and poetry and several superb novellas.*

THE PIAZZA

BY HERMAN MELVILLE

> *"With fairest flowers,*
> *Whilst summer lasts, and I live here, Fidele—"*

When I removed into the country, it was to occupy an old-fashioned farm-house, which had no piazza—a deficiency the more regretted, because not only did I like piazzas, as somehow combining the coziness of in-doors with the freedom of out-doors, and it is so pleasant to inspect your thermometer there, but the country round about was such a picture, that in berry time no boy climbs hill or crosses vale without coming upon easels planted in every nook, and sun-burnt painters painting there. A very paradise of painters. The circle of the stars cut by the circle of the mountains. At least, so looks it from the house; though, once upon the mountains, no circle of them can you see. Had the site been chosen five rods off, this charmed ring would not have been.

The house is old. Seventy years since, from the heart of the Hearth Stone Hills, they quarried the Kaaba, or Holy Stone, to which, each Thanksgiving, the social pilgrims used to come. So long ago, that, in digging for the foundation, the workmen used both spade and axe fighting the Troglodytes of those subterranean parts—sturdy roots of a sturdy wood, encamped upon what is now a long land-slide of sleeping meadow, sloping away off from my poppy-bed. Of that knit wood, but one survivor stands—an elm, lonely through steadfastness.

Whoever built the house, he builded better than he knew; or else Orion in the zenith flashed down his Damocles' sword to him some starry night, and said, "Build there." For how, otherwise, could it have entered the builder's mind, that, upon the clearing being

284

made, such a purple prospect would be his?—nothing less than Greylock, with all his hills about him, like Charlemagne among his peers.

Now, for a house, so situated in such a country, to have no piazza for the convenience of those who might desire to feast upon the view, and take their time and ease about it, seemed as much of an omission as if a picture-gallery should have no bench; for what but picture-galleries are the marble halls of these same limestone hills?—galleries hung, month after month anew, with pictures ever fading into pictures ever fresh. And beauty is like piety—you cannot run and read it; tranquillity and constancy, with, now-a-days, an easy chair, are needed. For though, of old, when reverence was in vogue, and indolence was not, the devotees of Nature, doubtless, used to stand and adore—just as, in the cathedrals of those ages, the worshipers of a higher Power did—yet, in these times of failing faith and feeble knees, we have the piazza and the pew.

During the first year of my residence, the more leisurely to witness the coronation of Charlemagne (weather permitting, they crown him every sunrise and sunset), I chose me, on the hill-side bank near by, a royal lounge of turf—a green velvet lounge, with long, moss-padded back; while at the head, strangely enough, there grew (but, I suppose, for heraldry) three tufts of blue violets in a field-argent of wild strawberries; and a trellis, with honeysuckle, I set for canopy. Very majestical lounge, indeed. So much so, that here, as with reclining majesty of Denmark in his orchard, a sly ear-ache invaded me. But, if damps abound at times in Westminster Abbey, because it is so old, why not within this monastery of mountains, which is older?

A piazza must be had.

The house was wide—my fortune narrow; so that, to build a panoramic piazza, one round and round, it could not be—although, indeed, considering the matter by rule and square, the carpenters, in the kindest way, were anxious to gratify my furthest wishes, at I've forgotten how much a foot.

Upon but one of the four sides would prudence grant me what I wanted. Now, which side?

To the east, that long camp of the Hearth Stone Hills, fading far away towards Quito; and every fall, a small white flake of something

peering suddenly, of a coolish morning, from the topmost cliff—
the season's new-dropped lamb, its earliest fleece; and then the
Christmas dawn, draping those dun highlands with red-barred
plaids and tartans—goodly sight from your piazza, that. Goodly
sight; but, to the north is Charlemagne—can't have the Hearth
Stone Hills with Charlemagne.

Well, the south side. Apple-trees are there. Pleasant, of a balmy
morning, in the month of May, to sit and see that orchard, white-
budded, as for a bridal; and, in October, one green arsenal yard;
such piles of ruddy shot. Very fine, I grant; but, to the north is
Charlemagne.

The west side, look. An upland pasture, alleying away into a
maple wood at top. Sweet, in opening spring, to trace upon the hill-
side, otherwise gray and bare—to trace, I say, the oldest paths by
their streaks of earliest green. Sweet, indeed, I can't deny; but, to
the north is Charlemagne.

So Charlemagne, he carried it. It was not long after 1848; and,
somehow, about that time, all round the world, these kings, they
had the casting vote, and voted for themselves.

No sooner was ground broken, than all the neighborhood, neighbor Dives, in particular, broke, too—into a laugh. Piazza to the
north! Winter piazza! Wants, of winter midnights, to watch the
Aurora Borealis, I suppose; hope he's laid in good store of Polar
muffs and mittens.

That was in the lion month of March. Not forgotten are the blue
noses of the carpenters, and how they scouted at the greenness of
the cit, who would build his sole piazza to the north. But March
don't last forever; patience, and August comes. And then, in the cool
elysium of my northern bower, I, Lazarus in Abraham's bosom, cast
down the hill a pitying glance on poor old Dives, tormented in the
purgatory of his piazza to the south.

But, even in December, this northern piazza does not repel—
nipping cold and gusty though it be, and the north wind, like any
miller, bolting by the snow, in finest flour—for then, once more, with
frosted beard, I pace the sleety deck, weathering Cape Horn.

In summer, too, Canute-like, sitting here, one is often reminded
of the sea. For not only do long ground-swells roll the slanting grain,
and little wavelets of the grass ripple over upon the low piazza, as

their beach, and the blown down of dandelions is wafted like the spray, and the purple of the mountains is just the purple of the billows, and a still August noon broods upon the deep meadows, as a calm upon the Line; but the vastness and the lonesomeness are so oceanic, and the silence and the sameness, too, that the first peep of a strange house, rising beyond the trees, is for all the world like spying, on the Barbary coast, an unknown sail.

And this recalls my inland voyage to fairy-land. A true voyage; but, take it all in all, interesting as if invented.

From the piazza, some uncertain object I had caught, mysteriously snugged away, to all appearance, in a sort of purpled breast-pocket, high up in a hopper-like hollow, or sunken angle, among the northwestern mountains—yet, whether, really, it was on a mountain-side, or a mountain-top, could not be determined; because, though, viewed from favorable points, a blue summit, peering up away behind the rest, will, as it were, talk to you over their heads, and plainly tell you, that, though he (the blue summit) seems among them, he is not of them (God forbid!), and, indeed, would have you know that he considers himself—as, to say truth, he has good right —by several cubits their superior, nevertheless, certain ranges, here and there double-filed, as in platoons, so shoulder and follow up upon one another, with their irregular shapes and heights, that, from the piazza, a nigher and lower mountain will, in most states of the atmosphere, effacingly shade itself away into a higher and further one; that an object, bleak on the former's crest, will, for all that, appear nested in the latter's flank. These mountains, somehow, they play at hide-and-seek and all before one's eyes.

But, be that as it may, the spot in question was, at all events, so situated as to be only visible, and then but vaguely, under certain witching conditions of light and shadow.

Indeed, for a year or more, I knew not there was such a spot, and might, perhaps, have never known, had it not been for a wizard afternoon in autumn—late in autumn—a mad poet's afternoon; when the turned maple woods in the broad basin below me, having lost their first vermilion tint, dully smoked, like smouldering towns, when flames expire upon their prey; and rumor had it, that this smokiness in the general air was not all Indian summer—which was not used to be so sick a thing, however mild—but, in great part, was blown from far-off forests, for weeks on fire, in Vermont; so that no wonder the sky was ominous as Hecate's cauldron—and two sportsmen, crossing a red stubble buck-wheat field, seemed guilty Macbeth and foreboding Banquo; and the hermit-sun, hutted in an Adullum cave, well towards the south, according to his season, did little else but, by indirect reflection of narrow rays shot down a Simplon pass among the clouds, just steadily paint one small, round, strawberry mole upon the wan cheek of northwestern hills. Signal as a candle. One spot of radiance, where all else was shade.

Fairies there, thought I; some haunted ring where fairies dance.

Time passed; and the following May, after a gentle shower upon the mountains—a little shower islanded in misty seas of sunshine; such a distant shower—and sometimes two, and three, and four of them, all visible together in different parts—as I love to watch from the piazza, instead of thunder storms, as I used to, which wrap old Greylock, like a Sinai, till one thinks swart Moses must be climbing among scathed hemlocks there; after, I say, that gentle shower, I saw a rainbow, resting its further end just where, in autumn, I had marked the mole. Fairies there, thought I; remembering that rainbows bring out the blooms, and that, if one can but get to the rainbow's end, his fortune is made in a bag of gold. Yon rainbow's end, would I were there, thought I. And none the less I wished it, for now first noticing what seemed some sort of glen, or grotto, in the mountain side; at least, whatever it was, viewed through the rainbow's medium, it glowed like the Potosi mine. But a work-a-day neighbor said, no doubt it was but some old barn—an abandoned one, its broadside beaten in, the acclivity its background. But I, though I had never been there, I knew better.

A few days after, a cheery sunrise kindled a golden sparkle in the same spot as before. The sparkle was of that vividness, it seemed as if it could only come from glass. The building, then—if building, after all, it was—could, at least, not be a barn, much less an abandoned one; stale hay ten years musting in it. No; if aught built by mortal, it must be a cottage; perhaps long vacant and dismantled, but this very spring magically fitted up and glazed.

Again, one noon, in the same direction, I marked, over dimmed tops of terraced foliage, a broader gleam, as of a silver buckler, held sunwards over some croucher's head; which gleam, experience in like cases taught, must come from a roof newly shingled. This, to me, made pretty sure the recent occupancy of that far cot in fairy-land.

Day after day, now, full of interest in my discovery, what time I could spare from reading the *Midsummer Night's Dream*, and all about Titania, wishfully I gazed off towards the hills; but in vain. Either troops of shadows, an imperial guard, with slow pace and solemn, defiled along the steeps; or, routed by pursuing light, fled broadcast from east to west—old wars of Lucifer and Michael; or the mountains, though unvexed by these mirrored sham fights in the sky, had an atmosphere otherwise unfavorable for fairy views. I was sorry; the more so, because I had to keep my chamber for some time after—which chamber did not face those hills.

At length, when pretty well again, and sitting out, in the September morning, upon the piazza, and thinking to myself, when, just after a little flock of sheep, the farmer's banded children passed, a-nutting, and said, "How sweet a day"—it was, after all, but what their fathers call a weather-breeder—and, indeed, was become so sensitive through my illness, as that I could not bear to look upon a Chinese creeper of my adoption, and which, to my delight, climbing a post of the piazza, had burst out in starry bloom, but now, if you removed the leaves a little, showed millions of strange, cankerous worms, which, feeding upon those blossoms, so shared their blessed hue, as to make it unblessed evermore—worms, whose germs had doubtless lurked in the very bulb which, so hopefully, I had planted: in this ingrate peevishness of my weary convalescence, was I sitting there; when, suddenly looking off, I saw the golden mountain-window, dazzling like a deep-sea dolphin. Fairies there, thought I, once more; the queen of fairies at her fairy-window; at any rate, some glad mountain-girl; it will do me good, it will cure this weariness, to look on her. No more; I'll launch my yawl—ho, cheerly, heart! and push away for fairy-land—for rainbow's end, in fairy-land.

How to get to fairy-land, by what road, I did not know; nor could any one inform me; not even one Edmund Spenser, who had been there—so he wrote me—further than that to reach fairy-land, it must be voyaged to, and with faith. I took the fairy-mountain's bearings, and the first fine day, when strength permitted, got into my yawl—high-pommeled, leather one—cast off the fast, and away I sailed, free voyager as an autumn leaf. Early dawn; and, sallying westward, I sowed the morning before me.

Some miles brought me nigh the hills; but out of present sight of them. I was not lost; for road-side golden-rods, as guide-posts, pointed, I doubted not, the way to the golden window. Following them, I came to a lone and languid region, where the grass-grown ways were traveled but by drowsy cattle, that, less waked than stirred by day, seemed to walk in sleep. Browse, they did nòt—the enchanted never eat. At least, so says Don Quixote, that sagest sage that ever lived.

On I went, and gained at last the fairy mountain's base, but saw yet no fairy ring. A pasture rose before me. Letting down five mouldering bars—so moistly green, they seemed fished up from some sunken wreck—a wigged old Aries, long-visaged, and with crumpled horn, came snuffing up; and then, retreating, decorously led on along a milky-way of white-weed, past dim-clustering Pleiades and Hyades, of small forget-me-nots; and would have led me further still his astral path, but for golden flights of yellow-birds —pilots, surely, to the golden window, to one side flying before me, from bush to bush, towards deep woods—which woods themselves were luring—and, somehow, lured, too, by their fence, banning a dark road, which, however dark, led up. I pushed through; when Aries, renouncing me now for some lost soul, wheeled, and went his wiser way. Forbidding and forbidden ground—to him.

A winter wood road, matted all along with winter-green. By the side of pebbly waters—waters the cheerier for their solitude; beneath swaying fir-boughs, petted by no season, but still green in all, on I journeyed—my horse and I; on, by an old saw-mill, bound down and hushed with vines, that his grating voice no more was heard; on, by a deep flume clove through snowy marble, vernal-tinted, where freshet eddies had, on each side, spun out empty chapels in the living rock; on, where Jacks-in-the-pulpit, like their Baptist namesake, preached but to the wilderness; on, where a huge, cross-grain block, fern-bedded, showed where, in forgotten times, man after man had tried to split it, but lost his wedges for his pains —which wedges yet rusted in their holes; on, where, ages past, in step-like ledges of a cascade, skull-hollow pots had been churned out by ceaseless whirling of a flintstone—ever wearing, but itself unworn; on, by wild rapids pouring into a secret pool, but soothed by circling there awhile, issued forth serenely; on, to less broken ground, and by a little ring, where, truly, fairies must have danced, or else some wheel-tire been heated—for all was bare; still on, and up, and out into a hanging orchard, where maidenly looked down upon me a crescent moon, from morning.

My horse hitched low his head. Red apples rolled before him; Eve's apples; seek-no-furthers. He tasted one, I another; it tasted of the ground. Fairy-land not yet, thought I, flinging my bridle to a humped old tree, that crooked out an arm to catch it. For the way now lay where path was none, and none might go but by himself, and only go by daring. Through blackberry brakes that tried to pluck me back, though I but strained towards fruitless growths of mountain-laurel; up slippery steeps to barren heights, where stood none to welcome. Fairy-land not yet, thought I, though the morning is here before me.

Foot-sore enough and weary, I gained not then my journey's end, but came ere long to a craggy pass, dipping towards growing regions still beyond. A zigzag road, half overgrown with blueberry bushes, here turned among the cliffs. A rent was in their ragged sides; through it a little track branched off, which, upwards threading that short defile, came breezily out above, to where the mountain-top, part sheltered northward, by a taller brother, sloped gently off a space, ere darkly plunging; and here, among fantastic rocks, reposing in a herd, the foot-track wound, half beaten, up to a little, low-storied, grayish cottage, capped, nun-like, with a peaked roof.

On one slope, the roof was deeply weather-stained, and, nigh the turfy eaves-trough, all velvet-napped; no doubt the snail-monks founded mossy priories there. The other slope was newly shingled. On the north side, doorless and windowless, the clap-boards, innocent of paint, were yet green as the north side of lichened pines, or copperless hulls of Japanese junks, becalmed. The whole base, like those of the neighboring rocks, was rimmed about with shaded streaks of richest sod; for, with hearth-stones in fairy-land, the natural rock, though housed, preserves to the last, just as in open fields, its fertilizing charm; only, by necessity, working now at a remove, to the sward without. So, at least, says Oberon, grave authority in fairy lore. Though setting Oberon aside, certain it is, that, even in the common world, the soil, close up to farm-houses, as close up to pasture rocks, is, even though untended, ever richer than it is a few rods off—such gentle, nurturing heat is radiated there.

But with this cottage, the shaded streaks were richest in its front and about its entrance, where the ground-sill, and especially the door-sill had, through long eld, quietly settled down.

No fence was seen, no inclosure. Near by—ferns, ferns, ferns; further—woods, woods, woods; beyond—mountains, mountains, mountains; then—sky, sky, sky. Turned out in aerial commons, pasture for the mountain moon. Nature, and but nature, house and all; even a low cross-pile of silver birch, piled openly, to season; up among whose silvery sticks, as through the fencing of some sequestered grave, spring vagrant raspberry bushes—willful assertors of their right of way.

The foot-track, so dainty narrow, just like a sheep-track, led through long ferns that lodged. Fairy-land at last, thought I; Una and her lamb dwell here. Truly, a small abode—mere palanquin, set down on the summit, in a pass between two worlds, participant of neither.

A sultry hour, and I wore a light hat, of yellow sinnet, with white duck trowsers—both relics of my tropic seagoing. Clogged in the muffling ferns, I softly stumbled, staining the knees a sea-green.

Pausing at the threshold, or rather where threshold once had been, I saw, through the open door-way, a lonely girl, sewing at a lonely window. A pale-cheeked girl, and fly-specked window, with wasps about the mended upper panes. I spoke. She shyly started, like some Tahiti girl, secreted for a sacrifice, first catching sight, through palms, of Captain Cook. Recovering, she bade me enter; with her apron brushed off a stool; then silently resumed her own. With thanks I took the stool; but now, for a space, I, too, was mute. This, then, is the fairy-mountain house, and here, the fairy queen sitting at her fairy window.

I went up to it. Downwards, directed by the tunneled pass, as through a leveled telescope, I caught sight of a far-off, soft, azure world. I hardly knew it, though I came from it.

"You must find this view very pleasant," said I, at last.

"Oh, sir," tears starting in her eyes, "the first time I looked out of this window, I said 'never, never shall I weary of this.'"

"And what wearies you of it now?"

"I don't know," while a tear fell; "but it is not the view, it is Marianna."

Some months back, her brother, only seventeen, had come hither, a long way from the other side, to cut wood and burn coal, and she, elder sister, had accompanied him. Long had they been orphans, and now, sole inhabitants of the sole house upon the mountain. No guest came, no traveler passed. The zigzag, perilous road was only used at seasons by the coal wagons. The brother was absent the entire day, sometimes the entire night. When at evening, fagged out, he did come home, he soon left his bench, poor fellow, for his bed; just as one, at last, wearily quits that, too, for still deeper rest. The bench, the bed, the grave.

Silent I stood by the fairy window, while these things were being told.

"Do you know," said she at last, as stealing from her story, "do you know who lives yonder?—I have never been down into that country—away off there, I mean; that house, that marble one," pointing far across the lower landscape; "have you not caught it? there, on the long hill-side: the field before, the woods behind; the white shines out against their blue; don't you mark it? the only house in sight."

I looked; and after a time, to my surprise, recognized, more by its position than its aspect, or Marianna's description, my own abode, glimmering much like this mountain one from the piazza. The mirage haze made it appear less a farm-house than King Charming's palace.

"I have often wondered who lives there; but it must be some happy one; again this morning was I thinking so."

"Some happy one," returned I, starting; "and why do you think that? You judge some rich one lives there?"

"Rich or not, I never thought; but it looks so happy, I can't tell how; and it is so far away. Sometimes I think I do but dream it is there. You should see it in a sunset."

"No doubt the sunset gilds it finely; but not more than the sunrise does this house, perhaps."

"This house? The sun is a good sun, but it never gilds this house. Why should it? This old house is rotting. That makes it so mossy. In the morning, the sun comes in at this old window, to be sure—boarded up, when first we came; a window I can't keep clean, do what I may—and half burns, and nearly blinds me at my sewing, besides setting the flies and wasps astir—such flies and wasps as only lone mountain houses know. See, here is the curtain—this apron—I try to shut it out with them. It fades it, you see. Sun gild this house? not that ever Marianna saw."

"Because when this roof is gilded most, then you stay here within."

"The hottest, weariest hour of day, you mean? Sir, the sun gilds not this roof. It leaked so, brother newly shingled all one side. Did you not see it? The north side, where the sun strikes most on what the rain has wetted. The sun is a good sun; but this roof, it first scorches, and then rots. An old house. They went West, and are long dead, they say, who built it. A mountain house. In winter no fox could den in it. That chimney-place has been blocked up with snow, just like a hollow stump."

"Yours are strange fancies, Marianna."

"They but reflect the things."

"Then I should have said, 'These are strange things,' rather than, 'Yours are strange fancies.' "

"As you will"; and took up her sewing.

Something in those quiet words, or in that quiet act, it made me mute again; while, noting, through the fairy window, a broad shadow stealing on, as cast by some gigantic condor, floating at brooding poise on outstretched wings, I marked how, by its deeper and inclusive dusk, it wiped away into itself all lesser shades of rock or fern.

"You watch the cloud," said Marianna.

"No, a shadow; a cloud's, no doubt—though that I cannot see. How did you know it? Your eyes are on your work."

"It dusked my work. There, now the cloud is gone, Tray comes back."

"How?"

"The dog, the shaggy dog. At noon, he steals off, of himself, to change his shape—returns, and lies down awhile, nigh the door.

Don't you see him? His head is turned round at you; though, when you came, he looked before him."

"Your eyes rest but on your work; what do you speak of?"

"By the window, crossing."

"You mean this shaggy shadow—the nigh one? And, yes, now that I mark it, it is not unlike a large, black Newfoundland dog. The invading shadow gone, the invaded one returns. But I do not see what casts it."

"For that, you must go without."

"One of those grassy rocks, no doubt."

"You see his head, his face?"

"The shadow's? You speak as if *you* saw it, and all the time your eyes are on your work."

"Tray looks at you," still without glancing up; "this is his hour; I see him."

"Have you, then, so long sat at this mountain-window, where but clouds and vapors pass, that, to you, shadows are as things, though you speak of them as of phantoms; that, by familiar knowledge, working like a second sight, you can, without looking for them, tell just where they are, though, as having mice-like feet, they creep about, and come and go; that, to you, these lifeless shadows are as living friends, who, though out of sight, are not out of mind, even in their faces—is it so?"

"That way I never thought of it. But the friendliest one, that used to soothe my weariness so much, coolly quivering on the ferns, it was taken from me, never to return, as Tray did just now. The shadow of a birch. The tree was struck by lightning, and brother cut it up. You saw the cross-pile out-doors—the buried root lies under it; but not the shadow. That is flown, and never will come back, nor ever anywhere stir again."

Another cloud here stole along, once more blotting out the dog, and blackening all the mountain; while the stillness was so still, deafness might have forgot itself, or else believed that noiseless shadow spoke.

"Birds, Marianna, singing-birds, I hear none; I hear nothing. Boys and bob-o-links, do they never come a-berrying up here?"

"Birds, I seldom hear; boys, never. The berries mostly ripe and fall—few, but me, the wiser."

"But yellow-birds showed me the way—part way, at least."

"And then flew back. I guess they play about the mountain-side, but don't make the top their home. And no doubt you think that, living so lonesome here, knowing nothing, hearing nothing—little, at least, but sound of thunder and the fall of trees—never reading, seldom speaking, yet ever wakeful, this is what gives me my strange thoughts—for so you call them—this weariness and wakefulness together. Brother, who stands and works in open air, would I could rest like him; but mine is mostly but dull woman's work—sitting, sitting, restless sitting."

"But, do you not go walk at times? These woods are wide."

"And lonesome; lonesome, because so wide. Sometimes, 'tis true, of afternoons, I go a little way; but soon come back again. Better feel lone by hearth, than rock. The shadows hereabouts I know—those in the woods are strangers."

"But the night?"

"Just like the day. Thinking, thinking—a wheel I cannot stop; pure want of sleep it is that turns it."

"I have heard that, for this wakeful weariness, to say one's prayers, and then lay one's head upon a fresh hop pillow—"

"Look!"

Through the fairy window, she pointed down the steep to a small garden patch near by—mere pot of rifled loam, half rounded in by sheltering rocks—where, side by side, some feet apart, nipped and puny, two hop-vines climbed two poles, and, gaining their tip-ends, would have then joined over in an upward clasp, but the baffled shoots, groping awhile in empty air, trailed back whence they sprung.

"You have tried the pillow, then?"

"Yes."

"And prayer?"

"Prayer and pillow."

"Is there no other cure, or charm?"

"Oh, if I could but once get to yonder house, and but look upon whoever the happy being is that lives there! A foolish thought: why do I think it? Is it that I live so lonesome, and know nothing?"

"I, too, know nothing; and, therefore, cannot answer; but, for your sake, Marianna, well could wish that I were that happy one of the happy house you dream you see: for then you would behold him now, and, as you say, this weariness might leave you."

—Enough. Launching my yawl no more for fairy-land, I stick to the piazza. It is my box-royal; and this amphitheatre, my theatre of San Carlo. Yes, the scenery is magical—the illusion so complete. And Madam Meadow Lark, my prima donna, plays her grand engagement here; and, drinking in her sunrise note, which, Memnon-like, seems struck from the golden window, how far from me the weary face behind it.

But, every night, when the curtain falls, truth comes in with darkness. No light shows from the mountain. To and fro I walk the piazza deck, haunted by Marianna's face, and many as real a story.

◇◇◇*Martin Anderson Nexo (1869–1954). Danish novelist and short-story writer. The most widely famous Danish author of his time, he wrote moving accounts of his bitter childhood and of the lives of the socially oppressed in Denmark. See Pelle the Conqueror, Ditte, Days in the Sun, Under the Open Sky.*

BIRDS OF PASSAGE

BY MARTIN ANDERSEN NEXO

Peter Nikolai Ferdinand Baltasar Rasmussen Kjöng, whose name—following inviolable phonetic laws not to be explained here—in the course of time took the form of Nebuchadnezzar, was a man who had seen the world and knew the human race.

By trade he was a shoemaker; by nature, a wandering journeyman. He was one of those people in whose blood the rotation of the earth has become an urge, and who therefore feel themselves compelled to rotate around our globe like so many satellites. The desire to set out for the unknown was the moving power of his life; and he knew nothing finer than to break away, no matter from what. Thus he broke away from happiness several times, and felt all the happier for it.

He had wandered through the greater part of the civilized world, clearly and firmly defining civilization as synonymous with the wearing of leather shoes. He knew all the ins and outs of the German hostelries and the French highways, had walked across the Pyrenees and Alps more than once, and had stood with one foot in Switzerland and the other in France, spitting far down the Italian slopes. He had been in Sicily, at Gibraltar, in Asia Minor.

On his travels he had become acquainted with all the mysteries of modern traffic. He knew where it was possible to hang between the wheels of a freight car, and where it was more advisable to pretend having lost a ticket or to appeal to the generosity of the

From *Denmark's Best Stories*. (Translated by Lida Siboni Hanson.) By permission of W. W. Norton & Co. Copyright 1928 by The American-Scandinavian Foundation.

conductor. He slipped to Sicily from Gibraltar, by hiding in the cable-hold of a big steamer. After a while his hunger drove him to the deck, where he received a sound thrashing and countless threats of being thrown overboard to the sharks. But, after all, he reached his destination.

From Sicily he was to go as a stoker on another steamer, thereby earning his passage to Greece. But as it was soon discovered that he knew nothing about stoking, he was put ashore in Brindisi. Here he rubbed his feet with tallow, and walked north through the country, around the Adriatic, and down on the other side. It took him months, but this time also he gained his end. And what better use could he make of his time? King Nebuchadnezzar possessed some of the patience of a planet: he wandered for the sake of wandering, without any other purpose and without seeking other distractions. In the Balkans he had the pleasure of being captured by brigands who, however, rejected him with the greatest contempt after discovering the condition of his clothes. Afterward he used to say, with a magnificent gesture, "A mouse saved the king of the animals, but a louse saved King Nebuchadnezzar."

He took a short trip to California to have a look at the gold; but there he quickly came to the conclusion that gold was too heavy an article for a wandering journeyman, and he hurried back to New York, hanging between the axles of a coal car. On this occasion he made the discovery that the Americans really were practical people. In Germany the railroad employees would go peering under the trains with lanterns in search of tramps, who were then pulled out and dragged to the police court. There they were questioned, and often solemnly expelled from the district because of their criminal use of the benefits of society. But in America a man would run back and forth with a hose, and simply squirt cold water under the train. That made one's clothes freeze when the train put on its hellish speed, and for the rest of his life a fellow would have rheumatism in his left shoulder.

In New York he tried to get a job, first as chief cook and then as deck hand, in order to earn his passage back to Copenhagen. As both plans failed, he had a stroke and fell over in the street. All he then had to do was to open his eyes a little at the right moment and whisper, "Dane." He was taken to the Danish consulate, and from there transported back to Denmark.

He had indeed seen life and mankind! His trade had carried him over half the earth. He had worked in all big cities, as short a time as possible in each so as to get around and see them all. He had, as it were in passing, wheedled every secret out of his trade. He did not spend much time working, but what he produced was masterly. His work stood out among that of thousands of others as long as there was one whit left of it.

He thought with a smile of the greasy little shop where he had learned his trade. Now he was going to make things hum. It was his plan to settle down in Denmark and profit by his experience in the great world, following the maxim that a man owes his best to his own country. He hung around for about a month, so as to accustom his digestive organs to home cooking, whereupon he went to work in a shoemaker's shop.

But King Nebuchadnezzar was used to moving in big spaces, according to great simple laws. On his wanderings he had learned to eliminate and discard. Life had taught him thoroughly that most of the accessories which were burdening the shops were unnecessary baggage—at least to him who had the unique talent of simplification. The big apparatus set in motion by a Danish shoemaker before beginning his work could not but seem comical to a man who more than once had turned out first-class products, sitting by the wayside and only equipped with an awl, a knife, a small amount of shoemaker's thread, and the broken leg of a chair for the final polishing.

The result was that he did not hesitate to sell the superfluous tools wherever he went. But although this did not impair his work, his bosses did not like it, and deducted the cost from his wages. They even fired him and threatened to turn him over to the police.

He began to work in his lodging, and extended his economy from tools to material. Moreover, he knew the value of cardboard, and thus was able to save a surprisingly big part of the leather delivered by the bosses according to exact measurement. He sold this, and used the money to stretch his Blue Monday to Wednesday evening.

His comrades considered him a genius, by which they meant a person who could turn out a marvelously neat piece of work with the speed of lightning and out of almost nothing, and who loved idleness and hunger and little drams above anything else in this world.

Doubtless King Nebuchadnezzar was a genius. When he worked, he worked—nobody could say that his fingers acted like thumbs. A howling blue flame—zip! Two pair of ladies' shoes done before five. Then he would drink up his double wages, sleep off his debauch on a pile of paving-stones or behind a fence, and at a pinch be ready to resume work next morning.

But he did not like to do this. He preferred to hustle three pair together in one day, instead of working two days in succession.

While at work, he was lost to the world. But when he would straighten his back to go on a spree, he would sometimes find that he had to go alone. Time after time the most ridiculous of all phenomena spoiled his plans: people had no time. The Lord help us, no time to carouse! He could not understand it, but it was a fact.

It was comical beyond words. It took him some time to have his laugh and finally discover that he was a lonely man. His comrades had simply gone back on him and his firm convictions, and had—perhaps a little sheepishly—continued their drudgery so as not to fall behind. They had become useful citizens, petty respectable members of society with stomachs and earnest political consciences. They jogged to work at seven in the morning and went home at six in the evening—he could have set his watch by them if he had had one. In the evening they went to political meetings. They even married and shuffled to the circus with wives and children on Sunday afternoons. They called that enjoying life—phew!

Those that went on sprees were no longer men of his kind who felt the need of hammering out the dents given them by drudgery. More and more the magnificent debauches passed into the hands of professional toughs. King Nebuchadnezzar was not a tough. He was simply a free man who happened to have moved around and seen the world while his colleagues continued being slaves.

Well, that was their own funeral—if they were willing to be drummed together in factories and big workshops at the stroke of the clock, all right! King Nebuchadnezzar went on working in his lodging, refusing to work in the shops. He was his own boss. He was not going to have a foreman standing around watching all his doings. And as to being a member of the Union and having to obey all its orders down to the very air one breathed—the devil, no!

King Nebuchadnezzar was quite able to look after his own affairs.

He wanted the right to do three days' work in one and spend the next two days enjoying life. No need to worry about the prices. One day he learned that the Union had succeeded in prohibiting all home work. He was unspeakably scornful. "They can't touch *me*," he said, and continued working in his own way. Thanks to his efficiency, the bosses employed him whenever they needed an especially good man.

However, they could only employ him secretly, and ordinarily they preferred to follow the rules laid down by the Union. One never knew what to expect from King Nebuchadnezzar: right in the middle of a piece of pressing work ordered by some prominent person he might suddenly become possessed by the devil. Nor could he live on air while the few notabilities Denmark could boast were wearing the shoe leather that came from his hand.

Like all geniuses, he finally came to the conclusion that conditions in Denmark were too narrow. He would have to turn his back on his miserable country once more. He had kept the great world in mind, and always thought of it with gratitude and joy. Once more he broke away.

But he had lost the exhilaration of former days when his bones, like those of the birds, had been filled with air, and he felt that he must flit from one place to the other. The centrifugal force had left him; only gravity remained and bound him to the earth. He could not understand it; still it was so. It was an effort for him to set out on his flight, whereas it had formerly been an effort to remain quiet.

One no longer flew out at random—one sat down soberly and thought the matter over. The rotation of the earth no longer whirled mountains and rivers and unending white roads through one's brain. Now the question was whether or not one could stand the wear and tear. Certain things were required, especially strong feet; and it was advantageous to have a stomach that could crush stones. In the course of time he had lost these two assets. Then there was the general feeling of heaviness as if one were glued to the earth. The great world with its eternal restlessness and tension no longer tempted him. He had become afraid of it. A bit of a home with soft boiled food, warm clothes, a room with a clean bed, was all he aspired to now.

He tried to realize his wishes and keep the wolf from the door by allowing himself to be supported by a feeble-minded woman who lived on what the day might bring. They were always squabbling except when they were drunk. But a year or two of this life cured him thoroughly of all desire for a home and family. Let others enjoy domesticity as much as they wanted to; he knew now what it meant!

He tried to take up his trade again, but the door was irrevocably closed to a vagrant like him. Finally he resolved to accept what great men in antiquity had accepted before him: meals at the cost of the community. To this end he sought and received admittance to the prytaneum situated on Aaboulevard between Örstedsvej and Svineryggen—sometimes referred to as the public workhouse.

He was at once given awl and waxed end, and shown his seat among the shoemakers. But he had not entered the place in order to create any unfair competition with the outer world. Neither had he revolted against fixed working hours and workshop rules in order to sit as a slave with cropped hair in the workroom of the inmates and be granted one hour's liberty in the yard, dressed in the uniform of the institution and walking at the regulation pace. He loved liberty still more than his art, and, thanks to the rheumatism in his shoulder and his sadly trembling hands which were utterly unable to hold the point of the knife away from the vamps, he was declared impossible as an artisan.

The officials then tried him on the light brigade which every day swarms over the bridges and markets of Copenhagen, armed with brooms and shovels. He would saunter along and pass his broom indolently over the pavement, while the sparrows fluttered wildly in the sweepings, and life around him pulsated in a restless, feverish chase. He would watch the passionate hurry with a mild, sedate smile like one who knows the stakes but is safely out of the game. He had lived as deeply and fully as any of the rest, therefore it tempted him no longer. But when he saw a street-worker stride over piles of stone or gravel to his coat and take a clear, little bottle out of his pocket, he would feel a faint pang and a longing to lift it caressingly to his mouth. But otherwise he was quite satisfied and envied nobody—not a mother's soul!

One afternoon as he was sweeping Höjbroplads, lost in quiet, happy content, he saw something which robbed his philosophical heart of its calm and made it pound and flutter.

A woman came shuffling from Köbmagergade, crossed Höjbroplads, and walked toward the Bourse. She wore a black, shiny straw hat, the brim of which had become detached from the crown and was jolting on the bridge of her nose so that she was peering over it as through a visor. Besides this, she wore the remains of an old French shawl, a thin, scant skirt, and prunella shoes. Her cheeks and nose were protruding like three red pippins. She leaned forward and wriggled her hips coquettishly, not lifting her feet, but sliding them over the pavement. His expert eye saw at once that she did this so as not to lose her shoes: both vamps were split.

His wildly pounding heart told him that the woman was Malvina, his lady, his last and only great—but also unhappy—love, the woman who had shared her bed and her liquor with him, whom he had beaten and who had returned his blows, according to their relative states of drunkenness—the lady whom he had bidden a heart-rending farewell the day when they had knocked at the door of the workhouse, and had been admitted respectively to the female and male departments.

Evidently she had a free afternoon and was going out on a jaunt —Malvina who from the time of her confirmation to her eighteenth year had been the mistress of a decrepit count!—Malvina who with all her hoarseness could lisp so genteelly, who smacked a bit of all strata, from court to gutter!—the only being he had ever met who, like him, had some of the rotation of the universe in her blood.

And now she was going on a jaunt!

An irrepressible impulse to go along once more, to have just one more fling, awakened in him. He was on the point of throwing his broom aside and calling to her to wait and take him with her. But a remnant of his old presence of mind shot up in him. He dropped the broom, became quite pale, and staggered over to the overseer, Petersen, whom he asked for permission to steal away quietly as he felt sick to his stomach.

Overseer Petersen knew that King Nebuchadnezzar had no greater wish than to spend the rest of his days in the workhouse. He looked doubtfully first at his watch, then at the policeman under "the Clock," and finally at the patient. Really the man looked alarmingly ill.

"Do you think you can manage to get home by yourself?" he asked.

"Oh yes! But, of course, if I had ten öre I could ride right to the door."

"Well, see that you catch that bus!"

But King Nebuchadnezzar did not catch the bus, he was too feeble to hurry. He staggered over to Thorvaldsen's Museum where the street car was standing, but it started before he reached it, whereupon he followed it at an anxious trot, beckoning sadly to the conductor.

Overseer Petersen shook his head with misgivings. Nebuchadnezzar must be sick indeed if he thought he could catch up with an electric car. Oh well, there would be another in a minute, there were enough of them.

When King Nebuchadnezzar's calculation told him that there were houses between him and the overseer, he slackened his pace and turned from the Stormbridge into the Palace yard. It was important not to be suspected and caught on account of his uniform. Behind the Bourse he bought a huge yellow envelope for three öre and a newspaper for two öre. The remaining money was spent for a quid of tobacco. He never chewed tobacco, but simply felt uncomfortable with money in his pocket. It occurred to him that he could give the quid to his comrades. Later he realized that he might have spent the money for a milk toddy, but he was not the man to deplore his actions. He stuffed the newspaper into the envelope, put it carefully under his arm, and left the Palace yard walking as straight as an orderly on a confidential mission. The policemen on Knippelsbro looked askance at him, but he went ahead with the assurance born of an easy conscience.

He sauntered around in the bystreets behind Christianshavn market until he caught sight of Malvina, who disappeared through the door of a many-windowed house in Dronningensgade. He knew her errand at once, and went straight up to the third floor where many one-room apartments opened into a long, pitch-dark corridor.

Upon hearing Malvina's clothes rustle in the dark, he said solemnly, "Good day, Lady," and took hold of both her ears and kissed her.

"Mercy, how you scared me, little Nezzar! It might have been a strange fellow for all one can see here," she said coquettishly.

"Are you looking for the Prince, dear Lady? I shouldn't wonder if he had been ditched."

"No, I heard him cry a minute ago. But there is no key in the door."

King Nebuchadnezzar examined the lock with expert fingers and peered through the keyhole. "That is as simple as they make 'em," he said in an undertone, "if one only had a bit of wire." He thought for a moment. Then he tiptoed a few steps down the corridor to a door behind which a woman was scolding and some children were yelling. He picked the key out of the door and returned. The key fitted exactly.

"You are a great fellow, Nezzar," Malvina simpered.

"No, the landlord is a stingy louse who has had one kind of key made for the whole shootingmatch," he answered modestly, and put the key back as noiselessly as he had taken it. "That's what he is."

"Oh, you," said Malvina, rapping his fingers with small, genteel blows, faintly suggestive of aristocracy. "You always want to joke about nasty things. In our department we change every week, I want you to know."

King Nebuchadnezzar did not understand her. When she was acting the countess, the meaning of her words was sometimes hazy to him. But he knew that the origin of her refinement was genuine enough.

"Lady—" he said, and solemnly held the door open for her.

They entered a small room with one and a half narrow windows. The other half of the second window belonged to the kitchen, which measured six feet each way, and was separated from the room by a partition. Through this arrangement an alcove was formed in a corner of the room, just big enough to hold an old wooden bed, which was covered with rags. The space under it was filled with bottles. Half a table stood on its two legs leaning against the opposite wall, and in a dirty wicker cradle under the window slept a six-months-old baby sucking a pacifier made of an old curtain. The curtain had been tied into many pacifiers, which had been sucked and discarded in their turn, and were now dragging on the floor. The baby slowly pulled its present pacifier in and out while sleeping. Each time the whole heavy row was lifted and lowered; it looked like a ball fringe. The unused end of the curtain was thrown over a nail.

On the only chair in the room sat a boy of two or three years. He was tied to the chair and was evidently supposed to be looking out of the near-by window. On the window-sill before him lay the gnawed-off crusts of some lard sandwiches. The boy was asleep, his heavy head hanging down inertly to one side. His feeble breathing sounded like soft whistling. He opened two big eyes and stared at them.

"My stars, Sonny, Sonny!" cried King Nebuchadnezzar in a delighted falsetto, and stretched out his hands with a stage gesture, "don't you know your own father, eh?"

Between them they untied him, and Malvina placed him on her knees and began to clean him a little. Meanwhile the happy father strode around, giving vent to his delight in short exclamations— "You look fine that way, girl! You look mighty fine being good to him! If you could only see for yourself how fine you look with him on your lap!"

The child let them fuss with him without showing any noticeable interest. He seemed strangely dull and apathetic, breathed heavily and audibly, and evidently was not in the least impressed by the course of events. It was as if he had once for all made the resolution to walk through life unaffected by its ups and downs. There was a certain drowsiness over him. He did not by any movement help Malvina in her work, but went on breathing with a heavy, snoring sound which might well be interpreted as a purring of content.

"He makes himself heavy," said Malvina, "he just wants to be petted. And do see how plump he is, Nezzar!"

"He doesn't jabber any too much, does he?" said Nebuchadnezzar musingly. "I wonder if he can talk at all? How old did you say he was?"

"Three years, Nezzar—three years and then some. Mercy, that you could forget that!"

"Why—a man has so many more important things to think of."
Three years—oh, well, then there was time enough for him to

have his say, even if he should turn out to be a Rigsdag deputy.

"He may still learn to talk the leg off an iron pot. By the way, have you ever thought of what profession he is going to take up?"

"Lord, no," said Malvina in a frightened voice.

"Still that is as important as anything I know of! There are all kinds of possibilities in such a little body. He is a human seed, to express it nicely. Who knows, maybe some day he will sit astraddle of the whole cake!—It would be grand to see that day."

"Well, I think he is going to be a confectioner," said Malvina, in response to the word cake. Besides, she was fond of sweets.

"I don't mean any offense, Lady, but you women have no imagination. No—the time of handicraft is over. Or did you ever know a finer craftsman than King Nebuchadnezzar? And what did he get for it? Nowadays you've got to have *head*—brains are what tell in our day, see? And his head is big enough, Lord knows!—The little brat!"

King Nebuchadnezzar had taken the child's head between his big hands. "Is the yeast working in there? Is it, Sonny?" he said, laughing through tears. The thought of the boy's great future stirred him and made his hands tremble. "He doesn't say a word, he doesn't even blink. I tell you, there is backbone in him. And do you know, Malvina, I can feel the workings up here in his blessed little dome. His mind is busy even now. He'll be a good one, I tell you! Just see how calm and cool he is! Small as he is, he acts like our Lord himself, knowing the ins and outs of the whole thing. I guess nothing will hang too high for *him!*"

King Nebuchadnezzar began to whistle softly, gazing into the unknown. With his thoughts in the far future he did not hear Malvina ask him for his handkerchief. Anyway, he could not have given her any. Out there in the future his own existence was being repeated in a bigger and more successful way. He himself had beaten the record, but only in a matter which already was doomed. He had won the race hundreds of times, but he did not feel victorious. But when Sonny grew up, things were going to hum. He could sense the turmoil and bustle, and had taken part in enough of it to feel dizzy for Sonny.

His thoughts were gradually released from the future, and with a sigh he came back to earth and discovered that his throat was dry.

He took a few turns around the room and sent his restless eyes investigating in all corners. "I wonder how the wine cellar is getting on?" he said, pulling out the bottles from under the bed and holding them to the light. "Bone dry all along the line! Fine state of affairs! See here, don't you think your sister has an account somewhere around here?"

Malvina shook her head. She was busy cleaning the boy's nose with a corner of her handkerchief.

"But, my goodness, they live in style! Here she is supporting the family, and he has his sixteen crowns a week and can spend every öre of it! And you think they would have no account where one could charge a drop of liquor?" Such nonsense was incomprehensible. "Sonny, can you say 'Daddy'? My, now you look pretty! The Lord help us, I think he takes after both of us, Lady. That is what comes from agreeing in everything!"

He took a turn into the kitchen, which was the size of an ordinary table.

"They can afford running water, the spendthrifts!—Ah!"

He came back to Malvina and the child.

"Sonny, can you say 'Daddy'? Well, give me a smack, girl! You look fine with a little one on your knees! If you could only see yourself!"

But Malvina was pouting.

"You always find fault with my relatives. And yet they are grand to Sonny, keeping him here for nothing."

"Oh yes, they are good enough according to their lights," said King Nebuchadnezzar appeasingly. "Don't get on your hind legs, Mally!—Sonny!" He fumbled in his vest pocket for some gift for the boy and got hold of the tobacco quid. The deuce take it! Here he might have spent that darned five öre on something for the boy —cream, for instance. Cream was not a bit too grand for such a prince. He sauntered back to the kitchen and began to look over the plate rack, driven by some desperate hope.

Suddenly he gave a little surprised whistle: he had found a ten-öre piece under one of the cups.

He came back to Malvina with joyful, dancing steps.

"See here, Malvina, girl of my heart! run down and get five öre's worth of cream for the Prince, and brandy with the rest of the money. Tell them it is for a sick person, and they will give you better measure."

Nobody on earth, least of all Malvina herself, could help buying brandy with all the money. For one thing, the cream was sour at this time of day, also there was none to be had, and finally one could not buy brandy with less than ten öre. King Nebuchadnezzar was not the person to utter reproaches after hearing these altogether satisfactory reasons; and Sonny was already man enough to feel sufficiently compensated by a few drops of brandy on a crust of bread.

But after the drink it was as if the coziness of home life had vanished. King Nebuchadnezzar no longer felt the quiet satisfaction of dwelling in the bosom of his assembled family. Every now and then he went to the window and looked out. Some of his old flourish had returned. He was still buoyant, and felt the need of some personal outlet—the need of one more bout with the world, to say it nicely.

It was an unusually beautiful day, one of the few days when the sun triumphantly pierces the veil of smoke generally hanging over the city, and pours a flood of light over the streets. The sky, a marvelous blue between the trees on the old rampart, seemed to be nothing but limitless, immaterial space, resting in lucidity and peace. It was like looking into limpid infinity.

King Nebuchadnezzar shook himself.

"Such a day ought to be celebrated," he said, "and not be spent sitting here moping. Besides, Sonny is sleepy. I think I'll go out and get a breath of air.—If one could only have raised a few coins."

He sighed and cast a searching glance at the bare room.

"You can't show yourself publicly in that outfit!" said Malvina.

"No, of course, it would be better to be in plain clothes, but there are clothes enough in the wardrobe—any amount of them."

They examined the contents of the bed, and unanimously chose the least ragged pair of trousers and the remnants of a brown overcoat. King Nebuchadnezzar donned the finery, and contemptuously threw the tell-tale garb of the workhouse inmate on the bed.

"Now when I take a stitch here and there, you will look fine," said Malvina, and stroked him caressingly.

"Yes, that isn't half bad," he said delighted, "but they'll nab me anyhow when they see my socks."

"You'll have to let down the pants, Nezzar."

"That won't be enough! But never mind, it'll be all right to go barefoot in wooden shoes this time of year."

"I shall certainly not go with you if you are barefoot. There are plenty of others I can go with!"

"Did you think I meant it?" he said hurriedly. "We are not that far gone yet." He spoke swaggeringly, yet remained irresolute.

"You might try the attic," suggested Malvina.

"That was just what I was thinking of," he answered calmly, anxious to maintain as much as possible of his superiority over his lady. He went out quickly, and returned soon after, carrying a shabby high silk hat and a pair of worn-out boots with side inserts of elastic. "Look at the mud boats," he said, showing them triumphantly. "Of course it's a bum piece of work—still they are always better than wooden shoes. I hate wooden shoes more than anything. They ruin the profession. And think of the club-footed walk they give!"

The clothes looked like crumped paper that had been unfolded. But the couple only heeded the actual holes, and Malvina searched in vain for needle and thread. The baby in the cradle now began to move and cry, and they realized that Malvina's sister would soon come back. With much petting, they again placed Sonny on the chair near the window, and tied him so that he would not tumble out.

"It's fine for Sonny to sit there and look at the sky," said King Nebuchadnezzar, patting him gently on his thin hair. But Sonny preferred to sleep. His head dropped heavily down to one side, and he began once more to whistle softly.

The baby was angry. She had lost her pacifier, and was crying furiously, raising her naked stomach till her little body formed a bridge resting on her head and feet.

"She is hungry, poor thing," said King Nebuchadnezzar and looked around for an inspiration, "look how she humps her stomach. Would you like something poured into your little tummy, eh?"

He shyly patted her tense little drum. Then he took the empty bottle and held it to the light for inspection, but not the least particle was left. The last drop had been poured on Sonny's crust.

"It does seem a shame," said Malvina, "of course, she's not ours, still it does seem a shame."

She found a few morsels of bread which she held under the faucet, to moisten them before tying the lump into the curtain above the other knots. The baby stopped crying and began to doze, moving the whole machinery up and down with her small pumping apparatus, without realizing that she had now one more ball to keep going.

For a while King Nebuchadnezzar stood and looked at her patient drudgery. "She goes at it like a regular steam engine," he said musingly. "She'll be great when she grows up! Whew—I should hate to be the man that crosses her way. But shan't we cut all that old stuff off? It's a pity for her to lie there working at the whole mess."

"No, we better not; perhaps Sister wants to use the curtain," answered Malvina.

They sauntered aimlessly down the street. Malvina took her Nezzar's arm and walked along mincingly. "You'll take us to a nice place, won't you? Not to anything low-down? There are good places enough where *you* can get in." She spoke with such conviction that King Nebuchadnezzar felt extremely poor and powerless.

She left all details about the choice of a place entirely to him. Now and then she threw a rapt glance at him, but otherwise kept her eye modestly to the ground. It was so long since she had gone out with a man that she felt as if it were the first time. She felt as bashful as a young girl, and that was a lovely sensation. This, however, did not prevent her from stealthily watching the stores from which people turned their heads to look after the couple. King Nebuchadnezzar looked fine in a silk hat, and she knew that they created admiration of all by their appearance.

"I know where you are going to take us," she said gaily and hung heavily on his arm. But she did not know, and did not care to know. She only said it to express her blind faith in him. She wanted most of all to hang on his arm and with closed eyes walk straight into the light. Then, when they were in the full illumination, she would open her eyes quickly, and let herself be hurt and dazzled by the sudden radiance which would make her cry out.

How beautiful life could be!

King Nebuchadnezzar felt a little uneasy. When they reached the bridge leading to the heart of the city, he turned, and a minute later he turned again. Certainly, there were places enough. The whole city, brimful of splendors, was offering itself. The difficulty was to be sure of choosing the right place, so as not to sit there and be sorry afterward. He himself would have preferred to begin at one end and "do" the whole town lengthwise and crosswise. But that was out of the question if one had a lady along. He was just waiting for an idea which might save the day, a "darned good little hunch," such as he had had hundreds of times before. Meanwhile one simply had to keep going, and King Nebuchadnezzar varied his maneuvers like a skipper who tries to kill time while tacking in wait for the pilot.

Malvina began to take notice. "It seems to me we are going in a circle," she said surprised.

"But really, the first thing is to get needle and thread," mumbled King Nebuchadnezzar offended. "A gentleman—"

Malvina hugged his arm and looked innocently up to him astonished at his angry tone. And Nebuchadnezzar felt with a pang his responsibility toward this woman who walked by his side looking forward to a merry evening. She knew perfectly well that he had not a red öre, but she simply believed in him. And under normal conditions this would have been the right thing to do, for King Nebuchadnezzar was ordinarily not without resources when planning for a good time. But today his genius didn't seem to be at home. He did not feel a trace of that play of intelligence which in ways numerous and varied had supplied him with cash when he had needed it.

"We might go and dance in 'The Decanter,' " he said crestfallen, "only they won't let us in." He had the sad sensation that he was failing in the main issue. Sure, the world was chock full of excitement and fun, but what was the good if one no longer knew how to nab them? He had never quite realized the value of money, but now it began to dawn on him. Money was all right after all, when one was worn out and could think of nothing else.

Rather downcast, they sauntered up on the old rampart and sat down on a bench. The sun was setting. The dying day enveloped the city in a purple mist, which was wafted in and out among the trees on the rampart like voluptuous exhalations from a glowing, joy-sated world.

A short distance away some children were singing and dancing rounds under the trees, and at the end of the street the tower of Our Saviour's Church shone in its golden luster. It was impossible to be sad, and gradually they forgot their grudge against life and began to chat innocently about nothing and everything. The evening filled them with well-being and gentleness. With a tinge of melancholy they watched the sun take its leave, unhindered, as something too great to have its right disputed. Before it disappeared, it kissed their vapid faces and made them blush once more in giddy anticipation. Their eyes had perhaps never before shone so beautifully; far away over the city hovered the festive glow that was kindled again in them. For a short while ineffable joy—happiness unknown to the world—flowed into them and inflated their shriveled hearts.

Malvina had persuaded a little girl to go home for needle and thread. Eagerly she mended her big beautiful man here and there, surrounded by a crowd of open-mouthed children. King Nebuchadnezzar had to lie down on the bench to make the work go more quickly, and was told to turn round so as to be mended on all sides. He lay tossing about like a frolicsome puppy, overdoing everything, and making monstrous puns in order to amuse the children. In spite of the dying light, Malvina used her needle deftly and completed her work in the twinkling of an eye.

"There, Nezzar," she said, looking into his eyes elated. The last obstacle was overcome.

He gave her a humble and impotent look in return. Alas, the obstacles were overcome; there was no longer any hiding-place. Behind this careful mending, a secret hope had been lying in wait for him—for why make one's self so smart? Surely, there must be a reason! Now this hope failed before their very eyes, and revealed man's miserable poverty when deserted by his intelligence.

All his life King Nebuchadnezzar had kept his faith in himself. It had been present as a gigantic ruin in his dream of this very day, and had lured him into the attempt to revive his youth for one evening, to make a journey round the world on a small scale. That ought to be a mere trifle for a man who had tramped comfortably and easily through three continents without having a red öre in his pocket, and had partaken of all that life had to offer. And now the miserable end of it all was that he was sitting here, in the most self-evident place in the world, and had to admit his inability to pay fifty öre for admission to a dance-hall!

Of course one could always do something or other without money. Even the poorest bum must have connections enough to get a glad evening out of them without spending any money. Malvina hinted as much—after all, the women expected to hang on and get a good time out of the men. But King Nebuchadnezzar was not of the kind that sponged on his acquaintances. He much preferred to play the returned American. He had not gone out today to nibble a crumb here and there, but to visit once more the happy hunting grounds of his youth. If he found himself pushed out of the game—well, then he could call it square and return to the Institution if need be. But sit and lick the plates after the banquet— no, he couldn't do that. Leave that to those who had never been at the festive board themselves. "One has obligations toward the other fellows in the Institution," he argued aloud, thinking that even a woman would understand that. "One represents them all, so to say. But you go ahead, Lady! You will always find some guy—you with your face!"

But Malvina only clung still tighter to him and declared that she cared for nobody else in this world and wanted to stay with him. She could always find somebody else some day when he was not along.

"I expected as much of you," said King Nebuchadnezzar with emotion. "You answered as I should have done in your place."

Malvina accepted his praise with a brave smile, but suddenly burst out crying. She let herself go like a young girl, as if this were the first time her world had broken down around her. King Nebuchadnezzar did not try to console her with words, but put his arm gently round her. With her head on his shoulder she sobbed herself to sleep.

The evening had set in. Darkness was gathering under the trees of the rampart, and in the streets the lamps were lighted one by one, twinkling in the dusk. King Nebuchadnezzar's eyes had assumed a strange far-away expression.

He was gazing into the distance, farther than anyone could see. He had not the heart to stir and possibly awake Malvina, and he felt frightfully lonesome—so lonesome that he had to let things take their course and confess to himself that it was all over. He was absolutely good for nothing. He had grown old. It was a relief to acknowledge this at last, instead of trying to prop up the impossible by putting a tired shoulder to it. Well, now it was over. Life could no longer be snatched in passing. It lurched by so swiftly that, if he tried to jump on board, he only split his skull against the pavement.

But he had had his day. He had been no common trash. Gosh almighty, how he had made things hum! What precious memories he had! He could not restrain himself any longer, but felt that he must have a partaker in his reminiscences. When Malvina awoke, however, and looked at him, his whole glory faded before the disillusion in her eyes. Perhaps she had dreamed that she was in the midst of splendor.

They sat huddled close together, neither feeling the need of words. King Nebuchadnezzar wondered that Malvina did not scold him. A while ago he would have wished her to do so. It would have led to a brawl, and he could have withdrawn from it with the air of a man who would have redeemed everything if, woman-like, she had not spoiled the game by her squabble. But now he had surrendered to decrepitude, and was grateful to her for not throwing it up to him.

There were thickets growing on the slopes of the rampart, in which children and tramps had made little paths. The darkness put a soft shroud over the foliage, and here and there through the bushes the glimmering of ripples and the rustling of reeds told of the near-by water in the moat.

Something about all this went softly to King Nebuchadnezzar's heart, like a greeting from his great and good days. Here he could still in his present poor condition taste the sweetness of our great earth. A night in the open was something which he could still afford, and at the same time the gist of the whole thing. All he had attained in his life, nay, Life itself was founded on the furtive thrill he had felt when sleeping under the stars and awaking drenched by the morning dew, in the center of the whole universe. Surely, he was yet equal to as much as that!

But Malvina jumped up offended. She wasn't going to make her bed in the open air like she wouldn't say what kind of a woman. They were not used to that in her department. "We have decent beds, with all comforts—but I can certainly take myself away if you are going to be vulgar."

King Nebuchadnezzar gave her a despairing look while she carried on. She needn't have put on her aristocratic airs for his sake. He had felt the pain and loneliness of old age, and was not going to quarrel with anybody.

"You are acting so Spanish this evening," he said with a bitter smile. "One might think that one of the overseers had begun to make eyes at you."

"Why, Nezzar, for shame!" she exclaimed, offended, "you know very well that I am no scab."

Well, why not?—If that would lead to one or two small concessions. He, too, began to realize the importance of concessions, and was already slowly adapting himself to his new and humbler existence. This called to his mind the hayloft of Jensen, the livery man. He was now tired and longed for a rest, and such a hayloft could be perfectly splendid—the best thing next to a haystack in the open air.

He made his suggestion meekly, and to his surprise Malvina did not object, but rose silently. For a short time they walked southward on the rampart, then descended and crossed an empty lot where there was quite an accumulation of old boilers, rusty iron plates, and heavy, half corroded cables. Through an opening in the fence they entered a yard surrounded on three sides by low buildings and wooden barns. A black, factory-like building stood on the fourth side. King Nebuchadnezzar had taken Malvina's hand and was pulling her with him. They walked in the shadow of wagons and lumber piles, and were steering toward a low building from which was heard the steady sound of champing horses.

King Nebuchadnezzar stuck his head through the open upper half of the door and whistled softly. A youthful tension had come over his movements. He stood there straining every sense, ready to light out or change his tactics at the faintest sound. After all, this tasted magnificently of old times and the outer world. He turned and signaled to Malvina with his eyes while he stealthily unhooked the door. Then he entered the stable on tiptoe, and Malvina shuffled after him.

"Here is the hotel," he whispered, and looked around in delight. "Look, Malvina! Horses, and beautiful hay. No ordinary draught-horses either—just notice the manure; you smell the difference at once. The stable boy has gone out—fine fellow! Well, get up in the hay, Lady!"

He climbed up the ladder to the hayloft, and Malvina followed him. It was hard for her, and she held her dress together with unnecessary tightness in order to show her disapproval of Nezzar's vulgar exclamations.

That night King Nebuchadnezzar dreamed of the big plains and the starry skies. He had prepared for next day's hike by rubbing his feet with tallow and lacing his stomach firmly. Now he was resting in the finest haystack, gazing toward the distant mountains, and quietly anticipating what was to be found on the other side of them. Overhead the universe was moving to its eternal music. He sensed the unending melody of the vast night, and knew from this that he was alone. But it did not make him sad.

Malvina, dreaming too, was in "The Decanter" and was dancing the old dance called "The Crested Hen." She daintily lifted her dress far up on one side, for her leg was covered in its whole length with yellow silk.

Overseer Petersen had returned with his light brigade, and learned to his surprise that King Nebuchadnezzar had not yet arrived. It happened now and then that one or another of the inmates made themselves scarce for a couple of days, but they generally returned of their own accord. Even if not, they were always easy to trace, so the event did not arouse much concern.

Yet the authorities began to take a few leisurely steps to find Nezzar, and at a certain point his trail converged with Malvina's. She, too, was missed, and as their former relations were known, the matter began to look a bit more serious. Their connection with the family on Christianshavn was also known, and the investigations were started in Dronningensgade.

Here the man had come back and found the inmate's uniform in his bed. He saw at once how matters stood, and, knowing that they would be bothered by the police, he preferred to report his find at once to the station.

This double alarm stirred the police to action. Search was made, and all trails led to the Christianshavn rampart. But there they ended.

In some way or other the eloping of the indigent couple gradually changed its aspect and appeared romantic instead of comical. The beautiful summer night spun its mystic web around them. Perhaps the air was filled with love that night. Be this as it may, little by little their excursion took the shape of a love drama. The daily papers were notified, and the moat examined as far as possible during the night.

At dawn a policeman who knew all the ins and outs of the haunts of Christianshavn took it upon himself to investigate them one by one. A little later in the morning the sun rose over the distant mountains and tickled King Nebuchadnezzar's nose. He rubbed his eyes and awoke to the most odious of all sights, a red-haired policeman! However, he had by long experience learned to deal cordially with the archfiend, and said yawning—after having extricated himself from Malvina's arms— "Well, are we to beat it?"

The sergeant nodded.

"We would have come anyway by ourselves, but of course it's nicer to be sent for. You have a cab, I suppose?"

"There is one waiting in the square," said the sergeant laughing.

They found it, and all three stepped in. Malvina and King Nebuchadnezzar were equally delighted. They had received permission to have the top down, and were now leaning elegantly back in their seats. They were driving home from the banquet, a little dizzy from the splendor. The light and music were still pulsating through them and made them exuberant. King Nebuchadnezzar waved his hand condescendingly at the passers-by, and Malvina threw kisses at them with her fingers. Then they both laughed, and the policeman pretended not to notice.

"After all, that was a worthy ending," said King Nebuchadnezzar, as they swung up before the gate of the workhouse.

Malvina said nothing, but graciously put her finger to her closed lips and bowed slowly. King Nebuchadnezzar took this as it was meant—it was the high, aristocratic world's way of saying "Thanks for buns and chocolate," and he respected her silence. He lifted his old silk hat, made a deep bow to Madame, and entered his prison like a high-born guest from Belgrade who deigns to taste the food of the poor.

It turned out to be their last fling. Malvina had caught cold in the night and died shortly afterward, and King Nebuchadnezzar never again had the courage to compete by himself with the big world. Scenting future defeats, he preferred to live in his memories of the glorious days in which he had held his own so valiantly.

◇◇◇*Luigi Pirandello (1867-1936). Italian playwright, short-story writer and novelist. Nobel Prize, 1934. James Joyce in 1915 called attention to Pirandello's works. He was a prolific writer of short stories marked by a subtle and rather grim humor.*

HORSE IN THE MOON

BY *LUIGI PIRANDELLO*

In September, upon that high and arid clayey plain, jutting perilously over the African sea, the melancholy countryside still lay parched from the merciless summer sun; it was still shaggy with blackened stubble, while a sprinkling of almond trees and a few aged olive trunks were to be seen here and there. Nevertheless, it had been decided that the bridal pair should spend at least the first few days of their honeymoon in this place, to oblige the bridegroom.

The wedding feast, which was held in a room of the old deserted villa, was far from being a festive occasion for the invited guests. None of those present was able to overcome the embarrassment, or rather the feeling of dismay inspired in him by the aspect and bearing of that fleshy youth, barely twenty years of age, with the purplish face and with the little darting black eyes, which were preternaturally bright, like a madman's. The latter no longer heard what was being said around him; he did not eat, and he did not drink, but became, from moment to moment, redder and more purple of countenance.

Everyone knew that he had been madly in love with the one who now sat beside him as his bride, and that he had done perfectly mad things on her account, even to the point of attempting to kill himself. He was very rich, the sole heir to the Bernardi fortune, while she, after all, was only the daughter of an infantry colonel who had come there the year before, with his regiment, from Sicily. But in spite of this, the colonel, who had been warned against the inhabitants of the island, had been reluctant about giving his consent to this

(Translated by Samuel Putnam.)

match, for the reason that he had not wanted to leave his daughter there among people that were little better than savages.

The dismay which the bridegroom's aspect and actions inspired in the guests increased when the latter came to contrast him with his extremely young bride. She was really but a child, fresh, vivacious and aloof; it seemed that she always shook off every unpleasant thought with a liveliness that was, at once, charming, ingenuous, and roguish. Roguish as that of a little tomboy who as yet knows nothing of the world. A half-orphan, she had grown up without a mother's care; and indeed, it was all too evident that she was going into matrimony without any preparation whatsoever. Everyone smiled, but everyone felt a chill, when, at the end of the meal, she turned to the bridegroom and exclaimed:

"For goodness' sake, Nino, why do you make those little tiny eyes? Let me—no, they burn! Why do your hands burn like that? Feel, Papa, feel how hot his hands are— Do you suppose he has fever?"

The colonel, on pins and needles, did what he could to speed up the departure of the countryside guests. He wanted to put an end to a spectacle that impressed him as being indecent. They all piled into a half-dozen carriages. The one in which the colonel and the bridegroom's widowed mother rode proceeded slowly down the lane and lagged a little behind, for the reason that the bridal couple, one on one side and one on the other, holding hands with the mother and father, had wanted to follow a short distance on foot, down to where the highway which led to the distant city began. At that point, the colonel leaned down and kissed his daughter on the head; he coughed and muttered: "Good-bye, Nino."

"Good-bye, Ida," said the bridegroom's mother with a laugh; and the carriage rattled away at a good pace, in order to overtake the others.

The two stood there for a moment gazing after it. But it was really only Ida who gazed; for Nino saw nothing, was conscious of nothing; his eyes were fastened upon his bride as she stood there, alone with him at last—his, all his— But what was this? Was she weeping?

"Daddy—" said Ida, as she waved her handkerchief in farewell. "There, do you see? He, too—"

"No, Ida—Ida dear—" and stammering, almost sobbing, trembling violently, Nino made an effort to embrace her.

Ida pushed him away.

"No, let me alone, please."

"I just wanted to dry your eyes—"

"Thanks, my dear; I'll dry them myself."

Nino stood there awkwardly. His face, as he looked at her, was pitiful to behold, and his mouth was half-open. Ida finished drying her eyes.

"But what's the matter?" she asked him. "You're trembling all over— No, no, Nino, for heaven's sake, no; don't stand there like that! You make me laugh. And if I once start laughing—you'll see— I'll never stop! Wait a minute; I'll wake you up."

She put her hands on his temples and blew in his eyes. At the touch of those fingers, at the breath from those lips, he felt his legs giving way beneath him; he was about to sink down on one knee, but she held him up and burst into a loud laugh:

"Upon the highway? Are you crazy? Come on, let's go! Look at that little hill over there! We shall be able to see the carriages still. Let's go look!"

And she impetuously dragged him away by one arm.

From all the countryside round about, where so many weeds and grasses, so many things dispersed by the hand of time lay withered, there mounted into the heat-ridden air something like a dense and ancient drouth, mingling with the warm, heavy odor of the manure that lay fermenting in little piles upon the fallow fields, and with the sharper fragrance of sage and wildmint. Of that dense drouth, those warm and heavy odors, that piercing fragrance, he alone was aware. She, as she ran, could hear how gaily the wood-larks sang up to the sun, from behind the thick hedges and from between the rugged yellowish tufts of burnt-over stubble; she could hear, too, in that impressive silence, the prophetic crow of cocks from distant barnyards; and she felt herself wrapped, every now and again, in the cool, keen breath that came up from the neighboring sea, to stir the few tired and yellowed leaves that were left on the almond trees, and the close-clustering, sharp-pointed, ashen-hued olive leaves.

It did not take them long to reach the hilltop; but he was so exhausted from running that he could no longer stand; he wanted to sit down, and tried to make her sit down also, there on the ground beside him, with his arm about her waist. But Ida put him off with "Let me have a look first."

She was beginning to feel restless inside, but she did not care to show it. Irritated by a certain strange and curious stubbornness on his part, she could not, she would not stand still, but longed to keep on fleeing, still farther away; she wanted to shake him up, to distract him, to distract herself as well, so long as the day lasted.

Down there, on the other side of the hill, there stretched away a devastated plain, a sea of stubble, amid which one could make out occasionally the black and meandering traces of wood-ashes that had been sprinkled there; now and again, too, the crude yellow gleam was broken by a few clumps of caper or of liquorice. Away over there, as if on the other shore of that vast yellow sea, the roofs of a hamlet rose from the tall dark poplars.

And now Ida suggested to her husband that they go over there, all the way over to that hamlet. How long would it take? An hour or less. It was not more than five o'clock. Back home, in the villa, the servants must still be busy clearing away the things. They would be home before evening.

Nino made a feeble attempt at opposition, but she took him by the hands and dragged him to his feet; in a moment, she was running down the side of the hill and was off through that sea of stubble, as light and quick as a young doe. He was not fast enough to keep up with her, but, redder-faced than ever and seemingly stunned by it all, ran after her, pantingly and perspiringly, and kept calling to her to wait and give him her hand.

"Give me your hand, at least! At least, give me your hand!" he shouted.

All of a sudden, she uttered a cry and stopped short. A flock of cawing ravens had just flown up from in front of her. And there in front of her, stretched out upon the earth, was a dead horse. Dead? No, no, it wasn't dead; it had its eyes open. Heavens, what eyes! What eyes! A skeleton, that was what it was. And those ribs! And those flanks!

Nino came up, fuming and fretting;

"Come on, let's go—let's go back—at once!"

"It's alive, look!" cried Ida, shivering from compassion. "Lift its head—heavens, what eyes! Look, Nino!"

"Yes, yes," said he, panting still. "They've just put it out here— Leave it alone; let's go! What a sight! Don't you smell—?"

"And those ravens!" she exclaimed with a shudder. "Are those ravens going to eat it alive?"

"But, Ida, for heaven's sake!" he implored her, clasping his hands.

"Nino, that will do!" she cried. It was more than she could endure to see him so stupid and so contrite. "Answer me: what if they eat it alive?"

"What do I know about whether or not they'll eat it? They'll wait—"

"Until it dies here, of hunger, of thirst?" Her face was all drawn with horror and pity. "Just because it's old? Because it can't work any more? Ah, poor beast! What a shame! What a shame! Haven't they any heart, those peasants? Haven't you any heart, standing there like that?"

"Excuse me," he said, losing his temper, "but you feel so much sympathy for an animal—"

"And oughtn't I to?"

"But you don't feel any for me!"

"And are you an animal? Are you dying of hunger and thirst as you sit there in the stubble? You feel— Oh, look at the ravens. Nino, look, up there, circling around— Oh, what a horrible, shameful, monstrous thing! —Look— Oh, the poor beast—try to lift him up! Come, Nino, get up; maybe he can still walk—Nino, get up, help me—shake yourself out of it!"

"But what do you expect me to do?" he burst out, exasperatedly. "Do you expect me to drag him back? Put him on my shoulders? What's a horse more or less? How do you think he is going to walk? Can't you see he's half-dead?"

"But if we brought him something to eat?"

"And to drink, too!"

"Oh, Nino, you're wicked!" And the tears stood in Ida's eyes. Overcoming her shudders, she bent over very gently to caress the horse's head. The animal, with a great effort, had managed to get to its knees; and even in its last degrading agony, it showed the traces of a noble beauty in head and neck.

Nino, owing possibly to the blood that was pounding in his veins, possibly owing to the bitterness and contempt she had manifested, or to the perspiration that was trickling from him, now suddenly felt his breath failing him; he grew giddy, his teeth began chattering, and he was conscious of a weird trembling all over his body. He instinctively turned up his coat collar, and with his hands in his pockets, went over and huddled down in gloomy despair upon a rock some distance away.

The sun had already set, and from the distant highway could be heard the occasional sound of horses' bells.

Why were his teeth chattering like that? For his forehead was burning up, the blood in his veins stung him, and there was a roaring in his ears. It seemed to him that he could hear so many faraway bells. All that anxiety, that spasm of expectation, her coldness and caprice, that last foot-race, and that horse there, that cursed horse— Oh, God! was it a dream? A nightmare within a dream? Did he have a fever? Or perhaps, a worse illness? Ah! How dark it was, God—how dark! And now, his sight was clouding over. He tried to call "Ida! Ida!" but he could not get the words out of his parched throat.

Where was Ida? What was she doing?

She had gone off to the distant hamlet, to seek aid for that horse; she did not stop to think that the peasants had brought the animal there to die.

He remained there, alone upon the rock, a prey to those growing tremors; and as he sat there, huddled to himself like a great owl upon a perch, he suddenly beheld a sight that seemed— Ah, yes— he could see it plainly enough now—an atrocious sight, like a vision from another world. The moon. A huge moon, coming slowly up from behind that sea of stubble. And black against that enormous, vapory copper disk, the headstrong head of that horse, waiting still with its neck stretched out—it had, perhaps, been waiting like that always, darkly etched upon that copper disk, while from far up in the sky could be heard the caw of circling ravens.

When Ida, angry and disillusioned, came groping her way back over the plain, calling "Nino! Nino!" the moon had already risen;

the horse had dropped down as if dead; and Nino—where was Nino? Oh, there he was over there; he was on the ground, too.

Had he fallen asleep there?

She ran up to him, and found him with a death-rattle in his throat. His face, also, was on the ground; it was almost black, and his eyes, nearly closed, were puffed and bloodshot.

"Oh, God!"

She looked about her, as if in a swoon. She opened her hands which held a few dried beans that she had brought from the hamlet over there to feed to the horse. She looked at the moon, then at the horse, and then at the man lying on the ground as if dead. She felt faint, assailed as she was by the sudden suspicion that everything she saw was unreal. Terrified, she fled back to the villa, calling in a loud voice for her father, her father—to come and take her away. Oh, God! away from that man with the rattle in his throat—that rattle, the meaning of which she did not understand! away from that horse, away from under that mad moon, away from under those cawing ravens in the sky—away, away, away——

◇◇◇*Edgar Allan Poe (1809-1849). The famous American poet and short-story writer.*

THE IMP OF THE PERVERSE

BY EDGAR ALLAN POE

In the consideration of the faculties and impulses—of the *prima mobilia* of the human soul, the phrenologists have failed to make room for a propensity which, although obviously existing as a radical, primitive, irreducible sentiment, has been equally overlooked by all the moralists who have preceded them. In the pure arrogance of the reason, we have all overlooked it. We have suffered its existence to escape our senses, solely through want of belief—of faith; —whether it be faith in Revelation, or faith in the Kabbala. The idea of it has never occurred to us, simply because of its supererogation. We saw no *need* of the impulse—for the propensity. We could not perceive its necessity. We could not understand, that is to say, we could not have understood, had the notion of this *primum mobile* ever obtruded itself;—we could not have understood in what manner it might be made to further the objects of humanity, either temporal or eternal. It cannot be denied that phrenology and, in great measure, all metaphysicianism have been concocted *a priori*. The intellectual or logical man, rather than the understanding or observant man, set himself to imagine designs—to dictate purposes to God. Having thus fathomed, to his satisfaction, the intentions of Jehovah, out of these intentions he built his innumerable systems of mind. In the matter of phrenology, for example, we first determined, naturally enough, that it was the design of the Deity that man should eat. We then assigned to man an organ of alimentiveness, and this organ is the scourge with which the Deity compels man, will-I nill-I, into eating. Secondly, having settled it to be God's will that man should continue his species, we discovered an organ of amativeness, forthwith. And so with combativeness, with ideality, with causality, with constructiveness,—so, in short, with

328

every organ, whether representing a propensity, a moral sentiment, or a faculty of the pure intellect. And in these arrangements of the *principia* of human action, the Spurzheimites, whether right or wrong, in part, or upon the whole, have but followed, in principle, the footsteps of their predecessors; deducing and establishing everything from the preconceived destiny of man, and upon the ground of the objects of his Creator.

It would have been wiser, it would have been safer, to classify (if classify we must) upon the basis of what man usually or occasionally did, and was always occasionally doing, rather than upon the basis of what we took it for granted the Deity intended him to do. If we cannot comprehend God in his visible works, how then in his inconceivable thoughts, that call the works into being? If we cannot understand him in his objective creatures, how then in his substantive moods and phases of creation?

Induction, *a posteriori*, would have brought phrenology to admit, as an innate and primitive principle of human action, a paradoxical something, which we may call *perverseness,* for want of a more characteristic term. In the sense I intend, it is, in fact, a *mobile* without motive, a motive not *motivirt.* Through its promptings we act without comprehensible object; or, if this shall be understood as a contradiction in terms, we may so far modify the proposition to say, that through its promptings we act, for the reason we should *not.* In theory no reason can be more unreasonable; but, in fact, there is none more strong. With certain minds, under certain conditions, it becomes absolutely irresistible. I am not more certain that I breathe, than that the assurance of the wrong or error of any action is often the one unconquerable *force* which impels us to its prosecution. Nor will this overwhelming tendency to do wrong for the wrong's sake, admit of analysis, or resolution into ulterior elements. It is a radical, a primitive impulse—elementary. It will be said, I am aware, that when we persist in acts because we feel we should *not* persist in them, our conduct is but a modification of that which ordinarily springs from the *combativeness* of phrenology. But a glance will show the fallacy of this idea. The phrenological combativeness has, for its essence, the necessity of self-defence. It is our safeguard against injury. Its principle regards our well-being; and thus the desire to be well is excited simultaneously with its

Edgar Allan Poe

development. It follows, that the desire to be well must be excited simultaneously with any principle which shall be merely a modification of combativeness, but in the case of that something which I term *perverseness,* the desire to be well is not only not aroused, but a strongly antagonistical sentiment exists.

An appeal to one's own heart is, after all, the best reply to the sophistry just noticed. No one who trustingly consults and thoroughly questions his own soul, will be disposed to deny the entire radicalness of the propensity in question. It is not more incomprehensible than distinctive. There lives no man who at some period has not been tormented, for example, by an earnest desire to tantalize a listener by circumlocution. The speaker is aware that he displeases; he has every intention to please; he is usually curt, precise, and clear; the most laconic and luminous language is struggling for utterance upon his tongue; it is only with difficulty that he restrains himself from giving it flow; he dreads and deprecates the anger of him whom he addresses; yet, the thought strikes him, that by certain involutions and parentheses this anger may be engendered. That single thought is enough. The impulse increases to a wish, the wish to a desire, the desire to an uncontrollable longing, and the longing (to the deep regret and mortification of the speaker, and in defiance of all consequences) is indulged.

We have a task before us which must be speedily performed. We know that it will be ruinous to make delay. The most important crisis of our life calls, trumpet-tongued, for immediate energy and action. We glow, we are consumed with eagerness to commence the work, with the anticipation of whose glorious result our whole souls are on fire. It must, it shall be undertaken to-day, and yet we put it off until tomorrow; and why? There is no answer, except that we feel *perverse,* using the word with no comprehension of the principle. Tomorrow arrives, and with it a more impatient anxiety to do our duty, but with this very increase of anxiety arrives, also, a nameless, a positively fearful, because unfathomable, craving for delay. This craving gathers strength as the moments fly. The last hour for action is at hand. We tremble with the violence of the conflict within us, —of the definite with the indefinite—of the substance with the shadow. But, if the contest has proceeded thus far, it is the shadow which prevails, we struggle in vain. The clock strikes, and is the knell of our welfare. At the same time, it is the chanticleer-note to the ghost that has so long overawed us. It flies—it disappears—we are free. The old energy returns. We will labor *now*. Alas, it is *too late!*

We stand upon the brink of a precipice. We peer into the abyss—we grow sick and dizzy. Our first impulse is to shrink from the danger. Unaccountably we remain. By slow degrees our sickness and dizziness and horror become merged in a cloud of unnamable feeling. By gradations, still more imperceptible, this cloud assumes shape, as did the vapor from the bottle out of which arose the genius in the Arabian Nights. But out of this *our* cloud upon the precipice's edge, there grows into palpability, a shape, far more terrible than any genius or any demon of a tale, and yet it is but a thought, although a fearful one, and one which chills the very marrow of our bones with the fierceness of the delight of its horror. It is merely the idea of what would be our sensations during the sweeping precipitancy of a fall from such a height. And this fall—this rushing annihilation—for the very reason that it involves that one most ghastly and loathesome of all the most ghastly and loathesome images of death and suffering which have ever presented themselves to our imagination—for this very cause do we now the most vividly desire it. And because our reason violently deters us from the brink, *therefore* do we the most impetuously approach it. There is no passion in nature so demoniacally impatient, as that of him who, shuddering upon the edge of a precipice, thus meditates a plunge. To indulge, for a moment, in any attempt at *thought,* is to be inevitably lost; for reflection but urges us to forbear, and *therefore* it is, I say, that we *cannot.* If there be no friendly arm to check us, or if we fail in a sudden effort to prostrate ourselves backward from the abyss, we plunge, and are destroyed.

Examine these similar actions as we will, we shall find them resulting solely from the spirit of the *Perverse.* We perpetrate them because we feel that we should *not.* Beyond or behind this there is no intelligible principle; and, we might, indeed, deem this perverseness a direct instigation of the arch-fiend, were it not occasionally known to operate in furtherance of good.

I have said this much, that in some measure I may answer your question—that I may explain to you why I am here—that I may assign to you something that shall have at least the faint aspect of a cause for my wearing these fetters, and for my tenanting this cell of the condemned. Had I not been thus prolix, you might either have misunderstood me altogether, or, with the rabble, have fancied me mad. As it is, you will easily perceive that I am one of the many uncounted victims of the Imp of the Perverse.

It is impossible that any deed could have been wrought with a more thorough deliberation. For weeks, for months, I pondered upon the means of the murder. I rejected a thousand schemes, because their accomplishment involved a *chance* of detection. At length, in reading some French memoirs, I found an account of a nearly fatal illness that occurred to Madame Pilau, through the agency of a candle accidentally poisoned. The idea struck my fancy at once. I knew my victim's habit of reading in bed. I knew, too, that his apartment was narrow and ill-ventilated. But I need not vex you with impertinent details. I need not describe the easy artifices by which I substituted, in his bed-room candle-stand, a waxlight of my own making for the one which I there found. The next morning he was discovered dead in his bed, and the coroner's verdict was—"Death by the visitation of God."

Having inherited his estate, all went well with me for years. The idea of detection never once entered my brain. Of the remains of the fatal taper I had myself carefully disposed. I had left no shadow of a clue by which it would be possible to convict, or even to suspect, me of the crime. It is inconceivable how rich a sentiment of satisfaction arose in my bosom as I reflected upon my absolute security. For a very long period of time I was accustomed to revel in this sentiment. It afforded me more real delight than all the mere wordly advantages accruing from my sin. But there arrived at length an epoch, from which the pleasurable feeling grew, by scarcely perceptible gradations, into a haunting and harassing thought. It harassed because it haunted. I could scarcely get rid of it for an instant. It is quite a common thing to be thus annoyed with the ringing in our ears, or rather in our memories, of the burthen of some ordinary song, or some unimpressive snatches from an opera. Nor will we be the less tormented if the song in itself be good, or the opera air meritous. In this manner, at last, I would perpetually catch myself pondering upon my security, and, repeating, in a low undertone, the phrase, "I am safe."

One day, whilst sauntering along the streets, I arrested myself in the act of murmuring, half aloud, these customary syllables. In a fit of petulance, I remodelled them thus; "I am safe—I am safe—yes—if I be not fool enough to make open confession!"

No sooner had I spoken these words, than I felt an icy chill creep to my heart. I had had some experience in these fits of perversity (whose nature I have been at some trouble to explain), and I remembered well that in no instance I had successfully resisted their attacks. And now my own casual self-suggestion that I might possibly be fool enough to confess the murder of which I had been guilty, confronted me, as if the very ghost of him who I had murdered—and beckoned me on to death.

At first I made an effort to shake off this nightmare of the soul. I walked vigorously—faster—still faster—at length I ran. I felt a maddening desire to shriek aloud. Every succeeding wave of thought overwhelmed me with new terror, for alas! I well, too well, understood that to *think*, in my situation, was to be lost. I still quickened my pace. I bounded like a madman through the crowded thoroughfares. At length, the populace took the alarm, and pursued me. I felt *then* the consummation of my fate. Could I have torn out my tongue, I would have done it—but a rough voice resounded in my ears—and a rougher grasp seized me by the shoulder. I turned—I gasped for breath. For a moment I experienced all the pangs of suffocation; I became blind, and deaf, and dizzy; and then some invisible fiend, I thought, struck me with his broad palm upon the back. The long imprisoned secret burst forth from my soul.

They say that I spoke with a distinct enunciation, but with marked emphasis and passionate hurry, as if in dread of interruption before concluding the brief but pregnant sentences that consigned me to the hangman and to hell.

Having related all that was necessary for the fullest judicial conviction, I fell prostrate in a swoon.

But why shall I say more? To-day I wear these chains, and am *here!* Tomorrow I shall be fetterless!—*but where?*

◇◇◇*Katherine Anne Porter (1894-   ). American short-story and novella writer, distinguished for her fine style. See* The Leaning Tower, Flowering Judas *and* Pale Horse, Pale Rider.

FLOWERING JUDAS

BY KATHERINE ANNE PORTER

Braggioni sits heaped upon the edge of a straightbacked chair much too small for him, and sings to Laura in a furry, mournful voice. Laura has begun to find reasons for avoiding her own house until the latest possible moment, for Braggioni is there almost every night. No matter how late she is, he will be sitting there with a surly, waiting expression, pulling at his kinky yellow hair, thumbing the strings of his guitar, snarling a tune under his breath. Lupe the Indian maid meets Laura at the door, and says with a flicker of a glance towards the upper room, "He waits."

Laura wishes to lie down, she is tired of her hairpins and the feel of her long tight sleeves, but she says to him, "Have you a new song for me this evening?" If he says yes, she asks him to sing it. If he says no, she remembers his favorite one, and asks him to sing it again. Lupe brings her a cup of chocolate and a plate of rice, and Laura eats at the small table under the lamp, first inviting Braggioni, whose answer is always the same: "I have eaten, and besides, chocolate thickens the voice."

Laura says, "Sing, then," and Braggioni heaves himself into song. He scratches the guitar familiarly as though it were a pet animal, and sings passionately off key, taking the high notes in a prolonged painful squeal. Laura, who haunts the markets listening to the ballad singers, and stops every day to hear the blind boy playing his reed-flute in Sixteenth of September Street, listens to Braggioni with pitiless courtesy, because she dares not smile at his miserable performance. Nobody dares to smile at him. Braggioni is cruel to everyone, with a kind of specialized insolence, but he is so vain of his talents, and so sensitive to slights, it would require a cruelty and vanity greater than his own to lay a finger on the vast cureless wound of his self-esteem. It would require courage, too, for it is dangerous to offend him, and nobody has this courage.

Braggioni loves himself with such tenderness and amplitude and eternal charity that his followers—for he is a leader of men, a skilled revolutionist, and his skin has been punctured in honorable warfare —warm themselves in the reflected glow, and say to each other: "He has a real nobility, a love of humanity raised above mere personal affections." The excess of this self-love has flowed out, inconveniently for her, over Laura, who, with so many others, owes her comfortable situation and her salary to him. When he is in a very good humor, he tells her, "I am tempted to forgive you for being a *gringa. Gringita!*" and Laura, burning, imagines herself leaning forward suddenly, and with a sound back-handed slap wiping the suety smile from his face. If he notices her eyes at these moments he gives no sign.

She knows what Braggioni would offer her, and she must resist tenaciously without appearing to resist, and if she could avoid it she would not admit even to herself the slow drift of his intention. During these long evenings which have spoiled a long month for her, she sits in her deep chair with an open book on her knees, resting her eyes on the consoling rigidity of the printed page when the sight and sound of Braggioni singing threaten to identify themselves with all her remembered afflictions and to add their weight to her uneasy premonitions of the future. The gluttonous bulk of Braggioni has become a symbol of her many disillusions, for a revolutionist should be lean, animated by heroic faith, a vessel of abstract virtues. This is nonsense, she knows it now and is ashamed of it. Revolution must have leaders, and leadership is a career for energetic men. She is, her comrades tell her, full of romantic error, for what she defines as cynicism in them is merely "a developed sense of reality." She is almost too willing to say, "I am wrong, I suppose I don't really understand the principles," and afterward she makes a secret truce with herself, determined not to surrender her will to such expedient logic. But she cannot help feeling that she has been betrayed irreparably by the disunion between her way of living and her feeling of what life should be, and at times she is almost contented to rest in this sense of grievance as a private store of consolation. Sometimes she wishes to run away, but she stays. Now she longs to fly out of this room, down the narrow stairs, and into the street where the houses lean together like conspirators under a single mottled lamp, and leave Braggioni singing to himself.

Instead she looks at Braggioni, frankly and clearly, like a good child who understands the rules of behavior. Her knees cling together under sound blue serge, and her round white collar is not purposely nunlike. She wears the uniform of an idea, and has renounced vanities. She was born Roman Catholic, and in spite of her fear of being seen by someone who might make a scandal of it, she slips now and again into some crumbling little church, kneels on the chilly stone, and says a Hail Mary on the gold rosary she bought in Tehuantepec. It is no good and she ends by examining the altar with its tinsel flowers and ragged brocades, and feels tender about the battered doll-shape of some male saint whose white, lace-trimmed drawers hang limply around his ankles below the hieratic dignity of his velvet robe. She had encased herself in a set of principles derived from her early training, leaving no detail of gesture or of personal taste untouched, and for this reason she will not wear lace made on machines. This is her private heresy, for in her special group the machine is sacred, and will be the salvation of the workers. She loves fine lace, and there is a tiny edge of fluted cobweb on this collar, which is one of twenty precisely alike, folded in blue tissue paper in the upper drawer of her clothes chest.

Braggioni catches her glance solidly as if he had been waiting for it, leans forward, balancing his paunch between his spread knees, and sings with tremendous emphasis, weighing his words. He has, the song relates, no father and no mother, nor even a friend to console him; lonely as a wave of the sea he comes and goes, lonely as a wave. His mouth opens round and yearns sideways, his balloon cheeks grow oily with the labor of song. He bulges marvelously in his expensive garments. Over his lavender collar, crushed upon a purple necktie, held by a diamond hoop: over his ammunition belt of tooled leather worked in silver, buckled cruelly around his gasping middle: over the tops of his glossy yellow shoes Braggioni swells with ominous ripeness, his mauve silk hose stretched taut, his ankles bound with the stout leather thongs of his shoes.

When he stretches his eyelids at Laura she notes again that his eyes are the true tawny yellow cat's eyes. He is rich, not in money, he tells her, but in power, and this power brings with it the blameless ownership of things, and the right to indulge his love of small luxuries. "I have a taste for the elegant refinements," he said once, flourishing a yellow silk handkerchief before her nose. "Smell that? It is Jockey Club, imported from New York." Nonetheless he is wounded by life. He will say so presently. "It is true everything turns to dust in the hand, to gall on the tongue." He sighs and his leather belt creaks like a saddle girth. "I am disappointed in everything as it comes. Everything." He shakes his head. "You, poor thing, you will be disappointed too. You are born for it. We are more alike than you realize in some things. Wait and see. Some day you will remember what I have told you, you will know that Braggioni was your friend."

Laura feels a slow chill, a purely physical sense of danger, a warning in her blood that violence, mutilation, a shocking death, wait for her with lessening patience. She has translated this fear into something homely, immediate, and sometimes hesitates before crossing the street. "My personal fate is nothing, except as the testimony of a mental attitude," she reminds herself, quoting from some forgotten philosophic primer, and is sensible enough to add, "Anyhow, I shall not be killed by an automobile if I can help it."

"It may be true I am as corrupt, in another way, as Braggioni," she thinks in spite of herself, "as callous, as incomplete," and if this is so, any kind of death seems preferable. Still she sits quietly, she does not run. Where could she go? Uninvited she has promised herself to this place; she can no longer imagine herself as living in another country, and there is no pleasure in remembering her life before she came here.

Precisely what is the nature of this devotion, its true motives, and what are its obligations? Laura cannot say. She spends part of her days in Xochimilco, near by, teaching Indian children to say in English, "The cat is on the mat." When she appears in the classroom they crowd about her with smiles on their wise, innocent, clay-colored faces, crying, "Good morning, my ticher!" in immaculate voices, and they make of her desk a fresh garden of flowers every day.

During her leisure she goes to union meetings and listens to busy important voices quarreling over tactics, methods, internal politics. She visits the prisoners of her own political faith in their cells, where they entertain themselves with counting cockroaches, repenting on their indiscretions, composing their memoirs, writing out manifestoes and plans for their comrades who are still walking about free, hands in pockets, sniffing fresh air. Laura brings them food and cigarettes and a little money, and she brings messages disguised in equivocal phrases from the men outside who dare not set foot in the prison for fear of disappearing into the cells kept empty for them. If the prisoners confuse night and day, and complain, "Dear little Laura, time doesn't pass in this infernal hole, and I won't know when it is time to sleep unless I have a reminder," she brings them their favorite narcotics, and says in a tone that does not wound them with pity, "Tonight will really be night for you," and though her Spanish amuses them, they find her comforting, useful. If they lose patience and all faith, and curse the slowness of their friends in coming to their rescue with money and influence, they trust her not to repeat everything, and if she inquires, "Where do you think we can find money, or influence?" they are certain to answer, "Well, there is Braggioni, why doesn't he do something?"

She smuggles letters from headquarters to men hiding from firing squads in back streets in mildewed houses, where they sit in tumbled beds and talk bitterly as if all Mexico were at their heels, when Laura knows positively they might appear at the band concert in the Alameda on Sunday morning, and no one would notice them. But Braggioni says, "Let them sweat a little. The next time they may be careful. It is very restful to have them out of the way for a while." She is not afraid to knock on any door in any street after midnight, and enter in the darkness, and say to one of these men who is really in danger: "They will be looking for you—seriously—tomorrow morning after six. Here is some money from Vicente. Go to Vera Cruz and wait."

She borrows money from the Roumanian agitator to give to his bitter enemy the Polish agitator. The favor of Braggioni is their disputed territory, and Braggioni holds the balance nicely, for he can use them both. The Polish agitator talks love to her over café tables, hoping to exploit what he believes is her secret sentimental preference for him, and he gives her misinformation which he begs her to repeat as the solemn truth to certain persons. The Roumanian is more adroit. He is generous with his money in all good causes, and lies to her with an air of ingenuous candor, as if he were her good friend and confidant. She never repeats anything they may say. Braggioni never asks questions. He has other ways to discover all that he wishes to know about them.

Nobody touches her, but all praise her gray eyes, and the soft, round under lip which promises gayety, yet is always grave, nearly always firmly closed: and they cannot understand why she is in Mexico. She walks back and forth on her errands, with puzzled eyebrows, carrying her little folder of drawings and music and school papers. No dancer dances more beautifully than Laura walks, and she inspires some amusing, unexpected ardors, which cause little gossip, because nothing comes of them. A young captain who had been a soldier in Zapata's army attempted, during a horseback ride near Cuernavaca, to express his desire for her with the noble simplicity befitting a rude folk-hero: but gently, because he was gentle. This gentleness was his defeat, for when he alighted, and removed her foot from the stirrup, and essayed to draw her down into his arms, her horse, ordinarily a tame one, shied fiercely, reared and plunged away. The young hero's horse careered blindly after his stable-mate, and the hero did not return to the hotel until rather late that evening. At breakfast he came to her table in full charro dress, gray buckskin jacket and trousers with strings of silver buttons down the leg, and he was in a humorous, careless mood. "May I sit with you?" and "You are a wonderful rider. I was terrified that you might be thrown and dragged. I should never have forgiven myself. But I cannot admire you enough for your riding!"

"I learned to ride in Arizona," said Laura.

"If you will ride with me again this morning, I promise you a horse that will not shy with you," he said. But Laura remembered that she must return to Mexico City at noon.

Next morning the children made a celebration and spent their playtime writing on the blackboard, "We lov ar ticher," and with tinted chalks they drew wreaths of flowers around the words. The young hero wrote her a letter: "I am a very foolish, wasteful, impulsive man. I should have first said I love you, and then you

would not have run away. But you shall see me again." Laura
thought, "I must send him a box of colored crayons," but she was
trying to forgive herself for having spurred her horse at the wrong
moment.

A brown, shock-haired youth came and stood in her patio one
night and sang like a lost soul for two hours, but Laura could think
of nothing to do about it. The moonlight spread a wash of gauzy
silver over the clear spaces of the garden, and the shadows were
cobalt blue. The scarlet blossoms of the Judas tree were dull purple, and the names of the colors repeated themselves automatically
in her mind, while she watched not the boy, but his shadow, fallen
like a dark garment across the fountain rim, trailing in the water.
Lupe came silently and whispered expert counsel in her ear: "If
you will throw him one little flower, he will sing another song or
two and go away." Laura threw the flower, and he sang a last song
and went away with the flower tucked in the band of his hat. Lupe
said, "He is one of the organizers of the Typographers Union, and
before that he sold corridos in the Merced market, and before that,
he came from Guanajuato, where I was born. I would not trust any
man, but I trust least those from Guanajuato."

She did not tell Laura that he would be back again the next
night, and the next, nor that he would follow her at a certain fixed
distance around the Merced market, through the Zócolo, up Fran-
cisco I. Madero Avenue, and so along the Paseo de la Reforma to
Chapultepec Park, and into the Philosopher's Footpath, still with
that flower withering in his hat, and an indivisible attention in his
eyes.

Now Laura is accustomed to him, it means nothing except that he
is nineteen years old and is observing a convention with all propriety, as though it were founded on a law of nature, which in the
end it might well prove to be. He is beginning to write poems which
he prints on a wooden press, and he leaves them stuck like handbills
in her door. She is pleasantly disturbed by the abstract, unhurried
watchfulness of his black eyes which will in time turn easily towards
another object. She tells herself that throwing the flower was a mistake, for she is twenty-two years old and knows better; but she refuses to regret it, and persuades herself that her negation of all ex-

ternal events as they occur is a sign that she is gradually perfecting herself in the stoicism she strives to cultivate against that disaster she fears, though she cannot name it.

She is not at home in the world. Every day she teaches children who remain strangers to her, though she loves their tender round hands and their charming opportunist savagery. She knocks at unfamiliar doors not knowing whether a friend or a stranger shall answer, and even if a known face emerges from the sour gloom of that unknown interior, still it is the face of a stranger. No matter what this stranger says to her, nor what her message to him, the very cells of her flesh reject knowledge and kinship in one monotonous word. No. No. No. She draws her strength from this one holy talismanic word which does not suffer her to be led into evil. Denying everything, she may walk anywhere in safety, she looks at everything without amazement.

No, repeats this firm unchanging voice of her blood; and she looks at Braggioni without amazement. He is a great man, he wishes to impress this simple girl who covers her great round breasts with thick dark cloth, and who hides long, invaluably beautiful legs under a heavy skirt. She is almost thin except for the incomprehensible fullness of her breasts, like a nursing mother's, and Braggioni, who considers himself a judge of women, speculates again on the puzzle of her notorious virginity, and takes the liberty of speech which she permits without a sign of modesty, indeed, without any sort of sign, which is disconcerting.

"You think you are so cold, *gringita!* Wait and see. You will surprise yourself some day! May I be there to advise you!" He stretches his eyelids at her, and his ill-humored cat's eyes waver in a separate glance for the two points of light marking the opposite ends of a smoothly drawn path between the swollen curve of her breasts. He is not put off by that blue serge, nor by her resolutely fixed gaze. There is all the time in the world. His cheeks are bellying with the wind of song. "O girl with the dark eyes," he sings, and reconsiders. "But yours are not dark. I can change all that. O girl with the green eyes, you have stolen my heart away!" then his mind wanders to the song, and Laura feels the weight of his attention being shifted elsewhere. Singing thus, he seems harmless, he is quite harmless, there is nothing to do but sit patiently and say "No," when the moment comes. She draws a full breath, and her mind wanders also, but not far. She dares not wander too far.

Not for nothing has Braggioni taken pains to be a good revolutionist and a professional lover of humanity. He will never die of it. He has the malice, the cleverness, the wickedness, the sharpness of wit, the hardness of heart, stipulated for loving the world profitably. *He will never die of it.* He will live to see himself kicked out from his feeding trough by other hungry world-saviors. Traditionally he must sing in spite of his life which drives him to bloodshed, he tells Laura, for his father was a Tuscany peasant who drifted to Yucatan and married a Maya woman: a woman of race, an aristocrat. They gave him the love and knowledge of music, thus: and under the rip of his thumbnail, the strings of the instrument complain like exposed nerves.

Once he was called Delgadito by all the girls and married women who ran after him; he was so scrawny all his bones showed under his thin cotton clothing, and he could squeeze his emptiness to the very backbone with his two hands. He was a poet and the revolution was only a dream then; too many women loved him and sapped away his youth, and he could never find enough to eat anywhere, anywhere! Now he is a leader of men, crafty men who whisper in his ear, hungry men who wait for hours outside his office for a word with him, emaciated men with wild faces who waylay him at the street gate with a timid, "Comrade, let me tell you . . ." and they blow the foul breath from their empty stomachs in his face.

He is always sympathetic. He gives them handfuls of small coins from his own pocket, he promises them work, there will be demonstrations, they must join the unions and attend the meetings, above all they must be on the watch for spies. They are closer to him than his own brothers, without them he can do nothing—until tomorrow, comrade!

Until tomorrow. "They are stupid, they are lazy, they are treacherous, they would cut my throat for nothing," he says to Laura. He has good food and abundant drink, he hires an automobile and drives in the Paseo on Sunday morning, and enjoys plenty of sleep in a soft bed beside a wife who dares not disturb him, and he sits pampering his bones in easy billows of fat, singing to Laura, who knows and thinks these things about him. When he was fifteen, he tried to drown himself because he loved a girl, his first love, and she laughed at him. "A thousand women have paid for that," and his tight little mouth turns down at the corners. Now he perfumes his hair with Jockey Club, and confides to Laura: "One woman is really as good as another for me, in the dark. I prefer them all."

His wife organizes unions among the girls in the cigarette factories, and walks in picket lines, and even speaks at meetings in the evening. But she cannot be brought to acknowledge the benefits of true liberty. "I tell her I must have my freedom, net. She does not understand my point of view." Laura has heard this many times. Braggioni scratches the guitar and meditates. "She is an instinctively virtuous woman, pure gold, no doubt of that. If she were not, I should lock her up, and she knows it."

His wife, who works so hard for the good of the factory girls, employs part of her leisure lying on the floor weeping because there are so many women in the world, and only one husband for her, and she never knows where nor when to look for him. He told her: "Unless you can learn to cry when I am not here, I must go away for good." That day he went away and took a room at the Hotel Madrid.

It is this month of separation for the sake of higher principles that has been spoiled not only for Mrs. Braggioni, whose sense of reality is beyond criticism, but for Laura, who feels herself bogged in a nightmare. Tonight Laura envies Mrs. Braggioni, who is alone, and free to weep as much as she pleases about a concrete wrong. Laura has just come from a visit to the prison, and she is waiting for tomorrow with a bitter anxiety as if tomorrow may not come, but time may be caught immovably in this hour, with herself transfixed, Braggioni singing on forever, and Eugenio's body not yet discovered by the guard.

Braggioni says: "Are you going to sleep?" Almost before she can shake her head, he begins telling her about the May-day disturbances coming on in Morelia, for the Catholics hold a festival in honor of the Blessed Virgin, and the Socialists celebrate their martyrs on that day. "There will be two independent processions, starting from either end of town, and they will march until they meet, and the rest depends . . ." He asks her to oil and load his pistols.

Standing up, he unbuckles his ammunition belt, and spreads it laden across her knees. Laura sits with the shells slipping through the cleaning cloth dipped in oil, and he says again he cannot understand why she works so hard for the revolutionary idea unless she loves some man who is in it. "Are you not in love with someone?" "No," says Laura. "And no one is in love with you?" "No." "Then it is your own fault. No woman need go begging. Why, what is the matter with you? The legless beggar woman in the Alameda has a perfectly faithful lover. Did you know that?"

Laura peers down the pistol barrel and says nothing, but a long, slow faintness rises and subsides in her; Braggioni curves his swollen fingers around the throat of the guitar and softly smothers the music out of it, and when she hears him again he seems to have forgotten her, and is speaking in the hypnotic voice he uses when talking in small rooms to a listening, close-gathered crowd. Some day this world, now seemingly so composed and eternal to the edges of every sea shall be merely a tangle of gaping trenches, of crashing walls and broken bodies. Everything must be torn from its accustomed place where it has rotted for centuries, hurled skyward and distributed, cast down again clean as rain, without separate identity. Nothing shall survive that the stiffened hands of poverty have created for the rich and no one shall be left alive except the elect spirits destined to procreate a new world cleansed of cruelty and injustice, ruled by benevolent anarchy: "Pistols are good, I love them, cannon are even better, but in the end I pin my faith to good dynamite," he concludes, and strokes the pistol lying in her hands. "Once I dreamed of destroying this city, in case it offered resistance to General Ortíz, but it fell into his hands like an overripe pear."

He is made restless by his own words, rises and stands waiting. Laura holds up the belt to him: "Put that on, and go kill somebody in Morelia, and you will be happier," she says softly. The presence of death in the room makes her bold. "Today, I found Eugenio going into a stupor. He refused to allow me to call the prison doctor. He had taken all the tablets I brought him yesterday. He said he took them because he was bored."

"He is a fool, and his death is his own business," says Braggioni, fastening his belt carefully.

"I told him if he had waited only a little while longer, you would have got him set free," says Laura. "He said he did not want to wait."

"He is a fool and we are well rid of him," says Braggioni, reaching for his hat.

He goes away. Laura knows his mood has changed, she will not see him any more for a while. He will send word when he needs her to go on errands into strange streets, to speak to the strange faces that will appear, like clay masks with the power of human speech, to mutter their thanks to Braggioni for his help. Now she is free, and she thinks, I must run while there is time. But she does not go.

Braggioni enters his own house where for a month his wife has spent many hours every night weeping and tangling her hair upon her pillow. She is weeping now, and she weeps more at the sight of him, the cause of all her sorrows. He looks about the room. Nothing is changed, the smells are good and familiar, he is well acquainted with the woman who comes toward him with no reproach except grief on her face. He says to her tenderly: "You are so good, please don't cry any more, you dear good creature." She says, "Are you tired, my angel? Sit here and I will wash your feet." She brings a bowl of water, and kneeling, unlaces his shoes, and when from her knees she raises her sad eyes under her blackened lids, he is sorry for everything, and bursts into tears. "Ah, yes, I am hungry, I am tired, let us eat something together," he says, between sobs. His wife leans her head on his arm and says, "Forgive me!" and this time he is refreshed by the solemn, endless rain of her tears.

Laura takes off her serge dress and puts on a white linen nightgown and goes to bed. She turns her head a little to one side, and lying still, reminds herself that it is time to sleep. Numbers tick in her brain like little clocks, soundless doors close of themselves around her. If you would sleep, you must not remember anything, the children will say tomorrow, good morning, my teacher, the poor prisoners who come every day bringing flowers to their jailor. 1-2-3-4-5 it is monstrous to confuse love with revolution, night with day, life with death—ah, Eugenio!

The tolling of the midnight bell is a signal, but what does it mean? Get up, Laura, and follow me: come out of your sleep, out of your bed, out of this strange house. What are you doing in this house?

Without a word, without fear she rose and reached for Eugenio's hand, but he eluded her with a sharp, sly smile and drifted away. This is not all, you shall see—Murderer, he said, follow me, I will show you a new country, but it is far away and we must hurry. No, said Laura, not unless you take my hand, no; and she clung first to the stair rail, and then to the topmost branch of the Judas tree that bent down slowly and set her upon the earth, and then to the rocky ledge of a cliff, and then to the jagged wave of a sea that was not water but a desert of crumbling stone. Where are you taking me, she asked in wonder but without fear. To death, and it is a long way off, and we must hurry, said Eugenio. No, said Laura, not unless you take my hand. Then eat these flowers, poor prisoner, said Eugenio in a voice of pity, take and eat: and from the Judas tree he stripped the warm bleeding flowers, and held them to her lips. She saw that his hand was fleshless, a cluster of small white petrified branches, and his eye sockets were without light, but she ate the flowers greedily for they satisfied both hunger and thirst. Murderer! said Eugenio, and Cannibal! This is my body and my blood. Laura cried No! and at the sound of her own voice, she awoke trembling, and was afraid to sleep again.

◇◇◇*Marcel Proust (1871-1922). French novelist, author of* Remembrance of Things Past, *one of the great novels of the world. An enormously sensitive and psychologically penetrating writer. A chronic asthmatic condition early set him apart from the world. He was tremendously attached to his mother, and after her death in 1905 he withdrew from the world and secluded himself in a dark cork-lined room.*

FILIAL SENTIMENTS
OF A PARRICIDE

BY MARCEL PROUST

When M. van Blarenberghe the elder died several months ago, I remembered that my mother had known his wife very well. Since the death of my parents I am (in a sense which it would be irrelevant to describe here) less myself, more their son. Without giving up my own friends, I turn more readily to theirs. And the letters I write now are for the most part ones I think they would have written, ones they can write no longer, letters of congratulation or condolence to friends of theirs whom I often scarcely know. So when Mme. van Blarenberghe lost her husband, I wished to tell her of the grief my parents would have felt. I recalled that some years earlier I had occasionally dined with her son at the houses of mutual friends. To him I wrote, speaking more for my late parents than for myself. I got in reply the following beautiful letter, conspicuous for great filial love. I think that this document should be made public because of the meaning given it by the drama that followed so shortly, especially the meaning it gives to the drama. Here is the letter:

LES TIMBRIEUX, PAR JOSSELIN (MORBIHAN)
September 24, 1906

I deeply regret, dear sir, that I was unable to thank you sooner for the sympathy you showed me in my sorrow. But my grief has been so great

From *Partisan Review*, January, 1948. (Translated by Barbara Anderson.) Copyright 1950 by Charles Neider.

that on the advice of doctors I have been traveling for the past four months. I am only now, and with painful effort, beginning to take up my regular life again. Surely you will forgive me.

I wish to tell you, however belatedly, that I was much moved by your remembering our old and excellent relations and profoundly touched by the sentiment that inspired you to write me and my mother in the name of your parents, who left us so prematurely. I did not have the honor of knowing them well, but I remember how much my father appreciated your father and what a pleasure it was for my mother to see Mme. Proust. It was most considerate of you to send us their message from beyond the grave. I will soon return to Paris and if I succeed at all in overcoming the need for isolation which I have felt since the death of him who absorbed my every interest and inspired my every joy, I would be very happy to meet you and talk with you of the past.

Very affectionately,

H. van Blarenberghe

This letter touched me very much. I pitied one who suffered so, I pitied him, yet I envied him: he still had his mother. In consoling her he would console himself. I could not agree to his suggestion of a meeting, only because I was prevented by practical details. But above all the letter wrought a favorable change in my memory of him. The good relations to which he alluded were really of the most banal social kind. At the tables where we sometimes dined, I had scarcely had a chance to talk with him, but the great intellectual distinction of our hosts on those occasions remained for me, and still remains, a guaranty that Henri van Blarenberghe, under his rather conventional exterior—the index, perhaps, of his surroundings rather than of his real personality—hid an original and lively nature. Besides, among those strange flashes of the memory which our brain, so small and yet so vast, stores in prodigious number, if I seek those which represent Henri van Blarenberghe, the flash which always remains most vivid to me is of a face smiling in a way that was particularly fine, the lips still parted after having thrown off some witty remark. Pleasant and rather distinguished, so I "resaw" him, as one might say. Our eyes have more part than we can believe in this active exploration of the past which we call memory. If you look at someone while his mind is intent upon bringing back something from the past, restoring it to life for an instant, you will see that his eyes go suddenly blind to the surrounding objects which they reflected an instant before. "Your eyes are blank, you are somewhere else," we say; however, we see only the external signs of the phenomenon that takes place in the mind. At such a moment the most beautiful eyes in the world no longer touch us with their beauty; they are, to change the meaning of a phrase of Wells's, no more than "machines to explore time," the telescopes of the invisible, which become at best measures to gauge one's advancing age. One feels indeed, when one sees the unsteady gaze of old men, the gaze worn out with endless adaptation to a time so different, often so distant from their own, blindfold itself in order to recall the past, one feels indeed that the curve of their gaze, crossing "the shadow of the days" they have lived, comes to rest several feet before them, so it seems, but in reality fifty or sixty years behind. I remember how the enchanting eyes of Princess Mathilde were transformed when they fixed themselves on images of the great men and magnificent scenes of the beginning of the century. Such images, emanating from her memories, she saw and we shall never see. At the moments when my eyes met hers, I had a sense of the supernatural; her gaze, by some feat of resurrection, firmly and mysteriously joined the present to the past.

Pleasant and rather distinguished, I said, and it is thus that, in one of the more vivid images my memory had stored of him, I resaw Henri van Blarenberghe. But after receiving this letter, I retouched the image in the depths of my memory by interpreting, in terms of a profounder sensibility, a mind less mundane, certain details of his glance and bearing which could, indeed, permit of a more sympathetic and arresting meaning than I had at first allowed. Then, recently, at the request of a friend, I asked him for information concerning an employee of the Chemins de fer de l'Est (M. van Blarenberghe was president of the Board of Directors). Because he had ignored my change of address, his reply, written on the twelfth of last January, did not reach me until the seventeenth, not fifteen days ago, less than eight days before the drama.

48, RUE DE LA BIENFAISANCE
January 12, 1907

DEAR SIR,

I have asked the Compagnie de l'Est for the whereabouts of X, but they have no record of him. Are you right about the name?—if so, the man has disappeared from the company without a trace; he must have had a very provisional and minor connection.

I am distressed at the news of your health since the sad and untimely death of your parents. If it is any consolation to you, I have suffered many physical and moral ailments in attempting to recover from the shock of my father's death. One must always hope. . . . I do not know what the year 1907 holds for me, but let us pray that it may bring some improvement to us both, and that in several months we shall be able to see each other.

Please accept, I beg you, my deepest sympathy.

H. VAN BLARENBERGHE

Five or six days after getting this letter, I recalled, on waking up in the morning, that I had meant to answer it. The day had brought one of those unexpected cold spells which, like high tides of the air, wash over the dykes raised between ourselves and nature by great towns, and battering our closed windows, reaching into our very rooms, make our chilly shoulders feel, through a quickening touch, the furious return of the elements. Days troubled by brusque barometric changes, by shocks even more grave. No joy, after all, in so much violence. We weep for the snow which is about to fall and, as in the lovely verse of André Rivoire, things have the air of "waiting for the snow." Scarcely does "a depression move towards the Balearics," as the newspapers say, or Jamaica begin to quake, when at the same instant in Paris the sufferers from migraine, rheumatism, asthma, no doubt the insane too, reach their crises; the nerves of so many people are united with the farthest points of the universe by bonds which the victims often wish less tight. If the influence of the stars on at least some of them shall one day be recognized (Framery, Pelletan, quoted by M. Brissaud), to whom does the poet's line apply better than to such nervous ones?—

Et de longs fils soyeux l'unissent aux étoiles.

On getting up I prepared to answer Henri van Blarenberghe. But before writing him I wanted to glance at *Figaro*, to proceed to that abominable and voluptuous act called "reading the newspapers," thanks to which all the world's misfortunes and cataclysms of the last twenty-four hours, the battles costing fifty thousand lives, the crimes, the strikes, the bankruptcies, the fires, the poisonings, the suicides, the divorces, the crude emotions of statesman and actor, transmuted for our personal consumption, make for us, who are not involved, a fine little morning treat, an exciting and tonic accompaniment to the sipping of *café au lait.* The fragile thread of *Figaro,* soon enough broken by an indolent gesture, alone divides us from all the world's misery. From the first sensational news of so many people's grief, news we shall soon enjoy relating to friends who have not yet read the paper, we are brought briskly back to the exist-ence which, at the first moment of waking, we had felt it futile to recapture. And if at moments we melt into tears, it is at a phrase like this one: "An impressive silence gripped all hearts, drums sounded on the field, the troops presented arms, a tremendous cry rose up: 'Three cheers for Fallières!'" For this we weep, as we refuse to weep for misfortunes closer to our hearts. Base hypocrites who weep only for the anguish of Hercules or the travels of a President of the Republic! Nevertheless, that morning I did not enjoy reading *Figaro.* I had just skimmed with delight through the volcanic erup-tions, the ministerial crises, the duels of *apaches,* and I was calmly beginning to read a column whose title, "A Drama of Madness," was peculiarly adapted to quicken my morning energies, when sud-denly I saw that the victim was Mme. van Blarenberghe; that the murderer, who had presently killed himself, was her son, Henri van Blarenberghe, whose letter lay near me waiting to be answered: *"One must always hope. . . . I do not know what 1907 holds for me, but let us pray it will bring improvement,"* etc. One must always hope! I do not know what 1907 holds for me! Life had not been long in answering him. 1907 had not cast off her first month before she brought him her present: musket, revolver, and dagger, and a veil for his mind such as Athena fitted on that of Ajax so that he would slaughter the shepherds and flocks in the Greek camp without knowing what he did. "I it was who put the false images in his eyes. And he rushed upon them, striking here and there, thinking that with his own hand he killed the Atrides, hurling himself now on the sheep, now on the shepherds. I made him the prey of raging madness; I forced him into the snares. He came back, his head dripping with sweat and his hands red with blood." As long as the mad strike they know nothing; then, the fit having passed, what anguish! Tekmessa, Ajax's wife, described it: "His madness is over, his frenzy has fallen like the breath of Motos. But, having recov-ered his wits, he is now tormented by a new affliction; for to con-template his own evil deeds when he alone has caused them bitterly

increases his anguish. Once he knows what has happened, he cries
out in lamentation, he who used to say that a man was ignoble to
weep. He sits immobile, shrieking, plotting, no doubt, some dark
design against himself." But when the madness is over for Henri
van Blarenberghe, it is not butchered sheep and shepherds he has
before him. The anguish does not die at once since he himself is not
yet dead when he sees his murdered mother before him; since he
himself is not yet dead when he hears his dying mother say to him,
like Prince Andrey's wife in Tolstoy: "Henri, what have you done
to me! What have you done to me!" "When they reached the landing between the first and second floors," says *Le Matin*, "the servants saw Mme. van Blarenberghe, her face distorted by terror,
descend two or three steps, crying: 'Henri! Henri! what have you
done!' Then the poor woman, covered with blood, threw her arms
in the air and fell on her face. . . . The horrified servants went out
to get help. A little later, four policemen whom one of them had
found forced open the murderer's door. Besides slashing himself
with a dagger, he had ripped open the whole left side of his face
with a bullet. *His eye lay on the pillow*." Here I no longer think of
Ajax. In that eye "which lay on the pillow" I recognize the eye of
the miserable Oedipus, torn out in the most terrible act in the history of human suffering! "Oedipus bursts in with loud cries, goes,
comes, demands a sword. . . . With a dread shriek he throws himself against the double doors, pulls the boards from the hinges,
rushes into the room where he sees Jocasta hanging by the cord
which had strangled her. Seeing her thus, the wretch trembles with
horror, looses the cord; his mother's body falls to the ground. He
rips the gold brooches from Jocasta's garments, with them he tears
his wide-open eyes, saying that they shall no longer see the evil he
has suffered and the disaster he had caused, and, shouting curses,
again he strikes his eyes, the lids open, and from his bloody eyeballs
a rain, a hail of black blood flows down his cheeks. He cries that the
parricide must be shown to all the Cadmeans. He wants to be driven
from the land. Ah, their old felicity was a true felicity; but from this
day on they shall know all the evils that have a name. Lamentations,
ruin, death, disgrace." And in thinking of Henri van Blarenberghe's
pain when he saw his dead mother, I think of another mad man,
of Lear clasping the body of his daughter Cordelia. "Oh! she's

gone forever! She's as dead as earth. No, no, no life! Why should a dog, a horse, a rat, have life, and thou no breath at all? Thou'lt come no more, never, never, never, never, never! Look on her, look, her lips, look there, look there!"

In spite of his horrible wounds Henri van Blarenberghe did not die at once. And I cannot help finding very harsh (although perhaps necessary; can one be sure what really constituted the drama? Remember the brothers Karamazov) the act of the superintendent of police. "The unfortunate man was not dead. The superintendent took him by the shoulders and said: 'Do you hear me? Answer.' The murderer opened his one eye, blinked for an instant and fell back in a coma." To this cruel superintendent I want to speak the words used by Kent in the scene from *King Lear* which I quoted just now to stop Edgar from arousing the already fainting Lear: "Vex not his ghost: O! let him pass; he hates him that would upon the rack of this tough world stretch him out longer."

If I have insisted on repeating these great tragic names, especially those of Ajax and Oedipus, the reader should understand why, and also why I have published these letters and written this page. I wished to show in what a pure and religious atmosphere of moral beauty, bespattered but not defiled, occurred this explosion of madness and blood. I wished to open the room of crime to the air of heaven, to show that this commonplace event was exactly one of those Greek dramas, the presentation of which was almost a religious ceremony and that the poor parricide was not a criminal brute, a being outside humanity, but a noble example of humanity, a man of enlightened soul, a tender and dutiful son whom the most ineluctable fatality—let us say pathological fatality, as the world would say—has thrown, most unfortunate of mortals, into a crime and an expiation worthy of fame.

"I do not easily believe in death," says Michelet in an admirable passage. It is true that he says it of a sea nettle, whose death, so little different from its life, is scarcely notable; and one might also wonder whether Michelet's phrase may not be simply one of those "basic recipes" which great writers soon acquire, thanks to which they are sure of being able to serve up to their clientele at a moment's notice the particular feast which it demands of them. Although I believe without difficulty in the death of a sea nettle, I cannot easily believe in the death of a person, even in the simple eclipse, the simple decay of his reason. Our sense of the soul's continuity is very strong. What! this spirit which, a moment ago, controlled life by its views, controlled death, inspired in us so much respect, there it is, controlled by life, by death, weaker than our own spirit which, however much it may desire, can no longer bow before what has so quickly become little more than a nonentity! It is with madness as with the impairment of faculties in the old, as with death. What? The man who yesterday wrote the letter quoted above, so noble, so intelligent, this man today. . . . ? And also, for the smallest details are important here, the man who was attached so wisely to the small things of life, who answered a letter so elegantly, who met an overture so correctly, who respected the opinion of others, who desired to appear to them, if not influential, at least amiable, who conducted his game on the social exchequer with such finesse and integrity! . . . I say that all this is very important, and if I have quoted the whole first part of the second letter which, to tell the truth, may seem interesting to no one but myself, it is because that practical good sense seems still more remote from what has happened than the beautiful and profound sadness of the last lines. Often, in a ravaged spirit, it is the main branches, the crown, which survive the longest, after disease has already cleared away all the lower branches. Here, the spiritual plant is intact. And just now, as I was copying these letters, I would have liked to be able to communicate the extreme delicacy, and more, the incredible preciseness of the hand which had written so clearly and neatly.

"What have you done to me! What have you done to me!" If we think of it, perhaps there is no truly loving mother who would not be able, on her last day and often long before, to reproach her son with these words. At bottom, we make old, we kill all those who love us, by the anxiety we cause them, by that kind of uneasy tenderness we inspire and ceaselessly put in a state of alarm. If we can see in a beloved body the slow work of destruction side by side with the painful fondness which rouses it, see the faded eyes, the hair long rebelliously black at last vanquished like the rest and growing white, the arteries hardened, the kidneys choked up, the heart strained, courage gone before life, the walk slackened and heavy, the spirit knowing it can hope for nothing yet unwearingly rebounding with invincible hopes, the gaiety even, innate and seemingly immortal, which made such a pleasant companion for sadness, now finally exhausted, perhaps the one who can see this, in that tardy moment of lucidity which even lives most bewitched by idle fancies may have, for even Don Quixote had such a moment, perhaps that one, like Henri van Blarenberghe when he had dispatched his mother with a blow of the dagger, would shrink from the horror of his life and rush for a revolver so that he might die at once. In most men a vision so painful (supposing that they are able to rise to it) blots out immediately the slightest rays of the joy of living. But what joy, what reason for living, what life can withstand this vision? Which, the vision or the joy of living, is true, which is "the Truth"?

◇◇◇*Alexander Pushkin (1799-1837). The great national poet of Russia. See* Russlan and Ludmilla, *a fairy tale in poetic form, which brought him acclaim;* Eugene Onegin, *a novel in verse, his masterpiece;* Boris Godunov, *drama; and such prose works as* The Queen of Spades, The Captain's Daughter *and* Egyptian Nights. Boris Godunov *furnished the libretto for Moussorgsky's opera, and* The Queen of Spades *and* Eugene Onegin *inspired two of Tchaikovsky's operas.*

THE UNDERTAKER

BY ALEXANDER PUSHKIN

> *Are coffins not beheld each day,*
> *The gray hairs of an aging world?*
>   Derzhavin

The last of the effects of the undertaker, Adrian Prokhorov, were piled upon the hearse, and a couple of sorry-looking jades dragged themselves along for the fourth time from Basmannaya to Nikitskaya, whither the undertaker was removing with all his household. After locking up the shop, he posted upon the door a placard announcing that the house was for sale or rent, and then made his way on foot to his new abode. On approaching the little yellow house, which had so long captivated his imagination, and which at last he had bought for a considerable sum, the old undertaker was astonished to find that his heart did not rejoice. When he crossed the unfamiliar threshold and found his new home in the greatest confusion, he sighed for his old hovel, where for eighteen years the strictest order had prevailed. He began to scold his two daughters and the servants for their slowness, and then set to work to help them himself. Order was soon established; the ikon-case, the cupboard with the crockery, the table, the sofa, and the bed occupied the corners reserved for them in the back room; in the kitchen and parlor were placed the master's wares—coffins of all colors and of all sizes, together with cupboards containing mourning hats, cloaks and torches.

(Translated by T. Keane; revised by Avrahm Yarmolinsky.)

Over the gate was placed a sign representing a plump Cupid with an inverted torch in his hand and bearing this inscription: "Plain and colored coffins sold and upholstered here; coffins also let out on hire, and old ones repaired."

The girls retired to their bedroom; Adrian made a tour of inspection of his quarters, and then sat down by the window and ordered the samovar to be prepared.

The enlightened reader knows that Shakespeare and Walter Scott have both represented their grave-diggers as merry and facetious individuals, in order that the contrast might more forcibly strike our imagination. Out of respect for the truth, we cannot follow their example, and we are compelled to confess that the disposition of our undertaker was in perfect harmony with his gloomy métier. Adrian Prokhorov was usually sullen and pensive. He rarely opened his mouth, except to scold his daughters when he found them standing idle and gazing out of the window at the passers-by, or to ask for his wares an exorbitant price from those who had the misfortune—or sometimes the pleasure—of needing them. And so Adrian, sitting near the window and drinking his seventh cup of tea, was immersed as usual in melancholy reflections. He thought of the pouring rain which, just a week before, had commenced to beat down during the funeral of the retired brigadier. Many of the cloaks had shrunk in consequence of the downpour, and many of the hats had been put quite out of shape. He foresaw unavoidable expenses, for his old stock of funeral apparel was in a pitiable condition. He hoped to compensate himself for his losses by the burial of old Trukhina, the merchant's wife, who for more than a year had been upon the point of death. But Trukhina lay dying in Razgulyay, and Prokhorov was afraid that her heirs, in spite of their promise, would not take the trouble to send so far for him, but would make arrangements with the nearest undertaker.

These reflections were suddenly interrupted by three masonic knocks at the door.

"Who is there?" asked the undertaker.

The door opened, and a man, who at first glance could be recognized as a German artisan, entered the room, and with a jovial air advanced toward the undertaker.

"Pardon me, good neighbor," said he in that Russian dialect which to this day we cannot hear without a smile: "pardon me for disturbing you. . . . I wished to make your acquaintance as soon as possible. I am a shoemaker, my name is Gottlieb Schultz, and I live across the street, in that little house just facing your windows. Tomorrow I am going to celebrate my silver wedding, and I have come to invite you and your daughters to dine with us."

The invitation was cordially accepted. The undertaker asked the shoemaker to seat himself and take a cup of tea, and thanks to the open-hearted disposition of Gottlieb Schultz, they were soon engaged in friendly conversation.

"How is business with you?" asked Adrian.

"So so," replied Schultz; "I can't complain. But my wares are not like yours: the living can do without shoes, but the dead cannot do without coffins."

"Very true," observed Adrian; "but if a living person hasn't anything to buy shoes with, he goes barefoot, and holds his peace, if you please; but a dead beggar gets his coffin for nothing."

In this manner the conversation was carried on between them for some time; at last the shoemaker rose and took leave of the undertaker, renewing his invitation.

The next day, exactly at twelve o'clock, the undertaker and his daughters issued from the wicket-door of their newly purchased residence, and went to their neighbor's. I will not stop to describe the Russian *caftan* of Adrian Prokhorov, nor the European toilettes of Akulina and Darya, deviating in this respect from the custom of modern novelists. But I do not think it superfluous to observe that the two girls had on the yellow hats and red shoes, which they were accustomed to don on solemn occasions only.

The shoemaker's little dwelling was filled with guests, consisting chiefly of German artisans with their wives and apprentices. Of the Russian officials there was present but one, Yurko the Finn, a constable, who, in spite of his humble calling, was the special object of the host's attention. Like Pogorelsky's postman, for twenty-five years he had faithfully discharged his duties. The conflagration of 1812, which destroyed the ancient capital, destroyed also his little yellow booth. But immediately after the expulsion of the enemy, a new one appeared in its place, painted gray and with little white Doric columns, and Yurko again began to pace to and fro before it, *with his ax and armor of coarse cloth.* He was known to the greater part of the Germans who lived near the Nikitskaya Gate, and some of them had even spent Sunday night beneath his roof.

Adrian immediately made himself acquainted with him, as with a man whom, sooner or later, he might have need of, and when the guests took their places at the table, they sat down beside each other. Herr Schultz and his wife, and their daughter Lotchen, a young girl of seventeen, did the honors of the table and helped the cook to serve. The beer flowed in streams; Yurko ate like four, and Adrian in no way yielded to him; his daughters, however, stood upon their dignity. The conversation, which was carried on in German, gradually grew more and more noisy. Suddenly the host requested a moment's attention, and uncorking a sealed bottle, he said loudly in Russian:

"To the health of my good Louise!"

The imitation champagne foamed. The host tenderly kissed the fresh face of his partner, and the guests drank noisily to the health of the good Louise.

"To the health of my amiable guests!" exclaimed the host, uncorking a second bottle; and the guests thanked him by draining their glasses once more.

Then followed a succession of toasts. The health of each individual guest was drunk; they drank to Moscow and to a round dozen of little German towns; they drank to the health of all guilds in general and of each in particular; they drank to the health of the masters and apprentices. Adrian drank with assiduity and became so jovial, that he proposed a facetious toast himself. Suddenly one of the guests, a fat baker, raised his glass and exclaimed:

"To the health of those for whom we work, our customers!"

This proposal like all the others, was joyously and unanimously received. The guests began to salute each other; the tailor bowed to the shoemaker, the shoemaker to the tailor, the baker to both, the whole company to the baker, and so on. In the midst of these mutual congratulations, Yurko exclaimed, turning to his neighbor:

"Come, little father! Drink to the health of your corpses!"

Everybody laughed, but the undertaker considered himself insulted, and frowned. Nobody noticed it, the guests continued to drink, and the bells had already rung for vespers when they rose from the table.

The guests dispersed at a late hour, the greater part of them in a very merry mood. The fat baker and the bookbinder, whose face seemed as if bound in red morocco, linked their arms in those of Yurko and conducted him back to his booth, thus observing the proverb: "One good turn deserves another."

The undertaker returned home drunk and angry.

"Why is it," he argued aloud, "why is it that my trade is not as honest as any other? Is an undertaker brother to the hangman? Why did those heathens laugh? Is an undertaker a buffoon? I wanted to invite them to my new house and give them a feast, but now I'll do nothing of the kind. Instead of inviting them, I will invite those for whom I work: the orthodox dead."

"What is the matter, master?" said the servant, who was engaged at that moment in taking off his boots: "why do you talk such nonsense? Make the sign of the cross! Invite the dead to your new house! What nonsense!"

"Yes, by God! I will invite them," continued Adrian, "and that, too, for tomorrow! . . . Do me the favor, my benefactors, to come and feast with me tomorrow evening; I will regale you with what God has sent me."

With these words the undertaker turned into bed and soon began to snore.

It was still dark when Adrian was roused out of his sleep. Trukhina, the merchant's wife, had died during the course of that very night, and a special messenger was sent off on horseback by her clerk to carry the news to Adrian. The undertaker gave him ten copecks to buy brandy with, dressed himself as hastily as possible, took a *droshky* and set out for Razgulyay. At the gate of the house in which the deceased lay, the police had already taken their stand, and the trades-people were busily moving back and forth, like ravens that smell a dead body. The deceased lay upon a table, yellow as wax, but not yet disfigured by decomposition. Around her stood her relatives, neighbors and domestic servants. All the windows were open; tapers were burning; and the priests were reading the prayers for the dead. Adrian went up to the nephew of Trukhina, a young shopman in a fashionable jacket, and informed him that the coffin, wax candles, pall, and the other funeral accessories would be immediately delivered in good order. The heir thanked him in an absent-minded manner, saying that he would not bargain about the price, but would rely upon his acting in everything according to his conscience. The undertaker, in accordance with his custom, swore that he would not charge him too much, exchanged significant glances with the clerk, and then departed to commence operations.

The whole day was spent in passing to and fro between Razgulyay and the Nikitskaya Gate. Toward evening everything was finished, and he returned home on foot, after having dismissed his driver. It was a moonlight night. The undertaker reached the Nikitskaya Gate in safety. Near the Church of the Ascension he was hailed by our acquaintance Yurko, who, recognizing the undertaker, wished him good night. It was late. The undertaker was just approaching his house, when suddenly he fancied he saw some one approach his gate, open the wicket, and disappear within.

"What does that mean?" thought Adrian. "Who can be wanting me again? Can it be a thief come to rob me? Or have my foolish girls got lovers coming after them? It means no good, I fear!"

And the undertaker thought of calling his friend Yurko to his assistance. But at that moment, another person approached the wicket and was about to enter, but seeing the master of the house hastening toward him, he stopped and took off his three-cornered hat. His face seemed familiar to Adrian, but in his hurry he was not able to examine it closely.

"You are favoring me with a visit," said Adrian, out of breath. "Walk in, I beg of you."

"Don't stand on ceremony, sir," replied the other, in a hollow voice; "you go first, and show your guests the way."

Adrian had no time to spend upon ceremony. The wicket was open; he ascended the steps followed by the other. Adrian thought he could hear people walking about in his rooms.

"What the devil does all this mean!" he thought to himself, and he hastened to enter. But the sight that met his eyes caused his legs to give way beneath him.

The room was full of corpses. The moon, shining through the windows, lit up their yellow and blue faces, sunken mouths, dim,

half-closed eyes, and protruding noses. Adrian, with horror, recognized in them people that he himself had buried, and in the guest
who had entered with him, the brigadier who had been buried
during the pouring rain. They all, ladies and gentlemen, surrounded
the undertaker, with bowings and salutations, except one poor man
lately buried gratis, who, conscious and ashamed of his rags, did
not venture to approach, but meekly kept to a corner. All the others
were decently dressed: the female corpses in caps and ribbons, the
officials in uniforms, but with their beards unshaven, the tradesmen
in their holiday *caftans*.

"You see, Prokhorov," said the brigadier in the name of all the
honorable company, "we have all risen in response to your invitation.
Only those have stopped at home who were unable to come, who
have crumbled to pieces and have nothing left but fleshless bones.
But even of these there was one who hadn't the patience to remain
behind—so much did he want to come and see you. . . ."

At this moment a little skeleton pushed his way through the
crowd and approached Adrian. His skull smiled affably at the undertaker. Shreds of green and red cloth and rotten linen hung on him
here and there as on a pole, and the bones of his feet rattled inside
his big jackboots, like pestles in mortars.

"You do not recognize me, Prokhorov," said the skeleton. "Don't
you remember the retired sergeant of the Guard, Pyotr Petrovich
Kurilkin, the same to whom, in the year 1799, you sold your first
coffin, and a deal one at that, instead of oak, as agreed?"

With these words the corpse stretched out his bony arms toward
him; but Adrian, collecting all his strength, shrieked and pushed
him away. Pyotr Petrovich staggered, fell and crumbled to pieces.
Among the corpses arose a murmur of indignation; all stood up for
the honor of their companion, and they overwhelmed Adrian with
such threats and curses, that the poor host, deafened by their shrieks
and almost crushed to death, lost his presence of mind, fell upon the
bones of the retired sergeant of the Guard, and swooned away.

For some time the sun had been shining upon the bed on which
the undertaker lay. At last he opened his eyes and saw before him
the servant attending to the samovar. With horror, Adrian recalled
all the incidents of the previous day. Trukhina, the brigadier,
and the sergeant Kurilkin, rose vaguely before his imagination. He

waited in silence for the servant to open the conversation and inform him of the events of the night.

"How you have slept, Adrian Prokhorovich!" said Aksinya, handing him his dressing-gown. "Your neighbor, the tailor, has been here, and the constable also called to inform you that today is his name-day; but you were so sound asleep, that we did not wish to wake you."

"Did anyone come for me from the late Trukhina?"

"The late? Is she dead, then?"

"What a fool you are! Didn't you yourself help me yesterday to prepare the things for her funeral?"

"Have you taken leave of your senses, master, or have you not yet recovered from the effects of yesterday's drinking-bout? What funeral was there yesterday? You spent the whole day feasting at the German's, and then came home drunk and threw yourself upon the bed, and have slept till this hour, when the bells have already rung for mass."

"Really!" said the undertaker, greatly relieved.

"Yes, indeed," replied the servant.

"Well, since that is the case, make tea as quickly as possible and call my daughters."

◇◇◇*Wladyslaw Stanislaw Reymont (1867-1925). Polish short-story writer and novelist. He turned to peasant themes for his work, deploring urbanization. Nobel Prize, 1924. See his classic,* The Peasants.

TWILIGHT

BY WLADYSLAW STANISLAW REYMONT

Sokol lay dying. He had been lying this way a long time. He had fallen sick and was now kicked about like a useless carcass. Good people said it would be wrong to kill him, even though his handsome hide would make fine leather. Yes, good people let him die slowly, alone and forgotten. The same good souls rewarded him occasionally with a kick to remind him that he was dying too slowly. But they took no other notice of him. Once in a while the hunting dogs, with whom he used to leap in the chase, came to visit him. But dogs have ugly souls . . . (from too much contact with human beings). And at every call of their masters they left Sokol precipitously. Only Lappa, an old blind Siberian hound, stayed with him longer than the others. He lay dozing under the feed trough, oppressed with sorrow at the sight of Sokol, whose large, pleading, tearful eyes frightened him.

So the old horse was left to his solitary misery. The days kept him company . . . golden, rosy days, or gray and harsh and painful ones, filling the stall with their weeping. . . . They peered into his eyes, then silently departed, as if awe-stricken. . . .

But Sokol was afraid only of the nights, the short, fearful, silent, stifling nights of June. It was then that he felt he was surely dying. . . . And he became almost frantic with terror. He would tear at his halter, and beat with his hoofs against the wall . . . he wanted to escape . . . to run, and run. . . .

One day, as the sun was setting, he jumped up, stared at the flecks of light that filtered in through the cracks in the walls, and began to neigh long and plaintively. Not a single voice answered him from the close heavy stillness of the departing day. Swallows flitted by, or chirped from their nests, or darted like feathered arrows among the golden insects that buzzed in the sun's last rays. From the distant meadows was heard the sharp ringing and swishing of busy scythes. And from the fields of grain and flowers came a rustling, and humming, and whispering.

But about Sokol there was a deep, awful silence, that made him shiver. Somber panic seized him; he began to tug frenziedly at his halter . . . it broke, and he fled into the yard.

The sun blinded him and a wild pain gnawed at his entrails. He lowered his head, and stood motionless, as if stunned. Little by little, however, he came to himself again; dim memories of fields, forests, meadows, floated through his brain. . . . There awoke in him a resistless desire to run . . . a longing to conquer vast distances . . . a craving thirst to live again. . . . He began to seek eagerly for an exit from the yard. It was a square yard, three sides of which were shut in by various buildings. He searched in vain. He tried again and again, though he could barely stand on his legs, though every movement caused him indescribable pain, though the blood kept flowing from his old sores. . . .

At last he struck a wooden fence from which he could see the manor-house. He gazed at the flower-covered lawn before it, where dogs were basking, at the house itself with its windows glittering golden in the sun, and began to neigh pleadingly, piteously. . . .

If anyone had come and said a kind word to him, or smoothed his coat caressingly, he would willingly have laid down and died. But all about was deserted, drowsy, still. . . .

In despair he began to bite the rails, and wrench the gate, leaning against it with all his weight. It burst open, and he walked into the garden. He approached the verandah, still neighing plaintively; but no one heard him. He stood there a long time, gazing at the curtained windows, and even tried to climb up the steps. Then he walked all round the house.

Suddenly he seemed to forget everything. . . . He saw only visions of vast grain-fields, as limitless as the sea, stretching away to a distant, endlessly distant, horizon. Bewitched by these alluring fancies he began to stagger and stumble forward with all his waning might. . . .

Sokol shivered. His eyes grew glazed with suffering. He breathed heavily and nosed the damp grass to cool his heated nostrils. . . .

He was very thirsty . . . but he kept staggering onward, impelled by his somber panic and resistless impulse to escape. As he stumbled among the stalks of wheat and corn his feet grew heavier and heavier. The furrows were like pit-falls; the grass entangled his feet and dragged him down. The bushes barred his path. The whole earth seemed to pull him eagerly toward itself. Often the grain hid the horizon from his gaze.

His poor dumb soul sank deeper and deeper into the darkness of terror. Recognizing nothing, he kept staggering blindly forward as in a fog. A partridge, leading her brood, flew up suddenly between his legs, causing him to start in fright and remain motionless, not daring to stir. Crows that flew silently across the fields stopped on observing him, and sat down on a pear-tree, cawing and croaking evilly.

He dragged himself into the meadow and sank exhausted to the ground. He stretched out his legs, looked up into the sky, and sighed piteously. The crows flew down from the trees and hopped along the ground nearer and nearer. The corn bent over and stared at him with its red poppy-eyes. Still nearer came the crows, sharpening their beaks in the hard grass-tufts. Some flew over him, cawing ravenously, lower and lower, till he saw their terrible round eyes and half-open beaks. But he could not stir. He struck his paws into the ground and fancied he was up again, galloping across the field . . . in the chase . . . the hounds beside him barking . . . flying like the wind. . . .

His agony grew so intense that he gave one savage neigh and sprang to his feet. The crows flew away, screeching. . . .

But now he saw nothing . . . understood nothing. . . . Everything wavered about him . . . spun, tossed, crashed. . . . He felt himself sinking, as in a deep mire. . . . A cold shiver ran over his body, and he lay still. . . .

The sun sank. Obliterating twilight covered everything with a silent mantle. The barking of a dog grew audible in the distance.

Lappa ran up to his friend, but Sokol did not recognize him. The old dog licked him, pawed at the ground, ran barking across the field hither and thither, calling for help but no one came. . . .

The grass looked into Sokol's wide-open eyes. . . . The trees approached him, and reached out their sharp claw-like twigs to him. The birds grew still. Thousands of living things began to crawl over his body, to pinch, and claw, and rend his flesh. . . . The crows cawed frightfully.

Lappa, bristling with terror, moaned and howled weirdly. . . .

◇◇◇*Rainer Maria Rilke (1875-1926). German poet, born in Prague.*

THE STRANGER

BY RAINER MARIA RILKE

A stranger has written me a letter. Not of Europe has the stranger written me, nor of Moses, nor of the great or the small prophets, nor of the Emperor of Russia, nor of the Tsar, Ivan the Terrible, his awful ancestor. Not of the mayor or of our neighbor the cobbler, not of the nearby town, not of the far towns; and even the forest with the many deer, in which every morning I lose myself, is not mentioned in his letter. He tells me nothing about his little mother or about his sisters, who have probably married long ago. Perhaps his little mother is dead; how else could it be that in a four-page letter I find her nowhere mentioned! He shows a much, much greater confidence in me; he makes me his brother, he tells me of his need.

In the evening the stranger comes to see me. I light no lamp; I help him off with his coat and beg him to drink tea with me, for it is just the hour at which I daily drink my tea. And on such intimate visits one may be at ease. As we are about to sit down, I notice that my guest is restless; his face is full of fear and his hands tremble. "Quite so," say I, "here is a letter for you." And then I begin to pour out the tea. "Do you take sugar? And lemon perhaps? In Russia I learned to drink tea with lemon. Will you try?" Then I light a lamp, and place it in a far corner, rather high, so that really twilight remains in the room, only somewhat warmer than before, a rosy twilight. And therewith my guest's face seems more certain, warmer and by far more familiar.

I welcome him once more with the words: "You know, I have been expecting you for a long while." And before the stranger has time to be astonished, I explain: "I know a story which I would like to tell no one but you; do not ask me why, only tell me whether your chair is comfortable, whether the tea is sweet enough and whether you want to hear the story."

My guest had to smile. Then he said simply: "Yes."

"To all three questions: yes?"

"To all three."

We both leaned back simultaneously in our chairs so that our faces became shadowy. I put my glass down, rejoiced at the golden glint of the tea, slowly forgot this joy again and asked suddenly: "Do you still remember God?"

The stranger reflected. His eyes sank deep into the darkness, and with the little points of light in the pupils they resembled two long tree-lined avenues in a park, over which summer and sun lie luminous and broad. These too begin so, with round twilight, stretching in always narrower darkness up to a distant, shimmering point—the exit on the far side to a perhaps still brighter day. While I was realizing this, he said, hesitating and as though he only reluctantly used his voice: "Yes, I still remember God."

"Good," I thanked him, "for it is with him that my story deals. But first tell me, do you sometimes talk to children?"

"Well, yes, occasionally, just in passing, at least—"

"Perhaps you know that God, in consequence of some horrid disobedience of his hands, does not know what a finished man really looks like?"

"I heard that once somewhere, but I don't know from whom—" my guest replied, and I saw uncertain memories driving across his brow.

"No matter," I broke in, "listen to the story:

"A long time God endured this uncertainty. For his patience is great as his strength. Once, however, when dense clouds had lain between him and the earth for many days, so that he hardly knew any more whether he had not merely dreamed everything—the world and men and time—he called his right hand, which had so long been banished from his sight and hidden in small, insignificant works. It came willingly; for it believed that God wanted at last to forgive it. When God saw it there before him in its beauty, youth and strength, he was indeed tempted to forgiveness. But he remembered in time and commanded without looking at it: 'You are to go down to earth. You are to take on the form you will see there among men, and to stand, naked, upon a mountain, so that I can observe you closely. As soon as you arrive below, go to a young woman and say to her, but quite softly: I want to live. At first there will be a little darkness about you and then a great darkness, which is called childhood, and then you will be a man, and climb the mountain as I have commanded you. All this will last but a moment. Farewell.'

"The right hand then took leave of the left, called it many pleasant names—indeed, it has even been declared that it suddenly bowed down before it and said: 'Hail, Holy Ghost.' But here St. Paul stepped up and smote off God's right hand; and an archangel caught it up and bore it away under his wide mantle. But God held the wound to with his left hand, so that his blood should not stream over the stars and thence fall down in sorrowful drops on the earth. A short time after, God, watching attentively all that went on below, saw that men in iron garments were busying themselves about one mountain more than all others. And he expected to see his hand climb up there. But there came only a man in, as it seemed, a red cloak, who was dragging upwards some black swaying thing. At the same instant, God's left hand, lying over his open wound, began to grow restless, and suddenly, before God could prevent it, it left its place and rushed about madly among the stars, crying: 'Oh poor right hand, and I cannot help you!' Therewith it tugged hard at God's left arm, on the very end of which it hung, and tried to tear itself free. And the whole earth was red with God's blood, and it was impossible to see what was happening beneath it. At that time God had very nearly died. With a last effort he called his right hand back; it came pale and trembling and lay down in its place like a sick animal. And even the left hand, which already knew a good deal, since it had recognized the right down on earth as it toiled up the mountain in a red cloak, could not learn from it what had further happened on that hill. It must have been something terrible. For God's right hand has not yet recovered from it, and suffers under its memories no less than under the old wrath of God, who has still not yet forgiven his hands."

My voice took a little rest. The stranger had covered his face with his hands. Thus everything stayed for a long time. Then the stranger said, in a voice I had long known: "And why have you told me this story?"

"Who else would have understood me? You come to me without rank, without office, without temporal honors, almost without a name. It was dark as you came in, yet I noticed in your features a resemblance—"

The stranger looked up, questioning.

"Yes," I answered his silent gaze, "I often think perhaps God's hand is again on its way . . ."

The children have heard this story, and apparently it was told them in such a way that they could understand everything; for they love this story.

◇◇◇*Antoine de Saint Exupéry (1900-1944). French writer and aviator. He was reported missing over southern France in 1944. See* Night Flight; Wind, Sand, and Stars; Flight to Arras.

LETTER TO A HOSTAGE

BY *ANTOINE DE SAINT EXUPERY*

When, in December, 1940, I passed through Portugal on my way to the States, Lisbon seemed to me a sort of Paradise, bright but sad. People there were talking a good deal then of an impending invasion, and Portugal was clinging grimly to the illusion of its good luck. Lisbon, which had set up the most enchanting of Exhibitions, smiled a bit wanly as mothers do with no news of a fighting son, who try to save him by their faith. "My son's alive, you see I'm smiling" . . . And so Lisbon said: "See how happy, how peaceful, how well-lit I am." . . . The whole of the Continent loomed over Portugal like some menacing mountain, teeming with beasts of prey. Lisbon prinked out, was challenging Europe: "Who could take me for a target when I make such efforts not to hide! When I am so vulnerable! . . ."

At night, the towns at home were ash grey. I had got unused to light of any kind and this gleaming capital made me feel ill at ease. In districts where lights are dim, diamonds in a too bright window draw suspicious characters. You feel them around. I felt the night of Europe looming over Lisbon, a night peopled by bomber squadrons, as though sensing this treasure from afar.

But Portugal blinded herself to the greed of the monster. She would not credit the evil signs. Portugal talked art with a faith that was frantic. Who would dare smash her in her cult of art? Portugal had brought out all her wonders. She had produced her great men. Lacking guns and lacking an army, she had erected all her sentinels of stone—poets, conquistadors, explorers—to oppose the invader's old iron. All Portugal's past, for lack of guns and an army, barred the

---

From *Modern French Short Stories*. (Translated by John Rodker.) By permission of New Directions.

road. Who would dare smash her with all her heritage from a glorious past?

And so, every night, with melancholy, I would roam among the marvels of this Exhibition, where all was in perfect taste, where everything bordered on perfection, even to the very discretion of the music, selected with so much tact, which flowed unpretentiously through the gardens like the simple ripple of a stream. Would they wipe out this wondrous sense of proportion?

And I found Lisbon, under its smile, sadder than my blacked-out cities.

I have known, you too may have known, families a bit odd, which always at their tables keep a place for someone dead. They denied the irreparable. But it did not seem to me that this challenge comforted them. The dead should be treated as such. Then, as the dead, they regain another kind of being. But such families hold up their return. They turn them into the eternally missing, into eternally late guests. They barter mourning for hollow expectation. And such homes seem to me whelmed in a sort of endless wretchedness far more stifling than distress. For air pilot Guillaumet, the last friend I lost, Guillaumet who was shot down in the postal air service, Lord yes! for him, I was willing to go into mourning. Guillaumet will not change any more. He will never again be present, but neither will he ever be absent. I have sacrificed his place at my table, however futile the snare, and turned him into a true dead friend.

But Portugal strove to believe in happiness, leaving it its place at the table, its illuminations, its music. They acted being happy in Lisbon, so that God might believe in it too.

Lisbon also owed its atmosphere of sadness to certain refugees. I do not mean the banned in search of a refuge. I do not mean the immigrants in quest of a land to fecundate with their toil. I mean those who expatriated themselves far from the misery of their near ones to get their money safe.

Unable to get in anywhere in the city, I lived at Estoril, near the Casino. I had just come out of solid fighting: my own Air Squadron which, for nine whole months, had flown uninterruptedly over Germany, had again, in the one German offensive, lost three-quarters of its crews. Back home, I had experienced the drear atmosphere of slavery and the menace of starvation. I had experienced the

dense night of our cities. And now, a step away, Estoril Casino
thronged nightly with ghosts. Silent luxurious cars, as though bound
for some destination, set them down on the fine sand at the porch.
They were dressed for dinner, as in the past. They displayed their
shirt-fronts or their pearls. They had invited each other to stage
meals at which they would have nothing to say to each other.

Then they played at baccarat or roulette, according to their
means. Sometimes I went to look on. It was not indignation I felt,
nor irony, but a sort of anguish. The kind one feels at the Zoo before
the survivors of some extinct species. They took places round the
tables. They crowded up to some stern-looking croupier and strove
to feel hope, despair, alarm, envy and jubilation. Like the living.
They staked fortunes that, possibly, at that moment, had lost any
meaning. They used money that perhaps was obsolete. The shares
in their strong-boxes were perhaps backed by factories already con-
fiscated or being shattered by bombs. They drew their bills on some
distant planet. They strove to believe, by reliving the past, that nothing for so and so many months had started to crack in the world,
that their excitement was real, that their cheques were backed, that
their conventions were eternal. It was hallucinatory. Like a ballet
of dolls. But it depressed one.

Possibly, they really felt nothing. I gave them up, I went for air
to the seashore. And the Estoril sea, that tamed and seaside-place
sea, seemed also part of the play. Like an outmoded dress with a
train, it thrust one languorous, moon-glittering wave into the gulf.

I

I found my refugees again on the steamer. And the steamer, too,
diffused a sort of apprehension. This steamer was transplanting these
rootless plants from one continent to another. And I thought to myself: "I like being a traveller, but I should hate being an emigrant.
I learnt so much at home that anywhere else would be useless." But
here were my emigrants taking their little address books out of their
pockets, their identity shreds and tatters. They were still acting at
being somebody. They clung with all their might to whatever might
signify something. "Yes, I'm so and so, they would say . . . from
such and such city . . . the friend of . . . do you happen to
know . . . ?"

And they told you the story of a friend, or something they were responsible for, some lapse, or anything at all that would link them with anything whatever. Yet nothing of that past, since they were expatriating themselves, would be of further use to them. It was still warm, fresh, palpitating, as keepsakes are at first. You tie up the tender letters. You add a token or two. You wrap it all up very carefully. And a melancholy charm emanates from it all. Then some blue-eyed blonde passes by, and that's the death of the relic. And the friend, too, the responsibility, the native town and memories of home, all pale if they no longer serve any purpose.

They knew it, of course. Just as Lisbon simulated being happy, they pretended to believe they would soon return. It is pleasant—the exile of the prodigal son! But it is not a true exile, because, back at home, the paternal house still remains. Whether one be absent in the next room or on the other side of the planet, there is no essential difference. The presence of the friend who is seemingly distant may become more intense than that presence itself. So too with prayer. Never did I love home more than when I was in the Sahara. Never were betrothed closer to each other than when the sixteenth-century Breton sailors doubled Cape Horn, eternally struggling with contrary winds. From the minute they sailed, their return had already begun. And it was their return they were preparing as their massive hands raised the sails. The shortest road from Breton port to the sweetheart's house lay around Cape Horn. But here my emigrants seemed like Breton sailors whose sweethearts had been spirited away. No Breton sweetheart would ever again set for them her humble lamp at her window. They were not prodigal sons. They were prodigal sons with no home to which to return. Then the real journey begins, the journey outside oneself.

How remake oneself? How re-knot the weighty hank of memories in oneself? This phantom boat was full as Limbo with souls to be born. Real only, so real one would have liked to touch them with a finger, were those who, part of the vessel and ennobled by real tasks, bore dishes, polished brass, brushed shoes, and vaguely scornful, ministered to the dead. It was not poverty that gained these emigrants that faint scorn from the crew. It was not money they lacked, but density. They were no longer men of this or that family, friend or responsibility. They acted the part, but it was no longer true. No one needed them. What a miracle that telegram is that breaks in on your peace, gets you up in the night and urges you to the station. "Hurry! I need you." We quickly discover the friends who help. But we only slowly deserve those who demand to be helped. Yes, no one hated these ghosts of mine, no one envied them, no one pestered them. But no one loved them with the only love that mattered. I told myself: the minute they get ashore they'll be deep in cocktail parties to welcome them, in dinners to console them. But who will bang on their doors demanding admittance? "Open, it's me!" One must nurse a child at the breast a long time before it learns to demand. One must nurse a friend a long time before he demands his due of friendship. One must have ruined oneself for generations to keep the tottering manor in repair, before one learns to love it.

II

And so I said to myself: "The main thing is that somewhere, what one has lived through, should remain. The customs. The family reunions. Home and all one remembers it by. The main thing is to live for the return." And I felt menaced through and through by the fragility of those distant poles on which I depended. I was on the verge of refinding myself in a real desert and began to understand a mystery that had puzzled me for years.

I lived three years in the Sahara. I, too, like so many others, pondered its magic. Whoever has known life in the Sahara where everything, it seems, is but solitude and dearth, nevertheless laments those years as the finest in his existence. The words, "pining for the desert, pining for solitude and space" are but literary and explain nothing. But now, for the first time, on board this steamer packed tight and crawling with passengers, it seemed to me I understood the desert.

True, as far as eye can see, all the Sahara offers is uninterrupted sand, or rather, since dunes are rare, the aspect of a pebbly beach. There, one is eternally immersed in the very stuff of boredom. And yet, invisible divinities create for one a network of directions, of declivities and signs, a musculature hidden and vibrant. The monotony disappears. Everything drops into place. Even a silence there is not like other silences.

There is a silence of peace when the tribes are conciliated: when the evening brings its coolness back and it seems, sails furled, that one has moored in some quiet harbour. There is a silence of noon when the sun suspends all thought and movement. There is a false silence when the north wind drops and insects suddenly arrive, torn like pollen from the inland oases, heralding the sand-storm from the East. There is a silence of conspiracy, when one knows that some distant tribe is fomenting rebellion. There is a silence of mystery, when the Arabs start holding their unintelligible palavers. There is a taut silence when the messenger delays in returning; a piercing silence when at night one holds back one's breath to listen: a silence of melancholy if one remembers whom one loves.

Everything becomes polarized. Every star determines a precise direction. They are all stars of the Magi. Each serves its proper god. This points the direction of a distant well, hard to win. And the distance that separates you from this well crushes you like some overwhelming crag. This points the direction of a dried-up well. And the very star seems arid. And the distance between you and the dried-up well is all dead level. The other star serves as a guide to a secret oasis, whose praises the nomads have sung, but the tribes in revolt bar you from it. And the sand between you and that oasis is fairy greensward. That other again points to some white town in the South, delectable as a fruit under one's teeth. That other, to the sea.

Thus, almost unreal poles magnetize this desert from afar: the house where one lived as a child and still in memory vivid! A friend of whom one knows naught, save that he is living!

And so you feel yourself tensed and vitalized by the magnetic field that draws or repels you, solicits or resists you. You find yourself solidly based, fixed and installed in the midst of cardinal directions.

And as the desert offers no tangible riches, as there is naught to see or hear in the desert, one is forced to admit, since one's inner life, far from being lulled into insensibility there grows stronger, that man is animated primarily by invisible drags. Man is governed by the spirit. In the desert I am worth as much as my gods.

So, if, on board my sad steamer, I felt myself rich in orientations that were still fertile, if I inhabited a planet that still lived, it was, thanks to certain friends lost behind me in the night of France, friends I began to feel essential.

France, indeed, for me was neither an abstract goddess nor some historian's concept, but well and truly living flesh on which I depended, a network of ties which determined my actions, an arrangement of poles which fixed the trends of my heart. I had a need to feel that those whom I needed to give me direction were solider and more enduring than myself. To know where to return. To exist.

In them, my country dwelt in its entirety and lived through them in myself. For him who navigates the seas a continent epitomizes itself in the simple flash of some beacons. A beacon gives no measure of distance. Its light appears to the eye and that is all. Yet all the wonders of the continent dwell in that star.

And so to-day, when France, after the total occupation, with all its cargo, has passed wholly into silence, like a ship steaming without lights, of which no one knows whether or no it survives the perils of the sea, the fate of each of those I love tortures me more than some incurable disease. I find myself menaced to the core by their fragility.

He who, tonight, haunts my memory, is fifty. He is ill. And a Jew. How will he survive the German terror? To imagine he still breathes I must make myself think him unknown to the invader, secretly sheltered behind the fine rampart of silence of the peasants of his village. Then, only, do I believe he lives still. Then only, strolling off into the realm of his friendship, which no frontiers bound, can I let myself feel no emigrant, but a traveller. For the desert is not where one thinks it is. The Sahara is more alive than a metropolis and the city that most swarms with life grows empty if the essential poles of existence are demagnetized.

III

How then does life build these magnetic lines by which we live? Whence comes the weight that draws me towards the house of this friend? What then are those high moments that made this presence one of the poles I need? With what hidden happenings then must personal affections be moulded, and through them, the love of one's land?

The real miracles, how little noise they make! Cardinal events, how simple they are! Of that moment I wish to relate, so little is there to be said that I have to ponder on it and talk to this friend.

It was on a day before the war, on the banks of the Saône, near

Tournus. We had picked a restaurant for lunch whose wooden balcony overhung the river. Our elbows resting on a plain wood table, scored by customers' knives, we had ordered two Pernods. Your doctor had forbidden you spirits, but on big occasions you cheated. This was one. We did not know why, but it was one. What was rejoicing us was more impalpable than the quality of the light. And so, you decided for the Pernod that marked important occasions. And as, a few steps away, two men were unloading a barge, we invited the bargees. We had beckoned them from the balcony. And they came. Perfectly naturally. It seemed so obvious to invite these friends, perhaps because of this invisible heyday we were feeling. They saw it so well that they immediately responded. And so we drank together.

The sun felt good. The poplars on the farther bank, the plain to the very horizon, were bathed in its warm honey. And we went on getting more and more cheerful without knowing why. Everything assured us: the clear sunlight, the river flowing, the meal, the bargees for having responded, the maid who served us with a sort of consummate grace, as though in charge of some eternal feast. We were wholly at peace, tucked well away from all confusion in a finite civilization. We savoured a sort of state of perfection, in which, every wish vouchsafed, nothing remained to reveal to each other. We felt we were pure, upright, lambent, indulgent. We could not have said what truth was thus being manifested. But the dominant feeling was certainly that of assurance. Of an assurance almost proud.

Thus, the universe, through us, showed its kindness. The nebulae condensed, the planets hardened, the first amoeba came into being and life's gigantic labour pains led the amoeba to man in order that all should converge harmoniously, through us, in this quality of pleasure! It was not so bad, as an achievement.

And so we relished this mute communion and these almost religious rites. Lulled by the movements of the hieratic maid, the bargees and ourselves drank together like worshippers of the same religion, though none of us would have said which. One of the bargees was Dutch. The other, German. In the past, he had fled from the Nazis, who had been after him as a Communist, or a Trotskyist, or a Catholic or a Jew. (I have forgotten the label under which the man was outlawed.) But at this moment the bargee was something very different from a label. It was what was inside that counted. The human leaven. He was a friend, pure and simple. And we were agreed, as among friends. You, I, the bargees and the maidservant. Agreed about what? The Pernod? The meaning of life? The mellow sunlight? That too, we could not have said. But this agreement was so complete, so deep rooted, and its whole substance, though impossible to formulate in words, was based so clearly on a faith, that we would willingly have set to fortify the chalet, sustaining a siege and dying behind machine guns to preserve that substance.

What substance? . . . And this is just where it is difficult to express what one means! I run the danger of capturing only the reflections, not the essence. Inadequate words will allow my truth to escape. I should be being obscure if I claim that we would easily have fought to rescue a certain something in the bargees' smile, in your smile, in mine and in the maid's, some miracle of that sun, which, with so much effort, for so many millions of years, had managed to achieve through us the quality of a smile that was pretty satisfactory.

Essentials, most often, are imponderable. The essential here, apparently, was but a smile. Often, the essential is a smile. One is paid by a smile. One is repaid by a smile. One is animated by a smile. And the quality of a smile may lead to one's death. Yet, since this quality freed us so completely from the anguish of these times, vouchsafed us certitude, hope, peace; to-day, in order to try to express myself better, I feel the need to tell the story of another smile too.

IV

It was when I was reporting the Civil War in Spain. I had been indiscreet enough, round three a.m., to witness some secret stuff being loaded at a goods yard. The bustle of the gangs and the obscurity seemed to lend a certain collusion. And some anarchist militiamen thought me suspect.

It happened very simply. Before I had any idea of their springy, silent approach, they were already gently closing around me, like fingers. Their gun barrel pressed lightly against my abdomen, in a silence that seemed to me fateful. At last I raised my arms.

I noticed that they gazed not at my face, but at my tie (fashions in anarchist districts did not recommend this artistic appendage). My muscles twitched. I waited for the report: those were the days of prompt judgments. But there was no report. After some seconds of complete vacuum, in which the gangs at work seemed to be dancing a dream ballet in some other world, my anarchists, with a nod, beckoned me forward in front of them and we set off, without haste, across the sidings. My capture had taken place in absolute silence and with not one unnecessary movement. Submarine life must be like that too.

Soon I penetrated into a basement converted into a guardroom. Under the dim light of a cheap oil lamp, other militiamen dozed, their rifles between their knees. They exchanged some words, in expressionless tones, with the patrol which had brought me in. One of them searched me.

I talk Spanish, but Catalan I don't know. I understood, however, that they were demanding my papers. I had forgotten them at the hotel. I answered: "Hotel . . . journalist . . ." without knowing whether my language conveyed anything. The militiamen passed my camera from hand to hand as though proof of my guilt. Some of the yawners, collapsed on their rickety chairs, got up with a sort of boredom and leaned against the wall.

For the main impression was of boredom. Boredom and sleep. These men's capacity for attention, it seemed to me, was worn threadbare. I could almost have welcomed some sign of hostility, to establish a human contact. But they did not honour me with any sign of anger, nor even of blame. At various times I tried to protest in Spanish. But my protests fell on deaf ears. They looked at me, unresponsive, as they would have looked at a goldfish in a glass bowl.

They were waiting. What were they waiting for? For one of them to return? Dawn? I said to myself: "They're waiting, perhaps, to be hungry . . ."

And then I said to myself: "They'll do something stupid: it's absolutely ridiculous!" . . . What I felt—much more than feeling anxious—was disgust at the absurdity of it all. I said to myself: "If they unfreeze, if they want to do something, they'll fire!"

Was I, yes or no, really in danger? Were they still unaware that I was not a saboteur, not a spy, but a journalist? That my identity papers were at the hotel? Had they made a decision? What?

I knew nothing about them, except that they shot people without worrying particularly. It is not their fellows (the man himself does not interest them) that revolutionary vanguards hunt, whatever the party to which they belong, but symptoms. Adverse truth, to them, was like an epidemic. Given some dubious symptoms, the pestilent one was hurried to the isolation hospital. The graveyard. That was why this cross-examination which from time to time descended on me in vague monosyllables, and of which I understood nothing, seemed sinister. My life was at stake as though at roulette. That was why, too, I felt the strange need to impress them with my reality, to shout out something about myself that would convince them how real I was. My age, for instance! That, a man's age, makes an impression. It epitomizes all his life. It has come about slowly, this maturity of his. It has come about in spite of all the obstacles vanquished, the grave illnesses healed, the many pains soothed, the despairs surmounted and the risks that beset him, of most of which he knows nothing.

It has come about by way of so many desires, hopes, regrets, forgettings: so much love. What a cargo of experience, of memories, a man's age represents. In spite of pitfalls, jolts, ruts, one has still managed to struggle along, like a good wagon. And now, thanks to a determined convergence of lucky changes, there one is. One is thirty-seven. And the good wagon, if it please God, will bear its load of memories yet further. And so I said to myself: "This is where I've got. I'm thirty-seven." I would have liked to burden my judges with this confession. . . . But they had stopped questioning me.

Then it was that the miracle happened. Oh, a very modest miracle. I had no cigarettes. And as one of my jailers was smoking, I motioned to him to let me have one and gave a faint smile. First, the man stretched, then slowly passed his hand over his brow, raised his eyes towards me, no longer at my tie, but at my face, and to my stupefaction, he too, faintly smiled. It was like daybreak.

The miracle did not provide a solution to the play: it just wiped it out, as light does darkness. No drama had taken place. This miracle changed nothing that was visible. The cheap oil lamp, the paper-strewn table, the men leaning against the wall, the colour of things, the smell, everything remained. But everything was changed in its very essence. That smile released me. It was a token as final, as clear in its immediate consequences, as irreversible as the apparition of the sun. It opened a new era. Nothing had changed, everything had changed. The paper-strewn table became alive. The oil lamp became alive. The walls were alive. The boredom exuded by the dead things in this cellar dissipated as by enchantment. As though an invisible blood had again begun to flow, reconnecting all parts of the same body and restoring significance to them.

Yet the men had not moved either, but, whereas a second before they had seemed remoter than some prehistoric species, now they emerged into a continuous existence. I felt with extraordinary keenness their presence. Yes, that was it: their presence. And I felt my kinship to them.

The young man who had smiled, and who, a second earlier, had been but a task, a tool, a sort of monstrous insect, now appeared a bit gawky, almost timid, with a wonderful timidity. Not that this terrorist was less brutal than another, but the advent of the man in him so illumined all that was vulnerable! We put on great airs, we men, but deep in our hearts there is the hesitancy, the doubt, the fret that we feel.

Still nothing had been said. Yet all was settled. I put my hand, in thanks, on the militiaman's shoulder when he handed me my cigarette. And then, this ice having been broken, the other militiamen, too, became men again . . . and I entered their general smiles as into a new free country.

I entered into their smiles, as, in the past, into the smiles of our rescuers in the Sahara. The friends who had found us after days of searching, who had landed as close as they could, would come striding towards us with huge steps, swinging the water skins as prominently as they could. That smile of the rescuers if I were the castaway, that smile of the castaways if I were the rescuer, I remember, too, as though it were a homeland in which I felt infinitely happy. True pleasure is in the pleasure of sharing. Being rescued was but its excuse. Water could not bind spells were it not, first and foremost, the free gift of men.

Ministrations to the sick, the welcome offered to the outlaw, pardon itself, mean nothing save for the smile that illumines the occasion. In smiles we come together beyond language, caste or political party. We are all, me and mine, worshippers of one religion, it and its rites.

V

Is not this quality of joy the most precious fruit of the civilization which is ours? A totalitarian tyranny, too, might satisfy us in our material needs. But we are not beasts to be fattened. Prosperity and comfort could never of themselves wholly satisfy our needs. For us, brought up to believe in human respect, simple meetings which sometimes change into wonderful occasions are heavy with meaning.

Human respect! Human respect! . . . There is the touchstone! When the Nazi respects only what resembles him, he is respecting nothing but himself. He rejects creative contradictions, shatters all hope of man's ascent, and for a thousand years, in place of man, creates an antheap robot. Order for order's sake gelds man of his essential power, which is to transform both the world and himself. Life creates order, but order does not create life.

To me, far otherwise, it seems that our ascent is not completed, that to-morrow's truth feeds on yesterday's error and that the contradictions to be overcome are the very compost of our growth. We recognize as ours those even who differ from us. But what a strange kinship! It is based on the future, not on the past. On the objective, not on origins. We are pilgrims to each other who, along different roads, all toil towards the same rendezvous.

But to-day, human respect, the very condition of our ascent, is in danger. The creakings of the modern world have drawn us into darkness. The problems have no coherence, the solutions are contradictory. Yesterday's truth is dead, to-morrow's still to be erected. There is no valid synthesis perceptible, and each of us holds only a bit of the truth. Lacking proof to make them convincing, the political religions resort to violence. And so, by being divided as to methods, we risk no longer realizing that we are hastening towards the same end.

The traveller crossing the mountain, following a star, risks forgetting the star that guides him if too engrossed in pondering ways of reaching the top. If his only reason for action has become action, he will get nowhere. The pew-opener, too keenly pursuing her job, runs the risk of forgetting she serves a god. So, by absorbing myself too closely in some party passion, I risk forgetting that politics are meaningless unless they serve some spiritual truth. In wonderful moments we have savoured a certain quality in human relations: there, for us, is truth.

However urgent action may be, it is forbidden to us to forget, failing which such action must be sterile, that vocation must determine it. We wish to establish human respect. Why should we hate each other inside the same camp? None of us has a monopoly in pure intentions. I may dispute, in favour of my road, the road that someone else has chosen. I may criticize the way his mind works. Minds work erratically. But I ought to respect the man, as far as spirit is concerned, if he toils towards the same star.

Human respect! Human respect! . . . If human respect is established in men's hearts, men will certainly end by establishing in return the social, political or economic system that will sanctify this respect. A civilization first establishes itself on matter. It is, at first, in man, the blind desire for a certain warmth. Thereafter, man, from error to error, discovers the road that leads to fire.

VI

And that is why, no doubt, my friend, I so much need your friendship. I thirst for a companion who, superior to the disputations of reason, respects in me the pilgrim of that fire. I must sometimes savour, in advance, the promised warmth and rest, outside myself a little, in that rendezvous that is to be ours.

I am so weary of controversy, of the opinionated, of fanaticism. I can visit you without donning a uniform, without having to recite some Koran, without renouncing anything whatever of my homeland inside. With you, I do not have to exonerate myself, to plead, to prove: I find peace, as at Tournus. Beyond my clumsy words, beyond the reasonings that may lead me astray, you regard in me the Man simply. You honour in me the ambassador of a faith, of customs, of special affections. If I differ from you, far from injuring you, I augment you. You cross-question me as one does a traveller.

I, who, like each of us, feel the need to be recognized, in you I feel pure and I go to you. There is a need in me to go where I am pure. It is not my formulae nor the things I do that ever enlightened you as to the man I am. It is the acceptance of who I am which made you, at need, indulgent to these things as to these formulae. I am grateful to you for accepting me as you find me. What do I want with a friend who judges me? If I welcome a friend to a meal, I ask him to sit down if he limps, and do not ask him to dance.

My friend, I need you as one needs a height on which to breathe! I need to sit close beside you, once again, on the banks of the Saône, at some little gimcrack inn table where we could ask two bargees to drink and where we would all sit together in the peace of a smile at daybreak.

If I am still fighting, I shall fight a little for you. I need you in order to have more faith in the advent of that smile. I need to help you to live. I see you so weak, so menaced, dragging your fifty years, for hours on end, outside some wretched grocer's, merely to go on living a day or two more, as you shiver under the doubtful protection of a threadbare overcoat. You so French, I feel you in doubly mortal peril, first as being French and then as a Jew. How I prize a community that does not encourage contention. We all derive from France as from a tree, and I will serve your truth as you would have served mine.

For us, Frenchmen outside, what is at issue, in this war, is how to free the reserves of seed frozen by the snows of the German presence. The issue is how to succour you: you, over there. How to make you free in the land where you have the basic right to spread out your roots. You are forty million hostages. It is always in the caves of oppression that the new truths develop: forty million hostages ponder their new truth. We, in advance, submit to that truth.

For it is you from whom we will learn. It is not for us to bear the spiritual flame to those who feel it already with their very beings, as though wax. Maybe you will scarce look at our books. Maybe you will scarce listen to our talks. Our ideas, maybe, you will spew out. We are not building France. We can only serve her. We shall have no right, whatever we have done, to any gratitude. There is no common multiple between open combat and being crushed in darkness. There is no common multiple between the soldier's job and that of a hostage. You are the saints.

◇◇◇*Jean-Paul Sartre (1905-   ). French critic, novelist, dramatist and*
philosopher.

THE WALL

BY JEAN-PAUL SARTRE

They pushed us into a big white room and I began to blink because
the light hurt my eyes. Then I saw a table and four men behind the
table, civilians, looking over the papers. They had bunched another
group of prisoners in the back and we had to cross the whole room
to join them. There were several I knew and some others who must
have been foreigners. The two in front of me were blond with round
skulls; they looked alike. I supposed they were French. The smaller
one kept hitching up his pants; nerves.

It lasted about three hours; I was dizzy and my head was empty;
but the room was well heated and I found that pleasant enough:
for the past 24 hours we hadn't stopped shivering. The guards
brought the prisoners up to the table, one after the other. The four
men asked each one his name and occupation. Most of the time they
didn't go any further—or they would simply ask a question here
and there: "Did you have anything to do with the sabotage of muni-
tions?" Or "Where were you the morning of the 9th and what were
you doing?" They didn't listen to the answers or at least didn't seem
to. They were quiet for a moment and then looking straight in front
of them began to write. They asked Tom if it were true he was in
the International Brigade; Tom couldn't tell them otherwise because of the papers they found in his coat. They didn't ask Juan
anything but they wrote for a long time after he told them his name.

"My brother José is the anarchist," Juan said, "you know he isn't
here any more. I don't belong to any party, I never had anything
to do with politics."

They didn't answer. Juan went on, "I haven't done anything. I don't want to pay for somebody else."

His lips trembled. A guard shut him up and took him away. It was my turn.

"Your name is Pablo Ibbieta?"

"Yes."

The man looked at the papers and asked me, "Where's Ramon Gris?"

"I don't know."

"You hid him in your house from the 6th to the 19th."

"No."

They wrote for a minute and then the guards took me out. In the corridor Tom and Juan were waiting between two guards. We started walking. Tom asked one of the guards, "So?"

"So what?" the guard said.

"Was that the cross-examination or the sentence?"

"Sentence," the guard said.

"What are they going to do with us?"

The guard answered dryly, "Sentence will be read in your cell."

As a matter of fact, our cell was one of the hospital cellars. It was terrifically cold there because of these drafts. We shivered all night and it wasn't much better during the day. I had spent the previous five days in a cell in a monastery, a sort of hole in the wall that must have dated from the middle ages: since there were a lot of prisoners and not much room, they locked us up anywhere. I didn't miss my cell; I hadn't suffered too much from the cold but I was alone; after a long time it gets irritating. In the cellar I had company. Juan hardly ever spoke: he was afraid and he was too young to have anything to say. But Tom was a good talker and he knew Spanish well.

There was a bench in the cellar and four mats. When they took us back we sat and waited in silence. After a long moment, Tom said, "We're screwed."

"I think so too," I said, "but I don't think they'll do anything to the kid."

"They don't have a thing against him," said Tom. "He's the brother of a militiaman and that's all."

I looked at Juan: he didn't seem to hear. Tom went on, "You

know what they do in Saragossa? They lay the men down on the road and run over them with trucks. A Moroccan deserter told us that. They said it was to save ammunition."

"It doesn't save gas," I said.

I was annoyed at Tom: he shouldn't have said that.

"Then there's officers walking along the road," he went on, "supervising it all. They stick their hands in their pockets and smoke cigarettes. You think they finish off the guys? Hell no. They let them scream. Sometimes for an hour. The Moroccan said he damned near puked the first time."

"I don't believe they'll do that here," I said. "Unless they're really short on ammunition."

Day was coming in through four airholes and a round opening they had made in the ceiling on the left, and you could see the sky through it. Through this hole, usually closed by a trap, they unloaded coal into the cellar. Just below the hole there was a big pile of coal dust; it had been used to heat the hospital but since the beginning of the war the patients were evacuated and the coal stayed there, unused; sometimes it even got rained on because they had forgotten to close the trap.

Tom began to shiver. "Good Jesus Christ I'm cold," he said. "Here it goes again."

He got up and began to do exercises. At each movement his shirt opened on his chest, white and hairy. He lay on his back, raised his legs in the air and bicycled. I saw his great rump trembling. Tom was husky but he had too much fat. I thought how rifle bullets or the sharp points of bayonets would soon be sunk into this mass of tender flesh as in a lump of butter. It wouldn't have made me feel like that if he'd been thin.

I wasn't exactly cold, but I couldn't feel my arms and shoulders any more. Sometimes I had the impression I was missing something and began to look around for my coat and then suddenly remembered they hadn't given me a coat. It was rather uncomfortable. They took our clothes and gave them to their soldiers leaving us only our shirts—and those canvas pants that hospital patients wear in the middle of summer. After a while Tom got up and sat next to me, breathing heavily.

"Warmer?"

"Good Christ, no. But I'm out of wind."

Around eight o'clock in the evening a major came in with two *falangistas*. He had a sheet of paper in his hand. He asked the guard, "What are the names of those three?"

"Steinbock, Ibbieta and Mirbal," the guard said.

The major put on his eyeglasses and scanned the list: "Steinbock . . . Steinbock . . . Oh yes . . . You are sentenced to death. You will be shot tomorrow morning." He went on looking. "The other two as well."

"That's not possible," Juan said. "Not me."

The major looked at him amazed. "What's your name?"

"Juan Mirbal," he said.

"Well, your name is there," said the major. "You're sentenced."

"I didn't do anything," Juan said.

The major shrugged his shoulders and turned to Tom and me. "You're Basque?"

"Nobody is Basque."

He looked annoyed. "They told me there were three Basques. I'm not going to waste my time running after them. Then naturally you don't want a priest?"

We didn't even answer.

He said, "A Belgian doctor is coming shortly. He is authorized to spend the night with you." He made a military salute and left.

"What did I tell you," Tom said. "We get it."

"Yes," I said, "it's a rotten deal for the kid."

I said that to be decent but I didn't like the kid. His face was too thin and fear and suffering had disfigured it, twisting all his features. Three days before he was a smart sort of kid, not too bad; but now he looked like an old fairy and I thought how he'd never be young again, even if they were to let him go. It wouldn't have been too hard to have a little pity for him but pity disgusts me, or rather it horrifies me. He hadn't said anything more but he had turned grey; his face and hands were both grey. He sat down again and looked at the ground with round eyes. Tom was good hearted, he wanted to take his arm, but the kid tore himself away violently and made a face.

"Let him alone," I said in a low voice, "you can see he's going to blubber."

Tom obeyed regretfully; he would have liked to comfort the kid, it would have passed his time and he wouldn't have been tempted to think about himself. But it annoyed me: I'd never thought about death because I never had any reason to, but now the reason was here and there was nothing to do but think about it.

Tom began to talk. "So you think you've knocked guys off, do you?" he asked me. I didn't answer. He began explaining to me that he had knocked off six since the beginning of August; he didn't realize the situation and I could tell he didn't *want* to realize it. I hadn't quite realized it myself, I wondered if it hurt much, I thought of bullets, I imagined their burning hail through my body. All that was beside the real question; but I was calm: we had all night to understand. After a while Tom stopped talking and I watched him out of the corner of my eye; I saw he too had turned grey and he looked rotten; I told myself "Now it starts." It was almost dark, a dim glow filtered through the airholes and the pile of coal and made a big stain beneath the spot of sky; I could already see a star through the hole in the ceiling: the night would be pure and icy.

The door opened and two guards came in, followed by a blond man in a tan uniform. He saluted us. "I am the doctor," he said. "I have authorization to help you in these trying hours."

He had an agreeable and distinguished voice. I said, "What do you want here?"

"I am at your disposal. I shall do all I can to make your last moments less difficult."

"What did you come here for? There are others, the hospital's full of them."

"I was sent here," he answered with a vague look. "Ah! Would you like to smoke?" he added hurriedly, "I have cigarettes and even cigars."

He offered us English cigarettes and *puros*, but we refused. I looked him in the eyes and he seemed irritated. I said to him, "You aren't here on an errand of mercy. Besides, I know you. I saw you with the fascists in the barracks yard the day I was arrested."

I was going to continue, but something surprising suddenly happened to me; the presence of this doctor no longer interested me. Generally when I'm on somebody I don't let go. But the desire to talk left me completely; I shrugged and turned my eyes away. A little later I raised my head; he was watching me curiously. The guards were sitting on a mat. Pedro, the tall thin one, was twiddling his thumbs, the other shook his head from time to time to keep from falling asleep.

"Do you want a light?" Pedro suddenly asked the doctor. The other nodded "Yes": I think he was about as smart as a log, but he surely wasn't bad. Looking in his cold blue eyes it seemed to me that his only sin was lack of imagination. Pedro went out and came back with an oil lamp which he set on the corner of the bench. It gave a bad light but it was better than nothing: they had left us in the dark the night before. For a long time I watched the circle of light the lamp made on the ceiling. I was fascinated. Then suddenly I woke up, the circle of light disappeared and I felt myself crushed under an enormous weight. It was not the thought of death, or fear; it was nameless. My cheeks burned and my head ached.

I shook myself and looked at my two friends. Tom had hidden his face in his hands. I could only see the fat white nape of his neck. Little Juan was the worst, his mouth was open and his nostrils trembled. The doctor went to him and put his hand on his shoulder to comfort him: but his eyes stayed cold. Then I saw the Belgian's hand drop stealthily along Juan's arm, down to the wrist. Juan paid no attention. The Belgian took his wrist between three fingers, distractedly, the same time drawing back a little and turning his back to me. But I leaned backward and saw him take a watch from his pocket and look at it for a moment, never letting go of the wrist. After a minute he let the hand fall inert and went and leaned his back against the wall, then, as if he suddenly remembered something very important which had to be jotted down on the spot, he took a notebook from his pocket and wrote a few lines. "Bastard," I thought angrily, "let him come and take my pulse. I'll shove my fist in his rotten face."

He didn't come but I felt him watching me. I raised my head and returned his look. Impersonally, he said to me, "Doesn't it seem cold to you here?" He looked cold, he was blue.

"I'm not cold," I told him.

He never took his hard eyes off me. Suddenly I understood and my hands went to my face: I was drenched in sweat. In this cellar, in the midst of winter, in the midst of drafts, I was sweating. I ran my hands through my hair, gummed together with perspiration; at the same time I saw my shirt was damp and sticking to my skin: I had been dripping for an hour and hadn't felt it. But that swine of a Belgian hadn't missed a thing; he had seen the drops rolling down my cheeks and thought: this is the manifestation of an almost pathological state of terror; and he had felt normal and proud of being alive because he was cold. I wanted to stand up and smash his face but no sooner had I made the slightest gesture than my rage and shame were wiped out; I fell back on the bench with indifference.

I satisfied myself by rubbing my neck with my handkerchief because now I felt the sweat dropping from my hair onto my neck and it was unpleasant. I soon gave up rubbing, it was useless; my handkerchief was already soaked and I was still sweating. My buttocks were sweating too and my damp trousers were glued to the bench.

Suddenly Juan spoke. "You're a doctor?"

"Yes," the Belgian said.

"Does it hurt . . . very long?"

"Huh? When . . . ? Oh, no," the Belgian said paternally. "Not at all. It's over quickly." He acted as though he were calming a cash customer.

"But I . . . they told me . . . sometimes they had to fire twice."

"Sometimes," the Belgian said, nodding. "It may happen that the first volley reaches no vital organs."

"Then they had to reload their rifles and aim all over again?" He thought for a moment and then added hoarsely, "That takes time!"

He had a terrible fear of suffering, it was all he thought about: it was his age. I never thought much about it and it wasn't fear of suffering that made me sweat.

I got up and walked to the pile of coal dust. Tom jumped up and threw me a hateful look: I had annoyed him because my shoes squeaked. I wondered if my face looked as frightened as his: I saw he was sweating too. The sky was superb, no light filtered into the dark corner and I had only to raise my head to see the Big Dipper. But it wasn't like it had been: the night before I could see a great piece of sky from my monastery cell and each hour of the day brought me a different memory. Morning, when the sky was a hard, light blue, I thought of beaches on the Atlantic; at noon I saw the sun and I remembered a bar in Seville where I drank *manzanilla* and ate olives and anchovies; afternoons I was in the shade and I thought of the deep shadow which spreads over half a bull-ring leaving the other half shimmering in sunlight; it was really hard to see the whole world reflected in the sky like that. But now I could watch the sky as much as I pleased, it no longer evoked anything in me. I liked that better. I came back and sat near Tom. A long moment passed.

Tom began speaking in a low voice. He had to talk, without that he wouldn't have been able to recognize himself in his own mind. I thought he was talking to me but he wasn't looking at me. He was undoubtedly afraid to see me as I was, grey and sweating: we were alike and worse than mirrors of each other. He watched the Belgian, the living.

"Do you understand?" he said. "I don't understand."

I began to speak in a low voice too. I watched the Belgian. "Why? What's the matter?"

"Something is going to happen to us that I can't understand."

There was a strange smell about Tom. It seemed to me I was more sensitive than usual to odors. I grinned. "You'll understand in a while."

"It isn't clear," he said obstinately. "I want to be brave but first I have to know . . . Listen, they're going to take us into the court-yard. Good. They're going to stand up in front of us. How many?"

"I don't know. Five or eight. Not more."

"All right. There'll be eight. Someone'll holler 'aim!' and I'll see eight rifles looking at me. I'll think how I'd like to get inside the wall, I'll push against it with my back . . . with every ounce of strength I have, but the wall will stay, like in a nightmare. I can imagine all that. If you only knew how well I can imagine it."

"All right, all right!" I said, "I can imagine it too."

"It must hurt like hell. You know, they aim at the eyes and the mouth to disfigure you," he added mechanically. "I can feel the wounds already; I've had pains in my head and in my neck for the past hour. Not real pains. Worse. This is what I'm going to feel tomorrow morning. And then what?"

I well understood what he meant but I didn't want to act as if I did. I had pains too, pains in my body like a crowd of tiny scars. I couldn't get used to it. But I was like him, I attached no importance to it. "After," I said, "you'll be pushing up daisies."

He began to talk to himself: he never stopped watching the Belgian. The Belgian didn't seem to be listening. I knew what he had come to do; he wasn't interested in what we thought; he came to watch our bodies, bodies dying in agony while yet alive.

"It's like a nightmare," Tom was saying. "You want to think something, you always have the impression that it's all right, that you're going to understand and then it slips, it escapes you and fades away. I tell myself there will be nothing afterwards. But I don't understand what it means. Sometimes I almost can . . . and then it fades away and I start thinking about the pains again, bullets, explosions. I'm a materialist, I swear it to you; I'm not going crazy. But something's the matter. I see my corpse; that's not hard but *I'm* the one who sees it, with *my* eyes. I've got to think . . . think that I won't see anything any more and the world will go on for the others. We aren't made to think that, Pablo. Believe me: I've already stayed up a whole night waiting for something. But this isn't the same: this will creep up behind us, Pablo, and we won't be able to prepare for it."

"Shut up," I said. "Do you want me to call a priest?"

He didn't answer. I had already noticed he had the tendency to act like a prophet and call me Pablo, speaking in a toneless voice. I didn't like that: but it seems all the Irish are that way. I had the vague impression he smelled of urine. Fundamentally, I hadn't much sympathy for Tom and I didn't see why, under the pretext of dying together, I should have any more. It would have been different with some others. With Ramon Gris, for example. But I felt alone between Tom and Juan. I liked that better, anyhow: with Ramon I might have been more deeply moved. But I was terribly hard just then and I wanted to stay hard.

He kept on chewing his words, with something like distraction. He certainly talked to keep himself from thinking. He smelled of urine like an old prostate case. Naturally, I agreed with him, I could have said everything he said: it isn't *natural* to die. And since I was going to die, nothing seemed natural to me, not this pile of coal dust, or the bench, or Pedro's ugly face. Only it didn't please me to think the same things as Tom. And I knew that, all through the night, every five minutes, we would keep on thinking things at the same time. I looked at him sideways and for the first time he seemed strange to me: he wore death on his face. My pride was wounded: for the past 24 hours I had lived next to Tom, I had listened to him, I had spoken to him and I knew we had nothing in common. And now we looked as much alike as twin brothers, simply because we were going to die together. Tom took my hand without looking at me.

"Pablo, I wonder . . . I wonder if it's really true that everything ends."

I took my hand away and said, "Look between your feet, you pig."

There was a big puddle between his feet and drops fell from his pants-leg.

"What is it," he asked, frightened.

"You're pissing in your pants," I told him.

"It isn't true," he said furiously. "I'm not pissing. I don't feel anything."

The Belgian approached us. He asked with false solicitude, "Do you feel ill?"

Tom did not answer. The Belgian looked at the puddle and said nothing.

"I don't know what it is," Tom said ferociously. "But I'm not afraid. I swear I'm not afraid."

The Belgian did not answer. Tom got up and went to piss in a corner. He came back buttoning his fly, and sat down without a word. The Belgian was taking notes.

All three of us watched him because he was alive. He had the motions of a living human being, the cares of a living human being; he shivered in the cellar the way the living are supposed to shiver; he had an obedient, well-fed body. The rest of us hardly felt ours— not in the same way anyhow. I wanted to feel my pants between my legs but I didn't dare; I watched the Belgian, balancing on his legs, master of his muscles, someone who could think about tomorrow. There we were, three bloodless shadows; we watched him and we sucked his life like vampires.

Finally he went over to little Juan. Did he want to feel his neck for some professional motive or was he obeying an impulse of charity? If he was acting by charity it was the only time during the whole night.

He caressed Juan's head and neck. The kid let himself be handled, his eyes never leaving him, then suddenly, he seized the hand and looked at it strangely. He held the Belgian's hand between his own two hands and there was nothing pleasant about them, two grey pincers gripping this fat and reddish hand. I suspected what was going to happen and Tom must have suspected it too: but the Belgian didn't see a thing, he smiled paternally. After a moment the kid brought the fat red hand to his mouth and tried to bite it. The Belgian pulled away quickly and stumbled back against the wall. For a second he looked at us with horror, he must have suddenly understood that we were not men like him. I began to laugh and one of the guards jumped up. The other was asleep, his wide open eyes were blank.

I felt relaxed and over-excited at the same time. I didn't want to think any more about what would happen at dawn, at death. It made no sense. I only found words or emptiness. But as soon as I tried to think of anything else I saw rifle barrels pointing at me. Perhaps I lived through my execution twenty times; once I even thought it was for good: I must have slept a minute. They were dragging me to the wall and I was struggling; I was asking for mercy. I woke up with a start and looked at the Belgian: I was afraid I might have cried out in my sleep. But he was stroking his moustache, he hadn't noticed anything. If I had wanted to, I think I could have slept a while; I had been awake for 48 hours. I was at the end of my rope. But I didn't want to lose two hours of life: they would come to wake me up at dawn, I would follow them, stupefied with sleep and I would have croaked without so much as an "Oof!"; I didn't want that, I didn't want to die like an animal, I wanted to understand. Then I was afraid of having nightmares. I got up, walked back and forth, and, to change my ideas, I began to think about my past life. A crowd of memories came back to me pell-mell. There were good and bad ones—or at least I called them that *before*. There were faces and incidents. I saw the face of a little *novillero* who was gored in Valencia during the *Feria*, the face of one of my uncles, the face of Ramon Gris. I remembered my whole life: how I was out of work for three months in 1926, how I almost starved to death. I remembered a night I spent on a bench in Granada: I hadn't eaten for three days. I was angry, I didn't want to die. That made me smile. How madly I ran after happiness, after women, after liberty. Why? I wanted to free Spain, I admired Pi y Margall, I joined the anarchist movement, I spoke in public meetings: I took everything as seriously as if I were immortal.

At that moment I felt that I had my whole life in front of me and I thought, "It's a damned lie." It was worth nothing because it was finished. I wondered how I'd been able to walk, to laugh with the girls: I wouldn't have moved so much as my little finger if I had only imagined I would die like this. My life was in front of me, shut, closed, like a bag and yet everything inside of it was unfinished. For an instant I tried to judge it. I wanted to tell myself, this is a beautiful life. But I couldn't pass judgment on it; it was only a sketch; I had spent my time counterfeiting eternity, I had understood nothing. I missed nothing: there were so many things I could have missed, the taste of *manzanilla* or the baths I took in summer in a little creek near Cadiz; but death had disenchanted everything.

The Belgian suddenly had a bright idea. "My friends," he told us, "I will undertake—if the military administration will allow it—to send a message for you, a souvenir to those who love you . . ."

Tom mumbled, "I don't have anybody."

I said nothing. Tom waited an instant then looked at me with curiosity. "You don't have anything to say to Concha?"

"No."

I hated this tender complicity: it was my own fault, I had talked about Concha the night before, I should have controlled myself. I was with her for a year. Last night I would have given an arm to see her again for five minutes. That was why I talked about her, it was stronger than I was. Now I had no more desire to see her, I had nothing more to say to her. I would not even have wanted to hold her in my arms: my body filled me with horror because it was grey and sweating—and I wasn't sure that her body didn't fill me with horror. Concha would cry when she found out I was dead, she would have no taste for life for months afterward. But I was still the one who was going to die. I thought of her soft, beautiful eyes. When she looked at me something passed from her to me. But I knew it was over: if she looked at me *now* the look would stay in her eyes, it wouldn't reach me. I was alone.

Tom was alone too but not in the same way. Sitting cross-legged, he had begun to stare at the bench with a sort of smile, he looked amazed. He put out his hand and touched the wood cautiously as if he were afraid of breaking something, then drew back his hand quickly and shuddered. If I had been Tom I wouldn't have amused myself by touching the bench; this was some more Irish nonsense, but I too found that objects had a funny look: they were more obliterated, less dense than usual. It was enough for me to look at the bench, the lamp, the pile of coal dust, to feel that I was going to die. Naturally I couldn't think clearly about my death but I saw it everywhere, on things, in the way things fell back and kept their distance, discreetly, as people who speak quietly at the bedside of a dying man. It was *his* death which Tom had just touched on the bench.

In the state I was in, if someone had come and told me I could go home quietly, that they would leave me my life whole, it would have left me cold: several hours or several years of waiting is all the same when you have lost the illusion of being eternal. I clung to nothing, in a way I was calm. But it was a horrible calm—because of my body; my body, I saw with its eyes, I heard with its ears, but it was no longer me; it sweated and trembled by itself and I didn't recognize it any more. I had to touch it and look at it to find out what was happening, as if it were the body of someone else. At times I could still feel it, I felt sinkings, and fallings, as when you're in a plane taking a nosedive, or I felt my heart beating. But that didn't reassure me. Everything that came from my body was all cockeyed. Most of the time it was quiet and I felt no more than a sort of weight, a filthy presence against me; I had the impression of being tied to an enormous vermin. Once I felt my pants and I felt they were damp; I didn't know whether it was sweat or urine, but I went to piss on the coal pile as a precaution.

The Belgian took out his watch, looked at it. He said, "It is three-thirty."

Bastard! He must have done it on purpose. Tom jumped; we hadn't noticed time was running out; night surrounded us like a shapeless, somber mass, I couldn't even remember that it had begun.

Little Juan began to cry. He wrung his hands, pleaded, "I don't want to die. I don't want to die."

He ran across the whole cellar waving his arms in the air then fell sobbing on one of the mats. Tom watched him with mournful eyes, without the slightest desire to console him. Because it wasn't worth the trouble: the kid made more noise than we did, but he was less touched: he was like a sick man who defends himself against his illness by fever. It's much more serious when there isn't any fever.

He wept: I could clearly see he was pitying himself; he wasn't thinking about death. For one second, one single second, I wanted to weep myself, to weep with pity for myself. But the opposite happened: I glanced at the kid, I saw his thin sobbing shoulders and I felt inhuman: I could pity neither the others nor myself. I said to myself, "I want to die cleanly."

Tom had gotten up, he placed himself just under the round opening and began to watch for daylight. I was determined to die cleanly and I only thought of that. But ever since the doctor told us the time, I felt time flying, flowing away drop by drop.

It was still dark when I heard Tom's voice: "Do you hear them?"

Men were marching in the courtyard.

"Yes."

"What the hell are they doing? They can't shoot in the dark."

After a while we heard no more. I said to Tom, "It's day."

Pedro got up, yawning, and came to blow out the lamp. He said to his buddy, "Cold as hell."

The cellar was all grey. We heard shots in the distance.

"It's starting," I told Tom. "They must do it in the court in the rear."

Tom asked the doctor for a cigarette. I didn't want one; I didn't want cigarettes or alcohol. From that moment on they didn't stop firing.

"Do you realize what's happening," Tom said.

He wanted to add something but kept quiet, watching the door. The door opened and a lieutenant came in with four soldiers. Tom dropped his cigarette.

"Steinbock?"

Tom didn't answer. Pedro pointed him out.

"Juan Mirbal?"

"On the mat."

"Get up," the lieutenant said.

Juan did not move. Two soldiers took him under the arms and set him on his feet. But he fell as soon as they released him.

The soldiers hesitated.

"He's not the first sick one," said the lieutenant. "You two carry him; they'll fix it up down there."

He turned to Tom. "Let's go."

Tom went out between two soldiers. Two others followed, carrying the kid by the armpits. He hadn't fainted; his eyes were wide open and tears ran down his cheeks. When I wanted to go out the lieutenant stopped me.

"You Ibbieta?"

"Yes."

"You wait here; they'll come for you later."

They left. The Belgian and the two jailers left too, I was alone. I did not understand what was happening to me but I would have liked it better if they had gotten it over with right away. I heard shots at almost regular intervals; I shook with each one of them. I wanted to scream and tear out my hair. But I gritted my teeth and pushed my hands in my pockets because I wanted to stay clean.

After an hour they came to get me and led me to the first floor, to a small room that smelt of cigars and where the heat was stifling. There were two officers sitting smoking in the armchairs, papers on their knees.

"You're Ibbieta?"

"Yes."

"Where is Ramon Gris?"

"I don't know."

The one questioning me was short and fat. His eyes were hard behind his glasses. He said to me, "Come here."

I went to him. He got up and took my arms, staring at me with a look that should have pushed me into the earth. At the same time he pinched my biceps with all his might. It wasn't to hurt me, it was only a game: he wanted to dominate me. He also thought he had to blow his stinking breath square in my face. We stayed for a moment like that, and I almost felt like laughing. It takes a lot to intimidate a man who is going to die; it didn't work. He pushed me back violently and sat down again. He said, "It's his life against yours. You can have yours if you tell·us where he is."

These men dolled up with their riding crops and boots were still going to die. A little later than I, but not too much. They busied themselves looking for names in their crumpled papers, they ran after other men to imprison or suppress them; they had opinions on the future of Spain and on other subjects. Their little activities seemed shocking and burlesqued to me; I couldn't put myself in their place, I thought they were insane. The little man was still looking at me, whipping his boots with the riding crop. All his gestures were calculated to give him the look of a live and ferocious beast.

"So? You understand?"

"I don't know where Gris is," I answered. "I thought he was in Madrid."

The other officer raised his pale hand indolently. This indolence was also calculated. I saw through all their little schemes and I was stupefied to find there were men who amused themselves that way.

"You have a quarter of an hour to think it over," he said slowly. "Take him to the laundry, bring him back in fifteen minutes. If he still refuses he will be executed on the spot."

They knew what they were doing: I had passed the night in waiting; then they had made me wait an hour in the cellar while they shot Tom and Juan and now they were locking me up in the laundry; they must have prepared their game the night before. They told themselves that nerves eventually wear out and they hoped to get me that way.

They were badly mistaken. In the laundry I sat on a stool because I felt very weak and I began to think. But not about their proposition. Of course I knew where Gris was; he was hiding with his cousins, four kilometers from the city. I also knew that I would not reveal his hiding place unless they tortured me (but they didn't seem to be thinking about that). All that was perfectly regulated, definite and in no way interested me. Only I would have liked to understand the reasons for my conduct. I would rather die than give up Gris. Why? I didn't like Ramon Gris any more. My friendship for him had died a little while before dawn at the same time as my love for Concha, at the same time as my desire to live. Undoubtedly I thought highly of him: he was tough. But it was not for this reason that I consented to die in his place; his life had no more value than mine; no life had value. They were going to slap a man up against a wall and shoot at him till he died, whether it was I or Gris or somebody else made no difference. I knew he was more useful than I to the cause of Spain but I thought to hell with Spain and anarchy; nothing was important. Yet I was there, I could save my skin and give up Gris and I refused to do it. I found that somehow comic; it was obstinacy. I thought, "I must be stubborn!" And a droll sort of gaiety spread over me.

They came for me and brought me back to the two officers. A rat ran out from under my feet and that amused me. I turned to one of the *falangistas* and said, "Did you see the rat?"

He didn't answer. He was very sober, he took himself seriously. I wanted to laugh but I held myself back because I was afraid that once I got started I wouldn't be able to stop. The *falangista* had a moustache. I said to him again, "You ought to shave off your moustache, idiot." I thought it funny that he would let the hairs of his living being invade his face. He kicked me without great conviction and I kept quiet.

"Well," said the fat officer, "have you thought about it?"

I looked at them with curiosity, as insects of a very rare species. I told them, "I know where he is. He is hidden in the cemetery. In a vault or in the gravediggers' shack."

It was a farce. I wanted to see them stand up, buckle their belts and give orders busily.

They jumped to their feet. "Let's go. Molés, go get fifteen men from Lieutenant Lopez. You," the fat man said, "I'll let you off if you're telling the truth, but it'll cost you plenty if you're making monkeys out of us."

They left in a great clatter and I waited peacefully under the guard of *falangistas*. From time to time I smiled, thinking about the spectacle they would make. I felt stunned and malicious. I imagined them lifting up tombstones, opening the doors of the vaults one by one. I represented this situation to myself as if I had been someone else: this prisoner obstinately playing the hero, these grim *falangistas* with their moustaches and their men in uniform running among the graves; it was irresistibly funny. After half an hour the little fat man came back alone. I thought he had come to give the orders to execute me. The others must have stayed in the cemetery.

The officer looked at me. He didn't look at all sheepish. "Take him into the big courtyard with the others," he said. "After the military operations a regular court will decide what happens to him."

"Then they're not . . . not going to shoot me? . . ."

"Not now, anyway. What happens afterwards is none of my business."

I still didn't understand. I asked, "But why . . . ?"

He shrugged his shoulders without answering and the soldiers took me away. In the big courtyard there were about a hundred prisoners, women, children and a few old men. I began walking around the central grass-plot, I was stupefied. At noon they let us eat in the mess hall. Two or three people questioned me. I must have known them, but I didn't answer: I didn't even know where I was.

Around evening they pushed about ten new prisoners into the court. I recognized Garcia, the baker. He said, "What damned luck you have! I didn't think I'd see you alive."

"They sentenced me to death," I said, "and then they changed their minds. I don't know why."

"They arrested me at two o'clock," Garcia said.

"Why?" Garcia had nothing to do with politics.

"I don't know," he said. "They arrest everybody who doesn't think the way they do. He lowered his voice. "They got Gris."

I began to tremble. "When?"

"This morning. He messed it up. He left his cousin's on Tuesday because they had an argument. There were plenty of people to hide him but he didn't want to owe anything to anybody. He said, 'I'd go and hide in Ibbieta's place, but they got him, so I'll go hide in the cemetery.' "

"In the cemetery?"

"Yes. What a fool. Of course they went by there this morning, that was sure to happen. They found him in the gravediggers' shack. He shot at them and they got him."

"In the cemetery!"

Everything began to spin and I found myself sitting on the ground: I laughed so hard I cried.

◇◇◇*Ignazio Silone (1900-   ). Italian novelist and critic. See* **Fontamara,**
Bread and Wine, The Seed Beneath the Snow.

MR. ARISTOTLE

BY IGNAZIO SILONE

If anyone is having trouble with his sweetie and wants to straighten
matters out with a well-written letter, he goes to see Mr. Aristotle
Caramella. The latter lives somewhere between New Town and
Purgatory, in an unprepossessing street that is always damp and
smelly, for the reason that it gets little sun, while the women there
have the habit of emptying their household slops in front of their
doors.

There is no use in seeking an interview with Mr. Aristotle of an
evening, since he is always drunk then; nor of a morning, seeing
that he naps until eleven. It is better to look him up in the afternoon.

His house is a one-story affair, boasting neither bricks nor stone
by way of floor. As you come in, you catch sight over in one corner
of a chain, suspended from a spike; and from this chain there hangs
a kettle which is given a washing once a year, on the Saturday before Easter. The fire under the kettle is kindled from cornstalks; and
the smoke, after circling about the room, finds its way out the door.
In the corner opposite the fire there is a bed, that is to say, a pallet
stuffed with cornhusks and covered with a red woolen blanket. In
the center of the room there is a small table, with three little wooden
benches standing about. It is here that Mr. Aristotle sees his
clients.

If Mr. Aristotle has been reduced to living like a beggar, between New Town and Purgatory, it is all owing to a youthful in-
discretion. As a lad, he had received a good education, and had
later found work as town clerk and in a lawyer's office. It was Mr.

Reprinted by permission of the publishers, Robert M. McBride & Company. (Translated by Samuel Putnam.)

Aristotle's job to make the rounds of the neighboring villages in search of cases for his employer; after which, it was up to him to get or invent the right kind of evidence. He accomplished this task zealously and ingeniously, and was duly esteemed by the better class of people as one of Justice's humble but valuable servants.

In his labors Mr. Aristotle was assisted by three or four poor devils who from time immemorial had been known as grave-diggers, dog-shearers, or house-to-house-peddlers; but on Tuesday morning, which was court day, they placed themselves at his disposition as possible witnesses. Mr. Aristotle commonly referred to them as the Mouthpieces of Truth. Those who were taken as witnesses would shave, pare their nails, and learn from Mr. Aristotle what it was they were supposed to say to the judge. They would then go to court and swear, as usual, "to tell the truth, the whole truth, and nothing but the truth," before reciting their lesson. If their testimony happened to conflict with that of witnesses on the other side, they remained unshaken and proceeded to strengthen their case with so fervent an appeal to the wrath of God that the others would almost invariably end by becoming confused and would take back or change the testimony they had previously given.

Among these Mouthpieces of Truth was one Toto, who had specialized in denial, and one Rufino, who had a particular talent for affirmation. If Toto was charged with replying No to a question of the judge, nothing in the world could have made him say Yes; and if Rufino had had his orders to respond with a Yes, no amount of threats or cajoling could have induced him to change that Yes to a No.

As the law provides, the witnesses thereupon received a fee of two and a half lire. In addition to this, the Mouthpieces of Truth had the price of a drink from Mr. Aristotle. If one stops to think that they never got more than a lira for a funeral, it is not hard to understand why these same Mouthpieces of Truth should have preferred, on a Tuesday, to serve Justice rather than the Church. If someone died on a Monday, he accordingly had to wait until Wednesday to be taken to the cemetery. People gradually came to realize this, and as a result, they stopped dying on Monday.

The short of it is, Mr. Aristotle had every reason to look forward to a comfortable and self-respecting future, when sentiment took a hand, and he lost it all.

It was that business with Faustina, the dressmaker. This dressmaker person was attacked one day by a couple of large dogs belonging to the Baron of Pescina. It happened in front of the baronial residence. The Baron was on the balcony at the time, with other young members of the nobility; and it would appear that he set the dogs on Faustina, to amuse his guests. Alarmed by her cries and the yelping of the dogs, some of the neighbors came running up; but no one dared to go to Faustina's assistance, from fear of offending the Baron. It was only when the Baron went back into the house that she was rescued. It left her lame.

No sooner was Faustina able to be up and about than she went to the authorities and lodged a complaint against the Baron. Everything possible was done to get her to withdraw it, but she refused to listen to reason.

"I want justice!" was her answer.

Now, among those who had witnessed the scene in front of the baronial residence was Rufino; and so, on Mr. Aristotle's advice, Faustina had him summoned as a witness. On Tuesday morning, before court, Rufino came to Mr. Aristotle.

"What story am I to tell today?" he asked.

"The truth!" Mr. Aristotle replied.

"That's all right," said Rufino, "I'll swear to tell the truth, the whole truth, and nothing but the truth; but after that, what am I supposed to say?"

"After that"—Mr. Aristotle was firm—"you will tell the truth, the whole truth, and nothing but the truth!"

Rufino was beginning to be afraid. He had told lies many times; he had told them every time he had ever testified before the judge; but this was the first time he had ever been instructed to tell the truth. No wonder, he was afraid—

As he faced the judge, Rufino shook like a leaf. He took oath in an unsteady voice and then went on to describe what had happened in front of the Baron's residence, being specific as to the Baron's having set the dogs on Faustina. The Baron himself was not present in court, but the room was packed with his dependents, who filed before the judge, one by one, to contradict flatly Rufino's testimony. But it was Toto who clinched with matter.

"Is it true that your friend, Rufino, was in front of the Baron's residence?" the judge asked him.

And Toto's answer was: "No."

Rufino was at once placed under arrest for perjury, and a pair of police officers took him off to jail. He offered no resistance. He realized that he had made a mess of things; but his excuse was, that he had been ill advised by Mr. Aristotle. And so it was that the latter, through having yielded to a silly sentimental impulse, lost his job with the municipality and with the lawyer and was reduced to living on the brink of Purgatory, between the peasants whom he despised and the landed gentry whom he loathed.

Mr. Aristotle still writes a fine hand, but his epistolary style is a trifle antiquated, which is one reason why the young folks now resort to him only in the gravest emergencies.

The peasants ordinarily used to fall in love in church, in wintertime. In front of the church, before or after mass, the young fellows would lie in wait for the girls, to snowball them. To hit a girl with a snowball was the first way of letting her know that you were interested in her. After church came the fountain. In the evening, before the Hail Mary, all the girls would come out of the house with a copper pail, to go to the public fountain for a supply of water. On the way down, they dangled the pails from their arms; but coming back, they carried them on their heads, like antique water-jugs. And all along the way, coming and going, each peasant lad would follow, ardent-eyed but at a respectful distance, the object of his affections. After the fountain, especially if the girl, by a smile or two, had shown that the young man's suit was not displeasing to her, there would come a letter written by Mr. Aristotle.

"This ritual was once unvarying," Mr. Aristotle says to me. "First came the church, then the fountain, then the letter. If the letter met with an encouraging response, there was a serenade under the window. Very little of it all is left now. And what is the life of man without a ritual? A drab thing, indeed. But this is only one instance. Many another of the old ceremonious forms has gone by the board.

Human relations have become crude and unadorned with any niceties—"

"Human relations," I venture at this point, "have become more straightforward and direct. Between men and women, between rich and poor, they may be harsher, but they are at least more straightforward! If the priest, the public letter-writer, the witch and the fortune-teller suffer from it, it is all the better—"

"All the better for the revolution, is what you mean," Mr. Aristotle replied, "but not for the Public Welfare. The Public Welfare calls for ceremonies. To keep man bound to woman and peasant to his master, the priest, the public letter-writer, witches, and fortune-tellers are indispensable. I am well aware that they have tried to replace all these things with other means, but those means have proved unsatisfactory. The new government has not been able to create a new ritual acceptable to the masses, as a substitute for that old one of ours which has fallen into decay. The only thing left is Force; but Force without ritual cannot last very long."

Mr. Aristotle is an avowed enemy of universal and compulsory education. Only a minority should be able to read and write. He speaks with loathing of our present civilization, in which all are capable of wielding a pen, and thinks back longingly to that golden age when the majority of the population was illiterate. For the importance of the public letter-writer was never greater than then. That individual was everybody's private secretary, and clients stood in line in front of his desk.

"The saddest part of all," says Mr. Aristotle, "is that they try to justify the thing in the name of progress. What do they mean by progress? We haven't gone forward; we've gone backward! All you have to do is to read a love-letter written today by the party concerned, and compare it with one written in the old days by the public letter-writer.

"You hear a lot of talk about the family's not being what it used to be, and about the decrease in the number of marriages; but they don't dare go to the bottom of the matter and look for the root of the evil. The real root of the evil is the idiotic habit that the majority of women today have, of trying to write their own love-letters. It is not that women nowadays are any more stupid than they ever were. They've always been silly. But at least, in the old days, they didn't know how to read and write and so had to come to the public letter-writer, who, with his education and knowledge of life, could turn out an epistle that would stir the hardest-hearted man alive, which could patch up a broken engagement, and create in the man the illusion that the woman of his choice was not a simpleton, as she was in reality, but the most refined of beings, at once cultivated and burning with passion."

"And you mean to tell me that marriage didn't come as a disillusionment?"

"Never," Mr. Aristotle insists, "never. For it wasn't only the girl, you know, who came to the public letter-writer; the prospective bridegroom came also; and it was often one and the same letter-writer who served the two of them, who inspired in each of them in turn sentiments of whose existence they had not before been aware, in the guise of poetry and romance. The handwriting would have indicated that the letters on each side had been composed by the same person; but human beings like nothing better than to be deceived. And furthermore, you must remember that the public letter-writer was also a public letter-reader, and was used to having brought to him by the recipient the missives which he himself had indited, which gave him a chance to compute the effect, in the way of sighs and tears, which his eloquence had had. Knowing thus the two correspondents, being in their confidence and acquainted with their innermost desires, their tastes and longings, it was not hard for him to draw ever tighter a bond which in the beginning had seemed a wavering one, and to bring the couple to the point of matrimony."

Mr. Aristotle loved to tell of the hundreds of amorous barks which he had steered safely into harbor; for even after it had put him out of office, the public did not disdain to come to him with its private troubles.

"But don't you think, Mr. Aristotle, that letters are more sincere when they are written by the party concerned, and that the girl who knows how to write is better able to express her feelings than a public letter-writer who is getting along in years?"

"Don't talk nonsense!" exclaimed Mr. Aristotle. "If the girl came to the public letter-writer, it was not only because she didn't know how to write, but also, because she didn't know what to say, because she was inexperienced and ignorant in affairs of the heart. A girl would come and say, 'Mr. Aristotle, I want you to write a very passionate letter for me.' Those are all the instructions she would give me. 'Passionate in what way?' I would ask. 'Well, if you don't know,' she'd answer, 'how do you expect me to?' No, don't think for a minute that the public letter-writer simply took dictation. That rarely happened. Usually the party would provide him with the general theme, and leave it to him to develop. Something like this for example: 'A young man has just proposed to me. I don't want to say yes right away, for that wouldn't be nice; I just want to say enough to let him know that, if he keeps on, his chances are good.' And with this as a theme, the letter-writer would turn out four pages, with numerous asterisks."

Naturally, in the days when he had a host of clients, Mr. Aristotle did not greatly rack his brain in thinking up new phrases for each occasion; he had, so to speak, a permanent repertory of them. The only thing that was personal and individual in a letter had to do with the color of the loved one's eyes, her hair, the amplitude of her bosom, or similar anatomical details; but the rest was pretty much the same. The consequence was, a letter sometimes had an annoyingly familiar ring, as when a man received a "passionate" communication which was worded the same as those he had had from a number of previous sweethearts.

"But he seldom noticed it," Mr. Aristotle commented; "love is blind, you know!"

The truth is, Mr. Aristotle has not been able to adapt himself to the new tenor of relationship between men and women; he knows very little about the new forms that have come in; and accordingly, if any one still comes to him for aid and advice, the old letter-writer continues to be governed by the code of former years. Liberato Boccella, the butcher, is a case in point.

Boccella, the butcher, had been eying the notary's daughter. He was quite smitten with her.

"Be sure and wait for her outside the church," Mr. Aristotle advised him, "and then follow her when she goes to the fountain—"

"But she doesn't go to the fountain. They have water in the house at the notary's," said Boccella, mournfully.

"Water in the house!" Mr. Aristotle was taken unawares.

At this moment the notary's daughter went past.

"How do you do, Miss?" said the butcher. "Nice day for a walk!"

She looked at him contemptuously, without answering. A short while later, she came back with a girl friend. The notary's daughter carried daisies in her hand and did not so much as glance in the direction of the butcher-shop.

"Did you see that?" Mr. Aristotle was quick to note. "It's plain that she's in love with you! Daisies mean: 'Be persevering, and have faith in me!'"

Mr. Aristotle was thoroughly versed in the language of flowers.

"The sunflower means: 'Even though you change, I am true to you'; white gillyflowers mean: 'I am waiting for a letter'; white lilacs: 'I can't sleep on account of you'; yellow gillyflowers: 'There is a jealous woman who pretends to be a friend, but who would like to part us'; the red rose: 'Without you, I cannot go on living' —But daisies mean only one thing: 'Be persevering, and have faith in me!'"

Poor Boccella was beside himself with joy and made Mr. Aristotle a present of a soup-bone. A butcher is always a good client to have.

"What shall I do now?" Boccella asked.

"Keep some jasmines within arm's reach," Mr. Aristotle advised him, "and the next time you see her, put them to your lips. In the language of flowers, that means: 'Very well, I will persevere and have faith in you.'"

It would have been impossible to find more expert counsel. Every time the notary's daughter went out for a stroll, there was the butcher with a bunch of jasmines at his mouth. The girl would look the other way. Only once she stared him straight in the face.

"You big silly!" she said with a laugh.

On her way home, she had a bouquet of violets. Boccella at once ran to tell Mr. Aristotle. A butcher client is always a good one to have, and the old letter-writer did not mean to let this one slip through his fingers.

"It's as plain as day," said Mr. Aristotle. "In the language of flowers, a cluster of violets means: 'Don't look at appearances; look at my heart.'"

It was decided to draw up a letter. Mr. Aristotle labored at it one whole day and filled eight pages. It was a touching epistle. Mr. Aristotle was proud of it.

"If a cow could read," he assured the butcher, "it would bring tears to her eyes."

The notary's daughter, however, was not a cow; for that very day there came back a letter containing only these words: "Stop being so stupid, and leave me in peace!" It was a terrible blow for poor Boccella, but not for Mr. Aristotle.

"Take a good look at the envelope," he urged. "A stamp turned upside down, in sign language, always means: 'Don't believe what's in this letter, but just the contrary.' She probably had to write that way, on account of her father; but in putting the stamp on, she tried to warn you not to believe what the letter says."

The butcher was greatly pleased with this explanation and presented Mr. Aristotle with a big soup-bone this time. By way of reply to the loved one's note, a plain postal card was dispatched, with the stamp pasted sidewise, the head to the right.

"In sign language," Mr. Aristotle expounded, "that means: 'I understand perfectly.'"

It was then decided to give a serenade under the windows of the notary's house. The butcher put on a new suit for the occasion; the barber, who played the guitar very well, was engaged to furnish the music; and Mr. Aristotle, although he was a little hoarse, was to do the singing. At midnight the trio appeared at the notary's, and to the guitar accompaniment, Mr. Aristotle began:

> It's thirty days
> That I care for you,
> It's thirty nights
> That I cannot sleep—

A second-floor window opened, and Mr. Aristotle and the barber fell back a short distance to leave the butcher alone with his inamorata. Through the window came a man's arm and a huge thunder-mug; the thunder-mug was inverted, and the butcher found himself drenched with urine. The poor fellow thought of that brand-new suit of his; but his grief over this was as nothing to the sudden anger he felt toward Mr. Aristotle.

"It's all your fault!" he shouted. "You tricked and wheedled me, just for what you could get out of me—"

"Silence!" said Mr. Aristotle and raised a hand. Coming up to the butcher, he sniffed all around him for a minute or so.

"Cheer up," he finally said, "it's hers!"

Mr. Aristotle motioned to the barber. The latter now approached and in turn did some prolonged sniffing about the butcher's drenched garments.

"That's the truth," he announced; "you can believe me, on my word of honor; it's hers!"

"How do you know that?" asked the butcher.

"It's something you can't explain," the pair between them replied; "it's a matter of sense—and scent—you either get it, or you don't."

The episode just related goes to show that Mr. Aristotle's erudition is of no great service in this age of ours. All the old ritual has been lost. Men and women have learned to read and write, but they are none the happier for it, according to him.

"One of the evils resulting from popular education," he observes, "is the alarming increase in the number of suicides. You hear a great deal of discussion of this subject, and the explanation given is invariably a trite and stupid one. No one has stopped to compare the proportion of those who are able to read and write with the number who commit suicide. They will tell you that, if there are more suicides, it is on account of the greater poverty today. But there has always been poverty in the world. There are many who are poor, and yet they don't kill themselves. Stop and think a minute. What is the one thing that every suicide does? He writes letters; always without fail, every person who commits suicide writes a letter—to mother, sweetheart, the chief of police, his creditors, etc. The simplest bit of logic will show that, if he couldn't write a letter, he wouldn't commit suicide."

I glance at Mr. Aristotle in surprise.

"What are you getting at?"

"Just this," he says. "A system of society that cannot assure the well-being of all has no business popularizing education. If it weren't for education, poverty would be endurable. It has lasted for centuries, and men were able to bear it. But with education extended to all, no one wants to go hungry any longer. The weak commit suicide. The others—"

Mr. Aristotle breaks off. An old woman from New Town has need of his services. She is the only client he has had today.

"Mr. Aristotle," the old woman is saying, "I want you to write an anonymous letter for me; I want the one who gets it to cry with rage for twenty-four hours."

"Twenty-four hours?" Mr. Aristotle repeats. "Why not twelve?"

"No," replies the old woman, "it must be twenty-four!"

And so, tomorrow, in New Town, for twenty-four hours, some-one will weep and wait and gnash his teeth.

◇◇◇*Robert Louis Stevenson (1850–1894). English novelist, essayist and short-story writer. He abandoned the study of engineering for law. Tuberculosis caused him to travel widely for his health. He became famous in 1883 with the publication of* Treasure Island. *Noted as a superb stylist, he wrote poetry and collaborated with W. E. Henley in a number of plays. In 1890 he settled in Samoa and partly recovered his health. He died there suddenly of a brain hemorrhage.*

MARKHEIM

BY ROBERT LOUIS STEVENSON

"Yes," said the dealer, "our windfalls are of various kinds. Some customers are ignorant, and then I touch a dividend of my superior knowledge. Some are dishonest," and here he held up the candle, so that the light fell strongly on his visitor, "and in that case," he continued, "I profit by my virtue."

Markheim had but just entered from the daylight streets, and his eyes had not yet grown familiar with the mingled shine and darkness in the shop. At these pointed words, and before the near presence of the flame, he blinked painfully and looked aside.

The dealer chuckled. "You come to me on Christmas Day," he resumed, "when you know that I am alone in my house, put up my shutters, and make a point of refusing business. Well, you will have to pay for that; you will have to pay for my loss of time, when I should be balancing my books; you will have to pay for a kind of manner that I remark in you to-day very strongly. I am the essence of discretion, and ask no awkward questions; but when a customer cannot look me in the eye, he has to pay for it." The dealer once more chuckled; and then, changing to his usual business voice, though still with a note of irony, "You can give, as usual, a clear account of how you came into the possession of the objects?" he continued. "Still your uncle's cabinet? A remarkable collector, sir!"

And the little pale, round-shouldered dealer stood almost on tiptoe, looking over the top of his gold spectacles, and nodding his head with every mark of disbelief. Markheim returned his gaze with one of infinite pity, and a touch of horror.

"This time," said he, "you are in error. I have not come to sell, but to buy. I have no curios to dispose of; my uncle's cabinet is bare to the wainscot; even were it still intact, I have done well on the Stock Exchange, and should more likely add to it than otherwise, and my errand to-day is simplicity itself. I seek a Christmas present for a lady," he continued, waxing more fluent as he struck into the speech he had prepared; "and certainly I owe you every excuse for thus disturbing you upon so small a matter. But the thing was neglected yesterday; I must produce my little compliment at dinner; and, as you very well know, a rich marriage is not a thing to be neglected."

There followed a pause, during which the dealer seemed to weigh this statement incredulously. The ticking of many clocks among the curious lumber of the shop, and the faint rushing of the cabs in a rear thoroughfare, filled up the interval of silence.

"Well, sir," said the dealer, "be it so. You are an old customer after all; and if, as you say, you have the chance of a good marriage, far be it from me to be an obstacle.—Here is a nice thing for a lady now," he went on, "this hand glass—fifteenth century, warranted; comes from a good collection, too; but I reserve the name, in the interests of my customer, who was just like yourself, my dear sir, the nephew and sole heir of a remarkable collector."

The dealer, while he thus ran on in his dry and biting voice, had stooped to take the object from its place; and, as he had done so, a shock had passed through Markheim, a start both of hand and foot, a sudden leap of many tumultuous passions to the face. It passed as swiftly as it came, and left no trace beyond a certain trembling of the hand that now received the glass.

"A glass," he said hoarsely, and then paused, and repeated it more clearly. "A glass? For Christmas? Surely not?"

"And why not?" cried the dealer. "Why not a glass?"

Markheim was looking upon him with an indefinable expression. "You ask me why not?" he said. "Why, look here—look in it—look at yourself! Do you like to see it? No! nor I—nor any man."

The little man had jumped back when Markheim had so suddenly confronted him with the mirror; but now, perceiving there was nothing worse on hand, he chuckled. "Your future lady, sir, must be pretty hard-favoured," said he.

"I ask you," said Markheim, "for a Christmas present, and you give me this—this damned reminder of years, and sins and follies—this hand-conscience! Did you mean it? Had you a thought in your mind? Tell me. It will be better for you if you do. Come, tell me about yourself. I hazard a guess now, that you are in secret a very charitable man?"

The dealer looked closely at his companion. It was very odd, Markheim did not appear to be laughing; there was something in his face like an eager sparkle of hope, but nothing of mirth.

"What are you driving at?" the dealer asked.

"Not charitable?" returned the other, gloomily. "Not charitable; not pious; not scrupulous; unloving, unbeloved; a hand to get money, a safe to keep it. Is that all? Dear God, man, is that all?"

"I will tell you what it is," began the dealer, with some sharpness, and then broke off again into a chuckle. "But I see this is a love-match of yours, and you have been drinking the lady's health."

"Ah!" cried Markheim, with a strange curiosity. "Ah, have you been in love? Tell me about that."

"I," cried the dealer. "I in love! I never had the time, nor have I the time to-day for all this nonsense. Will you take the glass?"

"Where is the hurry?" returned Markheim. "It is very pleasant to stand here talking; and life is so short and insecure that I would not hurry away from any pleasure—no, not even from so mild a one as this. We should rather cling, cling to what little we can get, like a man at a cliff's edge. Every second is a cliff, if you think about it—a cliff a mile high—high enough, if we fall, to dash us out of every feature of humanity. Hence it is best to talk pleasantly. Let us talk of each other; why should we wear this mask? Let us be confidential. Who knows we might become friends?"

"I have just one word to say to you," said the dealer. "Either make your purchase, or walk out of my shop."

"True, true," said Markheim. "Enough fooling. To business. Show me something else."

The dealer stooped once more, this time to replace the glass upon the shelf, his thin blond hair falling over his eyes as he did so. Markheim moved a little nearer, with one hand in the pocket of his greatcoat; he drew himself up and filled his lungs; at the same time many different emotions were depicted together on his face—terror, horror, and resolve, fascination and a physical repulsion; and through a haggard lift of his upper lip, his teeth looked out.

"This, perhaps, may suit," observed the dealer; and then, as he began to re-arise, Markheim bounded from behind upon his victim. The long, skewerlike dagger flashed and fell. The dealer struggled like a hen, striking his temple on the shelf, and then tumbled on the floor in a heap.

Time had some score of small voices in that shop, some stately and slow as was becoming to their great age; others garrulous and hurried. All these told out the seconds in an intricate chorus of tickings. Then the passage of a lad's feet, heavily running on the pavement, broke in upon these smaller voices and startled Markheim into the consciousness of his surroundings. He looked about him awfully. The candle stood on the counter, its flame solemnly wagging in a draught; and by that inconsiderable movement, the whole room was filled with noiseless bustle and kept heaving like a sea: the tall shadows nodding, the gross blots of darkness swelling and dwindling as with respiration, the faces of the portraits and the china gods changing and wavering like images in water. The inner door stood ajar, and peered into that leaguer of shadows with a long slit of daylight like a pointing finger.

From these fear-stricken rovings, Markheim's eyes returned to the body of his victim, where it lay both humped and sprawling, incredibly small and strangely meaner than in life. In these poor, miserly clothes, in that ungainly attitude, the dealer lay like so much sawdust. Markheim had feared to see it, and, lo! it was nothing. And yet, as he gazed, this bundle of old clothes and pool of blood began to find eloquent voices. There it must lie; there was none to work the cunning hinges or direct the miracle of locomotion —there it must lie till it was found. Found! ay, and then? Then would this dead flesh lift up a cry that would ring over England, and fill the world with the echoes of pursuit. Ay, dead or not, this was the enemy. "Time was that when the brains were out," he thought; and the first word struck into his mind. Time, now that the deed was accomplished—time, which had closed for the victim, had become instant, and momentous for the slayer.

The thought was yet in his mind, when, first one and then another, with every variety of pace and voice—one deep as the bell from a cathedral turret, another ringing on its treble notes the prelude of a waltz—the clocks began to strike the hour of three in the afternoon.

The sudden outbreak of so many tongues in that dumb chamber staggered him. He began to bestir himself, going to and fro with the candle, beleaguered by moving shadows, and startled to the soul by chance reflections. In many rich mirrors, some of home designs, some from Venice or Amsterdam, he saw his face repeated and repeated, as it were an army of spies; his own eyes met and detected him; and the sound of his own steps, lightly as they fell, vexed the surrounding quiet. And still as he continued to fill his pockets, his mind accused him, with a sickening iteration, of the thousand faults of his design. He should have chosen a more quiet hour; he should have prepared an alibi; he should not have used a knife; he should have been more cautious, and only bound and gagged the dealer, and not killed him; he should have been more bold, and killed the servant also; he should have done all things otherwise; poignant regrets, weary, incessant toiling of the mind to change what was unchangeable, to plan what was now useless, to be the architect of the irrevocable past. Meanwhile, and behind all this activity, brute terrors, like the scurrying of rats in a deserted attic, filled the more remote chambers of his brain with riot; the hand of the constable would fall heavy on his shoulder, and his nerves would jerk like a hooked fish; or he beheld, in galloping defile, the dock, the prison, the gallows, and the black coffin.

Terror of the people in the street sat down before his mind like a besieging army. It was impossible, he thought, but that some rumour of the struggle must have reached their ears and set on edge their curiosity; and now, in all the neighbouring houses, he divined them sitting motionless and with uplifted ear—solitary people, condemned to spend Christmas dwelling alone on memories of the past, and now startlingly recalled from that tender exercise; happy family parties, struck into silence round the table, the mother still with raised finger: every degree and age and humour, but all, by their own hearts, prying and hearkening and weaving the rope that was to hang him. Sometimes it seemed to him he could not move too softly; the clink of the tall Bohemian goblets rang out loudly like a bell; and alarmed by the bigness of the ticking, he was tempted to stop the clocks. And then, again, with a swift transition of his terrors, the very silence of the place appeared a source of peril, and a thing to strike and freeze the passer-by; and he would step more boldly, and bustle aloud among the contents of the shop, and imitate, with elaborate bravado, the movements of a busy man at ease in his own house.

But he was now so pulled about by different alarms that, while one portion of his mind was still alert and cunning, another trembled on the brink of lunacy. One hallucination in particular took a strong hold on his credulity. The neighbour hearkening with white face beside his window, the passer-by arrested by a horrible surmise on the pavement—these could at worst suspect, they could not know; through the brick walls and shuttered windows only sounds could penetrate. But here, within the house, was he alone? He knew he was; he had watched the servant set forth sweet-hearting, in her poor best, "out for the day" written in every ribbon and smile. Yes, he was alone, of course; and yet, in the bulk of empty house above him, he could surely hear a stir of delicate footing—he was surely conscious, inexplicably conscious of some presence. Ay, surely; to every room and corner of the house his imagination followed it; and now it was a faceless thing, and yet had eyes to see with; and again it was a shadow of himself; and yet again beheld the image of the dead dealer, reinspired with cunning and hatred.

At times, with a strong effort, he would glance at the open door which still seemed to repel his eyes. The house was tall, the skylight small and dirty, the day blind with fog; and the light that filtered down to the ground story was exceedingly faint, and showed dimly on the threshold of the shop. And yet, in that strip of doubtful brightness, did there not hang wavering a shadow?

Suddenly, from the street outside, a very jovial gentleman began to beat with a staff on the shop-door, accompanying his blows with shouts and railleries in which the dealer was continually called upon by name. Markheim, smitten into ice, glanced at the dead man. But no! he lay quite still; he was fled away far beyond ear-shot of these blows and shoutings; he was sunk beneath seas of silence; and his name, which would once have caught his notice above the howling of a storm, had become an empty sound. And presently the jovial gentleman desisted from his knocking and departed.

Here was a broad hint to hurry what remained to be done, to get forth from this accusing neighbourhood, to plunge into a bath of London multitudes, and to reach, on the other side of day, that haven of safety and apparent innocence—his bed. One visitor had come: at any moment another might follow and be more obstinate. To have done the deed, and yet not to reap the profit would be too abhorrent a failure. The money, that was now Markheim's concern; and as a means to that, the keys.

He glanced over his shoulder at the open door, where the shadow was still lingering and shivering; and with no conscious repugnance of the mind, yet with a tremor of the belly, he drew near the body of his victim. The human character had quite departed. Like a suit half stuffed with bran, the limbs lay scattered, the trunk doubled, on the floor; and yet the thing repelled him. Although so dingy and inconsiderable to the eye, he feared it might have more significance to the touch. He took the body by the shoulders, and turned it on its back. It was strangely light and supple, and the limbs, as if they had been broken, fell into the oddest postures. The face was robbed of all expression; but it was as pale as wax, and shockingly smeared with blood about one temple. That was, for Markheim, the one displeasing circumstance. It carried him back, upon the instant, to a certain fair day in a fisher's village: a grey day, a piping wind, a crowd upon the street, the blare of brasses, the booming of drums, the nasal voice of a ballad-singer; and a boy going to and fro, buried over head in the crowd and divided between interest and fear, until coming out upon the chief place of concourse, he beheld a booth and a great screen with pictures, dismally designed, garishly coloured: Brownrigg with her apprentice; the Mannings with their murdered guest; Weare in the death-grip of Thurtell; and a score besides of famous crimes. The thing was as clear as an illusion; he was once again that little boy; he was looking once again, and with the same sense of physical revolt, at these vile pictures; he was still stunned by the thumping of the drums. A bar of that day's music returned upon his memory; and at that, for the first time, a qualm came over him, a breath of nausea, a sudden weakness of the joints, which he must instantly resist and conquer.

He judged it more prudent to confront than to flee from these considerations; looking the more hardily in the dead face, bending his mind to realise the nature and greatness of his crime. So little a while ago that face had moved with every change of sentiment, that pale mouth had spoken, that body had been all on fire with governable energies; and now, and by his act, that piece of life had been arrested, as the horologist, with interjected finger, arrests the beating of the clock. So he reasoned in vain; he could rise to no more remorseful consciousness; the same heart which had shuddered before the painted effigies of crime looked on its reality unmoved. At best, he left a gleam of pity for one who had been endowed in vain with all those faculties that can make the world a garden of enchantment, one who had never lived and who was now dead. But of penitence, no, not a tremor.

With that, shaking himself clear of these considerations, he found the keys and advanced towards the open door of the shop. Outside, it had begun to rain smartly; and the sound of the shower upon the roof had banished silence. Like some dripping cavern, the chambers of the house were haunted by an incessant echoing, which filled the ear and mingled with the ticking of the clocks. And, as Markheim approached the door, he seemed to hear, in answer to his own cautious tread, the steps of another foot withdrawing up the stair. The shadow still palpitated loosely on the threshold. He threw a ton's weight of resolve upon his muscles, and drew back the door.

The faint, foggy daylight glimmered dimly on the bare floor and stairs; on the bright suit of armour posted, halbert in hand, upon the landing; and on the dark wood-carvings and framed pictures that hung against the yellow panels of the wainscot. So loud was the beating of the rain through all the house that, in Markheim's ears, it began to be distinguished into many different sounds. Footsteps and sighs, the tread of regiments marching in the distance, the chink of money in the counting, and the creaking of doors held stealthily ajar, appeared to mingle with the patter of the drops upon the cupola and the gushing of the water in the pipes. The sense that he was not alone grew upon him to the verge of madness. On every side he was haunted and begirt by presences. He heard them moving in the upper chambers; from the shop, he heard the dead man getting to his legs; and as he began with a great effort to mount the stairs, feet fled quietly before him and followed stealthily behind. If he were but deaf, he thought, how tranquilly he would possess his soul! And then again, and hearkening with ever fresh attention, he blessed himself for that unresting sense which held the outposts and stood a trusty sentinel upon his life. His head turned continually on his neck; his eyes, which seemed starting from their orbits, scouted on every side, and on every side were half rewarded as with the tail of something nameless vanishing. The four-and-twenty steps to the first floor were four-and-twenty agonies.

On that first story, the doors stood ajar, three of them like three ambushes, shaking his nerves like the throats of cannon. He could never again, he felt, be sufficiently immured and fortified from men's observing eyes; he longed to be home, girt in by walls, buried among bed-clothes, and invisible to all but God. And at that thought he wondered a little, recollecting tales of other murderers and the fear they were said to entertain of heavenly avengers. It was not so, at least, with him. He feared the laws of nature, lest, in their callous and immutable procedure, they should preserve some damning evidence of his crime. He feared tenfold more, with a slavish, superstitious terror, some scission in the continuity of man's experience, some wilful illegality of nature. He played a game of skill, depending on the rules, calculating consequence from cause; and what if nature, as the defeated tyrant overthrew the chess-board, should break the mould of their succession? The like had befallen Napoleon (so writers said) when the winter changed the time of its appearance. The like might befall Markheim: the solid walls might become transparent and reveal his doings like those of bees in a glass hive; the stout planks might yield under his foot like quicksands and detain him in their clutch; ay, and there were soberer accidents that might destroy him: if, for instance, the house should fall and imprison him beside the body of his victim; or the house next door should fly on fire, and the firemen invade him from all sides. These things he feared; and, in a sense, these things might be called the hands of God reached forth against sin. But about God himself he was at ease; his act was doubtless exceptional, but so were his excuses, which God knew; it was there, and not among men, that he felt sure of justice.

When he had got safe into the drawing-room, and shut the door behind him, he was aware of a respite from alarms. The room was quite dismantled, uncarpeted besides, and strewn with packing-cases and incongruous furniture; several great pier-glasses, in which he beheld himself at various angles, like an actor on a stage; many pictures, framed and unframed, standing, with their faces to the wall; a fine Sheraton sideboard, a cabinet of marquetry, and a great old bed, with tapestry hangings. The windows opened to the floor; but by great good-fortune the lower part of the shutters had been closed, and this concealed him from the neighbours. Here, then, Markheim drew in a packing-case before the cabinet, and began to search among the keys. It was a long business, for there were many; and it was irksome, besides; for, after all, there might be nothing in the cabinet, and time was on the wing. But the closeness of the occupation sobered him. With the tail of his eye he saw the door—even glanced at it from time to time directly, like a besieged commander pleased to verify the good estate of his defences. But in truth he was at peace. The rain falling in the street sounded natural and pleasant. Presently, on the other side, the notes of a piano were wakened to the music of a hymn, and the voices of many children took up the air and words. How stately, how comfortable was the melody! How fresh the youthful voices! Markheim gave ear to it smilingly, as he sorted out the keys; and his mind was thronged with answerable ideas and images; church-going children and the pealing of the high organ; children afield, bathers by the brookside, ramblers on the brambly common, kite-fliers in the windy and cloud-navigated sky; and then, at another cadence of the hymn, back again to church, and the somnolence of summer Sundays, and the high genteel voice of the parson (which he smiled a little to recall) and the painted Jacobean tombs, and the dim lettering of the Ten Commandments in the chancel.

And as he sat thus, at once busy and absent, he was startled to his feet. A flash of ice, a flash of fire, a bursting gush of blood, went over him, and then he stood transfixed and thrilling. A step mounted the stair slowly and steadily, and presently a hand was laid upon the knob, and the lock clicked, and the door opened.

Fear held Markheim in a vice. What to expect he knew not, whether the dead man walking, or the official ministers of human justice, or some chance witness blindly stumbling in to consign him to the gallows. But when a face was thrust into the aperture, glanced round the room, looked at him, nodded and smiled as if in friendly recognition, and then withdrew again, and the door closed behind it, his fear broke loose from his control in a hoarse cry. At the sound of this the visitant returned.

"Did you call me?" he asked, pleasantly and with that he entered the room and closed the door behind him.

Markheim stood and gazed at him with all his eyes. Perhaps there was a film upon his sight, but the outlines of the new-comer seemed to change and waver like those of the idols in the wavering candle-light of the shop; and at times he thought he knew him; and at times he thought he bore a likeness to himself; and always, like a lump of living terror, there lay in his bosom the conviction that this thing was not of the earth and not of God.

And yet the creature had a strange air of the commonplace, as he stood looking on Markheim with a smile; and when he added: "You are looking for the money, I believe?" it was in the tones of every-day politeness.

Markheim made no answer.

"I should warn you," resumed the other, "that the maid has left her sweetheart earlier than usual and will soon be here. If Mr. Markheim be found in this house, I need not describe to him the consequences."

"You know me?" cried the murderer.

The visitor smiled. "You have long been a favourite of mine," he said; "and I have long observed and often sought to help you."

"What are you?" cried Markheim: "the devil?"

"What I may be," returned the other, "cannot affect the service I propose to render you."

"It can," cried Markheim; "it does! Be helped by you? No, never; not by you! You do not know me yet; thank God, you do not know me!"

"I know you," replied the visitant, with a sort of kind severity or rather firmness. "I know you to the soul."

"Know me!" cried Markheim. "Who can do so? My life is but a travesty and slander on myself. I have lived to belie my nature. All men do; all men are better than this disguise that grows about and stifles them. You see each dragged away by life, like one whom bravos have seized and muffled in a cloak. If they had their own control—if you could see their faces, they would be altogether different, they would shine out for heroes and saints! I am worse than most; my self is more overlaid; my excuse is known to me and God. But, had I the time, I could disclose myself."

"To me?" inquired the visitant.

"To you before all," returned the murderer. "I supposed you were intelligent. I thought—since you exist—you would prove a reader of the heart. And yet you would prose to judge me by my acts! Think of it; my acts! I was born and I have lived in a land of giants; giants have dragged me by the wrists since I was born out of my mother—the giants of circumstance. And you would judge me by my acts! But can you not look within? Can you not understand that evil is hateful to me? Can you not see within me the clear writing of conscience, never blurred by any wilful sophistry, although too often disregarded? Can you not read me for a thing that surely must be common as humanity—the unwilling sinner?"

"All this is very feelingly expressed," was the reply, "but it regards me not. These points of consistency are beyond my province, and I care not in the least by what compulsion you may have been dragged away, so as you are but carried in the right direction. But time flies; the servant delays, looking in the faces of the crowd and at the pictures on the hoardings, but still she keeps moving nearer; and remember, it is as if the gallows itself was striding towards you through the Christmas streets! Shall I help you; I, who know all? Shall I tell you where to find the money?"

"For what price?" asked Markheim.

"I offer you the service for a Christmas gift," returned the other.

Markheim could not refrain from smiling with a kind of bitter triumph. "No," said he, "I will take nothing at your hands; if I were dying of thirst, and it was your hand that put the pitcher to my lips, I should find the courage to refuse. It may be credulous, but I will do nothing to commit myself to evil."

"I have no objection to a death-bed repentance," observed the visitant.

"Because you disbelieve their efficacy!" Markheim cried.

"I do not say so," returned the other; "but I look on these things from a different side, and when the life is done my interest falls. The man has lived to serve me, to spread black looks under colour of religion, or to sow tares in the wheat-field, as you do, in a course of weak compliance with desire. Now that he draws so near to his deliverance, he can add but one act of service—to repent, to die smiling, and thus to build up in confidence and hope the more timorous of my surviving followers. I am not so hard a master. Try me. Accept my help. Please yourself in life as you have done hitherto; please yourself more amply, spread your elbows at the board; and when the night begins to fall and the curtains to be drawn, I tell you, for your greater comfort, that you will find it even easy to compound your quarrel with your conscience, and to make a truckling peace with God. I came but now from such a death-bed, and the room was full of sincere mourners, listening to the man's last words: and when I looked into that face, which had been set as a flint against mercy, I found it smiling with hope."

"And do you, then, suppose me such a creature?" asked Markheim. "Do you think I have no more generous aspirations than to sin, and sin, and sin, and, at last, sneak into heaven? My heart rises at the thought. Is this, then, your experience of mankind? or is it because you find me with red hands that you presume such baseness? and is this crime of murder indeed so impious as to dry up the very springs of good?"

"Murder is to me no special category," replied the other. "All sins are murder, even as all life is war. I behold your race, like starving mariners on a raft, plucking crusts out of the hands of famine and feeding on each other's lives. I follow sins beyond the moment of their acting; I find in all that the last consequence is death; and to my eyes, the pretty maid who thwarts her mother with such taking graces on a question of a ball, drips no less visibly with human gore than such a murderer as yourself. Do I say that I follow sins? I follow virtues also; they differ not by the thickness of a nail, they are both scythes for the reaping angel of Death. Evil, for which I live, consists not in action but in character. The bad man is dear to me; not the bad act, whose fruits, if we could follow them far enough down the hurtling cataract of the ages, might yet be found more blessed than those of the rarest virtues. And it is not because you have killed a dealer, but because you are Markheim, that I offered to forward your escape."

"I will lay my heart open to you," answered Markheim. "This crime on which you find me is my last. On my way to it I have learned many lessons; itself is a lesson, a momentous lesson. Hitherto I have been driven with revolt to what I would not; I was a bond-slave to poverty, driven and scourged. There are robust virtues that can stand in these temptations; mine was not so: I had a thirst of pleasure. But to-day, and out of this deed, I pluck both warning and riches—both the power and a fresh resolve to be myself. I become in all things a free actor in the world; I begin to see myself all changed, these hands the agents of good, this heart at peace. Something comes over me out of the past; something of what I have dreamed on Sabbath evenings to the sound of the church organ, of what I forecast when I shed tears over noble books, or talked, an innocent child, with my mother. There lies my life; I have wandered a few years, but now I see once more my city of destination."

"You are to use this money on the Stock Exchange, I think?" remarked the visitor; "and there, if I mistake not, you have already lost some thousands?"

"Ah," said Markheim, "but this time I have a sure thing."

"This time, again, you will lose," replied the visitor quietly.

"Ah, but I keep back the half!" cried Markheim.

"That also you will lose," said the other.

The sweat started upon Markheim's brow. "Well, then, what matter?" he exclaimed. "Say it be lost, say I am plunged again in poverty, shall one part of me, and that the worst, continue until the end to override the better? Evil and good run strong in me, haling me both ways. I do not love the one thing, I love all. I can conceive great deeds, renunciations, martyrdoms; and though I be fallen to such a crime as murder, pity is no stranger to my thoughts, I pity the poor; who knows their trials better than myself? I pity and help them; I prize love, I love honest laughter; there is no good thing nor true thing on earth but I love it from my heart. And are my vices only to direct my life, and my virtues to lie without effect, like some passive lumber of the mind? Not so; good, also, is a spring of acts."

But the visitant raised his finger. "For six-and-thirty years that you have been in this world," said he, "through many changes of fortune and varieties of humour, I have watched you steadily fall. Fifteen years ago you would have started at a theft. Three years back you would have blenched at the name of murder. Is there any

crime, is there any cruelty of meanness, from which you still recoil?
—five years from now I shall detect you in the fact! Downward,
downward, lies your way; nor can anything but death avail to stop
you."

"It is true," Markheim said huskily, "I have in some degree complied with evil. But it is so with all: the very saints, in the mere
exercise of living, grow less dainty and take on the tone of their
surroundings."

"I will propound to you one simple question," said the other;
"and as you answer, I shall read to you your moral horoscope. You
have grown in many things more lax; possibly you do right to be so;
and at any account, it is the same with all men. But granting that,
are you in any one particular, however trifling, more difficult to
please with your own conduct, or do you go in all things with a
looser rein?"

"In any one?" repeated Markheim, with an anguish of consideration. "No," he added, with despair, "in none! I have gone down in
all."

"Then," said the visitor, "content yourself with what you are, for
you will never change; and the words of your part on this stage are
irrevocably written down."

Markheim stood for a long while silent, and indeed it was the
visitor who first broke the silence. "That being so," he said, "shall I
show you the money?"

"And grace?" cried Markheim.

"Have you not tried it?" returned the other. "Two or three years
ago, did I not see you on the platform of revival meetings, and was
not your voice the loudest in the hymn?"

"It is true," said Markheim; "and I see clearly what remains
for me by way of duty. I thank you for these lessons from my soul;
my eyes are opened, and I behold myself at last for what I am."

At this moment, the sharp note of the door-bell rang through the
house; and the visitant, as though this were some concerted signal
for which he had been waiting, changed at once in his demeanour.
"The maid!" he cried. "She has returned, as I forewarned you, and
there is now before you one more difficult passage. Her master, you
must say, is ill; you must let her in, with an assured but rather serious countenance—no smiles, no over-acting, and I promise you

success! Once the girl within, and the door closed, the same dexterity that has already rid you of the dealer will relieve you of this last danger in your path. Thenceforward you have the whole evening—the whole night, if needful—to ransack the treasures of the house and to make good your safety. This is help that comes to you with the mask of danger. Up!" he cried: "up, friend; your life hangs trembling in the scales: up, and act!"

Markheim steadily regarded his counsellor. "If I be condemned to evil acts," he said, "there is still one door of freedom open—I can cease from action. If my life be an ill thing, I can lay it down. Though I be, as you say truly, at the beck of every small temptation, I can yet, by one decisive gesture, place myself beyond the reach of all. My love of good is damned to barrenness; it may, and let it be! But I have still my hatred of evil; and from that, to your galling disappointment, you shall see that I can draw both energy and courage."

The features of the visitor began to undergo a wonderful and lovely change: they brightened and softened with a tender triumph; and, even as they brightened, faded and dislimned. But Markheim did not pause to watch or understand the transformation. He opened the door and went down-stairs very slowly, thinking to himself. His past went soberly before him; he beheld it as it was, ugly and strenuous like a dream, random as chance-medley—a scene of defeat. Life, as he thus reviewed it, tempted him no longer; but on the further side he perceived a quiet haven for his bark. He paused in the passage, and looked into the shop, where the candle still burned by the dead body. It was strangely silent. Thoughts of the dealer swarmed into his mind, as he stood gazing. And then the bell once more broke out into impatient clamour.

He confronted the maid upon the threshold with something like a smile.

"You had better go for the police," said he: "I have killed your master."

◇◇◇*Italo Svevo (1861-1928). Italian novelist and short-story writer. His real name was Ettore Schmitz. He was born and educated in Trieste. He worked in a bank and then became a manufacturer, remaining in business until his death. James Joyce, who taught him English, was his discoverer. See* The Hoax, The Confessions of Zeno, The Nice Old Man and the Pretty Girl.

GENEROUS WINE

BY ITALO SVEVO

A niece of mine married at the age when girls cease to be girls and degenerate into old maids. The poor thing had renounced the world a little time before, but family pressure had induced her to return to it, giving up her desire for purity and religion; and she had consented to receive the addresses of a young man chosen by the family because he was a good match. Almost immediately there was an end of religion, an end to dreams of virtuous solitude. The date of the marriage was fixed even sooner than the relations had wished. And now they were seated at the supper for the eve of the wedding.

Being a licentious old fellow, I laughed. What had the young man done to induce her to change her mind so quickly? Probably he had taken her in his arms to make her feel the pleasure of living, and had seduced her instead of convincing her. That is why they needed so many good wishes. All people when they marry need good wishes, but this girl more than anyone. It would be disastrous if one day she had cause to regret having let herself be induced to return to the path which she had instinctively abhorred. And I even accompanied some of my glasses with wishes that I actually managed to invent for this particular case: "May you be contented for a year or two, then you will endure the other long years more easily, thanks to your gratitude for having enjoyed. The regret for joy remains, and this is also a pain, but a pain covered by the fundamental pain, the real pain of living."

The bride did not appear to feel the need of so many good wishes. Indeed, her face seemed to me to be absolutely crystallised into an expression of confident abandonment. But it was the same expression she had worn when she announced her desire to retire into a convent. Once again she was making a vow, this time a vow to be happy for her whole life. Some people always make vows in this way. Would she keep this one better than the other?

Everyone else at that table was thoroughly natural in his merriment, as onlookers always are. There was a complete lack of naturalness in me. It was a memorable evening for me. My wife had induced Dr. Paoli to let me eat and drink like everyone else for this once. Such liberty was all the more precious from the warning that it would be revoked immediately afterwards. And I behaved exactly like a young man who has been given a latchkey for the first time. I ate and drank, not because I was hungry or thirsty, but from a craving for liberty. Every mouthful, every sip was to be an assertion of my independence. I opened my mouth more widely than necessary to take in each individual mouthful. The wine passed from the bottle to my glass to overflowing, nor did I leave it there more than a single moment. I felt a longing to move and there, glued to my seat, I knew that I had the feeling of running and jumping like a dog slipped from his chain.

My wife made matters worse by telling a neighbour about the diet to which I usually had to keep, while my daughter Emma, aged fifteen, listened to her and put on an air of importance as she supplemented her mother's information. So they could remind me of my chain even now that it had been undone, could they? All my torture was described; how they weighed the little meat I was allowed at midday, taking all taste from it, and how at night there was nothing to weigh, because supper consisted of a roll with a morsel of ham and a glass of hot milk without sugar, which nauseated me. And while they were talking I was criticising the doctor's science and their affection. If my system was in such a bad way, how was it possible to allow, because they had brought off their *coup* of making someone marry who would never have done so from choice, that this evening it could suddenly endure so much harmful and indigestible stuff? And as I drank I prepared for rebellion on the morrow. They should see.

The others stuck to champagne, but, after taking a few glasses to drink the various toasts, I had gone back to ordinary wine, a dry and pure Istrian wine, which a friend of the family had sent for the occasion. I liked that wine, as one likes memories, and I felt confidence in it, nor was I surprised when, instead of bringing me gaiety and forgetfulness, it only increased the ire in my heart.

How could I help being in a passion? They had made a period of my life a burden to me. Frightened and depressed, I had let all my generous instincts die to make room for pastilles, drops and powders. No more socialism. What could it matter to me that the land, contrary to all the most enlightened scientific ideas, was still private property? What if on that account many people did not get their daily bread and the modicum of liberty that should adorn every day of a man's life? Had I either the one or the other?

That blessed evening I tried to be quite my old self. When my nephew, Giovanni, a huge man weighing seventeen stone, began in his stentorian voice to tell stories about his own smartness and other people's gullibility in business, I felt the old altruism stir in my heart. "What will you do," I cried, "when the struggle between man is no longer one for money?"

For a moment Giovanni was dumbfounded by my pregnant remark, which came quite unexpectedly to upset his world. He stared fixedly at me with his eyes magnified by his spectacles. He was looking for explanations in my face to give him his bearings. Then, while everyone was looking at him, expecting to be made to laugh by the answer of this ignorant, yet clever materialist, his mind a mixture of simplicity and cunning, a mind which always surprises, though it existed even before Sancho Panza, he gained time by saying that wine alters every man's outlook on the present, but in my case it was altering the future. This was something, but then he thought he had found something better and shouted: "When everyone ceases to struggle for money, I shall have it all without struggling, all, all." There was a long laugh, especially at a frequent gesture of his huge arms, which he first spread out to their full extent, then drew in, clenching his fists to give the idea that he had seized all the money that would flow to him from every direction.

The discussion went on, and no one noticed that when I was not talking, I was drinking. And I drank much and said little, being wholly wrapped up in studying my inner self, to see whether it would overflow with benevolence and altruism. I began to burn slightly inside, but it was a burning that would afterwards spread in a gradual glow, in the feeling of youth that wine produces, if only for a space all too brief.

And in expectation of this I called to Giovanni: "If you collar the money the others refuse, they will run you in."

But Giovanni shouted back readily enough: "And I will bribe the gaolers and have the people who have not got any money to bribe them run in."

"But money will not bribe anybody any more."

"Then why not let me have it?"

I grew violently angry: "We will hang you," I shouted. "You don't deserve anything else. A rope round your neck and weights on your feet."

I paused in astonishment. It seemed to me that I had failed to express my thoughts accurately. Was I really like that? No, certainly not. I reflected: How to recover my love for all living creatures, among whom must be included even Giovanni? I smiled at him at once, making a great effort to master myself and excuse and love him. But he prevented me, because he paid not the slightest attention to my kindly smile, and said, as if resigning himself to pointing out the existence of a monstrosity: "Yes, in practice all socialists end by calling in the executioner."

He scored off me, but I hated him. He poisoned my whole life, even those years before the intervention of the doctor, upon which I looked back with pride and regret. He had scored off me by raising the very doubt which I had felt so poignantly before he spoke.

And immediately afterwards another punishment was visited upon me. "How well he looks," my sister had remarked, gazing at me approvingly. The remark was unfortunate, because as soon as my wife heard it she felt that the exuberant good health that beamed from my face might possibly degenerate into its equivalent in illness. She was as frightened as if someone had just warned her of an approaching danger and attacked me fiercely: "Stop that," she shouted. "Down with that glass." She appealed to my neighbour, a certain Alberi, for help, one of the tallest men in the town, thin, dried up and healthy, but spectacled like Giovanni. "Be so good as to snatch that glass out of his hand." Seeing that Alberi hesitated, she became excited and anxious: "Signor Alberi, be good enough to take away his glass."

I tried to laugh, or rather I guess that a well-bred person ought to laugh, but I could not. I had planned my rebellion for the morrow, and it was not my fault if it broke out at once. These quarrels in public were really shameful. Alberi, who did not care twopence for me or my wife or any of these people who were entertaining him, made things worse by turning my position to ridicule. He looked over his spectacles at the glass I was clutching, moved his hands towards it as if he was really going to snatch it from me, then ended by drawing them comically back, as if he were afraid of me, for I was looking at him. Everybody laughed at me, Giovanni with a particularly noisy laugh of his, that took away his breath.

My daughter Emma thought her mother needed help. In tones that seemed to me absurdly pleading she said: "Daddy, don't drink any more."

And it was on this innocent child that I vented my wrath. I used a hard and threatening word to her, the effect of the resentment of the old man and the father. Her eyes filled with tears, and her mother, being engrossed in comforting her, paid no more attention to me.

Just then my son Ottavio, a boy of thirteen, ran up to his mother. He had seen nothing, neither his sister's tears, nor the quarrel that had caused them. He wanted to be allowed to go to the pictures with some friends, who had just proposed it, on the following evening. But my wife paid no attention to him, being too busy comforting Emma.

Eager to recover my self-respect by asserting my authority, I shouted my permission to him: "Yes, of course you shall go to the pictures. I give you my permission, and that is enough." Without waiting for more, Ottavio went back to his friends after saying: "Thank you, Papa." A pity he was in such a hurry. If he had stayed with us, his happiness, due to my assertion of authority, would have cheered me.

Good humour had vanished from that table for a few minutes,

and I felt that I had failed in my duty even towards the bride, with whom that good humour stood for good wishes and a good omen. And yet she was the only person who understood my feelings, or so it seemed to me. She looked at me quite maternally, ready to excuse me and be nice to me. That girl had always given an impression of confidence in her own opinions. Just as when she was longing for a cloistered life, so now she regarded herself as superior to everyone else in having renounced it. Now she was looking down upon me, upon my wife and upon my daughter. She pitied us, and her beautiful grey eyes rested serenely upon us, to see where the fault lay, for, in her opinion, there could be no doubt where the suffering was.

This increased my rancour towards my wife, whose conduct was humiliating us in this way. She was degrading us below everyone, even the meanest, at that table. Down at the end even my sister-in-law's children had stopped talking and were putting their small heads together, discussing what had happened. I seized my glass, wondering whether I should empty it or hurl it at the wall or, better, against the windows opposite. I ended by draining it at a draught. This was the surest proof of energy, because it was an assertion of my independence. I thought it the best wine I had tasted that evening. I prolonged the action by pouring more wine into my glass and drinking a little of it. But joy refused to come and all the life, now even too intense, that fired my system, was rancour. I was seized with a strange idea. My rebellion was not enough to put things right. Could not I suggest to the bride that she should join me in rebelling? By good luck at that very moment she smiled sweetly at the man who sat confident by her side. And I thought: "She does not know yet, and she is convinced that she knows."

I remember again that Giovanni said: "But let him drink. Wine is the milk of the old." I looked at him, wrinkling my face into the semblance of a smile, but I could not like him. I knew that all he cared about was the good humour, and he wanted to quiet me like a bad-tempered child who was spoiling a gathering of grown-ups.

After that I drank little, and then only when people were looking at me, nor did I open my mouth. Everyone around me was shouting merrily and this annoyed me. I did not listen, but it was difficult not to hear. Alberi and Giovanni had begun to argue, and everyone enjoyed watching the duel between the fat man and the thin. What they were quarreling about, I do not know, but I heard pretty aggressive words from both parties. I noticed Alberi on his feet, leaning towards Giovanni and bringing his spectacles almost over the middle of the table, quite close to his opponent. Giovanni, with his seventeen stone, stretched comfortably upon an armchair, which had been given him by way of a joke at the end of the meal, was gazing intently at him, like the good fencer he was, as if looking for an opening for his rapier thrust. But Alberi was also fine, woefully thin, indeed, but healthy, active and serene.

And I remember also the endless good wishes and greetings at the moment of parting. The bride kissed me with a smile that still seemed maternal. I received her kiss absent-mindedly. I was wondering when I should have an opportunity of telling her something about this life.

At that moment a name was mentioned by someone, that of a friend of my wife and an old friend of mine, Anna. I don't know by whom or in what connection, but I know it was the last name I heard before being left in peace by the guests. For years I had been used to seeing her often with my wife, and greeting her with the friendly indifference of people who have no reason to remark that they have been born in the same town and about the same time. Now, however, I remembered that many years ago she had been my one offence against love. I had courted her almost up to the moment of marrying my wife. But no one had ever made a remark about my treacherous behaviour, which had been so brusque that I had not attempted to attenuate it even by a single word, because she had also married very soon after and had been very happy. She had not been at the supper on account of a slight attack of influenza, which had kept her in bed—nothing serious. But it was strange and serious that I now remembered my offence against love, which came to weigh upon my conscience, already sufficiently troubled. I actually felt that at that moment my former offence was being punished. From her bed, where she was probably convalescent, I heard my victim protest: "It would not be fair for you to be happy." I went to my bedroom very depressed. I was rather confused, because it did not seem fair to me that my wife should be commissioned to avenge one whom she had supplanted.

Emma came to wish me good-night. She was smiling, rosy and fresh. Her short outbreak of crying had given way to a reaction of joy, as is usual with healthy and youthful systems. I had recently learnt to understand other people's characters, and then my daughter was as transparent as glass. My outburst had served to give her importance in the eyes of everyone, and she enjoyed it in all innocence. I gave her a kiss, and I am sure that I thought it was lucky for me that she was so happy and contented. For her own good it would, of course, have been my duty to point out to her that she had not treated me with becoming respect. But I could not find the words and I held my tongue. She went off, and the only result of my attempt to find words that remained was a preoccupation, a confusion, an effort which did not leave me for some time. To quiet myself I thought: "I will speak to her to-morrow. I will give her my reasons." But it was useless. I had offended her and she had offended me. But it was a further offence that she had forgotten all about it, whereas I never ceased brooding over it.

Ottavio also came to bid me good-night. A strange boy. He said good-night to his mother and myself almost without noticing us. He had already left the room when I called after him: "Are you glad to be going to the pictures?" He stopped and made an effort to remember and before going further said dryly: "Yes." He was very sleepy.

My wife handed me the box of pills. "Are these they?" I asked with a mask of ice on my face.

"Yes, of course," said she gently. She looked inquiringly at me, and, not being able to guess my thoughts in any other way, asked hesitatingly: "Are you well?"

"Perfectly well," I answered firmly, as I took off one of my boots. And at that very moment my stomach began to burn horribly. "This is what she wanted," I thought, with a logic about which I am only now doubtful.

I swallowed the pill with some water and experienced a slight relief. I kissed my wife mechanically upon the cheek. It was a kiss such as might go with the pills. I could not have avoided it if I wanted to escape discussions and explanations. But I could not settle down to rest without clearing up my position in the struggle which was not yet over for me, and I said just as I snuggled down in bed: "I think the pills would have been more effective taken with the wine."

She put out the light, and very soon the regularity of her breathing told me that her conscience was at rest, that is to say, I thought at once, she is completely indifferent to all that concerns me. I had anxiously awaited that moment, and immediately said to myself that I was at last free to breathe noisily, as the condition of my system seemed to demand, or even to sob, as, in my depression, I should have liked to do. But the suffering, the moment I was free, became even more intense. This was no liberty. How was I to vent the anger that raged within me? All I could do was to think over what I should say to my wife and daughter next day. "You are very anxious about my health when it is a question of nagging me before other people." It was so true. Here was I raging alone in my bed while they slept in peace. What a burning! A huge tract of it had invaded my system and was trying to vent itself through my throat. There should be a bottle of water on the little table by my bedside. I reached out for it, but knocked the empty glass and the slight noise was enough to wake my wife. Yes, she slept with one eye open.

"Are you ill?" she asked in a low voice. I could not believe my ears, and refused to rouse myself. I tried to understand for a little, but ended by thinking that her strange purpose was to gloat over my illness, which was merely the proof that she was right. I gave up the idea of the water, and settled down comfortably once more. At once she fell back into that light slumber of hers, which enabled her to keep watch over me.

Clearly, if I was not to get the worst of it in my quarrel with my wife, I must go to sleep. I shut my eyes and turned over on my side, but I was obliged to change my position at once. However, I was obstinate, and did not open my eyes. But every position meant the sacrifice of a part of my body. I thought: "With a body like this sleep is out of the question." I was all movement, all wakefulness. A man running cannot think of sleep. I had the breathlessness of a man running and also the sound of my steps in my ears; and my boots were large and heavy. I thought that, perhaps, I turned too gently in my bed to hit upon the right position for all my limbs at once. It was useless to search for it. I must let every part of me find the place that suited it. I flung myself back as violently as possible. At once my wife whispered: "Are you ill?" If she had used different words, I would have answered by asking her to help me. But I refused to answer those particular words, which referred offensively to our quarrel.

Yet to lie still should be so easy. What trouble can there be in lying, just lying in bed? I went over all the great difficulties that beset our path in this world and found that really, compared with any of these, to lie still was nothing. Any worn-out old horse can stand still. In my determination I discovered a position that was complicated, but incredibly tenacious. I fixed my teeth into the upper part of the pillow and twisted myself in such a way that my chest also rested on the pillow, while my right leg was outside the bed and almost touching the ground, and the left was stiff on the bed, pinning me to it. Yes, I had discovered a new way. It was not that I held the bed, but the bed held me. And this conviction of my inert state was such that even when the oppression increased, I refused to yield. When at last I had to give way, I comforted myself with the thought that at least a part of that dreadful night was over, and I was also rewarded by feeling, once I had freed myself from the bed, as exhilarated as a wrestler who has shaken off the clutch of his adversary.

I don't know how long I then kept still. I was tired. To my amazement I noticed in my closed eyes the strange brilliance of a whirlwind of flames which I supposed to be caused by the fire I felt inside me. They were not real flames, but colours like them. Then they diminished and shaped themselves into circular forms, or rather into drops of a viscous liquid, which soon became all blue, mild, but surrounded by a luminous red line. They fell from a point above, grew longer and, becoming detached, disappeared below. It was I who first thought that these drops could see me. Immediately, to see me better, they were transformed into so many huge eyes. As they grew longer in falling a little circle formed in their centre, which, as it shed the blue covering, displayed a real eye, evil and malevolent. I was actually followed by a crowd that hated me. I rebelled in my bed, groaning and calling out: "My God!"

"Are you ill?" asked my wife at once.

Some time must have gone by before I answered. But then it happened that I realised that I was not lying in my bed any longer, but was clinging to it, and that it had been transformed into a slope, down which I was slipping. I called out: "I am ill, very ill."

My wife had lit a candle and was standing by me in her pink nightdress. The light reassured me, and I even had the clear conviction that I had slept and had only then waked up. The bed had straightened and I was lying on it quite comfortably. I looked at my wife in surprise, because now, realising that I had been asleep, I was no longer certain that I had called for her help. "What do you want?" I asked her.

She looked at me half asleep and tired. My call had been sufficient to make her jump out of bed, but not to rob her of her longing for sleep, which was so great that she did not even care whether she was right or not. Not to waste time she asked: "Would you like those drops the doctor gave you to make you sleep?"

I hesitated, strong though my desire to feel better was. "If you like," I said, trying to appear only resigned. To take the drops was not by any means an admission that I was unwell.

Then there followed a moment during which I enjoyed perfect peace. It lasted while my wife in her pink nightdress, by the slender light of the candle, stood by me counting the drops. The bed was a real horizontal bed and my eyelids, when I closed them, were sufficient to shut out all light from my eyes. From time to time I opened them and that light and the pink of the nightdress gave me as much relief as complete darkness. But she did not want to go on helping me for a single moment more, and I was once again plunged into the night to fight for peace alone.

I remembered that, when I was young, to send myself to sleep, I used to force myself to think of a hideous old woman who helped me to forget the lovely visions that haunted me. Now, however, I might call up beauty without danger and it would certainly help me. It was an advantage, and the only one, of old age. I thought of several beautiful women, the loves of my young days, of a time when beautiful women had abounded in extraordinary numbers, and called upon them by name. But they did not come. Not even then did they yield themselves. And I called and called them continuously until out of the night there rose up a single lovely face; Anna, yes, she, as she had been many years before, but her face, her beautiful pink-complexioned face, was wearing an expression of pain and reproof. For she meant to bring me not peace, but remorse. That was clear. And as she was there I talked to her. I had jilted her, but she had immediately married someone else, which was only fair. And she had brought into the world a daughter, now fifteen, who was like her in her delicate colouring, her golden hair and blue eyes; but then her face was spoilt by the intervention of the father who had been chosen for her. The gentle wave of the hair had been turned into a mass of tight curls, the cheeks were large, the mouth broad, the lips much too full. The mother's colouring combined with the lines of the father produced the effect of a shameless kiss, in public. What did she want of me now, after she had let me see her so often arm-in-arm with her husband?

It was the first time that evening that I could feel that I had won. Anna became more gentle, almost changing her mind. And then her company was no longer distasteful to me. She might stay. And I fell asleep, admiring her, good and beautiful and won over to my view. I soon fell asleep.

A horrible dream. I was in a complicated building, which I understood at once, as though I had been a part of it. It was a huge cave, rugged, without any of those ornaments which nature amuses herself creating in caves, and therefore certainly the work of man, and it was dark. There I sat on a three-legged stool beside a glass chest, feebly illuminated by a light which I considered must be a quality of itself, the only light there was in the vast structure, though it was strong enough to illuminate myself, a huge wall consisting of great, rough stones and below it a cemented wall. How vivid are the constructions of dreams! You will reply that this is because their architect can easily understand them, and it is true. But the surprising fact is that the architect is not aware of having made them, and does not remember having done so even when awake, and as he turns his thoughts back to the world which he has left, where these constructions sprung up so easily, it may surprise him that everything is understood there without the need of a single word.

I knew at once that the cave had been built by men who were

using it for a cure invented by themselves, a cure that would prove fatal to one of those who were imprisoned in it—there must have been a number of people down there in the dark—but highly beneficial to all the others. Yes, a sort of religion which required a victim, and naturally I was not surprised.

It was even more easy to guess that, since they had put me so close to the glass chest in which the victim was to be asphyxiated, I had been chosen to die for the sake of all the others. And already I endured in anticipation the pain of the ugly death in store for me. I breathed with difficulty and my head ached and was heavy, so that I rested it on my hands, my elbows on my knees.

Suddenly everything I already knew was said by a number of people concealed in the darkness. My wife appeared first: "Be quick, the doctor has said that it is you who must get into that chest." I thought it painful, but perfectly natural, so I made no protest, but pretended not to hear. And I thought: "I always considered my wife's love silly." A number of other voices shouted imperiously: "Will you make up your mind to obey?" Among them I distinguished clearly that of Dr. Paoli. I could not protest, but thought: "He is doing it for money."

I raised my head to examine once again the glass chest that was waiting for me. Then I discovered seated on the top of it the bride. Even in that position she kept her perennial air of calm self-possession. I heartily despised the silly woman, but I was suddenly aware that she was very important for me. I should have found this out in real life as well as from seeing her seated on the instrument that was to compass my death. And then I looked at her and fawned. So abject was I that I felt like one of those tiny little dogs that make their way through life by fawning.

Then the bride spoke. Without any violence, as if it were the most natural thing in the world, she said: "Uncle, the chest is for you."

I should have to fight for my life singlehanded. That also I guessed. I had the feeling of knowing how to make an enormous effort without anyone being able to realise it. Just as at first I had felt within me an organ that enabled me to win the favour of my judge without opening my mouth, so now I discovered within me another organ, though I do not know what it was, with which I could fight without moving and thus fall upon my enemies when off their guard. And the effort immediately took effect. There was Giovanni, fat Giovanni, seated in the luminous glass chest on a wooden chair like mine and in the same position. He was leaning forward, as the chest was too low, and holding his glasses in his hand to prevent them from falling off his nose. In this attitude he looked rather as if he were engaged on a business problem and had taken off his glasses to be able to think better without seeing anything. And in fact, though he was bathed in perspiration and already very short of breath, he was not thinking of his approaching death, but was full of evil, as was clear from his eyes, by which I saw that he meant to make the same effort that I had made a little while previously. Hence I could feel no pity for him, for I was afraid of him.

Giovanni also made the effort successfully. Soon afterwards his place was taken by Alberi, the long, thin and healthy Alberi, in the same position that Giovanni had been in, but he was worse off owing to his height. He was actually bent double and would really have awakened my compassion, if he also, in addition to his suffering, had not displayed the same malice. He looked me up and down with an evil smile, knowing that he could, whenever he chose, escape death in the chest.

Once again the bride spoke from the top of the chest: "Now, of course, it will be your turn, Uncle." She pronounced each syllable with pedantic distinctness. Her words were accompanied by another sound, very distant, far overhead. From the prolonged noise made by a person who is hurriedly moving to go away I learnt that the cave ended in a steep passage leading to the surface of the earth. It was only a hiss, but a hiss of consent, and it came from Anna, who once more let me see her hate. She had not the pluck to put it into words, because I had really convinced her that she had been more guilty towards me than I towards her. But this conviction means nothing when it is a question of hate.

I was condemned by everyone. Some way from me, in another part of the cave, my wife and the doctor were walking up and down, waiting, and I knew by intuition that my wife's face wore a resentful expression. She was gesticulating violently as she described my crimes, the wine, the food and my rough treatment of herself and my daughter.

I felt myself drawn towards the chest by the look of triumph

Alberi was turning upon me. I drew slowly towards it with my seat, barely an inch at a time, but I knew that when I was within a yard of it—this was the law—I should be carried right up to it at a single bound, gasping.

But there was still a hope of escape. Giovanni, quite recovered from the effects of his hard struggle, had appeared close to the chest, which he could no longer fear, since he had been in it already. This also was the law there. He was standing erect in the full light, looking now at Alberi, who was gasping and threatening, now at me, as I slowly drew near the chest.

I shouted: "Giovanni, help me to keep him inside. I will pay you money." The whole cave echoed to my cry, and it sounded like a mocking laugh. I understood. It was useless to implore mercy. It was not the first, nor the second who found himself inside the chest who was to die there, but the third. This also was a law of the cave, which, like all the others, was bringing about my undoing. But it was hard that I had to realise that it had not been made at that moment deliberately to harm me. This also was a result of that darkness and that light. Giovanni did not even answer and shrugged his shoulders to show his regret at not being able to save me, and at not being able to sell me my safety.

And then I shouted again: "If there is no other way, take my daughter. She is asleep here close by. It will be easy." These cries were also sent back to me by a loud echo. Useless though it was, I shouted again to call my daughter: "Emma, Emma, Emma!"

And from the depths of the cave there actually came Emma's answer, the sound of her voice, still so childish: "Here I am, Daddy, here I am."

It seemed to me that she did not answer at once. Then there was a violent convulsion, which I thought was the result of my leap into the chest. Again I thought: "That girl is always so slow in obeying." This time her slowness was the cause of my undoing, and I was full of injured bitterness.

I woke up. That was the convulsion, the leap from one world into the other. My head and the top part of my body were out of the bed, and I should have fallen, if my wife had not run up to save me. She asked me: "Have you been dreaming?" And then, moved:

"You were calling for your daughter. You see how you love her."

At first I was dazzled by the reality where everything seemed to me out of focus and false. And I said to my wife, who also ought to have known everything: "How shall we be able to win our children's pardon for having brought them into this world?"

But she answered, in her simplicity: "Our children are happy to be alive."

The world which I then felt to be the real one, the dream-world, was still all round me, and I wanted to proclaim it: "Because they don't know anything yet."

Then I stopped and took refuge in silence. The window by my bed was growing light, and in that light I understood at once that I must not describe my dream, because I must conceal the shame of it. But soon, as the soft, bluish, but commanding light of the sun continued to flood the room, I ceased to feel the shame any more. The dream-world was not my world, nor was I the man who fawned and who was ready to sacrifice his own daughter to save himself.

However, at all costs I must never return to that horrible cave. And that is how I became submissive and ready to obey the doctor's orders. Should it happen that, from no fault of mine, that is, not as a result of excessive potations, but owing to the last fever, I had to go back to the cave, I would jump straight into the glass chest, if it was there, rather than fawn or betray.

◇◇◇*Rabindranath Tagore (1861-1941). Indian poet and short-story writer. He wrote mainly in Bengali, but also in English. Many of his poems have been translated into English. See his collections of stories,* The Hungry Stones *and* Broken Ties.

THE HUNGRY STONES

BY RABINDRANATH TAGORE

My kinsman and myself were returning to Calcutta from our Puja trip when we met the man in a train. From his dress and bearing we took him at first for an up-country Mahomedan, but we were puzzled as we heard him talk. He discoursed upon all subjects so confidently that you might think the Disposer of All Things consulted him at all times in all that He did. Hitherto we had been perfectly happy, as we did not know that secret and unheard-of forces were at work, that the Russians had advanced close to us, that the English had deep and secret policies, that confusion among the native chiefs had come to a head. But our newly-acquired friend said with a sly smile: "There happen more things in heaven and earth, Horatio, than are reported in your newspapers." As we had never stirred out of our homes before, the demeanour of the man struck us dumb with wonder. Be the topic ever so trivial, he would quote science, or comment on the *Vedas,* or repeat quatrains from some Persian poet; and as we had no pretence to a knowledge of science or the *Vedas* or Persian, our admiration for him went on increasing, and my kinsman, a theosophist, was firmly convinced that our fellow-passenger must have been supernaturally inspired by some strange "magnetism" or "occult power," by an "astral body" or something of that kind. He listened to the tritest saying that fell from the lips of our extraordinary companion with devotional rapture, and secretly took down notes of his conversation. I fancy that the extraordinary man saw this, and was a little pleased with it.

When the train reached the junction, we assembled in the waiting-room for the connection. It was then 10 P.M., and as the train, we heard, was likely to be very late, owing to something wrong in the lines, I spread my bed on the table and was about to lie down for a comfortable doze, when the extraordinary person deliberately set about spinning the following yarn. Of course, I could get no sleep that night.

When, owing to a disagreement about some questions of administrative policy, I threw up my post at Junagarh, and entered the service of the Nizam of Hyderabad, they appointed me at once, as a strong young man, collector of cotton duties at Barich.

Barich is a lovely place. The *Susta* "chatters over stony ways and babbles on the pebbles," tripping, like a skilful dancing girl, in through the woods below the lonely hills. A flight of 150 steps rises from the river, and above that flight, on the river's brim and at the foot of the hills, there stands a solitary marble palace. Around it there is no habitation of man—the village and the cotton mart of Barich being far off.

About 250 years ago the Emperor Mahmud Shah II had built this lonely palace for his pleasure and luxury. In his days jets of rose-water spurted from its fountains, and on the cold marble floors of its spray-cooled rooms young Persian damsels would sit, their hair dishevelled before bathing, and, splashing their soft naked feet in the clear water of the reservoirs, would sing, to the tune of the guitar, the *ghazals* of their vineyards.

The fountains play no longer; the songs have ceased; no longer do snow-white feet step gracefully on the snowy marble. It is but the vast and solitary quarters of cess-collectors like us, men oppressed with solitude and deprived of the society of women. Now, Karim Khan, the old clerk of my office, warned me repeatedly not to take up my abode there. "Pass the day there, if you like," said he, "but never stay the night." I passed it off with a light laugh. The servants said that they would work till dark, and go away at night. I gave my ready assent. The house had such a bad name that even thieves would not venture near it after dark.

At first the solitude of the deserted palace weighed upon me like a nightmare. I would stay out, and work hard as long as possible, then return home at night jaded and tired, go to bed and fall asleep.

Before a week had passed, the place began to exert a weird fascination upon me. It is difficult to describe or to induce people to believe; but I felt as if the whole house was like a living organism slowly and imperceptibly digesting me by the action of some stupefying gastric juice.

Perhaps the process had begun as soon as I set my foot in the house, but I distinctly remember the day on which I first was conscious of it.

It was the beginning of summer, and the market being dull I had no work to do. A little before sunset I was sitting in an arm-chair near the water's edge below the steps. The *Susta* had shrunk and sunk low; a broad patch of sand on the other side glowed with the hues of evening; on this side the pebbles at the bottom of the clear shallow waters were glistening. There was not a breath of wind anywhere, and the still air was laden with an oppressive scent from the spicy shrubs growing on the hills close by.

As the sun sank behind the hill-tops a long dark curtain fell upon the stage of day, and the intervening hills cut short the time in which light and shade mingle at sunset. I thought of going out for a ride, and was about to get up when I heard a footfall on the steps behind. I looked back, but there was no one.

As I sat down again, thinking it to be an illusion, I heard many footfalls, as if a large number of persons were rushing down the steps. A strange thrill of delight, slightly tinged with fear, passed through my frame, and though there was not a figure before my eyes, methought I saw a bevy of joyous maidens coming down the steps to bathe in the *Susta* in that summer evening. Not a sound was in the valley, in the river, or in the palace, to break the silence, but I distinctly heard the maidens' gay and mirthful laugh, like the gurgle of a spring gushing forth in a hundred cascades, as they ran past me, in quick playful pursuit of each other, towards the river, without noticing me at all. As they were invisible to me, so I was, as it were, invisible to them. The river was perfectly calm, but I felt that its still, shallow, and clear waters were stirred suddenly by the splash of many an arm jingling with bracelets, that the girls laughed and dashed and spattered water at one another, that the feet of the fair swimmers tossed the tiny waves up in showers of pearl.

I felt a thrill at my heart—I cannot say whether the excitement was due to fear or delight or curiosity. I had a strong desire to see them more clearly, but naught was visible before me; I thought I could catch all that they said if I only strained my ears; but however hard I strained them, I heard nothing but the chirping of the cicadas in the woods. It seemed as if a dark curtain of 250 years was hanging before me, and I would fain lift a corner of it tremblingly and peer through, though the assembly on the other side was completely enveloped in darkness.

The oppressive closeness of the evening was broken by a sudden gust of wind, and the still surface of the *Susta* rippled and curled like the hair of a nymph, and from the woods wrapt in the evening gloom there came forth a simultaneous murmur, as though they were awakening from a black dream. Call it reality or dream, the momentary glimpse of that invisible mirage reflected from a far-off world, 250 years old, vanished in a flash. The mystic forms that brushed past me with their quick unbodied steps, and loud, voiceless laughter, and threw themselves into the river, did not go back wringing their dripping robes as they went. Like fragrance wafted away by the wind they were dispersed by a single breath of the spring.

Then I was filled with a lively fear that it was the Muse that had taken advantage of my solitude and possessed me—the witch had evidently come to ruin a poor devil like myself making a living by collecting cotton duties. I decided to have a good dinner—it is the empty stomach that all sorts of incurable diseases find an easy prey. I sent for my cook and gave orders for a rich, sumptuous *moghlai* dinner, redolent of spices and *ghi*.

Next morning the whole affair appeared a queer fantasy. With a light heart I put on a *sola* hat like the *sahebs*, and drove out to my work. I was to have written my quarterly report that day, and expected to return late; but before it was dark I was strangely drawn to my house—by what I could not say—I felt they were all waiting, and that I should delay no longer. Leaving my report unfinished I rose, put on my *sola* hat, and startling the dark, shady, desolate path with the rattle of my carriage, I reached the vast silent palace standing on the gloomy skirts of the hills.

On the first floor the stairs led to a very spacious hall, its roof stretching wide over ornamental arches resting on three rows of massive pillars, and groaning day and night under the weight of its own intense solitude. The day had just closed, and the lamps had not yet been lighted. As I pushed the door open a great bustle seemed to follow within, as if a throng of people had broken up in confusion, and rushed out through the doors and windows and corridors and verandas and rooms, to make its hurried escape.

As I saw no one I stood bewildered, my hair on end in a kind of ecstatic delight, and a faint scent of *attar* and unguents almost effaced by age lingered in my nostrils. Standing in the darkness of that vast desolate hall between the rows of those ancient pillars, I could hear the gurgle of fountains plashing on the marble floor, a strange tune on the guitar, the jingle of ornaments and the tinkle of anklets, the clang of bells tolling the hours, the distant note of *nahabat*, the din of the crystal pendants of chandeliers shaken by the breeze, the song of *bulbuls* from the cages in the corridors, the cackle of storks in the gardens, all creating round me a strange unearthly music.

Then I came under such a spell that this intangible, inaccessible, unearthly vision appeared to be the only reality in the world—and all else a mere dream. That I, that is to say, Srijut So-and-so, the eldest son of So-and-so of blessed memory, should be drawing a monthly salary of Rs. 450 by the discharge of my duties as collector of cotton duties, and driving in my dog-cart to my office every day in a short coat and *sola* hat, appeared to me to be such an astonishingly ludicrous illusion that I burst into a horse-laugh, as I stood in the gloom of that vast silent hall.

At that moment my servant entered with a lighted kerosene lamp in his hand. I do not know whether he thought me mad, but it came back to me at once that I was in very deed Srijut So-and-so, son of So-and-so of blessed memory, and that, while our poets, great and small, alone could say whether inside or outside the earth there was a region where unseen fountains perpetually played and fairy guitars, struck by invisible fingers, sent forth an eternal harmony, this at any rate was certain, that I collected duties at the cotton market at Barich, and earned thereby Rs. 450 per mensem as my salary. I laughed in great glee at my curious illusion, as I sat over the newspaper at my camp-table, lighted by the kerosene lamp.

After I had finished my paper and eaten my *moghlai* dinner, I put out the lamp, and lay down on my bed in a small side-room. Through the open window a radiant star, high above the Avalli hills skirted by the darkness of their woods, was gazing intently from millions and millions of miles away in the sky at Mr. Collector lying on a humble camp-bedstead. I wondered and felt amused at the idea, and do not know when I fell asleep or how long I slept; but I suddenly awoke with a start, though I heard no sound and saw no intruder—only the steady bright star on the hilltop had set, and the dim light of the new moon was stealthily entering the room through the open window, as if ashamed of its intrusion.

I saw nobody, but felt as if someone was gently pushing me. As I awoke she said not a word, but beckoned me with her five fingers bedecked with rings to follow her cautiously. I got up noiselessly, and, though not a soul save myself was there in the countless apartments of that deserted palace with its slumbering sounds and waking echoes, I feared at every step lest any one should wake up. Most of the rooms of the palace were always kept closed, and I had never entered them.

I followed breathless and with silent steps my invisible guide—I cannot now say where. What endless dark and narrow passages, what long corridors, what silent and solemn audience-chambers and close secret cells I crossed!

Though I could not see my fair guide, her form was not invisible to my mind's eye,—an Arab girl, her arms, hard and smooth as marble, visible through her loose sleeves, a thin veil falling on her face from the fringe of her cap, and a curved dagger at her waist! Methought that one of the thousand and one Arabian Nights had been wafted to me from the world of romance, and that at the dead of night I was wending my way through the dark narrow alleys of slumbering Bagdad to a trysting-place fraught with peril.

At last my fair guide stopped abruptly before a deep blue screen, and seemed to point to something below. There was nothing there, but a sudden dread froze the blood in my heart—methought I saw there on the floor at the foot of the screen a terrible negro eunuch dressed in rich brocade, sitting and dozing with outstretched legs, with a naked sword on his lap. My fair guide lightly tripped over his legs and held up a fringe of the screen. I could catch a glimpse of a part of the room spread with a Persian carpet—some one was sitting inside on a bed—I could not see her, but only caught a glimpse of two exquisite feet in gold-embroidered slippers, hanging out from loose saffron-coloured *paijamas* and placed idly on the orange-coloured velvet carpet. On one side there was a bluish crystal tray on which a few apples, pears, oranges, and bunches of grapes in plenty, two small cups and a gold-tinted decanter were evidently awaiting the guest. A fragrant intoxicating vapour, issuing from a strange sort of incense that burned within, almost overpowered my senses.

As with trembling heart I made an attempt to step across the outstretched legs of the eunuch, he woke up suddenly with a start, and the sword fell from his lap with a sharp clang on the marble floor.

A terrific scream made me jump, and I saw I was sitting on that camp-bedstead of mine sweating heavily; and the crescent moon looked pale in the morning light like a weary sleepless patient at dawn; and our crazy Meher Ali was crying out, as is his daily custom, "Stand back! Stand back!!" while he went along the lonely road.

Such was the abrupt close of one of my Arabian Nights; but there were yet a thousand nights left.

Then followed a great discord between my days and nights. During the day I would go to my work worn and tired, cursing the bewitching night and her empty dreams, but as night came my daily life with its bonds and shackles of work would appear a petty, false, ludicrous vanity.

After nightfall I was caught and overwhelmed in the snare of a strange intoxication. I would then be transformed into some unknown personage of a bygone age, playing my part in unwritten history; and my short English coat and tight breeches did not suit me in the least. With a red velvet cap on my head, loose *paijamas*, an embroidered vest, a long flowing silk gown, and coloured handkerchiefs scented with *attar*, I would complete my elaborate toilet, sit on a high-cushioned chair, and replace my cigarette with a many-coiled *narghileh* filled with rose-water, as if in eager expectation of a strange meeting with the beloved one.

I have no power to describe the marvellous incidents that unfolded themselves, as the gloom of the night deepened. I felt as if in the curious apartments of that vast edifice the fragments of a beautiful story, which I could follow for some distance, but of which I could never see the end, flew about in a sudden gust of the vernal breeze. And all the same I would wander from room to room in pursuit of them the whole night long.

Amid the eddy of these dream-fragments, amid the smell of *henna* and the twanging of the guitar, amid the waves of air charged with fragrant spray, I would catch like a flash of lightning the momentary glimpse of a fair damsel. She it was who had saffron-coloured *paijamas,* white ruddy soft feet in gold-embroidered slippers with curved toes, a close-fitting bodice wrought with gold, a red cap, from which a golden frill fell on her snowy brow and cheeks.

She had maddened me. In pursuit of her I wandered from room to room, from path to path among the bewildering maze of alleys in the enchanted dreamland of the nether world of sleep.

Sometimes in the evening, while arraying myself carefully as a prince of the blood-royal before a large mirror, with a candle burning on either side, I would see a sudden reflection of the Persian beauty by the side of my own. A swift turn of her neck, a quick eager glance of intense passion and pain glowing in her large dark eyes, just a suspicion of speech on her dainty red lips, her figure, fair and slim, crowned with youth like a blossoming creeper, quickly uplifted in her graceful tilting gait, a dazzling flash of pain and craving and ecstasy, a smile and a glance and a blaze of jewels and silk, and she melted away. A wild gust of wind, laden with all the fragrance of hills and woods, would put out my light, and I would fling aside my dress and lie down on my bed, my eyes closed and my body thrilling with delight, and there around me in the breeze, amid all the perfume of the woods and hills, floated through the silent gloom many a caress and many a kiss and many a tender touch of hands, and gentle murmurs in my ears, and fragrant breaths on my brow; or a sweetly-perfumed kerchief was wafted again and again on my cheeks. Then slowly a mysterious serpent would twist her stupefying coils about me; and heaving a heavy sigh, I would lapse into insensibility, and then into a profound slumber.

One evening I decided to go out on my horse—I do not know who implored me to stay but I would listen to no entreaties that day. My English hat and coat were resting on a rack, and I was about to take them down when a sudden whirlwind, crested with the sands of the *Susta* and the dead leaves of the Avalli hills, caught them up, and whirled them round and round, while a loud peal of merry laughter rose higher and higher, striking all the chords of mirth till it died away in the land of sunset.

I could not go out for my ride, and the next day I gave up my queer English coat and hat for good.

That day again at dead of night I heard the stifled heart-breaking sobs of someone—as if below the bed, below the floor, below the stony foundation of that gigantic palace, from the depths of a dark damp grave, a voice piteously cried and implored me: "Oh, rescue me! Break through these doors of hard illusion, deathlike slumber and fruitless dreams, place me by your side on the saddle, press me to your heart, and, riding through hills and woods and across the river, take me to the warm radiance of your sunny rooms above!"

Who am I? Oh, how can I rescue thee? What drowning beauty, what incarnate passion shall I drag to the shore from this wild eddy of dreams? O lovely ethereal apparition! Where didst thou flourish and when? By what cool spring, under the shade of what date-groves, wast thou born—in the lap of what homeless wanderer in the desert? What Bedouin snatched thee from thy mother's arms, an opening bud plucked from a wild creeper, placed thee on a horse swift as lightning, crossed the burning sands, and took thee to the slave-market of what royal city? And there, what officer of the Badshah, seeing the glory of thy bashful blossoming youth, paid for thee in gold, placed thee in a golden palanquin, and offered thee as a present for the seraglio of his master? And O, the history of that place! The music of the *sareng*,[1] the jingle of anklets, the occasional flash of daggers and the glowing wine of Shiraz poison, and the piercing flashing glance! What infinite grandeur, what endless servitude! The slave-girls to thy right and left waved the *chamar*,[2] as diamonds flashed from their bracelets; the Badshah, the king of kings, fell on his knees at thy snowy feet in bejewelled shoes, and outside the terrible Abyssinian eunuch, looking like a messenger of death, but clothed like an angel, stood with a naked sword in his

---

[1] A sort of violin.
[2] *Chamar:* chowrie, yak-tail.

hand! Then, O, thou flower of the desert, swept away by the blood-stained dazzling ocean of grandeur, with its foam of jealousy, its rocks and shoals of intrigue, on what shore of cruel death wast thou cast, or in what other land more splendid and more cruel?

Suddenly at this moment that crazy Meher Ali screamed out: "Stand back! Stand back!! All is false! All is false!!" I opened my eyes and saw that it was already light. My *chaprasi* came and handed me my letters, and the cook waited with a *salam* for my orders.

I said: "No, I can stay here no longer." That very day I packed up, and moved to my office. Old Karim Khan smiled a little as he saw me. I felt nettled, but said nothing, and fell to my work.

As evening approached I grew absent-minded; I felt as if I had an appointment to keep; and the work of examining the cotton accounts seemed wholly useless; even the *Nizamat*[1] of the Nizam did not appear to be of much worth. Whatever belonged to the present, whatever was moving and acting and working for bread seemed trivial, meaningless, and contemptible.

I threw my pen down, closed my ledgers, got into my dog-cart, and drove away. I noticed that it stopped of itself at the gate of the marble palace just at the hour of twilight. With quick steps I climbed the stairs, and entered the room.

A heavy silence was reigning within. The dark rooms were looking sullen as if they had taken offence. My heart was full of contrition, but there was no one to whom I could lay it bare, or of whom I could ask forgiveness. I wandered about the dark rooms with a vacant mind. I wished I had a guitar to which I could sing to the unknown: "O fire, the poor moth that made a vain effort to fly away has come back to thee! Forgive it but this once, burn its wings and consume it in thy flame!"

Suddenly two tear-drops fell from overhead on my brow. Dark masses of clouds overcast the top of the Avalli hills that day. The gloomy woods and the sooty waters of the *Susta* were waiting in terrible suspense and in an ominous calm. Suddenly land, water, and sky shivered, and a wild tempest-blast rushed howling through the distant pathless woods, showing its lightning-teeth like a raving

---

[1] Royalty.

maniac who had broken his chains. The desolate halls of the palace banged their doors, and moaned in the bitterness of anguish.

The servants were all in the office, and there was no one to light the lamps. The night was cloudy and moonless. In the dense gloom within I could distinctly feel that a woman was lying on her face on the carpet below the bed—clasping and tearing her long disheveled hair with desperate fingers. Blood was trickling down her fair brow, and she was now laughing a hard, harsh, mirthless laugh, now bursting into violent wringing sobs, now rending her bodice and striking at her bare bosom, as the wind roared in through the open window, and the rain poured in torrents and soaked her through and through.

All night there was no cessation of the storm or of the passionate cry. I wandered from room to room in the dark, with unavailing sorrow. Whom could I console when no one was by? Whose was this intense agony of sorrow? Whence arose this inconsolable grief?

And the mad man cried out: "Stand back! Stand back!! All is false! All is false!!"

I saw that the day had dawned, and Meher Ali was going round and round the palace with his usual cry in that dreadful weather. Suddenly it came to me that perhaps he also had once lived in that house, and that, though he had gone mad, he came there every day, and went round and round, fascinated by the weird spell cast by the marble demon.

Despite the storm and rain I ran to him and asked: "Ho, Meher Ali, what is false?"

The man answered nothing, but pushing me aside went round and round with his frantic cry, like a bird flying fascinated about the jaws of a snake, and made a desperate effort to warn himself by repeating: "Stand back! Stand back!! All is false! All is false!!"

I ran like a mad man through the pelting rain to my office, and asked Karim Khan: "Tell me the meaning of all this!"

What I gathered from that old man was this: That at one time countless unrequited passions and unsatisfied longings and lurid flames of wild blazing pleasure raged within that palace, and that the curse of all the heart-aches and blasted hopes had made its every stone thirsty and hungry, eager to swallow up like a famished ogress any living man who might chance to approach. Not one of those who lived there for three consecutive nights could escape these cruel jaws, save Meher Ali, who had escaped at the cost of his reason.

I asked: "Is there no means whatever of my release?" The old man said: "There is only one means, and that is very difficult. I will tell you what it is, but first you must hear the history of a young Persian girl who once lived in that pleasure-dome. A stranger or a more bitterly heart-rending tragedy was never enacted on this earth."

Just at this moment the coolies announced that the train was coming. So soon? We hurriedly packed up our luggage, as the train steamed in. An English gentleman, apparently just aroused from slumber, was looking out of a first-class carriage endeavouring to read the name of the station. As soon as he caught sight of our fellow-passenger, he cried, "Hallo," and took him into his own compartment. As we got into a second-class carriage, we had no chance of finding out who the man was nor what was the end of his story.

I said: "The man evidently took us for fools and imposed upon us out of fun. The story is pure fabrication from start to finish." The discussion that followed ended in a lifelong rupture between my theosophist kinsman and myself.

THE THREE HERMITS

AN OLD LEGEND CURRENT IN THE VOLGA DISTRICT

BY LEO NIKOLAEVICH TOLSTOY

"And in praying use not vain repetitions, as the Gentiles do: for they think that they shall be heard for their much speaking. Be not therefore like them: for your Father knoweth what things ye have need of, before ye ask Him."

Matthew vi:7,8.

A Bishop was sailing from Archangel to the Solovétsk Monastery, and on the same vessel were a number of pilgrims on their way to visit the shrines at that place. The voyage was a smooth one. The wind favorable and the weather fair. The pilgrims lay on deck, eating, or sat in groups talking to one another. The Bishop, too, came on deck, and as he was pacing up and down he noticed a group of men standing near the prow and listening to a fisherman, who was pointing to the sea and telling them something. The Bishop stopped, and looked in the direction in which the man was pointing. He could see nothing, however, but the sea glistening in the sunshine. He drew nearer to listen, but when the man saw him, he took off his cap and was silent. The rest of the people also took off their caps and bowed.

"Do not let me disturb you, friends," said the Bishop. "I came to hear what this good man was saying."

"The fisherman was telling us about the hermits," replied one, a tradesman, rather bolder than the rest.

"What hermits?" asked the Bishop, going to the side of the vessel

---

Reprinted from *Twenty-three Tales* by Leo Tolstoy, World's Classics Series. (Translated by Louise and Aylmer Maude.) Used by permission of Oxford University Press.

and seating himself on a box. "Tell me about them. I should like to hear. What were you pointing at?"

"Why, that little island you can just see over there," answered the man, pointing to a spot ahead and a little to the right. "That is the island where the hermits live for the salvation of their souls."

"Where is the island?" asked the Bishop. "I see nothing."

"There, in the distance, if you will please look along my hand. Do you see that little cloud? Below it, and a bit to the left, there is just a faint streak. That is the island."

The Bishop looked carefully, but his unaccustomed eyes could make out nothing but the water shimmering in the sun.

"I cannot see it," he said. "But who are the hermits that live there?"

"They are holy men," answered the fisherman. "I had long heard tell of them, but never chanced to see them myself till the year before last."

And the fisherman related how once, when he was out fishing, he had been stranded at night upon that island, not knowing where he was. In the morning, as he wandered about the island, he came across an earth hut, and met an old man standing near it. Presently two others came out, and after having fed him and dried his things, they helped him mend his boat.

"And what are they like?" asked the Bishop.

"One is a small man and his back is bent. He wears a priest's cassock and is very old; he must be more than a hundred, I should say. He is so old that the white of his beard is taking a greenish tinge, but he is always smiling, and his face is as bright as an angel's from heaven. The second is taller, but he also is very old. He wears a tattered peasant coat. His beard is broad, and of a yellowish grey color. He is a strong man. Before I had time to help him, he turned my boat over as if it were only a pail. He too is kindly and cheerful. The third is tall, and has a beard as white as snow and reaching to his knees. He is stern, with overhanging eyebrows; and he wears nothing but a piece of matting tied round his waist."

"And did they speak to you?" asked the Bishop.

"For the most part they did everything in silence, and spoke but little even to one another. One of them would just give a glance, and the others would understand him. I asked the tallest whether they had lived there long. He frowned, and muttered something as if he were angry; but the oldest one took his hand and smiled, and then the tall one was quiet. The oldest one only said: 'Have mercy upon us,' and smiled."

While the fisherman was talking, the ship had drawn nearer to the island.

"There, now you can see it plainly, if your Lordship will please to look," said the tradesman, pointing with his hand.

The Bishop looked, and now he really saw a dark streak—which was the island. Having looked at it a while, he left the prow of the vessel, and going to the stern, asked the helmsman:

"What island is that?"

"That one," replied the man, "has no name. There are many such in this sea."

"Is it true that there are hermits who live there for the salvation of their souls?"

"So it is said, your Lordship, but I don't know if it's true. Fishermen say they have seen them; but of course they may only be spinning yarns."

"I should like to land on the island and see these men," said the Bishop. "How could I manage it?"

"The ship cannot get close to the island," replied the helmsman, "but you might be rowed there in a boat. You had better speak to the captain."

The captain was sent for and came.

"I should like to see these hermits," said the Bishop. "Could I not be rowed ashore?"

The captain tried to dissuade him.

"Of course it could be done," said he, "but we should lose much time. And if I might venture to say so to your Lordship, the old men are not worth your pains. I have heard say that they are foolish old fellows, who understand nothing, and never speak a word, any more than the fish in the sea."

"I wish to see them," said the Bishop, "and I will pay you for your trouble and loss of time. Please let me have a boat."

There was no help for it; so the order was given. The sailors trimmed the sails, the steersman put up the helm, and the ship's course was set for the island. A chair was placed at the prow for the

Bishop, and he sat there, looking ahead. The passengers all collected at the prow, and gazed at the island. Those who had the sharpest eyes could presently make out the rocks on it, and then a mud hut was seen. At last one man saw the hermits themselves. The captain brought a telescope and, after looking through it, handed it to the Bishop.

"It's right enough. There are three men standing on the shore. There, a little to the right of that big rock."

The Bishop took the telescope, got it into position, and he saw the three men: a tall one, a shorter one, and one very small and bent, standing on the shore and holding each other by the hand.

The captain turned to the Bishop.

"The vessel can get no nearer in than this, your Lordship. If you wish to go ashore, we must ask you to go in the boat, while we anchor here."

The cable was quickly let out; the anchor cast, and the sails furled. There was a jerk, and the vessel shook. Then, a boat having been lowered, the oarsmen jumped in, and the Bishop descended the ladder and took his seat. The men pulled at their oars and the boat moved rapidly towards the island. When they came within a stone's throw, they saw three old men: a tall one with only a piece of matting tied round his waist: a shorter one in a tattered peasant coat, and a very old one bent with age and wearing an old cassock—all three standing hand in hand.

The oarsmen pulled in to the shore, and held on with the boat-hook while the Bishop got out.

The old men bowed to him, and he gave them his blessing, at which they bowed still lower. Then the Bishop began to speak to them.

"I have heard," he said, "that you, godly men, live here saving your own souls and praying to our Lord Christ for your fellow men. I, an unworthy servant of Christ, am called, by God's mercy, to keep and teach His flock. I wished to see you, servants of God, and to do what I can to teach you, also."

The old men looked at each other smiling, but remained silent.

"Tell me," said the Bishop, "what you are doing to save your souls, and how you serve God on this island."

The second hermit sighed, and looked at the oldest, the very ancient one. The latter smiled, and said:

"We do not know how to serve God. We only serve and support ourselves, servant of God."

"But how do you pray to God?" asked the Bishop.

"We pray in this way," replied the hermit. "Three are ye, three are we, have mercy upon us."

And when the old man said this, all three raised their eyes to heaven, and repeated:

"Three are ye, three are we, have mercy upon us!"

The Bishop smiled.

"You have evidently heard something about the Holy Trinity," said he. "But you do not pray aright. You have won my affection, godly men. I see you wish to please the Lord, but you do not know how to serve Him. That is not the way to pray; but listen to me, and I will teach you. I will teach you, not a way of my own, but the way in which God in the Holy Scriptures has commanded all men to pray to Him."

And the Bishop began explaining to the hermits how God had revealed Himself to men; telling them of God the Father, and God the Son, and God the Holy Ghost.

"God the Son came down on earth," said he, "to save men, and this is how He taught us all to pray. Listen, and repeat after me: 'Our Father.'"

And the first old man repeated after him, "Our Father," and the second said, "Our Father," and the third said, "Our Father."

"Which art in heaven," continued the Bishop.

The first hermit repeated, "Which art in heaven," but the second blundered over the words, and the tall hermit could not say them properly. His hair had grown over his mouth so that he could not speak plainly. The very old hermit, having no teeth, also mumbled indistinctly.

The Bishop repeated the words again, and the old men repeated them after him. The Bishop sat down on a stone, and the old men stood before him, watching his mouth, and repeating the words as he uttered them. And all day long the Bishop labored, saying a word twenty, thirty, a hundred times over, and the old men repeated it after him. They blundered, and he corrected them, and made them begin again.

The Bishop did not leave off till he had taught them the whole of the Lord's Prayer so that they could not only repeat it after him, but could say it by themselves. The middle one was the first to know it, and to repeat the whole of it alone. The Bishop made him say it again and again, and at last the others could say it too.

It was getting dark and the moon was appearing over the water, before the Bishop rose to return to the vessel. When he took leave of the old men they all bowed down to the ground before him. He raised them, and kissed each of them, telling them to pray as he had taught them. Then he got into the boat and returned to the ship.

And as he sat in the boat and was rowed to the ship he could hear the three voices of the hermits loudly repeating the Lord's Prayer. As the boat drew near the vessel their voices could no longer be heard, but they could still be seen in the moonlight, standing as he had left them on the shore, the shortest in the middle, the tallest on the right, the middle one on the left. As soon as the Bishop had reached the vessel and got on board, the anchor was weighed and the sails unfurled. The wind filled them and the ship sailed away, and the Bishop took a seat in the stern and watched the island they had left. For a time he could still see the hermits, but presently they disappeared from sight, though the island was still visible. At last it too vanished, and only the sea was to be seen, rippling in the moonlight.

The pilgrims lay down to sleep, and all was quiet on deck. The Bishop did not wish to sleep, but sat alone at the stern, gazing at the sea where the island was no longer visible, and thinking of the good old men. He thought how pleased they had been to learn the Lord's Prayer; and he thanked God for having sent him to teach and help such godly men.

So the Bishop sat, thinking, and gazing at the sea where the island had disappeared. And the moonlight flickered before his eyes, sparkling, now here, now there, upon the waves. Suddenly he saw something white and shining, on the bright path which the moon cast across the sea. Was it a seagull, or the little gleaming sail of some small boat? The Bishop fixed his eyes on it, wondering.

"It must be a boat sailing after us," thought he, "but it is overtaking us very rapidly. It was far, far away a minute ago, but now it is much nearer. It cannot be a boat, for I can see no sail; but whatever it may be, it is following us and catching us up."

And he could not make out what it was. Not a boat, nor a bird, nor a fish! It was too large for a man, and besides a man could not be out there in the midst of the sea. The Bishop rose, and said to the helmsman:

"Look there, what is that, my friend? What is it?" the Bishop repeated, though he could now see plainly what it was—the three hermits running upon the water, all gleaming white, their grey beards shining, and approaching the ship as quickly as though it were not moving.

The steersman looked, and let go the helm in terror.

"Oh, Lord! The hermits are running after us on the water as though it were dry land!"

The passengers, hearing him, jumped up and crowded to the stern. They saw the hermits coming along hand in hand, and the two outer ones beckoning the ship to stop. All three were gliding along upon the water without moving their feet. Before the ship could be stopped, the hermits had reached it, and raising their heads, all three as with one voice, began to say:

"We have forgotten your teaching, servant of God. As long as we kept repeating it we remembered, but when we stopped saying it for a time, a word dropped out, and now it has all gone to pieces. We can remember nothing of it. Teach us again."

The Bishop crossed himself, and leaning over the ship's side, said:

"Your own prayer will reach the Lord, men of God. It is not for me to teach you. Pray for us sinners."

And the Bishop bowed low before the old men; and they turned and went back across the sea. And a light shone until daybreak on the spot where they were lost to sight.

◇◇◇*Ivan Turgenev (1818-1883). One of the great Russian novelists. Much of his mature life was spent abroad and he became more westernized than most of his compatriots. See* Fathers and Sons, Virgin Soil, Smoke.

THE DISTRICT DOCTOR

BY IVAN TURGENEV

One day in autumn on my way back from a remote part of the country I caught cold and fell ill. Fortunately the fever attacked me in the district town at the inn; I sent for the doctor. In half-an-hour the district doctor appeared, a thin, dark-haired man of middle height. He prescribed me the usual sudorific, ordered a mustard plaster to be put on, very deftly slid a five-ruble note up his sleeve, coughing drily and looking away as he did so, and then was getting up to go home, but somehow fell into talk and remained. I was exhausted with feverishness; I foresaw a sleepless night, and was glad of a little chat with a pleasant companion. Tea was served. My doctor began to converse freely. He was a sensible fellow, and expressed himself with vigour and some humour. Queer things happen in the world: you may live a long while with some people, and be on friendly terms with them, and never once speak openly with them from your soul; with others you scarcely have time to get acquainted, and all at once you are pouring out to him or he to you—all your secrets, as though you were at confession. I don't know how I gained the confidence of my new friend—anyway, with nothing to lead up to it, he told me a rather curious incident; and here I will report his tale for the information of the indulgent reader. I will try to tell it in the doctor's own words.

"You don't happen to know," he began in a weak and quavering voice (the common result of the use of unmixed Berezov snuff); "you don't happen to know the judge here, Mylov, Pavel Lukich?

From *Best Russian Short Stories*, edited by Thomas Seltzer. (Translator unidentified.) By permission of Random House, Inc. Copyright 1925 by Modern Library, Inc.

. . . You don't know him? . . . Well, it's all the same." (He cleared his throat and rubbed his eyes.) "Well, you see, the thing happened, to tell you exactly without mistake, in Lent, at the very time of the thaws. I was sitting at his house—our judge's, you know —playing preference. Our judge is a good fellow, and fond of playing preference. Suddenly" (the doctor made frequent use of this word, suddenly) "they tell me, 'There's a servant asking for you.' I say 'What does he want?' They say 'He has brought a note—it must be from a patient.' 'Give me the note,' I say. So it is from a patient—well and good—you understand—it's our bread and butter. . . . But this is how it was: a lady, a widow, writes to me; she says, 'My daughter is dying. Come, for God's sake!' she says, 'and the horses have been sent for you!' . . . Well, that's all right. But she was twenty miles from town, and it was midnight out of doors, and the roads in such a state, my word! And as she was poor herself, one could not expect more than two silver rubles, and even that problematic; and perhaps it might only be a matter of a roll of linen and a sack of oatmeal in payment. However, duty, you know, before everything: a fellow-creature may be dying. I hand over my cards at once to Kalliopin, the member of the provincial commission, and return home. I look; a wretched little trap was standing at the steps, with peasant's horses, fat—too fat—and their coat as shaggy as felt; and the coachman sitting with his cap off out of respect. Well, I think to myself, 'It's clear, my friend, these patients aren't rolling in riches.' . . . You smile; but I tell you, a poor man like me has to take everything into consideration. . . . If the coachman sits like a prince, and doesn't touch his cap, and even sneers at you behind his beard, and flicks his whip—then you may bet on six rubles. But this case, I saw, had a very different air. However, I think there's no help for it; duty before everything. I snatch up the most necessary drugs, and set off. Will you believe it? I only just managed to get there at all. The road was infernal: streams, snow, watercourses, and the dyke had suddenly burst there—that was the worst of it! However, I arrived at last. It was a little thatched house. There was a light in the windows; that meant they expected me. I was met by an old lady, very venerable, in a cap. 'Save her!' she says; 'she is dying.' I say, 'Pray don't distress yourself— Where is the invalid?' 'Come this way.' I see a clean little room, a lamp in

the corner; on the bed a girl of twenty, unconscious. She was in a
burning heat, and breathing heavily—it was fever. There were two
other girls, her sisters, scared and in tears. 'Yesterday,' they tell me,
'she was perfectly well and had a good appetite; this morning she
complained of her head, and this evening, suddenly, you see, like
this.' I say again: 'Pray don't be uneasy.' It's a doctor's duty, you
know—and I went up to her and bled her, told them to put on a
mustard plaster, and prescribed a mixture. Meantime I looked at
her, you know—there, by God! I had never seen such a face!—she
was a beauty, in a word! I felt quite shaken by pity. Such lovely
features; such eyes! . . . But, thank God! she became easier; she
fell into a perspiration, seemed to come to her senses, looked round,
smiled, and passed her hand over her face. . . . Her sisters bent
over her. They ask, 'How are you?' 'All right,' she says, and turns
away. I looked at her; she had fallen asleep. 'Well,' I say, 'now the
patient should be left alone.' So we all went out on tiptoe; only a
maid remained, in case she was wanted. In the parlour there was a
samovar standing on the table, and a bottle of rum; in our profession
one can't get on without it. They gave me tea; asked me to stop the
night. . . . I consented: where could I go, indeed, at that time
of night? The old lady kept groaning. 'What is it?' I say, 'she will
live; don't worry yourself; you had better take a little rest yourself;
it is about two o'clock.' 'But will you send to wake me if anything
happens?' 'Yes, yes.' The old lady went away, and the girls too went
to their own room; they made up a bed for me in the parlour. Well,
I went to bed—but I could not get to sleep, for a wonder! for in
reality I was very tired. I could not get my patient out of my head.
At last I could not put up with it any longer; I got up suddenly;
I think to myself, 'I will go and see how the patient is getting on.'
Her bedroom was next to the parlour. Well, I got up, and gently
opened the door—how my heart beat! I looked in: the servant was
asleep, her mouth wide open, and even snoring, the wretch! but the
patient lay with her face towards me, and her arms flung wide apart,
poor girl! I went up to her . . . when suddenly she opened her
eyes and stared at me! 'Who is it? who is it?' I was in confusion.
'Don't be alarmed, madam,' I say; 'I am the doctor; I have come
to see how you feel.' 'You the doctor?' 'Yes, the doctor; your mother
sent for me from the town; we have bled you, madam; now pray

go to sleep, and in a day or two, please God! we will set you on your feet again.' 'Ah, yes, yes, doctor, don't let me die . . . please, please.' 'Why do you talk like that? God bless you!' She is in a fever again, I think to myself; I felt her pulse; yes, she was feverish. She looked at me, and then took me by the hand. 'I will tell you why I don't want to die; I will tell you. . . . Now we are alone; and only, please don't you . . . not to anyone . . . Listen . . . ! I bent down; she moved her lips quite to my ear; she touched my cheek with her hair—I confess my head went round—and began to whisper. . . . I could make out nothing of it. . . . Ah, she was delirious! . . . She whispered and whispered, but so quickly, and as if it were not in Russian; at last she finished, and shivering dropped her head on the pillow, and threatened me with her finger: 'Remember, doctor, to no one.' I calmed her somehow, gave her something to drink, waked the servant, and went away."

At this point the doctor again took snuff with exasperated energy, and for a moment seemed stupefied by its effects.

"However," he continued, "the next day, contrary to my expectations, the patient was no better. I thought and thought, and suddenly decided to remain there, even though my other patients were expecting me. . . . And you know one can't afford to disregard that; one's practice suffers if one does. But, in the first place, the patient was really in danger; and secondly, to tell the truth, I felt strongly drawn to her. Besides, I liked the whole family. Though they were really badly off, they were singularly, I may say, cultivated people. . . . Their father had been a learned man, an author; he died, of course, in poverty, but he had managed before he died to give his children an excellent education; he left a lot of books too. Either because I looked after the invalid very carefully, or for some other reason; anyway, I can venture to say all the household loved me as one of the family. . . . Meantime the roads were in a worse state than ever; all communications, so to say, were cut off completely; even medicine could with difficulty be got from the town. . . . The sick girl was not getting better. . . . Day after day, and day after day . . . but . . . here. . . ." (The doctor made a brief pause.) "I declare I don't know how to tell you." . . . (He again took snuff, coughed, and swallowed a little tea.) "I will tell you without beating about the bush. My patient . . . how should I say? . . . Well she had fallen in love with me . . . or, no, it was not that she was in love . . . however . . . really, how should one say?" (The doctor looked down and grew red.) "No," he went on quickly, "in love, indeed! A man should not over-estimate himself. She was an educated girl, clever and well-read, and I had even forgotten my Latin, one may say, completely. As to appearance" (the doctor looked himself over with a smile) "I am nothing to boast of there either. But God Almighty did not make me a fool; I don't take black for white; I know a thing or two; I could see very clearly, for instance, that Aleksandra Andreyevna—that was her name—did not feel love for me, but had a friendly, so to say, inclination—a respect or something for me. Though she herself perhaps mistook this sentiment, anyway this was her attitude; you may form your own judgment of it. But," added the doctor, who had brought out all these disconnected sentences without taking breath, and with obvious embarrassment, "I seem to be wandering rather —you won't understand anything like this. . . . There with your leave, I will relate it all in order."

He drank a glass of tea, and began in a calmer voice.

"Well, then. My patient kept getting worse and worse. You are not a doctor, my good sir; you cannot understand what passes in a poor fellow's heart, especially at first, when he begins to suspect that the disease is getting the upper hand of him. What becomes of his belief in himself? You suddenly grow so timid; it's indescribable. You fancy then that you have forgotten everything you knew, and that the patient has no faith in you, and that other people begin to notice how distracted you are, and tell you the symptoms with reluctance; that they are looking at you suspiciously, whispering. . . . Ah! it's horrid! There must be a remedy, you think, for this disease, if one could find it. Isn't this it? You try—no, that's not it! You don't allow the medicine the necessary time to do good. . . . You clutch at one thing, then at another. Sometimes you take up a book of medical prescriptions—here it is, you think! Sometimes, by Jove, you pick one out by chance, thinking to leave it to fate. . . . But meantime a fellow creature's dying, and another doctor would have saved him. 'We must have a consultation,' you say; 'I will not take the responsibility on myself.' And what a fool you look at such times! Well, in time you learn to bear it; it's nothing to you. A man has died—but it's not your fault; you treated him by the rules. But what's still more torture to you is to see blind faith in you, and to feel yourself that you are not able to be of use. Well, it was just this blind faith that the whole of Aleksandra Andreyevna's family had in me; they had forgotten to think that their daughter was in danger. I, too, on my side assure them that it is nothing, but meantime my heart sinks into my boots. To add to our troubles, the roads were in such a state that the coachman was gone for whole days together to get medicine. And I never left the patient's room; I could not tear myself away; I tell her amusing stories, you know, and play cards with her. I watch by her side at night. The old mother thanks me with tears in her eyes; but I think to myself, 'I don't deserve your gratitude.' I frankly confess to you—there is no object in concealing it now—I was in love with my patient. And Aleksandra Andreyevna had grown fond of me; she would not sometimes let any one be in her room but me. She began to talk to me, to ask me questions; where I had studied, how I lived, who are my people, whom I go to see. I feel that she ought not to talk; but to forbid her to—to forbid her resolutely, you know—I could not. Sometimes I held my head in my hands, and asked myself, 'What are you doing, villain?' . . . And she would take my hand and hold it, give me a long, long look, and turn away, sigh, and say, 'How good you are!' Her hands were so feverish, her eyes so large and languid. . . . 'Yes,' she says, 'you are a good, kind man; you are not like our neighbours. . . . No, you are not like that. . . . Why did I not know you till now!' 'Aleksandra Andreyevna, calm yourself,' I say. . . . 'I feel, believe me, I don't know how I have gained . . . but there, calm yourself. . . . All will be right; you will be well again.' And meanwhile I must tell you," continued the doctor, bending forward and raising his eyebrows, "that they associated very little with the neighbours, because the smaller people were not on their level, and pride hindered them from being friendly with the rich. I tell you, they were an exceptionally cultivated family, so you know it was gratifying for me. She would only take her medicine from my hands . . . she would lift herself up, poor girl, with my aid, take it, and gaze at me. . . . My heart felt as if it were bursting. And meanwhile she was growing worse and worse, worse and worse, all the time; she will die, I think to myself; she must die.

Believe me, I would sooner have gone to the grave myself; and here were her mother and sisters watching me, looking into my eyes . . . and their faith in me was wearing away. 'Well, how is she?' 'Oh, all right, all right!' All right, indeed! My mind was failing me. Well, I was sitting one night alone again by my patient. The maid was sitting there too, and snoring away in full swing; I can't find fault with the poor girl, though! she was worn out too. Aleksandra Andreyevna had felt very unwell all the evening; she was very feverish. Until midnight she kept tossing about; at last she seemed to fall asleep; at least, she lay still without stirring. The lamp was burning in the corner before the holy image. I sat here, you know, with my head bent; I even dozed a little. Suddenly it seemed as though someone touched me in the side; I turned round. . . . Good God! Aleksandra Andreyevna was gazing with intent eyes at me . . . her lips parted, her cheeks seemed burning. 'What is it?' 'Doctor, shall I die?' 'Merciful Heavens!' 'No, doctor, no; please don't tell me I shall live . . . don't say so. . . . If you knew. . . . Listen! For God's sake don't conceal my real position,' and her breath came so fast. 'If I can know for certain that I must die . . . then I will tell you all—all!' 'Aleksandra Andreyevna, I beg!' 'Listen; I have not been asleep at all . . . I have been looking at you a long while. . . . For God's sake! . . . I believe in you; you are a good man, an honest man; I entreat you by all that is sacred in the world—tell me the truth! If you knew how important it is for me. . . . Doctor, for God's sake tell me. . . . Am I in danger?' 'What can I tell you, Aleksandra Andreyevna pray?' 'For God's sake, I beseech you!' 'I can't conceal from you,' I say, 'Aleksandra Andreyevna; you are certainly in danger; but God is merciful.' 'I shall die, I shall die.' And it seemed as though she were pleased; her face grew so bright; I was alarmed. 'Don't be afraid, don't be afraid! I am not frightened by death at all.' She suddenly sat up and leaned on her elbow. 'Now . . . yes, now I can tell you that I thank you with my whole heart . . . that you are kind and good—that I love you!' I stared at her, like one possessed; it was terrible for me, you know. 'Do you hear, I love you!' 'Aleksandra Andreyevna, how have I deserved—' 'No, no, you don't—you don't understand me.' . . . And suddenly she stretched out her arms, and taking my head in her hands, she kissed it. . . . Believe me, I almost screamed aloud. . . . I threw myself on my knees, and buried my head in the pillow. She did not speak; her fingers trembled in my hair; I listen; she is weeping. I began to soothe her, to assure her. . . . I really don't know what I did say to her. 'You will wake up the girl,' I say to her; 'Aleksandra Andreyevna, I thank you . . . believe me . . . calm yourself.' 'Enough, enough!' she persisted, 'never mind all of them; let them wake, then; let them come in—it does not matter; I am dying, you see. . . . And what do you fear? Why are you afraid? Lift up your head. . . . Or, perhaps you don't love me; perhaps I am wrong. . . . In that case, forgive me.' 'Aleksandra Andreyevna, what are you saying! . . . I love you, Aleksandra Andreyevna.' She looked straight into my eyes, and opened her arms wide. 'Then take me in your arms.' I tell you frankly, I don't know how it was I did not go mad that night. I feel that my patient is killing herself; I see that she is not fully herself; I understand, too, that if she did not consider herself on the point of death she would never have thought of me; and, indeed, say what you will, it's hard to die at twenty without having known love; this was what was torturing her; this was why, in despair, she caught at me—do you understand now? But she held me in her arms, and would not let me go. 'Have pity on me, Aleksandra Andreyevna, and have pity on yourself,' I say. 'Why,' she says, 'what is there to think of? You know I must die.' . . . This she repeated incessantly. . . . 'If I knew that I should return to life, and be a proper young lady again, I should be ashamed . . . of course, ashamed . . . but why now?' 'But who has said you will die?' 'Oh, no, leave off! you will not deceive me; you don't know how to lie—look at your face.' . . . 'You shall live, Aleksandra Andreyevna; I will cure you; we will ask your mother's blessing . . . we will be united—we will be happy.' 'No, no, I have your word; I must die . . . you have promised me . . . you have told me.' . . . It was cruel for me—cruel for many reasons. And see what trifling things can do sometimes; it seems nothing at all, but it's painful. It occurred to her to ask me, what is my name; not my surname, but my first name. I must needs be so unlucky as to be called Trifon. Yes, indeed; Trifon Ivanich. Every one in the house called me doctor. However, there's no help for it. I say, 'Trifon, madam.' She frowned, shook her head, and muttered something in French—ah, something unpleasant, of course!—and then she laughed—disagreeably too. Well, I spent the whole night with her in this way. Before morning I went away, feeling as though I were mad. When I went again into her room it was daytime, after morning tea. Good God! I could scarcely recognise her; people are laid in their grave looking better than that. I swear to you, on my honour, I don't understand—I absolutely don't understand—now, how I lived through that experience. Three days and nights my patient still lingered on. And what nights! What things she said to me! And on the last night—only imagine to yourself—I was sitting near her, and kept praying to God for one thing only: 'Take her,' I said, 'quickly, and me with her.' Suddenly the old mother comes unexpectedly into the room. I had already the evening before told her—the mother—there was little hope, and it would be well to send for a priest. When the sick girl saw her mother she said: 'It's very well you have come; look at us, we love one another—we have given each other our word.' 'What does she say, doctor? what does she say?' I turned livid. 'She is wandering,' I say; 'the fever.' But she: 'Hush, hush; you told me something quite different just now, and have taken my ring. Why do you pretend? My mother is good—she will forgive—she will understand— and I am dying. . . . I have no need to tell lies; give me your hand.' I jumped up and ran out of the room. The old lady, of course, guessed how it was.

"I will not, however, weary you any longer, and to me, too, of course, it's painful to recall all this. My patient passed away the next day. God rest her soul!" the doctor added, speaking quickly and with a sigh. "Before her death she asked her family to go out and leave me alone with her."

" 'Forgive me,' she said; 'I am perhaps to blame towards you . . . my illness . . . but believe me, I have loved no one more than you . . . do not forget me . . . keep my ring.' "

The doctor turned away; I took his hand.

"Ah!" he said, "let us talk of something else, or would you care to play preference for a small stake? It is not for people like me to give way to exalted emotions. There's only one thing for me to think of; how to keep the children from crying and the wife from scolding. Since then, you know, I have had time to enter into lawful wedlock, as they say. . . . Oh . . . I took a merchant's daughter—seven thousand for her dowry. Her name's Akulina; it goes well with Trifon. She is an ill-tempered woman, I must tell you, but luckily she's asleep all day. . . . Well, shall it be preference?"

We sat down to preference for halfpenny points. Trifon Ivanich won two rubles and a half from me, and went home late, well pleased with his success.

◇◇◇*Mark Twain (1835-1910). The American humorist. His real name was Samuel Langhorne Clemens.*

A DOG'S TALE

BY MARK TWAIN

I

My father was a St. Bernard, my mother was a collie, but I am a Presbyterian. This is what my mother told me; I do not know these nice distinctions myself. To me they are only fine large words meaning nothing. My mother had a fondness for such; she liked to say them, and see other dogs look surprised and envious, as wondering how she got so much education. But, indeed, it was not real education; it was only show: she got the words by listening in the dining-room and drawing-room when there was company, and by going with the children to Sunday-school and listening there; and whenever she heard a large word she said it over to herself many times, and so was able to keep it until there was a dogmatic gathering in the neighborhood, then she would get it off, and surprise and distress them all, from pocket-pup to mastiff, which rewarded her for all her trouble. If there was a stranger he was nearly sure to be suspicious, and when he got his breath again he would ask her what it meant. And she always told him. He was never expecting this, but thought he would catch her; so when she told him, he was the one that looked ashamed, whereas he had thought it was going to be she. The others were always waiting for this, and glad of it and proud of her, for they knew what was going to happen, because they had had experience. When she told the meaning of a big word they were all so taken up with admiration that it never occurred to any dog to doubt if it was the right one; and that was natural, because, for one thing, she answered up so promptly that it seemed like a dictionary speaking, and for another thing, where could they find out whether it was right or not? for she was the only cultivated dog there was. By-and-by, when I was older, she brought home the word Unintellectual, one time, and worked it pretty hard all the week at different gatherings, making much unhappiness and despondency; and it was at this time that I noticed that during that week she was asked for the meaning at eight different assemblages, and flashed out a fresh definition every time, which showed me that she had more presence of mind than culture, though I said nothing, of course. She had one word which she always kept on hand, and ready, like a life-preserver, a kind of emergency word to strap on when she was likely to get washed overboard in a sudden way—that was the word Synonymous. When she happened to fetch out a long word which had had its day weeks before and its prepared meanings gone to her dump-pile, if there was a stranger there of course it knocked him groggy for a couple of minutes, then he would come to, and by that time she would be away down the wind on another tack, and not expecting anything; so when he'd hail and ask her to cash in, I (the only dog on the inside of her game) could see her canvas flicker a moment,—but only just a moment,—then it would belly out taut and full, and she would say, as calm as a summer's day, "It's synonymous with supererogation," or some godless long reptile of a word like that, and go placidly about and skim away on the next tack, perfectly comfortable, you know, and leave that stranger looking profane and embarrassed, and the initiated slatting the floor with their tails in unison and their faces transfigured with a holy joy.

And it was the same with phrases. She would drag home a whole phrase, if it had a grand sound, and play it six nights and two matinées, and explain it a new way every time,—which she had to, for all she cared for was the phrase; she wasn't interested in what it meant, and knew those dogs hadn't wit enough to catch her, anyway. Yes, she was a daisy! She got so she wasn't afraid of anything, she had such confidence in the ignorance of those creatures. She even brought anecdotes that she had heard the family and the dinner guests laugh and shout over; as a rule she got the nub of one chestnut hitched onto another chestnut, where, of course, it didn't fit and hadn't any point; and when she delivered the nub she fell over and rolled on the floor and laughed and barked in the most insane way, while I could see that she was wondering to herself why it didn't seem as funny as it did when she first heard it. But no harm was done; the others rolled and barked too, privately ashamed of themselves for not seeing the point, and never suspecting that the fault was not with them and there wasn't any to see.

You can see by these things that she was of a rather vain and frivolous character; still, she had virtues, and enough to make up, I think. She had a kind heart and gentle ways, and never harbored resentments for injuries done her, but put them easily out of her mind and forgot them; and she taught her children her kindly way, and from her we learned also to be brave and prompt in time of danger, and not run away, but face the peril that threatened friend or stranger, and help him the best we could without stopping to think what the cost might be to us. And she taught us, not by words only, but by example, and that is the best way and the surest and the most lasting. Why, the brave things she did, the splendid things! she was just a soldier; and so modest about it—well, you couldn't help admiring her, and you couldn't help imitating her; not even a King Charles spaniel could remain entirely despicable in her society. So, as you see, there was more to her than her education.

II

When I was well grown, at last, I was sold and taken away, and I never saw her again. She was broken-hearted, and so was I, and we cried; but she comforted me as well as she could, and said we were sent into this world for a wise and good purpose, and must do our duties without repining, take our life as we might find it, live it for the best good of others, and never mind about the results; they were not our affair. She said men who did like this would have a noble and beautiful reward by-and-by in another world, and although we animals would not go there, to do well and right without reward would give to our brief lives a worthiness and dignity which in itself would be a reward. She had gathered these things from time to time when she had gone to the Sunday-school with the children, and had laid them up in her memory more carefully than she had done with those other words and phrases; and she had studied them deeply, for her good and ours. One may see by this that she had a wise and thoughtful head, for all there was so much lightness and vanity in it.

So we said our farewells, and looked our last upon each other through our tears; and the last thing she said—keeping it for the last to make me remember it the better, I think—was, "In memory of me, when there is a time of danger to another do not think of yourself, think of your mother, and do as she would do."

Do you think I could forget that? No.

III

It was such a charming home!—my new one; a fine great house, with pictures, and delicate decorations, and rich furniture, and no gloom anywhere, but all the wilderness of dainty colors lit up with flooding sunshine; and the spacious grounds around it, and the great garden—oh, greensward, and noble trees, and flowers, no end! And I was the same as a member of the family; and they loved me, and petted me, and did not give me a new name, but called me by my old one that was dear to me because my mother had given it me—Aileen Mavourneen. She got it out of a song; and the Grays knew that song, and said it was a beautiful name.

Mrs. Gray was thirty, and so sweet and so lovely, you cannot imagine it; and Sadie was ten, and just like her mother, just a darling slender little copy of her, with auburn tails down her back, and short frocks; and the baby was a year old, and plump and dimpled, and fond of me, and never could get enough of hauling on my tail, and hugging me and laughing out its innocent happiness; and Mr. Gray was thirty-eight, and tall and slender and handsome, a little bald in front, alert, quick in his movements, businesslike, prompt, decided, unsentimental, and with that kind of trim-chiselled face that just seems to glint and sparkle with frosty intellectuality! He was a renowned scientist. I do not know what the word means, but my mother would know how to use it and get effects. She would know how to depress a rat-terrier with it and make a lap-dog look sorry he came. But that is not the best one; the best one was Laboratory. My mother could organize a Trust on that one that would skin the tax-collars off the whole herd. The laboratory was not a book, or a picture, or a place to wash your hands in, as the college president's dog said—no, that is the lavatory; the laboratory is quite different, and is filled with jars, and bottles, and electrics, and wires, and strange machines; and every week other scientists came there and sat in the place, and used the machines, and discussed, and made what they called experiments and discoveries; and often I came, too, and stood around and listened, and tried to learn, for the sake of my mother, and in loving memory of her, although it was a pain to me, as realizing what she was losing out of her life and I gaining nothing at all; for try as I might, I was never able to make anything out of it at all.

Other times I lay on the floor in the mistress's workroom and slept, she gently using me for a footstool, knowing it pleased me, for it was a caress; other times I spent an hour in the nursery, and got well tousled and made happy; other times I watched by the crib there, when the baby was asleep and the nurse out for a few minutes on the baby's affairs; other times I romped and raced through the grounds and the garden with Sadie until we were tired out, then slumbered on the grass in the shade of a tree while she read her book; other times I went visiting among the neighbor dogs,—for there were some most pleasant ones not far away, and one very handsome and courteous and graceful one, a curly haired Irish setter by the name of Robin Adair, who was a Presbyterian like me, and belonged to the Scotch minister.

The servants in our house were all kind to me and were fond of me, and so, as you see, mine was a pleasant life. There could not be a happier dog than I was, nor a gratefuller one. I will say this for myself, for it is only the truth: I tried in all ways to do well and right, and honor my mother's memory and her teachings, and earn the happiness that had come to me, as best I could.

By-and-by came my little puppy, and then my cup was full, my happiness was perfect. It was the dearest little waddling thing, and so smooth and soft and velvety, and had such cunning little awkward paws, and such affectionate eyes, and such a sweet and innocent face; and it made me so proud to see how the children and their mother adored it, and fondled it, and exclaimed over every little wonderful thing it did. It did seem to me that life was just too lovely to—

Then came the winter. One day I was standing a watch in the

nursery. That is to say, I was asleep on the bed. The baby was asleep in the crib, which was alongside the bed, on the side next the fireplace. It was the kind of crib that has a lofty tent over it made of a gauzy stuff that you can see through. The nurse was out, and we two sleepers were alone. A spark from the wood-fire was shot out, and it lit on the slope of the tent. I suppose a quiet interval followed, then a scream from the baby woke me, and there was that tent flaming up toward the ceiling! Before I could think, I sprang to the floor in my fright, and in a second was half-way to the door; but in the next half-second my mother's farewell was sounding in my ears, and I was back on the bed again. I reached my head through the flames and dragged the baby out by the waist-band, and tugged it along, and we fell to the floor together in a cloud of smoke; I snatched a new hold and dragged the screaming little creature along and out at the door and around the bend of the hall, and was still tugging away, all excited and happy and proud, when the master's voice shouted:

"Begone, you cursed beast!" and I jumped to save myself; but he was wonderfully quick, and chased me up, striking furiously at me with his cane, I dodging this way and that, in terror, and at last a strong blow fell upon my left fore-leg, which made me shriek and fall, for the moment, helpless; the cane went up for another blow, but never descended, for the nurse's voice rang wildly out, "The nursery's on fire!" and the master rushed away in that direction, and my other bones were saved.

The pain was cruel, but, no matter, I must not lose any time; he might come back at any moment; so I limped on three legs to the other end of the hall, where there was a dark little stairway leading up into a garret where old boxes and such things were kept, as I had heard say, and where people seldom went. I managed to climb up there, then I searched my way through the dark among the piles of things, and hid in the secretest place I could find. It was foolish to be afraid there, yet still I was; so afraid that I held in and hardly even whimpered, though it would have been such a comfort to whimper, because that eases the pain, you know. But I could lick my leg, and that did me some good.

For half an hour there was a commotion down-stairs, and shout-ings, and rushing footsteps, and then there was quiet again. Quiet for some minutes, and that was grateful to my spirit, for then my fears began to go down; and fears are worse than pains,—oh, much worse. Then came a sound that froze me! They were calling me— calling me by name—hunting for me!

It was muffled by distance, but that could not take the terror out of it, and it was the most dreadful sound to me that I had ever heard. It went all about, everywhere, down there: along the halls, through all the rooms, in both stories, and in the basement and the cellar; then outside, and further and further away—then back, and all about the house again, and I thought it would never, never stop. But at last it did, hours and hours after the vague twilight of the garret had long ago been blotted out by black darkness.

Then in that blessed stillness my terror fell little by little away, and I was at peace and slept. It was a good rest I had, but I woke before the twilight had come again. I was feeling fairly comfortable, and I could think out a plan now. I made a very good one; which was, to creep down, all the way down the back stairs, and hide behind the cellar door, and slip out and escape when the iceman came at dawn, while he was inside filling the refrigerator; then I would hide all day, and start on my journey when night came; my journey to—well, anywhere where they would not know me and betray me to the master. I was feeling almost cheerful now; then suddenly I thought, Why, what would life be without my puppy!

That was despair. There was no plan for me; I saw that; I must stay where I was; stay, and wait, and take what might come—it was not my affair; that was what life is—my mother had said it. Then—well, then the calling began again! All my sorrows came back. I said to myself, the master will never forgive. I did not know what I had done to make him so bitter and so unforgiving, yet I judged it was something a dog could not understand, but which was clear to a man and dreadful.

They called and called—days and nights, it seemed to me. So long that the hunger and thirst near drove me mad, and I recognized that I was getting very weak. When you are this way you sleep a great deal, and I did. Once I woke in an awful fright—it seemed to me that the calling was right there in the garret! And so it was: it was Sadie's voice, and she was crying; my name was falling from her lips all broken, poor thing, and I could not believe my ears for the joy of it when I heard her say,

"Come back to us—oh, come back to us, and forgive—it is all so sad without our—"

I broke in with *such* a grateful little yelp, and the next moment Sadie was plunging and stumbling through the darkness and the lumber and shouting for the family to hear, "She's found! she's found!"

The days that followed—well, they were wonderful. The mother and Sadie and the servants—why, they just seemed to worship me. They couldn't seem to make me a bed that was fine enough; and as for food, they couldn't be satisfied with anything but game and delicacies that were out of season; and every day the friends and neighbors flocked in to hear about my heroism—that was the name they called it by, and it means agriculture. I remember my mother pulling it on a kennel once, and explaining it that way, but didn't say what agriculture was, except that it was synonymous with intramural incandescence; and a dozen times a day Mrs. Gray and Sadie would tell the tale to new-comers, and say I risked my life to save the baby's, and both of us had burns to prove it, and then the company would pass me around and pet me and exclaim about me, and you could see the pride in the eyes of Sadie and her mother; and when the people wanted to know what made me limp, they looked ashamed and changed the subject, and sometimes when people hunted them this way and that way with questions about it, it looked to me as if they were going to cry.

And this was not all the glory; no, the master's friends came, a whole twenty of the most distinguished people, and had me in the laboratory, and discussed me as if I was a kind of discovery; and some of them said it was wonderful in a dumb beast, the finest exhibition of instinct they could call to mind; but the master said, with vehemence, "It's far above instinct; it's *reason*, and many a man, privileged to be saved and go with you and me to a better world by right of its possession, has less of it than this poor silly quadruped that's foreordained to perish"; and then he laughed, and said, "Why, look at me—I'm a sarcasm! Bless you, with all my grand intelligence, the only thing I inferred was that the dog had gone mad and was destroying the child, whereas but for the beast's intelligence—it's *reason*, I tell you!—the child would have perished!"

They disputed and disputed, and I was the very centre and subject of it all, and I wished my mother could know that this grand honor had come to me; it would have made her proud.

Then they discussed optics, as they called it, and whether a certain injury to the brain would produce blindness or not, but they could not agree about it, and they said they must test it by experiment by-and-by; and next they discussed plants, and that interested me, because in the summer Sadie and I had planted seeds—I helped her dig the holes, you know,—and after days and days a little shrub or a flower came up there, and it was a wonder how that could happen; but it did, and I wished I could talk,—then I would have told those people about it and shown them how much I knew, and been all alive with the subject; but I didn't care for the optics; it was dull, and when they came back to it again it bored me, and I went to sleep.

Pretty soon it was spring, and sunny and pleasant and lovely, and the sweet mother and the children patted me and the puppy good-bye, and went away on a journey and a visit to their kin, and the master wasn't any company for us, but we played together and had good times, and the servants were kind and friendly, so we got along quite happily and counted the days and waited for the family.

And one day those men came again, and said now for the test, and they took the puppy to the laboratory, and I limped three-leggedly along too, feeling proud, for any attention shown the puppy was a pleasure to me, of course. They discussed and experimented, and then suddenly the puppy shrieked, and they set him on the floor, and he went staggering around, with his head all bloody, and the master clapped his hands, and shouted:

"There, I've won—confess it! He's as blind as a bat!"

And they all said,

"It's so—you've proved your theory, and suffering humanity owes you a great debt from henceforth," and they crowded around him, and wrung his hand cordially and thankfully, and praised him. But I hardly saw or heard these things, for I ran at once to my little darling, and snuggled close to it where it lay and licked the blood, and it put its head against mine, whimpering softly, and I knew in my heart it was a comfort to it in its pain and trouble to feel its mother's touch, though it could not see me. Then it drooped down, presently, and its little velvet nose rested upon the floor, and it was still, and did not move any more.

Soon the master stopped discussing a moment, and rang in the footman, and said, "Bury it in the far corner of the garden," and then went on with the discussion, and I trotted after the footman, very happy and grateful, for I knew the puppy was out of its pain now, because it was asleep. We went far down the garden to the furthest end, where the children and the nurse and the puppy and I used to play in the summer in the shade of a great elm, and there the footman dug a hole, and I saw he was going to plant the puppy, and I was glad, because it would grow and come up a fine handsome dog, like Robin Adair, and be a beautiful surprise for the family when they came home; so I tried to help him dig, but my lame leg was no good, being stiff, you know, and you have to have two, or it is no use. When the footman had finished and covered little Robin up, he patted my head, and there were tears in his eyes, and he said, "Poor little doggie, you SAVED *his* child."

I have watched two whole weeks, and he doesn't come up! This last week a fright has been stealing upon me. I think there is something terrible about this. I do not know what it is, but the fear makes me sick, and I cannot eat, though the servants bring me the best of food; and they pet me so, and even come in the night, and cry, and say, "Poor doggie—do give it up and come home; *don't* break our hearts!" and all this terrifies me the more, and makes me sure something has happened. And I am so weak; since yesterday I cannot stand on my feet any more. And within this hour the servants, looking toward the sun where it was sinking out of sight and the night chill coming on, said things I could not understand, but they carried something cold to my heart.

"These poor creatures! They do not suspect. They will come home in the morning, and eagerly ask for the little doggie that did the brave deed, and who of us will be strong enough to say the truth to them: 'The humble little friend is gone where go the beasts that perish.'"

◇◇◇*Miguel de Unamuno (1864-1936). Spanish novelist, poet, essayist,
philosopher. Born in Bilbao, studied in Madrid. In 1892 became professor of Greek language and literature at Salamanca University. In
1900 he was made rector of the university. A fearless spokesman
against oppression. In 1924 he was exiled by the dictatorship of Primo
de Rivera to one of the Canary Islands. During the Spanish Republic,
he returned to his rectorship. See* The Tragic Sense of Life; Essays
and Soliloquies; The Life of Don Quixote and Sancho; Mist; Three
Exemplary Novels and a Prologue.

SOLITUDE

BY MIGUEL DE UNAMUNO

Solitude was born of the death of her mother. Leopardi sang that
birth is a hazard with death:

> *"nasce l'uomo a fatica*
> *ed e rischio di morte el nascimento"*—

hazard with death for the new-born, hazard with death for her who
gives birth.

Poor Sanctuary, Solitude's mother, had led for five years of marriage a life of shadowed and silent tragedy. Her husband was a man
impenetrable and apparently without feeling. The poor woman did
not know how she had ever come to marry him; she found herself
bound in matrimony with this man like somebody awakening from a
dream. All her maiden life was lost in a misty distance, and when
she thought of it she remembered herself, as she had been before
her marriage, as though she were remembering somebody else.

Whether her husband loved her or hated her she could not tell.
His home was to him merely a place for eating and sleeping, for all
the animal side of life. He worked outside of it, he talked outside of
it, he amused himself outside of it. He never raised his voice or said
a harsh word to his wife. He never contradicted her. When poor

---

(Translated by Warre B. Wells.)

Sanctuary asked him a question or sought his opinion about anything, she invariably got the same reply from him: "All right. Don't bother me. As you like."

That persistent "As you like" went to poor Sanctuary's sick heart like a sharp knife. "As you like!" the poor woman thought to herself; "that means that I'm not even worth contradicting." And then his "Don't bother me!"—that terrible "Don't bother me!" which embitters so many homes. In Sanctuary's home—in what should have been Sanctuary's home—that terrible refusal not to be bothered enshadowed everything at the hearth.

The first year that she was married Sanctuary had a son; but in the dreary desolation of her drab home she longed for a daughter. "A son," she thought, "a man! Men always have something to do outside their homes." So, when she became pregnant, she dreamed of nothing but a daughter; and her daughter must be called Solitude. The poor woman was taken gravely ill in her pangs. Her heart fluttered feebly. She realised that she would live only long enough to give birth to her daughter—to introduce her into that shadowed home. She called for her husband.

"Oh, Pedro," she said, "if it's a daughter, as I hope, you'll call her Solitude, won't you?"

"All right, all right," he replied; "time enough to think about that"; and he reflected that this day, this day of birth, he was going to miss his game of dominoes.

"But I'm going to die, Pedro; I haven't the strength to get over it."

"Nonsense!" he replied.

"It may be," Sanctuary insisted; "but if it is a daughter, you will call her Solitude, won't you?"

"All right. Don't bother me. As you like," he closed the conversation.

And she ceased to bother him forever. After she had given birth to her daughter she had only time to realize that it was a daughter; and her last words were: "Solitude, remember, Pedro—Solitude!"

The man was shocked, and would have been humbled if there had been anything of him to humble. A widower at his age, and with two small children! Who was going to look after his house now? Who was going to bring up his children—until his daughter was old enough to be able to take over the management of it? . . . Marry again? No, that he would not do. He knew now what marriage meant. If he had only known before! That was no solution. Very decidedly he would not marry again.

What he did was to send Solitude to a village to be reared away from home. He did not want the bother of an infant and the insolence of nurses. It was bad enough with the other child, little Peter, now three years old.

Solitude hardly remembered those first years of her infancy at all. Her earliest dim recollection was of that dreary, drab home, and of that hermetically sealed father of hers, that man who ate at the same table with her and whom she saw for a moment when she went to bed; and of his perfunctory, formal kisses.

Her only companionship was that of little Peter, her brother. But Peter played with her in the strictest sense of the word—that is to say, he did not play in company with her; he played with her as one plays with a toy. She, Solitude, Solita, was his plaything; and he, like the man he was going to be, was a brute. Since his fists were stronger than hers, he always had the right of it.

"You women are no good for anything. It is we men who give orders," he told her one day.

Solitude was by nature acutely receptive; she had a genius for sensitiveness. Women very often have this receptive genius; but, since it produces nothing, it languishes away without anybody noticing it. At first, crying and cut to the quick, Solitude used to go to that Sphinx of a father of hers, expecting justice; but that unswerving man received her with his cold: "All right, all right! Don't bother me! Give me a kiss, and see this doesn't happen again!"

That, he thought, settled everything, and saved him from further annoyance. The end of it was that Solitude ceased to complain to her father about her brother's brutality and bore everything in silence, leaving him in peace and sparing herself the humiliation of those perfunctory kisses.

The dreary drabness of her home grew more and more unbearable, and the shadows that it cast grew deeper. Her only relief from it was at school, where her father had made her a day-boarder, among other things in order to get her more off his hands. At school she learnt that all her companions had, or once had, mothers. One evening, at supper, she dared to bother her father with a question.

"Tell me, Father, didn't I have a mother?"

"Well, what a question!" her father replied; "of course, every-body has a mother. Why do you ask?"

"Then where is my mother, Papa?"

"She died when you were born."

"Oh, how sad!"

And then, just for once, her father abandoned his boorish taci-turnity, and told her that her mother had been called Sanctuary, and sketched for her an outline of that dead woman.

"How pretty she must have been!" said the child.

"Yes," her father agreed; "yes, but not as pretty as you are." This remark that he let slip went to the bottom of one of his little idiosyn-crasies. If his daughter was prettier than her mother, the fact, in his opinion, was due to himself.

"And what about you, Pedrín," Solitude, excited by this fugitive stirring of the embers of the family hearth, asked her brother; "do you remember her?"

"Now how could I remember her, when she died when I was only three years old?"

"Well, if I were in your place I should remember her," the girl replied.

"Oh, of course, you women are so clever!" cut in her would-be grown-up brother.

"No, we're not; but I think we have longer memories."

"All right, all right! Stop talking nonsense and don't bother me!"

And so ended that memorable night when Solitude learnt that she once had a mother.

It gave her so much to think about that she could almost remem-ber for herself. She peopled her solitude with maternal dreams.

The years went on, all just the same, all drab and ashen beside that hearth where the fire had gone out. Her father seemed to grow no older, to possess no capacity for growing older. He did the same things at the same times every day, with the regularity of a machine. But her brother began to get himself talked about until he became a byword in the town, and until finally he disappeared—whither, Solitude did not know. Father and daughter were left alone: alone, but separated; they merely ate and slept under the same roof.

At last it seemed that day had dawned in the sky of Solitude. A gallant youth, who for some time had been making eyes at her every time he saw her in the street, scraped an acquaintance with her and presented himself to her as a suitor on approval. Poor Solitude saw Life beginning to open its doors to her; and, despite some presentiments, which she tried in vain to scare away, she accepted him on this basis. It was like a spring-tide.

Solitude began to live—or, rather, she was really born for the first time. The meaning of many things which until now had had no meaning for her was revealed to her. She began to understand much that she had heard from her mistresses and companions at school, much that she had read. Everything seemed to sing inside her. But at the same time she realised all the emptiness of her home, and, if it had not been for that picture of her betrothed that was ever present to her, she would have turned into stone there to match that man of granite, her father.

For poor Solitude this betrothal was a regular dazzling of her eyes. But her father seemed to pay no attention to it, or at least to refuse to pay any attention to it. He never made the slightest allusion to it. If he met his daughter's betrothed hanging about the railings when he left home during those blissful hours when they arranged to meet, he pretended not to see him.

More than once poor Solitude intended to say something about it to her father when they were at the supper-table together; but the words stuck in her throat before she could utter them. So she said nothing, and kept on saying nothing.

Solitude began to read books which her betrothed gave her. Thanks to him, she began to know something of the world. This young man did not seem to be like other men. He was caressing, gay, unreserved, ironical and sometimes he even contradicted her. But about her father he never said a word.

It was her initiation into life—something to dream about at home. Solitude began, indeed, to glimpse what a real home might mean: homes such as those that her school-mates had. And this knowledge, or rather this sensing, increased her horror of the back-water in which she lived.

Then suddenly one day, when she least expected it, there came the crash. Her betrothed, who had been away for a month, wrote her a long letter, full of endearments, adorned with all kinds of trimmings and twistings, in which, amid all his protestations of affection, he made it clear that their relations must be regarded as at an end. He wound up with this terrible sentence: "Perhaps, some day, you will meet somebody who can make you happier than I could."

Solitude felt an awful shudder go through her very soul. She experienced once more all the brutality, all the indescribable brutality, of mankind—of men, of the male species. But she showed no sign, swallowing her humiliation and her pain in silence and with dry eyes. She would show no weakness in the presence of that Sphinx of a father of hers.

Why—why had her betrothed abandoned her? Had he got tired of her? Again, why? Could a man get tired of being in love? Was it possible that he should get tired? No; the truth was that he had never loved her. Solitude, who had been thirsting for affection since the day she was born, realised that this man had never really loved her. She took refuge in herself, in remembrance of her mother, in the worship of the Virgin. She did not weep. Her pain was too deep for tears; it was a pain that burned and dried up.

One night, at supper, the paternal Sphinx opened his mouth long enough to say: "Well, that seems to be the end of that!" Solitude felt as though he had plunged a sword into her heart. She got up from the table, and rushed to her own room. There, crying, "Mother, my mother!" she collapsed in a spasm of agony; and thereafter the world was a waste for her.

So two years passed, and then one morning they found her father, Don Pedro, dead in his bed. He had had a heart attack. But his daughter, now left alone in the world, did not weep for him.

Solitude was left alone—quite alone. So that her solitariness should be complete, she sold the property that her father had left her, and on the proceeds of this modest fortune she went to live far away, very far away, where nobody knew her and she knew nobody.

Solitude is that woman, to-day almost an old woman, that simple but dignified woman, whom you see every evening going to take the sun on the banks of the river—that mysterious little woman about whom nobody knows whence she came or who she is. She is that solitary benefactor who, doing good by stealth, relieves all those ills of others that she can relieve. She is that kind little woman from whom there sometimes escapes a bitter saying that betrays an affliction which she keeps to herself.

Nobody knows her history, and there has grown up a legend of a terrible tragedy in her life. But, as you can see for yourself, there was nothing that one could call a tragedy in her life—or, at most, merely that common, that very common tragedy, undramatic, undemonstrative, which destroys so many human lives: the tragedy of solitude.

It is recalled only that, some years ago, Solitude was sought out by a man who looked old, old before his years, bowed as though beneath the weight of vice, who a few days afterwards died in the house of that little old woman. "He was my brother!" That was all she said about him.

And now do you understand what solitude means in the soul of a woman—a woman thirsting for tenderness and hungering for a home? A man in our society has ample scope in which to escape from solitude. But a woman—unless she chooses to shut herself up in a convent—how solitary she can be among us!

That poor little woman, whom you see wandering by the river bank, without aim or object, has experienced all the weight of the brutality of the animal egotism of men. What does she think? What has she got to live for? What far-off hope keeps her going?

I have gained the acquaintanceship—I cannot say the friendship—of Solitude, and I have tried to glimpse her view of life and destiny: what one might call her philosophy. So far I have learned little or nothing about it. All that I have got for her is her story, which I have just told you.

Apart from that, I have heard nothing from her but observations which are full of common sense, but of a common sense that seems cold and ordinary. She is a woman of extraordinary range of literary culture, for she has read very widely, and she is very far-seeing. But she remains extraordinarily susceptible to offensiveness or brutality from any quarter. She leads a solitary life, alone and retired, to avoid the rude elbowings of humanity.

About us men she has a curious idea. Whenever I have succeeded in turning the conversation to the subject of men, all her answer is: "Poor little fellows!" It appears that she pities us, as though we were one of the lower order of crustaceans. But she has promised me that she will talk to me some time about men and about that great, that greatest, that supreme problem—the relationship between men and women.

"Not the sexual relationship," she said, "be clear about that; not that, but the general relationship between man and woman, whether they be mother and son, brother and sister, or merely friends, on the one hand; or husband and wife, betrothed, or lovers on the other. The important thing, the essential thing, is the general relationship—the question how a man regards a woman, whether she be his mother, his daughter, his sister, his wife, or his mistress; and how a woman regards a man, whether he be her father, her son, her brother, her husband, or her lover." I am still awaiting the day when Solitude will talk to me about this.

Once I was talking to her about the flood of erotic books with which we are overwhelmed to-day; for one can talk to Solitude about anything, as long as one is careful not to hurt her. When I turned the conversation in this direction she looked at me quizzically out of those big, bright eyes of hers, those perpetually virginal eyes, and, with a shadow of a smile on her lips, she asked me: "Tell me, you eat, don't you?"

"Well, of course, I eat," I replied, surprised at her question.

"Very well; if I caught you, a man who eats, reading a cookery book and I had my way, I would send you to the kitchen to scour frying-pans."

And that was all she would say.

◊◊◊*Virginia Woolf (1882-1941). English novelist and short-story writer. A fiction experimenter. See* The Voyage Out, Jacob's Room, Mrs. Dalloway, Orlando, Waves.

THE DUCHESS AND
THE JEWELLER

BY VIRGINIA WOOLF

Oliver Bacon lived at the top of a house overlooking the Green Park. He had a flat; chairs jutted out at the right angles—chairs covered in hide. Sofas filled the bays of the windows—sofas covered in tapestry. The windows, the three long windows, had the proper allowance of discreet net and figured satin. The mahogany sideboard bulged discreetly with the right brandies, whiskeys, and liqueurs. And from the middle window he looked down upon the glossy roofs of fashionable cars packed in the narrow straits of Piccadilly. A more central position could not be imagined. And at eight in the morning he would have his breakfast brought in on a tray by a manservant: the man-servant would unfold his crimson dressing-gown; he would rip his letters open with his long pointed nails and would extract thick white cards of invitation upon which the engraving stood up roughly from duchesses, countesses, viscountesses, and Honourable Ladies. Then he would wash; then he would eat his toast; then he would read his paper by the bright burning fire of electric coals.

"Behold Oliver," he would say, addressing himself. "You who began life in a filthy little alley, you who . . ." and he would look down at his legs, so shapely in their perfect trousers; at his boots; at his spats. They were all shapely, shining; cut from the best cloth by the best scissors in Savile Row. But he dismantled himself often and became again a little boy in a dark alley. He had once thought that the height of his ambition—selling stolen dogs to fashionable women in Whitechapel. And once he had been done. "Oh, Oliver," his mother had wailed. "Oh, Oliver! When will you have sense, my son?" . . . Then he had gone behind a counter; had sold cheap watches; then he had taken a wallet to Amsterdam. . . . At that memory he would chuckle—the old Oliver remembering the young. Yes, he had done well with the three diamonds; also there was the commission on the emerald. After that he went into the private room behind the shop in Hatton Garden; the room with the scales, the safe, the thick magnifying glasses. And then . . . and then. . . . He chuckled. When he passed through the knots of jewellers in the hot evening who were discussing prices, gold mines, diamonds, reports from South Africa, one of them would lay a finger to the side of his nose and murmur, "Hum-m-m," as he passed. It was no more than a murmur; no more than a nudge on the shoulder, a finger on the nose, a buzz that ran through the cluster of jewellers in Hatton Garden on a hot afternoon—oh, many years ago now! But still Oliver felt it purring down his spine, the nudge, the murmur that meant, "Look at him—young Oliver, the young jeweller—there he goes." Young he was then. And he dressed better and better; and had, first a hansom cab; then a car; and first he went up to the dress circle, then down into the stalls. And he had a villa at Richmond, overlooking the river, with trellises of red roses; and Mademoiselle used to pick one every morning and stick it in his buttonhole.

"So," said Oliver Bacon, rising and stretching his legs. "So . . ." And he stood beneath the picture of an old lady on the mantelpiece and raised his hands. "I have kept my word," he said, laying his hands together, palm to palm, as if he were doing homage to her. "I have won my bet." That was so; he was the richest jeweller in England; but his nose, which was long and flexible, like an elephant's trunk, seemed to say by its curious quiver at the nostrils (but it seemed as if the whole nose quivered, not only the nostrils) that he was not satisfied yet; still smelt something under the ground a little further off. Imagine a giant hog in a pasture rich with truffles; after unearthing this truffle and that, still it smells a bigger, a blacker truffle under the ground further off. So Oliver snuffed always in the rich earth of Mayfair another truffle, a blacker, a bigger further off.

Now then he straightened the pearl in his tie, cased himself in his smart blue overcoat; took his yellow gloves and his cane; and swayed as he descended the stairs and half snuffed, half sighed through his long sharp nose as he passed out into Piccadilly. For was he not still a sad man, a dissatisfied man, a man who seeks something that is hidden, though he had won his bet?

He swayed slightly as he walked, as the camel at the zoo sways from side to side when it walks along the asphalt paths laden with grocers and their wives eating from paper bags and throwing little bits of silver paper crumpled up on to the path. The camel despises the grocers; the camel is dissatisfied with its lot; the camel sees the blue lake and the fringe of palm trees in front of it. So the great jeweller, the greatest jeweller in the whole world, swung down Piccadilly, perfectly dressed, with his gloves, with his cane; but dissatisfied still, till he reached the dark little shop, that was famous in France, in Germany, in Austria, in Italy, and all over America— the dark little shop in the street off Bond Street.

As usual, he strode through the shop without speaking, though the four men, the two old men, Marshall and Spencer, and the two young men, Hammond and Wicks, stood straight and looked at him, envying him. It was only with one finger of the amber-col- oured glove, waggling, that he acknowledged their presence. And he went in and shut the door of his private room behind him.

Then he unlocked the grating that barred the window. The cries of Bond Street came in; the purr of the distant traffic. The light from reflectors at the back of the shop struck upwards. One tree waved six green leaves, for it was June. But Mademoiselle had married Mr. Pedder of the local brewery—no one stuck roses in his buttonhole now.

"So," he half sighed, half snorted, "so—"

Then he touched a spring in the wall and slowly the panelling slid open, and behind it were the steel safes, five, no, six of them, all of burnished steel. He twisted a key; unlocked one; then another. Each was lined with a pad of deep crimson velvet; in each lay jewels—bracelets, necklaces, rings, tiaras, ducal coronets; loose stones in glass shells; rubies, emeralds, pearls, diamonds. All safe, shining, cool, yet burning, eternally, with their own compressed light.

"Tears!" said Oliver, looking at the pearls.

"Heart's blood!" he said, looking at the rubies.

"Gunpowder!" he continued, rattling the diamonds so that they flashed and blazed.

"Gunpowder enough to blow Mayfair—sky high, high, high!" He threw his head back and made a sound like a horse neighing as he said it.

The telephone buzzed obsequiously in a low muted voice on his table. He shut the safe.

"In ten minutes," he said. "Not before." And he sat down at his desk and looked at the heads of the Roman emperors that were graved on his sleeve links. And again he dismantled himself and became once more the little boy playing marbles in the alley where they sell stolen dogs on Sunday. He became that wily astute little boy, with lips like wet cherries. He dabbled his fingers in ropes of tripe; he dipped them in pans of frying fish; he dodged in and out among the crowds. He was slim, lissome, with eyes like licked stones. And now—now—the hands of the clock ticked on, one, two, three, four. . . . The Duchess of Lambourne waited his pleasure; the Duchess of Lambourne, daughter of a hundred Earls. She would wait for ten minutes on a chair at the counter. She would wait his pleasure. She would wait till he was ready to see her. He watched the clock in its shagreen case. The hand moved on. With each tick the clock handed him—so it seemed—pâté de foie gras, a glass of champagne, another of fine brandy, a cigar costing one guinea. The clock laid them on the table beside him as the ten minutes passed. Then he heard soft slow footsteps approaching; a rustle in the corridor. The door opened. Mr. Hammond flattened himself against the wall.

"Her Grace!" he announced.

And he waited there, flattened against the wall.

And Oliver, rising, could hear the rustle of the dress of the Duchess as she came down the passage. Then she loomed up, filling the door, filling the room with the aroma, the prestige, the arrogance, the pomp, the pride of all the Dukes and Duchesses swollen in one wave. And as a wave breaks, she broke, as she sat down, spreading and splashing and falling over Oliver Bacon, the great jeweller, covering him with sparkling bright colours, green, rose, violet; and odours; and iridescences; and rays shooting from fingers, nodding from plumes, flashing from silk; for she was very large, very fat, tightly girt in pink taffeta, and past her prime. As a parasol with many flounces, as a peacock with many feathers, shuts its flounces, folds its feathers, so she subsided and shut herself as she sank down in the leather armchair.

"Good morning, Mr. Bacon," said the Duchess. And she held out her hand which came through the slit of her white glove. And Oliver bent low as he shook it. And as their hands touched the link was forged between them once more. They were friends, yet enemies; he was master, she was mistress; each cheated the other, each needed the other, each feared the other, each felt this and knew this every time they touched hands thus in the little back room with the white light outside, and the tree with its six leaves, and the sound of the street in the distance and behind them the safes.

"And today, Duchess—what can I do for you today?" said Oliver, very softly.

The Duchess opened her heart, her private heart, gaped wide. And with a sigh but no word she took from her bag a long wash-leather pouch—it looked like a lean yellow ferret. And from a slit in the ferret's belly she dropped pearls—ten pearls. They rolled from the slit in the ferret's belly—one, two, three, four—like the eggs of some heavenly bird.

"All that's left me, dear Mr. Bacon," she moaned. Five, six, seven —down they rolled, down the slopes of the vast mountain sides that fell between her knees into one narrow valley—the eighth, the ninth, and the tenth. There they lay in the glow of the peach-blossom taffeta. Ten pearls.

"From the Appleby cincture," she mourned. "The last . . . the last of them all."

Oliver stretched out and took one of the pearls between finger and thumb. It was round, it was lustrous. But real was it, or false? Was she lying again? Did she dare?

She laid her plump padded finger across her lips. "If the Duke knew . . ." she whispered. "Dear Mr. Bacon, a bit of bad luck . . ."

Been gambling again, had she?

"That villain! That sharper!" she hissed.

The man with the chipped cheek bone? A bad 'un. And the Duke was straight as a poker; with side whiskers; would cut her off, shut her up down there if he knew—what I know, thought Oliver, and glanced at the safe.

"Araminta, Daphne, Diana," she moaned. "It's for *them*."

The ladies Araminta, Daphne, Diana—her daughters. He knew them; adored them. But it was Diana he loved.

"You have all my secrets," she leered. Tears slid; tears fell; tears, like diamonds, collecting powder in the ruts of her cherry blossom cheeks.

"Old friend," she murmured, "old friend."

"Old friend," he repeated, "old friend," as if he licked the words.

"How much?" he queried.

She covered the pearls with her hand.

"Twenty thousand," she whispered.

But was it real or false, the one he held in his hand? The Appleby cincture—hadn't she sold it already? He would ring for Spencer or Hammond. "Take it and test it," he would say. He stretched to the bell.

"You will come down tomorrow?" she urged, she interrupted. "The Prime Minister—His Royal Highness . . ." She stopped. "And Diana . . ." she added.

Oliver took his hand off the bell.

He looked past her, at the backs of the houses in Bond Street. But he saw, not the houses in Bond Street, but a dimpling river; and trout rising and salmon; and the Prime Minister; and himself too, in white waistcoat; and then, Diana. He looked down at the pearl in his hand. But how could he test it, in the light of the river, in the light of the eyes of Diana? But the eyes of the Duchess were on him.

"Twenty thousand," she moaned. "My honour!"

The honour of the mother of Diana! He drew his cheque book towards him; he took out his pen.

"Twenty—" he wrote. Then he stopped writing. The eyes of the old woman in the picture were on him—of the old woman his mother.

"Oliver!" she warned him. "Have sense! Don't be a fool!"

"Oliver!" the Duchess entreated—it was "Oliver" now, not "Mr. Bacon." "You'll come for a long week-end?"

Alone in the woods with Diana! Riding alone in the woods with Diana!

"Thousand," he wrote, and signed it.

"Here you are," he said.

And there opened all the flounces of the parasol, all the plumes of the peacock, the radiance of the wave, the swords and spears of Agincourt, as she rose from her chair. And the two old men and the two young men, Spencer and Marshall, Wicks and Hammond, flattened themselves behind the counter envying him as he led her through the shop to the door. And he waggled his yellow glove in their faces, and she held her honour—a cheque for twenty thousand pounds with his signature—quite firmly in her hands.

"Are they false or are they real?" asked Oliver, shutting his private door. There they were, ten pearls on the blotting-paper on the table. He took them to the window. He held them under his lens to the light. . . . This, then, was the truffle he had routed out of the earth! Rotten at the centre—rotten at the core!

"Forgive me, oh, my mother!" he sighed, raising his hand as if he asked pardon of the old woman in the picture. And again he was a little boy in the alley where they sold dogs on Sunday.

"For," he murmured, laying the palms of his hands together, "it is to be a long week-end."

◈◈◈*Saul Bellow (1915–   ). American novelist and short-story writer, whose style is intellectual yet often bawdy.* See Dangling Man, The Victim, The Adventures of Augie March, Herzog, Mr. Sammler's Planet.

A FATHER-TO-BE

BY SAUL BELLOW

The strangest notions had a way of forcing themselves into Rogin's mind. Just thirty-one and passable-looking, with short black hair, small eyes, but a high, open forehead, he was a research chemist, and his mind was generally serious and dependable. But on a snowy Sunday evening while this stocky man, buttoned to the chin in a Burberry coat and walking in his preposterous gait—feet turned outward—was going toward the subway, he fell into a peculiar state.

He was on his way to have supper with his fiancée. She had phoned him a short while ago and said, "You'd better pick up a few things on the way."

"What do we need?"

"Some roast beef, for one thing. I bought a quarter of a pound coming home from my aunt's."

"Why a quarter of a pound, Joan?" said Rogin, deeply annoyed. "That's just about enough for one good sandwich."

"So you have to stop at a delicatessen. I had no more money."

He was about to ask, "What happened to the thirty dollars I gave you on Wednesday?" but he knew that would not be right.

"I had to give Phyllis money for the cleaning woman," said Joan.

Phyllis, Joan's cousin, was a young divorcee, extremely wealthy. The two women shared an apartment.

"Roast beef," he said, "and what else?"

"Some shampoo, sweetheart. We've used up all the shampoo. And hurry, darling, I've missed you all day."

"And I've missed you," said Rogin, but to tell the truth he had been worrying most of the time. He had a younger brother whom he was putting through college. And his mother, whose annuity wasn't quite enough in these days of inflation and high taxes, needed money too. Joan had debts he was helping her to pay, for she wasn't working. She was looking for something suitable to do. Beautiful, well educated, aristocratic in her attitude, she couldn't clerk in a dime store; she couldn't model clothes (Rogin thought this made girls vain and stiff, and he didn't want her to); she couldn't be a waitress or a cashier. What could she be? Well, something would turn up and meantime Rogin hesitated to complain. He paid her bills—the dentist, the department store, the osteopath, the doctor, the psychiatrist. At Christmas, Rogin almost went mad. Joan bought him a velvet smoking jacket with frog fasteners, a beautiful pipe, and a pouch. She bought Phyllis a garnet brooch, an Italian silk umbrella, and a gold cigarette holder. For other friends, she bought Dutch pewter and Swedish glassware. Before she was through, she had spent five hundred dollars of Rogin's money. He loved her too much to show his suffering. He believed she had a far better nature than his. She didn't worry about money. She had a marvelous character, always cheerful, and she really didn't need a psychiatrist at all. She went to one because Phyllis did and it made her curious. She tried too much to keep up with her cousin, whose father had made millions in the rug business.

While the woman in the drugstore was wrapping the shampoo bottle, a clear idea suddenly arose in Rogin's thoughts: Money surrounds you in life as the earth does in death. Superimposition is the universal law. Who is free? No one is free. Who has no burdens? Everyone is under pressure. The very rocks, the waters of the earth, beasts, men, children—everyone has some weight to carry. This idea was extremely clear to him at first. Soon it became rather vague, but it had a great effect nevertheless, as if someone had given him a valuable gift. (Not like the velvet smoking jacket he couldn't bring himself to wear, or the pipe it choked him to smoke.) The notion that all were under pressure and affliction, instead of saddening him, had the opposite influence. It put him in a wonderful mood. It was extraordinary how happy he became and, in addition, clear-sighted. His eyes all at once were opened to what was around him. He saw with delight how the druggist and the woman who wrapped the shampoo bottle were smiling and flirting, how the lines of worry in her face went over into lines of cheer and the druggist's receding gums did not hinder his kidding and friendliness. And in the delicatessen, also, it was amazing how much Rogin noted and what happiness it gave him simply to be there.

Delicatessens on Sunday night, when all other stores are shut, will overcharge you ferociously, and Rogin would normally have been on guard, but he was not tonight, or scarcely so. Smells of pickle, sausage, mustard, and smoked fish overjoyed him. He pitied the people who would buy the chicken salad and chopped herring; they could do it only because their sight was too dim to see what they were getting—the fat flakes of pepper on the chicken, the soppy herring, mostly vinegar-soaked stale bread. Who would buy them? Late risers, people living alone, waking up in the darkness of the afternoon, finding their refrigerators empty, or people whose gaze was turned inward. The roast beef looked not bad, and Rogin ordered a pound.

While the storekeeper was slicing the meat, he yelled at a Puerto Rican kid who was reaching for a bag of chocolate cookies, "Hey, you want to pull me down the whole display on yourself? You, *chico*, wait a half a minute." This storekeeper, though he looked like one of Pancho Villa's bandits, the kind that smeared their enemies with syrup and staked them down on anthills, a man with toadlike eyes and stout hands made to clasp pistols hung around his belly, was not so bad. He was a New York man, thought Rogin —who was from Albany himself—a New York man toughened by every abuse of the city, trained to suspect everyone. But in his own realm, on the board behind the counter, there was justice. Even clemency.

The Puerto Rican kid wore a complete cowboy outfit—a green hat with white braid, guns, chaps, spurs, boots, and gauntlets—but he couldn't speak any English. Rogin unhooked the cellophane bag of hard circular cookies and gave it to him. The boy tore the cellophane with his teeth and began to chew one of those dry chocolate disks. Rogin recognized his state—the energetic dream of childhood. Once, he, too, had found these dry biscuits delicious. It would have bored him now to eat one.

What else would Joan like? Rogin thought fondly. Some strawberries? "Give me some frozen strawberries. No, raspberries, she likes those better. And heavy cream. And some rolls, cream cheese, and some of those rubber-looking gherkins."

"What rubber?"

"Those, deep green, with eyes. Some ice cream might be in order, too."

He tried to think of a compliment, a good comparison, an endearment, for Joan when she'd open the door. What about her complexion? There was really nothing to compare her sweet, small, daring, shapely, timid, defiant, loving face to. How difficult she was, and how beautiful!

As Rogin went down into the stony, odorous, metallic, captive air of the subway, he was diverted by an unusual confession made by a man to his friend. These were two very tall men, shapeless in their winter clothes, as if their coats concealed suits of chain mail.

"So, how long have you known me?" said one.

"Twelve years."

"Well, I have an admission to make," he said. "I've decided that I might as well. For years I've been a heavy drinker. You didn't know. Practically an alcoholic."

But his friend was not surprised, and he answered immediately, "Yes, I did know."

"You knew? Impossible! How could you?"

Why, thought Rogin, as if it could be a secret! Look at that long, austere, alcohol-washed face, that drink-ruined nose, the skin by his ears like turkey wattles, and those whisky-saddened eyes.

"Well, I did know, though."

"You couldn't have. I can't believe it." He was upset, and his friend didn't seem to want to soothe him. "But it's all right now," he said. "I've been going to a doctor and taking pills, a new revolutionary Danish discovery. It's a miracle. I'm beginning to believe they can cure you of anything and everything. You can't beat the Danes in science. They do everything. They turned a man into a woman."

"That isn't how they stop you from drinking, is it?"

"No. I hope not. This is only like aspirin. It's superaspirin. They called it the aspirin of the future. But if you use it, you have to stop drinking."

Rogin's illuminated mind asked of itself while the human tides of the subway swayed back and forth, and cars linked and transparent like fish bladders raced under the streets: How come he thought nobody would know what everybody couldn't help knowing? And, as a chemist, he asked himself what kind of compound this new Danish drug might be, and started thinking about various inventions of his own, synthetic albumen, a cigarette that lit itself, a cheaper motor fuel. Ye gods, but he needed money! As never before. What was to be done? His mother was growing more and more difficult. On Friday night, she had neglected to cut up his meat for him, and he was hurt. She had sat at the table motionless, with her long-suffering face, severe, and let him cut his own meat, a thing she almost never did. She had always spoiled him and made his brother envy him. But what she expected now! Oh, Lord, how he had to pay, and it had never even occurred to him formerly that these things might have a price.

Seated, one of the passengers, Rogin recovered his calm, happy, even clairvoyant state of mind. To think of money was to think as the world wanted you to think; then you'd never be your own master. When people said they wouldn't do something for love or money, they meant that love and money were opposite passions, and one the enemy of the other. He went on to reflect how little people knew about this, how they slept through life, how small a light the light of consciousness was. Rogin's clean, snub-nosed face shone while his heart was torn with joy at these deeper thoughts of our ignorance. You might take this drunkard as an example, who for long years thought his closest friends never suspected he drank. Rogin looked up and down the aisle for this remarkable knightly symbol, but he was gone.

However, there was no lack of things to see. There was a small girl with a new white muff; into the muff a doll's head was sewn, and the child was happy and affectionately vain of it, while her old man, stout and grim, with a huge scowling nose, kept picking her up and resettling her in the seat, as if he were trying to change her into something else. Then another child, led by her mother, boarded the car, and this other child carried the very same doll-faced muff, and this greatly annoyed both parents. The woman, who looked like a difficult, contentious woman, took her daughter away. It seemed to Rogin that each child was in love with its own muff and didn't even see the other, but it was one of his foibles to think he understood the hearts of little children.

A foreign family next engaged his attention. They looked like Central Americans to him. On one side the mother, quite old, dark-faced, white-haired, and worn out; on the other a son with the whitened, porous hands of a dishwasher. But what was the dwarf who sat between them—a son or a daughter? The hair was long and wavy and the cheeks smooth, but the shirt and tie were masculine. The overcoat was feminine, but the shoes—the shoes were a puzzle. A pair of brown oxfords with an outer seam like a man's, but Baby Louis heels like a woman's—a plain toe like a man's, but a strap across the instep like a woman's. No stockings. That didn't help much. The dwarf's fingers were beringed, but without a wedding band. There were small grim dents in the cheeks. The eyes were puffy and concealed, but Rogin did not doubt that they could reveal strange things if they chose and that this was a creature of remarkable understanding. He had for many years owned de la Mare's *Memoirs of a Midget*. Now he took a resolve; he would read it. As soon as he had decided, he was free from his consuming curiosity as to the dwarf's sex and was able to look at the person who sat beside him.

Thoughts very often grow fertile in the subway, because of the motion, the great company, the subtlety of the rider's state as he rattles under streets and rivers, under the foundations of great buildings, and Rogin's mind had already been strangely stimulated. Clasping the bag of groceries from which there rose odors of bread and pickle spice, he was following a train of reflections, first about the chemistry of sex determination, the X and Y chromosomes, hereditary linkages, the uterus, afterward about his brother as a tax exemption. He recalled two dreams of the night before. In one, an undertaker had offered to cut his hair, and he had refused. In another, he had been carrying a woman on his head. Sad dreams, both! Very sad! Which was the woman—Joan or Mother? And the undertaker—his lawyer? He gave a deep sigh, and by force of habit began to put together his synthetic albumen that was to revolutionize the entire egg industry.

Meanwhile, he had not interrupted his examination of the passengers and had fallen into a study of the man next to him. This was a man whom he had never in his life seen before but with whom he now suddenly felt linked through all existence. He was middle-aged, sturdy, with clear skin and blue eyes. His hands were clean, well formed, but Rogin did not approve of them. The coat he wore was a fairly expensive blue check such as Rogin would never have chosen for himself. He would not have worn blue suède shoes, either, or such a faultless hat, a cumbersome felt animal of a hat encircled by a high, fat ribbon. There are all kinds of dandies, not all of them are of the flaunting kind; some are dandies of respectability, and Rogin's fellow passenger was one of these. His straight-nosed profile was handsome, yet he had betrayed his gift, for he was flat-looking. But in his flat way he seemed to warn people that he wanted no difficulties with them, he wanted nothing to do with them. Wearing such blue suède shoes, he could not afford to have people treading on his feet, and he seemed to draw about himself a circle of privilege, notifying all others to mind their own business and let him read his paper. He was holding a *Tribune*, and perhaps it would be overstatement to say that he was reading. He was holding it.

His clear skin and blue eyes, his straight and purely Roman nose —even the way he sat—all strongly suggested one person to Rogin: Joan. He tried to escape the comparison, but it couldn't be helped. This man not only looked like Joan's father, whom Rogin detested; he looked like Joan herself. Forty years hence, a son of hers, provided she had one, might be like this. A son of hers? Of such a son, he himself, Rogin, would be the father. Lacking in dominant traits as compared with Joan, his heritage would not appear. Probably the children would resemble her. Yes, think forty years ahead, and a man like this, who sat by him knee to knee in the hurtling car among their fellow creatures, unconscious participants in a sort of great carnival of transit—such a man would carry forward what had been Rogin.

This was why he felt bound to him through all existence. What were forty years reckoned against eternity! Forty years were gone, and he was gazing at his own son. Here he was. Rogin was frightened and moved. "My son! My son!" he said to himself, and the pity of it almost made him burst into tears. The holy and frightful work of the masters of life and death brought this about. We were their instruments. We worked toward ends we thought were our own. But no! The whole thing was so unjust. To suffer, to labor, to toil and force your way through the spikes of life, to crawl through its darkest caverns, to push through the worst, to struggle under the weight of economy, to make money—only to become the father of a fourth-rate man of the world like this, so flat-looking with his ordinary, clean, rosy, uninteresting, self-satisfied, fundamentally bourgeois face. What a curse to have a dull son! A son like this, who could never understand his father. They had absolutely nothing, but nothing, in common, he and this neat, chubby, blue-eyed man. He was so pleased, thought Rogin, with all he owned and all he did and all he was that he could hardly unfasten his lip. Look at that lip, sticking up at the tip like a little thorn or egg tooth. He wouldn't give anyone the time of day. Would this perhaps be general forty years from now? Would personalities be chillier as the world aged and grew colder? The inhumanity of the next generation incensed Rogin. Father and son had no sign to make to each other. Terrible! Inhuman! What a vision of existence it gave him. Man's personal aims were nothing, illusion. The life force occupied each of us in turn in its progress toward its own fulfillment, trampling on our individual humanity, using us for its own ends like mere dinosaurs or bees, exploiting love heartlessly, making us engage in the social process, labor, struggle for money, and submit to the law of pressure, the universal law of layers, superimposition!

What the blazes am I getting into? Rogin thought. To be the father of a throwback to *her* father. The image of this white-haired, gross, peevish, old man with his ugly selfish blue eyes revolted Rogin. This was how his grandson would look. Joan, with whom Rogin was now more and more displeased, could not help that. For her, it was inevitable. But did it have to be inevitable for him? Well, then, Rogin, you fool, don't be a damned instrument. Get out of the way!

But it was too late for this, because he had already experienced the sensation of sitting next to his own son, his son and Joan's. He kept staring at him, waiting for him to say something, but the presumptive son remained coldly silent though he must have been aware of Rogin's scrutiny. They even got out at the same stop—Sheridan Square. When they stepped to the platform, the man, without even looking at Rogin, went away in a different direction in his detestable blue-checked coat, with his rosy, nasty face.

The whole thing upset Rogin very badly. When he approached Joan's door and heard Phyllis's little dog Henri barking even before he could knock, his face was very tense. I won't be used, he declared to himself. I have my own right to exist. Joan had better watch out. She had a light way of by-passing grave questions he had given earnest thought to. She always assumed no really disturbing thing would happen. He could not afford the luxury of such a carefree, debonair attitude himself, because he had to work hard and earn money so that disturbing things would *not* happen. Well, at the moment this situation could not be helped, and he really did not mind the money if he could feel that she was not necessarily the mother of such a son as his subway son or entirely the daughter of that awful, obscene father of hers. After all, Rogin was not himself so much like either of his parents, and quite different from his brother.

Joan came to the door, wearing one of Phyllis's expensive housecoats. It suited her very well. At first sight of her happy face, Rogin was brushed by the shadow of resemblance; the touch of it was extremely light, almost figmentary, but it made his flesh tremble.

She began to kiss him, saying, "Oh, my baby. You're covered with snow. Why didn't you wear your hat? It's all over its little head"—her favorite third-person endearment.

"Well, let me put down this bag of stuff. Let me take off my coat," grumbled Rogin, and escaped from her embrace. Why couldn't she wait making up to him? "It's so hot in here. My face is burning. Why do you keep the place at this temperature? And that damned dog keeps barking. If you didn't keep it cooped up, it wouldn't be so spoiled and noisy. Why doesn't anybody ever walk him?"

"Oh, it's not really so hot here! You've just come in from the cold. Don't you think this housecoat fits me better than Phyllis?

Especially across the hips. She thinks so, too. She may sell it to me."

"I hope not," Rogin almost exclaimed.

She brought a towel to dry the melting snow from his short black hair. The flurry of rubbing excited Henri intolerably, and Joan locked him up in the bedroom, where he jumped persistently against the door with a rhythmic sound of claws on the wood.

Joan said, "Did you bring the shampoo?"

"Here it is."

"Then I'll wash your hair before dinner. Come."

"I don't want it washed."

"Oh, come on," she said, laughing.

Her lack of consciousness of guilt amazed him. He did not see how it could be. And the carpeted, furnished, lamp-lit, curtained room seemed to stand against his vision. So that he felt accusing and angry, his spirit sore and bitter, but it did not seem fitting to say why. Indeed, he began to worry lest the reason for it all slip away from him.

They took off his coat and his shirt in the bathroom, and she filled the sink. Rogin was full of his troubled emotions; now that his chest was bare he could feel them even more and he said to himself, I'll have a thing or two to tell her pretty soon. I'm not letting them get away with it. "Do you think," he was going to tell her, "that I alone was made to carry the burden of the whole world on me? Do you think I was born to be taken advantage of and sacrificed? Do you think I'm just a natural resource, like a coal mine, or oil well, or fishery, or the like? Remember, that I'm a man is no reason why I should be loaded down. I have a soul in me no bigger or stronger than yours.

"Take away the externals, like the muscles, deeper voice, and so forth, and what remains? A pair of spirits, practically alike. So why shouldn't there also be equality? I can't always be the strong one."

"Sit here," said Joan, bringing up a kitchen stool to the sink. "Your hair's gotten all matted."

He sat with his breast against the cool enamel, his chin on the edge of the basin, the green, hot, radiant water reflecting the glass and the tile, and the sweet, cool, fragrant juice of the shampoo poured on his head. She began to wash him.

"You have the healthiest-looking scalp," she said. "It's all pink."

He answered, "Well, it should be white. There must be something wrong with me."

"But there's absolutely nothing wrong with you," she said, and pressed against him from behind, surrounding him, pouring the water gently over him until it seemed to him that the water came from within him, it was the warm fluid of his own secret loving spirit overflowing into the sink, green and foaming, and the words he had rehearsed he forgot, and his anger at his son-to-be disappeared altogether, and he sighed, and said to her from the water-filled hollow of the sink, "You always have such wonderful ideas, Joan. You know? You have a kind of instinct, a regular gift."

◇◇◇*Bernard Malamud (1914–   ). American novelist and short-story writer.* See The Magic Barrel, The Natural, The Assistant, The Fixer, Pictures of Fidelman.

IDIOTS FIRST

BY BERNARD MALAMUD

The thick ticking of the tin clock stopped. Mendel, dozing in the dark, awoke in fright. The pain returned as he listened. He drew on his cold embittered clothing, and wasted minutes sitting at the edge of the bed.

"Isaac," he ultimately sighed.

In the kitchen, Isaac, his astonished mouth open, held six peanuts in his palm. He placed each on the table. "One . . . two . . . nine."

He gathered each peanut and appeared in the doorway. Mendel, in loose hat and long overcoat, still sat on the bed. Isaac watched with small eyes and ears, thick hair graying the sides of his head.

"Schlaf," he nasally said.

"No," muttered Mendel. As if stifling he rose. "Come, Isaac."

He wound his old watch though the sight of the stopped clock nauseated him.

Isaac wanted to hold it to his ear.

"No, it's late." Mendel put the watch carefully away. In the drawer he found the little paper bag of crumpled ones and fives and slipped it into his overcoat pocket. He helped Isaac on with his coat.

Isaac looked at one dark window, then at the other. Mendel stared at both blank windows.

They went slowly down the darkly lit stairs, Mendel first, Isaac watching the moving shadows on the wall. To one long shadow he offered a peanut.

"Hungrig."

In the vestibule the old man gazed through the thin glass. The November night was cold and bleak. Opening the door he cautiously thrust his head out. Though he saw nothing he quickly shut the door.

"Ginzburg, that he came to see me yesterday," he whispered in Isaac's ear.

Isaac sucked air.

"You know who I mean?"

Isaac combed his chin with his fingers.

"That's the one, with the black whiskers. Don't talk to him or go with him if he asks you."

Isaac moaned.

"Young people he don't bother so much," Mendel said in afterthought.

It was suppertime and the street was empty but the store windows dimly lit their way to the corner. They crossed the deserted street and went on. Isaac, with a happy cry, pointed to the three golden balls. Mendel smiled but was exhausted when they got to the pawnshop.

The pawnbroker, a red-bearded man with black horn-rimmed glasses, was eating a whitefish at the rear of the store. He craned his head, saw them, and settled back to sip his tea.

In five minutes he came forward, patting his shapeless lips with a large white handkerchief.

Mendel, breathing heavily, handed him the worn gold watch. The pawnbroker, raising his glasses, screwed in his eyepiece. He turned the watch over once. "Eight dollars."

The dying man wet his cracked lips. "I must have thirty-five."

"So go to Rothschild."

"Cost me myself sixty."

"In 1905." The pawnbroker handed back the watch. It had stopped ticking. Mendel wound it slowly. It ticked hollowly.

"Isaac must go to my uncle that he lives in California."

"It's a free country," said the pawnbroker.

Isaac, watching a banjo, snickered.

"What's the matter with him?" the pawnbroker asked.

"So let be eight dollars," muttered Mendel, "but where will I get the rest till tonight?"

"How much for my hat and coat?" he asked.

"No sale." The pawnbroker went behind the cage and wrote out a ticket. He locked the watch in a small drawer but Mendel still heard it ticking.

In the street he slipped the eight dollars into the paper bag, then searched in his pockets for a scrap of writing. Finding it, he strained to read the address by the light of the street lamp.

As they trudged to the subway, Mendel pointed to the sprinkled sky.

"Isaac, look how many stars are tonight."

"Eggs," said Isaac.

"First we will go to Mr. Fishbein, after we will eat."

They got off the train in upper Manhattan and had to walk several blocks before they located Fishbein's house.

"A regular palace," Mendel murmured, looking forward to a moment's warmth.

Isaac stared uneasily at the heavy door of the house.

Mendel rang. The servant, a man with long sideburns, came to the door and said Mr. and Mrs. Fishbein were dining and could see no one.

"He should eat in peace but we will wait till he finishes."

"Come back tomorrow morning. Tomorrow morning Mr. Fishbein will talk to you. He don't do business or charity at this time of the night."

"Charity I am not interested—"

"Come back tomorrow."

"Tell him it's life or death—"

"Whose life or death?"

"So if not his, then mine."

"Don't be such a big smart aleck."

"Look me in my face," said Mendel, "and tell me if I got time till tomorrow morning?"

The servant stared at him, then at Isaac, and reluctantly let them in.

The foyer was a vast high-ceilinged room with many oil paintings on the walls, voluminous silken draperies, a thick flowered rug at foot, and a marble staircase.

Mr. Fishbein, a paunchy bald-headed man with hairy nostrils and small patent leather feet, ran lightly down the stairs, a large napkin tucked under a tuxedo coat button. He stopped on the fifth step from the bottom and examined his visitors.

"Who comes on Friday night to a man that he has guests, to spoil him his supper?"

"Excuse me that I bother you, Mr. Fishbein," Mendel said. "If I didn't come now I couldn't come tomorrow."

"Without more preliminaries, please state your business. I'm a hungry man."

"Hungrig," wailed Isaac.

Fishbein adjusted his pince-nez. "What's the matter with him?"

"This is my son Isaac. He is like this all his life."

Isaac mewled.

"I am sending him to California."

"Mr. Fishbein don't contribute to personal pleasure trips."

"I am a sick man and he must go tonight on the train to my Uncle Leo."

"I never give to unorganized charity," Fishbein said, "but if you are hungry I will invite you downstairs in my kitchen. We having tonight chicken with stuffed derma."

"All I ask is thirty-five dollars for the train ticket to my uncle in California. I have already the rest."

"Who is your uncle? How old a man?"

"Eighty-one years, a long life to him."

Fishbein burst into laughter. "Eighty-one years and you are sending him this halfwit."

Mendel, flailing both arms, cried, "Please, without names."

Fishbein politely conceded.

"Where is open the door there we go in the house," the sick man said. "If you will kindly give me thirty-five dollars, God will bless you. What is thirty-five dollars to Mr. Fishbein? Nothing. To me, for my boy, is everything."

Fishbein drew himself up to his tallest height.

"Private contributions I don't make—only to institutions. This is my fixed policy."

Mendel sank to his creaking knees on the rug.

"Please, Mr. Fishbein, if not thirty-five, give maybe twenty."

"Levinson!" Fishbein angrily called.

The servant with the long sideburns appeared at the top of the stairs.

"Show this party where is the door—unless he wishes to partake food before leaving the premises."

"For what I got chicken won't cure it," Mendel said.

"This way if you please," said Levinson, descending.

Isaac assisted his father up.

"Take him to an institution," Fishbein advised over the marble balustrade. He ran quickly up the stairs and they were at once outside, buffeted by winds.

The walk to the subway was tedious. The wind blew mournfully. Mendel, breathless, glanced furtively at shadows. Isaac, clutching his peanuts in his frozen fist, clung to his father's side. They entered a small park to rest for a minute on a stone bench under a leafless two-branched tree. The thick right branch was raised, the thin left one hung down. A very pale moon rose slowly. So did a stranger as they approached the bench.

"Gut yuntif," he said hoarsely.

Mendel, drained of blood, waved his wasted arms. Isaac yowled sickly. Then a bell chimed and it was only ten. Mendel let out a piercing anguished cry as the bearded stranger disappeared into the bushes. A policeman came running, and though he beat the bushes with his nightstick, could turn up nothing. Mendel and Isaac hurried out of the little park. When Mendel glanced back the dead tree had its thin arm raised, the thick one down. He moaned.

They boarded a trolley, stopping at the home of a former friend, but he had died years ago. On the same block they went into a cafeteria and ordered two fried eggs for Isaac. The tables were crowded except where a heavyset man sat eating soup with kasha. After one look at him they left in haste, although Isaac wept.

Mendel had another address on a slip of paper but the house was too far away, in Queens, so they stood in a doorway shivering.

What can I do, he frantically thought, in one short hour?

He remembered the furniture in the house. It was junk but might bring a few dollars. "Come, Isaac." They went once more to the pawnbroker's to talk to him, but the shop was dark and an iron gate—rings and gold watches glinting through it—was drawn tight across his place of business.

They huddled behind a telephone pole, both freezing. Isaac whimpered.

"See the big moon, Isaac. The whole sky is white."

He pointed but Isaac wouldn't look.

Mendel dreamed for a minute of the sky lit up, long sheets of light in all directions. Under the sky, in California, sat Uncle Leo drinking tea with lemon. Mendel felt warm but woke up cold.

Across the street stood an ancient brick synagogue.

He pounded on the huge door but no one appeared. He waited till he had breath and desperately knocked again. At last there were footsteps within, and the synagogue door creaked open on its massive brass hinges.

A darkly dressed sexton, holding a dripping candle, glared at them.

"Who knocks this time of night with so much noise on the synagogue door?"

Mendel told the sexton his troubles. "Please, I would like to speak to the rabbi."

"The rabbi is an old man. He sleeps now. His wife won't let you see him. Go home and come back tomorrow."

"To tomorrow I said goodbye already. I am a dying man."

Though the sexton seemed doubtful he pointed to an old wooden house next door. "In there he lives." He disappeared into the synagogue with his lit candle casting shadows around him.

Mendel, with Isaac clutching his sleeve, went up the wooden steps and rang the bell. After five minutes a big-faced, gray-haired bulky woman came out on the porch with a torn robe thrown over her nightdress. She emphatically said the rabbi was sleeping and could not be waked.

But as she was insisting, the rabbi himself tottered to the door. He listened a minute and said, "Who wants to see me let them come in."

They entered a cluttered room. The rabbi was an old skinny man with bent shoulders and a wisp of white beard. He wore a flannel nightgown and black skullcap; his feet were bare.

"Vey is mir," his wife muttered. "Put on shoes or tomorrow comes sure pneumonia." She was a woman with a big belly, years younger than her husband. Staring at Isaac, she turned away.

Mendel apologetically related his errand. "All I need more is thirty-five dollars."

"Thirty-five?" said the rabbi's wife. "Why not thirty-five thousand? Who has so much money? My husband is a poor rabbi. The doctors take away every penny."

"Dear friend," said the rabbi, "if I had I would give you."

"I got already seventy," Mendel said, heavy-hearted. "All I need more is thirty-five."

"God will give you," said the rabbi.

"In the grave," said Mendel. "I need tonight. Come, Isaac."

"Wait," called the rabbi.

He hurried inside, came out with a fur-lined caftan, and handed it to Mendel.

"Yascha," shrieked his wife, "not your new coat!"

"I got my old one. Who needs two coats for one body?"

"Yascha, I am screaming—"

"Who can go among poor people, tell me, in a new coat?"

"Yascha," she cried, "what can this man do with your coat? He needs tonight the money. The pawnbrokers are asleep."

"So let him wake them up."

"No." She grabbed the coat from Mendel.

He held on to a sleeve, wrestling her for the coat. Her I know, Mendel thought. "Shylock," he muttered. Her eyes glittered.

The rabbi groaned and tottered dizzily. His wife cried out as Mendel yanked the coat from her hands.

"Run," cried the rabbi.

"Run, Isaac."

They ran out of the house and down the steps.

"Stop, you thief," called the rabbi's wife.

The rabbi pressed both hands to his temples and fell to the floor.

"Help!" his wife wept. "Heart attack! Help!"

But Mendel and Isaac ran through the streets with the rabbi's new fur-lined caftan. After them noiselessly ran Ginzburg.

It was very late when Mendel bought the train ticket in the only booth open.

There was no time to stop for a sandwich so Isaac ate his peanuts and they hurried to the train in the vast deserted station.

"So in the morning," Mendel gasped as they ran, "there comes a man that he sells sandwiches and coffee. Eat but get change. When reaches California the train, will be waiting for you on the station Uncle Leo. If you don't recognize him he will recognize you. Tell him I send best regards."

But when they arrived at the gate to the platform it was shut, the light out.

Mendel, groaning, beat on the gate with his fists.

"Too late," said the uniformed ticket collector, a bulky, bearded man with hairy nostrils and a fishy smell.

He pointed to the station clock. "Already past twelve."

"But I see standing there still the train," Mendel said, hopping in his grief.

"It just left—in one more minute."

"A minute is enough. Just open the gate."

"Too late I told you."

Mendel socked his bony chest with both hands. "With my whole heart I beg you this little favor."

"Favors you had enough already. For you the train is gone. You shoulda been dead already at midnight. I told you that yesterday. This is the best I can do."

"Ginzburg!" Mendel shrank from him.

"Who else?" The voice was metallic, eyes glittered, the expression amused.

"For myself," the old man begged, "I don't ask a thing. But what will happen to my boy?"

Ginzburg shrugged slightly. "What will happen happens. This isn't my responsibility. I got enough to think about without worrying about somebody on one cylinder."

"What then is your responsibility?"

"To create conditions. To make happen what happens. I ain't in the anthropomorphic business."

"Whatever business you in, where is your pity?"

"This ain't my commodity. The law is the law."

"Which law is this?"

"The cosmic universal law, goddamit, the one I got to follow myself."

"What kind of a law is it?" cried Mendel. "For God's sake, don't you understand what I went through in my life with this poor boy? Look at him. For thirty-nine years, since the day he was born, I wait for him to grow up, but he don't. Do you understand what this means in a father's heart? Why don't you let him go to his uncle?" His voice had risen and he was shouting.

Isaac mewled loudly.

"Better calm down or you'll hurt somebody's feelings," Ginzburg said with a wink toward Isaac.

"All my life," Mendel cried, his body trembling, "what did I have? I was poor. I suffered from my health. When I worked I worked too hard. When I didn't work was worse. My wife died a young woman. But I didn't ask from anybody nothing. Now I ask a small favor. Be so kind, Mr. Ginzburg."

The ticket collector was picking his teeth with a match stick.

"You ain't the only one, my friend, some got it worse than you. That's how it goes in this country."

"You dog you." Mendel lunged at Ginzburg's throat and began to choke. "You bastard, don't you understand what it means human?"

They struggled nose to nose, Ginzburg, though his astonished eyes bulged, began to laugh. "You pipsqueak nothing. I'll freeze you to pieces."

His eyes lit in rage and Mendel felt an unbearable cold like an icy dagger invading his body, all of his parts shriveling.

Now I die without helping Isaac.

A crowd gathered. Isaac yelped in fright.

Clinging to Ginzburg in his last agony, Mendel saw reflected in the ticket collector's eyes the depth of his terror. But he saw that Ginzburg, staring at himself in Mendel's eyes, saw mirrored in them the extent of his own awful wrath. He beheld a shimmering, starry, blinding light that produced darkness.

Ginzburg looked astounded. "Who me?"

His grip on the squirming old man slowly loosened, and Mendel, his heart barely beating, slumped to the ground.

"Go." Ginzburg muttered, "take him to the train."

"Let pass," he commanded a guard.

The crowd parted. Isaac helped his father up and they tottered down the steps to the platform where the train waited, lit and ready to go.

Mendel found Isaac a coach seat and hastily embraced him. "Help Uncle Leo, Isaakil. Also remember your father and mother."

"Be nice to him," he said to the conductor. "Show him where everything is."

He waited on the platform until the train began slowly to move. Isaac sat at the edge of his seat, his face strained in the direction of his journey. When the train was gone, Mendel ascended the stairs to see what had become of Ginzburg.

◇◇◇*Vladimir Nabokov (1899–   ). Born in St. Petersburg, Russia; educated in England; became an American citizen and considers himself to be an American writer. Originally wrote in Russian, now
writes in English. In addition to being a poet, novelist and short-
story writer, he is a translator, chess master and lepidopterist.*

THE VANE SISTERS

BY VLADIMIR NABOKOV

I might never have heard of Cynthia's death, had I not run, that
night, into D., whom I had also lost track of for the last four years
or so; and I might never have run into D., had I not got involved in
a series of trivial investigations.

The day, a compunctious Sunday after a week of blizzards, had
been part jewel, part mud. In the midst of my usual afternoon stroll
through the small hilly town attached to the girls' college where I
taught French literature, I had stopped to watch a family of brilliant icicles drip-dripping from the eaves of a frame house. So
clear-cut were their pointed shadows on the white boards behind
them that I was sure the shadows of the falling drops should be
visible too. But they were not. The roof jutted too far out, perhaps,
or the angle of vision was faulty, or, again, I did not chance to be
watching the right icicle when the right drop fell. There was a
rhythm, an alternation in the dropping that I found as teasing as a
coin trick. It led me to inspect the corners of several house blocks,
and this brought me to Kelly Road, and right to the house where
D. used to live when he was instructor here. And as I looked up at
the eaves of the adjacent garage with its full display of transparent stalactites backed by their blue silhouettes, I was rewarded
at last, upon choosing one, by the sight of what might be described
as the dot of an exclamation mark leaving its ordinary position to
glide down very fast—a jot faster than the thaw-drop it raced. This
twinned twinkle was delightful but not completely satisfying; or

---

rather it only sharpened my appetite for other tidbits of light and shade, and I walked on in a state of raw awareness that seemed to transform the whole of my being into one big eyeball rolling in the world's socket.

Through peacocked lashes I saw the dazzling diamond reflection of the low sun on the round back of a parked automobile. To all kinds of things a vivid pictorial sense had been restored by the sponge of the thaw. Water in overlapping festoons flowed down one sloping street and turned gracefully into another. With ever so slight a note of meretricious appeal, narrow passages between buildings revealed treasures of brick and purple. I remarked for the first time the humble fluting—last echoes of grooves on the shafts of columns—ornamenting a garbage can, and I also saw the rippling upon its lid—circles diverging from a fantastically ancient center. Erect, dark-headed shapes of dead snow (left by the blades of a bulldozer last Friday) were lined up like rudimentary penguins along the curbs, above the brilliant vibration of live gutters.

I walked up, and I walked down, and I walked straight into a delicately dying sky, and finally the sequence of observed and observant things brought me, at my usual eating time, to a street so distant from my usual eating place that I decided to try a restaurant which stood on the fringe of the town. Night had fallen without sound or ceremony when I came out again. The lean ghost, the elongated umbra cast by a parking meter upon some damp snow, had a strange ruddy tinge; this I made out to be due to the tawny red light of the restaurant sign above the sidewalk; and it was then—as I sauntered there, wondering rather wearily if in the course of my return tramp I might be lucky enough to find the same in neon blue it was then that a car crunched to a standstill near me and D. got out of it with an exclamation of feigned pleasure.

He was passing, on his way from Albany to Boston, through the town he had dwelt in before, and more than once in my life have I felt that stab of vicarious emotion followed by a rush of personal irritation against travelers who seem to feel nothing at all upon revisiting spots that ought to harass them at every step with wailing and writhing memories. He ushered me back into the bar that I had just left, and after the usual exchange of buoyant platitudes came the inevitable vacuum which he filled with the random words: "Say, I never thought there was anything wrong with Cynthia Vane's heart. My lawyer tells me she died last week."

II

He was still young, still brash, still shifty, still married to the gentle, exquisitely pretty woman who had never learned or suspected anything about his disastrous affair with Cynthia's hysterical young sister, who in her turn had known nothing of the interview I had had with Cynthia when she suddenly summoned me to Boston to make me swear I would talk to D. and get him "kicked out" if he did not stop seeing Sybil at once—or did not divorce his wife (whom incidentally she visualized through the prism of Sybil's wild talk as a termagant and a fright). I had cornered him immediately. He had said there was nothing to worry about—had made up his mind, anyway, to give up his college job and move with his wife to Albany where he would work in his father's firm; and the whole matter, which had threatened to become one of those hopelessly entangled situations that drag on for years, with peripheral sets of well-meaning friends endlessly discussing it in universal secrecy—and even founding, among themselves, new intimacies upon its alien woes—came to an abrupt end.

I remember sitting next day at my raised desk in the large classroom where a mid-year examination in French Lit. was being held on the eve of Sybil's suicide. She came in on high heels, with a suitcase, dumped it in a corner where several other bags were stacked, with a single shrug slipped her fur coat off her thin shoulders, folded it on her bag, and with two or three other girls stopped before my desk to ask when would I mail them their grades. It would take me a week, beginning from tomorrow, I said, to read the stuff. I also remember wondering whether D. had already informed her of his decision—and I felt acutely unhappy about my dutiful little student as during one hundred and fifty minutes my gaze kept reverting to her, so childishly slight in close-fitting grey, and kept observing that carefully waved dark hair, that small, small-flowered hat with a little hyaline veil as worn that season and under it her small face broken into a cubist pattern by scars due to a skin disease, pathetically masked by a sun-lamp tan that hardened her features whose charm was further imparied by her having painted everything that could be painted, so that the pale gums of her teeth between cherry-red chapped lips and the diluted blue ink of her eyes under darkened lids were the only visible openings into her beauty.

Next day, having arranged the ugly copybooks alphabetically, I plunged into their chaos of scripts and came prematurely to Valevsky and Vane whose books I had somehow misplaced. The first was dressed up for the occasion in a semblance of legibility, but Sybil's work displayed her usual combination of several demon hands. She had begun in very pale, very hard pencil which had conspicuously embossed the blank verso, but had produced little of permanent value on the upper-side of the page. Happily the tip soon broke, and Sybil continued in another, darker lead, gradually lapsing into the blurred thickness of what looked almost like charcoal, to which, by sucking the blunt point, she had contributed some traces of lipstick. Her work, although even poorer than I had expected, bore all the signs of a kind of desperate conscientiousness, with underscores, transposes, unnecessary footnotes, as if she were intent upon rounding up things in the most respectable manner possible. Then she had borrowed Mary Valevsky's fountain pen and added: "*Cette examain est finie ainsi que ma vie. Adieu, jeunes filles*! Please, *Monsieur le Professeur*, contact *ma soeur* and tell her that Death was not better than D minus, but definitely better than Life minus D."

I lost no time in ringing up Cynthia who told me it was all over —had been all over since eight in the morning—and asked me to bring her the note, and when I did, beamed through her tears with proud admiration for the whimsical use ("Just like her!") Sybil had made of an examination in French literature. In no time she "fixed" two highballs, while never parting with Sybil's notebook— by now splashed with soda water and tears—and went on studying the death message, whereupon I was impelled to point out to her the grammatical mistakes in it and to explain the way "girl" is translated in American colleges lest students innocently bandy around the French equivalent of "wench," or worse. These rather tasteless trivialities pleased Cynthia hugely as she rose, with gasps, above

the heaving surface of her grief. And then, holding that limp note-
book as if it were a kind of passport to a casual Elysium (where
pencil points do not snap and a dreamy young beauty with an im-
peccable complexion winds a lock of her hair on a dreamy forefinger, as she meditates over some celestial test), Cynthia led me
upstairs, to a chilly little bedroom just to show me, as if I were the
police or a sympathetic Irish neighbor, two empty pill bottles and
the tumbled bed from which a tender, inessential body, that D.
must have known down to its last velvet detail, had been already
removed.

III

It was four or five months after her sister's death that I began
seeing Cynthia fairly often. By the time I had come to New York
for some vocational research in the Public Library she had also
moved to that city where for some odd reason (in vague connection, I presume, with artistic motives) she had taken what people,
immune to gooseflesh, term a "cold water" flat, down in the scale
of the city's transverse streets. What attracted me were neither her
ways, which I thought repulsively vivacious, nor her looks, which
other men thought striking. She had wide-spaced eyes very much
like her sister's, of a frank, frightened blue with dark points in a
radial arrangement. The interval between her thick black eyebrows
was always shiny, and shiny too were the fleshy volutes of her
nostrils. The coarse texture of her epiderm looked almost masculine, and, in the stark lamplight of her studio, you could see the
pores of her thirty-two-year-old face fairly gaping at you like something in an aquarium. She used cosmetics with as much zest as her
little sister had, but with an additional slovenliness that would result in her big front teeth getting some of the rouge. She was hand-
somely dark, wore a not too tasteless mixture of fairly smart heter-
ogeneous things, and had a so-called good figure; but all of her
was curiously frowsy, after a way I obscurely associated with left-
wing enthusiasms in politics and "advanced" banalities in art, although, actually, she cared for neither. Her coily hair-do, on a part-
and-bun basis, might have looked feral and bizarre had it not been
thoroughly domesticated by its own soft unkemptness at the vulnerable nape. Her fingernails were gaudily painted, but badly

bitten and not clean. Her lovers were a silent young photographer with a sudden laugh and two older men, brothers, who owned a small printing establishment across the street. I wondered at their tastes whenever I glimpsed, with a secret shudder, the higgledy-piggledy striation of black hairs that showed all along her pale shins through the nylon of her stockings with the scientific distinctness of a preparation flattened under glass; or when I felt, at her every movement, the dullish, stalish, not particularly conspicuous but all-pervading and depressing emanation that her seldom bathed flesh spread from under weary perfumes and creams.

Her father had gambled away the greater part of a comfortable fortune, and her mother's first husband had been of Slav origin, but otherwise Cynthia Vane belonged to a good, respectable family. For aught we know, it may have gone back to kings and soothsayers in the mists of ultimate islands. Transferred to a newer world, to a landscape of doomed, splendid deciduous trees, her ancestry presented, in one of its first phases, a white churchful of farmers against a black thunderhead, and then an imposing array of townsmen engaged in mercantile pursuits, as well as a number of learned men, such as Dr. Jonathan Vane, the gaunt bore (1780–1839), who perished in the conflagration of the steamer "Lexington" to become later an habitué of Cynthia's tilting table. I have always wished to stand genealogy on its head, and here I have an opportunity to do so, for it is the last scion, Cynthia, and Cynthia alone, who will remain of any importance in the Vane dynasty. I am alluding of course to her artistic gift, to her delightful, gay, but not very popular paintings which the friends of her friends bought at long intervals—and I dearly should like to know where they went after her death, those honest and poetical pictures that illumined her living-room—the wonderfully detailed images of metallic things, and my favorite "Seen Through a Windshield"—a windshield partly covered with rime, with a brilliant trickle (from an imaginary car roof) across its transparent part and, through it all, the sapphire flame of the sky and a green and white fir tree.

IV

Cynthia had a feeling that her dead sister was not altogether pleased with her—had discovered by now that she and I had conspired to break her romance; and so, in order to disarm her shade, Cynthia reverted to a rather primitive type of sacrificial offering (tinged, however, with something of Sybil's humor), and began to send to D.'s business address, at deliberately unfixed dates, such trifles as snapshots of Sybil's tomb in a poor light; cuttings of her own hair which was indistinguishable from Sybil's; a New England sectional map with an inked-in cross, midway between two chaste towns, to mark the spot where D. and Sybil had stopped on October the twenty-third, in broad daylight, at a lenient motel, in a pink and brown forest; and, twice, a stuffed skunk.

Being as a conversationalist more voluble than explicit, she never could describe in full the theory of intervenient auras that she had somehow evolved. Fundamentally there was nothing particularly new about her private creed since it presupposed a fairly conventional hereafter, a silent solarium of immortal souls (spliced with mortal antecedents) whose main recreation consisted of periodical hoverings over the dear quick. The interesting point was a curious practical twist that Cynthia gave to her tame metaphysics. She was sure that her existence was influenced by all sorts of dead friends each of whom took turns in directing her fate much as if she were a stray kitten which a schoolgirl in passing gathers up, and presses to her cheek, and carefully puts down again, near some suburban hedge—to be stroked presently by another transient hand or carried off to a world of doors by some hospitable lady.

For a few hours, or for several days in a row, and sometimes recurrently, in an irregular series, for months or years, anything that happened to Cynthia, after a given person had died, would be, she said, in the manner and mood of that person. The event might be extraordinary, changing the course of one's life; or it might be a string of minute incidents just sufficiently clear to stand out in relief against one's usual day and then shading off into still vaguer trivia as the aura gradually faded. The influence might be good or bad; the main thing was that its source could be identified. It was like walking through a person's soul, she said. I tried to argue that she might not always be able to determine the exact source since not everybody has a recognizable soul; that there are anonymous letters and Christmas presents which anybody might send; that, in fact, what Cynthia called "a usual day" might be itself a weak solution of mixed auras or simply the routine shift of a humdrum guardian angel. And what about God? Did or did not people who would resent any omnipotent dictator on earth look forward to one in heaven? And wars? What a dreadful idea—dead soldiers still fighting with living ones, or phantom armies trying to get at each other through the lives of crippled old men.

But Cynthia was above generalities as she was beyond logic. "Ah, that's Paul," she would say when the soup spitefully boiled over, or: "I guess good Betty Brown is dead"—when she won a beautiful and very welcome vacuum cleaner in a charity lottery. And, with Jamesian meanderings that exasperated my French mind, she would go back to a time when Betty and Paul had not yet departed, and tell me of the showers of well-meant, but odd and quite unacceptable bounties—beginning with an old purse that contained a check for three dollars which she picked up in the street and, of course, returned (to the aforesaid Betty Brown—this is where she first comes in—a decrepit colored woman hardly able to walk), and ending with an insulting proposal from an old beau of hers (this is where Paul comes in) to paint "straight" pictures of his house and family for a reasonable remuneration—all of which followed upon the demise of a certain Mrs. Page, a kindly but petty old party who had pestered her with bits of matter-of-fact advice since Cynthia had been a child.

Sybil's personality, she said, had a rainbow edge as if a little out of focus. She said that had I known Sybil better I would have at once understood how Sybil-like was the aura of minor events which, in spells, had suffused her, Cynthia's, existence after Sybil's suicide. Ever since they had lost their mother they had intended to give up their Boston home and move to New York, where Cynthia's paintings, they thought, would have a chance to be more widely admired; but the old home had clung to them with all its plush tentacles. Dead Sybil, however, had proceeded to separate the house from its view—a thing that affects fatally the sense of home. Right across the narrow street a building project had come into loud, ugly, scaffolded life. A pair of familiar poplars died that spring, turning to blond skeletons. Workmen came and broke up the warm-colored lovely old sidewalk that had a special violet sheen on wet April days and had echoed so memorably to the morning footsteps of museum-bound Mr. Lever, who upon retiring from business at sixty had devoted a full quarter of a century exclusively to the study of snails.

Speaking of old men, one should add that sometimes these posthumous auspices and interventions were in the nature of parody. Cynthia had been on friendly terms with an eccentric librarian called Porlock who in the last years of his dusty life had been engaged in examining old books for miraculous misprints such as the substitution of "l" for the second "h" in the word "hither." Contrary to Cynthia, he cared nothing for the thrill of obscure predictions; all he sought was the freak itself, the chance that mimics choice, the flaw that looks like a flower; and Cynthia, a much more perverse amateur of mis-shapen or illicitly connected words, puns, logogriphs, and so on, had helped the poor crank to pursue a quest that in the light of the example she cited struck me as statistically insane. Anyway, she said, on the third day after his death she was reading a magazine and had just come across a quotation from an imperishable poem (that she, with other gullible readers, believed to have been really composed in a dream) when it dawned upon her that "Alph" was a prophetic sequence of the initial letters of Anna Livia Plurabelle (another sacred river running through, or rather around, yet another fake dream), while the additional "h" modestly stood, as a private signpost, for the word that had so hypnotized Mr. Porlock. And I wish I could recollect that novel or short story (by some contemporary writer, I believe) in which, unknown to its author, the first letters of the words in its last paragraph formed, as deciphered by Cynthia, a message from his dead mother.

V

I am sorry to say that not content with these ingenious fancies Cynthia showed a ridiculous fondness for spiritualism. I refused to accompany her to sittings in which paid mediums took part: I knew too much about that from other sources. I did consent, however, to attend little farces rigged up by Cynthia and her two poker-faced gentlemen-friends of the printing shop. They were podgy, polite, and rather eerie old fellows, but I satisfied myself that they possessed considerable wit and culture. We sat down at a light little table, and crackling tremors started almost as soon as we laid our fingertips upon it. I was treated to an assortment of ghosts who rapped out their reports most readily though refusing to elucidate anything that I did not quite catch. Oscar Wilde came in and in rapid garbled French, with the usual anglicisms, obscurely accused Cynthia's dead parents of what appeared in my jottings as "*plagiatisme.*" A brisk spirit contributed the unsolicited information that he, John Moore, and his brother Bill had been coal miners in Colorado and had perished in an avalanche at "Crested Beauty" in January 1883. Frederic Myers, an old hand at the game, hammered out a piece of verse (oddly resembling Cynthia's own fugitive productions) which in part reads in my notes:

> What is this—a conjuror's rabbit,
> Or a flawy but genuine gleam—
> Which can check the perilous habit
> And dispel the dolorous dream?

Finally, with a great crash and all kinds of shudderings and jig-like movements on the part of the table, Leo Tolstoy visited our little group and, when asked to identify himself by specific traits of terrene habitation, launched upon a complex description of what seemed to be some Russian type of architectural woodwork ("figures on boards—man, horse, cock, man, horse, cock"), all of which was difficult to take down, hard to understand, and impossible to verify.

I attended two or three other sittings which were even sillier but I must confess that I preferred the childish entertainment they afforded and the cider we drank (Podgy and Pudgy were teetotallers) to Cynthia's awful house parties.

She gave them at the Wheelers' nice flat next door—the sort of arrangement dear to her centrifugal nature, but then, of course, her own living-room always looked like a dirty old palette. Following a barbaric, unhygienic, and adulterous custom, the guests' coats, still warm on the inside, were carried by quiet, baldish Bob Wheeler into the sanctity of a tidy bedroom and heaped on the conjugal bed. It was also he who poured out the drinks which were passed around by the young photographer while Cynthia and Mrs. Wheeler took care of the canapés.

A late arrival had the impression of lots of loud people unnecessarily grouped within a smoke-blue space between two mirrors gorged with reflections. Because, I suppose, Cynthia wished to be the youngest in the room, the women she used to invite, married or single, were, at the best, in their precarious forties; some of them would bring from their homes, in dark taxis, intact vestiges of good looks, which, however, they lost as the party progressed. It has always amazed me—the capacity sociable week-end revellers have of finding almost at once, by a purely empiric but very precise method, a common denominator of drunkenness, to which every-body loyally sticks before descending, all together, to the next level. The rich friendliness of the matrons was marked by tomboyish overtones, while the fixed inward look of amiably tight men was like a sacrilegious parody of pregnancy. Although some of the guests were connected in one way or another with the arts, there was no inspired talk, no wreathed, elbow-propped heads, and of course no flute girls. From some vantage point where she had been sitting in a stranded mermaid pose on the pale carpet with one or two younger fellows, Cynthia, her face varnished with a film of beaming sweat, would creep up on her knees, a proffered plate of nuts in one hand, and crisply tap with the other the athletic leg of Cochran or Corcoran, an art dealer, ensconced, on a pearl-grey sofa, between two flushed, happily disintegrating ladies.

At a further stage there would come spurts of more riotous gaiety. Corcoran or Coransky would grab Cynthia or some other wandering woman by the shoulder and lead her into a corner to confront her with a grinning embroglio of private jokes and rumors, whereupon, with a laugh and a toss of her head, she would break away. And still later there would be flurries of intersexual chummi-ness, jocular reconciliations, a bare fleshy arm flung around another woman's husband (he standing very upright in the midst of a swaying room), or a sudden rush of flirtatious anger, of clumsy pursuit—and the quiet half smile of Bob Wheeler picking up glasses that grew like mushrooms in the shade of chairs.

After one last party of that sort, I wrote Cynthia a perfectly harmless and, on the whole, well-meant note, in which I poked a little Latin fun at some of her guests. I also apologized for not hav-ing touched her whisky, saying that as a Frenchman I preferred the grape to the grain. A few days later I met her on the steps of the Public Library, in the broken sun, under a weak cloudburst, opening her amber umbrella, struggling with a couple of armpitted books (of which I relieved her for a moment). "Footfalls on the Boundary of Another World," by Robert Dale Owen, and something on "Spiritualism and Christianity"; when, suddenly, with no provocation on my part, she blazed out at me with vulgar vehemence, using poisonous words, saying—through pear-shaped drops of sparse rain—that I was a prig and a snob; that I only saw the gestures and disguises of people; that Corcoran had rescued from drowning, in two different oceans, two men—by an irrelevant coincidence both called Corcoran; that romping and screeching Joan Winter had a little girl doomed to grow completely blind in a few months; and that the woman in green with the freckled chest whom I had snubbed in some way or other had written a national bestseller in 1932. Strange Cynthia! I had been told she could be thunderously rude to people whom she liked and respected; one had, however, to draw the line somewhere and since I had by then sufficiently studied her interesting auras and other odds and ids, I decided to stop seeing her altogether.

VI

The night D. informed me of Cynthia's death I returned after eleven to the two-storied house I shared, in horizontal section, with an emeritus professor's widow. Upon reaching the porch I looked with the apprehension of solitude at the two kinds of darkness in the two rows of windows: the darkness of absence and the darkness of sleep.

I could do something about the first but could not duplicate the second. My bed gave me no sense of safety; its springs only made my nerves bounce. I plunged into Shakespeare's sonnets—and found myself idiotically checking the first letters of the lines to see what sacramental words they might form. I got fate (LXX), ATOM (CXX) and, twice, TAFT (LXXXVIII, CXXXI). Every now and then I would glance around to see how the objects in my room were behaving. It was strange to think that if bombs began to fall I would feel little more than a gambler's excitement (and a great deal of earthy relief) whereas my heart would burst if a certain suspi-

ciously tense-looking little bottle on yonder shelf moved a fraction of
an inch to one side. The silence, too, was suspiciously compact as if
deliberately forming a black back-drop for the nerve flash caused
by any small sound of unknown origin. All traffic was dead. In
vain did I pray for the groan of a truck up Perkins Street. The
woman above who used to drive me crazy by the booming thuds
occasioned by what seemed monstrous feet of stone (actually, in
diurnal life, she was a small dumpy creature resembling a mummi-
fied guinea pig) would have earned my blessings had she now
trudged to her bathroom. I put out my light and cleared my throat
several times so as to be responsible for at least *that* sound. I
thumbed a mental ride with a very remote automobile but it
dropped me before I had a chance to doze off. Presently a crackle
(due, I hoped, to a discarded and crushed sheet of paper opening
like a mean, stubborn night flower)—started and stopped in the
waste-paper basket, and my bed-table responded with a little click.
It would have been just like Cynthia to put on right then a cheap
poltergeist show.

I decided to fight Cynthia. I reviewed in thought the modern
era of raps and apparitions, beginning with the knockings of 1848,
at the hamlet of Hydesville, N.Y., and ending with grotesque phenomena at Cambridge, Mass.; I evoked the ankle-bones and other
anatomical castanets of the Fox sisters (as described by the sages
of the University of Buffalo); the mysteriously uniform type of
delicate adolescent in bleak Epworth or Tedworth, radiating the
same disturbances as in old Peru; solemn Victorian orgies with
roses falling and accordions floating to the strains of sacred music;
professional imposters regurgitating moist cheesecloth; Mr. Dun-
can, a lady medium's dignified husband, who, when asked if he
would submit to a search, excused himself on the ground of soiled
underwear; old Alfred Russel Wallace, the naïve naturalist, refusing to believe that the white form with bare feet and unperforated
earlobes before him, at a private pandemonium in Boston, could
be prim Miss Cook whom he had just seen asleep, in her curtained
corner, all dressed in black, wearing laced-up boots and earrings;
two other investigators, small, puny, but reasonably intelligent and
active men, closely clinging with arms and legs about Eusapia, a
large, plump elderly female reeking of garlic, who still managed

to fool them; and the sceptical and embarrassed magician, instructed by charming young Margery's "control" not to get lost in the bathrobe's lining but to follow up the left stocking until he reached the bare thigh—upon the warm skin of which he felt a "teleplastic" mass that appeared to the touch uncommonly like cold, uncooked liver.

VII

I was appealing to flesh, and the corruption of flesh, to refute and defeat the possible persistence of discarnate life. Alas, these conjurations only enhanced my fear of Cynthia's phantom. Atavistic peace came with dawn, and when I slipped into sleep, the sun through the tawny window shades penetrated a dream that somehow was full of Cynthia.

This was disappointing. Secure in the fortress of daylight, I said to myself that I had expected more. She, a painter of glass-bright minutiæ—and now so vague! I lay in bed, thinking my dream over and listening to the sparrows outside: Who knows, if recorded and then run backward, those birds sounds might not become human speech, voiced words, just as the latter become a twitter when reversed? I set myself to re-read my dream—backward, diagonally, up, down—trying hard to unravel something Cynthia-like in it, something strange and suggestive that must be there.

I could isolate, consciously, little. Everything seemed blurred, yellow-clouded, yielding nothing tangible. Her inept acrostics, maudlin evasions, theopathies—every recollection formed ripples of mysterious meaning. Everything seemed yellowly blurred, illusive, lost.

◇◇◇*Flannery O'Connor (1925–1964). Roman Catholic American writer, born and raised in Georgia, known especially for her short stories, in which her religious preoccupation plays an important role. See* A Good Man Is Hard To Find *and* Everything That Rises Must Converge.

EVERYTHING THAT RISES MUST CONVERGE

BY FLANNERY O'CONNOR

Her doctor had told Julian's mother that she must lose twenty pounds on account of her blood pressure, so on Wednesday nights Julian had to take her downtown on the bus for a reducing class at the Y. The reducing class was designed for working girls over fifty, who weighed from 165 to 200 pounds. His mother was one of the slimmer ones, but she said ladies did not tell their age or weight. She would not ride the buses by herself at night since they had been integrated, and because the reducing class was one of her few pleasures, necessary for her health, and *free*, she said Julian could at least put himself out to take her, considering all she did for him. Julian did not like to consider all she did for him, but every Wednesday night he braced himself and took her.

She was almost ready to go, standing before the hall mirror, putting on her hat, while he, his hands behind him, appeared pinned to the door frame, waiting like Saint Sebastian for the arrows to begin piercing him. The hat was new and had cost her seven dollars and a half. She kept saying, "Maybe I shouldn't have paid that for it. No, I shouldn't have. I'll take it off and return it tomorrow. I shouldn't have bought it."

Julian raised his eyes to heaven. "Yes, you should have bought it," he said. "Put it on and let's go." It was a hideous hat. A purple velvet flap came down on one side of it and stood up on the other; the rest of it was green and looked like a cushion with the stuffing out. He decided it was less comical than jaunty and pathetic. Everything that gave her pleasure was small and depressed him.

She lifted the hat one more time and set it down slowly on top of her head. Two wings of gray hair protruded on either side of her florid face, but her eyes, sky-blue, were as innocent and untouched by experience as they must have been when she was ten. Were it not that she was a widow who had struggled fiercely to feed and clothe and put him through school and who was supporting him still, "until he got on his feet," she might have been a little girl that he had to take to town.

"It's all right, it's all right," he said. "Let's go." He opened the door himself and started down the walk to get her going. The sky was a dying violet and the houses stood out darkly against it, bulbous liver-colored monstrosities of a uniform ugliness though no two were alike. Since this had been a fashionable neighborhood forty years ago, his mother persisted in thinking they did well to have an apartment in it. Each house had a narrow collar of dirt around it in which sat, usually, a grubby child. Julian walked with his hands in his pockets, his head down and thrust forward and his eyes glazed with the determination to make himself completely numb during the time he would be sacrificed to her pleasure.

The door closed and he turned to find the dumpy figure, surmounted by the atrocious hat, coming toward him. "Well," she said, "you only live once and paying a little more for it, I at least won't meet myself coming and going."

"Some day I'll start making money," Julian said gloomily—he knew he never would—"and you can have one of those jokes whenever you take the fit." But first they would move. He visualized a place where the nearest neighbors would be three miles away on either side.

"I think you're doing fine," she said, drawing on her gloves. "You've only been out of school a year. Rome wasn't built in a day."

She was one of the few members of the Y reducing class who arrived in hat and gloves and who had a son who had been to college. "It takes time," she said, "and the world is in such a mess. This hat looked better on me than any of the others, though when she brought it out I said, 'Take that thing back. I wouldn't have it on my head,' and she said, 'Now wait till you see it on,' and when she put it on me, I said, 'We-ull,' and she said, 'If you ask me, that hat does something for you and you do something for the hat, and besides,' she said, 'with that hat, you won't meet yourself coming and going.'"

Julian thought he could have stood his lot better if she had been selfish, if she had been an old hag who drank and screamed at him. He walked along, saturated in depression, as if in the midst of his martyrdom he had lost his faith. Catching sight of his long, hopeless, irritated face, she stopped suddenly with a grief-stricken look, and pulled back on his arm. "Wait on me," she said. "I'm going back to the house and take this thing off and tomorrow I'm going to return it. I was out of my head. I can pay the gas bill with that seven-fifty."

He caught her arm in a vicious grip. "You are not going to take it back," he said. "I like it."

"Well," she said, "I don't think I ought . . ."

"Shut up and enjoy it," he muttered, more depressed than ever.

"With the world in the mess it's in," she said, "it's a wonder we can enjoy anything. I tell you, the bottom rail is on the top."

Julian sighed.

"Of course," she said, "if you know who you are, you can go anywhere." She said this every time he took her to the reducing class. "Most of them in it are not our kind of people," she said, "but I can be gracious to anybody. I know who I am."

"They don't give a damn for your graciousness," Julian said savagely. "Knowing who you are is good for one generation only. You haven't the foggiest idea where you stand now or who you are."

She stopped and allowed her eyes to flash at him. "I most certainly do know who I am," she said, "and if you don't know who you are, I'm ashamed of you."

"Oh hell," Julian said.

"Your great-grandfather was a former governor of this state," she said. "Your grandfather was a prosperous landowner. Your grandmother was a Godhigh."

"Will you look around you," he said tensely, "and see where you are now?" and he swept his arm jerkily out to indicate the neighborhood, which the growing darkness at least made less dingy.

"You remain what you are," she said. "Your great-grandfather had a plantation and two hundred slaves."

"There are no more slaves," he said irritably.

"They were better off when they were," she said. He groaned to see that she was off on that topic. She rolled onto it every few days like a train on an open track. He knew every stop, every junction, every swamp along the way, and knew the exact point at which her conclusion would roll majestically into the station: "It's ridiculous. It's simply not realistic. They should rise, yes, but on their own side of the fence."

"Let's skip it," Julian said.

"The ones I feel sorry for," she said, "are the ones that are half white. They're tragic."

"Will you skip it?"

"Suppose we were half white. We would certainly have mixed feelings."

"I have mixed feelings now," he groaned.

"Well let's talk about something pleasant," she said. "I remember going to Grandpa's when I was a little girl. Then the house had double stairways that went up to what was really the second floor —all the cooking was done on the first. I used to like to stay down in the kitchen on account of the way the walls smelled. I would sit with my nose pressed against the plaster and take deep breaths. Actually the place belonged to the Godhighs but your granfather Chestny paid the mortgage and saved it for them. They were in reduced circumstances," she said, "but reduced or not, they never forgot who they were."

"Doubtless that decayed mansion reminded them," Julian muttered. He never spoke of it without contempt or thought of it without longing. He had seen it once when he was a child before it had been sold. The double stairways had rotted and been torn down. Negroes were living in it. But it remained in his mind as his mother had known it. It appeared in his dreams regularly. He would stand on the wide porch, listening to the rustle of oak leaves, then wander through the high-ceilinged hall into the parlor that opened onto it and gaze at the worn rugs and faded draperies. It occurred to him that it was he, not she, who could have appreciated it. He preferred its threadbare elegance to anything he could name and it was because of it that all the neighborhoods they had lived in had been a torment to him—whereas she had hardly known the difference. She called her insensitivity "being adjustable."

"And I remember the old darky who was my nurse, Caroline. There was no better person in the world. I've always had a great respect for my colored friends," she said. "I'd do anything in the world for them and they'd . . ."

"Will you for God's sake get off that subject?" Julian said. When he got on a bus by himself, he made it a point to sit down beside a Negro, in reparation as it were for his mother's sins.

"You're mighty touchy tonight," she said. "Do you feel all right?"

"Yes I feel all right," he said. "Now lay off."

She pursed her lips. "Well, you certainly are in a vile humor," she observed. "I just won't speak to you at all."

They had reached the bus stop. There was no bus in sight and Julian, his hands still jammed in his pockets and his head thrust forward, scowled down the empty street. The frustration of having to wait on the bus as well as ride on it began to creep up his neck like a hot hand. The presence of his mother was borne in upon him as she gave a pained sigh. He looked at her bleakly. She was holding herself very erect under the preposterous hat, wearing it like a banner of her imaginary dignity. There was in him an evil urge to break her spirit. He suddenly unloosened his tie and pulled it off and put it in his pocket.

She stiffened. "Why must you look like *that* when you take me to town?" she said. "Why must you deliberately embarrass me?"

"If you'll never learn where you are," he said, "you can at least learn where I am."

"You look like a—thug," she said.

"Then I must be one," he murmured.

"I'll just go home," she said. "I will not bother you. If you can't do a little thing like that for me . . ."

Rolling his eyes upward, he put his tie back on. "Restored to my class," he muttered. He thrust his face toward her and hissed, "True culture is in the mind, the *mind*," he said, and tapped his head, "the mind."

"It's in the heart," she said, "and in how you do things and how you do things is because of who you *are*."

"Nobody in the damn bus cares who you are."

"I care who I am," she said icily.

The lighted bus appeared on top of the next hill and as it approached, they moved out into the street to meet it. He put his hand under her elbow and hoisted her up on the creaking step. She entered with a little smile, as if she were going into a drawing room where everyone had been waiting for her. While he put in the tokens, she sat down on one of the broad front seats for three which faced the aisle. A thin woman with protruding teeth and long yellow hair was sitting on the end of it. His mother moved up beside her and left room for Julian beside herself. He sat down and looked at the floor across the aisle where a pair of thin feet in red and white canvas sandals were planted.

His mother immediately began a general conversation meant to attract anyone who felt like talking. "Can it get any hotter?" she said and removed from her purse a folding fan, black with a Japanese scene on it, which she began to flutter before her.

"I reckon it might could," the woman with the protruding teeth said, "but I know for a fact my apartment couldn't get no hotter."

"It must get the afternoon sun," his mother said. She sat forward and looked up and down the bus. It was half filled. Everybody was white. "I see we have the bus to ourselves," she said. Julian cringed.

"For a change," said the woman across the aisle, the owner of the red and white canvas sandals. "I come on one the other day and they were thick as fleas—up front and all through."

"The world is in a mess everywhere," his mother said. "I don't know how we've let it get in this fix."

"What gets my goat is all those boys from good families stealing automobile tires," the woman with the protruding teeth said. "I told my boy, I said you may not be rich but you been raised right and if I ever catch you in any such mess, they can send you on to the reformatory. Be exactly where you belong."

"Training tells," his mother said. "Is your boy in high school?"

"Ninth grade," the woman said.

"My son just finished college last year. He wants to write but he's selling typewriters until he gets started," his mother said.

The woman leaned forward and peered at Julian. He threw her such a malevolent look that she subsided against the seat. On the floor across the aisle there was an abandoned newspaper. He got up and got it and opened it out in front of him. His mother discreetly continued the conversation in a lower tone but the woman across the aisle said in a loud voice, "Well that's nice. Selling typewriters is close to writing. He can go right from one to the other."

"I tell him," his mother said, "that Rome wasn't built in a day."

Behind the newspaper Julian was withdrawing into the inner compartment of his mind where he spent most of his time. This was a kind of mental bubble in which he established himself when he could not bear to be a part of what was going on around him. From it he could see out and judge but in it he was safe from any kind of penetration from without. It was the only place where he felt free of the general idiocy of his fellows. His mother had never entered it but from it he could see her with absolute clarity.

The old lady was clever enough and he thought that if she had started from any of the right premises, more might have been expected of her. She lived according to the laws of her own fantasy world, outside of which he had never seen her set foot. The law of it was to sacrifice herself for him after she had first created the necessity to do so by making a mess of things. If he had permitted her sacrifices, it was only because her lack of foresight had made them necessary. All of her life had been a struggle to act like a Chestny without the Chestny goods, and to give him everything she thought a Chestny ought to have; but since, said she, it was fun to struggle, why complain? And when you had won, as she had won, what fun to look back on the hard times! He could not forgive her that she had enjoyed the struggle and that she thought *she* had won.

What she meant when she said she had won was that she had brought him up successfully and had sent him to college and that he had turned out so well—good looking (her teeth had gone unfilled so that his could be straightened), intelligent (he realized he was too intelligent to be a success), and with a future ahead of him (there was of course no future ahead of him). She excused his gloominess on the grounds that he was still growing up and his radical ideas on his lack of practical experience. She said he didn't yet know a thing about "life," that he hadn't even entered the real world—when already he was as disenchanted with it as a man of fifty.

The further irony of all this was that in spite of her, he had turned out so well. In spite of going to only a third-rate college, he had, on his own initiative, come out with a first-rate education; in spite of growing up dominated by a small mind, he had ended up with a large one; in spite of all her foolish views, he was free of prejudice and unafraid to face facts. Most miraculous of all, instead of being blinded by love for her as she was for him, he had cut himself emotionally free of her and could see her with complete objectivity. He was not dominated by his mother.

The bus stopped with a sudden jerk and shook him from his meditation. A woman from the back lurched forward with little steps and barely escaped falling in his newspaper as she righted herself. She got off and a large Negro got on. Julian kept his paper lowered to watch. It gave him a certain satisfaction to see injustice in daily operation. It confirmed his view that with a few exceptions there was no one worth knowing within a radius of three hundred miles. The Negro was well dressed and carried a briefcase. He looked around and then sat down on the other end of the seat where the woman with the red and white canvas sandals was sitting. He immediately unfolded a newspaper and obscured himself behind it. Julian's mother's elbow at once prodded insistently into his ribs. "Now you see why I won't ride on these buses by myself," she whispered.

The woman with the red and white canvas sandals had risen at the same time the Negro sat down and had gone further back in the bus and taken the seat of the woman who had got off. His mother leaned forward and cast her an approving look.

Julian rose, crossed the aisle, and sat down in the place of the woman with the canvas sandals. From this position, he looked serenely across at his mother. Her face had turned an angry red. He stared at her, making his eyes the eyes of a stranger. He felt his tension suddenly lift as if he had openly declared war on her.

He would have liked to get in conversation with the Negro and to talk with him about art or politics or any subject that would be above the comprehension of those around them, but the man remained entrenched behind his paper. He was either ignoring the change of seating or had never noticed it. There was no way for Julian to convey his sympathy.

His mother kept her eyes fixed reproachfully on his face. The woman with the protruding teeth was looking at him avidly as if he were a type of monster new to her.

"Do you have a light?" he asked the Negro.

Without looking away from his paper, the man reached in his pocket and handed him a packet of matches.

"Thanks," Julian said. For a moment he held the matches foolishly. A NO SMOKING sign looked down upon him from over the door. This alone would not have deterred him; he had no cigarettes. He had quit smoking some months before because he could not afford it. "Sorry," he muttered and handed back the matches. The Negro lowered the paper and gave him an annoyed look. He took the matches and raised the paper again.

His mother continued to gaze at him but she did not take advantage of his momentary discomfort. Her eyes retained their battered look. Her face seemed to be unnaturally red, as if her blood pressure had risen. Julian allowed no glimmer of sympathy to show on his face. Having got the advantage, he wanted desperately to keep it and carry it through. He would have liked to teach her a lesson that would last her a while, but there seemed no way to continue the point. The Negro refused to come out from behind his paper.

Julian folded his arms and looked stolidly before him, facing her but as if he did not see her, as if he had ceased to recognize her existence. He visualized a scene in which, the bus having reached their stop, he would remain in his seat and when she said, "Aren't you going to get off?" he would look at her as at a stranger who had rashly addressed him. The corner they got off on was usually deserted, but it was well lighted and it would not hurt her to walk by herself the four blocks to the Y. He decided to wait until the time came and then decide whether or not he would let her get off by herself. He would have to be at the Y at ten to bring her back, but he could leave her wondering if he was going to show up. There was no reason for her to think she could always depend on him.

He retired again into the high-ceilinged room sparsely settled with large pieces of antique furniture. His soul expanded momentarily but then he became aware of his mother across from him and the vision shriveled. He studied her coldly. Her feet in little pumps dangled like a child's and did not quite reach the floor. She was training on him an exaggerated look of reproach. He felt completely detached from her. At that moment he could with pleasure have slapped her as he would have slapped a particularly obnoxious child in his charge.

He began to imagine various unlikely ways by which he could teach her a lesson. He might make friends with some distinguished Negro professor or lawyer and bring him home to spend the evening. He would be entirely justified but her blood pressure would rise to 300. He could not push her to the extent of making her have a stroke, and moreover, he had never been successful at making any Negro friends. He had tried to strike up an acquaintance on the bus with some of the better types, with ones that looked like professors or ministers or lawyers. One morning he had sat down next to a distinguished-looking dark brown man who had answered his questions with a sonorous solemnity but who had turned out to be an undertaker. Another day he had sat down beside a cigar-smoking Negro with a diamond ring on his finger, but after a few stilted pleasantries, the Negro had rung the buzzer and risen, slipping two lottery tickets into Julian's hand as he climbed over him to leave.

He imagined his mother lying desperately ill and his being able to secure only a Negro doctor for her. He toyed with that idea for a few minutes and then dropped it for a momentary vision of himself participating as a sympathizer in a sit-in demonstration. This was possible but he did not linger with it. Instead, he approached the ultimate horror. He brought home a beautiful suspiciously Negroid woman. Prepare yourself, he said. There is nothing you can do about it. This is the woman I've chosen. She's intelligent, dignified, even good, and she's suffered and she hasn't thought it *fun*. Now persecute us, go ahead and persecute us. Drive her out of here, but remember, you're driving me too. His eyes were narrowed and through the indignation he had generated, he saw his mother across the aisle, purple-faced, shrunken to the dwarf-like proportions of her moral nature, sitting like a mummy beneath the ridiculous banner of her hat.

He was tilted out of his fantasy again as the bus stopped. The door opened with a sucking hiss and out of the dark a large, gaily dressed, sullen-looking colored woman got on with a little boy. The child, who might have been four, had on a short plaid suit and a Tyrolean hat with a blue feather in it. Julian hoped that he would sit down beside him and that the woman would push in beside his mother. He could think of no better arrangement.

As she waited for her tokens, the woman was surveying the seating possibilities—he hoped with the idea of sitting where she was least wanted. There was something familiar-looking about her but Julian could not place what it was. She was a giant of a woman. Her face was set not only to meet opposition but to seek it out. The downward tilt of her large lower lip was like a warning sign DON'T TAMPER WITH ME. Her bulging figure was encased in a green crepe dress and her feet overflowed in red shoes. She had on a hideous hat. A purple velvet flap came down on one side of it and stood up on the other; the rest of it was green and looked like a cushion with the stuffing out. She carried a mammoth red pocketbook that bulged throughout as if it were stuffed with rocks.

To Julian's disappointment, the little boy climbed up on the empty seat beside his mother. His mother lumped all children, black and white, into the common category, "cute," and she thought little Negroes were on the whole cuter than little white children. She smiled at the little boy as he climbed on the seat.

Meanwhile the woman was bearing down upon the empty seat beside Julian. To his annoyance, she squeezed herself into it. He saw his mother's face change as the woman settled herself next to him and he realized with satisfaction that this was more objectionable to her than it was to him. Her face seemed almost gray and there was a look of dull recognition in her eyes, as if suddenly she had sickened at some awful confrontation. Julian saw that it was because she and the woman had, in a sense, swapped sons. Though his mother would not realize the symbolic significance of this, she would feel it. His amusement showed plainly on his face.

The woman next to him muttered something unintelligible to herself. He was conscious of a kind of bristling next to him, a muted growling like that of an angry cat. He could not see anything but the red pocketbook upright on the bulging green thighs. He visualized the woman as she had stood waiting for her tokens—the pon-

derous figure, rising from the red shoes upward over the solid
hips, the mammoth bosom, the haughty face, to the green and purple hat.

His eyes widened.

The vision of the two hats, identical, broke upon him with the
radiance of a brilliant sunrise. His face was suddenly lit with
joy. He could not believe that Fate had thrust upon his mother
such a lesson. He gave a loud chuckle so that she would look
at him and see that he saw. She turned her eyes on him slowly.
The blue in them seemed to have turned a bruised purple. For a
moment he had an uncomfortable sense of her innocence, but it
lasted only a second before principle rescued him. Justice entitled
him to laugh. His grin hardened until it said to her as plainly as if
he were saying aloud: Your punishment exactly fits your pettiness.
This should teach you a permanent lesson.

Her eyes shifted to the woman. She seemed unable to bear looking at him and to find the woman preferable. He became conscious again of the bristling presence at his side. The woman was
rumbling like a volcano about to become active. His mother's mouth
began to twitch slightly at one corner. With a sinking heart, he
saw incipient signs of recovery on her face and realized that this
was going to strike her suddenly as funny and was going to be no
lesson at all. She kept her eyes on the woman and an amused smile
came over her face as if the woman were a monkey that had
stolen her hat. The little Negro was looking up at her with large
fascinated eyes. He had been trying to attract her attention for
some time.

"Carver!" the woman said suddenly. "Come heah!"

When he saw that the spotlight was on him at last, Carver drew
his feet up and turned himself toward Julian's mother and giggled.

"Carver!" the woman said. "You heah me? Come heah!"

Carver slid down from the seat but remained squatting with his
back against the base of it, his head turned slyly around toward
Julian's mother, who was smiling at him. The woman reached a
hand across the aisle and snatched him to her. He righted himself
and hung backwards on her knees, grinning at Julian's mother.
"Isn't he cute?" Julian's mother said to the woman with the protruding teeth.

"I reckon he is," the woman said without conviction.

The Negress yanked him upright but he eased out of her grip and shot across the aisle and scrambled, giggling wildly, onto the seat beside his love.

"I think he likes me," Julian's mother said, and smiled at the woman. It was the smile she used when she was being particularly gracious to an inferior. Julian saw everything lost. The lesson had rolled off her like rain on a roof.

The woman stood up and yanked the little boy off the seat as if she were snatching him from contagion. Julian could feel the rage in her at having no weapon like his mother's smile. She gave the child a sharp slap across his leg. He howled once and then thrust his head into her stomach and kicked his feet against her shins. "Be-have," she said vehemently.

The bus stopped and the Negro who had been reading the newspaper got off. The woman moved over and set the little boy down with a thump between herself and Julian. She held him firmly by the knee. In a moment he put his hands in front of his face and peeped at Julian's mother through his fingers.

"I see yoooooooo!" she said and put her hand in front of her face and peeped at him.

The woman slapped his hand down. "Quit yo' foolishness," she said, "before I knock the living Jesus out of you!"

Julian was thankful that the next stop was theirs. He reached up and pulled the cord. The woman reached up and pulled it at the same time. Oh my God, he thought. He had the terrible intuition that when they got off the bus together, his mother would open her purse and give the little boy a nickel. The gesture would be as natural to her as breathing. The bus stopped and the woman got up and lunged to the front, dragging the child, who wished to stay on, after her. Julian and his mother got up and followed. As they neared the door, Julian tried to relieve her of her pocketbook.

"No," she murmured, "I want to give the little boy a nickel."

"No!" Julian hissed. "No!"

She smiled down at the child and opened her bag. The bus door opened and the woman picked him up by the arm and descended with him, hanging at her hip. Once in the street she set him down and shook him.

Julian's mother had to close her purse while she got down the bus step but as soon as her feet were on the ground, she opened it again and began to rummage inside. "I can't find but a penny," she whispered, "but it looks like a new one."

"Don't do it!" Julian said fiercely between his teeth. There was a streetlight on the corner and she hurried to get under it so that she could better see into her pocketbook. The woman was heading off rapidly down the street with the child still hanging backward on her hand.

"Oh little boy!" Julian's mother called and took a few quick steps and caught up with them just beyond the lamp-post. "Here's a bright new penny for you," and she held out the coin, which shone bronze in the dim light.

The huge woman turned and for a moment stood, her shoulders lifted and her face frozen with frustrated rage, and stared at Julian's mother. Then all at once she seemed to explode like a piece of machinery that had been given one ounce of pressure too much. Julian saw the black fist swing out with the red pocketbook. He shut his eyes and cringed as he heard the woman shout, "He don't take nobody's pennies!" When he opened his eyes, the woman was disappearing down the street with the little boy staring wide-eyed over her shoulder. Julian's mother was sitting on the sidewalk.

"I told you not to do that," Julian said angrily. "I told you not to do that!"

He stood over her for a minute, gritting his teeth. Her legs were stretched out in front of her and her hat was on her lap. He squatted down and looked her in the face. It was totally expressionless. "You got exactly what you deserved," he said. "Now get up."

He picked up her pocketbook and put what had fallen out back in it. He picked the hat up off her lap. The penny caught his eye on the sidewalk and he picked that up and let it drop before her eyes into the purse. Then he stood up and leaned over and held his hands out to pull her up. She remained immobile. He sighed. Rising above them on either side were black apartment buildings, marked with irregular rectangles of light. At the end of the block a man came out of a door and walked off in the opposite direction. "All right," he said, "suppose somebody happens by and wants to know why you're sitting on the sidewalk?"

She took the hand and, breathing hard, pulled heavily up on it and then stood for a moment, swaying slightly as if the spots of light in the darkness were circling around her. Her eyes, shadowed and confused, finally settled on his face. He did not try to conceal his irritation. "I hope this teaches you a lesson," he said. She leaned forward and her eyes raked his face. She seemed trying to determine his identity. Then, as if she found nothing familiar about him, she started off with a headlong movement in the wrong direction.

"Aren't you going on to the Y?" he asked.

"Home," she muttered.

"Well, are we walking?"

For answer he kept going. Julian followed along, his hands behind him. He saw no reason to let the lesson she had had go without backing it up with an explanation of its meaning. She might as well be made to understand what had happened to her. "Don't think that was just an uppity Negro woman," he said. "That was the whole colored race which will no longer take your condescending pennies. That was your black double. She can wear the same hat as you, and to be sure," he added gratuitously (because he thought it was funny), "it looked better on her than it did on you. What all this means," he said, "is that the old world is gone. The old manners are obsolete and your graciousness is not worth a damn." He thought bitterly of the house that had been lost for him. "You aren't who you think you are," he said.

She continued to plow ahead, paying no attention to him. Her hair had come undone on one side. She dropped her pocketbook and took no notice. He stooped and picked it up and handed it to her but she did not take it.

"You needn't act as if the world had come to an end," he said, "because it hasn't. From now on you've got to live in a new world and face a few realities for a change. Buck up," he said, "it won't kill you."

She was breathing fast.

"Let's wait on the bus," he said.

"Home," she said thickly.

"I hate to see you behave like this," he said. "Just like a child. I should be able to expect more of you." He decided to stop where he was and make her stop and wait for a bus. "I'm not going any farther," he said, stopping. "We're going on the bus."

She continued to go on as if she had not heard him. He took a few steps and caught her arm and stopped her. He looked into her face and caught his breath. He was looking into a face he had never seen before. "Tell Grandpa to come get me," she said.

He stared, stricken.

"Tell Caroline to come get me," she said.

Stunned, he let her go and she lurched forward again, walking as if one leg were shorter than the other. A tide of darkness seemed to be sweeping her from him. "Mother!" he cried. "Darling, sweetheart, wait!" Crumpling, she fell to the pavement. He dashed forward and fell at her side, crying, "Mamma, Mamma!" He turned her over. Her face was fiercely distorted. One eye, large and staring, moved slightly to the left as if it had become unmoored. The other remained fixed on him, raked his face again, found nothing and closed.

"Wait here, wait here!" he cried and jumped up and began to run for help toward a cluster of lights he saw in the distance ahead of him. "Help, help!" he shouted, but his voice was thin, scarcely a thread of sound. The lights drifted farther away the faster he ran and his feet moved numbly as if they carried him nowhere. The tide of darkness seemed to sweep him back to her, postponing from moment to moment his entry into the world of guilt and sorrow.

tl